THE EVANGELINE MANUSCRIPT

BY

WALKER CHANDLER

PIKE PUBLISHING   *   ZEBULON, GEORGIA

Manufactured in the United States by:
            VISION PUBLISHING GROUP
                    Griffin Georgia

            Edited by Bonnie Bilyeu Gordon
            Proofreading by Elizabeth Suber
            Cover Design by Arthur Willis

        Quote from the play *Sappho* by Lawrence Durrell reproduced
with permission of Curtis Brown Ltd, London on behalf of The Estate
of Lawrence Durrell. Copyright Lawrence Durrell, 1950

        Library of Congress Catalog Number: 97-092621

        ISBN 0-9661246-1-8

        First Edition: March, 1998

To those who love liberty
&
fearlessly seek after truth

RES IPSA LOQUITUR

To Cora Shackelford
With Best Wishes
from Walter Chandler

Christmas, 2012

J. Walton Forsyth
Attorney at Law
425 Court House Square
Eatonton, Georgia 31024

Telephone   706-485-44°°
Fax   706 485-44°°

July 4, 1997

Mr. Walker Chandler
Pike Publishing Company
Post Office Box 311
Zebulon, Georgia 30295

                        Re: Weathers Manuscript

Dear Walker,

        First let me congratulate you once again on
your recent success in the U.S. Supreme Court. Thanks
for standing up against the foolishness of the
legislature.

        As we discussed on the phone yesterday, some
months ago I received the enclosed manuscript
(complete with a copy of it on a disk) from
Evangeline Weathers, a woman I used to live with when
I was in law school. I believe you met her once or
twice. Anyway, I have decided that I would like for
you to consider publishing it for me.

        I have gone to some length to break it into
chapters and to write introductory passages in the
third person so that I might describe how the
manuscript came to me. Whether or not I did so
effectively is for others to judge. Out of an
abundance of caution, I have changed Evangeline's
last name. I will expect you to conceal my identity,
too.

        Be that as it may, the letter that Eva wrote
was incredible, but she enclosed with it certain
tangible proofs which I have had authenticated. I
have not heard from her since receiving the
manuscript, but as you will read, she has granted me
all rights in it. I in turn grant to you all rights
to it on the sole condition that you publish it
within 10 months of the date of receipt.

        Publication may involve certain risks and
embarrassments to you and your company, but this is a
story that ought to be told. Apparently, you have the
nerve to publish it. I don't. I trust you will give
it your immediate attention.

                        Sincerely yours,

                        Walton

Contents

Prologue

Dressed in a housecoat and slippers, her reddish blonde hair still wet from the shower, and sipping on hot, sweet tea, the woman sat down in front of her new computer, sighed, and flipped a switch, then watched its screen come to life. Beside the keyboard lay a loaded .45 automatic, cold in the winter sunlight. The room was quiet except for the whirr of the computer's fan.

Fingering the thin, raised scar on the top of her right shoulder, she remembered how the arrow had looked as it sped toward her and how she had not felt it slicing her flesh as she took aim at the man who had shot it.

When the screen upon which she could at last begin to write appeared, she took her grandmother's old Bible down from the shelf, opened it at random, and read the first passage upon which her glance fell. Smiling, she closed it and began to type.

One year later she printed all she had written and tied it with ribbon. She put the neat stack of paper in a box with some other carefully selected items and wrote a short note by hand. Then she sealed it all up, addressed it to a man she once knew, and sent it off to him. Then she went away from that place.

***

Two days later the man that once she had known and loved was walking back to his office. A jury had reached its verdict that morning, and he had just minutes before been standing with his client before the judge when the sentence was pronounced. 49-year-old Walton Forsyth trudged back through the cold wind toward his office on the Square, his briefcase heavy in his hand. In his rush that morning he had left his overcoat at home. The short, thin hair around the central dome of his bald head and the edges of his suit coat played in the bitter wind. It was in the low thirties but felt colder. Fortunately, he didn't have far to go.

"Mr. Forsyth has represented you well," Judge Eichmann had said, throwing the small town lawyer a tidbit from his judicial table, "but we cannot—no: we shall not tolerate what you have done. Counsel has forcefully argued that you should be allowed to do what you want to do, Son, but we

live in an orderly society, a society of laws and not of men! You cannot flaunt the law even if you disagree with it, at least not in this Circuit!"

The judge had a lot of other things to say to the boy—things that Walton would soon forget, but the import of his declarations would stick. They had the power and they were going to use it.

When the judge finished his little tirade, making the boy tremble, Walton worry, and the courtroom full of next week's jury pool—voters one and all—suitably impressed with his stand against any who would dare break the Laws of Georgia in that county, "Adolph" Eichmann had not laid the hammer down on the client too hard, certainly not as hard as he used to. Like Walton, he, knew that the War on Drugs was lost. Nevertheless, he gave the boy some time to serve, plus a big fine.

"One more boy on de plantation," thought Walton, contemplating his client's life on parole after Corrections got through with him.

When he had begun his law practice some 20 years before, he had been possessed of the fire. He had argued and had fought many courtroom battles with the judges, the prosecutors, and the police, wondering how men could, in good conscience, keep on prosecuting that war to carry out the government's edicts to whip the rednecks, blacks, and the young people into line, year after year.

Then he got older, and he got married. He did less criminal law work and less worrying about his society's more obvious injustices. He learned to accept that which he could not change. He became less outspoken, keeping his opinions to himself unless he was asked—and even then he might obfuscate. Imperceptibly, he moved into denial, finally keeping silent altogether about things he had once believed. He quit talking about how people should not be owned by the government, about the things he had done in college and law school, and about the women he had known. Eventually he had even quit talking about the books and music he had once cherished and of the ambitions he had once nurtured.

His metamorphosis helped him get clients and fit into the life of the rural community where he practiced. He had become a man with many friends. Other men recognized in him a fellow conservative, a man solid and reliable, a good fellow—

in short, one of them. The local Republican Party was thinking of running Walton as its candidate for the State Senate against the long-time Democrat incumbent. He had developed, he thought, into the kind of man they thought he was, and he was proud of their respect and their confidence in him. The only thing that had not gone particularly well was his relationship with his wife. They had begun arguing with increasing frequency, but he had learned to live with it. Most men did, he thought.

But then his self-perception had come up short one evening at his judicial circuit's annual bar party. Through his own alcoholic haze, he heard a drunk talking to Judge Eichmann, District Attorney Blair, and some other, highly respected lawyers who were standing with them. He had heard the man's voice sycophantically agreeing with whatever insupportable ideas they expressed. He heard the man braying eloquent, commonplace opinions. "Who is this ass?" he thought. Then he knew it was himself. He looked away from them and he saw himself.

Although the light was dim and he was drunk, Walton could see himself rather clearly in the mirror behind the bar. He saw a middle-aged man whose well-cut suit could not conceal the bloated stomach which had sneaked up on him over the years, as had so many other things: gray hair, receding hairline, children who were his but who seemed like strangers when he met them after long days at the office.

Becoming a fool who gave up his own ideas to please the men who held the real power in the county had sneaked up on him, too, as had the alcoholism which he had not recognized until that very moment. Alcohol, he realized, had been the lubricant which allowed the worst parts of his character to dominate him to the extent that they had. It had almost completely overthrown the man he had been and the ideals that he had once held dear.

Standing there in that circle of men, but no longer talking, he had leered at the fat man in the mirror who leered back at him and hated him. He knew that it was the second—or was it the third?—time he'd been drunk that week. Something in him snapped. He walked away without a word to the others.

He staggered toward the main dining room, found his

wife talking to some other lawyers' wives, and asked her to drive him home, saying he was sick. Relieved to have an excuse to return to her home and children, she didn't argue. She knew him so well! She could see that he was sick. Thanks to the mirror, he could, too.

Since that night just one year before, he had not drunk anything more than an occasional glass of wine with dinner or a beer with a friend. He had lost thirty pounds, taken his children camping at least once a month, and watched the dust gather on the half-full bottles of whiskey and gin in his liquor cabinet.

He didn't tell his wife why he did what he did and why he started jogging and cycling. After a while, he realized that his arguments with her had almost ceased and that somehow she was prettier and nicer than she had been in years.

Without making an issue of it, he never went back into the country club's dark, little alcohol den, even for the Bar's biannual parties. He managed to maintain most of the friendships he had made over the years, but he often found himself once again biting his tongue around people with whom he disagreed. At least he no longer agreed with them in order to be liked.

In front of juries, though, when the circumstances were right, he did not hold back. He was reaching for a voice and was beginning to find it, and it was a voice with some of the old fire in it. It was the voice of liberty, of the right of free men and women to make their own decisions and to accept responsibility for their own acts. When appropriate—as in the drug case he had just lost—he tried to tell the jury that it could, if it chose, judge not only the facts of the case but also the law itself. Each juror, he told them, had an individual right and a duty to think about the particular law which his client was said to have violated. He urged each juror to decide for himself whether or not that law should even exist, much less be enforced against his particular client in that particular case.

Once again, though, his voice had not been heard. The fire he had hoped to rekindle in at least one of the twelve hearts had not lasted through the night when the judge had let the jury go home before resuming deliberations in the morning.

"How can you hope to have liberty yourselves if you will not grant it to another? If you will not let Billy here make his own decisions in life, how can you in good conscience demand

any similar rights for yourselves and your children?" he had argued. He knew he was skating on the thin ice of the Judge's patience as he urged that most dangerous and constitutional of notions—that of jury nullification which was preserved in the Georgia Constitution by long-dead men who knew just how dangerous a government-- particularly a democracy-- could be.

Flame and voice had failed him again, he thought sadly as he leaned into the bitter wind that lifted a fine curtain of sand against him as he stood waiting for the light to turn green.

He looked across the street at the steamy, inviting glass of Becky's Grill and thought of stopping in. Drinking coffee and talking to Becky's husband, Wolfgang, as they watched the town loafers shooting pool in the back of the long room was one way to postpone going back to the office. He dreaded sitting down behind his desk and trying to forget that another boy was going to jail for something that shouldn't even be illegal and that it was his own fellow citizens who had sent him there.

His body made an almost imperceptible move toward Becky's, but when he saw a neighbor of his who had served on the jury go in, he headed straight to his office. Within minutes he was busy reading his mail, returning calls, dictating letters, and reviewing a long set of interrogatory responses, the jury's verdict a dark, receding cloud.

Promptly at 11:30, Kenny Remmington, the UPS man, showed up with a bulky cardboard box that looked as if it might contain either a transcript he was expecting or some books the firm had ordered. When the secretaries left for lunch and the office was quiet, he opened it. He was surprised to find that it contained, first, a smaller box which held a carefully packed iron costume-type helmet with hinged cheek flaps and a red horsehair crest. Then he lifted out from the main box a long, hard object wrapped in a towel. Unrolling it he found that it contained a short-sword.

Beneath the next layer of packing he found a second cardboard box which contained a stack of paper tied with a ribbon. On top of it was a small envelope upon which a vaguely familiar woman's hand had written, "This is all real. Keep it safe for me. —E."

When he opened the envelope, three small coins slid out

upon the top of the stack of paper. The first one was of gold. On the coin, a standing figure held a child out to a seated man. At the bottom was stamped "IMPXIII".

The second, apparently of silver, was shiny. On one side was the profile of a man surrounded by lettering. On its other side was a seated woman facing the word "Pontif". Behind her was stamped "VIIXVVI".

The third coin, also of sliver, had a portrait of a man with a straight nose, curly hair, and a lion's head helmet. On the other side was a seated figure with a hawk or falcon. Its lettering was Greek.

He lifted the pages from their box and began to read.

****

I

Christmas, 1995

Dear Walton,

I have begun this letter several different times. I trust your kind and forgiving nature to relieve me of any further indecision concerning the manner in which I ought to couch this story. Today is different. It is Christmas Day and I am alone here in Charlottesville, your old stomping grounds. For the last several weeks, I have been a recluse. I've spent my time hiking in the mountains, walking around Washington, and thinking about all the things that I have been through since we last saw one another on the last day of October in the year you graduated from law school.

I am staying on a farm where I have a big gelding hunter, and on my morning ride across the rolling, snow-covered pastures, it became clear how I could go ahead with this. I realized that I should just write a letter to you, telling you everything as best I could.

After reading it you can decide what to do with it. I must make one thing plain though: it is possible that I may need to call you at some time in the future to bear witness to the fact that I did write this all down for you and that I mailed it on a particular date.

You must already be wondering, *Why is this woman writing to me?*

I imagine you grown stout and graying. The UPS man brings you a package, and you are, well: astonished! This woman who hasn't been in touch with you for years, who wore out your patience when you lived with her and who returned your letters unopened after the relationship was over: she writes! She even sends a huge manuscript!

What does she want out of me? you ask. You weigh the stack of paper and presume that she is going to try to get you to help her publish a book. Trained by years of law practice, you'll think of the billable hours you'll lose skimming the book and fending her off. She's read the novel you wrote and wants you to help her get hers published, no doubt.

Don't worry. That's not what I want. First of all, I hereby grant you all rights everywhere in and to these words. You can do with them what you wish, but I hope you'll safeguard at least this original copy.

Why then do I write?

In short, I am accepting your offer.

You will recall, I trust, how on that Halloween night the last time we were together we stood on the platform at the Brookwood Station in Atlanta waiting for my train. It was over and we both knew it, but there we stood looking lovingly into one another's eyes, kissing and lying. As I recall, you even cried a little—from sheer relief unless I miss my guess. Letting go was easier then than it might be these days: all of that "you-go-your-way, I'll-go-mine" nonsense must have been a form of generational insanity.

But if we had little understanding, at least we had drama, and that goes a long way with me. I remember that scene at the station better than I remember most of the other things that happened during the year which preceded it: that year when your love for me failed to grow into the marriage I thought I wanted but which would have probably failed.

This very morning, though, when I rode out on my horse, Thucydides, that great leave-taking of ours came back to me as clearly as the sound of the morning bell ringing across the snow from a distant church. I recalled how with great sincerity you said that if I ever needed you, I should call on you.

This, then, is that call. It is made not from need but desire—the desire to be heard, to be remembered, and to be recorded. I know, too, that it must be done. Nature itself compels me. For example, after I came in from riding this morning, all set to start this letter, I took a shower, fixed tea and sat down in front of the computer. I opened the Bible to a place at random, and read the following:

"Thus speaketh the Lord God of Israel, saying, Write thee all the words I have spoken to you in a book."
(Jeremiah 30)

So I am going to do just that, or at least I shall try. I may not get finished. I may be silenced, but if not, I shall stay with it until I am done. Then when I am finished, I shall go back underground. As in previous times I shall try to keep myself and my doings shrouded in the strictest secrecy and once again live in some fear that the government will learn about my airplane, what I have been up to, and where I've been.

This is a history, but more: it is a story of my travels and what I have seen and done. I shall write the truth and then— perhaps unfairly—I shall lay it on you to believe or not believe it, and either to publish or to hide it. Discretion may indeed be the better part of valor. But I don't think so.

**

A postscript on hope & pity:

One last thing is this, Walton: it will sadden you to know that during the year after we parted, both my sister and my parents died. Since then I have also had a husband who was killed and have gone through other hardships of which I shall write.

I do not, though, relate these things to evoke your pity, for I have hope, too, and say to you that hope has always been the dominant theme in the developing world. Without it, no progress could have occurred. Without it, all of our efforts, futile and frustrating as they may be, would be stillborn. Hope is one of the gifts of God.

There is something we used to kid about in our family, a characteristic you will recall. It was our Scottish thrift. We were descendants of a stubborn ancestor who got off the ship in Willmington and walked across the state to be with his kin in the mountains 'though he had money enough to buy a horse. Well, that was one side of our Scots nature.

The other was a religious one, but it was a side that usually appeared, if ever, later on in life. I'm not old yet, but events moved for me in such a way that I now suppose that I am become, once again, the Presbyterian and the Calvinist. One thing *is* clear: I know that I am surely one of the Elect.

****

II

Mark

I learned to fly planes when I was in graduate school at the University of Virginia. I went there after my parents' deaths in an attempt to lose myself in the study of classics. At that time I was still battling intermittent bouts of depression and was in the process of trying to establish a normal life. Never a particularly popular or outgoing person, I had few close friends at that time and was out of touch with the people you and I had hung out with. At any rate, all that was normal enough, and my advent in Charlottesville was not in and of itself remarkable, nor was it what we might call the beginning of my story.

Actually, it might be more accurate to say that it began on a certain Wednesday morning in October of 1979 in Greek class when I noticed another student surreptitiously looking at me in the way that a man looks at a woman he wants. I met his look with one of my own and a silent flirtation began. He was definitely interested.

Just having him interested in me lifted my spirits. As I recall, I was also somewhat embarrassed and probably blushed some that first day. In the days that followed I returned his looks with enigmatic smiles of my own—ones I had practiced as a teenager standing in front of my mirror. Boys never found me to be very seductive-looking, but I tried.

The man who was interested in me, though, was no boy. About 28 or 30 and rather handsome in that lithe way of Englishmen, he had jet black hair he combed straight back in an old-fashioned style that suited his accent and demeanor. I knew nothing about him, and until those days began I had heard him speaking Greek more often than I had heard him speaking English. He was clean-shaven, had dark blue eyes, and dressed very conservatively in crisp and expensive clothes. In short, he really wasn't exactly my type—but he was definitely interested. *He just thinks I'll be easy*, I thought.

That particular morning was the first time I had paid much attention to him. Prior to that time, I had written him off as being a dullard and perhaps something of a snob. Older than the rest of us and always dressed in an expensive coat-and-tie outfit, he didn't seem the type to be studying classics. Quite naturally I assumed that he was some sort of lazy, rich boy hiding out in the world of academia and living on his inheritance. But then, that was what I was doing, wasn't it? I had no plan--just pain and a certain amount of profound loneliness. Maybe the same was true of him. Suddenly I was intrigued, interested, and even flattered. It had been a long time since a man other than my boyfriend had shown much interest in me. At 28 and lonely, I had put on still more weight. I was often depressed and felt the years closing in.

Finally, one day when our class was over, he asked me to have lunch with him. I agreed, expecting him to take me to one of the places on The Corner. Surprising me by speaking in Greek, he asked, "Shall we walk to my chariot?" This set an almost formal tone that did not invite much conversation.

It felt good, though, to meet a man slowly and to engage only in small talk in our rough Greek as we walked out to the parking lot near the stadium. I don't know what I was expecting him to be driving—an older sports car, perhaps—but he stopped at a new, black Buick that had UVA and UNC stickers and North Carolina plates on it. I tried not to look surprised, and I rather thoughtlessly asked him if his father was a Republican. "No, He was a Labourite and a soldier, and now he's dead," he said.

Naturally I quickly told him I was sorry and assumed that he felt his loss as keenly as I felt the loss of my own parents.

"No matter," he said lightly. "That was so long ago that it's hard even to remember if I ever had a dad. I was just a lad when it happened. He was killed in the War," he concluded as he started the car. By my quick math, I concluded he was at least 34 and possibly older, but he didn't look it.

We drove out to Farmington and dined very well indeed. We had good wine and good conversation, but as if by mutual consent we held back from one another many of the facts of our lives. For example, I certainly didn't tell him about my current boyfriend. It was too nice a luncheon to spoil with such a small detail.

You may recall having once met Brad Miller, a fellow who had been my neighbor for about six years when we were children. At the time you met him, he was home for the summer after having finished his first year of law school. He was a big, heavy guy with thinning brown hair, blue eyes, and a self-confident, blustering, almost pushy manner. When he was a senior in high school and I was a junior, we had gone out once or twice. Years later—when I was home selling the house after my parents' deaths—we met again, and I started dating him again as part of my ongoing effort to fight off the blues.

Right off the bat, Brad had started talking about marriage in a vague, preliminary sort of way. I didn't discourage him, but after the first week or two of sleeping with him, I knew his fatal flaw. As my sister would have said, he was *bore-ring*. Still, it was easier to keep seeing him than to be alone or to find somebody else. I will confess, too, that we gave each other no small amount of pleasure, and you will recall that – all my other shortcomings aside—I did like my pleasures.

And he was steady. He was so steady that he thought it "perfect" for me to go to UVA while he went to work for the government in Washington. People like him belong in D.C.

Our relationship, then—at least from my point of view—was rather utilitarian. We would get together and cook great meals, get stoned, and have good and sometimes even great sex. It was a perfect 70s sort of relationship, I suppose.

Another good thing (or so I thought) about Brad was that he wasn't promiscuous and skittish like you were, for example. His predictable dullness seemed almost a virtue. I had begun to equate dullness with loyalty.

A young woman, though, can stand only so much boredom and virtue. Mark, the mysterious Englishman who knew how to feed me and how to intrigue me, was not boring. Therefore I thought it best not to allude to Brad.

We talked for hours, and our conversation was like fencing: thrust and parry. I tried to match his reticence with reticence of my own, but over the course of the afternoon, I realized that he knew much more about me than I did about him. I tried to dig out more of what Castanada might have termed his *personal history*, but he skillfully evaded me.

I assumed, of course, that he had a wife. What else could I think under the circumstances? I thought about that possibility and realized that I might sleep with him anyway—if he asked and if the spark of interest grew into something warmer. At that point I was interested, but hardly turned on.

So although we sat and talked all that long afternoon, all I knew about him was that he was from England, his parents were dead, and he lived with his uncle, Ned, in North Carolina. He said he had an airplane parts business of his own and that he had his own plane at the Charlottesville airport. Oddly enough, though, he didn't offer to take me flying. Obviously, most men would have done so had seduction been their object. Perhaps he, too, I concluded, was just lonely and wanted someone to talk with. *No harm in that*, I thought.

Finally, though, I began to be somewhat uneasy about him. His story—what little of it he told me—seemed not to fit together. Even his evasiveness seemed to have about it something profound, if not unsavory. Early in the meal I had thought about going to bed with him right away. By midafternoon something had slipped away—my trust, I guess. He felt it leave, too, and we got up to go. He left a huge tip on the table, and I knew or thought I knew: he was either married or he was a drug dealer. Or both.

Don't get me wrong: I hadn't become opposed to dealers who sold grass. For that matter, Brad dealt some and always liked for me to get high with him. Of course I did, but sometimes when we smoked he took on new dimensions of creepiness which would make me recoil from him. I never felt that with you, by the way.

Mark and I drove back to my apartment in silence. He walked me to the door and neither of us needed to say anything: he wasn't going to ask to come in. After a brief, awkward moment he tried to say what was on his mind.

"Eva," he started out in a rather high-pitched, indecisive voice, "perhaps I ought not to have asked you out today, but I couldn't help it." He broke off eye contact as he struggled through his embarrassment for the right words. I suddenly had the impression confirmed that he certainly was no ladies' man. Well, I was no Mata Hari myself.

He continued by saying something like, "I think you are very attractive and nice. Maybe you're too nice to get involved with me, and until you know me better, if you ever do, I should hope that you will reserve your judgement of me."

In the instant before he turned to go, he looked as if he might cry. He walked a step or two, then turned, and stammered,

"You're... you're lovely."

As the girl in *Oklahoma!* asked, *Whatcha gonna do when he talks that way? Spit in his eye?*

At that moment I knew that he was probably just another guilt-ridden married man, but I liked him anyway, and it *had* been a great lunch and an interesting afternoon. And he *was* quite handsome. All that, and he said I was lovely. Up to that point in my life not many men beside you had told me that, and we both knew you were lying.

So what could I do?

I stepped forward and kissed him. For a long minute, I pressed my lips softly to his and let him put his arms around me and squeeze me up against himself. I could feel his hunger for me, and I started feeling that old, warm, familiar hunger inside me, too.

I think it would almost be appropriate to say that we *tore ourselves apart from one another,* but that overstates things. It would be more accurate to say that neither of us wanted intellectually that which both of our bodies were beginning to demand.

I had learned some lessons about relationships prior to that time. Between the time I lived with you and the death of my parents, it had been altogether too easy for me to sleep with men. At one point I made a list of every "lover" I had known, but it embarrassed me and I threw it out.

After my sister and my parents died, though, something in me died, too, it seemed. I went for six months without even dating anyone and finally started seeing Brad. I must admit he helped me escape that deep feeling of disconnectedness I had felt, and for that I shall always be grateful to him.

During those promiscuous days before The Accident, though, I had learned some harsh lessons that made me want to keep my distance from Mark. I had been in love with a married man before.

It was two weeks before Mark finally confessed to me why he had been so reluctant with me that first day, and it hadn't been because he was married.

What happened was that I got tired of waiting for him to ask me out again, particularly since we kept looking at one another in class. Finally, I invited him over for supper. When I did, he seemed relieved, and he accepted. I wore a white blouse and a plaid skirt with flats that night. I was being conservative and cautious, you see.

At first we talked about our classes and some of our fellow students. This was not just a matter of avoiding a discussion of our "relationship", for we shared a deep fascination for the life and languages of the ancient Mediterranean world. We had read many of the same books and were hopelessly addicted to watching movies that depicted classical times. *Cleopatra* and *Ben Hur* were among our favorites. I cooked spaghetti, and we drank red wine in moderation. He was more comfortable with me than he had been before and I was beginning to more attracted to him even if he was still being mysterious.

After two hours of pleasant talk, we knew that the Big Issue would have to be discussed, one way or another.

I had more or less presumed that we would end up on the sofa, but he never made the moves to get me away from the table.

"There are great barriers between us," he said at last, when we had temporarily exhausted conversation.

That remark grated on me. I was in the mood for love.

"Damnit! Please don't tell me now that you are gay or something," I blurted out. I had stepped on that nail before, too.

Even in the candlelight I could see his blush. "Certainly not!" he exclaimed with some anger in his voice. The record had stopped and it was suddenly very quiet in the house. He stood up rather suddenly as if he might leave. I arose, and he stepped toward me.

"I didn't mean to..." I began to say, touching his arm lightly with my fingertips for emphasis.

Suddenly he was up against me and his arms were around me. We kissed, but I pulled my head back from his. "Wait," I said without conviction. I felt his hands slip up under my shirt behind me. They were warm, smooth, and strong, more powerful than I had thought they would be. His fingers did their offices on my hooks and buttons, and as we looked in one another's eyes, gently he pushed my shirt off of my shoulders. I shrugged off my bra. Then he held me by my upper arms and softly we kissed again as we pressed tenderly against each other. I started breathing more rapidly as I switched on to "automatic".

All I could do, it seemed, was to respond to him, even though I still knew that I wasn't ready for him emotionally. I kissed back, enjoying the feel of his hands as they began to explore my body. The whole apartment was cozy and warm from the oven, and was rich with the fragrances of food, perfumes and candles.

Of course I had that sort of vague notion that I could stop him if he went too far, but he sure hadn't gotten that far yet, I thought. But he made no move to go farther and we just stood there kissing in the half-light of the candles, me stripped to the waist. Finally we stopped and I looked in his face. He was fighting back tears.

"I think we have to have a serious talk," I said, backing away from him. Reluctantly he let me go, and looked at my body quite frankly across the yard that separated us.

"Yes we do, Eva," he said looking into my eyes. He was in turmoil, and he turned to the window.

I bent down to pick up my clothes in the silence. I started to put on my blouse. "Leave it off, please," he said hoarsely without turning around. "You look so beautiful in the nude. Shall we have some music and some more wine?"

Again, it may sound silly as I recount it now years later: how I put on another record and poured more wine. I took him his glass. By the time I gave it to him, he was calm and in control of himself once again. He turned to me and gave me a quick, cheerful kiss. When I didn't back off from him, he smiled the warmest of his smiles. He could see that he hadn't spoiled things between us—and that I was still waiting for kisses and explanations. He kept telling me over and over how lovely I was. Normally I would have felt big, fat and dumpy, and would have partly hidden myself with my hands. But as we stood there he kept looking at and touching my face, my skin and my hair as if I were some amazing beauty. Finally he let me go. There was a look of despair on his face.

We sat down across the table from one another. I was sensitive in the extreme to the damp, cool spots where he had kissed my breasts and I could feel goose bumps and a certain stiffening all over.

I start off with the commonplace—a man meeting a woman at grad school. Then there is the sublime: the kiss. Then there is the ridiculous: me sitting half-naked in my apartment with a man who is not yet even my lover, drinking wine.

"You have me at a disadvantage—conversationally speaking, that is," I said to him. "You take your shirt off, too." I didn't know whether to fold my arms, sit up straight, or what. I settled for lounging back on the chair with my chin up. He didn't argue with me. He was lean and smooth with just a little chest hair.

"Now that we are settled down a bit," he began, "I can't say much, but I am not in any kind of trouble with the law. I haven't a wife or children. I have some money and intend to be very careful about it and very private in my life generally."

"I can accept that."

"I should also tell you that because of my business interests I could quit school and go abroad—perhaps as soon as next spring."

I sipped some wine. "I can accept that. Spring is a long time off," I added.

"And I am quite lonely. I don't have a lover or a girlfriend of any kind these days, except for you, and haven't had one for a painfully long time. You see, I take all that sort of thing very seriously."

He reached across the table and took my hand. As I leaned forward to take his, my breast knocked over a water glass. We laughed.

"A drawback of being big," I said, thankful for levity. I blushed a little, I suppose, then thought about my face with its large, straight nose and wished I was prettier.

"Who knows?" I offered. "Maybe it's time for being serious about this sort of thing."

"Maybe so," he said, "We can't go any farther with all of this; this dining together, holding hands, kissing, and sitting around like this. I hate to say such things, but I must be fair."

His face looked so serious that I felt sorry for him.

"I haven't been leading you on or anything like that," he continued. "I just can't help myself, I want you so badly. But it wouldn't be fair to you, maybe not even to me, if we slept together."

"I'm a big girl; I can handle it," I said, practically feeling the surge of his sex in his fingertips. It was a facile thing for me to say, and yet I knew that maybe I wasn't such a big girl after all, and maybe there was something I really couldn't handle. I was beginning to realize that there was something dangerous about Mark, and I had always thought of myself as a coward, at least in matters involving physical danger. Suddenly I found myself much more attracted to him. I imagined he was a man who could kill if he needed to.

"Maybe you could handle it," he said. "Just maybe you could," he added for emphasis. "You must clearly see that I am falling in love with you, of course."

"I can handle that."

I could practically feel a current pass between us. My motor was running and he knew it. I was his on a plate, secrets and all. I could feel the goosebumps on my breasts and thighs. I imagined that he was already erect. A long minute passed in silence as looked into one another's eyes.

"I must leave now," he suddenly declared as his rose quickly from his chair. I was too astonished to say anything. I guess I'd never before had a man get to that stage with me only to turn me down. He was putting on his shirt.

"Don't leave now, for Christ's sake!" I exclaimed, standing up. It made me sound weak but I didn't care. "You can't just get me here like this and *leave!* What's fair about that?" I asked, holding his arm.

"Look, Eva, I told you I'm falling in love with you. I told you everything I could, all right? It just won't work, but I want us to be friends."

"No, it's not *all right!*" I said sharply. "You owe me something better than this."

"Yes I do. And I'm sorry. I truly am," he said. He was convincing, even pitiful.

"O.K." I said, letting him go. "Just leave!"

I started to cry big, copious tears that squirted out like a child's. I turned to go to the bedroom and he reached for me. "Just leave," I repeated bitterly as I snatched myself away and ran down the hall.

I threw myself face down on the bed in a fit of self-pity. I cried about Mark and about my relationship with Brad, about my parents and my sister. I cried because I wasn't prettier or happier or less lonely.

All the while I could hear noises in the dining room and knew he hadn't left. For all I cared, he could have been tearing the place up or getting drunk. Presently, though, he came and sat beside me on the bed, where I was lying face down. He didn't say anything, just stroked my hair and my back as he would have stroked a cat. It was dark in the room and we stayed like that for a long time. I would not turn to face him, but he didn't ask me to.

"I'm going to go now," he finally said, "but only because I don't want to put you into any kind of danger. You could get in trouble associating with me. Just remember that the only reason I'm leaving is because if I don't leave now, I won't be able to later."

I wasn't watching his face, but I believed him. I knew that he was making some sort of sacrifice for my benefit and protection and not his own.

He got up and left the room. I got up and followed and watched from the darkened hallway as he put on his coat. I could see that he had cleaned off the table and done the dishes while I had been crying. He was not looking back at me, but he looked sad and beaten. He opened the door and went out.

I called out his name when it shut. I ran to the door, opened it and ran outside where his car was parked. It was his turn to be astonished.

"You forgot to thank me for the dinner," I said as he opened his arms for me. I kissed him again, then whispered in his ear, "Let's not give up—not yet. I'll wait."

He whispered in mine. "I won't wait if there is a next time. I won't be able to. But it could mean your life. You'd better think about that first!"

We looked into each other's eyes. "Everything has a price," I said before kissing him again. I let him go and crossed my arms.

"Even knowledge," he said in Greek.

He walked down to the curb to his car and drove away. The chill wind blew and reminded me that I was in the front yard of the apartments without a shirt on. I crossed my arms over myself. As I went back inside I noticed that my next door neighbor, a woman in her 30s, was watching me from her front window. Cheerfully letting go of myself, I waved.

For a week I waited and watched. Mark and I were

friendly to one another, but distant, like two predators circling a common kill. It amused me to see that he started paying attention to another student in our class, one who was very pretty, very slender, and very married. In the lounge I would see them together and hear their amiable chatter, replete with flirtation and sexual innuendo. I remember you reading *Women in Love* in bed one night and exclaiming "meretricious persiflage!" when you came across Lawrence's use of that phrase. That's all it was between them, and anyone could have seen through it. His eyes kept coming back to mine. Almost imperceptibly, I would square back my shoulders so that my sweaters would look even more full and his eyes would flicker down.

So I circled and thought and watched.

Although he had said that he was not in trouble with the law, I thought he might be a dealer or perhaps something more sinister, like a bank robber. It also occurred to me that he might work for the DEA or the CIA or some other governmental agency or perhaps even a foreign government. My curiosity grew daily, and I knew in my heart that he wasn't one of those kinds of men who pretended to dangerous things. He had been too personal with me for that, and too concerned with my welfare.

I saw Brad over the weekend. Being with him exacerbated my craving for something more from life than his type of man he could offer me. Then, too, his block-headed self-satisfaction threw Mark's torment into bolder relief. As soon as he left on Sunday afternoon, I took a long shower to wash him off of me. I wanted to talk to Mark. No, I wanted Mark, and I knew it, but I didn't know his phone number or where he lived.

I knew what I wanted. I wanted action, reality, danger, and sex. I thought of my family and how I might soon be gone, too. Why not then, I pondered, live closer to the edge? When I was 11—before I became a woman—I dreamed of high adventure, of Africa and safaris and mountain climbing. I can remember that even before I had my first period, I had started disliking my oncoming womanliness for the restraints that it might put upon me and for the dreams it might make impossible to fulfill.

I studied Latin in high school and read Plutarch late into

the night, particularly enjoying re-reading his account of the last days of Antony and Cleopatra. Those were the days, and through Mark, they had returned. I was bold again and it felt good.

On the Monday after Brad visited, I took Mark aside and told him that I had thought about what he had said. I told him I thought we ought to discuss it more at my house over supper on Wednesday evening.

"We have said all that we can say without your going over a precipice with me, Eva," he said in a way that made him seem older and wiser than I was.

I quoted one of the Greeks: *Those who would live, must. The fearful, too, must die.*

He smiled and replied in Latin: *Caveat Emptor!*

"That does not tell me whether or not you will come to dinner Wednesday."

"You mean 'come for you,' don't you?"

"Yes, that's exactly what I mean," I replied. His face was close to mine. We were conversing in low voices in the hallway. The beautiful, married girl was waiting down the hallway for him to join her.

"Then the answer is No."

"Then I'll have it ready at seven," I said, smiling at him and knowing with a warm, familiar feeling in my stomach that men in love are weak creatures.

Tuesday was a study day with no classes. On Wednesday, we did not speak to each other at all, and only exchanged glances once or twice. Beneath his facade of diffidence, he looked like a hungry puppy. I started cooking at 6 p.m.

At 6:30 the doorbell rang and I went with my apron on and floured hands, thinking it would be my neighbor. It was Mark. He squared his shoulders back and bravely said, "I just came by to tell you I'm leaving town for a few days."

"Oh, did you?" I asked with a smile, happy that he had in fact arrived. I could see him waver and I waited. I knew what he was going to do. He came in, defeated and relieved, reluctant yet eager. I took his hand in mine and led him to my bedroom.

As if we were pleasantly drowning together, we went down into one of those confusions of senses and flesh that humans love so much. Eventually we came up for air.

"Even now, it's not too late," he said, as we lay upon the bed beneath the blankets.

I kissed him again. "Oh, yes: it is too late, far too late, Mark," I said as I looked into his eyes. "Now you must tell me what you need to tell me even if you must kill me because I then know too much. It is only the Way of the World. I would understand."

"No, my Sweet Love," he said tenderly. "I would never harm you. But many others would, if you join with me."

"What are you, then, Mark?" I asked. "A bank robber, a spy, a dealer, or what? Remember: You can tell me, then kill me."

I already knew he wouldn't kill me. Nevertheless, I reached across him to the bedside table and pulled out my father's .38. I put it on his chest, cold and heavy, pointed in my direction. I laid down beside him again, propped myself up on one elbow, and looked in his eyes.

It was too much for him: he began to cry out of pure happiness and emotion.

He put the gun aside, and we held each other close. His tears wet my forehead and rolled into my eyes.

"This either hurts so badly or feels so well that I can hardly bear it," he said at last. "I have never been in love before. I'm practically a virgin, at least in some ways," he continued. I just held him.

"Now that finally I am in love, though, I bring with me to my beloved the seeds of her own destruction."

"I am not afraid of possibilities. Everything is a possibility: even love."

Carefully he gathered his words.

"I have lived with great secrets too long, Eva, and now if you insist, I will share them with you.

"I am not a bank robber, nor a spy, but I am a pilot, and I have made a lot of money bringing in marijuana over the last four years. I am pretty much retired from that now."

I was so relieved, I couldn't believe it.

"Well, it's hard work but somebody's got to do it," I kidded. "Your secret is safe with me."

"That's not the secret."

"So, you *are* married, then."

"No, I am not married," he insisted. "I told you I was practically a virgin."

"So?" I kidded again. "Lots of married people are practically virgins. Anyway, I find that hard to believe. You're too healthy and normal for that."

He kissed me and got out of bed. "Yes, I'm normal in that way. Oh, I've had some women down in South America from time to time, and I used to pick up an occasional one-night stand here, but that was too dangerous."

"Yeah, I'll bet!"

"No, I don't mean disease and all that, I mean discovery and danger. Like the kind of danger you'll be in if you stay with me," he said.

He arose to put on his clothes. His body was so smooth in the subdued light that it looked like a moving marble statue.

"Mark," I said, sharply enough to get his attention, "I'm going with you all the way. I mean, if you're not a real criminal or just insane or a real shitass."

He looked at me and smiled. He pulled up a chair and sat next to the bed and held my hand between his.

"Except for being a dope smuggler and a tax evader and an illegal immigrant, I'm really not a criminal," he said, gently smiling at me in a way that I would have found condescending, except that he was being so open and without guile.

"Now as to whether or not I'm a shitass: well, that's something for you to decide.

"But if I tell you everything," he said, "then you will think I'm crazy, and you'll think that I am a liar and a forger."

"I might, but I don't think so," I said. He was almost completely dressed. "Don't leave," I added, throwing aside the covers for emphasis.

What's he going to do when *you* act that way? He leaned down and kissed my body in several places.

"Don't you worry about that," he said. "I'm just going to get some things out of the car. By the way, would you like to smoke a number?"

"Maybe just a little one. Shall I put on dinner, get dressed, or what?"

"No. Stay like that. I'll be right back." He seemed like a happy boy who has finally gotten something he wants.

So I stayed there until he came back with an old blue leather dispatch pouch that had "RAF" and golden wings embossed on it. He set it down on the bed beside me.

Silently we smoked half a joint, and drank some ice water. Then he took off his clothes again and came to me. He moved on top of me, gently supporting most of his weight on his elbows, caressing me and holding my face in his hands. I had no idea what he was going to say or do, but I was practically melted back down into the bed with loving anticipation of our encore lovemaking. I could feel him stiffen on my belly. I was aroused. He had my full attention.

"Do you trust me to tell you the truth?" he asked.

Yes I said. I could feel that he was already hard.

"Will you hear me out and reserve judgement until I'm finished?" he asked.

I nodded. I could feel him throbbing against my abdomen. I was surprised to discover that I was deeply aroused by the sense of danger and foreboding that he brought with him.

"Yes," I said, half choking.

"And whether you believe me or not, do you swear on the graves of your parents and sister never to tell anyone what I am about to tell you so long as either I or my uncle is alive?"

I nodded.

"No: *Swear!*" He knew that keeping one's word meant a lot to me.

Looking straight into his blue eyes, I said, "I swear on the graves of my sister and my parents that I shall not tell a living soul what you are about to tell me—even if I don't believe it—so long as either you or your uncle Ned is alive. So help me God!"

He brought himself into position and I opened for him.

"Do you love me enough to keep loving me no matter what I say?"

I said *yes*, and he entered me.

He and his uncle are dead now, and I am released from my oath.

****

III

The Truth

Perhaps I should say, it felt wonderful to have him that time, but the significant thing about that second time was the story that came with it. In a very real sense, what we did that second time was not sex at all—at least not to begin with. It was ceremony. Like a willing victim in some ancient fertility rite, I was impaled, and although we lay gently joined together in a side-by-side position and talked, it was sexual mainly because that which had been separating us emotionally was about to dissolve. Then I would be, he said, in great danger. His voice was as thick with emotion as his body was with his blood.

"My Christian name *is* Mark. My surname is Powell. I was born in Kent in 1915. My mother was from Cambridge and died in the 1940 Blitz. My father died in 1918 in France. That would, of course, make me 64 years old, which, as you can plainly see, I am not.

"I have told you of my uncle, Ned. He was born in 1895, which would, of course, make him 84 years old, which he is not.

"You are astonished and think that I am insane. It's not enough for me to say that I am not, nor to show you my RAF papers and my original passport, but here they are."

"No one but you has seen them since 1939. That's when we made what we call 'The Jump'."

I glanced at both the small flight book and the passport. They looked authentic. He was about 20 in the pictures. I looked at his face. *Go on*, I said gently.

"I have thought how I should tell you all of this: how we should...*position* ourselves first. I have practiced what I should say, and in what order, should this time come. Here we are.

"My Uncle Ned is a scientist of the highest caliber. Before the War—the Great War, that is—he was already at Oxford. He flew planes in 1916 and was wounded several times and ended up working in secret weapons projects of various sorts. He has worked with some of the greatest geniuses of the 20th century, including Neils Bohr and Einstein.

"Because of the nature of his work—which continued right up to the Second War—he never gained recognition for his discoveries and his work on Wave Theory.

"By 1938 I was flying for the RAF and working on what was supposed to be primitive radar evasion equipment that Ned had installed on an airplane. We worked together, just the two of us, testing Ned's secret airborne apparatus. The first time we tested it skipped us forward in time for an instant.

"Later--in April of 1939-- we tried it again and made a dreadful miscalculation. We skipped forward, not for a day as we had planned, but for three decades, and we landed not off the West Coast of Wales, but in the United States."

I said nothing. If he was crazy, then he had me, I thought. But he had me from the start of the evening and now, even if he were totally insane, I could help him, I could share in it and ease his heart. I closed my eyes and felt a strange, overwhelming compassion for him. I kissed him again and urged him to lose himself in me, which he did. Then he slept.

As he slept, I thought about all he had said with a feeling of pathos. I looked at the faint wrinkles around his eyes and recalled something of the past in them. With a start I thought, *pilot's eyes*! And I saw in his sleeping features the faces of Earhart and Lindberg and my Uncle Joseph who was lost in Viet Nam.

Then I saw it. Across his chest from me lay the blue book with the golden, winged seal. Suddenly I felt a cold chill as it dawned upon me that neither the log book, nor the cover of it, nor the little wrinkles around the naked young pilot's closed eyes were forgeries. As I reached for the booklet I remembered what he had said.

I opened it and there was Mark, but younger and without the little crinkles of a thousand bright runways. If the book was forged, it was an excellent job, but I knew the truth, and I am telling it to you in this roundabout way because I had to lead you into it even as Mark led me into it:

They had skipped forward in time.

I lay back upon the pillow looking at every page, at

every notation and stamp, at the watermarks of the paper and the printer's name on the leather.

As they saying goes, *his papers were in order.*

I could not really comprehend it all. My heart pounded heavily in my chest and my blood roared in my ears. I don't know how long I was like that. I must have fainted or somehow fallen asleep. Then I woke and stared at the ceiling.

I was startled when he spoke.

"Don't even say whether you believe me fully yet or not. Reserve your judgement until you meet Ned and have seen the plane," he offered with his fingertips upon my lips. "Of course, he will be very cross that I've told you."

I kissed his fingers and took them away from my face. "Do you mind if I ask some questions--just for the sake of argument?" I asked warily.

"Not at all," he said. "I expect questions and more questions from you until there is nothing left to question. I accepted that some time back when I knew I loved you and thought about what I would have to tell you."

"Well, first," I said, shifting about to rest my head upon my hand so that I could look in his eyes for any speckle of insanity that might glimmer there, "assuming two men did what you said, why would they be in danger? Wouldn't such a feat be considered to be a marvelous scientific accomplishment? "

"Like the atomic bomb, perhaps?"

"I was thinking more of Lindberg's crossing the Atlantic," I countered.

"A thrilling stunt, you mean? It was thrilling— Lindberg's flight, that is. It sure excited me back in '27," he said, looking into my eyes, doubtlessly to see if fear of him came into them. "I had just turned 12," he reminded me.

"Continue."

"No: this is deep, serious danger: Not only would men kill us for what we know, but so would governments— particularly yours. If the CIA or the Army knew about us—and that includes *you* now—they would arrest us immediately. The three of us would just disappear, and it would all be in the interests of National Security."

I started to object, to say that the American government

wasn't that kind of a government. Even if he did have such a plane and had done such a thing, everything would be all right, and he ought not have such fears. But you don't have to be much of an historian to know that we *do* have that kind of a government, and that they could and would do all of those sorts of things, and that Mark and Ned would be in danger, if it was true. And if it was true—this story—then obviously I had just stepped out of society and into the most select group of potential fugitives in the world. Suddenly a wave of fear swept over me and I almost threw up. I turned way from him as my mind tried to grasp all the implications of what he had told me. *Perhaps he is just crazy*, I hoped.

He let me think about the things he had said for a few minutes. Then he reached out and pulled me back against him, turning me as he did so that my face was against his smooth chest. He stroked my hair as if I were a child, and I began to feel better. I became aware that a peculiar roaring in my ears was subsiding.

"And so you discover at last," he continued gently, "that you have indeed gotten into something very dangerous. You are from this hour on a woman without a country. I can absolutely prove everything I am saying—and you know it. You can go with me to North Carolina this weekend to meet Ned. You can see the plane. You can decide whether or not you want to go with us when we leave. But there's no turning back for you—not now."

I knew he was right. I could see clearly that there wasn't any turning back, any pretending as if I hadn't heard what he had told me. If he was crazy enough to invent such a tale and the forgeries that supported it, he would be crazy enough to kill me to defend it.

"If you were to 'turn us in'," he continued, "they will take you in, too. To them the truth would be too dangerous. You would be locked away." I knew he was right about that.

"Where will you go?" I asked. "Where in the wide world could you hide?"

"There is nowhere in this world that is safe—and nowhere that we want to go. No, we are leaving forever, and not to the future. After all," he said wistfully, "we've already done that and we lost ground."

"What do you mean, *'lost ground'*?" I asked, turning to face him. He looked sad.

"My Darling, the world of 1939 England was in many ways far better than that of the 1972 America into which we came. Perhaps I should never be able to explain it, nor you to feel it, but there it is. Have you read many accounts of the War? We missed out on the war."

"But you could have been killed!"

"Yes, I could have, but at least I would have died in a fight for a great cause and in the defense of what was then my country. Better that than in some secret American prison or by the hand of a government thug.

"You have no idea how it has been for me since 1972, for since the day I arrived, I've been living with the constant fear of capture. You'll soon feel that way, too, now that you're in it with us.

"And the modern world isn't all it's cracked up to be either. Why do you think the older generation looks back with such nostalgia? Something has been lost, and I don't know how it's happened or what have been the causes.

"I suspect that the War itself lies at the heart of things, ending with America and the British Empire allied with the Soviets. All that blood and all that waste!

"Now your world of spies and acronyms, your CIA, FBI, NSA, KGB, DEA! It's all one piece to your intrepid time travelers, you see.

"And, God knows, television and mass marketing, and global communications and all that flotsam of the modern world's ideologies make men limp with exhaustion when they try to find some decency and civilization in it. All modern man seems to get out of it is more sexual promiscuity, x-rated movies, and penicillin.

"And the future looks worse," he concluded bitterly.

I had to agree with him.

I suggested that perhaps women were better off.

"Don't bet on it. At least the middle and upper class girls I knew in England in the '30s were happier by far than girls are today. For one thing, men treated them better. Oh, am I supposed to say 'women' these days?" I shrugged my shoulders.

"So what are you going to do now? Or, rather, what are

we going to do now?" I asked. "In addition to enjoying modern promiscuity, that is," I added snuggling into his chest.

"That is the real question," he told me. "We do have a plan of escape; the question is not *where* but *when*? Ned has now modified his device so that the airplane can probably take us back in time."

"I thought that, too, was impossible," I said. "What do you mean by *probably*?"

"The world thought traveling forward in time was impossible. Then Einstein introduced his theories, and it learned that through the mechanics of speed one can bypass time, as it were.

"But Ned Powell has found another way of traveling through time. By manipulating tangible objects in fields or something like that, we can move relative to the seemingly slow, waving pulse of time. I don't understand it and don't want to. He assures me that it is the most obscure notion imaginable. He also thinks it's incredibly dangerous. It holds out the possibility of historical tampering."

"Tampering?"

"Of course. Going back and killing Hitler in 1919. That sort of thing. Who could trust the CIA or KGB with such an invention?

"After five years of thought and computerization of our old controls, Ned has come to the conclusion that we can go back in time if we chose to try it.

"Naturally, that may be impossible, don't you see: How could the very atoms of which we consist exist at the same time but in different places, for example?

"That's just one theoretical consideration, but we are convinced that to stay here is to continue to risk capture and imprisonment. We've been skillful and lucky so far.

"What we do assume is that it would be impossible to go back to a time during this century, for we couldn't conceivably exist in two places at once, could we? Also, what's done is done. They won the war without us or our machine. Everything is resolved, for better or worse.

"Even if the plane goes backward in time perfectly there is no guarantee that we would not breakup in flight or upon reentry. Then, too, there is always a great possibility that if we survive the time travel, we might find ourselves in space, or far out to sea, or under it, for that matter."

Needless to say, I had never contemplated these questions before. Once again it was all sounding absurd.

"Well, even if all you say is true and your machine will work again—where will you go?" I asked.

"Where would you go if it was one way and you should have to live out your life there?"

I thought about that long and hard, but came back to my original inspiration.

"To ancient Greece," I said.

"Periclean Greece, to be exact," he said.

****

IV

The Short of It

Ned Powell had known from the beginning what he was about when he invented the machine that had brought him and Mark forward in time. His discoveries and inventions were not accidental but came about as a result of his diligence, persistence, and hard work. For two decades he had worked out the theoretical physics and practical electronic and mechanical problems of forward time travel. To his credit, and after having witnessed firsthand many examples of the misapplication of scientific knowledge, he had not neglected to consider the political and social ramifications of time travel. He therefore had predetermined his course of action should his invention finally work, and it was to further that plan that he had insisted on having his nephew as his pilot when experimentation finally began.

I should explain that during 1938 as it belatedly prepared for war, the British government began providing Ned a

Coastal Command flying boat as a test platform for his radar avoidance experiments. Since 1937 it had been obvious to the developers of the first radar sets that since it was possible to locate distant aircraft by radio detection waves, then it was at least theoretically possible to develop countermeasures. As one of the country's leading physicists, Ned was part of the research and development efforts, and after having made numerous theoretical and practical contributions to the developing science of radar, he began working independently on the family's small estate east of London. The Powell family's electronics business financed all of the development costs of the apparatus, and thus Ned was free to work in secrecy without having to submit to government oversight. Finally, too, he had the time and the means to develop his own device—one which he thought might make forward time travel possible.

One should understand that the acquisition of the flying boat was an essential part of the plan since as I understand such things, being aloft at the time of the jump is absolutely critical— as is being able to come back down safely.

By 1939, Mark's once-large, immediate family consisted only of him, his mother, and Ned, his uncle on his father's side. They had a home in London as well as an estate in Surrey as well as an electronics and radio factory in Coventry that had been in the family since 1905. The firm had been highly successful during the First World War and provided the technological and financial basis for Ned's scientific work.

Like most boys of his class and generation, Mark had attended an English public school—a painful and brutal experience designed, one must suppose, to fit Englishmen to a life of duty and service to the nation. As a child he had been standoffish and painfully shy and had excelled only in Greek, Latin, and Art. At eighteen he began taking private flying lessons and was, according to Ned, quite a natural-born pilot. At the age of twenty he had used his connections to secure a commission in the RAF. As I have said, he flew combat missions against the fascists during the Spanish Civil War. By 1938 he was back in England assigned to work with Ned on their highly secret project.

On a rainy Spring day in 1939, they carried out their first test of what was called an RDA or Radio Detection

Avoidance apparatus. An invention Ned had been working on for some six years, it seemed simple enough. Hardly larger than a console television of the 1970s, the basic "black box" from which the wires and antenna ran was mounted in the cargo area of an RAF twin-engine Short Flying Boat, a much smaller version of the huge, four-engine Short Sunderland that was used for patrol work during the Second World War. For power, Ned's machine drew directly upon the airplane's own electrical system to provide the surge of current that supposedly was meant to cloak it from radar detection.

At first glance, the external appearance of the plane was unaltered, but upon closer inspection, one could see it was covered with a fine mesh of thin gold-plated copper wire that looked like chickenwire. The netting completely encased the plane except for the propellers that were themselves gold-plated. Although the wire was light enough, it caused so much aerodynamic drag that the efficiency of the airplane was severely compromised.

For security reasons, only Ned and Mark flew the plane during its tests. Like many men in England, they were acutely aware of the imminence of war with Germany and knew the importance of air defense measures in general and of the newly-developed science of radar in particular. Adherents of the foreign policies urged by Eden, Churchill, and others, they had been deeply ashamed of Chamberlain's 1938 sellout of Czechoslovakia at Munich, a sellout they knew committed Britain either to war or eventual, ignominious capitulation.

Ned knew that he was working on the greatest project of his career, but he kept the true nature of his invention and the theories upon which it was based secret even from Mark. His explanations of how the proposed electronic cloaking would work were so vague that neither Mark nor his colleagues believed that the machine would work.

On that first, fateful trip, they took the Short up to about 15,000 feet before heading on a bearing southeasterly over the English Channel. At a precise, prearranged moment while they were still in radio contact with a coastal RDF station that was tracking the flight, Ned went back and "bumped" the RDA's control switch. There was a flash of light, but the plane flew on. Mark assumed that the mesh had shorted out instantaneously.

Immediately after the flash, though, the Short experienced a brief but violent turbulence. After checking the instruments and making sure that the plane was once again flying normally, Mark looked out at the sky and was astonished to see that below him there had been a vast change in the types of cloud formations from those over which he had been flying. After a bit more confusion that came as a result of checking the sun's position against the compass reading, he reached forward to toggle the switch to send a routine message to the RDF station.

Ned's hand stopped his. In his eyes was excitement and something akin to passion and even tears. The older man took off his flying mask.

"I have done it!" he shouted over the noise of the engines. "I have done it—what no other man has ever done!"

Mark was astonished at the older man's uncharacteristic display of enthusiasm and told him to put his mask back on.

But instead of doing as Mark asked, Ned checked the compass and other instruments, then picked up binoculars and scanned the horizon.

"The bloody hell you say," he shouted to the younger man. "I've done it! Look again at the magnetic compass. It's not broken. Here," he said, as he handed Mark the binoculars, "take her down and tell me where we are."

They descended to 10,000 feet and Mark scanned the horizon himself. To the southeast in the distance he could see what appeared to be tall snow-capped mountains.

"What is that? A mirage?" he asked dumbly.

"Nephew, if I do not miss my guess, those are the Alps!"

Mark was skeptical, of course, but it was the Alps he saw, for in that brief moment they had skipped lightly over a wave of time and had come out some 300 miles east of the English Channel.

It was not difficult for Ned to convince him of what had happened, for the proofs of what they had done were obvious. The implications were more ominous—particularly since they were over Germany.

"Righto:" Ned confirmed as he took the wheel and put the plane into a long shallow dive, "and now we must scurry back to school before we are caught out!"

They had skipped through time. Not a lot of time: just a brief flash of it, just a speck of it. But they had disappeared entirely from the Folkestone RDF radar screen and "waited" while the earth turned "beneath" them.

Naturally enough, on their return to England, they did not tell the truth of what they had done to anyone, but invented a story that explained how they had gotten lost and had spent the night floating on the sea.

Their second time travel was carefully planned to involve a skip forward of longer duration that was supposed to pass them "over" a few thousand miles. They planned for all contingencies except for the one that occurred.

During the weeks before the second attempt was to be made, they converted much of their savings to gold coins and five-pound notes in case they landed far away, and they loaded up extra fuel, survival rations, and both arctic and tropical clothing and gear. They carried aerial navigation charts of practically the entire world.

According to Ned's calculations—which were really just wild guesses—they could easily emerge from a brief flight through time in an inverted position, flying directly into a mountain, or irredeemably lost over some vast continent or ocean. He also admitted that there was a possibility that the Short might emerge in outer space, left behind by a speeding solar system. Therefore they also prepared for the possibility that they might not ever return.

Ned did so by writing a will and giving other complete instructions to his solicitor. Mark's preparations consisted primarily of seducing his fiancée and withdrawing all of his meager savings from the bank.

When the day finally came for their second and more ambitious test—the one that was to have taken them around the world in a twinkling of an eye—they flew out once again from Dover. They climbed to 17,000 feet, going above the clouds to a clear and sunny sky. After a final radio contact with 1939, Ned toggled the switch.

Almost immediately something went wrong. After the initial flash, they felt the heavy g-pressures that one identifies with steep banking and sharp turns in flight. Mark switched on the instrument lights. He realized that the plane was losing electrical power and that his engines were dying from having instantly sucked the cabin's atmosphere free of oxygen. Instantaneously the plane filled with exhaust gasses. Both men turned on emergency oxygen.

Shifts in air pressure caused both men to howl with pain as their eardrums surged out. Mark watched in awe as Ned calmly threw the paddle switch. The whole incident took only a few seconds.

Suddenly they were back in time, the fuselage filled with smoke. The engines were still rotating and came back to life. The plane was in a slight bank relative to the direction of its travel, and as the tail bit into the air, they were snatched about roughly as the airframe corrected for pitch, yaw, and roll. A glance told them that the Short's airspeed was approximately the same as it had been when they had left England. They were back in time, but it wasn't their time and they didn't yet realize it.

Experienced pilots, they first got the plane under control and checked for damage. They opened the windows to clear the cabin. Then, excitedly, they looked down to see that they were flying above a heavily forested, hilly land.

"Are we over Russia?" Mark asked.

"No," said Ned. "Look there. We must be over Germany again. Is that not what they call *der autobahn?*"

Then they saw their first jet airliner, and, over their radio, began hearing traffic in English—unmistakable American English.

They descended, changing radio channels, listening to it, and seeing with their eyes that which was obvious. They had flown forward into time—perhaps several years—and they were over the southeastern United States.

The implications bore down on them as they descended. They did not talk with one another just then, but thought of all they had left behind: their country in its time of peril, their friends, and Mark's mother and fiancée. But what could be done about that?

They landed the plane in an empty arm of a large reservoir somewhere in North Carolina. Ned stayed with the plane while Mark walked to a town they had seen from the air. Wearing civilian clothes—outdated though they were—he walked through the woods to a two-lane highway and started walking eastward.

As he walked, the sights he saw amazed him—particularly the cars and trucks. Soon he came to the town. Keeping to himself as he walked down the main street, he found what he was looking for—a newspaper box with the current edition behind clear plastic. It was the Asheville newspaper: July 15, 1972! Thirty-three years! He was horrified and overwhelmed and could not decide whether to laugh or cry. Two hours before he had taken off from 1939 England. He comforted himself with the fact that he had at least landed in an English-speaking country.

To passersby he must have appeared to be somewhat odd or lost. A middle-aged black man, obviously concerned about his condition, offered aid in a dialect he could only barely understand. "No. No. I'm all right," he said, waving him off.

He sat on a public bench thinking. He wanted to run up to people he saw and ask, "Was there a war?" and "Who won?" He had other questions to ask, too, but those were the main ones. He stiffened when he saw a policeman looking at him. He looked at his watch as if he were waiting for someone, then casually strolled off down the street. The cop didn't follow him.

He came upon the town bank. He entered it and approached a young woman behind a desk.

"I'd like to change some old money—English money—if I might," he asked.

"Let me get Mr. Jackson," she said, smiling sweetly at him. He resisted the urge to run. He did not know whether or not his fivers had value or, for that matter, whether the bank could take gold coins. But he did know that he would need money before he could take his next step.

"May I help you?" a pleasant, 40ish man asked.

"What can you give me for these, please? I haven't had them valued," Mark said, passing four five-pound notes to the man.

"Why, these are from before the war! Sir, you might get more for them from some kind of collector than from a bank."

"I should rather have some cash for them now, sir," he replied, realizing that perhaps he had spoken in too much haste and that the banker might think that he had stolen them.

"Who won the war?" was what he wanted to shout.

"They belonged to my family," he said vaguely.

"Well, yes. An they certainly are in good condition: just like new! We'll see what we can do. Frankly, we don't even have a way of knowing whether they are genuine or not. I think the Germans made up counterfeit during the war." *So there had been a war.*

"Could you take a couple of these, then?" Mark asked as he produced two gold sovereigns.

He could see the banker's eyes light up when the money gleamed before them. He called over another, younger banker over to admire the coins, drawing unwelcome attention to the transaction.

"May I examine them?" Jackson asked politely. He dropped them on the desk and listened to the clear sounds they made.

"I know something about coins, young man," he said with a smile, "and these are as good as, well, gold. I'll buy these myself."

Mark was prepared to be swindled—or at least to be taken advantage of. He was, however, pleasantly surprised when the American took him to an office and called a coin dealer in Asheville, described the condition of the coins, and wrote down their values on paper. He bought them for their full numismatic value less a small discount that he explained and which seemed to Mark to be quite fair.

As they concluded the transaction, the banker began to make some polite inquiries. Mark instinctively continued to be evasive, giving him a false name and finally telling him that he was a tourist who was thinking of settling locally. He said he wanted Jackson to be his own banker—if he could have assurances of discretion and probity. That was the beginning, as it turned out, of what Mark later called a beautiful relationship. For the moment, though, it cut off what seemed to be a growing nosiness, and Mark was able to leave the bank without answering further questions.

He was almost struck by a car as he walked into the street after looking the wrong way. He remembered how Winston Churchill had almost been killed making the same mistake when he had visited America some four—no 40—years before. He wondered what had become of the old man with whom he had dined at his estate, Chartwell, just six months (no:

36 years!) before. Extraordinary man! And so war had come after all. Well, that was no surprise to him. But who won, he wondered?

He went to a bookstore, and in an hour's time, had many of the answers he sought. He bought books about the war, airplanes, and modern history, then walked back out to where Ned anxiously awaited his return. They ate cold rations and read books, astonished at the changes that the world had experienced.

One would read and interrupt the other's reading. "They've landed men on the *moon!*" Mark shouted.

"China's gone bloody Communist." Ned announced.

"Plastics!"

"Hydrogen bombs!"

"Television!"

In that way they spent many hours in the main cargo hold of the aircraft as they bobbed about there on the lake in North Carolina. They pondered their position, and discussed their options.

How strange it was for the two Englishmen who came so uniquely to this country and who I eventually met under such extraordinary circumstances! They were careful—so very careful—about every thing they did. To move about was to risk exposure, so they ended up staying there in North Carolina and coping with all of those thousands of problems and inconveniences that were dictated by their circumstances. They had to forge new identities, establish a residence, get driver's licenses, and deflect curiosity. They had to learn how to function in the modern world and—perhaps most importantly—they had to learn how to avoid being arrested. This sounds like a simple matter to the average person, but once I became a part of their lives, I understood just how critical to their safety this was.

Of course, in order to do all of it, they had to spend all of the money they had, and early on they had to involve themselves with those who make a living preparing false identifications. Unbeknownst to the American government, they became U.S. citizens—at least according to the birth certificates and passports they soon possessed. They made a little money selling some of their uniforms and insignia, and they considered selling the plane, but they didn't because it was their ticket out— if they needed it.

The Short quickly became their prime source of income. Through the connections they made with those who provided false identifications, they soon learned that smuggling marijuana from offshore freighters involved exactly the skills and equipment they had. Within six months of their arrival in North Carolina, they were making $80,000 a flight twelve times a year.

As you can imagine, although Mark was constantly terrified of the legal and physical dangers inherent in smuggling, he had no moral qualms about it since he enjoyed smoking dope himself and thought the laws against it were ridiculous.

His fear of getting caught was offset by his conclusion that he was living on borrowed time anyway, for he assumed— quite rightly, I believe—that if for any reason at all his true identity was discovered, he would be arrested. They needed lots of money, and Mark brought it in.

With the help of their underworld friends they faked a Bahamian purchase of the plane so that they could get it registered in the United States. They obtained pilot's licenses and bought the most modern navigational and radar equipment available. To a limited extent, they armed themselves. They bought a farm and studied electronics, history, and computer science, and everything they did was in furtherance of their two goals: avoiding capture and going back in time to ancient Greece. Of course, Mark's meeting me was not part of the plan. As things worked out, because of me the first goal was imperiled and the second was thwarted. But let me not get ahead of myself.

Of course, they had considered whether or not they ought go forward into the future, but they had already done that and as Mark had explained, they hadn't liked what they had found. The current age threatened them personally. They could see the writing on the wall. With more computerization and more crowding, the world of the near future would become even less free and more difficult for them.

There was no point in trying to go back to their England of 1939 either. It was a closed chapter, and it hadn't ended badly, with or without them. Their loved ones had been few and, with the aid of a London detective agency, they had been able to trace out the fates of most of them. They learned that Mark's mother had died in the Blitz in '40 and that his fiancée—his only other strong link to those days—had married a soldier who was killed in France. After the war she had inherited a small hotel in

Brighton. Three cousins had been killed in the war, and one, the fourth and youngest, a girl, had married an American and moved to Australia. At the time of the inquiries—in 1976—Mark was 28 and she, the cousin, was 57. Neither Mark nor Ned ever went back to England.

They decided on trying to fly back to ancient Greece for reasons that must surely be obvious. Nothing more need be said about it other than to repeat the fact that when faced with the same choices, I agreed with theirs wholeheartedly.

By 1979, when I came into the picture, they had been here for seven very busy years. Interestingly, once I became Mark's lover and made the final decision to go with them, my whole life seemed to fall in order and attain a sense of purpose. There is nothing like having some direction to make a person happy!

It also made me to happy to be loved, even if my lover was someone from another world. He was, after all, practically a virgin and had strange ways and mannerisms. At least initially he was terribly devoted to me, and that was something I needed in those days. I immediately broke things off with my boyfriend, of course, and gave myself over totally to the intense and private world which Mark and I soon shared.

For security's sake, as long as I stayed in Charlottesville we continued to keep separate apartments and appeared to be just casually dating one another. In fact we were almost always together. In addition to the business aspects of his importing operations, Mark taught me to fly his Cessna and the flying boat. We also continued our joint studies of Greek language and history.

You must remember that by Ned's calculations, there appeared to be a distinct possibility that even if the Short could emerge into time during the right era, it might be wrecked during the violent reemergence or lost at sea thereafter. Nevertheless, studying Greek took on a new excitement that had little to do with the knowledge or abilities of the professors. After all, there was a chance—albeit only a slight one—that we might soon actually meet the men whose lives and works we studied.

I would be less than candid if I said or implied that it was for me a year of sexual and domestic bliss, because it wasn't. At least for the first month or so we were very active.

All those years of pent-up loneliness and sexual starvation that Mark had known ended, literally, in me. It would be indecent of me to quantify and qualify all the things we did, but I will say that after a while, I tired of the new, the different and the kinky. Finally I forced him to settle for a sexual normalcy with which I could live comfortably. I should have done so sooner, because, frankly, his excesses set a negative tone in our relationship in the months that followed.

Some of our problems arose from unavoidable cultural differences, I'm sure. After all, he grew up in English public schools complete with whippings, cold showers and a too intimate contact with other boys. The only woman he had ever had prior to 1972 had been his fiancée during the final few days before his departure, and apparently she hadn't made too much of an impression on him. I would not write of such matters but for the ramifications they had upon later events.

The walls of secrecy that Mark had so necessarily maintained were so profound that it had been impossible for him to have a normal relation with any woman prior meeting me. So there I was. I didn't ask him much about the few women he had known, other than about his fiancée, and he didn't offer much. I realize now that there was probably much in his life about which he was ashamed to talk.

In the final analysis, I might not have treated him as well as I should have. After all, he was very resourceful, brave, and handsome. Sometimes even all that is not enough when one is young. As you will remember, I had my share of needs, too: the need for affection. The need for real passion. Perhaps I was too pushy in demanding simple, straightforward satisfaction. But what's a girl to do?

Notwithstanding those sorts of growing disappointments, I feel that during that year I lived each day to the fullest. Such living makes time seem to expand; it is as if I can remember every day. We took trips down to North Carolina to visit with Ned and make plans. I took advanced flying lessons and learned to handle the Short, becoming so good at it that I went on two dope flights as a co-pilot and to help with the off-loading. It was exciting, but I worried terribly about getting caught. On those trips we made a $100,000 on each flight. I should point out in passing that we never hauled anything but grass. I believed then as I do now that there *is*, in fact, an obvious moral line between it and things like coke and heroin.

Among all the other things we did during those months, I met Mark's contacts in "the business", went with him as his wife to meet his banker, his lawyer and his CPA, and went on shopping trips to buy things we thought we might need on the proposed trip. I studied petroleum refining by posing as a journalist in a refinery in Texas for two weeks, then purchased a laboratory-grade, stainless steel refining apparatus. It weighed about 400 pounds, but we thought it might eventually prove to be very important to us. Without it we could never have hoped to make more fuel should the passage through time prove successful.

I also went to Europe for two and a half months during the summer of 1980, spending thousands of dollars on a whirlwind trip to the major capitals and sights I had always wanted to see and might not ever have another chance to visit. I stayed in Athens for a week, rented a car, and drove out to Delphi. I went by ferry to Crete.

I came back through Great Britain and rode trains through England, Scotland, Wales, Ireland, and the Lake District. I saw the Victory, the Tower, and Oxford. I stood on the white cliffs of Dover, the banks of Loch Lomond, and Glastonbury Tor. It was a marvelous trip, and I was all by myself except for a week that I spent with Cathy Simons, a friend from college days who lived in London and who you may remember as a slender artist with long brown hair and a single, blue eye.

Ned and Mark wanted me to check on some things and people for them while I was in England. I took many pictures while I was there—pictures that confirmed that the England they had known was long gone. The house in which Mark had grown up had been replaced by a supermarket, and the family home in Surrey had been hemmed in on three sides by typical 1960's-type development.

I also went to Brighton to see Mark's fiancée.

****

V

Brighton

I took that trip down to the little English seacoast city primarily to satisfy my own curiosity. Mark hadn't asked me to go there and I certainly hadn't mentioned to him that I might do so out of fear of his disapproval. After all, it was his past, not mine, and if he wasn't interested in it, why should I be?

The very idea of Brighton as being some sort of a bygone kind of place made we want to go there. So did the idea of the bygone woman I was going to look up there. At that point in my strange life, my curiosity about the possibilities of my own aging held a great fascination for me, and I had a notion that to see Mark's fiancé would be somehow to see myself at her age.

I expected to find someone gray and boring and quiet, someone who I would become if I lived on and did not go with Mark on the journey we were planning. Perhaps I wanted to see her to fortify myself so that I would rather take the risk of dying than to chose safety, survival, and the ravages of age.

I had her address from the detective agency's file, but nothing more—nothing about the woman herself. After telephoning from London to reserve a room at her bed-and-breakfast, I took the morning train down and walked from the station. It was a simple thing to do, really, but like so many things that seem simple, it became complex in ways I could not have anticipated.

On the rainy day that I arrived, I walked along house-crowded streets that seemed straight out of an Agatha Christie novel. Wearing rain poncho, boots, and jeans, and carrying a backpack, I thought of your travels in Europe and how proud you would have been of mine.

I found the place quite easily. Like many others in Brighton, the small hotel had been an upper-middle-class house at the turn of the century, but its elegance had been traded in for several smallish sleeping rooms, add-on closets and antiquated sinks. It was quite second-rate, but pleasantly so, and it offered a slight view of the sea from the dining room. The lady at the desk—who looked every minute of her 64 years—introduced herself as Mrs. Parker-Lane. The fiancé.

She may have been as wrinkled as a prune and as gray as limestone under her hair coloring, but she was trying. Through her piles of makeup and harsh laugh, she came across as brave. I supposed from her appearance that she had probably been a good-looking, slender girl in the late 'thirties, and I imagined that at her tallest she had been about 5'7". When I met her, she stood no more than 5'4" and was beginning to show signs of arthritis. Her fingers had brown-yellow tobacco stains, and her teeth were shockingly crooked and yellow. On the other hand, she had a beautiful, closed-lip smile that was full of mischief and mystery, and her eyes were a beautiful sky-blue.

Another immediate impression that I got of her—confirmed during the following two days of observation—was that the old girl had been around some and had known more than a few men in her day. She really enjoyed looking at and talking about men, and I quickly realized that the hotel business had probably suited her rather well during the years, having provided a more or less steady stream of male admirers as well as, perhaps, of occasional extra income. It was quite easy to bring her out. I asked if I could have tea with her in the afternoon, and she was delighted to have my company.

We spoke for many hours and on into the night. More accurately, she spoke and I listened, ingratiating myself with her merely by paying attention to her and by appearing to be interested in who she was and what she had seen and done in her life. A lot of people will like you if you put up with them.

On the surface of things, her life had been commonplace, and if one listened to her long enough, she would have begun a course of repetition that would have moved rapidly from the tedious to the excruciating. For long parts of that first conversation, it was interesting to discern various truths from what she omitted or alluded to. Naturally, she never suspected the reasons behind my patience, much less my curiosity.

She was quite vivid in her descriptions of her life and talked openly about her admirers. As she warmed to me and we switched from tea to tea-and-brandy, she became more bold, as people will, and spoke of her lovers and their wives and of her son.

I recalled from the report I had read that she had been married, but I was surprised to learn that she had a son. Soon I knew more about him than I want to know. Born during the war; his father had been killed in France, she said—a victim of that first great onslaught of Germans in May of 1940 when the British were obliged to fall back on Dunkirk. She took me into the parlor and showed me his picture and the pictures of their son when he was a baby. Somehow the wartime pictures were all out of focus and old, and it made me sad to see how she had been and to think of her as a young woman who like so many in Europe that year had lost their husbands.

She had a difficult time raising the child by herself, she said, and I gathered that a strain existed between her and her son. He had grown to manhood with her in the small hotel by the sea—a place filled with her memories, her stories and her admirers. One could understand the strain without sitting through a thousand meals at which she would have presided.

Her son, Julian, was tall and handsome, she told me. He had done well in school, and after completing university, he had become a priest in the Anglican Church. In it he was prospering, moving steadily up through its hierarchy despite his few connections. She said that he was at that time making a name for himself as an evangelical. He apparently preached like some sort of English Baptist.

Although one could hear Doris speak of him with pride, there existed behind her words an obvious burden of resentments that separated them, and she did not have a picture of him on display as one might have expected her to.

"Oh, he's very righteous, he is," she would say rather more often than she should. "A real servant of the Lord, and always busy with His work."

Too busy, it would seem, to visit with his mother regularly.

On the second day of my stay, we went from tea to straight brandy right away and became much more sociable.

Just on the verge of being hopelessly in her cups, she spoke for the first time of Mark.

I pushed the subject. Instinctively feeling guilty, I nevertheless inquired who was the "First Love" to whom she had briefly referred. Her eyes grew wistful.

"He was a flyer," she said. "A rather strange lad in his

way, but terribly handsome and dashing."

I didn't think of Mark as being all *that* handsome. I suppose it was a sample of the way time distorts one's memories or of how tastes change through the years.

"Have you a picture of him?" I asked, and of course she did. She brought out a small, black album from her desk. It was full of clippings, mementos and pictures. One could readily glean from it, a view of those strivings for social approval and probity of the middle class of yesteryear: reports of teas, socials, school plays, and, of course, of the engagement. There were many pictures of her and Mark together, for their families and friends had money and could afford photographers as well as cameras of their own.

Satisfied at last, I read through all of it as we sat there drinking brandy and smoking cigarettes. She spoke from time to time to annotate what I saw and read, but she also allowed silences during which I read and she pondered.

"So you were engaged?" I asked lightly at the right time.

"Yes, but read on," she said, and I did until I came to the last page of the book, and there it was: the newspaper clipping with Mark's picture on it—the same picture I had seen in his RAF book the first time we made love. *Flyer Lost At Sea*, it read. There was no mention of Ned.

For an instant, I felt as if I had taken away that old woman's young man, but it wasn't my fault. It was just the way it was: amazing, irredeemable, and sad.

"Did you love him very much?" I asked her.

"Well, I don't know, really," she replied with amazing frankness. "It was so long ago and far away. All of that seems like a dream now, or something that happened in someone else's life in an old novel. It's so easy, don't you know, to let one's imagination run rampant about such things and to forget the truth altogether. Life goes on."

And I could plainly see that it had. I had to admire her candor even if she sounded cold.

"And what about your husband," I asked?

"Actually, he caught me on the rebound that summer and got shipped off to France in October of '39 right after the war broke out. He was a sergeant—a fine, big-chested brute with a hearty laugh and a big smile. Now he was a *man*. Quite the thing to drive out sad memories and teach a woman some tricks, he was!"

"Did he know his son before he died?"

"Oh, yes! I took the child over to France in the Spring of 1940. That was during what we called the Phony War: no fighting going on, you see."

She showed me pictures of them together in France. He was indeed a big, burly, blond man. She was fashionably slim in a long polka dot dress with puffed shoulders. Her hair was long, blonde, and curled under.

"A fine looking man," I commented. "And you were so pretty," I added, which made me feel an instant pang of regret since those days for her were long past.

She rested her hand on mine as we sat there in her cozy little room. "Thank you, Dear. Yes I was. But it's all right: Every dog has her day."

Oddly enough, although she meant well, I took some offense of my own at that. After all, unlike her, I had never had my day. I had never been either fashionable or pretty, and she knew it, too. I had always been too chunky and too athletic and had this big, straight nose. No one had ever considered me beautiful, except, of course, for my father, Mark, and—in moments of weakness—you.

We sipped brandy in silence.

"My boy missed having a father, you know," she said after a while. "Boys need fathers."

Silently we smoked.

"Of course, there were always men around. After I lost my husband, another RAF lad caught me, then he got killed, too. On September 15th, 1940, to be exact. There were altogether too many of us girls rebounding all around Britain in those days."

"It must have been terrible," I offered.

"Well, yes it was, but it was terribly romantic, too—lots of what people later called 'Free Love'," she explained with a nudge of her bony elbow. "Much nicer in some ways than before the war, you know. Much freer."

She leaned forward and there was a sparkle in her eyes.

"Love! My friends and I positively lived for it!" she said cheerfully, raising her brandy glass. "Here's a toast to the boys who went off to save our country, and to the girls who sent them off with smiles on their faces," she added with a wink.

I was mildly astonished, but I joined her in the toast.

"What with the training going on everywhere, the men off at air bases and in the Navy and in North Africa, we women were about to run out of precious natural resources. Plenty of fellows were having to do double or even triple duty, if you know what I mean. Then the Yanks saved us again: they sent us a fresh crop of the most virile, fun-loving men the country had seen since Queen Elizabeth's time!

"Here's to your father's generation:" she added tipsily. "Long may they wave!"

So we drank to them, too, and I thought about my Dad who flew bombers out of England during 1944. He could have been one of her fun-loving young admirers.

Later on that evening, when we were both about drunk, she spoke of Julian, her son, who was—sadly as she saw it—a bachelor and a pious misfit. In the midst of expressing the wish that he could meet a "good woman," I could see the idea dawning in her face that I just might be that woman. In her eyes I was a likely enough prospect. Not only was I female—an important point, to be sure—but she liked me. And I was single.

I had told her that I was divorced and traveling around Europe before entering graduate school and that my parents were alive and well in Alabama. I painted a picture of myself as a rather normal, young American woman—which in most ways, of course, I was. Naturally I had been using a false name, and so the other fabrications came easily enough: it was fun to see how willingly people let themselves be fooled. I was fooling myself, too, of course: it was altogether too easy to weave that particular net.

Doris asked me to stay for another day so that I might meet her son, and in my intoxicated condition I agreed since I was not in a hurry and since I felt sorry for her. After a bit more conversation we went to bed. I slept until noon the next day, which was a Saturday.

I spent the afternoon away from the hotel, walking around the town and sightseeing in a nearby village. When I returned at six, she called me up the stairs to her rooms to meet her right reverend son.

I have seldom been so surprised in my life, for upon seeing him, I knew at once that Julian was Mark's son. It was obvious not only because he looked so much like Mark but also because he looked like neither his mother nor the burly sergeant. He was big—fat actually—and much more placid-looking than either Mark or his mother, but his face, though heavier and jowly, and particularly his eyes, were identical to Mark's. It was very distressing to me—so much so that I could not speak. I almost fainted.

"What is it, My Dear?" she asked, and without thinking I said, "He looks just like...my husband! You know," I added, catching myself, "my former husband, I mean. Except for the clerical clothes and collar."

"Is that so distressing, Mrs. Johnson?" the man asked tartly, raising his brow as if he had already decided to dislike me.

"Oh, no!" I protested. "It's just, well...it surprised me. He was a nice man and all that," I added weakly.

"Cathy, let me introduce my son, Julian," Doris said in an attempt to overcome the initial awkwardness. "Julian, Cathy Johnson."

"Delighted," he said insincerely as he took my hand rather formally before we all sat down for an afternoon chat. Doris had tea and pastries, and we made small talk as we ate. His manners were excellent, if somewhat fastidious and fussy—just what one might expect—but they did not disguise the fact that he was an habitual overeater who was in poor physical shape for a man of his age. At least he was well-educated and knew how to behave and carry on an intelligent conversation. In some ways he seemed like his mother and the building: out-of-date.

It was obvious, too, that he knew that I was "a girl" his mother wanted him to like. Unobserved by her, he made a subtle effort to demonstrate to me that he knew what her scheme was and that he was having no part of it. I could understand his defensiveness, but his distaste went beyond that almost to the point of rudeness. He looked at me with ill-concealed disdain, and I couldn't tell what it was he disliked—Americans, women, me, or people in general. But the dislike was palpable. It was also apparent that he didn't trust me. He had a suspicious nature and he seemed to see through parts of my act.

He was at that time 40 years old. He was exactly Mark's height—six feet—and had the same jet black hair, combed more or less straight back the way Mark combed his. Unlike Mark, though, his hair was beginning to thin quite noticeably and it was streaked with white. Except for his fat cheeks, he looked quite distinguished. Also like his father, he was a careful dresser. His clothes were expensive and so well-fitted that they minimized his stoutness.

He had Mark's same startling blue eyes, long, sensuous eyelashes and aquiline nose, but his skin was pallid from lack of sunlight. His turned-down mouth and dimpled chin were his mother's, as were his lips. Probably full and soft when he was a youth, they terminated at their corners in hard wrinkles that gave him a petulant look that absolutely spoiled what could have been a strikingly handsome face. I immediately wondered whether or not he was homosexual.

We all had dinner together that evening, and his better sides eventually came through. He was, after all, an Anglican priest, and was quite adept at engaging in conversation with total strangers. He knew Greek and Latin, but his main area of study had been Hebrew. Much to the obvious chagrin of his mother, he was devout to the point of priggishness and constantly interlaced his conversation with comments designed not so much to profess his faith as to nettle her.

He did drink sherry with us, though, and under its leavening influence, brought himself to tell several rather dry English jokes. One could sense that he was not a great speaker, for he had neither the voice nor the presence for effective public speaking. It didn't surprise me that he was an academic who specialized in translations and interpretations of ancient works, particularly of the Gospels and the Dead Sea Scrolls.

Our conversation began to leave Doris out, for she had little interest in such matters and was beginning to pine for her "telly." She loved to talk about game shows.

Julian began to be much more charming, even friendly. After a glass or two of sherry, he surprised me by asking if I would go for a walk in town with him. Doris almost fainted with pleasure when I accepted and we left together.

It was a fine, late-summer evening and the streets were busy with tourists and young people on holiday. I felt vigorous and free, and happy to be out and about. I felt happy, confident and even a bit tipsy, and I wanted to know more about Julian—that strange man whose father was my lover. My mind was racing with thoughts. It had already occurred to me, for example, to consider whether or not I would even tell Mark about him, for such information might change our plans in ways I couldn't foresee and might not want.

As we walked along the bustling sidewalks, Julian skillfully steered our conversations away from trivial matters and discussions about his mother and toward the topic which interested him the most: me and my background. I was flattered, I suppose, to have the attentions of an educated man who was obviously not paying attention to me as a mere prelude to trying to sleep with me.

Blithely, then, I repeated for him the fabrications I had told his mother. Feigning interest, he led me into embellishment after new embellishment for over an hour. By then we had settled down in a quiet pub and eaten some snacks. He ordered another sherry for himself and a whiskey for me. As you may remember, I never was much of a drinker and it was drink that began my downfall that night.

I had already formed the conclusion that Julian had missed his calling in life. He didn't in the least seem cut out to be a minister of God. For one thing, he was too self-centered actually to consider what others might think. He also appeared to lack basic human compassion for normal human needs and frailties--particularly his mother's. I know now that he should have been a detective. His nose for crime and deception was acute, and no false nuance or gesture escaped his notice nor faded from the marvelous catalogue of his memory. Like a policeman well aware of deception and sin in others, he was perfectly capable of hiding from others his own deceptions and sins. And like a good detective he was relentless and remorseless.

Even though I was 29 years old and had been around some, in the final analysis I was still quite young and inexperienced in the ways of the world, but I was too arrogant to realize it. I thought myself as being so very clever. To a limited extent, the deceptions and forgeries that I was using were ones Mark and Ned had very carefully worked out over the years or had prepared for me during the preceding months, but in actually using them I was just an amateur. The main rules were these: Never get close too anybody. Never give references that could be checked. Never get drunk and start making up things.

Little did I recall the rules that evening. I broke all of them, when, like a fool, I sat in a pub and drank whiskey with a curious and intelligent man who urged me to drink more. More and more cheerfully I talked as during the second hour he began to lead me gently back through the small inconsistencies with which my story had been replete.

Now—with the benefit of hindsight—I realize that being something akin to a spy was only a game at which I was playing. Practically anyone who caught Mark, Ned, or me out, and who had the time and the inclination to dig about for the truth and to accept the truth he found, could have uncovered it all. It would have taken only that first hint of something awry. So there we sat in the pub: me talking and going awry, Julian leading me down the primrose path.

I was not drunk, but close to it, when finally I began to feel confused and uncomfortable under his increasingly accusing cross-examination. Suddenly I was once again coldly aware of him, and my initial dislike of the man resurfaced. Through the alcoholic haze, I began to sense danger.

"Let's go," I said rather suddenly, bolting up from the table.

Grabbing my wrist, he exclaimed, "Not just yet!" rather too brutally. His grip was cold and clammy but hard. I hate for a man to grab my wrists, even in play. I seem to recall that you made that mistake once.

I snatched my hand away from him with such force that he was pulled forward across the table top, knocking over glasses and a napkin holder. Instantly the room was silent as my heavy shot glass bounded twice off the tile floor then broke with a loud, pretty tinkle. There were about 30 people in the room, and they all looked at us. We were acutely aware of the tableau that they thought they saw: an Anglican priest trying unsuccessfully to put the make on a drunk American girl.

Julian sat back in his chair, trying to recover a bit of his dignity, but I did not offer to sit back down myself. I looked down at him and saw a look of rage and hate in his eyes. Here was a man to whom appearances were important—even before strangers—but here, too, was a man who could carry a grudge, a dangerous man.

A waitress came to clean up the glass. Julian mumbled something to her as I turned and went to the ladies' room. I did not get sick like I thought I might, but I do recall looking into the mirror at the big woman there who stared back: light blue eyes, long, reddish-blonde hair and light makeup, wearing a blue work shirt open at the neck—your typical drunk American graduate student. I didn't dislike her—after all, she had stood up for herself when the man had grabbed her. The bouncing glass had been the perfect touch.

There are in life many false pleasantries to which in the name of civilization we bow. When I returned to the public room, I said nice things to Julian and he said nice things to me, even apologizing to me in a sincere and almost credible way for interrogating me as well as for grabbing me. I accepted his apology and apologized for my own rudeness, and we soon left in an a public show of cordiality and good will that barely concealed the ugliness of that sharp little moment in time at the table.

"I'm drunk," I exaggerated as we walked down the street. "Forgive me for causing that little mess in there," I added. "My husband used to abuse me," I lied, "and I can't stand to have someone grab me by the arms."

"Ah, yes: your husband!" he said. "Well, I never should have done that; it was rude and I did not think first. American girls are sensitive about such things."

"All women are," I said. He agreed with me only to be polite.

He offered to hail a cab, but as the distance was short, I said I needed the air, and we walked back to the hotel. Doris was still up when we came in. I greeted her then went straight up to bed, where I fell into a deep and dreamless sleep.

Sunday was my last day in Brighton. I woke to the loud flapping of pigeons on the roofs. Bright rays of the sun poured through my open windows, and I realized that I had no hangover at all and felt glad to be alive. I thought about the night before and how I had related to Julian, what I had learned about him, and what I might tell Mark about him when—and if—the time came.

Doris and I had breakfast together. It was a subdued occasion, for not only was it to be my last day with her, but also she knew that Julian and I had gotten along badly the night before. It was plain that once again the little flame of matchmaking that she had harbored had been snuffed out. For all her time-worn flashiness, she was a motherly type and would have loved grandchildren. It was becoming all too obvious to her that Julian was not likely to give her any.

Julian had been invited to deliver a sermon that very day in one of the town's largest churches, and he had already gone out before I got up. Before leaving, though, he had told her enough about our little date—from his standpoint, of course-- so that she knew it had been something of a disaster. She was polite enough not to mention it, but finally I brought up the subject.

"What did Julian tell you about last night?" I asked, looking her in the eye from across the little table with its array of cups, silverware, and condiments.

"Well, I won't lie to you," she said. "He said some things about you—you know: that you drank too much, that you were too fast, too loose, and all that sort of thing." I could see tears welling up in her eyes, and she started dabbing at them with her paper napkin, smearing her make-up.

"It's O.K." I said, putting my hand across to touch her and lightly resting my fingertips on the soft, wrinkly skin at her elbow. "It's all true, you know!" I added cheerfully.

She started crying. I would have been embarrassed to watch had I not felt pity for her.

"He never really likes any girls," she cried. "He doesn't really like anybody, for that matter," she continued on, adding through her sobs, "including me." Little tears dropped out of the corners of her eyes.

"He didn't have a father, you know. Little boys so need their fathers."

I knew. More than she would ever know, I knew. Little girls need their fathers, too. I remembered my own parents at that moment, and my tears came up hot and sad as I thought about Daddy out in our yard playing with me in the jonquils. I thought of how I cried and cried when I was 13 and the boy next door had made fun of me, and Daddy tried to comfort me. I remembered the look of love and pride in his eyes as I went out the door to my senior prom—my first real date—and the terrible loneliness of my parents' house after he and Mom died.

"I'm so sorry," I offered through my own sadness. "So many boys without fathers..." I added. "He must have been proud that his father was a brave soldier."

She looked queerly at me for a moment. Then, wiping her eyes and sniffing, she said, "Oh, that man—my sergeant—wasn't his real father. I lied to you about that. The pilot I told you about—the one who was lost at sea—was his father, but we were never married—just engaged. I told everybody I was married to the sergeant to cover up the fact that I had a little bastard. Lots do it these days, but that was back in 1940.

"Julian found out, of course," she continued, looking down at her hands. "He was 12 years old. Oh, cruelty!"

It was an odd turn of phrase, but I felt its bitterness and thought of the boy and how perhaps he had been taunted and made to feel resentful not only toward his tormentors but also toward the principal villain—his mother.

"It must have been hard on him," I offered in sympathy.

"Oh, it was. It was. He lost a father and a mother in just a few words spoken by a cruel cousin. He never trusted me again, you see."

I saw.

"The pilot?" I asked for some reason.

"Yes, the bloody pilot. Julian looked just like him when he was 25."

She looked sad. "It's odd, you know."

"What?" I asked.

"Oh, it's just odd how something that's just a small thing can seem to slide along unnoticed and unremembered, seemingly for weeks, before it surfaces like a boil once again."

I remained quiet while she poured herself more tea.

"It was so *unfair* of that young man to get himself killed like that," she continued after sipping at the tea. "You see, we had been sweethearts for some time before we were engaged. He was so insistent—as men are, you know—and we had been somewhat intimate whenever we could arrange things. I was still a virgin, and, well," she said with a wry smile, "since we were engaged and he was so ardent, I gave in to him."

"Of course you did," I said sympathetically. "We all did sooner or later. After all, we're all just human. And we humans like doing that sort of thing, don't we?"

She smiled, knowing that in me she had if not a co-conspirator, then at least a friend.

We finished our breakfast and I agreed to go with her to the church were Julian was preaching that morning. It seemed the least I could do.

That was the first time I had been in a church since my parents' funeral; it felt good to be there. The sonorous organ, the sweet anthems of the choir, and the beautiful architecture almost made me feel religious again like I did when I was a girl sitting with my sister and my parents. Then Julian began to deliver his message.

Before beginning he fixed upon me a glaring look that made me realize that he probably thought I was some sort of confidence crook trying to curry favor with his mother in furtherance of some criminal scheme. Well, let him think what he will, I thought.

It was easy to tell that he departed from his awkward, prepared text—a departure which probably improved his sermon enormously for those to whom it was not specifically tailored.

After thumbing through his Bible for the passage he wanted, he read from one of Paul's writings—I forget which one—and began rather quietly to talk about deception and mistrust, and somehow led into a condemnation of some of the more specific sexual sins . He read from The Book again.

By the time he read Paul's injunctions to "Flee fornication!" and to "Marry or burn!" he was shouting like an Appalachian revivalist. It would have been humorous had it not seemed to be so directly addressed to me and to his mother where we sat in one of the closer rows. His performance was quite ludicrous, really, and I felt embarrassed for Doris as her own son stood there in the archetypal position of moral authority and condemned her as he did. There were, it is true, motes in our eyes, but in our astonishment and defensiveness, we could not see the beams in his. Nor could he.

Having started with deception and wallowed in sin, he finished with salvation. It brought back memories of a Baptist church back home that I used to visit with friends—a church whose preacher was caught having sex in the sanctuary with the organist. As my father sardonically noted, at least the organist was a woman.

Julian began to speak with a passionate vehemence that seemed out of character for him. When speaking of sin he sounded priggish, but when he began talking of redemption, his message improved. Although I can only paraphrase what he said, I do remember the gist of it fairly well. It went something like this:

"Christ," he said, "is a personal savior. Even though He was sent to redeem the world, and masses and nations are under His sway and dominion, His message and His loving embrace is addressed to you and to me personally.

"His is not the announcement in the press or the loud game show on the telly. His voice is not the announcer's at the match, nor are his footsteps loud like the treading of soldiers or the beating of drums.

"No: His announcement of His coming is a slow and spreading thing that goes from man to man, from woman to woman, and passes among us like a gentle breeze in myriad acts of Christian charity and righteousness.

"The telly cannot package Him for half an hour. Even in America, He cannot sell soap.

"His voice quietly and lovingly whispers to you alone in the night. His footsteps are but the subtle slip of sandals in the hallway or the almost-silent padding of bare feet across the floor as he comes to you and me in the dark hours of our lives.

"His face is not the comely one, nor does his raiment place him among the Elect of the City. He wears only the simplest of garments, and they are not for show or for power. The simple robe he wears hides not His nakedness but His perfection. His face is that of a man who has lived the life of a man and has known its joys and sorrows—yes, and even its desires and temptations. It is too mature a face to have the unflawed, untested mien of youth that in our times passes for beauty.

"And his embrace! Ah, yes! His loving embrace is not the in-gathering of nations or groups or families. Not a bit of it! We may think we know Him in that collective way," he continued with an astonishing look of passion, "but we do not. We are not a crowd of kiddies bunched together in His arms feeling good together.

"Each of us stands or sits alone here in this place. Isolated are we from one another and from God. Yet our human nature demands that we feel otherwise, does it not? We want those feelings of collective union with one another.

"Yes, we want that feeling of union. We want not to be alone. Willingly and even against the laws of God, we enter into small co-conspiracies of the flesh with other individuals and give ourselves over to carnal pleasures and licentiousness.

"That being insufficient and unsatisfactory, gladly we join ourselves into groups and then our groups into larger groups. We follow our leaders like sheep. As nations we rise up and fight one another in the perfect frenzy of togetherness. We call it nationalism, but it is nihilism. Truly it is written: All we like sheep are gone astray!

"All this and more! Is there any wonder, then, that even what we call the best of men turn to the bottle that gives not absolution but at least oblivion? Where does it all end, this despair? Is the grave that waits upon us late or soon the only bitter termination?

"All of this despair and gloom and hopelessness and war that dogs our days is a result of the very things we pursue. But what we really want and need is not union with man or woman or country, but union with God. What we really need is not the communion of the flesh, but of the Holy Spirit.

"And how in our need and our despair can this salvation of the Holy Spirit come to us? It comes to us when we ask for it. When in that darkness we are alone and quiet, even as it came to Mary who was alone and inexplicably with child. There she was despairing in the garden while unknown to her the Hope of the World was growing in Her precious Womb.

" 'Well, that was Mary,' is our poor lament and excuse. 'She was the Chosen of God.'

"Maybe this was so and that those who are not God's chosen people will never hear his subtle approach. But on the other hand, maybe in His infinite wisdom He has not given many people the wherewithal to listen, to hope, and to pray. Those who can't listen are doomed. Their lives are spent in drunkenness, licentiousness, and joining up with clubs and parties and fashions and political parties or causes.

"But we can *try* to listen, can't we? We can *try* to pray, can't we? We can be still in the nighttime of our despairs and ask for help.

"But perhaps we are in fact God's Chosen People, you and I. Perhaps His plan includes you and me, and we have but to listen and to follow or to stand and wait.

"Clearly that Jesus Christ Who is Our Savior is not for everybody. How could the tumultuous world even notice his approach? Yet *you* can, if you but listen. Softly in the night He comes. At first you may hear only the subdued slip of sandals or the even more subtle padding of bare feet, but then there is His touch. It is the touch which shocks but does not surprise. And then comes His embrace, His loving embrace!

"Let us pray."

And he prayed for us all and pronounced the benediction. The mighty organ played and we went out into the sunlight with the crowd without speaking to him. Out on the street again, still astonished by the message that had seemed so odd and disjointed but which Julian had delivered with such vehemence and screwball conviction, I looked at Doris. She was lighting up a cigarette.

"What a blowhard!" she said with a chuckle. "Always did take himself a mite too seriously, that boy. Her Holy Womb, my ass!" she sniggered. "He uses that in every bloody sermon he preaches. Gets a mite tiresome, what!"

But as it was all very interesting to me. The first and last of his sermons I ever heard, I thought about it quite a lot in the years since. He had pulled forth from the morning some fascinating lines. I remembered most particularly Julian's references to 'His loving embrace.' It had an unmistakable tinge of the English public school about it.

A few days after the trip to Brighton, I flew back to the States to put my affairs in order and to make my final preparations for the trip. The projected departure date was now only two months away: the 15th of October, 1980.

****

VI

Uncle Ned

I found these unfinished, handwritten notes Ned made in 1977. He buried them in a box in Beaufort County, North Carolina. I retrieved them recently and after some editing include them here:

I, Edward Manwarring-Powell, Scientist,
write this, my story:

It must be said: this is your age, not mine. In it, yet I am not of it, just as I am English but have no country. Though I am not old, I feel very old sometimes only in that I share with a dwindling handful of octogenarians memories of bygone times and share with them the estrangement that the old feel in this rapidly changing world. He who vividly remembers his trips to Kenya and New York in 1913, who saw service in the trenches and in the skies of France, and who carries in him the sharp bits of metal and resentments that left their marks on so many of my generation, must necessarily be an alien in your more modern world of opulence, abundance, and decadence. The horrors of that four year struggle, now largely forgotten, are barely even imaginable by moderns. The weighty drama of chance, destruction, and death which we acted out in France week after week for years had its effects on the kind of men the survivors came to be. After all of that, for the common run of us everything else has been as pleasant as it has been meaningless. Were it not for my science, I should have gone crazy or become a drunk like so many others did, but, as a matter of fact, I did not.
Like most young Englishmen of my generation, I took part in what I shall always call the Great War, serving first in the infantry and later in the air corps. This story is not about those dreadful times, but I shall recount the more salient points of my experiences and observations for the years between 1915 and 1924 which did so much to shape the outlook with which all

life thereafter has been lived.

As a child I started out frail and sickly. Baden-Powell's Scouting for Boys *was first published when I was nine years old, and in those days just after the Boer War he and Teddy Roosevelt were my idols. As I grew into manhood I modeled myself upon them. I practiced riding, boxing, scouting, and marksmanship until I became quite proficient in all. At the same time I was proving to be what in these times is called a prodigy in mathematics and applied electronics.*

Still thinking of me as a sickly child, however, my parents kept me from the service in 1914, and thus I continued my extraordinary education in the sciences and was spared some of the worst of the fighting in the first two years of struggle. When I was at home during those dark days and wanted so much to join up, my mother would say, "God has spared you so that you, in His proper Time, can perform some extraordinary service to Him and to Mankind. I know this is so, my son." That may have been what she thought, but I have never believed that there is a God, and if one ever did exist, He certainly must have left here prior to 1914. In any event, I missed what was optimistically called the Big Push on the Somme in July and August of 1916, when 60,000 fell on the first day. Such incredible slaughter!

But I was at Arras, Ypres, and Passchendaele in 1917, and saw the mad elephant of war for months on end before I was wounded and sent to England. Better words than mine have described what went on out there in the trenches during those times, but those books seem sadly ignored by a generation that cannot, it seems, begin to grasp the memory, much less the magnitude of events 60 years in the past. It is all as fresh in my mind as if it had happened a month ago. I can still see bits of men hanging on the wire in front of machine gun positions. I can smell the gas still. Even now I recall how my mother and my brother's widow came to the hospital in Kent to see me. Mark was two years old then.

In April of 1918, I went back to the front as a pilot of an observation plane. I had, I think, about 30 hours of flying time when I first went up over enemy territory. In the following two weeks, I got in 30 hours more and was shot down twice, losing my observers both times. It was a wonder I survived those six months of flying: most of my class didn't. It was the longest six months of my life, even though I spent much of it dead drunk. Then the war ended.

Science was my first love, and in particular I have always been fascinated with radio waves of all descriptions. Even before the war, I was an avid radio enthusiast. My father owned a radio factory, and employed the best men he could find to help develop wireless sets for the war effort. He was particularly interested in wireless apparatus for airplanes and ships, and made a good bit of money filling government contracts.

At the end of the war, I joined the firm but spent a great deal of my time in theoretical studies which took me all over Europe. So intense was my devotion to our work that I had no time for a wife and family, although I did eventually make a long-term arrangement with a war-widow who worked for us at our main factory. She was a sweet and intelligent woman some ten years my senior, and 'though we were often together, no children were born of our unconventional union.

On the other hand I had my nephew, Mark, the child of my older brother who had been killed in 1915. When we were together, I acted more as if Mark were my younger brother than my nephew. He was a pretty but melancholy child, and despite my offers to have him privately tutored, his mother sent him off to school, presumably to make him into a typical English automaton. He would have received a much better education had he come into the firm. By the time he finished his schooling, however, the light of science and discovery in him had been most thoroughly suppressed and he was socially quite awkward. But he knew his Greek and Latin—for all the good that does a man! Like many of his generation—and mine, for that matter— he toyed with socialism and even went off to Spain to fight for the Loyalists. He soon returned, thoroughly disillusioned with communists, commanders, and causes.

I had taken him under my wing and secured him a commission in the RAF so that he could help me in my work. He was not a daring, brilliant pilot, but he was a good one— careful, meticulous, and calm. He liked flying quite a lot, but the English schools and the social system had dampened his enthusiasm. He was beginning to recover it when we began the airborne phase of my experiments in 1938. He found himself a girlfriend and got engaged.

I did not make him aware of the true nature of my theories. Perhaps it was not fair of me to make him an unwitting subject of a test for the safety of which I could not vouch. The device I created worked. By using it we passed through an instant of time. Thereafter, during the course of a second experiment, we skipped forward in time not a day as we had planned, but 32 years.

To the best of my knowledge, all of my prewar notes, diagrams, and calculations were destroyed during the second war or were lost thereafter. All I have done before and since our great jump froward from 1939 to 1972 has been carried out in a secrecy so complete that such knowledge as I have will pass away—or fly away--with me.

This is my testament. It is brief and I am no writer...

***

About 50 years old when I met him, Ned was still in the prime of his life. About 5'7" tall and very fit, he had a big, hairy chest, large, strong arms covered in scars left by shrapnel, and delicate, almost feminine hands. He had a massive, almost totally bald head. His heavy, dark eyebrows were shot through with white so that the total effect of the man was quite astonishing. His eyes were dark brown and seemed to flash and burn when he was angry or excited.

He was not a handsome man. His lower face was partially scarred from burns he received when he was shot down in 1918, and his lips were slightly distorted from the surgeries that had repaired them. He was not pretty, but I have seen much worse. He looked like a short, scared bricklayer whose hobby was nuclear physics.

Nor was he a lovable man. When we first met he treated me especially poorly, resenting as he did Mark's involvement with me, and he continued to dislike me even after I proved to him my willingness to work toward their common goal.

He was not a misogynist, and yet he seemed not to be very interested in female companionship, complaining that women were too curious, too demanding, too extravagant, and too cowardly. Only after many months did he come around to admitting a grudging respect for me, particularly since I am a pretty good cook and careful with my money.

His work always came first. He spent practically all of his time learning about computers, studying scientific theories and working on the Short. Consequently, he was not very active in the smuggling operation although he was every bit as much at risk as was Mark. *In for a penny, in for a pound* was his attitude, and he was not at all averse to the various operations themselves.

"My family were all smugglers in Cornwall in the 1700s," I can recall him saying. "It is ever this way: the Crown always makes things illegal so that it can have its obscene tariffs and levies and maintain the monopolies of the wealthy! What's most shocking about this new Prohibition is how a free people would impose it upon themselves. Hemp illegal! How absurd! Alcohol, maybe. But *hemp*? Ridiculous!"

Occasionally he would sit out on the dock with us and smoke a big pipeful of dope between bowls of his homegrown Carolina tobacco. Notwithstanding his contempt of its politicians, its drug laws, and its police, Ned loved North Carolina in general and his lovely, little, backwater farm beside the estuary near the coast in particular.

"Where else can you have mountains, the sea, neighbors who mind their own business, and fields of the very best tobacco?" he would ask as if in rapture. He loved his pipe and his hand-rolled cigarettes.

****

VII

Preparations & Other Problems

During those months of preparation, we thought of thousands of things that had to be done and hundreds of things we needed to buy. Even after all of their investments in land, aircraft, smuggling equipment, and in the Short Flying Boat itself, Mark and Ned had a lot of money. In addition to the 200-acre farm, they owned several cars, a twin-engine Beechcraft, a speedboat, a small house in Wilmington, a small commercial aircraft repair business, and two tractor-trailer trucks. We liquidated practically everything.

Of course, although we expected never to return to this time, we had to prepare for several eventualities. Fortunately, we had enough money to make some provision for each possible outcome of our attempt to pass through time.

There was, of course, a chance that the Short wouldn't work again and we would have been "stuck" in the present with all of its dangers. One of those dangers, of course, was the IRS. It was already investigating Mark. Up to that point he had been highly successful in putting it off.

There was also a chance that Ned could be completely wrong in his calculations and that we could only go forward in time. Such travel would seem to be mandated by Einsteinian relativity, at least as I understand it, and the idea that we could only travel to the future suggested a prospect that was very unpleasant. After all, things are bad enough right now. We imagined how much worse it might well be if some future world government could keep track of every man, woman, and child on earth. Even the gold we would be taking with us might not be sufficient to protect us in such an uncertain future.

And modern weapons? What good would they be against the weapons of the future?

Travel to the future seemed to us worse than death, but Ned thought that we should prepare for that possibility, too. He thought that he might be able to abort an in-progress transition to the future and bring the Short out before we had gone more than a few days, weeks, or years into the future. Therefore, in addition to our other preparations we chose not to divest ourselves completely of all of our assets and instead made provisions for the possibility that we might "skip forward" for ten years or less. The farm was put into a trust with Mark's banker serving as its well-paid trustee, and all the other mobile—and replaceable—assets were systematically sold off during September and early October.

Each of us had a will drawn up. You will be pleased to know that I included you as a legatee of the $25,000 certificate of deposit I bought to be here when—and if—I got back. I also took the precaution of burying $20,000 in gold and silver coins on the farm. I either spent or took with me all the rest of the money from my parents' estate.

You may recall that in those days I used a Copper 7 IUD for birth control. I had always liked it because it never gave me any trouble, but I knew that should we succeed, it might be a dangerous thing to have inside me. I therefore had it removed and went on the pill—which might have been a mistake. I put a three-year supply of pills aboard the Short along with our other medical supplies.

Medical supplies! What could we have been thinking about? We couldn't have carried enough with us if we had tried, and none of us took even so much as a refresher first aid course. None of us could have performed field dentistry, midwifery, or even minor surgery, and we took only those medical supplies an organizer of a small safari might take. There again, we had to weigh everything and make sure the plane could carry it.

We took $175,000 in gold and silver coins, three rubber rafts, aircraft repair tools and replacement parts, three extra propeller blades, the lightweight, collapsible oil-refining apparatus for cracking petroleum, cases of motor oil, fabric-patching equipment, and three small short wave radio transceivers.

For armament, we took two .308 bolt-action rifles, 2 Ruger .22 automatic rifles, two sawed-off shotguns, one Thompson sub-machinegun, four .45 automatic pistols, some .45 derringers, a .50-caliber flintlock rifle and some reloading equipment. Because all that stuff was so heavy and we had to take so much else, we could carry only a limited supply of ammunition. We also had the foresight to take along some forty pounds of high explosives complete with blasting cord, caps, trip wire detonators and fuse. In addition to everything else, we put aboard a very minimal selection of winter and summer clothing, mosquito netting, two tents, three sleeping bags, cooking utensils, a propane stove, and enough light-weight emergency rations for two months. It was rapidly becoming a very crowded and heavily-laden plane—too heavily laden for the carrying of much extra fuel.

On September 1st, the young man who was Mark's main contact in the marijuana-smuggling business came to the farm in his cabin cruiser for what was ostensibly a social visit. Actually he was there to buy out all of Mark's remaining avionics and radar-avoidance gear.

George was the closest thing we had to a friend. Since we were living so secretively it could hardly have been any other way. Be that as it may, Mark and George had learned to trust each other through the years, but even then, in the dope business one can never know whom to trust since the government so often captures people and forces them to turn on their friends.

George and I liked each other quite a lot. We had worked together closely on the two deals on which I had flown, and I had discovered that he was really my kind of guy. We both knew that there was a certain chemistry between us, and even though we had never been alone together, I wanted to reach out to him. He made me feel sexy and desirable. Blond, handsome, rugged, and decent, he radiated a certain funny but unmistakable virility that--quite frankly—I wanted a bit of.

That last weekend with George was very memorable, but as one can imagine, *memorable* does not always equal *pleasant* in the smuggling business.

On Saturday night George and I had flirted outrageously with one another—particularly when Mark and Ned weren't around. George must have figured I was reasonably fair game and that Mark probably wouldn't be able to object to his trying to be with me. It was obvious to him that I was some sort of partner in the operation and not just an out-of-bounds hanger-on.

At that point in my relationship with Mark, I didn't much care whether or not he might be irritated by some of the things I did. Part of that was Mark's fault, I suppose. Although initially he had been intense, interesting, and intellectual, as the months wore on, I began to think of him as being something of a prig and something of a pervert.

Another factor that was at work on me was the stress and callousness which living outside the law had brought in upon us all. We constantly went about armed and ready to defend ourselves and our property, which is to say, our independence. Each of us was ready—at least intellectually—to defend his freedom.

And you know me: I was always a sucker for flirtation. It was nice once again to feel desirable and naughty, and to have a man of broad experience want to experience me, too. My own weakness led me to make what soon proved to be a mistake.

Over Mark's implied objections, on Sunday morning I

went water-skiing with George on his boat. We cruised several miles down the estuary to a wide-open area of flat water where we got stoned, skied, and fixed an elegant little luncheon.

We had just begun to get into some heavy petting on the front deck of the boat when a county police boat approached us. As I scrambled to put on my bathing suit top, two leering cops jumped aboard, ostensibly to "check our registrations." Obviously, though, they were just checking me out. Almost immediately, they spotted a big roach George had carelessly left in the ash tray.

So it was that one of North Carolina's most successful dope dealers and I were busted together—for simple misdemeanor possession.

The cops searched the boat and found three legally-owned guns and $10,000 in cash. Had I not been there, they probably would have stolen the money, but since I was, they had to content themselves with asking us whose it was. Naturally, George claimed it, and as you can well imagine, we were both glad that he had not already put his newly-acquired avionics aboard. George was very friendly to the cops. I wasn't.

We said nothing more and by the time I was booked, I had figured out what information I would give them about my address. They kept his money, of course, as "evidence", and charged us both with possession. Since they didn't like my silence or my attitude, they also charged me with public indecency.

George's brother, a lawyer, came from Wilmington to bail us out. We were given a December court date.

Naturally, I had avoided giving my true address, so the authorities had no idea that I was staying with Mark and Ned just up the river. We took the boat back home in the failing light of late afternoon. We were lucky. Had the arrest taken place later on in the 1980s, under the Regan-era policy of "Zero Tolerance the cops would have taken—which is to say, stolen--the boat, too.

When we arrived, Mark came down to the dock, furious. He assumed that I had had sex with George—which I would have done if the police had stayed away. He looked capable of killing us.

We quickly told him what had happened and why we

hadn't called. His fury gave way to a sickening, palpable fear. George loaded the boat with his new acquisitions and left.

One of the biggest drawbacks in dealing is the paranoia it inspires. One loses a trusting nature first, then decency, then niceness. It can slip away over time or it can all go in the twinkling of an eye.

So it was that Mark almost fell apart that night. He said terrible things about me, about George, and even about Ned. I wanted to contradict him and to defend myself. All that is natural, but any defense or apology I might have offered would not have concealed the fact that I had jeopardized all of us for the sake of a little fun. Now it had become even more possible that our preparations to leave might be thwarted by the authorities.

I sat in our little living room and was silent as Mark raved on into the night. I bore it, too, as Ned made bitter remarks about Mark's involvement with me. It was a terrible night, and for my penance, I sat there with them in the little house beside the river long after George had left, and took their abuse and wept and apologized. Though I kept my own counsel, I blushed with shame because I knew that George and I could have avoided it all had I kept my clothes on and had he thrown the roach overboard.

Mark drove his unhappiness into the ground and almost killed what little love I had left for him. Although I continued to live with him and share his bed, I seldom again felt for him anything more than friendship.

It is tempting to ascribe that final failure of our love to my own actions and to draw from this little story some lesson that finds me justly caught and justly condemned for my infidelity to Mark. Such a facile lesson, though, would ignore what really happened that day. Simply put, the bonds of affection, having frayed for months, broke. I could just as easily have made some other blunder—gotten a speeding ticket, perhaps—which would have set off similar tirades and resulted in the same recriminations.

What proved to be the worst aspect of my arrest was the publicity that came with it. Not only was George's brother an attorney in Wilmington, but his was a family prominent in North Carolina. His grandfather had been governor, and there is nothing that the press likes so much as a fall from grace by the high and mighty.

At first there was just a small article in the local paper giving our names and the offenses with which we were charged. Then the Wilmington paper picked up the story and sent a reporter to do a follow-up that included more details, including why I was charged with public indecency. The article gave the Greenville address of the house I had sold two years before. Then the Greenville paper picked it up, too, wrote about "The Love Boat," and ran a college picture of me.

Some of our North Carolina neighbors realized that I was the one caught on the boat, and they started making excuses to drop by to see us. I was developing into a minor celebrity and had to quit going into town.

Then the local sheriff paid us a courtesy call late one afternoon. He knew Ned to be a wealthy, retired Englishman, but obviously now wanted to know more about us and pretended to be just a good old boy come for a social visit. Ever so politely he insisted on seeing our antique flying boat. We had not done the final packing yet, but he nevertheless got a good view of our preparations. At long last, all smiles and handshakes, he and Ned drove off together for a while in his car. Ned came back $5,000 poorer and furious.

"I'd have given him $50,000 and some of the gold," he said to Mark angrily, "if he'd been more of a gentleman. As it was, the son-of-a-bitch should be glad for the pin money and that I didn't listen to you and kill him. Perhaps I ought to have done just that."

That's how serious it was. I knew at that moment that either he or Mark would have murdered the sheriff had it come down to a choice between killing him or being captured. To fully appreciate how they felt about the morality of such a thing, you must understand that they saw themselves as above the law. They were practically like downed aviators behind the lines of an enemy.

The real weight of things started pressing in on me. I wanted no part of a murder—even the murder of an extortionist. If they had killed that sheriff, half the blood would have been on my hands. I have since gotten more used to such responsibility.

By October 1, we were all completely on edge and decided that we would make our big attempt to leave in five days. I called you that night from a pay phone in town at about 10 p.m., and I have often wondered whether or not you remember our last conversation. We spoke for ten minutes about nothing of consequence. I recall that I had interrupted something you were doing, but you were kind enough about it and patiently listened to me. I was saying good-bye and you were trying to arrange for us to meet somewhere. I could tell that you still loved me—at least in your way.

On October 2, I went to see George's lawyer. He was preparing a suppression motion, and I insisted on giving him an affidavit even though he said that I would have to appear in court in late October. I called a few distant friends and relatives and wrote a few notes.

The months of our feelings of exhilaration toward the prospective journey had given way to a feeling of imminent doom. It was impossible not to fear that we would be captured or killed. Those few days flew.

Ned and Mark had told neighbors that they were going back to England. They had given away the dogs, their extra guns, and practically everything else that wasn't sold or stored. We even had the power turned off on our last day. The farm had never been a show place. The house was a very plain, small 1940s block structure which had once served as the office of a third-rate aviation business . The grass had grown up on the airstrip, and around the hangars and outbuildings, things looked abandoned and lonely—all except for the Short which floated neatly by the dock, clean, waxed, and loaded. It was ready, but I can't say that I was.

In the late afternoon of our last day, Mark insisted that he and I go for a walk. It was a beautiful day. Beyond the fields that went down to the water's edge there were deep woods of old oak trees, and we went there. He led me to a small clearing beside a large rock, a place where we sometimes picnicked and made love.

"We may die tomorrow," he said to me after a long silence, "and it will be my fault if you're killed."

"No, Mark," I said, "I go where I will and do what I want. You are not responsible for me."

"Perhaps it would be better were that not the case," he said with a tone that mixed regret and petulance.

Here was a man, I thought, who no woman could satisfy.

My heart judged him harshly, but my head counseled compassion for him once again. No other men had ever been through what he and Ned had been through. They were unique. I felt sorry for him and wanted to make love with him right there, to expunge our records and allay—if only temporarily—our doubts, discords, and fears.

"This is where we buried our gold," he said, pointing to a mark on the rock. "Three feet down. Don't tell Ned I told you. I thought it only fair since we know where you buried yours."

Then we kissed each other. It took a long time, but finally we could feel the barriers melting. We were like an estranged couple on a sinking ship, finding some common ground just before the long slide into the dark sea. I began crying and laughing in the tumult of my emotions.

"But I am not strong like you. I'm afraid," I admitted.

"I'm afraid, too. But I'm more afraid to stay than to go," he said, "and at least you're going with me." He loved me still.

We kissed me again and I held him tightly, trying to pull our souls together, but just then Ned interrupted us.

"Isn't this a pretty sight," he saidas he entered the small glade. "Undoubtedly you have told her of our little treasure. Well, it can't be helped—perhaps it's all for the best: one way or another we'll never be here again."

"Well, that's what I thought, too, Ned," Mark told him as we stood there in the gathering darkness. "I'm half a mind to ask Eva to pray for us."

Ned's voice took on a kindly tone. "If either of us were a Believer, I might myself pray--if only in passing and to cover all bases, Lad."

He turned to me. "Perhaps later you can pray for me: just in case."

The things we said that evening stuck in my memory for years. Ned was trying to be kind and personal with me. It was in the tone of his voice. And he was speaking to both of us, not just to Mark as he usually did.

"We'll do all right," I offered. "It has been so easy to forget that tomorrow the greatest adventure in history will begin."

"If we aren't killed," Mark responded needlessly.

"Yes. That's possible, too," I said. "Ned, our fate is in

your hands."

"Then why don't you pray for us all right now, all right?" Ned said. "I'll go along with that."

Agnostic though I was, I offered up a prayer as we bowed our heads beside the rock in the woods. I remembered prayers from church and said something to the effect of this:

Lord who has created the heavens and the earth and set each of us in his particular pathway, be with us now and on the morrow. Bless our endeavors; uphold the wings of our plane; bear us over the tumultuous seas and the rough places. Give us your guidance, help us to do what you would have us do and live or die as you decree, and to listen when you speak. Be with us all the rest of our lives and in the life or lives to come, and help us to understand that it is your will and not ours, that will prevail. Amen.

"Amen," Mark said.
"Amen!" Ned added.

We stood there for a minute or two. Then Ned walked back toward the house, and we strolled down deeper into the woods. We spoke very little. There was nothing more to say, and we listened to the night sounds and savored the melancholy feeling of being alive one last evening.

A short time later, Ned came running back to us.

"There's someone at the house," he said as he breathed heavily.

"The police?" Mark asked nervously.

"I don't think so. It's a man—apparently alone. I was down at the Short and watched him through binoculars. He's in a rented car. Never seen him before."

"Maybe a nark," I suggested.

"Maybe so," Ned agreed. I could see he was wearing his shoulder holster. He drew the pistol and operated the slide to put a round in the chamber, then put it back. He meant business, but it looked strange to see a kindly, 52-year-old scientist preparing to meet another man, gun at the ready.

I remembered he had fought in the trenches in 1917. He had told me he had killed men face-to-face with both a pistol and a bayonet, and I knew that he could do it again if he had to.

As we trotted back to the Short, we could see that the

man was leaving it, flashlight in hand, and walking up to the house. We slipped into the plane and went to the gun locker.

"Let's go find out what the bugger wants," Ned said as he handed us two pistols. "You circle around the back," he said to Mark, who nodded and immediately moved away as silently as an Indian scout.

Ned and I took our time getting back to the house. Without the dogs, it was hard to tell whether or not our visitor was really alone, so we split up and carefully reconnoitered the area around the house, hangar, and airfield but found no one else. My heart was in my throat as I slipped about, cocked pistol in hand, and listened for strange noises. It did not seem like anyone was about, but in the darkness, a small army of narcs could have concealed itself from us.

Whoever was in the house had gone about and lighted the kerosene lanterns and candles he found and was obviously making himself quite at home. We could tell that he was going from room to room in a casual but thorough manner. Clearly he was not a typical burglar. He could have been a friend of ours— if we had any—but we couldn't take chances.

Mark slipped around to the back door so he could enter silently if there was trouble. Ned and I entered through the front door, guns drawn.

I was shocked and amazed beyond speaking: *It was Julian!*

Obviously, he had followed me from England and, well, there he was— standing in our messy little living room. Even though he was wearing his black coat and a clerical collar, his resemblance to Mark was so close that subconsciously Ned relaxed his guard even as I shouted out his name.

"*Julian!* What are you doing here?"

"You know this man?" Ned asked loudly.

"Yes," I admitted. "I met him in England in August. He's... he's a priest."

"That's bloody obvious—perhaps too obvious," Ned said, his gun still half-pointed at Julian.

"But quite true, Sir," Julian said, proffering his hand to Ned. "Julian Parker-Lane, Sir, and you are...?"

"Name's Nigel Hampton," Ned lied, using his local alias that corresponded with his driver's license. He did not shake

Julian's hand but kept his gun at the ready, which is to say pointed near but not directly at our visitor.

"Oh, no, it's not," Julian said cheerfully, as he lowered his untaken hand. "No more than this lady's name is Cathy Johnson, which is what she was calling herself when she came to Brighton." He was smiling like a cat.

"As she suggests," he continued, remarkably coolly for a man more or less held at gunpoint, "Evangeline Weathers and I have met before, but under different circumstances."

"Why have you come here and what do you want?" I asked, amazed that he had found me and knew my real name.

"I have come because I want the truth. All of it. I'm very good about getting the truth, you know," he said.

"Take off your coat," Ned said with a gesture of his gun. Somewhat nervously, Julian complied.

"Search him," Ned said to me in Greek. "He might be armed."

I patted him down carefully, for we thought he might be wearing a body transmitter or tape recorder. I also looked around the room for one.

"This is not necessary," Julian said to him, also in Greek. It was Ned's turn to be astonished. I shrugged my shoulders in answer to his questioning glance. I found a voice-activated tape recorder in the inside coat pocket of his jacket. It was working. I took out the tape.

"We shall decide what is necessary and what is not," Ned said.

Julian affected calmness. "Mind if I sit?" he asked.

"Go right ahead," Ned responded rather too quickly as he gestured to an armchair with his pistol. "Where have I seen you before, Sir?" he inquired politely as the two of them sat down. Ned rested his arms on the arms of his overstuffed chair. The gun, still in his hand, was laying flat and sinister-looking on the top of one arm, negligently pointed about a yard to the side of Julian's head.

"Perhaps you have seen me in England. I preach there sometimes. Perhaps at Oxford?"

"Not bloody likely in either case."

I sat down in a straightback chair opposite the doorway to the kitchen. Julian's back was to that doorway—the one through which Mark might come if he was still behind the house.

We sat in silence for a few moments. Each of us was waiting for one of the others to say something. Ned—who would have made a great poker player—could have stayed that way forever. Julian, too, was playing a waiting game. Finally I spoke up.

"What truth do you want, Julian?"

"I thought you'd never ask," he replied. "I have rehearsed my little speech setting forth my not-so-little reasons for finding you, for tracking you down, so to speak."

Carefully, for Ned's sake, he lighted a pipe. It made him look even older than his 41 years. Then he continued.

"Look, I know you people are doing something really secret and all that. It's rather obvious, too, that you're all getting ready to leave here. I must conclude that you are simply moving from the local area and that possibly you're all involved in some sort of illegal business.

"Now if you are, then perhaps I have stepped in where I don't belong. Maybe I've gotten myself into big trouble, a jam, or a fix: whatever you Americans call it.

"But I still want the truth—or at least so much of it as touches me," he concluded—rather bravely I thought.

"I don't see that what we are doing is any of your business," Ned said. "Naturally we presume you are with the police or an extortionist of some sort, not to mention a burglar."

My heart was in my mouth. I felt that something terrible was going to happen and that, again, it would be my fault.

My heart began beating rapidly. I saw Mark slipping into the kitchen behind Julian. I tried to catch his eye and raised my hand to warn him, but I was speechless, almost paralyzed.

"Well, I'm certainly not a policeman nor am I working with them," Julian said quickly. "I am not an extortionist, either, Sir. I want nothing but the truth. Mainly, why did she," he said pointing at me, "come snooping around in England?"

Ned moved the pistol slightly more in our visitor's direction and said, "In this country we shoot first and ask questions later. Don't you think you are not in much of a position to be asking us anything?"

"Don't shoot him," I croaked, barely able to speak. "Please." I couldn't take my eyes off of them. Julian began to look worried again, but he still had pluck.

"I warn you, Sir, that I have taken certain precautions in case you are tempted to indulge in foul play. I would advise you to not to threaten me with that gun!"

Still unnoticed by Julian, Mark stopped some ten feet behind him.

"No one is threatening you," Ned said. He feared, no doubt, that Julian had planted a transmitter of some sort in the room before we came back. "And may I inquire as to what sort of 'precautions' you have deemed it prudent to take before coming here to commit burglary?"

"You may," Julian replied pompously, not realizing how superior Ned's intelligence was to his own.

"First, I have left certain sealed instructions with a trusted man in a nearby town—to be opened should I not return. Furthermore, noting that you appeared on the verge of leaving, I took the liberty of tampering with both your truck and your aircraft. You will tell me what I want to know."

Suddenly Mark exploded out of the kitchen doorway, furious, his eyes burning with the pure rage.

"You son-of-a-bitch!" he shouted loudly enough to wake the dead.

He startled us all and Julian dove from his seat and stumbled forward over a crate in pure fear of the redneck who was clawing his way toward him, gun in hand.

"Don't shoot him!" I screamed. It probably saved Julian's life; Mark paused in his headlong rush.

"No, don't shoot me!" Julian cried from the corner where he had ended up, huddled behind a chair. "I won't hurt you. I promise: I'll fix everything," he babbled quickly. "Just don't shoot!"

Pushing the chair aside and grabbing the terrified priest by the lapels with his left hand, Mark jammed his automatic under the man's chin. "Why are you butting into our business, asshole?" he shouted. I thought he had finally gone mad from the strain. He was almost out of control.

White with fear, Julian pointed to me. "Ask her," he said in a high-pitched whimper. "She came to Brighton. She looked up my mother, questioned her endlessly about all manner of things and gave a false name. For the Love of God, Man: ask her!"

Mark turned to me and for a few long seconds, I thought he was going to shoot me. I was beginning to tremble, but it was from some strange sense of excitement, not fear. Realizing that, suddenly I became cool and calm although my heart continued beating with such a power that I could hear the blood rushing in my ears.

It was all so simple: I had gone to Brighton, I had been unfaithful with George and I had jeopardized everything. Because of me, all the terrors would fall on Mark and Ned. And I? I would be dead, because Mark was just about to point the gun at me and kill me.

In that brief moment I had time enough to know that I was going to forgive him for shooting me: The strain of it all was clearly too much for him, and it was my fault. He had not yet turned the gun on me.

Coldly, he asked me: "Who is this bastard?"

"That bastard," I said slowly, *"is your son."*

****

VIII

The Father and The Son

The room was totally silent. The four of us were perfectly immobile. No one had the slightest idea what would happen next, and as the seconds ticked away, the absolute truth of what I had said sank into Mark and Ned. Julian was too afraid to move. He thought that I was speaking metaphorically in an effort to save him.

And I? I sat there without thought or volition. Coming together as it had, it was all too complex to comprehend. Only the truth could have come out of my mouth, and it had.

Finally, Ned broke the ice. "I guess we don't have to worry now about the police busting in on us. They'd 'a bloody well done that already." He looked at Julian in awe.

"The son-of-a-bitch really does look like you, old boy," he said to Mark.

Suddenly Mark let go of Julian's lapels as if they were hot. With a look of shock and incredulity he stepped back from him, staring at the face of an older man who, according to me, he had fathered. His eyes were wide and his mouth open. It was too much for him; he was dumbstruck.

Mark staggered backward and sat down--or rather collapsed--against the wall across from where Julian remained crouched down, stock-still and afraid to move. Absentmindedly he uncocked his gun and ejected the clip onto the floor then covered his face with his hands and tried to think.

With the possibility of immediate, violent death lifted from him, Julian regained some of his composure. He too, straightened up some, although he did not yet dare to stand up completely or take a chair. He shook himself slightly, trying to salvage some of his dignity. He straightened his lapels and his collar.

Then Ned began to find the situation amusing. Then he found it funny. For the first time in weeks, I heard him laugh, and when he laughed, he roared. He couldn't stop laughing, and he rose up out of his chair and went to the kitchen doorway laughing and leaned against the doorjam, pistol in hand.

I, too, was near madness, but I started giggling anyway. Suddenly it all seemed the silliest situation imaginable. Then Mark began laughing hysterically.

As our laughter increased, so did Julian's obvious discomfort, and that gave us even more cause for laughter. Ned was in tears and could barely stand up. Mark stole glances at the man—his son who was older than he was—sitting near him in those silly vestments. Mark pointed and said, *"My son!"* which urged us to further fits of laughter.

I was laughing as much from relief as from anything else, but also because finally—for the first time in months—there was laughter among the three of us together. It is amazing how badly one can miss some humor.

Julian found none of it amusing and was certain that we were laughing at him. At that point, too, he was quite naturally thinking we were all crazy and that we probably would kill him to cover our crimes. His response was to pretend to be amused, and he began to feign laughter of his own.

His attempts to join in were as obvious as they were hilarious. He was still terrified of Mark—as well he should have been—and was trying to laugh his way out of a shooting. When he brayed out a loud and very English, *"Ha, Ha, Ha!"* the three of us practically collapsed on the floor. He thought about making a grab for Ned's gun and holding us at gunpoint while he made good his escape, but since he was too scared and too unfamiliar with weapons to try such a thing, he attempted to humor us instead. And he did.

Over and over Mark asked, *"Who is this bastard?"* and Ned replied, *"Your son!"* Then both men nearly ruptured their spleens laughing at what was for Julian the most galling fact of his entire life—his illegitimacy.

He couldn't know that the two men knew that he was, in fact, a bastard, just as he did not know that one was his great-uncle and the other was his father. He hadn't yet noticed that Mark was English and looked very much like him. That soon changed.

He could not, however, miss that they were laughing at him. More importantly, he realized that his status as a clergyman added to their amusement, and to that he objected.

"See here," he said at last, getting to his feet, "that's clearly enough of that."

"See here! See here!" Mark and Ned began to repeat. They, too, stood up, then collapsed into two old armchairs as if exhausted from their efforts.

Julian sat down on a kitchen chair opposite mine, and so there we were, sitting in the dimly-lit room in a circle of chairs about eight feet in diameter, the three of us giggling like school girls at the perplexed priest.

Ned pulled out a half-bottle of whiskey from a box next to his chair.

"This calls for a drink," he said, holding the bottle by the neck and offering it to Julian.

"Ladies first," he said, taking the bottle and handing it to me.

I took a big slug of it. It burned but tasted good anyway. My eyes watered. I handed it back to him. He was still trying to placate us and got ready to drink it.

"Give us a toast," Ned said.

"To the Queen!" Julian said before sipping from the bottle.

Mark and Ned laughed almost hysterically. Julian passed the bottle to Ned.

"To the Queen!" Ned said as he downed a big swallow. Then he handed the bottle to Mark, who now toasted without thinking first.

"To Cookie!" he said, tipping the bottle to take a huge swallow that made him come up choking. He handed the bottle to Ned as he sputtered.

"To Cookie!" Ned said, tipping it up. I had no idea who Cookie was until I looked at Julian.

The color—which never had been very good—was draining away from his face. Ned was staring at him.

"How is old Cookie doing?" he asked Julian. "I should have thought she'd be dead by now. Eva doesn't share with us all of the things she does, you know."

"No, she doesn't," Mark added. "She can be quite secretive—and quite naughty. But things have a way of coming back to haunt her. Like you, for instance. I say you've come back to haunt us both." Mark's eyes were wide with madness. "No sin remains hidden."

Compared to what I had just been through, his criticisms of me were as nothing. Heck: I was, after all, still alive.

Julian had realized for the first time that Mark was not an American.

"You're English!" he exclaimed. Then: "How did you know my mother was once called Cookie?" He jumped to his feet and backed up a step, almost falling over his chair.

"You both called her Cookie!" he said wildly. "That was what she was called long ago—before I was born! Who are you?"

He backed up against the wall and looked at us again. There was still a chance that our deceptions could be carried off and we could leave as we had planned. It would have been best that way, we thought. But of course we were fooling ourselves to think that we had any control over events.

He was thinking, thinking, his eyes almost shifty as he tried to determine where the truths lay. Ned was trying to think faster.

"Show us, Father, what you have done to disturb the plane—if you have disturbed it, that is," Ned said at last in a kindly, patronizing way. Rarely one to say anything without a reason, he was trying to let Julian think that he could leave unscathed and thereby speed his exit. But Ned had only reminded Julian of the fact that he was a clergyman—something he had probably forgotten during the preceding ten extraordinary minutes.

"Give me a few moments to think...to pray, that is," he said, correcting himself. Astonishingly, he sank to his knees and began to pray silently. We had no idea what to do. We passed the bottle around while we waited.

When he arose and dusted off his knees after a two or three minutes, he was a new man. Not a better man, but a new one all the same.

"God works in mysterious ways His wonders to perform," he said prophetically. "This He hath said to me."

Then Mark, who had collected himself somewhat, spoke. "I'm sorry. I was rude to you. You said you damaged my plane. I lost my temper. Did you disable my plane?"

"Yes I did," Julian said. "but it can be easily corrected. I know quite a bit about mechanics myself."

"Then let's go fix it, Julian," I said, acting as if I was getting ready to get up.

He straightened his clothes in an officious manner, then seated himself once again. He paused. "Not until I have my truths," he said simply.

"We could force you," Ned said, but it sounded unconvincing.

"And Daniel was amid the lions and they opened not their mouths," Julian said. "Now, who are you?"

"Please, Julian, let us go," I pleaded. "Don't ask any questions. Just leave us alone. We'll give you money—enough for plane tickets and then some. Just go."

"You didn't leave me and my mother alone," he said to me angrily.

No one was laughing now.

It was then that Julian started fitting all the pieces of the puzzle together.

While he thought, Ned and Mark tried to cajole and

intimidate him, but to no avail. The three of us were left waiting on Julian.

It did not take him long to recount in his own mind the events which had led up to that point some twenty or thirty minutes before when all was crisis and violence, and his life and mine had lain in the balance.

I had sought him and his mother in England. I had used an alias with them, but he had gotten at my true identity by using a passkey and searching out my passport while I slept. He had tracked us down, but might never have found us in time without help from the Greenville newspaper that carried the "Love Boat" story about me and George getting busted.

We all saw it happen. Each of us had undergone his or her own epiphany in these events, and so we watched with rapt attention as his unfolded. We knew what he was thinking when he turned his eyes first on Mark and then on Ned.

He remembered the pictures on his mother's mantle and in her old newspaper clippings.

He kept reviewing it all. Always it came back to this: I had called him Mark's son.

Finally he said, "That's the very airplane, isn't it? How is this possible? What is this? Why didn't you ever come back?"

He knew. We said nothing.

"But if you were my father," he continued in astonishment, "how could you look so young and why didn't you let people know you weren't dead?"

Now it was Julian's turn to be the one who was feeling insane.

"I'm not your father. That's impossible," Mark lied.

"Nothing is impossible to God," he replied.

Julian turned to Ned and pointed his finger at him.

"And I know who you are, too! You're his uncle: the man who was lost with him, aren't you?" he said.

"I'd have to be 84 years old now, wouldn't I," Ned said without thinking first. He didn't know what a quick mind Julian had.

"How did you know how old that man would be now were you not him?" asked Julian.

And so it went on that way for a few minutes with Mark and Ned trying to carry out their deceptions in the face of a relentless cross-examination, all to no avail. Julian's questions kept coming at them one after another until at last they were defeated.

Finally Mark and Ned clamed up and he turned on me. I wouldn't talk, either; I had done enough damage already. On the other hand, neither could I leave that compelling scene. Where in the wide world would I have gone, anyway?

Then Julian summarized aloud all that he knew or could surmise about me, revealing that he had investigated my past and had been asking questions about us in town. That really upset us, but we said nothing.

The final, masterful conclusions he drew were completely correct, leaving out only the mechanism by which all had come to pass. He had cracked the nut intellectually, but not emotionally. He sat smiling with his fingertips together, looking like his favorite character in literature, Sherlock Holmes, whom he quoted: "When all else is excluded, that which remains must be true." There were but two possible truths, he finally deduced.

"You *are* Mark Powell, my mother's lover before the war. Don't bother trying to deny it! I have seen your picture. Either the two of you have discovered various techniques or substances to delay or hide aging or you, Sir," he said to Ned, "have discovered the means whereby to pass through time.

"As incredible as it may seem, I must therefore believe the latter of the two theories. I reject the former on many grounds. Firstly, nothing in your histories suggests that you intentionally went missing in 1939 and stayed away ever since, disloyal to your families, your country, and mankind--not to mention my mother, Mr. Powell."

Mark blushed deeply. Loyalty was the virtue he most cherished.

"Had you, for example," Julian continued, "been captured by the Germans, that would not account for your present youth. Perhaps, then, you found the mythical Shangri-la? I think not. Nothing would have prevented you from coming back, or at least from using the radio. After all, the plane is still intact.

"It is, of course, covered with a copper wire apparatus and has aboard a sophisticated computer system, not to mention all the supplies necessary for a long journey.

"I therefore surmise that you came forward in time in

that very same aircraft and that you could not go back, and that you are once again on the verge of leaving." He had searched after the truth and found it.

" Where will you go now?" he asked, looking at Ned.

"Wherever we want to go," Ned said.

"Not without my cooperation," Julian quickly reminded him.

By this time, Mark was beyond getting angry with him, and I was saying nothing.

Ned thought for a few moments. "All right, young man: You win." He looked at Mark. "We might as well tell him everything. He's in it as deep as we are now."

Mark nodded his assent.

"And how is that? What do you mean, *in deep*?" Julian asked uneasily, and so it was that Ned began to explain it all, including the accidental trip to the '70s, the dope smuggling, the preparations and even the grand plan to try to escape the present by going to the past using an untried technique.

In a brief, straightforward way, he told him of the dangers of the passage as well as the dangers of the present, and Julian listened with first wonder and then with outright admiration. He did not question our fears. Nor did he question hiding the invention from the world, particularly considering that it might be used to go backward in time. If it worked, the Short might possibly be used in an attempt to reverse the course of history—if such an alteration was possible. That is the ultimate question of time travel. It is one I can now answer.

Then Julian dropped two bombshells on us.

"We must leave at once," he said.

"You're not going anywhere with us," Mark said abruptly.

"Then you're not going anywhere either, *Father*," Julian said, adding in his second bombshell: "And there's going to be a change in the proposed destination. I must insist."

"Where away?" Ned asked. He knew Julian had him over a barrel. He knew that he would neither torture nor kill Julian.

"Isn't it obvious? If you can try for Greece, you can try for Rome. You said we'd probably all get killed anyway. And I am going with you.

"And that being the case—and it is the case, *Uncle*—we

are going to Palestine if it is God's will and if your crazy machine will convey us thither." An undeniable glow was in his eyes. "How could you not want to risk all for even the slightest opportunity to go there and to walk beside Our Lord and Savior when he dwelt among us? That is where we are going, and we'd better be quick about it if we're going at all."

We had, of course, thought previously of making exactly that particular attempt, but we had rejected it for many reasons. Primarily, of course, our own studies and interests had been of Greece. To us, the era of Christ seemed one of decline, decadence, and Roman domination.

On the other hand, there was only a slight chance that we could land in the right hemisphere. If we missed, it hardly mattered to us in what era we alighted even if we did "hit" the time-era at which Ned would aim us. There was also the possibility of death or of even something less appealing: a suspension outside of time, travelling endlessly backward or forward through time, never to emerge.

So it was that we had decided to go where our hearts directed. We argued with him, but he knew and we knew that we could not force him to say what, if anything, he had done to disable the plane. After his own fashion he was both brave and stubborn.

So it was that after long discussion, we agreed to readjust the master controls to 26 A.D.

Ned calculated that all he could do was "aim" at the desired year based on calculations of the characteristics and number of oscillations of the waves to be "ridden." Since the unfortunate second "jump" he had computerized the counting process, but supposed that the computing might be impaired while we were out of time, possibly distorting the start-up and shut-down of the apparatus and of our consequent reemergence into time. Be that as it may, we gave in to Julian.

At about midnight, we all trooped out to the airplane. Using batteries, Ned turned on the computer and explained briefly to Julian how it worked and Julian acted as if he understood everything. He watched as Ned dialed in the equivalent of 1,954 years, and the appropriate numbers appeared on the small display of what had been a transceiver.

"So much for optimism," Ned said. He had no way of knowing whether or not it would work.

I should say that in all honesty, by that point in time we no longer resented the sudden change of plans forced on us by Julian. We knew there might be advantages in the later target, and we just wanted to leave before something else went wrong.

Strangely enough, Julian's arrival and his complete faith in our ability to carry off the journey rekindled our excitement. So much for the plans of humans—of eight years of danger and work, eight years of studying the language, customs and personalities of the Greeks of 450 B.C.

"And now," asked Mark resentfully, "what have you done to the plane?" But Julian devised a plan to barricade himself behind the cargo in the rear of the plane before he would reveal the various mischiefs he had committed to disable the Short.

We spent the whole night getting ready. The precautions Julian had taken to assure his safety could have brought out the sheriff by morning.

Julian was prepared to go without even a note to his mother; at my insistence he called her. What could he say? What did he say? I don't know. I stayed in the car and watched him placing the call. I couldn't hear a thing. For all I know, he called someone else. I could not help thinking that now Doris might be losing a son to the same sea and the same instrumentality that had taken her fiancé some 41 years before.

When we got back to the farm, Julian left a note in the rented car saying that he had met some old friends and was going flying with them. Then he took up his place behind the cargo and revealed his sabotage. His easily-corrected damages had been cleverly done. They would have taken hours to unravel without his help.

We took off just at dawn. The heavy plane ate up two miles of flat, smooth water before it could finally lift off. Slowly, and using more gas than Mark liked, we climbed until we reached our maximum altitude. Our hearts were beating wildly on that cloudless morning.

****

IX

The Leap

"Ready?" asked Mark over the intercom. "Ready!" we replied, as we turned on the oxygen to our masks. The red light went on. Ten seconds to go. Mark killed the engines and lowered the nose to maintain airspeed. In the copilot seat, Ned lifted the safety cover to the wave machine control and flipped the paddle switch.

In an instant the scene outside disappeared as if it were a blank electronic screen. The sea, sky, and clouds were replaced by an eerie, greenish-white light that seemed like a viscous liquid in which we were suspended with no sense of motion. Everything was silence, and I realized that this was how time travel feels. Time seemed to slow greatly in the cabin. Taking what seemed to be minutes, I lowered my glance to my wristwatch and saw the second-hand dropping from one station to the next at a crawl, as if it were marking the heartbeat of a sleeping whale. A vague memory of your favorite Lawrence Durrell lines from the play, *Sappho*, went slowly through my mind:

> *Damned in effect and still neglecting cause,*
> *Soft brief and awkward as the kisses which combine*
> *To intersect with death till time follows us, time*
> *Finds and detains us here in time*
> *In this eternal pause,*
> *Fumbling outside immortality's immobile doors.*

We could see nothing outside the windows, not even the wing. Ahead of me, the back of Ned's head was as immobile as mine as we sat suspended in the odd glare. A slight electric haze seemed to cover everything, and I thought that we could be this way forever. There was no sound except that which came from within me—my heart beating and the faint, rushing sound of blood in the ear. I moved my mouth but couldn't seem to speak.

Sorrow and regret moved in on me like a sluggish tide.

The machine was surely working; it had taken us out of time. Whether it would put us back, and where and when, were questions we had considered many times before. But there in the soup of travel itself we were as if stunned. We were beyond pondering our future. It was eerie, and I was becoming frightened in a listless sort of way.

We stayed in that suspended state for only 13.695 minutes by our electric clocks, but it seemed as if we were there for hours.

Suddenly, a loud, bass drumbeat of sound shattered all of that, and I was thrown violently against the window beside me. My face hit it with so much force that I cracked the Plexiglas and came away dazed. My nose started to bleed and I was engulfed in noise: the restarting engines, the wind, a ringing in my left ear, and a loud flapping noise aft. The Short began to rise and dip and yaw.

Ned and Mark worked the controls and soon we were flying level. I looked out over an azure sea and a cloudless sky. Unbuckling my seat harness and holding a tee shirt to my nose, I staggered forward to the little jump seat beside Mark.

"What happened?" I yelled.

"I think we did it!" he yelled back.

And so we had. Naturally, we didn't know where or when we were, but we had survived and we believed that we had slipped through time. Ahead of us lay an open, empty sea and empty skies— no shipping, no aircraft. Mark spun the radio dials through the frequencies and found nothing.

We were ecstatic. Fools rush in.

Ned's face was shining with pride in what was the greatest scientific accomplishment of his life. He was a god in his own right that day, and he knew it.

Julian came forward, too, his eyes blazing with fervor. "God is with us!" he kept saying over and over.

Finally Mark yelled at him: "Then I wish he would bloody well fix the sodding rudder!" Julian was aghast.

"God will not be mocked!" he said as he moved back past me, his face red with rage. No one was too concerned about my injuries and the bleeding was beginning to slow. Finally it stopped.

To the southeast lay islands Ned and Mark hoped were

the Madeira group over which Mark had flown in the Winter of 1939. We continued toward the east. I relieved him and Ned from time to time, glad to have something to do and satisfied with my ability to handle the Short.

As the hours passed, we began to worry that we might be forced to land on the sea, and we were grateful that we had added extra fuel tanks to the plane.

As we droned on, my face began to hurt. I resisted the urge to take some of the morphine we had, and in the mirror I saw how my cheek had swollen and become purple. I had bled all over my shirt, too, but luckily my nose was not broken.

After long flying, low on fuel, we finally came to a long, sunny, and mostly empty coastline. Without hesitation Mark headed us straight in toward a small river delta where he set the plane down just up the main estuary from the sea. Before touching down in a long, smooth, slide across the glassy waters between tree-studded islands and peninsulas, we had seen some signs of human habitation north along the coast and a few sailboats with lanteen sails motionless off to the south.

We taxied to a large, heavily wooded island and shut off the engines. The sudden absence of noise seemed abnormal and unsettling, and yet we greeted it with relief as the Short slid to within 40 feet of the shore. Come what might, at least we had made land. Opening the main hatches and doors, we breathed the salt-rich air.

It was late afternoon. The sky was bright and the weather mild. Mark cast our small aluminum anchor while Ned and I pumped up the smallest of our rafts. Trailing a towline and armed with a pistol, Mark paddled in toward the large clearing ahead. Ned and I covered him with rifles as he searched for snags under the water. Finding none, he stepped ashore on a muddy beach and cast about for signs of recent human activity. Then he pulled the Short in while I worked the water rudder and Ned maintained his guard.

The island was about a half-mile long and seemed to be uninhabited. We landed, however, at a frequently used campsite complete with wooden racks probably meant for drying fish. Scattered about were bits of broken pots and other small litter. We ate some canned food, inspected the airplane, and camped on the shore beneath the towering trees.

We quickly learned that Julian was the kind of person who wouldn't work if there were others around to work for him. I found his inexhaustible supply of excuses amusing. Mark, on the other hand, was not so entertained. His dislike was growing for the son he had first met scant hours before, and I do not doubt that they would have had harsh words had not Julian taken the raft and gone fishing. As it turned out, he even managed to catch a large fish.

That night—thinking about you and our camping trips in the mountains—I cooked a meal of rice and fresh fish over an open fire while Mark and Ned took stock of the airplane. Part of the rudder was missing. Presumably it had been left somewhere outside of time, for there was no sign of tearing, just a surgically clean edge where the remaining tail ended.

Our first night on that island was uneventful but for an onslaught of mosquitoes that our repellents and screening just barely kept at bay. In spite of them, Ned stood watch most of the night. Julian slept in the plane, and Mark and I pitched a tent ashore.

Our initial jubilation had given way to worry. Depression and self-doubt had begun to set in, and we were reluctant to admit even to each other that we might have made a terrible mistake. After all, not everything that is possible to be done ought to be done. Sleepless, we lay there in the insect-loud night; together but alone with our thoughts. We had apparently done what no one had ever done. But had it been wise?

With a flawless dawn came relief from the mosquitoes, and our spirits lifted. After making fairly sure that there were no crocodiles or vicious fish in the water, I bathed, shampooed my hair, and put on a fresh safari-type shirt and shorts. The left side of my face was swollen and purple, but as long as I didn't use a mirror it didn't bother me much. I felt rough and ready. There's nothing like the combination of fresh underwear, clean socks, hiking boots, and a dramatic, honestly come-by and painless bruise to make a woman ready to take on the day.

The men revived, too. Talking like boys on an impromptu camping trip, they shaved, ate a hearty breakfast, and began to make plans to scout the area using the largest of the rubber boats. Somehow or another they had assumed that I would be the cook and the bottle-washer—which was, for the moment, all right with me.

As the plane had only 20 minutes of fuel left, it would have been pointless, even dangerous, to take it up, and so some of our discussions that day concerned getting it ready for mothballing even though we thought it would probably never be used again.

Mark and Ned organized and cleaned their supplies and weapons and set Julian about the only task to which he did not object—more fishing, a pastime which he apparently thought well fit for a clergyman. The estuary teemed with fish, and we were glad to have him busy and out of our way.

At midmorning we experienced a stroke of what might have been the greatest good fortune of our entire trip--outside of survival itself, of course. It came in the form of a white man in a small boat who sailed boldly toward us from the east and ran his craft ashore beside the beached plane. He jumped lightly from his craft, dragged it up a bit, and made the gesture of greeting and peace that we learned was universal in those times. As if surrendering, but to demonstrate that he was unarmed, he raised both palms toward us at shoulder level. His wide grin showed that he was missing the front left incisor.

He was about five and half feet tall and appeared to be about 50 years old. Deeply tanned and dressed in an old brown tunic with an embroidered edge and sandals, our visitor had light brown, short-cropped hair around a central bald area, and sharp, light blue eyes. He had many scars—particularly on his arms and calves. One real beauty ran across his bald spot. He carried no weapons, although he had left a bow, arrows, a short sword, and two long, slender fishing spears in the boat. We could see that he also had a basket of vegetables and three small jugs in his boat.

The boat itself was made of broad boards laid flush and caulked with black pitch and oakum. Similar in shape to a modern double-ended dory, it was about 20 feet long with a single mast, lanteen sail, and attached paddle-rudder on the starboard side aft. It also had double liftable lee boards amidships as well as oars. It was tidy and seaworthy, I thought, having learned to notice and respect such matters on numerous weekend sailing adventures in Charleston Harbor with my Uncle Tom.

Lowering his hands, the man began to speak in a tongue

none of us could recognize.

Ned replied to him in a slow, careful Latin, and the man immediately smiled, then began speaking in another language that sounded a little like modern French. We soon realized, however, that it *was* Latin, but it was a spoken Latin that used many slang words and grammatical constructions to which it took us some weeks to grow accustomed. It was as if one had learned Russian only to discover that it was pronounced and used like Spanish. The spoken Latin sounded prettier and flowed more smoothly than I had imagined it would, the language of the street being more dynamic than that used by the writers whose works have survived through the centuries.

Our visitor's name was Marcus, and he was obviously a daredevil. Who but a brave man would have approached us unarmed?

His intelligence, too, was obvious. I could see it in the way that his eyes glinted with interest as they darted over our clothing, our possessions, and the Short Flying Boat. He was impressed but tried not to appear overawed or afraid.

He laughed easily at anything, any little mishap or foible or joke. He later told us that he could see quickly that we were not a threat to him, and that he had found it easy to be brave when approaching us. He explained that he had been a soldier, a veteran of many combats, and he knew intuitively (and correctly) that we would have weapons far superior to his own, so that he was putting himself completely in our power even before he came ashore.

It was Julian who most quickly got the hang of talking to him. He had a superior ability with languages that we found useful but irritating. It meant that on many occasions he was able to exercise control over the tone and tenor of conversations and took upon himself a leadership role that had not been conceded to him. For that matter, the question of leadership within our group was never really settled, and the three men unconsciously vied with one another for control of even minor matters.

On that first day, our guest spoke and we listened as best we could, asking Julian to translate when necessary.

With hand gestures, we invited our guest to sit on the logs around our campfire underneath a large oak tree. As I served him some sweet, lightened coffee which he tried without hesitation, he glanced at my face. I realized he thought that one of the men had beaten me, and naturally enough, my embarrassment made me look even more a victim. I hoped there would be time later to explain that it was just an injury. There was no help for it. As he spoke to the men, there was not much point of my butting in.

"Who are you?" was his central question.

"Who do you think that we are?" Julian responded in a stylized but bold Latin inflected with the accents of our inquisitor.

"All I know is this," Marcus responded, "You're not from any country I have ever been in, and I've been in practically every land a Roman soldier has tramped in the last 20 years. You have all these amazing...things," he said looking around and sweeping his arm.

Julian translated for us. We were thrilled. We were beginning to understand him; he spoke as much with his hands as he did with words.

"And your boat," he continued when we did not offer anything, "It's of a type I've never seen, and I've seen them all. The fishermen from the village told me it flew through the air and roared like a lion, but they are an ignorant and superstitious lot."

Again Julian translated for us. After some discussion, he spoke for us.

"We are emissaries from a faraway land from which no man has ever come. We are travelers here to see your world."

"Then you are from that great land far to the West. It is the land, I have heard, where the truly ancient ones live in their matchless cities high on mountains which would dwarf those of Helvetia and Gaul," he said.

We presumed that he meant the Andes. Julian did not contradict him. "We are new to this land, and there is much we must learn. First, please tell us what is the name of this country."

He said that to the Romans this was known generally as Mauretania and more particularly as Tingitana. Mark pulled out one of his maps. The stranger tried not to be overly impressed by it. As soon as he realized what he was looking at and what the approximate scale was, he pointed things that might interest us.

We had landed on what is now called the Sebou River in Morocco. I was excited: It was another great good fortune.

Julian kept on talking, "And there is someone who we must meet and worship."

"Then you must go to him," the man replied. "I believe he lives these days some 150 miles south of Rome on an island. It is, of course, very far, but we have a saying here: 'All roads lead to Rome'."

Understanding him even as he spoke, we laughed. He looked puzzled.

Ned smiled and tried out his own Latin. "We have the same saying," he said.

"You were a soldier," he continued, baring his right arm to show his old scars from the First World War and pointing to the scars on his face. "So was I." Their eyes met.

Not wanting to be left out or underrated, Mark asked, "What is it that you want of us?"

"Only to serve you," the man responded, nodding his head downward as if bowing.

It was simple and straightforward enough.

"Or to trick us, perhaps?" Julian suggested.

Our guest showed not the least offence taken, but rather he smiled and gestured with outstretched hands. "But of course!" he readily admitted. "I could be an agent of Rome or of the king of this country. Or a pirate, for that matter; there are some around, after all.

"But I am not. I am willing to serve you for such rewards as your service may give me. Humble men must constantly make choices in this life: Who they will serve, who they will not serve. I served Octavian. I served Varus, I served Tiberias. Sometimes it came out to the good, sometimes not so good.

The mention of Tiberias affected Julian and he immediately wanted to know if Tiberias was now the emperor, and, if so, for how long had he been in charge?

"Why, you are from far off, aren't you?" Marcus said. "The Old Man has been head of the government of Rome since Octavian died, for... 13 years."

I was still trying to translate when Julian leaped up and shouted in English, "God be praised! We are in time! We are not too late! Even as we speak, God dwells among men!"

Our guest was as amused as the rest of us, and assumed that word of Tiberias' reign was the cause of Julian's jubilation.

"This is..." Julian said, grasping for words in English, "This is great! This is marvelous! This is the greatest thing that has ever happened in the history of Mankind!"

Well, maybe. But sitting there on that sunny March day beside the quiet waters on a littoral isle, he seemed silly to us. I had to stop myself from saying, "Of course it is, you fool! Has it just dawned on you what we've done?"

It's not that we took it for granted; it's just that the dancing, gesticulating priest (who was still dressed in a clerical collar) was simply insufferable. He irritated Mark most of all. Ned and I merely disliked him.

"Sit down, *Father*!" Mark told him a bit too coldly. Julian was flustered—but he sat down.

Realizing that he had been unnecessarily rude, Mark changed his tone and spoke to all of us. "Let's drink to Ned," he said in Latin, "the greatest engineer of all time." He stood up and went to a packing box. Marcus settled in.

"Why did you come here so boldly," Julian asked, "unarmed, defenseless, alone?"

"Simple: unarmed because you were many. Defenseless because I am not afraid: I am favored of the gods. And alone in case the gods have changed their hearts toward me. At my age— and after the life I have lived—death holds little terror for me."

His frankness was amazing. Later, after I got more friendly with death, I spoke like that, too.

"But I came here mainly because of my tragic flaw," he continued.

Julian translated for us. "Which is...?" he asked.

"Curiosity! I can't keep my nose away from things. How could one so afflicted as I stay away? Impossible! You are the most amazing people I have ever seen—if you are people, that is."

"What else would we be?" Julian again asked.

"Gods? Illusions? How could I know?" he said with a smile. "But you look flesh and blood. Maybe you are scouts for a great army sailing this way from your country. But I trust you to be good to me, and that's the whole point, isn't it? It doesn't matter what we say to one another, only how we treat each other. After all, one can never believe a stranger who may have reasons to lie," he said. "I have reasons to lie; you have reasons to lie."

"He who does not speak does not lie," I said in Greek quoting an aphorism I had learned.

That astonished our visitor and gave him an excuse to look more closely at me.

"By the Gods! Is that some dialect of Greek that you are speaking?" he asked me in Latin.

In Latin I answered him: "The cultures and languages of the Romans and the Greeks have made themselves known to the far corners of the earth."

"Then you all—who are so reluctant to say what nation you are from—come surely from that great nation across the seas whence so many ships have sailed but not returned."

"Pardon me," said Julian, "I can imagine many reasons you might lie, but why should we?"

"No wise men reveal their secrets to strangers," Marcus responded. "Julius Caesar once said that 'To know is to win; to reveal is to disarm oneself.'

"But you have the look of innocent men on your faces. You have a strange boat, wear marvelous clothes, and have all manner of strange things which I have never seen. You are not open about who you are, which is wise, of course."

"You are a friendly man and a wise one," Ned said. "We are happy to have you around the fire with us. Have a drink." With that he opened the bottle that Mark had fetched and poured it into tin cups that we passed around.

"We come as friends," he continued, "and we are curious, too, about you, your friends, and about everything else in the wide world. That's why we have come here."

We cautioned Marcus not to drink too much, but he wasn't careful enough. He got very drunk that first afternoon— as did Mark who matched him drink for drink. Finally he passed out, but not before he delivered himself of a long, rambling dissertation on who he thought we were, ending with a most memorable phrase that Julian translated.

"Therefore" Marcus concluded just moments before he slid from the log upon which he was sitting, " I must think you are stepchildren of the gods. Or castaways from lost Atlantis."

Perhaps we were.

****

X

Roughing It

Altogether we spent about ten days on the island. Among all the other things we were doing during that time, we worked on the missing part of the Short's tail—the four- square-foot section that we assumed was "lost in time." Why that part was lost and not, say, the unprotected propellers, we had no idea. That anything was lost gave us pause. It could just as easily have been all of us that went missing in time or high over the sea.

Against that background, life went well. We were kept busy taking in the vast amounts new information we were getting first from Marcus and later from his servants. With their help, we began making travel plans and practicing our use of Latin—so much so that we very quickly found ourselves using more Latin than English.

On the day after he had first landed on the island Marcus sailed back to his home, returning the following morning fully prepared to stay with us for several days. He brought with him a large supply of food and wine that he insisted we take.

We were still afraid that he might intend to poison us. The ancient world was notorious for its high incidence of poisonings, and what better way to rid oneself of foreign agents? Even after he ate his own food in our presence, we tried to play it safe by choosing one of our number by lot to be the guinea pig. After all, we couldn't live on our own rations forever. I drew the short straw, but I ate without trepidation. I trusted Marcus, and I was hungry for the vegetables he brought and the lamb he roasted.

Marcus was a blessing in so many ways that one can only describe his arrival in terms of *Deus ex machina*. Ideally suited to us in temperament, he had a rich knowledge of both the local area and the whole Roman Empire. He became our servant, guide, translator, and teacher, and he was free to spend a lot of time instructing us in the manners, customs, languages, and mores of his world. He had traveled over most of the ancient world and spoke some of at least six languages: Greek, Teutonic, Latin, Syrian, Celtic, and the Berber tongue of the local area. A direct descendant of Lucius Aemilius Paulus, the general whose army had defeated the army of Peseus at Pydna, he was well-versed in history too. His heritage didn't mean much to us early on, but we later learned how well the Romans revered such antecedents. Among his other exploits and experiences, he had fought in the legion led by Varus at the Teutoborg Forest disaster some 16 years before when an entire Roman army was defeated by a great German ambush.

My own knowledge of Roman history was weak, but the men were familiar with the general outline of the battle and listened with rapt attention to his tale of German cunning and his own assessment of Varus' arrogance and credulousness.

Storytelling was considered a much higher art form in those days and even the least literate people I heard used varying sentence structures and mythological allusions when putting together their tales. It took some getting used to, but we learned the pleasure of patient listening. In that regard, we were people who had conquered time but time still ruled us in everyday situations. As a species, we had become impatient, I supposed, and we missed some of the best parts of living because of it.

Of course, we had some of the medicine that ameliorates that disease. Mark had brought about ten or twenty pounds of it along with us in a special, weighted container that he could have jettisoned had the need to do so arisen if the jump failed and the narcs closed in. Be that as it may, all of us including even Julian got stoned together on the night we sat around the fire and heard the tale of the Teutoborg Forest told by an eyewitness.

After telling us how the Germans had lured Varus deep into the forests against the better judgement of his officers and troops, Marcus described the initial attacks and the Romans' responses to them. As in most pitched battles of those times, the Germans took heavy casualties, but their numbers were so great and the Romans were so impeded by the narrow woodland roadways that defeat soon became almost certain. Marcus was one of the few who survived, for his cohort commander led him and his comrades in a desperate night attack by which they managed to cut their way out of the encirclement. In the following days, pursued by their foes and losing comrade after comrade, they made their way back to the fortress from which they had departed a week earlier, bringing with them the first news of one of the greatest military disasters that was ever inflicted upon the Roman Empire. Marcus himself was unwounded throughout the fighting. "It was," he said, "like a sure sign from the gods that I was being saved for some greater purpose later on."

When he said that he looked at us in a way that we all recognized. He obviously believed that serving us was that purpose finally come to pass.

We were equally interested in his accounts of the lands we hoped to visit: Italy, Greece, Egypt, Asia Minor, and, of course, Palestine, where he had lived during his last hitch in the army some five years before our arrival. He had not liked it there and he almost got caught embezzling legion payrolls. He had skipped out in the nick of time with his life savings and taken a ship bound for Carthage just one step ahead of the military police.

In that regard, I should note that the Roman armies were so well organized and so experienced in the administration of large groups of men that a very complete system of record-keeping and identification had long been established. In addition to a regular system of "wanted" notifications that circulated throughout the empire, the legions used free-agent detectives and spies as well as special officers with summary arrest powers to chase after malefactors like Marcus. Although such practices helped to maintain order, they also explain why during the various power struggles and civil wars of somewhat earlier times there had been large unit desertions and loyalty changes. Those officers wanted by one army for malfeasance might well be recruited by an opponent's army. The very existence of *The System*, as it was called, also explained how Marcus had come to live where he did, which is to say, just beyond the reach of the Roman authorities.

So it was that we learned he was something of a criminal in the ancient world. I say "something of" because by modern standards, it would not be so clear who would be called a thief and who would be deemed honest. The Roman order was based on extortion and theft, the legality of which was determined primarily on the basis of political and military power.

We gave Marcus no demonstration of our weapons during those weeks that we knew him. He had, naturally, assumed that the guns we wore were, in fact, weapons, but he very tactfully asked no questions about them nor did he ask to handle them.

By the same token, at first we didn't crank up the plane, use the Polaroid camera or demonstrate the use of a tape player to him. We had wonders enough at hand for him to observe. He scrupulously avoided touching anything belonging to us without first asking permission to do so. He continued to respect the fact that we were being careful about explaining our origins. Undoubtedly that in turn gave him good reason to suspect us of being scouts or spies from some great foreign power across the sea--a power preparing to invade the known world. At least he would be on the winning side.

He spoke with Julian at length about Palestine, describing in some detail the religious strife that seemed to keep the people there in a state of constant turmoil. All of us were interested in these accounts, but I clearly recall our discussion when Julian asked him if he had ever heard rumors of a Jewish deliverer who was to come.

"Ever hear?" he said through his usual gap-toothed smile, "Of course! Almost all of those Jews are perfectly afflicted with obsessions about revolts, leaders, saviors—you name it. Their leaders are forever fighting amongst themselves, and about half of them hate the Romans and the other half have enough sense to tolerate us. Most of them give lip service to a one-God theory and, like most people, consider themselves to be The People chosen by their God to rule the world. They spend all their time trying to rule each other. It is said that they have ten commandments and ten thousand rules. They're always wanting to kill somebody for religious reasons. Most of the Jews who have any sense at all don't live there, though. They live in Egypt and Iberia, and most of them are good, decent people. Palestine is a land full of crazy fanatics."

All of us—even Julian—found that we enjoyed outdoor life. Out of pure self-defense, I became the chief cook of our outfit, and prepared some wonderful meals out in the open. Until Marcus provided me with a baked clay charcoal cooking brazier, I cooked on an inefficient open fire rather than use the small gas camping stove that we brought for emergencies. I had forgotten how balky fires can be and found that the brazier was a marvelously efficient instrument. Rarely did we need more than a handful or two of charcoal to make the stews and broths that were our staples. With Marcus' help, in just a few days, I learned what herbs I could collect locally and how to bake fish, hoecakes, and a local root. I learned how to make and use charcoal.

Marcus provided us with fresh food from his garden and gave Julian some pointers about how to fish for the species that lived in the estuary. We told him that we would pay for the food he provided us, and when he had come back more heavily laden than ever with fruit, wine and bread, he would accept only a few silver dimes.

"Masters," he said when we marveled at the abundance that the dimes had bought, "you are by my reckoning the richest people in all this part of the world. Anything can be yours for a price—a price you can easily pay."

He taught us the simple but effective rules of barter we used thereafter to make our way through the world. Every unusual thing we had—no matter how insignificant it was to us—a photo from a magazine, a bit of metal, a coin, a rivet or a tool, anything could be effectively traded so long as we could invest it with mystery or power. It was just the old law of supply and demand working like it always does. I recall stories of wooden sailing ships of the 1820s making landfalls in Polynesia where the native women would eagerly trade sexual favors for a bit of iron, and captains posted guards to keep crew members from dismantling the ships, nail by nail.

On the fourth day, Ned and Julian sailed off with Marcus and returned at dark after having seen his home and met his servants. It surprised us to learn that he had servants at all, for at first glance he seemed just a fisherman. He had, however, amassed some wealth during his army years, and he had cleverly loaned money to merchants here and there over the years and managed to call most of it back in before he left the army one step ahead of the auditors.

His home—which I first visited on the eighth day— might best be described as an isolated, fortified homestead on a low promontory overlooking the water, with a view off toward the sea. For defensive purposes, the land around it was cleared of trees and undergrowth. There were several stone-walled pastures and paddocks for horses and sheep around it, but all were so located as to prevent their being used for cover by attackers. There were what soldiers call "clear fields of fire" in every direction.

The whole place was quite tidy and well organized, with about 20 acres under the plough with another five planted in fruit trees and grapes.

The main building had been built along local lines similar to those of a modern Moroccan home only it had no large windows to the outside. Built around a central courtyard enclosing about two-thirds of an acre, it had thick, high walls of plastered adobe and stone and contained nearly 40 rooms including the storerooms and stables. Cool, bold and rather ideal, like many such fortresses of the time it could be defended fairly easily by a small number of determined men unless taken by surprise or attacked by an overwhelming foe equipped with siege machines. It was, in fact, the king's property and on the border of his domain, his capital being some 30 miles away to the north. It behooved him to lease Marcus' villa and a line of similar border outposts and forts to experienced fighting men so that the countryside would have a strong first line of defense against the barbarians to the south.

Such precautions were necessary, and the place had actually come under attack twice during the five years that Marcus had held it. On those occasions several other local men with their families had come to the small fortress while the raiding party ravaged the neighborhood. Under Marcus, the little militia had conducted counterattacks and sallies until both attacks were beaten off.

It could well be said that we were on the very outer fringe of the civilized world. We were outside of Rome's control. That would come later. Nevertheless, the Latin, Carthagenian, and even Greek influences had already impacted the area's architecture, civil and military organization, culture, and outlook.

Like many other retired military men in the area,

Marcus had a symbiotic relationship with the local king. In short, at the sufferance of the king and in return for his maintenance and defense of the promontory and surrounding area, he lived in comfortable retirement on the funds he had acquired while serving Rome, and he was free from any threat of extradition.

Two couples lived at the fortress and worked the place with him and his Alexandrian Greek consort, Naadia.

The younger of the two couples were locals. They were of dark-skinned Atlas Mountain Moroccan stock, and like the people of that region today, they were fiercely independent and tough. The husband, Bilau, was about 20 years old. He had remarkably dark, shining eyes and sharp, hawk-like features. He was clever and industrious, loved horses, and could ride better than anyone I have ever seen. He was thin, wiry, and always cheerful. Since he spoke practically no Latin, our conversations were limited.

His hot-blooded little wife was obviously held to be a great beauty among her people and had apparently grown up with servants to wait upon her day and night. It was amusing to see the disdain with which she approached manual labor, and I soon learned that she was the wayward daughter of a distant chieftain who was related to the king.

"They are the satrap's spies," Marcus explained to us quite frankly. "They are sent here to do a duty—which is to watch over me, of course—as well as to enjoy the passionate days of their youth together in the comparative beauty and isolation of this place. There are many distractions in the towns and cities. Here they have each other."

They did have each other—often and somewhat indiscreetly as far as I could tell. The girl was consumed by a young woman's first flush of lust and was insatiable—or at least, she wanted her husband to think so, much to our amusement. She often led him, grinning and eager, off to their rooms or to a little picnic place down by the water.

The other couple, Constatus and Marrilla, were in their early 50s. Like his master, Constatus was a retired soldier who had served in the legions for twenty years. He was let go from the service after wounds he received on the Parthian frontier left him blind in one eye and slightly crippled. Otherwise a fit man, he had huge hands and arms. The scar that ran down the side of his face and took in the dead eye gave him the formidable appearance of a great, baleful dog. A serious-minded man, he had a real love for the soil and was eager to learn from us anything he could about the agricultural practices of our countries.

Like everyone else on the place, Marrilla—which in her native tongue meant *Beautiful Morning*—seemed contented with her circumstances. Before meeting her husband she had spent most of her life as a slave and from the age of fifteen had been owned by a series of merchants in the Middle East by whom she had borne several children, all of whom had died in infancy. Constatus had bought her on a whim as he passed through Caesarea in Palestine four years earlier. Then, he fell in love with her, freed and married her. They had come to Mauretania in response to an inquiry from one of Marcus' bankers and had lived there ever since.

I spoke with Marrilla often in my slowly improving Greek. I liked her very much, and it was through her that I first became aware of the frank fatalism that dominated the thinking of the people of those times. I soon realized that men and women from all walks of life seemed capable of facing injury, dismemberment, and death with resignation and equanimity. It was a liberating experience to live among such people who both planned for the future and lived for the day.

Marrilla spoke Hebrew, too, having lived in Jerusalem for ten years with an old Jew. Julian was delighted. The rest of us knew no Hebrew, so we couldn't follow his attempted conversations with her in that language.

Marilla herself preferred to speak Greek. It was the *lingua franca* of the east, and as much a mark of being a cultured person as the speaking of French is today. She also hated the Jews.

"They are such nasty people:" she said, when Julian pressed her to talk about them, "full of rules and self-righteousness and constantly scheming to best one another in any way, great or small.

"They are famed for avariciousness, but it is a misplaced accusation," she continued in a Greek that I was only slowly beginning to understand. Even at that early stage, I could tell from listening to Naadia's more perfect Greek that Marrilla's was heavily laden with an unfamiliar, guttural sound. "They crave the advantages that money will convey, and more than any people of whom I know, they crave the adulation of others.

"They worship one god to whom they impute all god-like attributes. They despise foreigners, and they are even more proud—but with perhaps less cause—than are the Romans themselves."

Neither Marcus nor Constatus took offense at such remarks, for both were too cosmopolitan to discount another person's expressions, and even Romans joked at their own foibles.

"But what have you heard of the Jewish Messiah?" Julian asked her on our third or fourth evening at the farm. We were all craning forward to hear her reply, knowing he'd get around to asking that very question as soon as he could. We gloated about the fact that when he finally asked and when she answered it was in Greek.

"The Jewish Messiah! The Anointed One and all that crap!" Marrilla spat. "You can't believe how tired one gets of hearing about that. I've had it up to here!" she said, gesturing with a hand held at neck level.

"Always they want someone to lead them to the glory they think they deserve, and it's always a glory that involves them lording it over others and taking other people's land. In Judea one always is hearing of fellows claiming to be the Deliverer, the Messiah, the True King, or whatever. It's tiresome, is what it is! Some say Herod Antipas is to be the Messiah, and some say that a bandit in Lebanon is the long sought-after leader, but as far as I'm concerned," she said, pausing to spit the taste of Israel out of her mouth into the dust of the yard, "they can all just rot off into the sea!"

Her views were not uncommon among people I met. Jews were widely disliked as a group and generally loved as individuals. Even Marrilla spoke with gratitude and affection of a few Jewish women she had known—women who had been little better off than she.

Marcus and Naadia, on the other hand, had many Jewish friends and business contacts around the Mediterranean, but both of them had said that only a non-Palestinian Jew or what they referred to as an "Etruscan Roman" could be trusted with one's money.

We talked a good deal about finances and commerce during the time we were together, and I learned almost everything I knew about ancient business practices from them. Necessity made me very attentive, for I knew that if I were going to make my way in that world I needed to know as much about it as I could. I took notes and made lists of the friends and contacts they had made around the world. Later on during our first long sea voyages I committed the lists to memory, a practice that served me well later on.

As I have said, Julian was eager to be on his way to Palestine, but the rest of us thought otherwise, there being a lot of world to see: Athens, Rome, Egypt. We would travel as royalty—princely agents of the powerful and non-existent kingdom across the sea, people to be feared, respected and, yes, watched. We would see the sights, and Jerusalem would be one of them. If Jesus of Nazareth existed, if he was a living, breathing person, we would meet him, maybe, and talk with him. We would not to be disappointed if we found that the target of our journey was merely a peasant religionist deified into mythology after his death.

Of course, we could have made as our initial objective the location and exploitation of a petroleum source somewhere so as to be able to refuel the Short so that we might use it for traveling about. Naturally, too, we thought of how we might use it again some day in an attempt once again to pass through time if we became desperate. At any rate, without fuel no such attempt could be mounted. Ned had made one thing clear: setting off the wave on the ground would be fatal. We had to be airborne to do that, and at that point in time we certainly had no plans for taking one more such risk. Somehow, someday, we thought, we would be able to refuel the Short, but that could wait. We had a world to see.

Part of our reluctance to go to Palestine arose from our feeling that it would be a great disappointment, as when one plans to visit a long-lost relative, but fears to find her intolerable. There was something, too, about Christianity—particularly Julian's brand of it—that sickened us. Finally, after irrevocably casting our lot in the distant past, the beliefs of the distant future became irrelevant. After all, Ned and Mark had been atheists all their lives. Curiously, though, even at that early stage in our journey the two of them were beginning to show signs of becoming religious, which is to say, they began to embrace our hosts' paganism. It was easy to understand, for once we were divorced from clocks and schedules, the world seemed more alive and magical. One felt the presence of nymphs and gods and heroes It was ironic that the three of us found ourselves in that particular post-heroic age.

I had been raised a Presbyterian, which is to say, a believer, but one without unreasoning faith that "true" Christians so often insist upon. I had intellectual misgivings, too, with the gender problem that pervades the society and religion in which I was raised. Spiritually speaking, I was like charcoal with a small spark, but no heat. The Mauretanian air itself began fanning that spark and the heat began to build.

We said that we would go to Palestine, yes, but not before we were ready.

The person at the farm to whom I was most attracted was Naadia, Marcus's companion who he had purchased from a famous counting-house in Tyre. Counting-houses in those days were the ancient equivalents of combined accounting and law firms, and she was skilled at both professions. Marcus had therefore paid a lot for her. She was attractive, but he had bought her not because of her beauty, but because of her financial and linguistic abilities.

Born in Alexandria of Greek parents, she spoke eight languages and wrote in Latin and Persian as well as Greek. She had been a slave since she was 16 years old when her father's business had failed.

She was a rather small woman and had particularly fine, carefully-tended hands such as one might expect to find on a professional card-player. Her eyes were a violet blue and her hair was long and jet black—kept so, no doubt, by continuing dyes. Her shapely body was as trim as that of a much younger woman, for she had never borne children. Her skin was thin, white and clear, and she had a lovely, friendly smile that belied her straightforward, hard-nosed approach to business.

Customarily, she spoke very little and listened intently to all that was said. It was soon apparent to me that it was she, not Marcus, who ran things in paradise where, legally, she was a slave, a concubine, a chattel. It was a curious world.

Unlike the passionate and oversexed young woman, Azzia, the comfortably warm, voluptuous, and easy-going Marrilla, or me, Naadia seemed cool and professional. She was the sort of woman an intelligent man might want for a mistress, and for that reason alone, I gained respect for Marcus. He knew quality when he saw it and he was willing to pay for it. He had not so much wanted her as needed her, for his life had gotten complicated and his enemies and creditors had been moving in on him.

She had obviously been worth the investment, because due primarily to her knowledge and cunning they had managed to get out of the east with both his money and his head. She was the perfect agent, the consummate factor, and, like him, she had business contacts all around the Mediterranean. Unlike him, she could keep secrets—including, I suspect, the secrets of her heart. That she and Marcus lived as man and wife seemed almost an afterthought.

"Why does he not free you?" I asked her once.

"Freedom is nothing compared to honor," she said, chin high, "and the gods gave me the status in life to which I was destined. He could sell me tomorrow. It would be his right. I am content." I often heard such comments and rarely thought it polite to question the rationale behind them.

I believe—or would like to believe—that Ned fell in love with her at some point during our short stay at the villa. Something about the way he and she spoke to one another made me think the old bachelor scientist found himself once again in a position to trust and love a woman, even to hold her in awe. They were like two sides of the same coin: rational, scientific, and cool on the one side, passionate or at least deep-simmering on the other. A few things I saw gave me every reason to suspect that with Marcus's consent and knowledge, Ned visited her in her rooms late at night after all the rest of us were asleep.

From her I received extensive and valuable advice, all of which I solicited eagerly.

"You do not realize it yet," she said to me at sundown one day when we were alone together sitting on the flat roof over her quarters, "but you will find that you will be considered very beautiful in the eyes of men. You will stand out in any crowd and provoke the jealousy of women and, perhaps, even of the goddesses."

"What goddesses?" I asked, curious that she should even mention such a thing, for I saw among them few tokens of religious beliefs except for the almost obligatory small room of the household gods, a room that they rarely visited. "In what gods do you truly believe?"

"Well, I believe in very little of such stuff, actually," she responded with a smile, "except, of course, for the power of life, and the efficacy of interest and trade."

"But what goddesses do you worship?"

"None really, unless we count Athena, to whom I sacrifice occasionally."

I was curious, of course. "Tell me, then:" I asked, "why do anything for the gods if you do not believe in them?"

"It's not so much that I don't believe in the existence of powers beyond our ken; it's just that the gods don't speak to me. That is all right. Some people need their beliefs like ships need oars. But what, I ask, does it hurt, to worship the gods of one's forefathers? With no worship at all, we should fall into the trap of believing that there are no gods, and that we create ourselves."

"And what would be wrong with that belief?"

"Simple: It would be bad for business and would lead mankind into sorrows deeper than the sorrows caused by religious wars."

I had never thought of atheism as being bad for business. Maybe it is; maybe it isn't.

"What then of this beauty of mine?" I asked her. "In my country, I am not considered beautiful."

She arose from her couch and came to mine where she knelt on a mat and took my face in her hands, turning it from side to side in the last rays of afternoon sun as if she were contemplating a purchase. My bruises where almost gone by that time. "And why do the people of your country not think you are beautiful?" she asked.

"I'm too heavy, my hair is too thick and can't easily be managed, and my nose is too big and shaped funny."

"Each country has its own tastes, I suppose, but you will

find that here you will be held in great esteem—too much, perhaps," she concluded with a sigh.

"What do you mean?" I wondered aloud.

"Let me tell you this: Many women less beautiful than you have disappeared. On the sea, down some alleyway, even betrayed by suborned litter carriers or ship's captains. It can happen when a rich man decides he wants you or a jealous wife or queen wants you out of the way. Take some advice from an old woman: Don't flaunt that face in public. A woman's life is hard enough sometimes even without the burden of beauty."

"But you're beautiful!" I exclaimed trying to be gracious but aware as the young always are of the lines in her face and circling her neck.

"Thank you for saying so. It's true that I was in my day a beauty--a beauty who became the plaything of men far stupider than she. It was because of my looks that my father was ruined: the merchant who engineered his downfall wanted me, you see. Only through my father's bankruptcy could he get me."

"And how did it all end up?" I asked.

"Bad for all of us: my father, me, the rich man—even his family. Getting me was like getting a snake in his bed. He ruined my father. I ruined him. It took time, but I did it. I was ever so young, but I learned a great deal about the affairs of business in general and that man's business in particular. He got me when I was 16, and it took me four years to shatter his fortune and his family with it. I was sold off by his creditors when I was 21. That was all back in Alexandria, the city that mixes love, commerce, and dust together in a mad, eternal melee. I'm not complaining: it's been an entertaining life. But remember what I have told you: be careful with that face!"

Naadia also advised me how to dress and to comport myself at meals and in public. She helped me to prepare some clothes so that I could dress in the styles of the day and gave me a veil of the sort commonly worn by women with pocked faces, bad teeth, or possessive husbands. She coached me in table manners, speech, etiquette, and even the ways of feminine hygiene and birth control. She told me how to pick good doctors and good bankers. She said that I would be her secret walker who would go out into the world for her and showed me how to make an invisible ink from goat milk so that I could write to her privately and even Marcus wouldn't know. Finally, she told me how to detect and avoid the most common poisons of the day.

For my part, I showed her how some of our instruments worked and showed her all the pictures in the few magazines I possessed. In doing so, I made up a lot of wild explanations about how things worked, but all in all I was more honest with her than I would be with anyone else for a long time afterward. I stopped shy of telling her about flying and I didn't tell her about the nature and power of our weapons. I gave her something I know she cherished: my tape player with its rechargeable batteries, tapes, and solar recharger. The feeling of having music injected directly into the center of one's head always seemed like magic to me and it certainly seemed so to her. As I recall, I had only about 20 tapes of things like Vivaldi, the Beatles, the Allman Brothers and Chicago. I was tired of it all, but over time I missed that music about as much as I missed anything.

While I was busy learning how to conduct myself in the world of women, Mark was not idle. Having brought with him some two pounds of hemp seeds, he taught Constatus and Marcus all he knew about how it should be grown for both fiber and pleasure. He showed them how it should be retted and beaten for the one use and hung and cured for the other. As far as I know, hemp was unknown in the Roman world at that time. I think it was originally native to the region north of the Himalayas but I'm not sure of that, either. Be that as it may, the ancient world didn't lack for widely-available medicinal, recreational, and religious drugs. There was, for example, a locally-made, strangely-flavored wine akin to absinthe. It was thought to have almost mythical powers, but Marcus warned us that it was addictive and could cause dementia so we avoided it. Getting high is one thing, but irreversible brain damage is another. We merely drank the excellent local and Italian vintages of unadulterated wines and tried to smoke dope.

I say "tried" because early on Mark and I found that we almost always got paranoid when we were stoned. Although getting high was often pleasant enough, some constantly recurring themes were *very* negative: We could not turn back, we were vulnerable to a thousand kinds of death, we didn't really love each other, we were alone.

It was so bad for me, that I stopped smoking altogether.

I didn't miss it. There was so much else to do and to think about. If I could put aside those big negatives it was fairly easy to be, as the Bible-thumpers used to say, "high on life."

We stayed at Marcus's place a whole month while Mark and I planned our great journey. During that time Ned was completely at his leisure with our new-found friends--the first friends he had allowed himself since 1939. He sailed, rode horses, and went on long walks with them. He reveled in the simple pleasure of being alive and of speaking Greek and Latin.

Naturally, Julian was chafing at the bit to be gone. He was the pedant without an audience and the man without a friend. He read and spoke as often as possible with Marrilla, primarily so that he could perfect his Hebrew and he spent long hours fishing from Marcus' boat, a huge straw hat pushed down on his head. He always caught fish.

A lot of the work around the place came to a halt when we arrived, but of course there was always work to be done. Fortunately, Marcus could afford to hire help for the Spring planting and for the harvesting of the winter crops. As I recall, Ned forced on him two or three gold coins to pay for our keep and he assured us that it was more than enough to pay for the food we ate as well as the extra labor he brought in to help out around the place.

As I have said, his life was relatively secure in his adopted territory. His only real duty was to remain vigilant for pirates and for that other possibility: invaders from across the great sea, invaders who had never in recorded history bothered them, but for whom we might possibly be the scouts.

As Marcus loved to sail and Bilau loved to ride, they divided their sea-watching duties accordingly. The boy rode about on daily rounds to keep in touch with other farmers in the area and Marcus sailed about keeping in touch with the fishermen and their families. They had all kinds of signal systems involving fires, bells, and the like, as well as various hideouts and mini-fortresses. After all, the area was fairly sparsely settled and the few residents of the area had to have some means of self-defense if they were to live so far from the fortified towns to the north.

Early on, rather than abandoning it on the island, we had moved the flying boat to the farm, a process that took a full day and a half. After loading up literally everything we had left on the island, we invited Bilau and Marcus to come aboard. One would have thought they had been invited to be eaten by a great bird, but they got in. Mark and I started the engines and immediately began to taxi toward the farm, moving slowly to conserve fuel.

Although they had been warned about it, our two passengers were astounded at the terrific noise the engines made, and were terrified as we blistered along at thirty miles an hour. It was the only time I ever saw either of them show fear.

Every detail of the Short fascinated them, but it was also a sensory overload for them. Following that demonstration of our godlike power they were totally in awe of us, even when that power failed us when we ran out of gas three miles from our destination. We had to rig sails and paddles to continue.

Everyone at the farm was thrilled by the prospect of having the Short put in storage there, and I don't blame them. I love airplanes, and I'm *impressed* by them, too. With the Short at their home, they could sleep in it, examine it at leisure, and show it to their friends. If it could have been taken to Rome, it would have been the greatest tourist attraction in the world.

With their help, we put it into storage condition and provided enough money so that Marcus could afford to have it kept covered in our absence. We paid him in gold and promised a huge reward if it was safely kept in accord with our directions. That seemed to be the most sensible thing to do—particularly since there was a good chance that it would never fly again. We were careful to put oil in the cylinder heads, to drain, cover, and wrap the carburetors, and block up all the various ports and orifices in which insects might nest or build mud structures. We showed the men how to rotate the props by hand once a month, told them what they could and could not touch, and cautioned them about the danger of fire that fuel vapors might cause. We had already removed the copper netting from the fuselage and wings before we left the island, and now we disconnected the batteries and did everything else we could think of to prepare the Short for a storage that might last for years.

Fuel was not a particularly pressing issue anymore. We considered dismantling the plane and selling it piece by piece over the years. We also thought about sinking it at sea so that we might not be tempted to use it again. Better to burn our bridges, we thought, than to think that we could opt to go somewhere else to live out our lives. To destroy the plane would have been to destroy what we then thought of as a false hope that might limit happiness itself.

So it was that after four or five weeks of being there with our new-found friends our time to be on our way was at hand. The plan was simple enough. First we would go to the capital of the country, pay our respects to the king, and try to secure his cooperation in protecting the things and the new friends we were leaving behind. It was also the nearest seaport of any size and as there were no boats in the neighborhood large enough for all of our equipment, we had to go there to find one. Therefore, the first stage of our journey was to be by horseback and cart. Once we had a ship, our plan was to travel together to what is now Spain. There Julian would separate from us and sail on to Palestine by himself. Ned, Mark and I would go directly on to Rome, stay a while, then go to Greece and Egypt. We were ready and we were excited. Ned asked Marcus to go with us as our guide and translator, but he said that not even for love of us would he go back within the borders of the Roman Empire. He was, he said, too old to row boats—referring to the slave-powered galleys to which malefactors like himself were often sentenced. On the other hand, it was decided that Bilau would go with us on that fist stage of the journey—ostensibly as a guide, but in fact to report on us to the authorities. His would be a report we hoped would keep everyone at peace and the soldiers of the king at a distance.

Looking back on our travels I should note that many of the places I visited are gone now. Some have been altered beyond recognition by earthquakes, tides & Hoods. There were plenty of times during those years that even though I knew geography fairly well even as a child I couldn't recognize where I was or know the modern names of the islands, rivers, and bays I visited. I still can't exactly trace my travels on any modern maps. All I can do now is as I did then: I can try.

****

XI

On The Road

Finally, and after having sacrificed a goat to the gods the night before, we bade our hosts farewell and began the first leg of our journey on a fine March morning just as dawn was breaking. Our road ran along the high ground beside the estuary, weaving in and out from the water's edge to take advantage of the best terrain, but always the broad river and its delta were close at hand. The songs of hundreds of birds practically drowned out conversation.

I felt wonderful and healthy. Dressed in jeans and a khaki shirt, I rode out in front of our little entourage on a pretty little mare who tossed her head up and down as if she were leading a parade. Immediately behind us Mark was driving the larger of two heavily laden carts. Ned sat beside him on the narrow bench smoking his beloved pipe while Julian rode in the back of it reading his Bible. Behind them Bilau followed in the second cart. From time to time I could hear him singing some sort of local song which was oddly similar in style and tonal qualities to those of the birds.

After we had been on the road for a couple of hours, he stopped his cart and got down to relieve himself. We plodded on ahead slowly.

As we rounded the next turn, my horse twitched nervously and whinnied loudly. Before us the road narrowed down to a slightly elevated lane between low brush on either side beyond which lay open fields studded with occasional trees. Directly ahead of us in the middle of the road some fifty yards away, six or seven short, dark men dressed in rags were hobbling toward us, obvious victims of some misfortune. They were covered in dirt and bandages and were loudly bewailing their sufferings. An old man in the center of the group was being helped along by two of his companions on either side, his leg bandaged and his head lolling back and forth. They were all barefoot and looked pitiful as they waved and showed obvious signs of relief when we came into view. Mark and Ned's cart was just behind me. I pulled my horse to a halt.

Ned got down from the cart immediately, raised his hand in a gesture of peace and began walking toward them rapidly to render aid.

Mark yelled "*Stop!*" just as I first noticed some small commotion beginning behind the men. "Move out of the way, Eva!" he yelled at me as the little group ahead parted like a human curtain.

My horse and I shied out to the right as I saw what was happening. A wiry young man—hardly more than a boy—ran forward from his concealment behind the group. Smoothly and without hesitation he cast a light javelin at us as he and his companions gave a shout and began running toward us. Still others rose up from hiding on either side of the road and came at us. There were about 30 of them altogether.

For a long moment, though, it seemed as if all the world stood still as, fascinated, I watched the slender javelin rocket forward and up, then curve gracefully downward to strike Ned squarely in the chest. It passed halfway through him. I was too surprised to be horrified or even to try to defend myself. Charging men were just steps away, teeth and eyes white in black faces.

Then all hell broke loose. From behind me the incredibly loud hammering of the Thompson submachine gun began, and my horse bounded forward and to the right, running over the men in her way while ahead of us in the road, the men and the boy who threw the spear disintegrated in a hail of .45 bullets. Holding to the horse's mane for dear life as she broke into a dead run, I looked back.

Behind me the cart horse was leaping about in terror, frantically jerking at his traces as Mark leaped nimbly to safety, the submachine gun in one hand and his rifle in the other. Released from the reins, the cart horse fled from him, running down five or six of the same men I had just brushed through. They were screaming, everyone was shouting, and Mark began shooting again. Ned was on his knees, falling forward and to the side. I did not see Julian anywhere.

It was a miracle that I had not been left behind when my mare first bolted. Now, clear of the first group of men but not of the tumult, she was running full out. It was all I could do just to hang on and glance back from time to time.

The men on the left side of the road had stopped in their tracks in shock. Mark turned on them and mowed them all down with one sweep of the Tommy gun that had one of those large-capacity, round drums of bullets rather than a clip. It was a hell of a weapon.

I saw all this while my horse thundered forward down the road, then leaped about frantically in its effort to run from the writhing pile of bodies in the dirt. Madly she cut off to the right and ran through a large patch of small trees, and I forced her to circle back to the road only to find that we had come among some of the remaining bandits and were running in the same direction with them. Once again we passed the first group of dead and wounded men.

One terrified fellow grabbed the horse's mane and ran along beside us, but by then I had my own .45 out of its holster. Too wild with fear and excitement to chamber a round, I clubbed him viciously, first in the mouth, then in the forehead. He hardly noticed. Then I hit him hard, very hard, in the temple and he rolled off into the little ditch beside the road.

By then Mark was firing only aimed, single shots for fear of hitting me, and I signaled that I was going to the left into a big, open field. Kicking my horse and jerking her head violently to the side, I immediately found myself beside a pathetic pile of loot that obviously had been stashed there when the gang prepared its ambush. We leaped over it, and ran a short way down a shallow draw until, finally, I brought her to a halt. Then I turned her around and checked my pistol and was ready to rejoin the fight. We ran back up the draw and out onto the road.

By that time I was about 300 yards from Mark and Ned and our attackers were still running up the road in my direction. Now there was a new sound: an occasional, loud, cracking report as Mark began shooting the .308, dropping still more men as they fled from him. The rest kept running, sheer terror giving wings to their feet.

Because of a slight curve in the road I was somewhat out of Mark's line of fire. I steadied my horse, aimed at a man who was about 40 yards off and fired, hitting him in the knee and tumbling him into the dirt. The others broke away from me like a covey of quail. Terrified by the report of my .45 near her ear, my horse began bucking, then took off. I dropped the pistol and once again clung to her for dear life. Mark kept shooting.

After another brief spell of mad-horse pandemonium I was able once again to control the mare and make her go back to the roadway. Unarmed except for a derringer, I was careful not to get too close to any underbrush or to the bodies which were scattered about.

Suddenly, everything was quiet, save for the moans and screams of the wounded. Back down the road I could see Mark and Bilau kneeling beside Ned's body. In the other direction, where still more fields opened on either side, I could see Mark's cart stuck in a hole; its horse had begun to graze. Midway between me and Mark, sitting next to the corpse of one of his fellows and holding his ruined leg with both hands was the man I had shot. I rode toward him but he took no notice of me. He was about 35 years old. His ribs showed plainly as he breathed.

I searched about until I found my .45. Making sure there were no more bandits about, I dismounted, picked it up, then remounted as quickly as I could. I uncocked it, took out the clip and the chambered round, and made sure the barrel was not plugged up with dirt. Then I reloaded, put it back in the holster and trotted back toward Mark feeling strangely elated.

I rode right by the man I had shot and saw that a huge pool of blood was spreading out from the tissues where his knee had been. He was in shock and was beginning to get glassy-eyed with his oncoming death. It didn't even occur to me at the time to get down and put a tourniquet on him, but I did have one sharp, little moment of insight: but for our guns, that same man might have been at that very moment waiting his turn to rape me.

Off to the left, a completely naked man about my age had gotten up and was trying to hobble away, holding a big wound in his side with his bare hands. It was obvious that he wouldn't get far in that condition.

I made my nervous horse trot back past the wounded and dead men and rode up to Mark, who was still kneeling beside Ned's body. The spear was still in it and the face was turned away from me, which was good: I could not have borne to look at it. I turned my attention to Mark.

He looked up at me, and though the sun was at his back, I could see there was fire in his eyes as he looked into mine. He was not weeping, and his face was not contorted with grief. He had seen death before.

Slowly he stood up and stepped to my side and laid his hand upon my thigh. "So simple a thing, is Death," he said. Rifle in hand, he turned to Bilau.

Obviously afraid of the now-revealed, awesome power of our weapons, Bilau just stood there trying to comprehend everything. Even in that emotional moment it occurred to me that he had been absent at the moment of attack, and I suspected that he might have had a hand in it. Looking back on it, I now believe that his absence was, of course, the merest coincidence He must have been completely astonished at the scene that unfolded before him as he drove his cart around the bend and saw the boy casting the spear.

He also came into view just as Julian, screaming with terror, leaped away from the big cart at the first sign of trouble, then ran past him at a speed that was nothing short of amazing for a man so fat.

Bilau had watched as Mark took up the scoped .308 and began shooting down running men 200 yards off. I had no idea that he was such an excellent marksman, but of course to Bilau it was magic: Black Magic. When the shooting stopped, he led his horse forward and inspected Ned's body with Mark. That was just before I rode up.

He looked at Mark as if he were looking at some terrible god. Then he pointed off down the road at the man who was hobbling away holding his side. It was about 250 yards. Mark raised the rifle to his shoulder a last time and fired. The man threw up his arms and fell forward.

Bilau pulled the javelin out of Ned's body and covered it with a blanket. Then he walked forward with a short sword to slit the throats of the wounded men and retrieve the other cart. Mark took my horse and the rifle. Cramming his pockets full of ammunition, he went out after those few who had escaped. He left the Thompson with me, but I knew that I would be safe. Who in his right mind would have bothered us at that point? I sat on the second cart while they were gone, and when the adrenaline wore off I began shaking and crying, surrounded by the dead.

Mark was gone for half an hour. He had found none of the survivors and returned bitterly disappointed, for he wanted to kill every last one of them.

As it was, we had killed 25 men in about four long minutes.

That killing changed everything, even my relationship to Mark. Something about shooting all those men awakened in him a dormant characteristic that was sharp, brutal, and competent. He had acted first in self-defense and then in anger, but I am convinced that in the final analysis he *enjoyed* killing those men.

I, on the other hand, still cannot adequately describe how I felt once the shooting stopped. Although it is shameful to admit it, it was as if real life had stopped, too. Each of those few moments of action are even to this day more real to me than are the memories of whole months of my life prior to that time. I can recall each little detail right down to how my fingers looked twined in the mare's mane as I struck that man in the head and he rolled away. I remember the aftermath, too, when I watched helplessly and without protest as Bilau and Mark killed the wounded and piled their loot on the carts. I resisted the urge to inspect the corpse of the man I had shot.

Drained emotionally, I rode in the cart beside Ned's shrouded body as we returned to Marcus' villa. On the way we picked up the exhausted and relieved Julian. Mark could not bear to look at him. I went to sleep.

Marcus and Naadia took it hard. Of all of us Ned was their favorite, and they blamed themselves for not preparing us better and for failing to hire a bodyguard. Marcus said that he himself should have gone along, and Bilau set out to alert the militia about the presence of the surviving pirates.

I could tell that they were all worried, too, about the nature and extent of our arms' powers and the ramifications those powers might have on their lives. As I have said, for all they knew, we were the forerunners of a horde of similarly armed, unstoppable people who soon would follow us, killing all who got in the way.

We burned Ned's body that very evening, right there in the courtyard. The fire was hot and consumed the body as we looked on drinking wine and feeling ever so sorrowful. I remember even now the ugly Constatus telling us that the fast-rising smoke was going to heaven in the true, old Roman style. Ned would have liked that, the grieving Naadia told me. Over

Julian's objections, such rites as we performed were purely pagan. He had tried to get his own way about it, but Mark threatened to beat him to a pulp if he so much as uttered a Christian word. We were all convinced that Mark would have done just that, if not worse.

"If you wouldn't fight for him, I'll be damned if you'll get to pray over him!" Mark said as he took the torch from a wall socket and kindled the pyre himself. He shouldn't have been so hard on Julian. After all, he couldn't have saved Ned, either, and who knows but that Julian might have stood his ground had the attack been less a surprise.

After the fire had roared through its grisly duty and died down, we split up into little groups and retired for the night. Mark and I went up to the flat roof of one of the small corner towers. There we stayed up late drinking toasts to Ned's memory and recounting the exact details of the fight. Remembering what we had experienced and what we had sensed, we ourselves felt again that intoxicating and corrupting sense of power that comes from facing and overcoming danger and, yes, from killing armed men.

Somewhat ashamed of feeling those passions, I looked to Mark for guidance, but I could plainly see that he felt no such reservations. For him, Ned's loss was almost totally offset by the new sense of power and self-confidence that had come over him. He spoke with the voice of a soldier jubilant in victory, telling how he fired out of fear and instinct right at first. Then, almost bragging, he described shooting the others in cold blood.

When I spoke of the man I had shot, he rushed to assure me with a rough hug. "I was going to shoot him next, and at that distance, I could hardly have missed," he said, sounding like my Daddy, "but when I saw you aiming at him, I paused to see if you'd hit him. Good shot!"

So it was that in just those few moments, his killing of other men had gone from reaction to contest. The thought of Mark pausing like my father on a quail hunt so that I might make my first kill was distasteful.

We lay back on blankets. Overhead the eternal canopy of stars silenced us. Finally, we made love in a strange, wild, and wordless fury that somehow echoed the events of the day. It was satisfying and frightening and helped us drop off into a dreamless sleep. Sex was never again that good between us.

On the day of the fight we had not even considered trying to bury all the bodies, and so Bilau rounded up some local men to do the job and to hunt down the few pirates who had escaped. Mark went with him—armed to the teeth, of course.

Wild dogs, vultures, and locals had already found the corpses. The animals had eaten with relish, and the men had noted with interest the types of wounds they saw.

Bilau did not tell the locals how the battle had unfolded or how our astonishing weapons had done such terrible execution, but he didn't have to. Since Mark was a foreigner and was carrying unknown weapons and since Bilau avoided their questions, they knew. They were friendly enough, however, but they were scared, too. On the other hand, they were happy the thieves were dead and joined in eagerly in the effort to track down the survivors. Unfortunately, however, the four or five men Mark didn't kill made it back to their boat and got away.

On our second leave-taking, we had a three-man bodyguard who acted as mounted scouts, but we encountered no more bandits. As we traveled through that sparsely-populated region, curious families came to the road to watch our passing. Often they regarded us with suspicion and fear, but more often they were friendly or even reverent. After all, we *had* killed their enemies.

On the morning of the second day, we arrived in the capital, a city like many others I would see but can't locate on maps. It was small and low and white, clinging to a bluff along the side of a large river which was deep enough for ocean-going boats. Although it seemed to be quite a tidy little place glistening with whitewash and red awnings, it had no sewer system, and the weather was getting warm. It stank, but that was something I got used to rather quickly back then.

Word of what we had done to the brigands preceded us. Consequently, we were greeted by the king with terrified cordiality. We had told no one, not even Marcus, the comparatively limited capacities of our weapons. For all any of them knew, our guns threw thunderbolts without limit of time or distance, and we saw no reason to demonstrate otherwise.

Bilau found himself in a unique position and was quite uncertain of what use he could make of it. On the one hand, he was still the king's man and reported much of what he had observed. On the other, he was now totally devoted to us, as he had seen the weapons in action and had ridden on the taxiing Short. For all he knew, we had the powers of gods.

We were treated well in the capital, but left there within two days to avoid extensive questioning. We met privately with the king and demonstrated various miracles that we felt would keep him from trying to cross us or from bothering Marcus.

Then we took ship for Rome.

****

XII

Gibralter

"Behold: the Pillars of Hercules!" the captain of our ship said with a navigator's pride as we came on deck at dawn on our sixth day at sea.

There in the distance, as unmistakable as an image for a Prudential ad, dominating the flat line of the sea, lay The Rock. Known in those days as *Calpe,* the rock was the northernmost of the two "pillars". The southern cape or prominence was called Abyla . It lies on the southern or African shore at a point where the strait narrows to about nine miles. We plowed eastward through the low waves.

We were well out from shore and made straight toward Calpe, having declined the small seaport, Tingis, on the African side of the straits. In the late morning, mirrors atop the rock began to signal the distant Tingian towers which by that time we could only barely make out with the naked eye. Mark went to our baggage and brought back a pair of binoculars. Needless to say, they astonished the captain and the sailors--so much so that every man in the crew including the cook lined up to use them. For the rest of the trip, they were in constant demand. We were offered an enormous price for them, but Mark would not sell. When we finally parted from that ship, we took out the center pins and gave the captain one of the halves.

Struggling all day against contrary winds but swept along by the east-rushing currents, we finally landed at sunset at a small but almost impregnable town on the western side of the Rock. There a clever gate mechanism of wood and iron opened to permit our ship to pass inside, closing behind it as we entered a harbor so small that it could have held no more than ten ships the size of ours. There were only two other ships in port, however, and so all was roomy and calm. As I recall, the others were outbound—presumably to Britain—but one could never be sure since traders in those days were usually quite secretive about such things.

The purpose of the harbor gate was multiple. First, it provided protection from pirates on cutting-out expeditions. Such attempts to make off with whole ships that are lying at anchor are usually carried out at night. Accordingly, the gates and watch towers were studded with torches and other things that could be lighted in emergencies. It was also defensive in that it protected the harbor from fire-ships: boats carrying large amounts of hay, tar, and other inflammable materials that can be set afire purposely as they are being steered into enemy fleets and anchorages in times of war.

The gate also made it easier to collect the steep and strictly enforced harbor fees that were the town's main source of municipal income and ameliorated the effects of wave damage from storms driving in from the southwest. Although the gate itself had been damaged many times by such storms, the townsmen kept it in excellent repair, and it was always manned. Naturally, it required constant maintenance, and every citizen of the town—including the prefect and his wife—was required to contribute several days a year to stand guard or carry out repair duties. At night it was patrolled and lighted, even in times of peace, and from time to time live pigs were thrown into the water in front of the gate so as to encourage sharks and thereby discourage night attacks spearheaded by swimmers.

Obviously, docking was a service for which ships paid handsomely. Captains who could not justify the fees often would sail on by, going to Tingis instead, but necessity sometimes compelled even the reluctant to stop, and no honest ship and crew was denied. Some captains paid the fee by bringing in heavy replacement timbers for the sea gates lashed to the decks, for even then that part of Spain was denuded of old-growth forests.

No uninspected ships could enter the port, either, and all were required to use one of the port's pilots, whose duties included quick searches to guard against hidden storming parties. There were many other interesting facets of the small port's facilities and operations, and it was obvious that each precaution had been carefully thought out.

The use of such practical systems of revenue and crime control were widespread in those days. I have described the set-up in Gibraltar to illustrate how one port exploited its peculiar advantages as a way of showing how throughout the Roman world there was wide latitude for exploiting opportunities and anticipating and guarding against dangers.

Our own ship was well known to the authorities, and thereby we escaped a thorough search of our personal gear—a search that might have excluded us from the harbor. The gates' locks were undone and we backed into our slip. It all reminded me of putting a horse into a stall for the night.

Although Julian and most of the crew stayed aboard, Mark and I slept ashore that night in a tavern that was built onto side of a large, manmade cave. Our own little room was small, dark, and quiet, a delightful change from our little curtained-off area on the boat, but as I lay upon the padded rock shelf, I could still feel the roll of the sea and I missed the slap of the water against the ship's side.

Setting out before dawn on the following day and in the company of at least 20 other tourists, Mark and I clambered up the trails to the top of the highest point of the rock to view the most magnificent sunrise imaginable. From those windy heights some 1400 feet above the sea the whole world seemed to be spread out around us. Below us on the West side of the rock we could see the small town and our little ship in its snug berth. To the East the sun played on the water as if to make a highway of golden, calm sea leading off to great things and exciting adventures. To the South lay the rippling strait, Cape Ceuta, and the coast of Africa. To the West across a wide bay as well as to the North, farmlands and forests trailed out to low hills and distant haze. It was beautiful.

We stayed there all day, eating, drinking, and talking with other travelers. It was at once civilized and wild, and the wind was mild yet constant. We shared our food and, once again, we amazed those around us with our binoculars.

There were three Roman and two Gaulish families with us, two or three traveling priests, an unattached and sad-eyed woman of about 25, newly widowed, and three local soldiers wearing light armor who were on duty near the small stone guardhouse. It was they who kept the lookout and manned the signal mirrors, and we could tell that they enjoyed their work. To spend a day on the top of the rock with rich and food-laden tourists, sharing with them the views and holiday atmosphere was more a privilege than a duty.

It was also a place where lady tourists were known to share their favors with their lovers or even with the soldiers. One side of the summit had small niches cut into it suitable for trysting and mazes of trails covered the hillside. Unobservable from the heights above, there were scores of lovely picnic places which offered their own private vistas.

On the other sides of the summit the cliffs were much more dangerous and sheer, and for that reason they were sometimes used by suicides with a sense of flair. We could understand why. Standing up there made me think it would be a good day to pay one's debt to Death; better there than in some forgotten, dirty room, one thought.

No wonder the local people loved it. And no wonder the guards went up so readily. I could imagine that in bad weather and during lightning storms they might go up much more grudgingly even though there was a stout, stone guardhouse on the summit. But on that warm, Spring day it was quite ideal and even the light cloaks and coats in which we tourists had dressed were soon discarded. The women lifted their faces and bared their arms to the sun and the smaller children ran about naked.

We had still not encountered true Roman soldiers. The guards were paid members of the local militia, and 'though they wore Roman armor and were armed with short sword and pilum—an iron-tipped, wood-shafted spear about seven feet long, which was the standard infantry casting weapon of the Romans—they were not Italians. They actually reminded me of Swiss guides when carrying their arms and food, they led us up, long coils of rope hanging from their shoulders. At the top they had relieved the night watch which had duly taken down with it its own sets of ropes and weapons. That was how things were there in that small, cautious society which duly posted its guards aloft and alow around the clock, ready at all times to defend their town and its heights or to signal with sunlight, flags, or fire using signals remarkably similar to the Morse Code of 1800 years later.

All day long we talked and sunbathed and watched two of our companions paint landscapes on flat, wooden sheets. Even with no place in the world to develop film, I took black-and-white pictures with my small Leica. It was that sort of day. Eventually Mark and I wandered off to one of the little lovers' niches, enjoyed one another, and took a long nap.

Eventually, too, the young widow, made merry at last by wine, companionship, sunlight and song, went off down the trails with a handsome young soldier in the late afternoon. They must have had a good time, for she did not come down off the rock with us that night. It was such a place.

We stayed at Gibraltar for two nights, then sailed east toward the city now known as Cartagena on the southeast coast of Spain. There we planned to part company with Julian so that he could go directly upon his way to the Holy Land. I could hardly wait for him to be gone. For the most part he was civil toward me, but I could feel his hostility and contempt for those emotions always underlay his interactions with me. I tried to avoid him but aboard the little Mauretanian boat that was impossible.

It could have been me who was obnoxious, but I think not, for I always seemed to get along well with the other men around me. I was very popular among the crew—of that I am certain—and I spent many an hour sharing with them the delights of sea-life and making small trades of some of my less-valuable, trivial items. I should note that most seamen of those days were traders. All the 20 men on our ship, for example, were working on set shares of the earnings that were brought in by the cargoes and passengers. They were all free men from the same province and were bound to one another with ties of blood and marriage even though several were originally from other countries. Some of them had heavily tattooed faces--the mark of men who wanted to disguise themselves in foreign ports. Such tattoos were mostly reddish and laid out in geometric patterns, but it should be noted that for the most part such markings were rare, those particular ones being the only tattoos I ever saw in those days.

They got along with one another remarkably well. I certainly never saw any of them arguing or fighting. They worked together effortlessly and were to a man gentle, resourceful, and kind. Our 40-year-old captain assured us, though, that they could fight as well as they could sail, which was an important point since storms at sea were not the only dangers to be feared by travelers. One always had to bear in mind the possibility of piracy. Throughout time, many a ship's passenger has been a lady or a gentleman one day and a chattel or a corpse the next.

Although the Romans had largely succeeded in suppressing piracy throughout the Mediterranean, beyond Gibraltar to the West and the Suez and Byzantium to the East, the rule of the sea went to the strong and the intrepid. Along the northwest coast of Africa, we were assured, things were comparatively safe because suitable ports and offshore islands whereon pirates might rewater and refit were lacking. Nevertheless, the captain and crew kept careful lookouts day and night, kept their weapons to hand, and avoided other ships on the high seas. They told us Atlantic coast stories of pirates from the south—black men in long, low boats driven by sails and paddles, in fleets of 20 or more, racing along the beaches raiding villages and capturing women, livestock, and whole ships.

Even in the Mediterranean ships sometimes disappeared and piracy was common--particularly since large parts of the coasts of North Africa were not under Roman rule. Then as now, the law held terror only for those who it could reach, and often the only reach of the law out there was that which catapults and arrows might provide.

For defensive armament our particular ship had a powerful balista forward of the mast in the bow. It was essentially a large crossbow capable of shooting various types of long bolts, fire arrows and javelins. It could be rotated on its base so as to be fired forward, starboard, or port, and at Mark's request the captain and crew shot it for us on our first afternoon out of Gibraltar.

They fired an arrow that was as big around as my lower arm. To its tail was attached a stout line by which it could be retrieved or by which a heavier hawser or line could be worked over to another ship or even into a dock. It could also be used as a harpoon in the rare event that a whale might get too close. It was very powerful and was pulled back to full cock by four men working a horizontal capstan on a ratcheted shaft. With a resounding *Whack!* it shot the heavy bolt which flew away trailing its little line out to about 100 yards.

Their launching of a javelin was even more impressive. Perfectly balanced and launched upward at a 45-degree angle, it sailed effortlessly away from the ship, traveling at least 200 yards before slipping into the sea.

Two crew members were grandsons of a man who had fought at Atticum in 31 BC. From him, they had heard tales of the fearful effects that such javelins and arrows had upon the densely packed soldiery on the decks of ships that were still too far apart to permit ramming or boarding. In that battle which decided the fate of the empire for the next 100 years and put an end to the ambitions of Antony and Cleopatra, a single javelin had killed four unarmored men on that grandfather's ship as they held onto a mainstay. Many other ships were set ablaze by fire arrows and catapult-launched firepots.

Our double-masted boat was about 90 feet long and had oars so that it could be rowed by the crew if necessary. Normally they rowed only in performing docking maneuvers since it was almost pointless to do so at sea, the craft being too large and undermanned for such work. If the wind failed, therefore, the ship stopped. That happened on our second day out of Gibraltar when we were becalmed for two whole days. No one but Julian and Mark even suggested rowing, but they sure didn't offer to do it themselves.

I found that floating about on the empty sea was a memorable experience that most of us took in stride by sleeping, talking, and eating. Only the impatient Englishmen were anxious to be moving.

The rest of us acted as if on holiday. What else could we do? A few men got drunk, some gambled, and some fished. Most of them went swimming while we waited for a breeze to send us on our way, and, naturally, they swam nude. Diving and jumping from the bow and the main spar, they frolicked about like boys, often diving down deep in the clear water. Oddly, though they did do some fishing, neither Mark nor Julian swam, and I knew that Mark was not much of a swimmer anyway.

Not so me. By the second day I desperately wanted to join in the fun, so I asked the captain if it would be all right, knowing that he had the best judgment about the discipline and deportment of his crew. As soon as he gave me permission, I went straightaway to my cabin and squeezed into my nylon tank suit. It didn't occur to me that I should say anything to Mark.

When I emerged on deck, an astonished cry went up from the first man who saw me, and everyone came running. All eyes were on me. Suddenly I was surrounded by friendly, wet, and mostly naked men who were staring at me and talking with one another. They laughed, looked, and pointed at what seemed to them a second skin. Some of them even reached out to feel the cloth, unabashedly touching me wherever they pleased. The fabric fascinated them and they pulled at it without expressing embarrassment, asking permission, or tendering apology. Since it was very non-threatening and friendly, I found that I liked all that attention, even though I could feel myself blushing and my breasts stiffening with the beginning of sexual tension.

"Back away there!" Mark suddenly shouted in English, pushing himself angrily through the little crowd, then shoving and slapping away their hands. His face was filled with rage, and the mood immediately went from festive to unpleasant. I doubt if he could have held his own against any of those men in a fist or knife fight, and some of them were beginning to have the glint of fight in their eyes. He was wearing a .45.

"Go back to the cabin," he said sharply to me. "You look like a tart and you'll cause trouble. Have you no shame? You're practically naked!"

Standing there on the deck in shorts, L.L. Bean polo shirt and tennis shoes amid the tough, tanned, naked sailors, he looked terribly priggish and effeminate. Behind him, dressed in slacks and leather shoes, stood his son, the even more priggish

Julian. I could see in an instant that my future lay not with them, but was entirely in my own hands.

I told him, in English, what he could do with himself. It just came out. He looked shocked and Julian, who never had liked me anyway, smirked.

"And you, too, Preacher!" I said to him. It was unladylike, I know, but I shot him a bird, too. The crew couldn't understand us, of course, but they could tell what was going on and they howled with laughter. The obscene gesture was previously unknown to them. Perhaps I introduced it to the ancient world.

Prior to that time I had noted with interest that all of the sailors used side and breast strokes, and no one was using what I have always called the American crawl. Quickly I turned to the captain and spoke to him in Latin. "Tell the men that I'll give a silver coin to any one who can catch me before I reach that rock," I said, pointing to a large rock sticking out of the sea about 200 yards away. Mark tried to grab my wrist, but I snatched it away.

As the captain began to translate my challenge to the men and they began to smile, I ran lightly to the side and dove over into the cool water, then struck out for the rock. The better swimmers cheered and followed, but I had a lead and I kept it and the little silver dime I would have given to the winner.

By the time I reached my destination, only two of the men were still trying to catch me. Seeing that they had lost, but nearer to the rock than the boat, they swam on out and rested there with me. One was about 16—sleek, tanned and callow. The other was a weatherbeaten fellow of 40 who was burly and tough, but had a big grin and a hearty laugh. Neither could speak much Latin or Greek. Encouraged by my smile, they climbed out of the gentle swells, and the three of us sat on the rough stone in the warm sun, panting and trying to talk to one another in Latin. As the rock was small, we were very close to one another and I could not help but look at their bodies as they relaxed and revived. Except for their teeth, they were beautiful men. I should point out that other than Mark, all of the men I saw for the first two years back then—including the two on the rock—were uncircumcised, a fact that took some getting used to on my part from an aesthetic standpoint. I shall discuss that more at some later point. At any rate, as we sat there, the boy couldn't take his eyes off me, and 'though I tried not to notice, he soon had an interesting, curved erection that embarrassed me more than it embarrassed him. Frankly, I felt a little like reaching out and touching it, but of course I didn't.

I could, however, feel Mark watching me with the binoculars and for that reason alone I almost went ahead and touched the boy out of pure mischievousness and spite. Again I knew that Mark and I would have to split up sooner or later, and that when we did, I would be more alone than I had ever been in my life. For the time being he'd have to do, I thought. I wished my sister was with me.

I thought about friends and family a lot in those days, for we rarely miss a thing until it's too late to retrieve. It was certainly too late to regret having come on this journey, and I could only hope that my health would hold up.

I was often sad on that part of the trip, for I thought about the wonderful things and people I had left behind. Unlike Mark, who had left his own world behind in 1939, and had eight year in the States to get over it, I had just left my homeland only a few weeks before. Furthermore, though I was now engaged upon a great adventure, Ned's murder and the day-to-day reality of living bereft of modern conveniences were growing weights upon my heart.

I smiled at the men on the rock with me. They were good people. Marcus, Naadia, and the others had been good people, too. I would be all right. I could face the world. I put an arm around each of the sailors and clapped them on their backs like a good comrade would, and gave them a sisterly hug. We swam back to the waiting boat and my disgruntled lover.

****

XIII

Carthago Nova

Altogether it took about ten days to reach Carthago Nova, a city founded on the ruins of a still older city some 250 years earlier by the Carthaginian Hasdrubal. Conquered by the Romans in 210 BC., it was one of the most valuable of the empire's strategic and financial assets. Possessed of a fine harbor and numerous gold, silver, and lead mines in the area, it was bustling with activity and was well-garrisoned by troops unquestionably loyal to Tiberias. In many ways Spain was the most important and most jealously guarded province of Rome, for it had often demonstrated its potential for financial, industrial, and military independence during various civil wars.

We had discussed our plans with no one, but the authorities had anticipated our arrival. This came as no surprise to us because we were well aware that there was in existence a complete system of regular, written interprovincial intelligence sharing. Before we arrived reports about us had been circulated—reports which included identification of our ship as well as its probable destinations. As we were first beating, then rowing into port on that bright morning, there was ample time for the Roman governor to summon the guard, don suitable attire, and walk down to the waterfront.

Like most ships of the time, ours could not sail close to the wind and often had to employ the oars to come into port. On that particular day, the crew took almost three hours to bring us in. By the time we landed, it was midmorning.

Using the binoculars, we could see the governor and his retinue long before we landed. Although he was accompanied by five or six nervous soldiers in shiny armor, he himself was dressed in a white toga and soft leather sandals. Our captain took a long look at the receiving party and thought their attire and composure signaled a greeting worthy of respected ambassadors. Had our greeter been wearing armor, he told us, the unspoken message would have been one of military preparedness if not downright hostility.

Our captain could see that we were expected to dock at the premiere landing place in the center of the crescent harbor. With great skill and finesse, he had the crew row us forward with just the right amount of way. Just as we came up to the stone steps, he had them strike two quick back-strokes, then ship oars on the landward side as the seaward bank struck twice more then gently sculled us in. The long craft slid gently sideways into the dock, barely caressing the rope fenders. The big boat came to a dead stop. A single man in a rowboat couldn't have done better, and it was the perfect touch for us: We arrived in style. Our boat's hinged side panel was smartly swung down amidships and Mark and Julian stepped ashore to greet the provincial governor. I stayed back on the boat behind the gunwales where our Thompson submachine gun was propped up next to my hand out of the sight of those on shore.

As both of them were wearing modern shirts and long pants, Mark and Julian astonished all who saw them. An excited murmur went up from the crowd of about 300 people who had gathered at the quay and stood a loose semicircle behind the governor and the small group of his soldiers. As they mounted the steps, the crowd pressed forward but was immediately stopped by the men in the shiny armor who at a word from their centurion had turned and held them back with spears held as a sort of horizontal fence.

Mark had on a bullet-proof vest and was wearing his .45 automatic in a holster attached to a Sam Browne belt. To me he looked very dangerous. He was. One false or treacherous move on the part of the Romans and he would have skipped back for the Thompson and mowed them all down: men, women and children. To give him credit, though, he managed to come across as being quite peaceable. Smiling and raising his hand, palm forward, in a universal sign of peaceful intentions he stepped forward boldly.

Julian, on the other hand, looked not the least bit martial and had declined to carry Ned's pistol. In his increasingly worn-out clothes he looked like a nervous tourist following in Mark's wake. The crowd merely gawked at him, and it was obvious enough that Mark was the leader of our little band.

I turned my attention to the governor whose name was, as I recall, Antonious Cato, a noble member of that famous family, so our captain had told us. Even from my vantage point some fifteen or twenty feet from him I could tell, though, that such a man had not risen to his present position through birth alone. About 50 years old, he had white hair and carried more weight than perhaps suited him, but he was a fine figure of a man as well as an apparently competent soldier. During the short time we spent in Nova Cartago, he displayed a panoply of talents and graces that were hallmarks of noble men of that age.

As planned, I hung back aboard the boat as Mark and

Julian went forward toward our host and began speaking with him in the sort of loud, rhetorical manner that such occasions seen to demand. I could, however, hear only bits and pieces of that which was being said and I felt slighted, even left out as if I was of no importance. Dressed in the garment Naaida had made for me--a modified version of the common stola--I was covered almost completely with carefully draped folds of light linen. I was wearing a veil that hid the lower half of my face and so I looked much like a Mauritanian woman, albeit a tall one who was probably quite homely. As I have said, the use of veils was not uncommon in those days, particularly among those who had bad teeth or other imperfections. I felt dowdy in such a garment, but had heeded Naadia's warnings and donned that costume so as not to make too many enemies among the women or gain too many admirers among the men. Actually, at that point I was still not convinced that Naadia was right about me, but wore the outfit anyway—largely for the purpose of concealing my own .45.

I became miffed as the men continued to ignore me. Realizing that a sudden attack was very unlikely, I, too, stepped ashore and walked forward with as much grace and dignity as I could fake. Nonetheless, even after our ship's captain had introduced me as The Lady Evangeline, a personality in her own right, Antonious Cato politely ignored me, obviously assuming that I was a chattel of one of the two strangely-dressed men. They were telling him how they were emissaries from a friendly nation far across the seas, and I was rather pointedly being excluded from the conversation. I use the term "conversation" loosely, for as I have said, the men were posturing before one another and making speeches for the benefit of the crowd. When Julian was going on about something I caught Antonious' eye briefly and saw a sudden spark of interest arise in it. Even at his age he probably wondered what was under both the veil and the stola. He had looked me over briefly when we were introduced; in that instant his eye had missed little.

Having sized us up and listened to our stated business, he invited us to stay with him and to join him at a banquet he was planning for that very evening. Not without some worry and some discussion in English, we assented. After considering what we should take with us and whether or not we could trust the ship's captain, we followed him up the hill to his residence in open sedan chairs.

It was the first time that I had ridden in a litter. It was just like "in the movies," I thought, and I wondered whether the two men carrying me were slaves, soldiers, or freemen, for they were healthy, well-turned out fellows wearing what was apparently the household uniform of the governor's villa—brown tunics trimmed in yellow. I learned later that they were freemen and that litter carrying was just an ordinary task about which no one complained.

I found myself elevated above the crowds of people who parted to allow us a yard or so of space on either side as we passed along above their heads.

One quickly learned that sedan chairs were very useful to those who could afford to hire or own them. Not only could one keep one's dignity sitting up above the crowd like that, but also one could avoid stepping in filth, avoid being trampled, and avoid being an easy mark for cut purses and perverts. In large, dense crowds, there were often men who would think nothing of fondling women they passed. It was so commonplace that women—including me—often put up with it without making scenes. As I recall, some few women thought of such fondling as being complimentary. Imagine yourself in a milling, moving, stinking crowd of thousands, when unknown hands reach out to feel your genitals or search for your wallet. The first time that it happened to me was some weeks later when for the first time I was walking in Rome *incognito* in stola and veil. No sooner did I find myself in a large, pressing crowd, than three different men tried to grope me within a 20 minute period. One of them—a short, ugly fellow with only one eye—was passing by me going slowly in the opposite direction. As he passed, he put his outstretched hand directly upon my mons venus and rubbed it obscenely in the moment before I slapped it away. He mumbled something, sniggered, and was soon out of sight.

Another aspect of the use of litters was that, like clothes, they separated the classes. There were usually just two bearers per litter, but sometimes four or even six men carried one- and two-person rigs. Litter carriers also doubled as bodyguards in the event of trouble. Bearers were usually quite stout and tough. Most teams could trot or even run with their burdens, and once or twice a year during festivals, races would be held among the various teams—races often involving increasingly large rounds of wine between events.

At the governor's one and two story villa we were given a suite that consisted of a sitting room with three large, adjoining bedrooms. It was quite lavish by the standards of the time and place, and I was happy to have a room to myself. It was heavenly to have some privacy and to be away from men, if only for a few hours. I also wanted to sleep in a real bed and walk around nude in a room on dry land.

To my surprise, I was assigned my own personal servant. About my age, she was Italian and spoke Latin as well as the local language—a language which did not sound the least bit like modern Spanish. We got along well, for she was polite and seemed happy to be waiting on me. Although I knew her duties included spying on me and trying to discover as much about us as she could, I enjoyed having her around and happily indulged her curiosity concerning my wardrobe and toiletries.

I asked if I might take a bath and in a short time found myself in a marble bathroom some 15 feet in diameter, soaking in wonderfully hot water while my servant scrubbed my back and washed my hair. As she bathed me, two young, nude girls played music on lyre and flute.

It was luxurious, and I would have felt quite happy except for the knowledge that I had made myself vulnerable. Not only was I separated from Mark and Julian, but also I hadn't carried either of my guns with me to the bath. There again, I had already resolved early on to trust people as much as I could, and the girls seemed harmless and pleasant enough. I relaxed and gave myself over to the pleasure of the moment. While drinking delicious wine from a goblet of thin gold, I closed my eyes and let my servant massage my shoulders, face and scalp.

The girls spoke to me without artifice and with disarming candor. They told me how they admired my face and my body and ignoring my feeble protests, washed me all over using the small bar of scented soap that I had brought with me. After all, I had let other people—you included--wash me before. Of course, that with you was different, I suppose, but as anyone will understand, the bath that day was a sensual and arousing experience. Finally I closed my eyes and lay back in the water. Those girls were the first people other than Mark who had touched me in a long time, and their caresses, though erotic, were innocently given, lovely and smooth. I felt as if I were swimming through soft grasses or silk. Although I became quite aroused, their touches did not make me want a man. I was, rather, suffused with a warm feeling of well-being.

After I got out of the bath, limp with pleasure and slightly drunk, they gave me a thorough massage then led me back to my room. I slept through the afternoon in a silken bed.

Just before dark, my girl awakened me, arranged my hair, and she and her companions helped me to dress in my best outfit. The girls assured me that although I was wearing an old style still favored by rich Mauritanian women—light, white woolen garments trimmed in blue—I seemed a wonder to behold. The voluminous, floor length dress that was yet another variation of the Roman stola was really quite flattering, they said. Unlike many of the stolas I had seen and the one I had worn that morning, this one was cut well, its folds and drapes enhancing rather than concealing my rather large frame. Caught up with ties at the shoulders, it allowed pleasant, changing glimpses of my arms, neck, and ankles. I wore no bra with it, so it moved with me in ways that made me very conscious of the necessity of moving with graceful deliberation.

For makeup I wore only some light-blue eye shadow and darkened my lashes and brows. I didn't need any blush or similar enhancements of my cheeks since on the voyage there I had gotten enough sun to give even more color to the already reddish tones of my skin. As in other ages, true ladies were expected to protect themselves from the sun, and I was glad that at least I had not let myself get burned. As you will recall, my skin is so fair that I almost can't get a tan. I did not wear a veil.

At that time, my hair was rather long and I usually let it hang down more or less naturally in a simple, curly fall down over my shoulders. Sometimes I tied it back in a ponytail, but in those days such a practice was considered vulgar even in Mauretania. For that dinner, though, the girls insisted that I let them put it up in a fairly elaborate pile, the end of which ran through a gold fillet in the back so that my neck was exposed. They assured me that if I wore it in that manner mine would look more nearly like the hairstyles of the other women who would be at the dinner.

As I had no slippers or sandals which would go with the

that particular dress, I decided to go barefoot since the girls had told me that to do so was acceptable, particularly since, according to them, my feet were lovely, soft, and well shaped. All in all I felt rather sexy since I was obviously going to be once again the object of so much attention and was practically nude under a garment that resembled nothing so much as a lovely nightgown my mother used to wear when I was a girl. But I was a woman, and beneath that lovely garment, I wore my thin linen money-belt with its cache of gold coins and a .45 derringer in the small of my back. It pays to be careful.

I arrived at dinner rather late, but that was not considered a breach of etiquette under the circumstances. Quite to the contrary, being both a traveler and a guest I was expected to arrive somewhat after the men had been formally introduced.

My entrance caused a sensation. Everyone--including the servants and the three or four guards--turned to gape and stare at me as I paused in the doorway—everyone, that is, except Mark, Julian, and our host. The three of them were busy noting the effect that I was having on everyone else. In hindsight, I suspect that Antonious Cato either did not wish to show that he was impressed or else he had already gotten a good look at me through hidden apertures in the bathroom or my bedroom. He was polite but not smitten and used those precious minutes to observe the effect I had on others.

The rest of the Romans stared at me, though, and conversation came to a halt. Antonious rose and with an elegant gesture of his extended hand, he addressed me in the formal style.

"You do us great honor to join us, My Lady. We could have spared the expense of lamps: Your face would have been light enough for us all," he said, approaching me.

I took his proffered arm. He walked me around the inside of the ring of low tables, introducing me to each of his guests. As he did so, I noticed that Mark and Julian both were ignored, a fact that galled them, I'm sure. As he had invited several other local dignitaries and young people to join us, altogether there were about fifteen Romans there.

Antonious led me to my place: a low couch on the outside of one of the low tables which were arranged about the room. There was no one opposite me to block my view—or to block others' views of me. Obviously, I was on display.

The meal itself was served like many a meal that followed: with a show of pomp, wealth and luxury. We ate four or five types of fish, fowl, meat, and cheese, eight types of vegetables, breads, and pastries, soups, honeyed fruit, wine, beer, melons, and some other things I cannot identify.

The room was about 20 feet across, the tables arranged in an open square around a small pool in the center of the room where a small fountain splashed and sparkled in the light of a score of lamps hanging from the ceiling around the colonnade behind us. There was only a partial roof above us, a ten-by-ten foot square area being open to the sky. As the night was warm and the ventilation excellent, it felt refreshing and very pleasant as we lounged on the couches, ate, drank, and looked up at the stars.

There were many servants about. Waiters, cooks, musicians, and guards hustled back and forth or stood respectfully while the guests, reclining on low sofas, gorged themselves. As was the custom, Mark and Julian were seated on other sides of the square. During the main courses, I practically had to yell at them to be heard over the din.

I was seated beside the governor's wife, and after having made a bit of small talk with her, I turned my attentions to the food. Tired of the bland shipboard fare, I ate like a pig. It was held to be a sign of my appreciation as well as my trust in my hosts.

If I had not been so admired and, at the same time, amazed and interested in the other women and how they dressed and acted, I should have felt quite out of place. Of course, I *was* out of place as well as out of time, and therefore suffered not the least bit of embarrassment for being somewhat out of style.

The lady of the house was in her early 40's and had long gone to fat, but the clothes she wore hid her weight well. She had on a bright, pink stola over a voluminous red silk dress which was criss-crossed with golden ropes. There were various semi-precious stones hanging here and there upon her person in no particular order—something of a fad, I learned later. Her hair was pressed in flat, tight curls all over her head and was surmounted by a silver tiara that was beautifully worked and studded with what must have been diamonds, but could just as easily been quartz. She was doused in lilac perfume, and as she was seated to my left, she made an effort to befriend and to intoxicate me, a duty that had no doubt been imposed by custom and her husband.

Like many Roman women I met, she spoke in an artificial or superficial way and had mannerisms that seemed to me to be strange and even offensive. She seemed to be badly playing at some role, and her attempts to make me feel at ease with her were totally in vain.

Another female guest sitting to my far right was the wife of the head of town government. She wore her hennaed hair piled high upon her head in a multicurled fashion that must have taken hours to establish. Like our hostess, she wore heavy makeup that made no attempt to appear to be a natural enhancement of her looks. She was between 30 and 50 years old, but I couldn't tell exactly nor could I look at her without recoiling from the heavy mask of powder and paint that passed for her face. A thin woman dressed gorgeously in lime green and gold, she wore heavy rings of solid gold on her bony hands. I suspected that she was in the middle stages of some serious, wasting disease.

There were two attractive, young women seated on the right side of the square on either side of Julian. Apparently they were the wives or girlfriends of the young officers who were seated between him and me and had apparently been invited purely for their decorative effect, for both were quite lovely. I had the impression that theirs were the least important places at the tables, and I also assumed they had been strategically placed near Julian to enchant him if it were possible for them to do so.

As far as I had seen, though, he didn't seem to care for women at all. For that matter, I had not seen him show any sexual interest in men either. Truth to tell, I had very little experience in such matters at the time and could have been easily deceived in that regard.

No one including Julian paid much attention to those young women, a fact which didn't seem to bother them at all. Apparently they and the young men they came with were having a good time and obviously felt honored to be dining in company with the governor, his wife and senior officers, the mayor, and their exotic, foreign guests.

My own status as well as my placement was quite

ambiguous. Everyone kept looking at me—surreptitiously for the most part, but sometimes quite openly—and there were no cut flowers or decorations on the table before me to block their views. I was not just imagining being the center of such attention, but at least I was prepared for it after my experiences with the adoring servant girls that afternoon.

We soon realized that what we had heard from Marcus was true: It was considered poor etiquette to pay even the slightest attention to the cooks, servers, and guards in the room. To do so would have been to indicate that one was of low birth and unaccustomed to the ministrations of help. I nevertheless got a look at each of them, and noted that most of them were stealing looks at me, too. After so many years of being thought of as a wallflower or tomboy, it was pleasant, even heady, to be thought beautiful by others.

I ate a lot that night. It might have been better for me if I had eaten nothing, but as it was, I dug in like I was at a family reunion in Charleston, thereby dispelling immediately any notion of my possible divinity. I would have liked some sweet, iced tea, but nothing is perfect.

Our hosts tried to act naturally around us, but the conversation was fairly stiff until the wine took off the first edges of mutual distrust. After that our host's guests plied us with scores of questions. We, too, had many questions, but out of an abundance of caution, we tried to control ourselves. Since Julian was being excessively taciturn and I was thought politically unimportant, most of the seemingly random questions were addressed to Mark. It was an interrogation, but a polite one.

In slow Latin that we could easily follow, the older men made speeches and told anecdotes that were supposed to pass for conversation. We could not yet understand the subtleties of language that would have permitted us to enjoy the jests, mythological and historical references, epigrams, and jokes with which Romans entertained themselves—usually at one another's expense. In that way as in others, they were not unlike many educated people before or since.

Neither of the two young officers were treated with more than passing deference. Like the young women, they had been invited for a purpose which I soon assumed was to entertain and interrogate me. Clearly, their placement nearby was intentional. One was dark and very muscular, but the more handsome of the two—Valerius, was his name—was tall and lean and had light brown hair and clear, blue eyes. Something about him was very attractive to me. He seemed open, friendly, guileless, and, yes, sexy. He was not soft, though, for he was obviously in terrific physical condition and the deep scars on his right arm testified to the military training that he had undergone.

As was obvious from the untrimmed togas they wore, neither of the young men was an aristocrat. They were, rather, sons of men of the equestrian class and were, coincidentally, cavalry officers in the local garrison. I learned that they therefore had some status in the local community, but not much. Even with my limited command of Latin I could tell that their attempts at conversation with me were considered intrusions— particularly by the older ladies who, like women of their position throughout time, sought to elevate themselves largely through the artful denigration of others. Of course, it was not my place to say anything about such a state of affairs, but I had eyes.

The older men made out that they were an agreeable bunch of fellows, but we knew to be leery of their hospitality and sparing of their wine. Mark was more sparing than I. The stiff-necked Julian was more sparing still. After the first hour of drinking and feasting, I was in a garrulous mood. Tired of lounging about on the soft, low dining couches, I wanted to get up and run around or dance or something. Finally I went ahead and got up, stretched, and went out to powder my nose. Apparently the streatching part got to most of them, for as I learned later, it was considered naughty, almost vulgar. My maid giggled later when she told me how several of the men's mouths had dropped open when, towering over them like some great lioness, I had flexed myself so carelessly. Had I known it at the time, I might have done it a bit longer.

Following the main course when the speeches were over, a general din arose in the room, and I addressed Mark for the first time.

"Darling," I called out in English with a big smile that belied my true feelings for him at that moment, "Is this about what you had in mind when you suggested we take our little trip?"

It doesn't sound right now and it didn't sound right then when I said it, either, but he responded quickly enough.

"Yes, Eva! Quite outstanding! Quite wonderful, this place!" he said with a strange look on his face--a disapproving look, I thought: something we could discuss later.

Tired of him and his disapprovals, I turned to Julian. "Hey, Julian, old boy! What about it? This about what *you* had in mind?"

Well, needless to say, it wasn't, and he told me so with a forced smile on his face, too. "Like father, like son," I thought instantly.

"Degeneracy and wickedness! Gluttony, drunkenness, and paganism: That's all these people have to offer," he ranted with a tone in his voice that sounded as if he were saying, "Yes, I did have a good nap. And you?"

"They just want you to be happy," I said.

"They just want me to come down to their level," he replied with a sour smile. At least he had the good sense to try to conceal his hostility toward both our hosts and me.

"Cool it, Julian. Nobody here wants to hear your sermons. Ease up. Have a good time. Drink some wine," I said.

"Get thee from me, Satan," he said, with thinly disguised disdain.

With a smile as sweet as any debutante's, I responded to him, telling him what he could do with himself. Mark laughed when he heard me, and I saw approval and even affection for me in his eyes.

Julian turned red in the face, but what did I care? I was sick of him and sick, too , even of thinking about worry and fear. I was a young, healthy woman out on the town: I wanted to have a good time.

What good would worry do, anyway? Any fool could figure out that our hosts could poison us if they wanted to. Maybe they were afraid to harm us, and maybe not. Maybe they were just biding their time. My intuition, however, told me that we were safe and that intuition was good enough for me.

During the main course, Mark had proven himself to be a careful but brilliant diplomat from our imaginary country across the seas, speaking without revealing anything of significance to our host and his guests. Pursuant to the plans we had agreed upon, he told them that we were from an advanced civilization far across the seas—a civilization that was the successor of Atlantis. He told them that although we had developed weapons of astonishing capacity, we had learned how to live in peace with other nations based upon our military supremacy and goodwill—goodwill which was in turn based upon our monotheistic religion and a rigid class structure. He told them, too, that we could communicate with one another around the world. Ours was a peaceful empire that could conquer the world if it chose to do so, he said, but our history had taught us to be content with control over only our own vast lands.

By the use of this particular fiction and some proofs to sustain it, we thought we could secure our safety. We assumed that the Romans would be reluctant to abuse the emissaries of an empire that was more powerful than their own.

Our hosts were polite but skeptical. They, too, had played their roles that night in accord with a subtle but obvious plan. During what must have been the seventh or eighth course of the meal, one of the older men named Quintus, pretending the wine had given him leave to be familiar and to pry, addressed Mark in a friendly, blustering tone.

"Now see here," he said as if he were a straightforward sort of old soldier, "let's make plain with one another. I've heard you have something wonderful and terrible—weapons held in your hands that can kill men at great distances, tearing great holes in them. I'd like to see one of them work. How about it? I heard of a Greek, or maybe it was a Persian, who made such weapons, but I've never seen one."

He spoke too long—long enough for the rest of the company to notice and become silent in order to hear Mark's reply.

Mark looked at me and spoke in English. "The obvious question comes at last, what! How predictable! Shall we provide them some entertainment tomorrow?"

"Why not?" I said, confident by now in his judgment about such matters. "We are in the hands of the Fates anyway. Who knows what tomorrow will bring?" I concluded, satisfied that for the first time the group saw that I was being consulted about a matter of importance. He turned back to the old soldier.

"Maybe tomorrow—in the afternoon—after you have shown us your troops and your own machines of war," Mark said as if he, too, needed to learn more of them. "But for what I shall show you, let us go far off and in a small group—not, pray, where all the eyes of the town will be upon us. Ignorant people fear that which is different. Only our enemies have any reason to fear us." A glance and a subtle nod from Antonious to the general sealed the bargain.

I looked at the handsome, young officer who sat near me and could tell that he was falling for me or was pretending to fall for me. After all, in a society where marriage is both voluntary and important for financial and career goals, and where securing affection must be subordinated to those   aims, courtship becomes rather distorted. Passions, if unrequited within such arranged marriages, become the province and the cause of adultery.

Valerius, however, seemed callow and sincere enough, and the look in his eyes vacillated between a self-assured stare and puppy love. I hadn't had that effect on a boy since sixth grade when I was the tallest, most developed girl in the class, and something about him made me want to follow up on the little thrill he was giving me with his looks. I asked him whether or not he would be joining when we went out for a small demonstration of our weapons on the morrow. In that way that women have, I did not want to seem to forward or bold, so with an eye to the girl across from him I said something to the effect of, "If your lady will be so kind as to spare you, we would like your company." The pretty girl reclining between him and Julian blushed with pleasure at being addressed, for in the scheme of things, she was only a step above the servants.

He was taken by surprise. "Might I propose an alternative? " he asked smoothly, surprising me with his quick grasp of the possibilities.

"Might I call for you in the morning and show you the training grounds of my troop of cavalry" he asked, using a slight flourish of the hand for emphasis, "if your husband can spare you?"

"But, Sir," I said, perhaps too quickly, "you misunderstand. Lord Mark and I are not married to one another. I go where I will. I assure you: he can spare me." There was a slight stirring in the room, for prior to that point all had assumed that he and I were married or that he had at least some sort of claim over me.

Mark was busy talking to the older officer, making

arrangements for the demonstration, but he had caught the end of my conversation.

"I'd rather you not go off by yourself. In fact, I forbid it!" he said to me in English, using a pleasant tone to mask his irritation.

If anything, my voice was sweeter than his. "You forget yourself, Mark. You don't own me, and therefore you can forbid me nothing. I will do as I please, and it pleases me to go out riding. And so I shall."

"You trust too much," he tried to remind me.

"Yes. But if they wished to kill us? Nothing could stop them. *Tempis Fugit*."

"So you see?" I said in Latin, turning to the young people near me at our end of the table, "My countryman and I are at your disposal. He chooses martial plans with these friends. I, on the other hand, having spent too much time at sea, hope only to smell again fine horses. Let me say this, though: in my country, women don't just look at horses, they ride them."

"And do the women of your country ride horses in war?" asked another of the officers who was sitting off to the left. It was the sort of question that called for an answer not just to him but loud enough for all.

"In war, the women of my country do whatever is necessary, I assure you," I said. "More like the Germans than the Trojans, I think."

I could see the reaction among the men.

"Then you know of the Germans and of the Trojans?" asked one of the older men.

"Only what we have read in books and have heard about from people we have met."

"Then your people have studied our nations?" Quintus asked politely and without artifice.

"Oh, yes. I have read Homer and the account of Julius Caesar in Gaul."

They all seemed impressed. I thought it best to let them think that we knew more about them than they knew about us.

"Then you know of the power and extent of the Roman Empire," the magistrate said, "and of the invincibility of its armies."

"I don't know about that," I replied politely, "but I do

know something of the Punic Wars, of Cannae, and of the defeat of Varus in the Teutoborg Forest." Everyone was very quiet by that time.

"They fought to the last man and then, when all was hopeless, the last most honorably took their own lives!" blurted out the burly young officer. He seemed offended, as if I had questioned the valor of Roman arms.

"Please take no offense, centurion," I said to him with a smile that I hoped would convey friendliness, "but I have met a Roman who claims to have survived the battle. He told me that some 110 men under Cassius Chaerea cut their way out of the encirclement. Eighty survived. My acquaintance was one of them—or so he said," I concluded, remembering the story Marcus had told and acutely wishing he were here dining with us. I was surprised to have retained the name of the officer and the numbers of his band.

Needless to say, the Romans were more surprised by my story than I was. They may have thought, I realized, that we were German allies. I thought it might be best to change the subject and to deflect some attention away from myself.

"We are all avid readers of history, and our compatriot," I explained with a gesture toward Julian, "is a high priest who comes among you now to observe your ways and those of the people ruled by Rome."

Julian was suddenly pleased by this sudden shift of attentions toward him. He was used to having people watch him in the pulpit, and I think it galled him when in normal life their attentions wandered elsewhere.

The men began to ply him with questions concerning the nature of our nation's beliefs and religious practices. Mark and I were as amazed by his answers as Julian was.

"I have not come to talk about our religion but to study yours," he told them diplomatically in his good Latin. "If I were to discuss or attempt to explain our body of beliefs and the sacred writings upon which they are based, it would effect the way people talk to me and how they express their own beliefs and values. It is better that I don humble garb and travel among the people, quietly visiting the temples of all the major religions in the empire."

"One must be careful in doing that sort of thing," the mayor warned him. "There are many whose beliefs are exclusive. They are taught to hate foreigners and think of themselves as superior to others. From time to time wars have been fought over such trivia."

"Surely the relationship of Man and God is not a trivial matter, sir," Julian replied. "Is it not of prime importance?"

"Just so," Antonious interjected as if to shield his colleague from friction with Julian, but also to state the position of Rome. "But is it not also impious for men to suppose that they know the will off the gods completely? Some feel justified in killing of those with whom they disagree."

"Our history has been plagued by such religious wars," I interjected, with a glance at Julian. "Wars, revolutions, persecutions. All in the names of various gods." I said.

"The lady does not recognize that there is such a thing as Truth," explained Julian. "So it is with too many of our people. It will be enough for me, however, to seek out the greatest teacher of the age if only to kiss his foot and to look upon his face."

"Your priest has in him something that bears watching," said a thirtish officer across from me. I could tell that Julian had almost unwittingly fanned a spark of distrust, a spark that the older men kept hidden behind their outward cheerfulness.

"Oh, Julian is harmless enough. He's a player--a *dilettante* as we would say," I said this loudly enough so that the others could hear. I looked about with a gaiety I did not feel, preferring, perversely, to offend Julian rather than our hosts. "Or as you would put it, he loves to fight with wooden swords," I said, referring to soldiers and gladiators who trained with mock weapons.

"I once knew a man who was killed with a wooden sword," our host said. "As I recall, he who swung it was altogether too reckless during practice. He thought he could vary from the training book. I seem to remember that he was executed as an example to his legion."

Whatever else he was, Julian was not stupid. He knew a threat when he heard one, and he knew as well as we did that the Romans would kill potential enemies without hesitation. As much as he wanted to deliver a sermon, he knew his only hope of seeing Palestine lay in placating the minions of Imperial Rome. He knew, too, that our every word and plan would be reported to their superiors. Still he hated me for belittling him and his beliefs even though I had done it at least in part to save his skin.

"The lady is right," he finally conceded. "I like to fight with wooden swords, although not recklessly, I assure you. I am just a student of the beliefs of others and only want to taste the delights of the spiritual world."

He was trying to be gracious and non-threatening, but he sounded as if he were groveling. I would have felt sorry for him had I not remembered how he fled when we were attacked and Ned was killed.

The mayor put an end to it. "Well, noble traveler," he said, "enjoy your taste of the world's religions, but don't drink too deeply. Intoxication makes men stupid, as well as dangerous both to themselves and others. Although Rome tolerates other religions, it has its own pantheon of gods and cannot allow the fomentation of religiously inspired revolutions. We're too tired of revolutions to be tolerant of them."

"Not all revolutions are brought by the sword," Julian responded, unable to let the man have the last word.

"Not all ambassadors bring good tidings, either, but diplomacy bids us attend to them anyway, and see to their needs," Antonious said as a final word before his wife changed the conversation at his wordless signal. Music and dancing soon followed.

Later on, after setting a time for the morning's tour and after thanking my host and his wife for their abundant hospitality, I retired at about midnight. It did not occur to me to lock the door to my room even though all doors in the villa were provided with heavy slide bolts.

Though stuffed with food and mildly high from wine, I was not sleepy. A thunderstorm came on and rain beat down on the roof, making wonderful, distant noises on the tiles. The lightning lit everything with excitement and power. Irrationally, I felt secure. Calling my servant, I had more lamps brought, got in bed and, with her help, began reading a book from our host's library. As I recall, it was an account of the First Punic War, and it was engrossing. My ability to read Latin had improved so much by that time that I had difficulty only with unfamiliar vocabulary and kept my servant with me to explain any of the unfamiliar words. Sleepy though she was and illiterate, she appeared eager to stay up and help me.

After a half hour or so Mark came to the door and entered without knocking. I dismissed the girl with a glance.

I greeted him with mixed emotions. I was annoyed by his repeated attempts to dominate me, but he was still a good-looking man and we had been through a lot together. I was also in the mood for love.

He locked the door and sat down on the edge of the bed.

"We need to talk," he said in English.

"Later," I told him, as I blew out the lamps in case the walls had eyes. He came to me almost reluctantly, which surprised me, as it had been almost a week since our last time together. I recall that on that particular night I didn't go out of my way to try to please him, but I certainly made an effort to please myself.

"We need to plan," he said quietly when we were through and were spread in a tangle of flesh upon the bed.

"You go ahead and plan," I said drowsily, "and I'll go to sleep. You want to tell me what to do, I know. Just go to sleep, Mark. You'll feel better if you do."

He gave up trying to reason with me.

I snuggled in close to him and kissed his ear.

"I love you," I lied.

When I awoke at dawn Mark was gone, which was just as well. I summoned my servants. They came in giggling and eager to wait on me, as if it were they who would be going out with the young cavalryman. My principal servant was thrilled when I told her that I would take her along with us.

The girls brought in a breakfast of hot porridge and fruit and basins of warm water so I could wash. They stood around looking at me as if I was conveying a favor upon them by letting them be there. I asked for some privacy. They at least gave me time to urinate, but almost immediately returned and insisted on helping me dress. Laughing, they began by stripping off my camisole. How greatly they admired it! They passed it among themselves as I stood there naked and slightly shivering in the cool morning air. Although I soon got over the awkward feeling that I should cover myself with my hands, I never got used to having other women in clothes standing around and touching me when I bathed and dressed. Of course, it seemed natural enough to have others brush and set my hair, do my nails and so forth, but for the most part I often felt as if I were some big Barbie Doll with whose body and strange clothing other, shorter and less well-endowed women loved to play.

Like all the women I met, the servant girls were fascinated by my toothbrush, combs, and brushes as well as my swimsuit and underwear. Everything right down to the plastic handles on the brushes interested them, and even my small, day backpack was a marvel with its zippers, snaps and Velcro closures.

After eating and washing, I stood patiently as the girls dressed me in the best two-piece, chamois riding outfit they could find on such short notice. Probably someone had stayed up all night altering it, for it fitted almost perfectly and hugged my body like a golden glove, but, yes: I did wear proper underwear under it for decency's as well as comfort's sake. At first the costume may have looked quite odd to me, but it felt *very* sexy.

I put on just a bit of make-up and wore a thin circlet of gold in my hair. Except for where the ornament held together a hank in the middle of my head to keep it out of my face, my hair was free, curling against my back. I don't know what I looked like to others, but I surely liked the way I felt.

Leaving my .45 automatic in the pack I gave the maid to carry, I slipped my derringer into the top of my soft brown boots. There it made a firm but uncomfortable lump, and, irrationally, I worried all day that it might accidentally go off and blow away my ankle. I seldom carried it that way again. Nevertheless, after the attack in Tingitana, I felt defenseless if I didn't have at least one gun on me. Naturally, I was acutely aware that the little derringer provided almost no protection beyond the range of six feet, but it made me feel safer, and that was the important thing. A woman aware of her own defenselessness is a person whose life is already severely circumscribed. Better an illusion of security, I thought, than a debilitating feeling of insecurity.

Although I started out the day bareheaded, I also took a round-crowned straw hat so that when the brutal Spanish sun rose later in the day, I would have some protection. All of the Romans wore straw hats when they went out in the midday sun. To do otherwise invited sunstroke at that time of year. I recalled the advice of Naadia, and although I had no intention of trading upon my looks, I determined to be taken as a lady by staying as white as possible. Whiteness, she had told me, was indicative of one's wealth and racial purity.

About an hour after sunrise, my escort arrived. Accompanied by a small troop of mounted men and an extra chariot for my maidservant, he picked me up in front of the villa in a light chariot. It was pulled by two brown horses that could not have been more than 14 hands tall. Although I was no great judge of horseflesh, at first glance they seemed quite inferior, being shaggy and stubborn-headed like large Shetland ponies. I soon learned that they were of a stock then known as Britannia ponies. They were marvelously well-trained and intelligent animals and could be guided as much by voice command as by a light touch on the reins. They were both strong, willing, and fearless in combat, and although they had rough gaits that made them unsuitable as mounts, they were practically tireless.

There were long, half-stiff, lunge-type whips in sockets on either side of the car, but they were more for ornamentation than for driving and waved delicately like flags as the car moved along. I noticed that many of the chariots of those days were similarly equipped, and soon learned that, except for racing, such whips were used more for hitting flies than for disciplining horses.

The car or cockpit part of the chariot had a bowed front with small, folding, padded seats on either side. Valerius and I sat facing one another in the little compartment, our knees intermingled as we rested our forward arms on the low rail over the thin, wooden bulwark that was between us and the swiftly trotting horses. With as much nonchalance as he could manage, he rested his hand on my arm.

The morning air was cool and invigorating, and we moved along with a fine sense of hustle-bustle, overlaid by the rich smells of horses, leather, and men. Without even a word of command, we and the whole escort started off, passing by long rows of two-story buildings until at last we wheeled out onto a broad, open road lined with olive trees and stone walls.

Although more often than not war chariots were fitted with solid axles bolted directly to the pole and the floor of the chariot, light chariots usually employed a variety of suspensions to mediate between the feet or butt of the driver and the vagaries of the road surface. Our chariot had heavy, hickory-like springs and ropes between the floor and the axle so that it gave a remarkably smooth ride over both cobblestones and dirt. I noted that smoothness, and my companion pointed out that the roads were remarkably even owing to constant maintenance. Since chariot racing and driving was a popular pastime of the officers; the main roads were kept in almost perfect condition.

Just off the road, we saw small farmhouses surrounded by fields alive with crops, sheep, herdsmen, and farmers. All of them looked up at us as we passed. I was happy to be out and on my own, away from Mark and Julian. I wanted to keep on going.

After only a short mile or so we came to the entrance to his legion's main camp, an entrance which stood in the middle of a long, low wall atop a dirt-and-stone parapet that rose on the far side of a ditch that ringed the fort like a dry moat. A sturdy but easily-disassembled oak bridge crossed the ditch and provided access to the narrow gate.

It was the sort of pattern camp that was typical of the Romans. It was laid out exactly as all other legionary encampments on level ground were, except the wall was made of brick and stone rather than of wood as was common in the construction of less permanent field fortifications. New men learned their exact places in the Roman military so that whether in permanent camp or field camp, a man might, if awakened by the enemy, know exactly where he was and where he should go to form up even in complete darkness. It was all very well thought out. "Drill, march, fight, dig, and build" were the watchwords of the Roman armies, and the recruits were kept constantly busy at one or another of those assignments.

"Must we stop already?" I asked, as Valerius began to turn at the main gate of his unit's camp. He was flattered that I wanted to keep on going. Like most young men, he was eager and willing. He smiled at me and shook his head.

"Stop? Of course not! Venus may go where she wills," he said, using for the first time an appellation that was often given to me by Romans. Although I should have preferred to be called Athena, I did not demur. Being compared to a goddess of love was quite enough for the moment.

By giving a series of hand signals to his troop he dismissed all of them except for two mounted men who dropped back to follow us at a distance. We drove on up the road to the top of the large hill beyond the camp, and there we paused to take in the view. From that height I could look back across the grassy plain to see the camp below and the little farms and villages as well as Nova Carthago in the near distance. I could just make out the chariot with my maid in it as it moved about the camp and how, in various arrays and units, the soldiers were at work drilling or practicing at arms under the tutelage of their centurions.

"And now where?" he asked, as we continued on, cresting the hill. Before us spread the sea not a half mile off.

"To the beach!"

So leaving behind the two horsemen, we traveled down the steep road to the beach. After letting the horses rest while I let Valerius talk about a man's favorite subject—himself—we put them through their paces. At first we just trotted some, but as soon as he knew that I was not afraid of such a low speed, he urged them to run, and that they did: skimming along down the hard sand, moving across the water's edge where the surf curved in, cutting the thin sheets of advancing and retreating water with our narrow, iron-rimmed wheels and sending up sprays of water and sand behind them. The noises alone were magnificent. The panting horses and their splashing hooves, the squish of the wheels in the sand and their hiss through water, the calls of birds, and the surge of small waves combined to wipe out the past and future. I was wet and covered in sand, but what did I care?

The beach was rather narrow and formed a long crescent out to a point where it ended in some rocks. There we stopped, stood up, and threw our heads back and laughed. He handed me the reins and I turned us around. It was the first time I had ever driven horses, but it felt quite natural and manageable. When we started out he stood behind me, reaching around me to show me how to hold my hands in the proper positions and talking into my ear as the front of his body touched my back. I almost leaned back into him, but I didn't. Once I got the hang of things, he sat back down and I drove us back down the beach at a trot, standing up with my legs outspread to brace myself. As he continued to advise me how to stand and how to manage the reins, he clamped my legs between his knees. When we lurched a bit he reached his left arm around behind me to keep me from falling backward as he held on to the front bar with his right hand. I leaned down to listen to him over the noise.

"Make them go!" he urged me.

He did not seem to be the least bit afraid even though I could have easily made a mistake that might have overturned the chariot and injured or killed us both. I figured that if he wasn't worried, then I shouldn't be either. I put the team into a fast trot, then a canter. Our forward movement, combined with a slight headwind, gave us a wonderful sensation of great speed and set my hair sailing out behind me.

"Faster?" I asked, looking down at him and pressing his hand for emphasis.

"Faster!" he yelled out over the noise, with a look of pure joy in his eyes as they met mine and he pressed his left arm firmly in upon my thigh.

I covered that arm, too, with my hand for a moment, snuggling it up against my backside. Then, taking hold of the reins with both hands and shaking them for more speed, I looked down into his eyes with what must have been my best smile, for I felt the immediate, blunt and unmistakable nudge of his third leg against my right thigh. He was wearing a long tunic and, apparently, nothing else under it except his ardor. Surprised but a little thrilled, I looked down again to see the hot blush spreading across his face. I smiled a toothy smile to let him know I was not offended, and nudged back against him just a bit with my thigh. Then we were off, racing along up and down the beach, going all-out, pounding out something exciting and primal, leaning together as we skidded through the turns at either end in those little instances before the horses rocketed forth on the next lap.

When we got to the end of the final run, I could barely stop the horses in time to prevent crashing them upon the rocks, and fear came up in me like an orgasm. I doubt if they would have stopped had I urged them to go on.

We got out and walked the horses. Although I didn't look down, I knew that he was still excited, and, of course, he tried to kiss me. I almost let him, but knew that if I did, I might not stop and everyone in town would soon find out about it. I smiled at him but slipped away and scampered across the rocks, yelling back at him that I needed to pee and wanted to be left alone for a while. I was almost disappointed that he did not follow me.

Out behind the rocks I found a small spot, stripped down and washed off the sand. Before I hit the water, though, I could feel my body trembling with that feeling of tension that I sometimes have that comes of unrequited passion. The cold water washed it away. I took my time about going back to the beach, and by the time I did, all of us, including the horses, had cooled down considerably. Valerius knew that our moment had passed—at least for then--and yet he was very gracious about it. We spoke of trivial things and he joined me in a conspiracy of silence about what had passed between us. I imagine that we both lay awake that night thinking about it.

The rest of the day was pleasant but less memorable. Valerius took me back to the camp and we joined up with all the others for a trip farther out into the countryside. There we were treated to an elaborate luncheon before we displayed a few of our own little secrets and demonstrations which, of course, included a very impressive but gory show of Mark's marksmanship as he hit distant targets with the .308, then slaughtered a small herd of cattle with the Thompson. I begged out on that part by having Valerius take me for another drive. We got back just in time for Mark's real showstopper: he blew up a small wooden house.

All that seems like a long time ago, and yet that morning lives on so well in my mind's eye that I cannot shake it, and it had an important lesson for me that bears repeating. It made me realize that I was somehow beyond all sexual morality except for whatever I wished to impose upon myself. To begin with, I knew that I could have practically any man I wanted. I had certainly found myself wanting men a lot more than I ever had before. Ironically, if I started giving in to those impulses, I would probably have been thought of rather highly in that culture since I was somehow going to be held to be above the mores applied to mere mortals. But was that what I wanted for myself, I asked? Besides what the Romans might think of me—and they were an openly promiscuous bunch—I still had those Protestant vestiges of my Presbyterian youth, those precepts that make a person think that gluttony itself is a sin even if it does not lead to physical or moral obesity. But what is gluttony? How much is enough? How much love and sex, for that matter, is too much?

So throughout the day I reflected on that issue long and hard and resolved that I should try to understand myself better before I unbridled the woman in me who was almost eager to give and to take pleasure so casually. If I knew nothing else, I did know that even the greatest of pleasures could become humdrum if indulged too frequently, and I suspected that a constant barrage of pleasure can wear a person out spiritually and physically.

I realized, too, that practically anything I did would be reported on to the government and that I needed to preserve some secrecy about myself if I was to get by in the ancient world. My mother told me that a woman needs to have some mystery about her, and getting naked with lots of men involves a pretty high degree of demystification, to say the least.

On the other hand, what security was there in the cautious approach to living--an approach which I had long ago abandoned anyway? Acutely aware that I could die any day and for any number of reasons or for no reason at all, I thought that security was simply unattainable. I had no family, no friends but Mark, no home, no country, and no religion. The false security of modern life that I lost when I lost my family and then lost again when I met Mark, was triply lost when I lost even the era in which I had lived all my life.

Philosophically, I realized that a policy of chastity and reserve would most likely be a temporary one based upon expediency and caution. There I was, living in that great basin of passionate living, the Mediterranean. Then as now, it exerted a sensual influence on its young people: warm, romantic, hedonistic, clear-seeing, opulent.

You sometimes spoke of the Greece you knew when you were young—of its shores, clear seas, and sharp contrasts. You quoted Durrell's speaking of the world lying open like a ripe fig, a fruit to be pressed to the mouth. Imagine how it would be to live there if you had all the money you wanted and all the willing, eager companions you desired, and no country far away across the cold Atlantic to call you home. Without guilt, what would you do? What might you do?

I had also become more acutely aware of the fertile times during my own cycles, which is to say, the times I most probably might have gotten pregnant had I not been taking the Pill. I got the impression, though, that many of the men in those days were aware of that stage, too, and could actually smell when a woman was more or less in heat. I sometimes noticed how other women, often downright plain women, turned men's heads in their passing: was it not the scent of them that drew the attentions?

The sexual life was a natural part of existence, and was much celebrated, even worshipped. All about were the examples of the herds and of the fields and of the gods who smiled upon reproduction, birth, and lovemaking. Almost every home was adorned with a figurine of the Greek god Priapus, a sometimes-splendid little fellow with an exaggerated penis that stuck out from his loins. He was the god of many a farmer's home, and as we walked along the road, we saw many such idols in small altars by the road, serving as constant reminders of that aspect of the human experience. I often thought that men created that particular little god and those idols that symbolized him so that we women would be more constantly aware of our own carnal natures.

I found myself trying to satisfy my longings with Mark. Usually it was a vain effort that ended in frustration for both of us.

"You are with that young centurion," he accused me when he came to my bed on that second night in Carthago Nova.

"Maybe, Priapus," I said as I sat on the edge of the bed and slipped my hands up under his tunic, "but you'll do for now."

It was almost summer, it was Spain, and I was hungry, so I ate. But I couldn't kid myself; we were falling apart.

****

XIV

Julian's Farewell

As the preceding day had been long and exciting, Mark and I decided to sleep late. We told the servants not to bother us until Noon, but at midmorning an insistent knocking on the door to my room brought me out of a deep dream. I awoke as Mark rose, pulled on some pants and went to the door. It was Julian. I stayed under the covers, smiled and waved to him, trying to be polite. After all, it was my room.

He was up and dressed for travel, wearing a romanized version of his own clothes. Under a rather nice, new tunic. he had on the same trousers he had been wearing when he confronted us in North Carolina--trousers that were certainly ready for the rag man. Since he had left behind most of his clothes at his North Carolina motel and none of Ned's things fit him, he had finally broken down and was going native bit by bit. His dress shoes had not lasted long, and so he had some sandals made in Gibraltar. His two or three shirts had mostly fallen apart under rough washing, but he still had some socks and underwear.

So now he stood before us in a tunic with an ornate leather belt, the worn black trousers, leather sandals, and an all-weather cloak slung tastefully across one shoulder. Beside his half-naked, skinnier father, he looked massive and in good health, and I could not help thinking that he looked more handsome than I had ever seen him before. Despite all his complaining, I could see that the trip had done him a world of good. He had lost a little weight, firmed up, and gotten enough sun to drive away his sickly English pallor.

The bald dome of the top of his head, too, seemed different. No longer did it look like something naked that ought to be hidden, but rather rose like a mountain above the tree line formed by his side hair and his rather prominent eyebrows. He was beginning to look like a real man, which is to say, like one of our Roman hosts.

I took all of that in at a glance, and it was a startling

revelation. It was, however, an attraction that was quickly quelled when I saw his look of disdain for me: the self-righteous glance dismissing his father's whore. Barely acknowledging me—as if I were not an equal partner and he did not like to look at a woman lying naked in bed under thin linen—he addressed Mark brusquely.

"A boat bound for Alexandria leaves on the afternoon tide. I am going to be on that boat, and I suggest that you get on it, too," he said, rather more forcefully than I thought him capable of being. It was obvious that his use of the word "you" was meant in the singular and that he was indifferent or hostile toward me.

As much as we had looked forward to this moment, I had not really thought he had the gumption to make his own way in the world. I should have known better. He was, after all, the man who had followed me from England and tracked me down, patiently doing the work himself without relying on police or detectives. Also--and to give him his due--he was the same man who had the nerve to come onto our farm, disable the plane, and confront us with his demands. He was the man who, when faced with an incredible truth, had made a quick and final conclusion, and then had imposed a settlement upon us when *he*, not us, was literally under the gun. He was the man who for the sake of his beliefs risked his life to the Short and Ned's calculations.

However, experience teaches us that our palpable dislike of a person clouds our judgment of him and makes us not so capable of admitting his good points. Perhaps this is one of the reasons men so often underestimate their enemies or, for that matter, overrate their friends.

I stifled the urge to say something clever and hurtful to him, but was speechless with a growing rage. For that matter, Mark seemed to be ignoring me, too. Naked under the sheets, I just listened to them and thought, "You sons of bitches!."

Mark was taken aback, but soon collected himself. "And why," he asked, "should I do that?"

I was shocked by Mark's own use of "I" rather than "we". It was a portent of things to come, I knew.

"Because we have come by the divine will of God to bear witness to His presence on earth, to be by His side and to be the instruments of His will. This is for us not an option. It is what we must do! We have dallied here among the wicked. It is time to go. We are a long way yet from our destination and the hour of Our Lord is at hand."

"You mean *your* destination, Julian," he replied. "And just what do you think you're going to find there?" Mark asked as he sat down on the bed, then lay back against the bolsters beside me with his hands behind his head.

"The Son of Man, the Living God, the Messiah, Emmanuel, God With Us!" the older man said, with a firmness and conviction that carried a lot of weight. It was obviously a little speech that he had been rehearsing all night, or all of his life.

"What I think you're going to find is what the American cowboys will someday call 'a whole heap o' trouble,' Julian."

Mark had a smirk on his face that made him look like a small-time hoodlum. Almost involuntarily my body recoiled from him.

"That may well be, Mark," Julian said, using his father's name for the first time in weeks, "but nothing worth having comes easily. If there is to be travail, then I shall share it. But the joy I shall share also."

I thought it was a pretty good speech. It showed backbone and conviction, but Mark continued to sneer.

"And if all you think you know is true," he said, "and if He's really out there somewhere plodding down some dusty lane, old boy, then what're you going to do? Shake His Holy Hand? Take His picture?"

Mark thought it was all a big joke, and his flippant attitude irritated me almost as much as it did his son.

"I shall worship Him with all my heart and all my soul," Julian responded almost beatifically. Had it not been him I might have been truly moved.

"And what then?"

"Then I shall do as God wills."

"Well," Mark said, "have a nice trip. I'm not going to bloody Palestine, not straight away, at least. You go on ahead if you want. We'll catch up with you later, after we've seen a bit of the world and given our respects to the Emperor."

At least Mark was remembering me in his grandiose plans, I thought. Then I saw the look in Julian's eyes as he glanced again at me.

"I'm leaving and I'm telling you one last time!" he thundered as if from a pulpit. "The hour of Our Lord is at hand! We do not know whether the fullness of God's plan shall be in the coming year or the one after or the one after that. It could be, too, that even now we are too late. Whatever else you have done with your life," he said, "you may nevertheless be absolved of your sins by going to Him not only in the spirit but also in the flesh! *There* in Palestine. *Now. This year.* Think of it: Within a few weeks, I shall be there!"

"Oh, bull shit!" Mark said with his best Southern accent, drawing out the word "bull" to sound more like *bool.* "I'm going to Rome and Athens. I am certainly not going into some disappointing backwater looking for a preacher. And anyway: I've already been there. I spent four months there in 1938 and that was bloody well enough.

"If you even find somebody that remotely fits the description of the historical Jesus, you won't know him for sure because there'll be a lot of others out there, too. They'll all be holy men, they'll all be dirty and poor, and each bloody one of 'em will have some disciples with him. That's my prophecy, but what's more likely is that you'll die of some bloody plague or get leprosy or tuberculosis. Even if you survive all the cops, diseases, thieves, and disappointments, like any good disillusioned cleric of the Church of England, you'll turn to the bottle for consolation. In a year or two you're going to be either dead or dead drunk."

"I have tried," Julian declared to the heavens, rolling his eyes up to the ceiling. "I have come to him in the midst of his iniquity and his eyes are blind and his heart is closed!"

"Well, Julian," Mark said, "as they will one day say in England, bugger off!"

I felt as if I had to say something. I actually hated to see them parting on such bad terms.

"I'll come there soon enough, Julian. Keep in touch and tell us what and who you find. And be careful," I said.

"God speed," I added, trying to part on some positive note. I felt in my heart though that we would never see him again. It was particularly hard these days to let go of any part of the past—or the future.

He turned on me like a vicious dog. "You! Unrepentant

slut! I shall never see you again, thank God! It is you who has done this to him," he said, glaring at me and pointing at Mark who lay beside me calm and collected.

"You have insinuated yourself into his bed and taken away what was left of his purity to satisfy your own unbridled lusts! You have brought his soul to the brink of eternal destruction.

"Stay away from me, whore," he continued, so worked up that I was astonished at the depth of his obvious hatred for me, "For that you are: fornicating with him night after night onboard that ship, grunting with pleasure like a hog. You display yourself to other men and hold yourself out as an epitome of lust to a pagan people. I see it in you, and it's a growing thing, this lust. Soon you'll be little better than a barracks whore, or a bitch in heat, American!" he spat out, as if my nationality was a curse.

By then I was as angry as I ever had been in my life. It was a clear, ringing anger, and it was against both men—one for attacking me and the other for failing to defend me. Without trying to cover my nakedness at all I threw aside the sheets, jumped over to Julian, and slapped him as hard as I could. I had moved so quickly and deliberately that he was not able to block the blow. I almost knocked him down. He came up almost shocked from the pain. The side of his face began to redden with the imprint of my hand and I slapped the shit out of the other cheek. His own anger began to overcome his astonishment and pain, and I could tell that he was about to hit me, for he was balling up his fist and getting ready to strike. We were only about a pace apart.

"Just try it, Julian," I snarled at him, "and I'll beat the living shit out of you." I could have beaten him and he knew it, too. I was really pumped up. He'd have had a hundred forty or fifty pounds of naked wildcat on him, and he didn't have the balls for that kind of a fight. I could see the disgusting little flicker of fear in his eyes as he squared back his shoulders, unclenched his fists, and tried to salvage his dignity.

"I'm not going to fight you," he said, adding, "you *woman!*"

So I slapped his other cheek again as hard or harder than I had before. The blow spun him around.

"Now get out of my room," I told him, "and get your sorry, pompous ass on that boat, and go do your thing. I'm sick of your shit. You don't understand normal human life, much less normal human decency."

And, by God, he did just that: he got out.

He left the door wide open behind him and as I reached to close it I found myself face-to-face with an astonished male servant who had obviously been listening. Stark naked, I reached on out into the salon to grab the brass door-pull. He glanced down at my body. I paused, smiled, and said to him in Latin, "See: that's how you talk to those silly British bastards! Now get out of here!" He left in a hurry, too. I slammed the door.

Mark was still on the bed with his hands behind his head. "I say," he said as if to mock his own English background, "Good show, what!"

"You, too:" I said, "get out! And go make sure the sorry bastard doesn't steal anything of ours."

****

XV

The Slave

On the day following Julian's departure, I bought the first person I ever owned.

Having thought about buying a servant since Naadia suggested it, I approached the matter with a certain amount of confidence. I had some moral reservations about owning a slave, but she had helped me see another side of the matter.

"Before you reject the idea, ask yourself, 'Since the slave is already a slave, might she be better off with you rather than with another?' Better to be the handmaiden of a lady than the concubine of a merchant."

She had also explained that a slave might prove more loyal to me than anyone else since her fate would be intertwined with mine and suggested to me what I might look for in a servant and how to go about finding one in a typical commercial setting. She told me what I should avoid in the buying and selling of human beings, ending with the most basic advice. "Never," she said, "let another person chose for you either a horse or a slave. Pick her out yourself and even then beware!"

Recalling everything she told me, and knowing that I needed someone to count on beyond Mark, I lay awake half the night planning how I would acquire the type of servant I wanted. When dawn came, I breakfasted, sent an excuse to Valerius, who wanted to ride with me again, and went shopping with my maid.

Naturally, I had thought of asking our host to lend or sell her to me because she seemed so sweet and pleasant. On the other hand, she was illiterate and her loyalties might be divided. A person cannot serve two masters, and she already had one.

I already knew that it was legal for a foreigner to own a slave. Nevertheless I first consulted a sort of lawyer, a man who was learned in Roman and provincial law and who most helpfully referred me to a colleague of his who brokered slaves as a sideline business.

It is interesting to note that whereas slaves—particularly recent captives or manual laborers—were sometimes sold at public auction, most of them were traded in a far more subtle fashion. The slave himself, for example, might ask his master to negotiate a trade, perhaps one that might further his own particular vocational goals or might eventually lead to his being sent to live nearer his friends or family. Then, too, sometimes personal conflict or financial embarrassment might lead an owner to approach a broker to arrange the sale of a servant who if he knew what was in the works might become very upset or even belligerent. In short, there were many reasons for putting together tactful, private transactions, and the small fees charged by brokers to both buyers and sellers were generally considered well worth the money.

The broker to whom I was referred seemed to be a kind and considerate man. About 40 years old and completely bald, he had a regular office in four or five well-appointed, second-floor rooms that looked out over the forum of the town. Astonished to see me, one of the city's most celebrated visitors, he nevertheless maintained a professional decorum that I found very reassuring. In the best Latin we could manage (for he was originally a Gaul), we talked for an hour about my needs and his fees. It was a ridiculously low price, and I offered to double it on condition that he acted promptly and strictly in accord with my directions. I particularly stressed that he should operate with as much secrecy as possible so that others could not pre-select a servant who would spy upon me.

By the late afternoon, I was able to interview three different women for about 30 minutes each. Each seemed eager, almost desperate, to become my servant, and it was a difficult choice. As the price was low, I was tempted to buy two of them rather than just one. Finally, though, I made a choice. I passed the purchase money and the commission directly to the broker and immediately got from him the sealed ownership papers, which I duly recorded at a notary's office next door. I bought a girl named Propea.

At 20, she was younger than I had in mind at first, but when I met the other prospects and as I considered the sort of impression we would make as we traveled, I realized that I did not want to have an older woman along. I had to think of the image that I wanted to project. Propea was pretty enough and might, I thought, add to whatever aura of confidence and power that I might be able to give. Also I realized that I did not wish to appear to be chaperoned or to be traveling in the company of my mother. Both of the other two women were older than I was and didn't really seem to be up to the extensive traveling I told them I was anticipating.

Though Propea was short and thin, she was big-boned and healthy. She had all her teeth and was not, she assured me, either sick or pregnant. A native of Thrace, she spoke fluent Greek and Latin, although she was literate only in the latter, having been raised in Italy on a farm near what is now Turin. She was a brunette who wore her hair in braids coiled on either side of her head in the Gaulish fashion. From her and the broker I learned that her former owner had been a wealthy, older man who had bought her when she was 15 to use as a plaything during his declining years. Before then she had been trained to be a ladies' maid, but had been shifted into the scullery when she hit puberty, since it was thought that maids should be of a more delicate mold than hers.

As things turned out, the old man had done little more than play with her, but not for want of trying, she said. At any rate, he had gone on his way to Hades after some four years of such trying and his widow, finding Propea embarrassing and superfluous, had agreed to find her a different position should a suitable buyer be found. I turned out to be that buyer. It was considered good fortune by all that my purchase came at just the right time, for we all profited. I got a good servant, the widow recovered her husband's investment, the broker made his fee, and Propea found herself suddenly improving her station in life—from scullery maid and concubine to traveling companion and lady's maid. Her looks of veneration during our first three months together would have suggested to the casual observer that I had bestowed the greatest of favors upon her.

This is not to say I did not own her, for I did. Many a subtle hint and act on both our parts affirmed that relationship and all it implied. I had been warned by Naadia, that the distinction between mistress and slave had to be maintained for the benefit of both parties, and Propea "knew her place" as the saying goes. Custom and the law did not give me the power of life and death over her, but I clearly had the legal right to beat her and to have her brought to me by force if she tried to escape. As an aside I should note that as a matter of law, a man could not compel his slaves to have sex with him, but that was a law impossible to enforce.

The slavery of the Augustinian time was not, for the most part, a slavery of whip and chain. It was, rather, a system of slavery not unlike later-day "wage slavery," but for the fact that wages other than room and board were non-existent in most cases. Only rarely could a slave manage to strike out on his own in some fashion. They got away from their masters mainly through sales, and in the case of a woman or a girl, such sale was often to a man who wanted her for a concubine or even a wife. Then as now, there were many incentives for a woman to keep herself attractive and to increase her talents.

I am not trying to glorify slavery, but I don't see why it can't be spoken of in the frankest terms. For some reason, the slavery of antiquity seemed less brutal to me than the form of it practiced in South Carolina prior to the War Between The States might have seemed had we found ourselves there instead. In ancient times one's enslavement was not based on race but on chance. Therefore a master could truly separate himself not by type but only by condition from his slave.

I owned a girl and she had a new mistress, one who would take her out to see the world. She was very happy to make the change, and on that very first day, I spelled out exactly what I expected of her. Naadia had told me that it was absolutely necessary to lay down and enforce rules.

Fidelity was my first demand. I told her in no uncertain terms that she was to indulge in no spying and she was not to report my affairs to anyone, particularly not to other slaves or servants. I told her that my relationship to Mark was strictly my business, and she should speak of it to no one. Above all I told her that I would tolerate no stealing at all—not one dime, not one bit of paper, not one needle. I told her that she should never importune me for anything at all. She agreed to each and every point.

In exchange for her total cooperation and obedience, I promised that I would give her freedom in two years, but upon the slightest infraction of my rules, I would sell her without hesitation. She fell to her knees, kissed my feet, and wept with joy when I made my unexpected promise of freedom to her.

As I expected, Mark was astonished and displeased that I had bought her, but he was mollified when I explained the care that I had taken in selecting her. Also, the purchase was a *fait accompli* and he was beginning to learn that I would do what I wanted to do whether or not he liked it. Realizing that every great person took a servant along made him consider the efficacy of finding one for himself.

The thing that upset him most was that I had acted without his advice and consent. My competence in the matter bothered him, particularly in light of some of my demonstrations of incompetence in other matters. After all, I *had* made serious mistakes in the year we had been together. I should have never gone to Brighton and I should not have put myself in the position to be arrested in North Carolina. Hindsight being clearer still, had it not all been for the best anyway?

It was already obvious to us that we were probably better off here than we would have been some 400 years earlier, and so the choice that Julian had imposed upon us was probably not a bad one. The culture shock we experienced was terrific, but at least the world was at peace, the main roads were paved, and the larger cities had running water and good sewer systems. In time, other advantages over our original goal became clear, and our main regret about everything was how we had fallen into the ambush when Ned was killed.

Three days after I bought Propea, the three of us sailed for Italy aboard a fast military galley that the governor was sending over. As a cargo it carried gold and silver bullion and dispatches that no doubt included reports about us. Anticipating our need to travel in style and comfort, he ordered his best ship for us. It was a full-sized trireme 140 feet long. When there was no wind, it was rowed by some 130 slaves who were chained to their places below. I never went below to the rowing decks and I could hardly bear to think about them. As I learned to my dismay once we were out to sea, the smell of all those men made me sick, and I was glad I had arranged for a private cabin.

It was on the port side, aft below the main deck and had a small, unglazed but shuttered window that let in light and air and gave me a view of the sea from my bunk. The window was equipped with two removable iron bars and was just large enough to squeeze through in case of emergency.

The cabin had attached to it a small anteroom of about six feet by five where my maid had a fold-down cot that doubled as a seat or sofa, and between it and my room was a stout oaken door with heavy iron bolts on the inside. I measured my part of the cabin as being four by eight cubits with headroom of about a half cubit over my height of five feet, eight inches. It had a wash stand which doubled as a desk, a bookshelf filled with books in the form of scrolls and, best of all, a fixed chair that doubled as a toilet giving a straight shot out to the passing sea below.

I spent most of my time aboard that ship sleeping or thinking. The officers fell all over themselves attempting to talk with me whenever I came on deck, and in the evenings, we gathered together after supper and sang songs on the afterdeck. I wished I could remember songs like you could, but they were all happy enough just to hear the ones I knew or could make up on the spot.

Still, with all that crowd of manacled men below, it was hard to be jolly or to sleep without dreaming sad dreams, particularly when the wind was low and the torturous rowing began.

****

XVI

Ostia

We arrived in Ostia, the seaport of Rome, late one lovely afternoon. There we were greeted by an unofficial crowd similar to the one that had met us at Novo Carthago. As there were neither imperial officials nor soldiers present, we assumed that we were being officially ignored. There was always a large crowd down at the docks anyway--the loading and unloading of ships was a labor intensive activity in those days, and it was one worth watching. There were men and women everywhere, and they were busy, but not too busy to stop and look at us.

The harbor as well as the Tiber River were crammed with ships, barges, houseboats, lighters and fishing boats all the way to Rome, and the din of all that activity was terrific. As soon as we landed, we were besieged by merchants and onlookers. As at Nova Carthago, our arrival had been anticipated, and the mayor joined his fellow merchants to greet us in their sort of informal way. Several of them offered us the hospitality of their homes, but we decided to stay in the most expensive hotel along the quays. It was a large establishment not unlike a modern hotel. It was three stories tall and had a lobby, dining room, and kitchen out back. The guest rooms were small, clean, and unpretentious and we took three adjoining second floor rooms that shared a private bathroom and had a small balcony. We had a decent view of the harbor.

For a toilet, it had the sort of enameled hole-in-the-floor-with-foot-pads that one can still find in Europe. After use it was flushed by pouring down it a small bucket of perfumed water after which one stopped up the hole with a wooden plug. There was also cold, running water and a copper basin in which to heat it. As real baths could be had in an elegant building adjacent to the kitchen, Propea and I went there right away to wash our hair and cleanse away the smell of the galley slaves. At that time I still had a good supply of the toiletries I brought with me, but I knew it wouldn't be long before I would start running out of such things as soap and shampoo.

We dined that night at a nearby outdoor cafe where we held informal court and met many of the local merchants, including two very friendly Etruscan bankers who had been recommended to me by Marcus and Naadia. I still had my little notebook at that time and in a moment of privacy told them the names of our friends. That and our obvious wealth gained us immediate credibility with them. Mark was impressed. Knowing them to be trustworthy, I immediately decided to bank some of my money with them. I later had cause to wish I had left more.

Ostians thought of themselves as Romans--rich Romans who lived by the port of the city. As such they wanted us to share in their civic pride. They said that to arrive at Rome was to arrive at the center of the world. Of course, I have noticed that people throughout the world all seem to feel that way about their capital cities. They might be overawed by other nations militarily or even culturally, but the individual on the street thought of his native land as Americans think of theirs: the best, the preferable, and the font of most wisdom. One might suppose that until the advent of printing such provincialism might be reinforced by the lack of pictures and books, but then one would be wrong. At least within the empire the common people of that time understood foreign ways fairly well and they sometimes saw pictures of distant lands. In the homes of the wealthy, for example, there were always murals depicting foreign scenes. Oddly enough, though, the emphasis in such pictures was more often on the commonality of the human condition rather than on the world's geographical differences. Such landscapes or cityscapes as one saw were indifferently done and gave the viewer little urge to travel.

On the other hand, storytellers were commonplace even in out-of-the way villages. There were always people willing to relate, often as not in damning terms, their experiences in foreign lands. To walk somewhere in the company of strangers was much like it would be some 1200 years later when Chaucer walked to Canterbury. Travelers shared their tales over the long, easy miles and narrative was held in higher esteem.

I suppose that it is natural for the young expatriate to look homeward with growing nostalgia. Even amid the wonderful scenes I was witnessing, I was aware of how acutely I missed many of the people, comforts, and securities of my native land, and it is a wonder I was not more often despairing of what

I had done. I often thought that I had thrown away many of the good things of modern life without sufficient thought. Standing by the railing during long sea trips and plodding along day after day on foot or horseback, I had plenty of time to brood. I could usually dispel the gloom and despair of such thoughts by recalling the year before we left. It was beyond wishing even for something different. The big word "if" was at the beginning of every thought. If I had only ignored Mark's look in class or had been more faithful to Brad, I might still be at home. If my parents hadn't died I would never had enrolled at Virginia. If, if, if...

But it was all beyond wishing, though, and there was only one explanation of it: it was my destiny.

On the following day, we proceeded to Rome in chariots we had hired for the purpose. Propea and the owner of the two rigs rode in the larger, less impressive one. Mark and I took the other and, over his objections, I drove. That may have been a mistake, for as we came into the more built-up suburbs of the capital, the roads became increasingly congested with people in chariots, on litters, and on foot. On several occasions I almost ran down people before I got the hang of driving those docile horses in traffic. Eventually we were forced to slow from a trot to a walk, and I was growing tired and irritable. In direct proportion to my distress Mark grew more cheerful. For him it was a pleasant turn-about that I was vexed.

In order to keep its streets passable, Rome had an ordinance that forbade the use of animal-drawn vehicles on the public streets between dawn and dusk. Most deliveries were therefore made during the nights, and, consequently, we were being met by a lot of outbound traffic. Mark said the morning exodus made the road look like evacuations he had witnessed during the Spanish Civil War in the 1930s.

We encountered every conceivable type of person on the road, including several strings of slaves and one chained lot of what we heard were condemned criminals headed to the games, the galleys or the mines.

We intended to hire litter bearers when we arrived where animal traffic was turned back. At that place, we had been told, there was a great field in which a transportation market constantly thrived, and we planned to hire litter transport. As things worked out, though, when we finally arrived at the traffic-control station outside the city's walls, a hundred soldiers from the emperor's personal guard led by a mounted centurion met us. A handsome man in his mid-twenties dressed in bronze armor and wearing scarlet-crested helmet and a scarlet cloak, he told us in the most gracious of terms that he had been ordered to conduct us into the heart of the city. There, he said, we were invited to stay at the imperial residences. We had expected that sort of an honor, but not an honor guard. Accompanied by it, we were allowed to drive the chariots right on into the city and weren't obliged to shift to litters. Before we proceeded I freshened up a little at a small bathhouse and then was able to stand up and drive the horses. We went in over the Aventine Hill, passing the Temple of Diana, the Circus Maximus, and other temples and shrines too numerous to remember, much less to name, moving in a stately procession down along the streets amid the marching soldiers. In this manner we made a fairly grand appearance. Dressed in an elegant Grecian style, I wore neither a veil nor a hood, having been assured by Propea that I would astonish all who saw me.

Beside me, dressed in fresh, modern khaki and clean, shined shoes with his black hair combed straight back, Mark was about as handsome as he had ever been. He was wearing his .45 in the Sam Browne harness and so once again he had the look of a vigorous, young, English officer. I felt proud of him and drawn to him, a feeling that I welcomed.

We were the spectacle of the day. As the townsmen were unused to seeing chariots on the streets in broad daylight, much less a chariot escorted by imperial troops and driven by a big woman, they parted, stopped, and looked. I was having a good time, but Mark was worried and kept the Thompson at hand. We were altogether too vulnerable for his taste and he said so, but I think that what really bothered him was that he was not the center of attention, I was. He tried to look regal and at ease, but he had not yet grown used to having hundreds of people starring at him. Perhaps young women are more practiced at this. At any rate, the crowds began to cheer for us. Shouting to him as he rode beside us, I asked the centurion what was the cause of all the adulation. I cannot forget his uneasy answer.

"This is Rome, M'Lady, and Romans will cheer for

anything. They will just as easily howl for blood."

Rome was all I could have imagined and more. In the middle of a typical business day there were crowds in every street, crowds more akin to organic masses than collections of individuals. Words, feelings, rumors, and emotions rippled out through them in visible waves. This characteristic was most noteworthy in the main Forum, toward which we unerringly progressed. Our progress was marked by fast-changing emotions and, while the crowd parted in automatic deference, it did so only by a few feet and the endless succession of faces was unnerving.

After we passed the portals of the Forum, those who had watched us pass and seen Mark's unusual attire and accouterments and those who were within the forum itself who saw us arriving sent up a cheer that quickly overwhelmed us as it bounced around among the buildings and the surrounding hills.

Was I the subject of that adulation? At the time I supposed I was, but it only took a week in Rome to realize that the majority of people was affected by a mass hysteria not dissimilar from that which might affect modern urban populations were their circumstances more crowded and their entertainments fewer. There was an element of jaded pleasure-seeking among the people that manifested itself in brief but universal interest in novelties. We had achieved stardom by the time we entered the Forum and I must admit that there was something in my nature that made me respond positively to such massive, public acclaim. I basked in it. Only after the taste got bitter did I shun, then fear it.

As can be imagined, there were many soldiers around the forum. Mostly they seemed relaxed enough, but they stood about in pairs, ever vigilant for fights, thieves, or potential riots. I learned later that a small barracks was located nearby so that 100 additional men could be marched in on short notice to clear away even large crowds.

Set amid scores of temples and beautiful buildings, the Forum was a busy, exciting place at noon. We passed through the open central parts, moving among the splendid array of booths, people, temples, and colonnades. As I tried to look regal and not like a gawking tourist, I thought of how you and your brother would stand here nearly 2,000 years later. From behind fences and rails you would be the tourist then, but only to view the broken rubble into which that splendor would someday fall.

"Anyone who does not go first to the Forum is as a thief who comes in the night," was a saying of those days. It was as if one had to display herself and to see and be seen, when one visited Rome or returned from long journeys. We were expected to go there; our escort did not even ask us if we wanted to.

We proceeded to the steps of the building where the senate met. There we alighted from our chariot to be greeted by a delegation of important men in white togas. Seeing them made me look about for the statue of Pompey, at the base of which Julius Caesar, stabbed by senators, had died. I did not see it. They invited Mark to address the pressing crowd but he declined because he was well aware that his abilities were very limited compared to theirs. He was polite but firm.

"Then at least wave!" one of the senators urged him, nervously but in an urgent tone. "Give them something!"

So Mark leaped nimbly up upon a rostrum by the stairway and reached back down to give me a hand up. Then we just smiled and waved, and people cheered. We left before the novelty wore off.

****

XVII

Rome

During the three months I stayed in the Eternal City I saw everything I wanted to see, and many things I didn't. The powerful saw about as much of me as they wanted to see, too.

We were ensconced in the palace of the Caesars, with separate quarters that communicated through a private atrium. Roman villas and palaces were rarely taller than two stories and were open and airy to make summer living more pleasant. In winter they were less comfortable, particularly during rainy weather and as the art of glazing had not long been practiced, most windows were small and shuttered. During the day, the majority of light got in through doorways or through celestory openings near the ceiling. For those reasons, murals were often painted on the plastered brick walls of what would otherwise have been gloomy, interior rooms. This was true even in the homes of the poor. Those in the palace where we stayed were quite nice and covered a wide range of subjects, primarily mythical or allegorical. Because of the murals, no rooms were ever quite alike, and although muted colors of fairly equal intensities and values were the norm, sometimes the colors used were as vibrant as those one sees in Mexico or the Philippines.

At the palace, I had three spacious rooms with a private bath that was about 12 feet square with a sunken, marble tub, the water for which was heated by a hypocaust located beyond the wall in a service corridor. My main sleeping room measured about 14 cubits square and had a raised-dias, four-poster bed. The mattress was made of linen pulled over carefully laid hay that was arranged in patterns to make it most comfortable. In winter a thin down-filled undersheet or furs would overlie such a mattress. My walls were decorated with murals: florals, one of Roman ladies around the pool of a villa, and others of mountainous, allegorical scenes of nymphs and satyrs frolicking about.

Mark had two big rooms, bold and well appointed. The murals opposite his bed depicted sea battles, Atticum most likely, while the one behind his bed depicted various lascivious couplings between men and women on a picnic in the Apennines. Their positions and the expressions in their faces were almost charming. The posts of his bed were of heavy bronze spears that had been captured from a Greek phalanx 100 years before.

We were told that at one time Augustus and his wife, Livia, the mother of Tiberias, had occupied those very rooms, and, indeed, somewhat faded inscriptions painted over the lintels of the doors indicated that such was the truth. Of course, Romans were like everyone else in that they like to tell of such things: *Caesar slept here.* Well, of course: he had to sleep somewhere. It is a shame that the walls themselves could not speak! What stories they might have told: stories of intrigues, loves, infidelities, and murder. Livia would have been at the center of many of such tales, no doubt.

She herself was still alive at that time but was in

declining health. I was never invited to her quarters, and through Propea I heard rumors that she feared me and suspected that I might be able to undo all of her work which had resulted in her and her son's acquisition of the power of government. It was not a good thing to have her think such things about me. It was rumored that she had a hand in the deaths of several members of the imperial family who had stood between her son and what was, in effect, the throne. It was thought that she had poisoned even her husband, the great Augustus himself, rather than risk having him name a new heir other than his stepson Tiberias.

I never met him either, for his primary residence was on an island to the south. His presence, though, was constantly felt. In the banquet hall and in the smaller room where we most often dined, his place was always set as if at any moment he might come in and sit with us and begin telling us stories of his last campaign in Germany. This was his favorite topic as it illustrated his vigor, judgement, and ruthlessness. Be that as it may, we felt neither slighted nor ignored, for there was something about meeting him that we feared. We assumed we were safe so long as the old man hadn't gotten a good look at us.

It was always possible that he did get a good look at us at some point. Dressed as a servant, he could have come to Rome and watched us on the sly had he wanted to do so. It may sound strange, but such was not an unusual practice during those times. I heard several stories of men who caught their wives at adultery by insinuating themselves into the staffs of her lover's household. For that matter, I heard of men gaining access to other men's wives through the same expedient. In all likelihood, though, we would have known if Tiberias had come in disguise because Propea knew what he looked like. Having served at several banquets he had attended, she assured me that should he appear she would recognize him.

She also knew many other noble Romans by sight and name and had an astonishing memory that was always at my service. Such knowledge made her all the more valuable to me, and we keep it a secret even from Mark. She and I often slept in the same bed so that we could whisper in the night without fear that our words could be heard. Naturally enough, all that intimacy soon led to a sisterly affection between us as well as to rumors that we were lesbians.

I think that part of the reason Tiberias did not come to

Rome to see us or bid us come to him on Capri was that he feared we might harm him or undermine his power. Given the reports he had available to him, that was a fairly reasonable fear on his part. For all he knew, we could destroy Rome itself.

Mark had only about 5,000 rounds of .45 ammunition left for our pistols and the Thompson. The Thompson fired at 450 rounds a minute, and the Romans must have realized early on that one spent brass cartridge equaled one shot. On the other hand, we still had some of the explosives left, and they knew nothing of how limited we were in that regard.

During the time we were in Rome, Tiberias' subordinate, Lucius Aelius Sejanus, head of the Praetorian Guard, was running the government and was practically the dictator of the city if not of the empire. I met him on many occasions and disliked him completely, but for some reason, Mark enjoyed his company and often went out with him. Sejanus was tall, dark, and ugly.

Our main host was Tiberias' uncle by marriage, Claudius. I had many long talks and shared wonderful meals with him both in the palace and in the homes of his friends and scholarly acquaintances. It was through Claudius that I was able to confirm the tale that Tiberias was afraid of us. Upon reading the entrails of a sheep in his presence, a group of priests had unanimously agreed that I or some woman very similar to me would be the harbinger of the murder of someone great, most probably himself.

Upon consulting his own favorite prophetess, Claudius told us that she, too, said that it would be best for Rome and for us if Tiberias stayed at Capri. I suspected that particular divination had more to do with Roman politics than it did with our visit--Claudius wielded more influence in Tiberias' absence.

As can be imagined, the palace was elegant and staffed by scores of soldiers and servants. It held about 60 rooms, not counting pantries and closets. It had been built there on the Palatine Hill in stages over the preceding 200 years and was more like a modestly walled neighborhood than a large residence. Although its predominant color was white, some of the central buildings were painted in pastel hues of green and pink. It had ten or eleven courtyards with pools or fountains, no less than 20 bedrooms, two kitchens, four bathing rooms, numerous small studies or offices, and five conference or living rooms. Most of the servants and guards lived in barracks on the premises and there was also a carriage house with stalls for four horses as well as a central furnace room from which many of the buildings were heated.

Mark, Claudius, and I frequently went out in sedan chairs or on foot to see the sights. We visited temples, markets, the Senate, and the various seats of the imperial government. We also went with him to visit in the homes of people who were mostly, but not always, the rich. Claudius actually had some friends who were quite poor, and one could plainly see that either he was a miser or that he himself was not possessed of much personal wealth. Be that as it may, everywhere we went people greeted us—or at least me—with a degree of respect that bordered on worship. Naadia was right. Unbelievably, people were in awe of me. Men and women alike stared at me as if I were divine, but by then I had gotten used to it. Mark never did, and I could not help but feel that he was jealous of me. Yet when I looked in my little travelling mirror I saw the same young woman as I always had seen, and yet I could see a difference. There was something about my eyes that *was* more compelling. I had noticed, too, that when I walked about I held my head up and squared my shoulders back with some kind of animalistic pride in myself that I had never really known before. Having been away from America for two or three months (although it seemed like two years) and having eaten simpler fare and gottten much daily exercise in the form of walking, I was trimmer, too, although I was still rather heavy. In short, I felt more confident and more powerful; other people could feel it, too.

Sometimes, accompanied only by Propea and with the cheerful connivance of our host, I would go forth in disguise on foot or in a cheap sedan chair. That sort of stunt was a rather common practice among the members of the ruling classes of Rome. After all, from time to time one gets tired of the life at center stage and prefers simply to walk among her fellow humans, to shop and to poke about or to indulge one's vices unnoticed.

This is not to say that I was sneaking around in order to indulge in any particular vices, for at that particular time I wasn't doing anything I couldn't have written home about—assuming I had a home, that is. On several occasions I drank a little more wine than I should have, but for the most part, I was only a tourist. As such I learned, saw, and smelled much.

I think of Dr. Johnson's correction when a lady complained that he smelled. "No, Madam:," he said, "*you* smell. *I* stink!" Well, I could smell, and Rome stank. To be fair about things, though, due to its advanced sewage and waste collection systems, Rome stank less than any other inland city I ever visited. Nevertheless, the assault on the olfactory senses Rome presented in summer had to be experienced to be believed. It was a feast of fragrances and odors to which one could never grow accustomed. Naturally the rich and well to do spent most of the hotter months at their villas in the country. The poor, too, found ways to get out of town during the sweltering, stinking summers, either by working in the countryside or living in vast tent and cave cities on the seashores. In any case, the odors of the city were terrific, despite the fact that it was drained by a sewerage system the equal to which would not be seen for another 1700 years. Having insufficient water for constant flushing action, however, it had an unfortunate tendency to trap wastes in shallow pools below street level, pools that often gave distinctly different odors to the neighborhoods above them. During dry spells, crews of men pushed brooms through the drains to keep the plastered stonework drains free from pockets of sewerage that would otherwise have provided breeding places for mosquitoes.

Rain was the intermittent blessing. People prayed for it to give some relief from the heat at the same time it gave the streets and drains a thorough cleaning. Such was the relief brought by rain that it was not uncommon to see people happily walking in downpours conducting their business or coming out of tenements to bathe in the rain by standing under streams of water cascading from the rooftops. "The heavier the rain, the happier the Romans," was a popular saying.

At one point that summer we were without rain for ten days and the temperature was in the 90s. The humidity was unbearable. On the morning of the eleventh day Propea and I went on a day trip out of the city dressed in long, light stolas of the cheapest sort. We looked like two women headed to one of the suburbs to work or to bathe in a creek somewhere. Wearing straw hats, sandals, and veils, and carrying our picnic in common sacks slung over our shoulders, we had set out to go to a particular shrine to see the sights and to have our fortunes told by a famous astrologer. Like some sort of an attorney of the occult, he maintained a sort of temple in the front part of his small villa situated beside one of the roads that led east from the city.

It was a long walk, so we started early to avoid the crowds and the midday heat. As luck would have it, the sear was not there when we arrived. We had walked some eight or ten miles for little more than the sights we saw and some freedom from the heat and odors of the city.

We were, however, lucky enough to find a creek to wade in. Along with dozens of other people, we splashed about and cooled off for awhile. We dallied about, picnicking and playing a game that was rather like a big game of marbles in which we rolled round stones the size of softballs at a central area. We also bought two small amphora of an excellent local wine to take back with us. That soon seemed to be a mistake since the containers were heavy and awkward in our sacks on the long walk home.

Even though we had taken off our underclothes and loosened everything else, it was so hot that our clothes were soon dark with sweat and were clinging to our bodies. Dust stuck to us and we were tired. We probably looked pretty ragged and should have taken refuge in a tavern, but we walked on, glad at least to have the roadway mostly to ourselves. I can pretty well take heat.

Around 3 p.m., it began to look like it was going to rain. The sky clouded up and gusts of wind stirred up the dust and sand. Our hair became downright grimy.

By the time we got back into the city, the sky was very dark. Thunder began reverberating among the low hills, pierced by the occasional crack of lightning. Just as we arrived in a street full of three- and four-story apartment houses, a deluge began. My natural inclination was to get into a doorway or under shelter, but Propea laughed and, taking me by the hand, dragged me out into the shower. Except for my slight fear of being struck by lightning, I went willingly enough. The streets rapidly filled with crowds of people who lived in that neighborhood. They came out laughing and playing with one another or stood with arms outstretched and their faces lifted to the sky. The rain redoubled in its force, making a heavy, drumming sound on the roofs and a crackling, hissing noise on the pavement. Our clothes were immediately soaked through. We took off our hats, veils, and sandals and put them in the sacks with our underwear and gave away the two jugs of wine to the people around us. Soon there were wine bottles everywhere and groups of people joining hands and dancing in circles and singing. Here and there naked or nearly naked men, women, and children cavorted in the driving rain. It was as joyous a scene as I had ever seen.

It kept on raining hard until the stone street was clean beneath our bare feet, and we took turns with others standing under heavy streams of water pouring from the tile roofs above. When it was her turn under a column of water, Propea very unselfconsciously took off her top and quickly washed her body, her hair, and under her arms, slapping away merrily the hands of a young man who was teasing her and offering to wash her back.

I myself was not so immodest, but I took my turn under the pouring water and I joined hands in the dancing circles, drank wine, and laughed along with the mob of which I was a part. Here and there as the rain slacked off, I noticed men and women pairing off, exchanging glances, touches and, in one particular case, sexual caresses of the most obvious sort. Who could blame them? After all, they were clean! One strapping fellow about 20 years old walked about with a full erection, as if advertising his availability. Soon enough his offer was accepted by a woman in her 30s who led him off to her flat.

"You better hurry up, boy!" the man next to me shouted after them as they left. "Her husband will be back at dark and he carries a big knife!" The crowd of some 20 or 30 people around us laughed and made obscene gestures and jokes.

Against a wall under a small stream of water, Propea was talking in low tones with the boy who had tried to caress her while she washed. He leaned upon a wall with one hand while with the other he toyed with the ends of her hair. Their eyes met and he was making her giggle. She looked very cute. She was still bare to the waist and I could see that her breasts were taut and her breath was uneven.

What people did that day there on the streets seemed ever so natural to me at that time. There they were, relieved of the tensions and lassitude that such prolonged heat waves bring, happy to be alive and suddenly freed of the boredom of daily life. Freshly bathed, perhaps for the first time in a month, they let their animalistic selves come out in a riot of passion. Some things are just too good to be passed up!

After an hour we went on our way, for when the rain let up, so did the festivities. The partygoers who were left in the street, looking somewhat abashed, trickled back to their homes and their private lives. We turned our feet toward the palace, but not until Propea had enjoyed being kissed and petted by her young man in a little section of alley they had found. They were never far from me and so I had watched them from the corner of my eye. Typically, he had obviously wanted in right then and there. She wanted it, too, I could tell, but it wasn't the time nor the place.

She was young and lonely, and I thought she was entitled to a little fun in her life, and having done the same sort of thing before myself--though not so publicly--I did not criticize her. Actually, I envied her. That's how it is when we see lovers and are without real love ourselves.

****

XVIII

The Races

Most of my pleasures during those summer days were simple ones like that walk in the country, and for the most part I was more temperate than I wanted to be. For one thing, Mark spent less and less time with me every week, and as I was afraid to make myself too vulnerable to others, I avoided both heavy drinking and moon struck men—of which and of whom I should note in passing there were many. I was temperate, that is, until I attended my first chariot race with Claudius and a group of his friends.

Generally speaking, chariot races were not held during the summer months because the horses cannot run at full speed in such heat, and Romans loved their teams too much to risk killing them in such events. The mob and the owners valued their horses more than their gladiators—the latter were afforded little in the way of seasonal respites.

As I recall, the owners of the very best teams formed a sort of syndicate that leased the Circus from the state. As in modern professional sports, a complicated series of rules assured a division of the gate receipts and concession sales proceeds, regulated the races themselves, assured balanced competitions that would keep the crowds coming and betting, and operated pari-mutuel wagering operations.

The teams were divided into "colors:" blues, reds, yellows, and so forth. Within each team were several ranked chariots. Thus the Leek Greens, for example, might be a consortium of 15 or 20 teams, all carefully ranked. On a given race day, there might be a series of races wherein the chariots of equal rankings raced one another, building to an end-of-the-day event featuring all the chariots of the first rank.

The people of the city divided themselves into partisan groupings—often by districts—and roamed the streets or headed to races in swelling, scarf- and pennant-waving groups of men, women, and children. Race days were announced well in advance, and they were often preceded by other celebrations: impromptu parades by one or more group of fans, picnics and parties. Sometimes fights broke out and sometimes one group tried to maim or drug some of the horses and even kidnap the leading charioteers of another color. Such events could quickly lead to riots.

After a few weeks in Rome and before I had ever seen a race, I was tentatively making some friends among Claudius' small but influential group of writers, artists, and theater people. For some reason, they were mostly Greens during racing season. They supported the Leek Green race teams, wore ribbons and even full outfits of that color, hosted parties and country weekends for the charioteers and owners of Green teams, and otherwise acted like modern sports fans. It was commonplace for the women—and sometimes the men—to have affairs with the more successful charioteers.

The group that I visited with most often was centered around a woman named Calpurnia Julianus. Although she traced her lineage legitimately through married ancestors, she was said to be a natural granddaughter of Julius Caesar. A patroness of the arts, she was Claudius' lover. She had only some moderate, inherited wealth, but was an aristocrat. About 40 years of age and quite delicate and lovely, she was held to be both a poet and an epigramist of great renown.

As good as my Latin became I never was much taken by Roman poetry. It always seemed heavy and harsh to me. I have often sat in Latin poetry readings amid cynical women and hard-bitten men who wept copiously during presentations of verse that had failed utterly to move me. I later noticed that those who wept most easily were often those most inclined to go to those bloody spectacles referred to as "the Games."

The epigram was a favorite literary form and had its own special place in the social, political and cultural life of Rome. It was the verbal rapier used to cut opponents or rise above others in the esteem of the literate. I liked them better than I did the poetry I heard. As indirect as they often were, I could appreciate the jest, wit, and jab of most of them. One that I remember only in essence went something to the effect of "Even Claudius' goat's feet can grip well enough to scamper over walls when Demeter hails him."

In that one sentence reference was made to Claudius'

manipulative wife, his own over-sexed nature, his lameness, an infamous, adulterous escapade of his involving the walls of the palace as well as those of the city. Although we all found it most clever that first night, we might not have remembered it the next day but for the fact that Claudius usually brought along a scribe who took down as much of the conversations and repartee as he could.

As history has recorded, Claudius was an inveterate historian. As such, he contended that the price of maintaining a servant as an amanuensis was negligible compared to the "cost" of letting a priceless poem, witticism, or epigram slip away forever unrecorded for posterity. To my knowledge, not one of those transcriptions has survived down to the present. Claudius himself acknowledged the ultimate futility of making such writings, calling them "flowers" rather than "records" or "histories".

"What does it matter," he asked one night, "that so much has been lost through the ages and so little has been retained? What difference does it all make in the way man governs himself? Is the bear less ursine if his den is lined with writings?"

Under Augustus, historical revisionism had come into its own, and the ruling family had on several occasions confiscated books, altered public records, and commissioned the writing of new, correct histories, poems, and even agricultural tracts.

The reports of the discussions of the Calpurnian group had a more immediate political value. They had a way of leaking out to advertise to any who wished to know how clever and careful the Julio-Claudian family was, what it was up to, and what were the permissible limits on free speech among the literati, the senators, and the rest of the power-wielding classes. Copies of the remarks, poems, and epigrams heard within the group were often distributed within days if not hours of Calpurnia's gatherings. Slanders could be promulgated, careers in civil administration or the military could be enhanced or broken, and those in disfavor could be given fair warning—all through the use of ambiguous couplets that served to protect the speaker as well as the listener. The intention of the speaker, as well as his words, could easily be explained by the Roman coda: No harm meant, no harm done.

This is not to say that all of the wealthy people in Rome

set their sails to the Calpurnian breezes. There were other forces to consider such as the winds of Sejanus and the distant hurricane of Tiberias. If the metaphor can be extended, all of the rich people kept weather eyes out as much as possible to facilitate those eternal human enterprises known as getting and spending.

But if there was a great social leveler, it was the Circus, because there rich and poor—ostensibly separated by wooden walls and armed guards—all gathered as one. There they joined their hopes and fears together on the same colors, horses, and men, wishing ill or favor together as their interests and passions lay. At race's end it was not uncommon for fans of a common color to flow together like Latin American soccer fans in a mass around their victorious heroes, colors waving, their voices hoarse from cheering amid the mass hysteria.

Something almost like hysteria was common in the taverns and drawing rooms of the city in the weeks preceding big races like the one that I first saw. Scheduled to be held on a festival day in early July, it was advertised as being of five heats only, beginning in the late afternoon. It would be cancelled in the event of oppressive heat.

Like everyone else in the city, as the day of the race approached, Claudius' friends discussed the upcoming event with increasing passion. I was not infected until four or five days before the big race, when I went with Claudius to a farm just outside the city to watch the Leek Green horse teams at practice.

I have always liked horses, but nothing prepared me for such beautifully matched three- and four-horse teams, such tough, sleek chariots or such beautiful, sleek charioteers. The equestrian events at Camden, South Carolina, were as nothing compared to such scenes.

We weren't the only spectators at the Green practice fields that day, but merely a small group among a large throng of Leek Green supporters, spies, bookies, partygoers, and the general riff-raff that such places attracts. We watched and talked while men and horses trained in the early morning and late afternoon, running long, elegant laps around central fences, going fast, but never full out. There were mishaps but no crashes, and it was all quite exciting and lovely. Yet it was more than that. It was a taste of what was to come, like gentle foreplay or kisses after dinner. Here was elegance and bridled power. In a few days, would come that and more: the hard-driving, dangerous, crowded dash to the finish before 100,000 berserk partisans.

Claudius and I didn't have to mingle with the thousand people who were there but were treated to a special, late luncheon with Leek Green team owners and their two leading charioteers—handsome, identical twins about 25 years old. At that point in my visit, I did not find the average Roman man particularly physically attractive, but those two fellows were. About my age, 30, they were well built, blue-eyed and fair, and, most importantly, their faces showed something not often seen in those times: true kindness. As they were indistinguishably identical, they looked as if they had been chosen for their beauty and uniqueness instead of their ability. Like a bookie, I wondered whether or not they truly had the stuff to make the hard, sudden choices that racing demanded. I wondered whether either of them would push his horses beyond their limits or run over injured men who might have fallen in the way during the race.

The two brothers were flattered by the opportunity of dining with a member of the Emperor's family and his beautiful companion, and they behaved very well, never betraying the appearance of insolence that was so often the blemish of Italian beauty. Modest and taciturn, they were comfortable in their chairs, and their well-oiled arms rippled in the light that reflected off the atrium pool beside us. They were obviously used to having what and whom they wanted. At first my presence and my face daunted them, but during the hour we spent together, they became at first comfortable around me and then downright familiar. I realized that it was a game that they had played before and it turned me on. For the first time in my life I thought seriously about going to bed with two men at once, and I was certain they would have been up for it. Such are the thoughts of a warm Italian afternoon rich with horses, men, food and wine.

So I began to look forward to the race and share in the fervor that was growing in the city, a fervor that was dampened by a heat wave that threatened to postpone our date. Imagine, then, the jubilation for one and all, when heavy rains came the day and night before the races, and the day itself was overcast and cool. Businesses closed and the Forum emptied by noon. By four in the afternoon, noisy crowds began flowing toward the Circus.

A large U-shaped arena on the flats near the river, the Circus would have been ugly at any other time. On that day, with the sun glinting in from the west and the whole place decked out in bunting and flags, it was grand. The throb and roar of the crowds and the smells of horses, people, and food made me feel marvelous even before the first ceremonies. Then the races began. No longer was I a mere spectator. I was a fan. I was a Leek Green.

Seated with my kind, I watched the races with them and shared their emotions, not taking my eyes from even the horrible wrecks, and I gambled and cheered and screamed along with 100,000 people. I saw people begin fighting total strangers for no reason other than sheer madness, and women oblivious to their nakedness ripping at their clothes in frustration or frenzy. I saw people fall down—whether with fainting, epilepsy, or death, I'll never know. I saw huge wagers won and lost and three charioteers die in wrecks during the afternoon's five races.

Mark and I joined the Claudian family box that overlooked the finish line. The box had oak walls seven or eight feet tall and provided seating on padded chairs and fixed benches for 150 people. Not all in the box were Greens—far from it. Mark, in fact, was a Blue, the faction most favored by the 30ish officers and senators with whom Mark was associating and with whom he sat. The Reds had no representatives at all in our box, for Red was then, as now, the color of revolution. Most Reds, Claudius told me, were the descendants of those who had lost the Social Wars that had ended about 60 years before.

Generally speaking, Greens thought of themselves as the Dionysians, the artists, the joie-de-vie crowd. Our drivers were the handsomest, our horses the most graceful, and our fellow Greens the most fun. We thought we were cleverer that other colors because we lived while they only passed time.

Blues were considered by our crowd to be the militarists and the control freaks. They thought of their charioteers as the ideal representatives of the manly virtues and of the other teams as being effeminate and slothful. The Blue fans were most likely to attack the fans of other factions without apparent cause.

Yellows were the most underrepresented of the major groups for they were the types, for the most part, who thought of themselves as the intellectuals, the teachers, and the learned professionals. We thought them rather funny, for in the heat of the race, their pretensions were stripped away and, but for the color of their bunting and ribbons, one could not distinguish them from any of the rest of us.

The merchants, craftsmen and *proletari* were generally inclined to be big White fans, thinking themselves and their teams as being the best trained and most deserving of victory. They seemed to think that their wagers on White were more rational and less emotional than were the wagers that might be placed teams of other colors.

Maybe they were, but once the starter's flag waved and things got going down there on the track, it was anybody's race. Horses or chariots might break down, mistakes might be made, and wrecks almost always occurred. It was possible to win a race by the mere expedient of staying alive.

As I have said, Reds seemed to be a catchall of people who took themselves too seriously. It always seemed to us that Reds were the social misfits. Had I been born into the brutal, violent, and commercially unfair Roman society of those times, I might have been inclined to run with the Reds myself. It was certainly a natural enough predilection among female graduate students of my time.

In addition to the five main colors, there were several other colors that would appear from time to time, trying to break into the big time by garnering backers from the ranks of the other colors. The only color that was never used was purple. During that particular summer there were three extra racing colors—Orange, Pink, and Black—but none of them had sufficiently identifiable followings upon which we Greens might afix any useful prejudices.

At that time Mark and I were still living together even though we had separated our property once and for all. It had always been clear whose money was whose, but our experiences had made us realize that, just as Marcus had said, our prestige would be our most valuable commodity—if we parlayed it wisely.

We certainly parlayed our money wisely enough before

the races that day. Each of us making bets according to our guesses and prejudices, we placed trinkets as stakes against hard money. In that manner, prior to the final race of the day both of us had won big chunks of cash, Green having prevailed in the first race and Blue having taken the third.

The fifth and final race was run amid incredible hysteria. On the sixth lap of the eight, a terrific crash occurred when Red, attempting to pass on the outside, bumped another chariot and went out of control in front of the rest of the field. Every team was involved in the wreck except White, which was also on the outside, and Pink, which was 200 feet back. Right before our eyes the most incredible jumble of flesh, wood, and leather appeared, and we watched with amazement and even admiration as the Pink charioteer dashed his team over the smallest part of the mess, oblivious to any further injuries he might cause. We cheered ourselves hoarse as he went on to catch up with and pass White to win the race. I think the Green twin who was driving in that race escaped with only a broken leg. Two charioteers were killed.

As darkness began to fall, everyone hurried home, and the race area emptied in short time. We had an armed escort and nothing to fear from muggers, so we were at leisure to leave late and avoid the rush.

Mark and I stayed together that night, exuberant yet exhausted and glad to be alive.

****

XIX

The Games

Chariot races were one thing. Fights to the death by armed men were another, and I knew before I got to Rome that I had no wish to attend gladiatorial combats no matter how compelling such scenes might have be. As things worked out, though, I did go one time. I found it inescapably horrible, and I still have nightmares involving the scenes I witnessed. On the other hand it must be admitted that the memorable quality of those fights was part of their attraction. I remember that you had a book called *Those About To Die* that described the Games in lurid detail. You urged me to read it. Had I done so I might have been prepared for what I saw. For one thing, until that time, the only fight to the death I had ever seen was the one on the road when Ned was killed, and that wasn't the same sort of thing. It could hardly be called a fight, anyway. Once Mark started shooting, our attackers made no pretense of standing to fight.

Having experienced that violence, though, I thought I was ready enough to see whatever Rome might offer, including sword fights. Undoubtedly I had become a harder person. I often walked down the streets ignoring the truly wretched and, of course, I had seen the deadly chariot races. My experiences had inured me to the suffering of others and I had become increasingly fond of the life of those times.

Perhaps the most shocking thing about the gladiatorial fights was how socially acceptable they were. All classes and conditions of men and women attended Games, and their motives for going were perhaps as varied as are the motives people have for going to church or professional football games. Just as it is folly to contend that all Christians attend church to worship God, it would be erroneous to think that all of the ancients went to games to satisfy their blood lusts.

The ruling class, for example, supported and sponsored combats for reasons its members thought entirely conducive to the maintenance of a healthy and vigorous state. Just as football is thought to encourage and demonstrate bravery, planning, and teamwork, the Games were thought to demonstrate the same qualities, but with higher stakes. Just as a good tragic play can uplift the spirit, the Games evoked many of the great emotions. Unlike the theater, there was no play-acting involved.

Claudius was an occasional patron of games. By himself or in conjunction with some of his friends he might sponsor one or two exhibitions each year from his own funds, but as his money was limited, he never put on a show that included fights to the death since they were always more expensive. The rich were expected to put on reduced admission or even free shows from time to time.

There had been some Games held during the summer, but spring and fall were the seasons when the promoters and politicians packed in the crowds, using both town criers as well as posted signs throughout the city to advertise particular pairings of individuals. Games would also feature wild beasts fighting one another and men fighting animals. Be that as it may, some great festival or another was held about two weeks after the chariot races which I attended, and two days of bloody games duly were scheduled and the posters went up all around the city. Soon I found myself discussing the games at Calpurnia's table while at the officer's feasts where Mark often dined, all the men began discussing the same tiresome subject. I was still not interested in going, but Mark was and even considered going into the arena against a lion or a man--armed with the Thompson, of course. In that way, he said, all Rome might know what power we possessed. Had he been younger and less cautious, he would have done just that. I had little trouble dissuading him, though, for I pointed out that rather than being overawed, the people and their rulers might be so terrorized as to turn on us at their earliest convenience. It was enough, I told him, that he had fired some for the officers in Spain as well as for some of his soldier friends at Sejanus' villa. The people who counted knew enough already, I reasoned. Why press our luck?

The Censor (a public official akin to a mayor), hoping to gain support of the mob against Sejanus' growing power, sponsored those late summer Games at his own expense. Even though all of Claudius' friends bade me to attend, I said that I would not go. They implored me. Eventually I got the impression that some of our friends might have wanted me to go so that I might emerge as morally soiled by the games as they were.

Publius Cato, a young historian of Calpurnia's group, had been urging me to attend. At a dinner the night before the games, he asked if I were adamant about not going. I assured him that I had no desire to witness and endorse the killing.

"In my country," I told them, "it is not an accomplishment to kill even a powerful man. Even a frail woman can defend herself if she has the right weapon and sufficient determination."

"It is said that young Mars can hurl thunderbolts that kill. Is that true?" he asked, referring to Mark by his new nickname.

"In my country, even women can hurl thunderbolts that

kill and maim," I confirmed, "and that's why we put so little value on individual combats to the death."

They began plying me with questions about our country's armaments--questions that they had been dying to ask but had long withheld, probably at Claudius' bidding. Mark and I had long since figured out how not to answer such inquiries by pleading instructions from our government and from our god. And yet who could blame them for asking?

Certainly Claudius and Calpurnia could blame them, for it became obvious to me that they all had been treating me as a friend in order to pry information out of me. Now that they had given away their waiting game, I felt hurt.

I was never very good at disguising my emotions, and that night was no exception. I was on the verge of tears, and crying is not exactly the thing for a demi-goddess to do. Fortunately, Calpurnia sensed my unhappiness, and the party broke up early in response to an argument she staged between herself and Claudius--an argument that was sufficiently bitter to send even the most obtuse guests packing. By the way, I should note that even though Claudius was married, he never saw his wife who had been imposed on him during childhood. For the sake of some sort of appearances, he and Calpurnia pretended to be mere friends and literary collaborators.

When the big day came at last, I had already decided to spend it walking in town making inquiries that I wanted to keep secret from Claudius and his spies. Accompanied only by Propea and wearing a veil, I went out early dressed in common, middle-class raiment of a middling sort.

By mid-morning I had found the man for whom I was searching--a 45-year-old Greek physician named Aechelus the Younger. His practice was located in the front portion of his rather large villa two miles from the Palatine Hill on the Appian Way . I was pleased to discover that his offices were surprisingly modern in that they were clean, well lit, and carefully organized. He had several examination rooms and enough patient rooms for his place to function as a small hospital. Aechelus had a pretty receptionist and both male and female nurses. Not surprisingly, he was flourishing.

As it was a festival day, he had only a few patients waiting to see him when we arrived, so our wait was not a long one. Flashing some silver in proof of our ability to pay, we were soon ushered into his presence.

This doctor did credit to his calling, for although he might have been ignorant of many of the most basic medical concepts of my times, he was certainly an expert in his. He had an inquisitive mind and had studied in Athens and Alexandria, and consequentially, he had a vast knowledge of the medical practices and theories of those times.

Having introduced myself with a fictitious name, I kept my veil on while we talked. I began our interview by asking him about his education and experience. At first he was somewhat offended by my questioning, but as he soon realized that I knew something of medicine myself, he recited to me with pride the names of several of the more well-known of the men and women under whom he had studied.

It may sound strange or even callous, but I then asked him to give Propea a complete check-up, including a pelvic examination, in my presence so that I could observe his technique. He balked at that request until I pointed out that I was a foreigner and new to the city. I wanted to be sure that he knew his business before I entrusted the care of my body to him.

As Rome was practically overflowing with quacks, he knew my request was reasonable, and he readily admitted he would do the same thing were he in my position. With that and with Propea's assent—for he would not work on even a slave without that person's permission—he began by asking her questions as he pushed, probed, smelled, felt, and even tasted practically every part of her body.

All of this caused Propea considerable embarrassment, for even though not a virgin, she was completely unused to being handled by a man in such a fashion. Naturally, I had informed her about this, and having told her my purposes, had obtained her cooperation.

Watching him as he worked, I could see that he was thorough and gentle, taking care to speak to her in a kindly fashion as he thumped and probed, listened and observed.

I asked him to explain to me the purposes of his tests as he proceeded. At first he was hesitant to do so, and was rather obviously disdaining me as being ignorant and meddlesome. He soon realized, however, that my knowledge of medicine was considerable, and his explanations became more collegial and less forced.

He was soon done with her, and he turned to me to ask what else might I require. Taking down my veil, I astonished him by saying that I was she who was known in Rome as Venus Atlanticus. Having seen me in the Forum and at the Temple of Augustus not two weeks before, he recognized me at once. I was, he said, the most beautiful woman he had ever seen. I thanked him, and he proceeded to examine me.

It is always important to have a doctor you can trust, and as things worked out, I certainly learned to trust him. For example, having me numbered among his patients would almost certainly have helped him to expand his practice, but because I requested it, he agreed to keep our relationship secret. He agreed because he was professional and because he was going to get to examine the most beautiful and exotic woman in Rome. Even the most practical of older doctors like to have beautiful patients from time to time.

He took much more time with me than he had with Propea who at my insistence stayed to watch as Aechelus worked. I knew that I might need to have her work on me some day, and at any rate thought that she might learn something useful.

Just as in a modern examination, I was always partially clothed, moving this or that part of my garments as the need arose. To examine my heart and lungs, he placed his ear against the bare flesh of my back, under my arms on each side, and on my chest right above my sternum. In the same manner, he listened to my stomach and my abdomen. Even though he was very professional and talked to me constantly as he worked, I could not help but be aroused by him, particularly when he examined my breasts.

Lower down and using an ivory device that was remarkably like a modern speculum, he found a raw spot and asked a few tactful questions about my sex life. Having listened, he suggested that I avoid intercourse for a few days, use a salve he would provide, and make Mark aware that Rome was rife with venereal illnesses. Apparently, neither syphilis nor gonorrhea had yet made an appearance in Italy, although some very serious transmissible yeast infections were rampant. He suggested in the most tactful way that Mark might have given it to me.

He checked me over from stem to stern and kept remarking with some sort of professional awe that he had never examined a person quite like me before and noted many minute ways in which he contended my body differed from the thousands of others he had studied. He was especially interested in my eyes. He said had iris patterns unlike any he had ever seen.

Following all of that, we talked about medicine for nearly three hours during which time we had a wonderful luncheon with his staff. I shared with him as much medical knowledge as I felt I could. Naturally enough, he didn't believe much of what I told him since it was contrary to his own observations and education, but he recognized that it was possible that I knew more about some things than even his teachers had known.

We talked about the circulatory system, the nervous system, the spine, and germs, and before I knew it his attraction to me as a woman had given way to an attraction to me as a colleague. His opinion may have been helped along considerably by the wine, for by midafternoon we were all about half-drunk. We were talking—or rather, arguing--about the functions of the heart. That's what did it.

On some point or another he kept repeating, "No, that's not the way it works at all" and I kept replying "Of course it does: look for yourself! It's as plain as the nose on your face!"

Everyone including Aechelus laughed, for he had a particularly large, well-formed nose that was about an inch short of a Cyrano. I hadn't meant to poke fun at him and he knew it. We were just that drunk.

"How do you know?" he asked.

"'Because the doctors in my country cut up corpses and study every little thing about them. They've been doing that for hundreds of years," I said, noting how they were all getting a bit quiet. "Don't you?" I asked.

He said that he had studied a few cadavers in Alexandria, but not in detail and only so as to better understand the fixing of wounds, particularly broken bones. In Rome, he told me, dissection of humans was more or less illegal, and, for that matter, rigorous scientific study of most aspects of medicine was almost unknown. Philosophy, religion, speculation, and divination were constantly substituted for observation. The wildest theories on the organization and physiology of the body were propounded and asserted with passion by men who thought it foul to test for the accuracy of their ideas..

Some would-be Roman dissectionists had even been prosecuted for witchcraft and grave robbing. My host, though, had studied in Alexandria, where under the Ptolomies, the study of anatomy had been tolerated. He had also studied under men who had studied under the great Alexandrian, Marinus, author of several books on the subject. Aechelus therefore was conversant with many of the essential elements of human physiology.

I did the best I could to share with him everything I knew about medicine. His own knowledge was very extensive, and his abilities were probably unsurpassed in Rome. While he might not know the causal mechanisms behind a given condition, he most often would know appropriate treatments, and he had a large pharmacy on hand which experience and training helped him employ to good effect. He was also a believer in the efficacy of cleanliness and sunlight, which put him ahead of most other doctors of those times. Most importantly, he knew how to deal with people and how to get the information he wanted. Maybe that's why he plied us with so much wine that day. I was a treasure-trove of information.

I agreed to dissect a body with him and two of his colleagues, and that's how we went that very afternoon to the place where the fresh bodies were being made. Together with the man who assisted him we went to the hideous stadium on the edge of Mars Field that was packed with screaming, frenzied spectators and victims. We left Propea sleeping peacefully in the infirmary.

Neither Aechelus or his man had any use for the Games, but as what we were doing was both odd and illegal, we did not want to attract attention to ourselves. Since informers often brought people up on charges of witchcraft so they could share in the confiscated property of a convicted person, we went on in as if we were mere late arrivals, and I wore my veil and clothes borrowed from one of the nurses. Almost too drunk to walk, we had arrived in sedan chairs.

So it was that I drunkenly watched as wild cattle fought a pair of lions. Then four pairs of naked women viciously wrestled one another, biting, grabbing hair, using their fists, and screaming. The crowd loved it. Then scores of men fought one another with various sorts of weapons. Some just fenced and fought without serious consequences, but as the day drew on, more were wounded and two died prior to the final, mortal combats that produced the type of body we wanted: one not too badly mangled and one that nobody wanted. Portus, the nurse, slipped away to the darker recesses of the cages and arranged the secret purchase and transportation of the body. We left before the final fights.

But before we left, I got a good look at the Imperial Box where Mark sat with a woman on one side and his favorite officer on the other. Both of them were obviously fawning over him, but he paid them no mind. He was transfixed by the slaughter before him. I was some distance away from them and was glad that I could not see his face any clearer than I could because I didn't think I would have liked what I saw. After all, he was still my occasional lover.

Claudius and his friends were there, too, all of them feigning regal indifference as they laughed and betted with one another while men slew and were slain.

And Sejanus, ugly Sejanus, was in the box. He watched the spectators--they were *his* game.

In all fairness to him, it must be said that those spectators were something to watch. For example, on the row in front of us, a short, voluptuous woman about my age was having hysterics during a fight between a net-and-trident man and a swordsman. A total stranger moved to her, got behind her, and fondled her breasts with both of his hands as she joined her voice in the general tumult. I couldn't tell if that was what she wanted or whether she didn't notice. Both the man and the woman shouted out in unison when the man with the sword drove it into the other's stomach and killed him. He was the one we took home.

I don't think I need to write much about the dissections which began the next day except to say that at first—being cold sober and a bit hung over—it took some doing and some wine to get me started, but I did it. I did it so successfully, in fact, that my host and his colleagues at the Schola Medicorum where we worked were fascinated by my various explanations of the parts

WALKER CHANDLER   203

of the body. They looked upon me for what I was: a godsend. As a practical matter, the things they learned from me may not have helped them and their patients in any appreciable ways, but unlike the vast majority of men I met in those days, they had truly inquisitive minds and were interested in acquiring knowledge for its own sake. I wished I had known more about anatomy and medicine. At night we kept the body in vinegar, and eventually we had to get another one—that of a woman found drowned in the river. All in all, I worked with those men practically every day for three weeks and learned a great deal from them, including a lot about the best treatments of wounds, suturing, trepanning, and midwifery. So I guess the games weren't all bad.

****

XX

The Journey North

I grew tired of Mark and he of me. We could hardly bear to be together. Each of us had cultivated different circles of friends and we went for days without seeing one another. Increasingly I felt that with his new friends he had acquired new lovers because his desire for me had ended. That was all right with me, but while we were both still in Rome, we continued to occupy the same suite of rooms although as I have said Propea most often slept with me in my bed.

Yet Mark and I were still co-conspirators isolated from the sea of humanity in which we swam. We still had sex sometimes, but it was never very good. It never lasted very long, and it distressed us both as it emphasized rather than mended our estrangement. It also resulted, I think, in the small infection that Aechelus soon cured.

It would be nice to think the alienation was all Mark's fault, or came about as a result of his having changed so much. It seemed that in a twinkling of an eye he had changed from an insecure, paranoid smuggler into an acclaimed warrior. It would be too facile a thing, though, to say that it was only he who had been transformed.

I, too, had changed. For one thing, one cannot pass by the poor, the dying, and the leprous and look upon scenes of carnage and death without growing more callous. Neither can a plain woman suddenly become a beauty without having her frail ego leap at the chance for fame and the worship of men.

Nor can one face mortal peril without being changed. I often thought of the fight in Tingitana and particularly of shooting that man. How could we have helped but outgrow the people we left behind in the future?

During the last weeks I was in Rome I studied and worked with my physician friends almost every day, and I tried to share my excitement about our work with Mark. By that time, though, the disdain that he had for me had worn even at the bonds of friendship. At least I hid my disdain for him as best I could.

I felt sorry for him. Surrounded by imperial spies and false friends, he reveled in the role they conspired to let him play. More fit than he had been when we first crossed over through time, he was still no match for the soldiers and officers of the Praetorian Guard with whom he spent most of his time. Even though he was a head taller than most of them, they were men who filled out the beautiful bronze cuirasses they wore with muscles made hard from long campaigning and constant training in heavy armor, and although he had killed men with a gun, they had fought men with swords, spears, and knives. They knew what they were doing; they were seducing him.

Even though we were no longer lovers, Mark and I agreed to work together to find, refine, and store some fuel supplies for the Short. We thought it would be prudent at least to work toward that goal so as to be prepared if ever need for the Short arose. After all, we had lugged the distilling apparatus with us and we knew that we could actually find crude oil somewhere since surface seeps of it were already known in various places around the empire.

We also agreed that whenever we were separated, we would stay in touch with our short wave radios, agreeing that the nights of the new and full moons would be our set times to communicate. The radio sets we had were marvels of ingenuity.

No bigger than cigar boxes and capable of sending low power Morse code signals (but not voice transmissions) over vast distances, each had a rechargeable battery and a solar recharger. In the months that followed my departure from Rome we both grew quite proficient at sending and receiving code.

Julian had taken the third set with him, but in the many weeks since we had parted with him, he had contacted us only four times. In a ponderous, slow way he reported only his progress in a sentence or two like those of the brief telegrams of yesteryear. It was obvious that he wasn't putting any effort into learning code, and after the first ten weeks we no longer heard from him.

"I guess he's got new friends now," Mark joked. "Let's hope they don't have to depend on him in a pinch."

His last report had been from Alexandria. After that we didn't hear from him, but for that matter we really didn't care where he was or what he did. We assumed he had lost the set or that it had gotten broken. On the other hand, we knew that either he might have been prevented from using it, or simply didn't want to contact us. He could have been dead. Nevertheless, through long nights we listened.

Since the Short was Mark's plane, we decided that the fuel project would be his responsibility. Since he was planning on staying in Rome for the present and I was planning on leaving, we assumed that he would be in a better position to order supplies and put up the refining apparatus than I would be. His plan was to import crude oil from what is now Albania and to refine it somewhere nearby. It would be expensive, but he could afford it.

At any rate, that was all business and I wanted to get moving. I was tired already of the strange and dangerous world of intrigue and suspicion that prevailed in the city, and in spite of my new interest in things medical, there was something about those days in my life that made me want to push on. I wanted to see the next town, sample the next culture, and see the next vista.

In this I was not alone, for it was a time when tourism flourished. The opportunity to travel without too much fear of attack had revived the tourist industry. It had been reinvigorated throughout the Empire since Atticum--the advent of peace and

Roman order, the suppression of piracy and the existence and completion of the vast system of paved roads made travel very popular once again.

I had decided that for the next leg of my journeys I would go across Italy and take ship to the Dalmatian coast where there were small surface petroleum leaks that might be exploited. Mark and Claudius supported my wish to travel. Each had motives for wanting me gone, I suppose, and both thought that a trip to the Adriatic and Greece would be quite the thing for me to do. On the other hand, a little bird told Propea that Sejanus also wanted me to leave Rome, although he would rather have seen me going off to some place where he had many agents and few enemies. Spain was such a place, as was Syria; both were recommended to Propea as being healthy and exciting.

As things worked out, though, in the late summer of our first year, I gave most of my possessions to Mark for safekeeping and traveled up to the German frontier with a girl I had only recently met—a trip that probably worried Sejanus. After all, many an insurrection had started in the far north, and it was rumored that Mark and I had secret ties to both the Germans and the Celts.

My new friend and traveling companion, Messalina Lucretious, was a girl I met for the first time at my physician's villa during one of our dissections. A native of Pompey and just in from Ostia, she had come on over to the villa looking for our colleague who was her uncle. When I first saw her we were coming out of the surgery drying our hands with towels, and she made a ribald joke that got us all laughing. I felt an immediate attraction to her.

She was a pretty, petite girl about 22 years old. Blessed with dark eyelashes and luminous brown eyes, she carried herself well and wore her hair in a fashion that was rather normal by modern standards: long, with ringlets. She had a musical voice and fine lips beneath a neat, small nose. Her skin was flawless, and her hands were small, fine, and incredibly soft. It was a delight just to hear her talk, no matter what she might say. Her eyes, lips, hands, and the sound of her voice entranced me. I felt that next to her I looked like an awkward giantess.

As she had a great, fun-loving personality, met me purely by chance, and came from south of Naples, I had no reason to suspect that she might be a spy for Sejanus, Claudius, or Tiberias. It was easy for me to let down my guard and accept her as a friend. And fast friends we became, for we had such a strong natural affinity for one another that it bordered on infatuation. We spent a lot of time together in the weeks that followed.

For all her attractiveness, though, she was still single. At ten, she had been betrothed to the son of one of her father's wealthiest friends, but the boy had died at 15 and so, too, had a second fiancé. She joked about what bad luck it was for men to know her, but it wasn't a joke anymore—at least not to her parents and their acquaintances. They had begun to believe in the local rumor that she was bad luck. Fewer and fewer parents wanted her to marry their sons despite her father's great wealth, and at her age, she was considered a spinster. She had turned such a misfortune to her advantage by enjoying a freedom that few other women enjoyed, for her father doted on her and financed her every whim.

When we met, she was on the first leg of a long journey north to visit her principal lover, a centurion in the Tenth Legion on the German frontier. There was a chance that he and she might decide to get married if the negotiations between their families could be settled, she said, and in the meantime they had, as she put it, "already begun practicing." She really liked me as much as I liked her, and because of that she tarried in Rome for two weeks. As the summer was fast turning into fall, though, she had to press on if she was to get a few weeks with her man before the winter set in.

Rather than parting from her, I decided to go with her. It seemed to be a perfect opportunity to travel in the company of someone I really liked, and although I had been thinking of going to Greece, she helped me change my mind. Making a trip with her through France seemed like the thing to do at the time, and she had already made all the plans anyway. She told me that the trip would take 30 days in each direction, depending on what breaks we took along the way, and as she had family and friends all along the route, we assumed that our journey north would be quite a holiday—which it was.

I made final plans with Mark, and got Propea and myself ready to go. All that didn't take long to accomplish. Sometimes I think I was born ready, and I don't need heavy baggage.

We sailed out of Ostia on one of Messalina's father's ships on the first leg of the journey. The weather was excellent, complimenting our high spirits and the choice I had made. Rome fell behind us like a dream.

The ship was a large, slow, sail-powered transport on which Messalina and I shared a pleasant cabin aft; her maid and Propea shared a cabin beneath ours. As they were eager to get her married and had tentatively approved of the match--the centurion being the oldest son of one of the richest of the Neapolitan aristocrats-- she was going with her parents' blessings. I must say, though, that we had some worries: after all, there was the problem of her reputation for ill fortune and by that time I, too, was easily infected by local superstitions and beliefs. I was glad that the eyes on the bows had been newly painted.

The voyage up the Italian coast was marvelous. The views were beautiful, and the days were sunny and warm. Messalina was excellent company: witty, urbane, and worldly. Better than that, I had chosen her; I felt I could trust her.

It was fun to be with her around other people, too. She flirted with many of the young men we met and encouraged me to flirt with the older ones, a game we called "dividing the spoils".

It was such a new thing for me that I felt as if I was a teenager again, tossing out little smiles and making eye contacts that were filled with hints of possibility. It was just a game with me, though, for I was not ready to want a man. I was content.

Putting in at little port towns along the way, we stayed with different families—friends or relations of her family. Always we were invited into the best villas, for her family was one of the most prominent along the coast, and my own fame spread out before us like ripples on the water. So it was that all along the coast and until we made Marseilles, there were always feasts and handsome men and beautiful women, and we had various adventures and dinner parties too numerous to recount. We were like girls on holiday and for the five weeks it took us to arrive near what is now Mainz on the Rhine River, every day was a vacation. More than a few fellows were happy that we had passed their way if only because we had smiled at them, or walked with them in the twilight holding hands, or exchanged tender kisses with them in the moonlight.

We were able to go as far as Lugdunum (modern-day Lyon) by water, having stopped at Massilia (Marseilles) and Arelate (Arles) on the way. In Lugdunum we stayed two days with a family that had commercial ties to Messalina's family, and through them we met several of the town's leading citizens, all of whom had heard of me even before I left Rome.

The nature of our trip changed as we started up the long road to the frontier. Our retinue included the two of us and our two maids, one 12-year-old Gallic page and three older men-at-arms who were retainers to Mesallina's family. We all traveled in three light, horse-drawn, covered wagons much like the gypsy wagons of later times. One was for the maids and page, one was for the men, and one was for us. The word "wagon" is deceptive, for it evokes a vision of something ponderous and heavy. Ours were fairly light and fast, and as winter was approaching, our travel was not particularly leisurely. In addition to the two horses that pulled each wagon, we pulled behind us a string of three or four spare horses and often changed out those that tired during the long daily stages.

Messalina and I either drove or lounged in the wagons as we moved along, but more often than not we rode on horseback or even walked. Generally speaking, in the mornings we moved at a good clip, going at a trot for 30 minutes at a stretch, then walking 20. In the afternoons our pace was slower, but we commonly pushed on until dark even if that meant camping out and sleeping in the wagons.

From time to time we traveled in the company of others, either when they could keep up with us or when we had slowed down to their pace as we overtook them in the afternoon. From time to time we stayed in inns, and there were private homes along the road that took in travelers. There were also numerous horse paddocks and livery stables to service the needs of the traveling public.

The main, paved part was only about 12 feet wide and was slightly bowed in the center so that it would shed water. The paving cobbles were very well fitted and the joints all along the way were either mortared smooth or were filled with sand or packed dirt so as to prevent the sort of cobbled roughness we associate with similar, modern roads of inferior construction. Grass was allowed to grow where it could on the pavement for its padding softens the walk, and on one or both sides of the pavement there usually ran a level, dirt, foot-and-horse path another ten or fifteen feet wide. It was on that path that most people preferred to walk or ride. The roads were principally paved to prevent them from becoming impassible during wet weather.

We paid careful attention to the conditions of the paths and of the horses' hooves. The standard horseshoe used in those days was a thick, formed leather sheet fitted around the hoof and tired in place. Such a shoe worked well, but its drawback was its tendency to trap stones inside and cause immediate limping. When that happened we had to stop at once and remove the boot, a task that our menservants performed in less than two minutes. "Horseshoes" were also made in the same fashion out of both copper and lead, but the use of iron shoes, nailed on, was unknown. Frankly, having seen both methods in operation, I think the ancient one superior in many ways. The weakening effect of nails upon the hoof walls is circumvented, natural abrasion when the hoof is bare is encouraged, and the all-or-nothing choice imposed by the modern shoe is avoided.

Our wagon horses were of the small, wooly, large-headed type I had seen in Spain. Fractious as saddle animals, they were docile in harness and displayed the surprising strength and stamina I have noted earlier. They were not pleasant to ride, though, because they had terribly rough trotting gaits and seemed to object to being ridden. Because of their speed and eagerness to get ahead and win, most of the chariot-racing horses I had seen in Rome were Arabian, for with considerable work, they could be trained to race in harness. For war chariots, though, the shaggy horses were quite superior since they were steadier and, for that matter, fiercer. They could even be trained to bite enemy infantry and horses during an attack. Ours weren't that mean, but we were careful around them nonetheless.

In addition to the harness animals we had two saddle horses of the sleek, Arabian type. Messalina and I often used them for side trips or to ride on out ahead of the wagons. As delicate as she was, she loved to run her horse and could always best me. My horse was bigger, but he had to carry a lot more weight. I had put on the pounds in Rome and aboard ship. I could barely squeeze into some of my clothes.

With all that horseback riding I quickly began to rely completely upon my beautiful, golden chamois and deerskin riding outfits. They were comfortable, sleek, and gave a good purchase upon the stirrupless saddles that we used. They could be washed easily and most of the water wrung out of them so that I could put them back on damp and let the sun dry them. I quickly discovered that when I was dressed in those trouser-and-shirt outfits it was much nicer to go without wearing my regular underwear except when it was absolutely necessary to do so. For one thing, the outfits clung to me like second skins, and for the other they were a pain to put on and take off. Since riding without a bra--particularly trotting—was almost unendurable, over the chamois I wore leather vests that laced up the front. Although the vests were rather plain, they immobilized my breasts in a way that pushed them up and gave me even more cleavage. When we stopped or rode in the wagons, I could unlace some of the thongs but I usually keep the vest on for style and modesty. An alternate method of dealing with the problem was the one that the petite Messalina used. She wrapped a long, wide silk or linen band around herself horizontally in the same way one bandages for a broken rib. I was too large for that method to be of much use, and found it was too hot and cumbersome even in the cooler weather. Also I looked better in the vests—an important consideration, to be sure.

Although we had servants with us, both Messalina and I shared in many of the camp and travel duties such as caring for the horses, building fires, and setting up and breaking camp. Although pretty, rich, and seemingly delicate, Messalina had been trained all of her life to stay busy. Parents those days— even very wealthy parents like hers— almost universally recognized the benefits of having their children constantly employed in useful tasks. When he was a child, for example, although he was a weakling and was thought to be retarded, Claudius had been kept busy from dawn to dark studying Greek poetry and shoveling out stables. Similarly, starting at the age of three, Messalina had worked in her parent's villa's kitchen, weaving rooms, storage rooms, and gardens. Like all up-and-coming rich girls, she was expected to be capable of running huge domestic and agricultural establishments by the age of 19, and it was thought that one can only learn how to manage such complicated enterprises by starting at the bottom.

I myself had been somewhat raised that way. Even when I was a little girl, when we visited my grandparents farm I was expected to spend long hours in the gardens planting, hoeing, and harvesting. I worked in the kitchens and did housework. I didn't like it, but I did it, and I don't think it hurt me. So it was that it was natural that both Messalina and I should work alongside our servants much of the time. It seemed to me as if some of the normal resentments one expects to exist between master and servant are absent when they work side by side.

I think I should point out that it was not just the legal and social structure that helped a family maintain or better its financial and social position in ancient Rome. Clearly, the work ethic of the upper class was what kept families prosperous generation after generation. There was a harsh side of that coin, too. Those who did not keep up were allowed to fail.

An example of that could be seen in how the sons of rich men gamble away their wealth and find themselves penniless. Unsupported by their families, such men often turned to the expedient of selling themselves into gladiatorial contracts with promoters. Under such a contract a man might "belong" to a promoter for a period of two or three years. During that time, he could not refuse to fight. He might, however, refuse to fight more often than he was contracted to fight, or refuse to fight in certain types of fights. His contract might also specify whether or not he could be entered into fights to the death. If he survived his contract he might be much more careful about what he did with any other wealth he might acquire. On the other hand, some men never learn.

One of the most pleasant aspects of the trip was that we were received everywhere by the most generous and hospitable people imaginable. The ones I remember best were our hosts on a large farming estate in the valley of the Saone a day's journey north of the town of Cabillonum. The rolling countryside of that region reminded me of middle Georgia and the good times you and I had together there. But that was the past which was actually the future, and I was living in the present. And, Oh, did I feel *alive!*

It was harvest season and the whole region, too, was

alive with activity and commerce. Migrant workers found themselves in great demand for the labor-intensive harvesting of grapes and winemaking. During that particular season, there was a labor shortage, particularly in the northern valley district. When we stopped for the night at the estate alongside the main road, our harried hosts were friendly but in obvious need of help. They importuned us and we agreed to remain with them for a few days to join our 16 hands with theirs, and they agreed to pay our help. Our small retinue pitched in and worked with them from dawn to dark every day for a week.

We dressed, ate, and worked just like everyone else. It was the thing to do, and we loved it. It was enough just to do our jobs well in the company of good people, and every traveler must tarry awhile if she is to learn something of the people whose country she is visiting. The owners of the farm worked right beside us in the kitchens, vats, and fields, and all of us-- rich and poor, slaves and freedmen--ate standing up side-by-side at long tables of rough boards in the courtyard. When night came, even the rich and amorous Messalina slept the same satisfied sleep of the poorest field worker.

Our hosts were both Gauls who spoke fluent Latin. The husband was originally from another district, but the wife had been born on that very farm. Her family had been a relatively wealthy one that had long allied itself with the Romans even before Julius Caesar's great defeat of Vercingetorix at Alesia.

Her husband was an ex-legionnaire in his mid-40s. Although he was not a handsome man, he had a great deal of animal vigor that I found irresistible. An athletic sort, he had lost the lower part of his left leg fighting Germans near the Rhine some years before, but he shunned the use of crutches and instead wore a sort of prosthesis that allowed him to walk quite normally. I soon discovered that the rest of him was very much intact, for he was soon professing his desire for me with his eyes and in a hundred little kindnesses and attentions. Something about him brought out the twenty-year old in me, and I returned his looks and began blushing and feeling silly. I was embarrassed about his openness, for his attentions toward me were often tendered in his wife's presence.

She was a sweet woman, and had once been very pretty, but the years had not been kind to her. She had lost her figure to childbearing and a fondness for butter and honey. Naturally she could see her husband's interest in me, but she gave no signs of jealousy, and made no attempts to nip our attraction for one another.

After all, it was the harvest season. I broke my long fast one night in the quiet secrecy of a hayloft, quickly discovering that my host's lack of a lower limb was more than made up for by his surplus elsewhere. It was a very pleasant experience for both of us.

It seemed that it had been a very long time since I had felt a man's love. The simple pleasure of touching a man who was eager yet kind and affectionate toward me was wonderful. Because of all of my flirtations on the trip north and because I had been close at hand during Messalina's trysts on several occasions, I was more than ready for some lovemaking of my own. If she was enjoying herself, it seemed natural that I should enjoy myself, too. Then, too, ever since arriving in Spain I had traveled through a world rich in the celebration of carnal things and found myself thinking about sex more than I had since college. The places and people grew on me as on fertile ground, and infused me with their natures, and that was not all.

As I had learned in Mauretania, the wines we drank were different and were often infused with aphrodisiacs such as an extract of certain types of mushroom. There was also a type of wine fortified with powdered opium, but I never cared for that type as it made the drinker lapse quickly into a stupor every bit as ridiculous as pure alcohol. That kind of wine was quite cheap and popular among the lower classes and slaves. It was consumed not for its taste but for its effect.

Normal, unfortified wines were the most commonly consumed, of course, and varied greatly in taste from region to region, type to type, and even jug to jug. The trade in wine, mushrooms, amphorae, potions, and opium was active and diverse.

You will recall that in ancient times the wine was watered down before it was consumed. This was done not only to make it more palatable but also to control the level of intoxication it caused, but of course such control was difficult to perfect when other intoxicants were present. A mushroom-fortified wine might be indistinguishable by taste from a common table wine, and its effects might take ten minutes or two hours to come on so that a purely unintentional and sometimes unwelcomed experience could occur. Naturally enough, people often failed to keep themselves under control when drinking fortified wines. It was not uncommon for a party that started out being rather tame to turn into an orgy. People who would never consider intimate contact with one another when sober often mated wildly while intoxicated. The mistress might copulate with the slave, the master fondle his friend. Anything might happen, and when it all wore off by the next morning, all would be back to normal and the entire event would be talked about in the most forgiving terms. The Italians were a very forgiving people when it came to the things people did while intoxicated. The things they did when sober were different.

When thinking of those wines and that journey I recall with utmost clarity a picnic that Messalina and I went on with two of our admirers in Marseilles. They were about her age and were both shorter than I am, but they were sweet, exuberant, and fun loving. Like most of the people of that small city-state, they were Greeks and really knew how to treat us and had serenaded us on our first night in town. On the following day we went boating with them and let them talk us into going with them on a surprise adventure on the third and final day of our stay there.

When they came for us we were told that our adventure would consist of a simple walk into heaven. That and Messalina's eagerness and pleasure at hearing the proposal should have told me something, The four of us walked and climbed for two or three miles until we came to the top of a large grass-covered hill that overlooked the port. When we got to the crest, the view was sublime. We also discovered that a small banquet had been set out for us by their servants who had guarded the table until we arrived, then politely withdrawn and returned to the town by a second pathway.

It was a perfect afternoon—just as the men had planned it—and among the array of other foods and wines was a glass flask of wine that sparkled when they poured it into our glasses, for it had added to it a tiny a bit of gold dust. Each of us poured out a little libation to the gods, before we drank, and I asked Messalina what it was.

"*Magica:*" she said, "which brings you into the moment

and holds you in the eye of Apollo."

"It's not Apollo I'm worried about, it's Dyonisus over there. He looks mighty eager," I said to her in our secret distortion of Latin, which we used to speak privately. A bad joke perhaps: the original Pig Latin. Nevertheless, I drank the sparkling elixir.

"Don't worry: I'll handle him. You can be happy with Haephestus here," she said, nudging the more homely of the two guys who had attached himself to her when his much more handsome friend had attempted to claim me at the beginning of the walk. "I don't think he'll be more than you can handle," she concluded. He smiled at me and I, indulgently, smiled at him. One would have thought I had given him a great gift.

And so I drank and we all ate and talked and laughed and watched the sun begin its descent, and somehow during the course of things Messalina and I traded men. I sat with my increasingly handsome host, then lay down on my back on the blankets, resting my head on his thigh and looking up at the clouds while he played sweet tunes on a flute. He was quite good—or perhaps it was the drug. Quickly caught up in the music, Messalina rose and began to dance slowly and gracefully for us. Her short, diaphanous, silk gown floated and waved in the light airs as the drug in the wine came on. There was nothing but the music and the pretty girl with the smooth arms and legs who had such a happy face into which the afternoon sun poured. Her partner rose and began to dance with her in a similar fashion that soon took on the meaning of courting swans. One thing led to another. Soon there was no world outside of that happy, little one of love there on the hilltop. By then I was lying on my side watching them, my head resting still on my guy's thigh, and we watched contentedly while our companions began to touch their necks, chests and backs together as swans might do. They began to kiss with a tenderness which was lovely to behold, then fell into a more passionate series of caresses and embraces. Even though they were very stoned, I expected them to get up and go away to a private place, but they didn't. While my date continued to play his flute, they went right on ahead and made love not ten feet away from us. It seemed like the most natural thing in the world at that moment in time. While she was on top of him, Messalina turned her face to me with dazed and happy eyes, and smiled at me in a way that made me warm with pleasure.

It was the first time I had ever actually watched someone else making love, and it didn't seem vulgar or even particularly exhibitionistic. In fact, under the influence of that wine, I found it truly enchanting to watch them. They were a handsome couple, and went on for what seemed like a long time, gently moving slowly, ever so carefully, there in the golden rays of the afternoon sun.

My date played on and I just smiled and watched and snuggled up against his warm leg. I don't think it occurred to us to do anything ourselves until our companions finally lay still upon their backs, side-by-side on the soft wool blanket.

I rolled over on to my other side to look at my fellow as he stopped playing his flute. Only then did it occur to us that it was somehow our turn—if we wished it to be. More particularly, it occurred to my date's friend, Pirapus, who popped up right in front of me, unhooding himself like a saint to be admired. So in a lovely trance, I admired him, tickling him gently with my fingernails and tracing the lines of his veins. As I caressed him, my date slipped his hands up under my tunic and caressed me in return, his touch sending little, golden trills of pleasure through me. And it was obvious to me that such a clean, upright fellow deserved kissing, and so I kissed him, too, as we were held there outside of time under the indulgent eye of Apollo. We were happy enough just doing those sorts of things, and even that gentle stroking and those kisses were more than my guy had hoped for. Eventually it was more than he could stand. I was stoned, and so right there in front of my friend I did just what I felt like doing—but no more.

Hearing such an account, one may wonder, as I did, what forms of birth control girls like Messalina employed so that they could enjoy sexual freedom. There were several methods used, including ovulation-suppressing herbs, which affected the body like modern birth control pills do. Couples also practiced withdrawal and rhythm—that is to say, having sex only near or during menstruation. Some used a soft wool packing which acted as a barrier. As a last resort when all else failed, abortion was available.

In the days that had followed our outing at Marseilles, I often thought about that afternoon, and how beautiful and happy Messalina and that boy had looked as they made love. I thought about my own companion, his flute music, his smell, and the hard/soft feeling of his body. Those memories made sleep elusive sometimes and made me think that I perhaps should have done more with him than I had.

I was therefore more than ready to relieve my own tensions at the farm north of Cabillonum, and I was eager, almost desperate to have some satisfaction. Fortunately, I had chosen well, for my Gaul was adept at giving pleasure. Meeting during the moonless nights in the hayloft of a big barn he had, we came together quietly in the darkness. It was very, very intimate, and I soon found myself stifling my own noises when he aroused me to a fervor pitch with touches of his hands and his tongue. It was the best sex I had had since before Mark, and I thought I needed it. He certainly acted as if he did.

We tried to be discrete, but his wife found out about it anyway. Wives usually do, I suppose. At first I felt terrible, but then I learned a great lesson from her. As it turned out, she was not the least jealous about our lovemaking--particularly since I was just passing through. Even after that night and the ones that followed it, she remained friendly and cheerful toward me. Finally, as we worked side-by-side together on the fifth day, she told me how she felt about things.

When we were alone for a few minutes preparing the midday meal, she suddenly looked me in the eye and blurted out, "I thank you for being with Lucritus last night." I was surprised and embarrassed. I had not wanted her to find out about us in the first place. Certainly I had not wanted to hurt anyone who had treated me so well, nor did I want to come between her and her husband. I could not think of anything to say. She broke the silence.

Putting down her knife, she touched my arm and said, "When he was young, he was a veritable satyr, a goat. He was...everything a woman could want." She blushed and I could see how she had been everything a man could want: fine-figured, pretty, lusty, and eager. "A woman doesn't have so many children by weaving cloth," she said with a grin. She had borne 12 children of whom eight were still living; the youngest being three years old.

What could I say to her? Obviously I was caught.

"He's a good man," I said.

"One of the best," she agreed.

I felt sorry for her--for her lost youth and faded beauty. She had been very kind to us and I felt guilty. "What I want to say," she continued after waiting politely for me to continue, "was that whoever or whatever you are, for you to go to him was a blessing he will long remember. We have never seen as beautiful a woman as you in all our lives. It was said that Livia, wife of the divine Augustus, was the most beautiful woman in the world, but my mother saw her and said that it wasn't so. And my grandmother saw Cleopatra and said that her nose was too small and that she wasn't so terribly good-looking either. Grandmother thought she was a witch or a sorceress."

My hostess' name was Aemelia. She washed and wiped her hands while she talked, not looking at me directly.

"It is not an insult to a woman that her husband is attracted to such perfection as yours. When you are gone, he will turn to me again with renewed ardor, and the pride that will keep him hard and happy. When you are gone, I shall make a small figurine of you for our alae—the little room we showed you—a statuette by which our family can remember and revere you. We are honored by your visit. You have honored my husband."

"Aemelia," I began, "What do you mean by honored? Who do you think that I am?"

We were standing very close to one another, and as I looked down into her eyes, she seemed almost to bow before returning my look.

"I don't know," she said, "but then it is not given to us to always comprehend the acts and doings of the gods. I know that you are mortal, of course. You eat, pass wind, and make water like the rest of us." We smiled. "And make love, but of course, the gods do that, too."

"But what else is there?" I asked.

She raised her cool, clean hands to my cheeks and held me as if to examine my irises the same way that Aechelus had. "Yes, but it is what is in your face that tells me that you are not just a foreigner and a great beauty. You are an agent of the divine, I think—perhaps a child of Zeus, perhaps just a beautiful woman. But I tell you this: your destiny is not your own. You have no more power over it than I have over the rise and fall of the river."

"How do you know such things?"

"I read it in your palm last night, and I am descended from a Druid. I have The Gift of Sight," she said. "You are destined for great things, great sadness or great joy. You are a blessing to those you encounter. Again I say it: it is a great honor to have you in my house."

I could not disbelieve her. She looked at me practically in the same way her husband had looked at me during the preceding days: as grateful and loving as a dog, and I don't mean that in a derogatory sense. What could I say or do?

I placed my hands on the sides of her face as she was holding mine, and then I kissed her on the lips as one would kiss a sister. She trembled as we kissed. Her lips were warm and moist on mine, and both of our eyes watered with the pure, shared human tenderness. I did not feel uncomfortable with it.

"May the blessings of all the gods be with you and your house forever, Aemelia Who Has the Sight," I said as we released one another.

Astonishingly, she fell to her knees before me and bowed her head. "Thank you," she said simply.

Thus with her as with the youth in Marsallies I discovered the power that I had to make people happy simply by sharing myself with them at practically any level I chose. From being with Aemelia and her husband I realized that I was held to be so supernormal as to exempt me from the possessiveness of men or the jealousy of women.

Thereafter, like some traveling priestess of high renown, my advent was heralded before me and the curious would sometimes come out of their way to see me passing or to visit with me at taverns or villas were we stayed. My fame grew to the point that by the time we reached our destination, the winter quarters of the Tenth Legion at Mogantiacum, it seemed that I had almost no privacy of any kind. There were times when I couldn't even relieve myself in the woods near the roadside without having upon me the watchful eyes of little children. What little bathing I was able to accomplish when we were camping out along the road was so seldom private that I became almost used to having people gawk at me in various states of undress.

Time considerations and the purposes for which this manuscript are written prevent the rendering of even a cursory—

much less a detailed—account of the time I spent by the Rhine. Suffice it to say that things did not work out as we planned.

The first unplanned event was that almost immediately after we arrived I fell in love with one of the legion's principal officers.

I have thought a lot about whether or not to write his name in this account, and I am reluctant to do so for several reasons. To begin with, to the English-trained ear it has quite a silly sound, and he was not a silly man. He was, in fact, the finest man I had ever met. About thirty-four years old, he had lovely, creamy skin and abundant, soft, auburn hair over almost all of his muscular body except upon the very top of his head. There he was beginning to bald in a way that looked totally Roman and totally distinguished. Baldness never has bothered me, for my father was bald and as most women know, baldness is usually the mark of virility and intelligence.

He had a large, honest face that was not considered to be of the handsomest sort by the standards of those times—rather a reversal of my situation—and he had wonderful, reddish-brown eyes that entranced me from the very first moment I looked into them. Almost exactly my height, he outweighed me by at least forty pounds—all of which was muscle and bone. When I first met him he was wearing a beautifully-worked bronze lorica that fit him like a glove and emphasized his deep chest and powerful arms. I can still remember how I felt myself go weak in the knees when he smiled at me and touched my hand. From that moment on, for all intents and purposes I was his. A true gentleman, he never pushed me, but I fell anyway, and I fell hard. It was not long before we were lovers.

He had not been born into a particularly famous family, being an Italian from the farming country on the Adriatic coast near Brindisium. In that regard, a Roman of the upper classes might think that I had somehow lowered myself by becoming involved with him. I knew, for example, that Messalina felt that way until she knew him better and saw how his actions contrasted with those of many others of her countrymen. She finally came to realize that his only fault was that he was not very rich, but to her that was still a serious shortcoming. It was certainly one I could overlook. I could fall for a poor man, so long as he *was* a man.

And when I did fall down with him it was not in youthful heat but something far better—something that will stay undefined by anything more than that old, familiar word, which is love. It was a deep, abiding love, too, and one that grew rather than lessened, as the troubles came. At first, though, our happiness, though sufficient, was less than profound. We were each very well pleased with the other's looks. We were mature enough to know what we had found, and yet each of us was playful, willing, and skilled enough to be content the other as few are able to do.

So the second reason I don't want to call him by name is obvious: that I lost him to death, and the memory of him is such that the repetition of his name—silly perhaps to you—is fraught with pain for me. Is that not reason enough to leave you with "my lover" and all the simple nouns and pronouns which for him must suffice?

I cannot even elaborate on him or our relationship much because of the feeling I have that to do so violates something very personal. Let it be enough for me to say that we soon had our own little house in town and our own little circle of friends. We forged our own secret endearments.

He was about three years older than I and bore upon him the scars of many battles in which he had fought. I recall that he was the third or fourth highest-ranking officer in the town, his modern equivalent being something akin to a Major in charge of military intelligence. As such, he was the senior officer in charge of the garrison's detachment of scouts, and his duties had often taken him beyond the frontier on reconnaissance, spying and diplomatic missions into Germany. From him I learned some German as well as many other things of interest that later proved useful to me.

In case one wonders, I should note that even though I loved him, I kept from him most of my secrets, including those concerning my weapons of which at that time I had only three: a .45 pistol, a .45 derringer, and a .22 automatic rifle. I would have taken along one of the .308's and a sawed off shotgun, but at the time I left Rome I thought that would be overdoing it, and I didn't want to be burdened with the extra weight and bulk of them and their ammunition. As things worked out, of course, the roadway north had been as safe as one could have wished it to be and even the guns I carried seemed to be constant nuisances.

I did show him how my radio worked even though like most people I ever showed it to he didn't really believe me when I told him that I was using it to send signals to Rome. Nor did I tell him about the airplane, time travel, modern life and all the rest, and I modified the stories of my childhood so that they would be credible enough to him. I showed him the tattered magazine pictures I still had with me, and spoke with him of all manner of wonderful things. In the privacy of our home I showed him how to unzip my pants and proudly I paraded myself before him in my modern underwear. It was all very wonderful.

He worshiped the ground I walked on. Like the great coconspirators of the heart we were, we quickly fashioned a very intense private life for ourselves, knowing that somehow it would not—or could not—last. And we were right.

After about a month and a half-- which is to say, in early December when we should have been half way home according to our earlier plans—Messalina (who lived next door to us) became very ill with a serious disease that the local physician could neither diagnose nor treat. She wasted away over a two-week period but then slowly improved until she became well enough to travel. Her fiancé was given a six-month's furlough, and accompanied by him and after many tearful farewells to me, she went back to Italy.

Naturally, I did not go back with her. I was in love, and for the first time in my life I was pregnant. My birth control pills had somehow failed me—either that or life was trying to assert itself in spite of the pills. The pregnancy did not distress me at all, and in fact we were happy about the coming child even if we didn't know what would become of us. He asked me to marry him, and of course I agreed. He wrote home for his parents' blessing—a mere formality--and we laid our little plans for the future.

But then I got sick in the same way that Messalina had been sick. Each day was a little worse until finally I was so sick and so weak that we were all certain that I was dying. Soon I was too ill to travel—which was very ill indeed. It was that bad.

I was not able to hold food down, and I had constant, severe headaches accompanied by a completely immobilizing lassitude. My lover was with me almost constantly. He seemed to suffer as much as I did.

To make a long story short, I radioed my predicament to Mark from my bedside on the night of the full moon in what must have been early January. He reminded me that it was possible that I was not sick at all but rather that I was being poisoned—something which was instantly obvious to me even though I had not thought of it until just that moment.

The army doctor who had been treating me had not even mentioned that possibility to me. I realized through the haze of my suffering that if I were being poisoned he might be well aware of the plot—if not its agent. Indeed, in my weakened condition I realized the awful myriad of possibilities almost immediately, and suspected everyone—including my lover—of trying to kill me.

Primarily I suspected Propea since it was she who had the most ready access to my foods and medicines. I had her boil my water and cook my food, but if the medicines I had been given were themselves tainted, how could she know?

On the following afternoon I sent Propea away for the evening, telling her quite truthfully that I wanted to say good-bye to my paramour a final time. She did not question my judgement, and, weeping sorrowfully herself, she kissed me on the forehead and I thought, *The Kiss of Death.* Then she put on her boots and furs and went out into the oncoming snowstorm to spend the night next door. When my man came in from his duties about an hour later, we were alone.

It was at the very door of death, then, that I told him of Mark's and my suspicions. He was appalled—particularly when he realized that even he himself was not above those suspicions. He held me close and wept as only a mature man can weep, and he swore to me by every oath he could that if it were so he certainly had no part in it. Tearfully, though, he confessed that his superiors had ordered him to keep tabs on me and to report to them anything of interest that he might learn—which he had done.

By that time I was so close to death that I could not care, it seemed, whether or not he had been either the poisoner or a spy of the legate. As he wept, though, and put himself upon oath, and professed his love for me, I was so deeply moved that I too, wept some, but I was too weak to put my arms around him and hold him to my almost lifeless breast.

So it was that on that very night, without the slightest hesitation he went out into the driving snowstorm and came up with an escape plan for us that depended upon no one other than himself to carry out. In just an hour or two he obtained a two-horse sleigh, travelling furs, food, cash, and extra hay. He wrote a letter of resignation that he left with his clerk which had enough false information to mislead any pursuers, and he got a fellow officer to fill in for him for the next day's duties.

When he returned to our house he scribbled out a note for Propea and loaded into the sleigh only those of my things that he thought were most important. My death-lethargy was so profound that I was little help to him. I tried to stop him as he worked.

"It's no use," I whispered to him when he came to me. "Let me die in peace here in our home."

"You will not die, you cannot die, my Goddess, so long as I can prevent it," he said as he held me with a calm assurance that he did not really feel. "Our lives are as one. I shall not live without you. I must do what I think is best."

He continued the hurried packing. We forgot to take several things, including one of my money-belts and all of my toiletries, my famous tank suit, and half my ammunition. That done, he came back and lifted me up as if I were a feather and carried me out into the cold. Gently he put me in the sleigh and tucked me in under a fur robe. It was incredibly dark outside. Huge flakes of snow poured down out of the sky into the little pool of light given off by our shaded lantern. The bearskin robe was covered with snow even before we pulled away from that snug little house where we had shared so many happy hours during the previous weeks. I would have been sad, but I hardly knew what was going on.

In leaving like that, he gave up everything—his career, his family, his country, and, ultimately, his life—to save me. He was not my poisoner.

****

XXI

Into Germany

Not trusting either his own people or my servant, we crossed the Rhine River bridge and headed northeastward into Germany, not stopping until late the next afternoon when we were half-frozen and deep in the territory of the Hermandurii. Braving the cold wind, he built a large survival shelter of fallen tree limbs and fir boughs. When he got through, it was big enough for both of the ponies, a small fire-pit, and the sleigh. The shelter saved our lives, for soon the storm gave way to a true blizzard that snowed us in for several days. During that time we mostly stayed under the bearskins and slept. He cooked for us and tended the increasingly hungry horses as best he could. The snow got so deep that we couldn't go outside to relieve ourselves. The place might have stunk terribly, but because of the piles of snow that covered us, our tiny fires, and the body heat of the horses and ourselves, we stayed reasonably warm. I started getting better almost immediately.

On the fourth day we had to leave despite the depth of the snow, for we were out of hay and grain for the horses as well as food for us. Hindsight being clear, we probably should have killed the horses and eaten them, but as we were still too close to the frontier for comfort, my man thought it would be best if we continued to move farther east. I was in no condition to argue, much less to walk.

It took him half a day just to dig us out and get ready to leave, and when we finally got going the drifts were so deep that the horses could make little headway along the forest road. At midday we came upon a young deer struggling through the snow, and to my lover's amazement, I shot it with my .22, mortally wounding it from about sixty yards. He had never seen me use my guns before, but he knew what they were and hadn't forgotten to bring them along. As I have said, unfortunately he had left half of my ammunition behind.

That night we made a miserable, cold camp. I was still very weak and thought that I was getting sick from something else. From the slimy, freezing deer hide I tried to make a pair of snowshoes, but my hands couldn't take it, and such work takes more time and knowledge than I possessed. The horses were beginning to show signs of quitting, and when a horse quits, it stops working and waits for death.

We struggled along like that for a couple more days before being captured by a small, pathetically ignorant and dirty tribe of Germans. Had I been well, we might have been able to fend them off, but under the circumstances we had to take our chances with them or die in the forest. I have no doubt that my lover could have survived out there on his own, but he would not abandon me.

So it was that the little tribe plundered us and held us as prisoners for a week or two until they sold us to a larger tribe for what they judged was our hostage value. For all of their abuse of my lover and their looting of our possessions—most of which we got back later—they probably saved our lives. At the time of our capture it was about ten degrees out—so cold that our wine was frozen solid and our hungry horses were covered with ice. At least they fed us and kept us together in a warm house with their livestock and slaves. It was an altogether miserable and filthy place. To top off our sadness, although I had been feeling much better, I had a miscarriage. All is as God wills.

After about a month of privation, crowding and filth, we and most of our stuff were given over to a still more powerful chieftain whose much larger holding lay some thirty miles farther East. There we were treated better and were eventually able to bargain for our own freedom.

The Germans were not awed by my companion, for in their eyes he seemed to be just a deserter running away with a woman—possibly the wife of another man. Among Germans adultery was a forbidden thing punishable by death. They also refused to give him any credit for being an equal to them, much less their superior. No matter how often they interrogated him, their preconceived notions prevented them from believing that he held high rank in the Roman army.

In their opinion, too, he was obviously a coward, for circumstances had forced him to submit first to capture and then to various humiliations at the hands of the members of the two smaller tribes. He had submitted to indignities, of course, in order that he might live and thereby be able to protect me. Under any other circumstances he would have gladly chosen death to servility. Because it went so against his nature, I took my lover's obedience to his enemies as added proof of his devotion to me. "Better love hath no man than he would give up his life for his friend," it is written—a Greek sentiment, no doubt. A true Roman of the old, staunchly republican school, my man would rather have given up his own and his friend's lives together rather than to compromise his honor and his pride.

Eventually the Germans began to notice me as a person in my own right—a person distinct not only from him, but also from all of them. Initially I had been thought of as a sick, foreign woman. As I regained my health and began to converse in German, and as people in the chieftain's holding paid more attention to me, I began to be treated with more deference. For one thing, by their standards, too, I was held to be a beautiful woman. I wasn't looking too bad at that time. I had gotten back most of my health and most of my color. Due to the poisoning and the scanty rations we had been given during our captivity, I had lost almost thirty pounds. I hadn't been that slender since I was fifteen.

In addition to the advantage that my looks conferred, our captors could somehow tell that I was more like them than like a Roman. They came to realize that I was not even a European, for they had never met my type before. As rough and as pigheaded as they were, all of them had treated my radio and my guns with surprising care and respect, it being obvious even to them that those things could be broken easily. They also assumed correctly that the guns were weapons, and so they were kept from us.

I came to be regarded as someone akin to a captured queen and my lover to be my servant or bodyguard. It suited our purposes to let them think that, for it seemed to offer us greater protection from their strange ways than we might otherwise have had. Like the Britons, they held the occasional woman leader in high esteem. Their own women, I might add, were widely thought to be the most warlike in all the world.

Some of the Germans suspected that I was a barbarian princess from the outer reaches of Ireland or Scotland, but careful examination of my possessions outside my presence had made them reject that theory. Eventually they decided that I should be publicly examined by a group of their priests and priestesses in front of a large gathering in the main hall of the holding. Word duly went out that such an event was planned, and in the following days a crowd of newcomers arrived for the meeting.

I'm not sure if I could ever tell what the theological basis of their religion was, and I sometimes wonder if any one of them could, either. There was some sort of understanding of a single god who was referred to in a method that could be translated as *"Of Course!"* It was as if no question of the existence of the god was possible—God As Is: indefinable, inexorable, and yet with a thousand fragmented faces of demigods, gods, spirits, and nymphs. They did not appear to have any sort of universal truth—at least not one they tried to force on one another at spear point. We use the modern term *"theological"* loosely, I suppose. It certainly appeared to me that their *theo* was not logical.

At any rate, their religious practices were founded in part on the use of a certain mushroom that grew only in the forests of Northern Europe. The universal use of it imparted to that region a major spiritual bond that was not, in my opinion, particularly good. Although its use commonly evoked a feeling of unity with nature, apparently it also induced bizarre hallucinatory effects emphasizing visions of brutality, murder and cannibalism. Perhaps those characteristics were already present in the Teutonic human material waiting to be liberated. I don't know. What I do know was that there seemed to be a fascination with human skulls and the implements of death, primarily the javelin and the battle-axe.

The use of the mushroom, although purportedly jealously guarded by the would-be clergy, was universal, albeit seldom abused through frequent tripping. The Germans could have been wrong, but they believed that its excessive use— which is to say, more than once or twice a year—led to insanity and death. Their explanation for the behavior of the men among them who were the most violent and death-obsessed was that they "had eaten too often of the earth." These were the men who often had ritual scars covering large portions of their bodies and who were always spoiling for a fight. Such blood-and-guts warriors were widely admired, if not widely emulated, throughout the holdings.

For most people, then, the use of the Germanic

mushroom was a "special occasion" drug. For a wedding, childbirth, a death, or a big, pitched battle, a man or woman might eat a mushroom, and apparently, there was no such thing as a small dose. It was all or nothing. At all other times, though, they were big beer and mead drinkers. Men and women alike loved to get drunk and sing songs. Again: what changes?

When the formal examination was finally held one evening in late winter, a council of some 15 priests, priestesses, and augurs questioned me in the presence of the chieftain and his assembled "lords" and "ladies"—and whoever else could fit himself in the great hall. As he was so fluent in German, my lover acted as my translator.

It was a packed house, with kids in the rafters and dogs on the floor. For that special occasion, one of the priests and one of the priestesses ritually took the magic mushroom as the lengthy proceedings began. They sat on two special chairs on either side of a low, raised dais from which they could witness our faces as we stood before the entire assembly and responded to questions. On the surface of things, it was all very formal. Despite all the trappings of power and religion that our captors were trying to present, it was obvious to me that whole meeting was little more than an entertainment to break the end-of-winter doldrums and give all of the self-important "lords" and their womenfolk something to do. In a sense, it was like court before the advent of television.

The chieftain or headman of the country was himself not a particularly gifted or imposing man, and I suspect that he had been elected by the erstwhile nobility for that very reason. Possibly out of due regard to his own rather tenuous grip on power, he carried out his offices with a great deal of caution and tact. In the event of war, undoubtedly some stronger, more ruthless leader would have shouldered him aside.

The inquiry followed a feast to which we had not been invited, and when the tables were cleared of all but apples, breads, and beer, we were brought in.

I wore a long, simple, blue German woolen dress tied snugly against me with yellow ribbons that encircled my midsection and criss-crossed between my breasts. My hair was clean and fell in gentle waves down my back, and on my feet I wore warm, plum-colored felt slippers.

My lover wore what was left of his Roman uniform. It

consisted of the beautiful bronze lorica and his leather-clad kilt, but it was all rather tattered-looking. He was, however, the sort of man whose nobility of mind and strength of character would have shown through even the humblest clothes.

The case was: "Who are these people and what shall we do with them?" It began with a presentation of statements and a recitation of facts given by a man who was the equivalent of a state prosecutor. With a lot of help from my lover, I could follow him well enough to realize that intellectually most of our captors were little more than children.

Like police-types throughout the ages, our accuser's theme seemed to be that we were guilty of something—probably spying— even if he couldn't tell everybody what crime it was. He concluded that in all good judgement, we should be killed or at least sold off into slavery in the East somewhere. I almost laughed.

For some reason I did not feel at all threatened by the situation. My lover did, though, because he thought that we might be separated or that I might be killed. He could not see through and beyond the event—a limitation that hampered his enjoyment of it.

After the cop-type fellow spoke, an older, graver man rose and presented our case as though he was serving as our appointed counsel. This was like a smoky scene out of *Gulliver's Travels*. He had never even spoken with us.

Finally we spoke for ourselves—or rather I spoke to them through my lover since it was I who they wanted to understand and to judge. I stood up as I spoke. He sat beside me in a high-backed chair and translated.

I forget what I told them, but it was a fantastic rendition of the truth that kept them spellbound for over an hour. I told them that I had come from across the seas in the belly of a great bird that roared as it flew and that landed on the water like a great duck. I told them how my home country had been settled long before by people from all over the world—blacks from Africa, Asians, Britons, Italians, Scandinavians, and even Germans—and that ours was a powerful nation. I said that even with a small army we could defeat all the armies of Rome and all the tribes of Germany in a single, pitched battle. I heard loud, angry objections from the small groups of men with the scars.

I told them how the loud-roaring bird had landed on the edge of the sea and how we had been first befriended by a Roman and how we were then attacked by bandits who we had killed with our thunderbolts. I described the journey to Rome and thence to Gaul and Mogontiacum.

They listened so intently that I knew that most of them believed me. I paused for effect.

"And it was there that I met this man," I continued, putting my hand upon his shoulder, "who is the best of all the Romans: better than the legate, better than their emperor, better than their bravest gladiator. And here he is held in low esteem? Who could be so base as to close his eyes to greatness? But perhaps I am blind, perhaps my love for him makes me overlook some fault, some deep flaw in his character." I stepped away from him and made an histrionic gesture in his direction. "Well, if any man or woman here can find fault in him, let him do it now."

The great hall was silent but for the sobs of a few women made maudlin by beer and my tale. From the back of the room there was a stirring. A huge, blond man came forth, a man whose thick arms were covered in ornamental scars, and whose face and clothes proclaimed him to be a member of the Brotherhood of Death. It was obvious that he was one of those who had eaten of the earth too often.

"I hear that this man is a coward!" he said belligerently.

I had expected that. My man stood up and stepped forward without hesitation to face him, relieved, I think, by the simplicity of what was before him: kill or be killed.

"No real Roman officer is a coward," he said calmly in a loud voice heard by all.

The men, eager that the evening's spectacle should include at least one fight, began to clamor like boys on a playground.

But then from the chair where the Priestess of the Earth sat came a firm voice, her first speech of the night.

"Stop!" she said in a resonant, imperious tone that silenced the hall. She rose from the chair and came across the dais to where we stood. About 50 years old, she was thin and almost as tall as I. She had lovely, gray-blonde hair and sky-blue eyes that were alive in the torchlight. She was wearing a long dress of black wool from which were suspended hundreds of thin silver disks the size of dimes that made musical sounds when she moved. She went first to my lover and looked into his eyes for a minute. Then she looked in mine in much the same way that both Aemelia the Gaul and Aechelus the physician had. She was very drugged and very intent. Finally she turned to our challenger and to all the men who were on their feet and said, "Sit down!" and the entire assemblage sat right down like well-trained schoolchildren. Then she spoke to them:

"It is as she says. Other than his being a Roman, there is not fault in this man.

"And as to her," she said of me, "she does not lie, and the things she has told us are true!"

A hundred voices began speaking all at once, and my lover stood transfixed and dumb, for he had thought my tale so incredible that even the Germans would disbelieve it.

Then the Priest of the Sky rose and came forward, and he, too, silenced the crowd with a word. He examined each of us in the same way that the Priestess of the Earth had, and pronounced the same conclusion. He declared that our persons should be held inviolate among the Hermandurii, and that no man should offer to fight my lover, nor any woman insult me in any way. There were general nods of assent.

Then he bad me continue and I did, knowing that I was home free. I told them of how my friend had fallen ill and how she had recovered enough to return home. I spoke of my own illness and how I grew weaker and weaker. In a hushed voice, I spoke of how Death had been reaching out to claim me, and how I had contacted my fellow countryman when the moon was full by using the magic box. I told them how he reminded me of the possibility of poisoning, and they all shook their heads when they thought of the perfidy of Romans. I told them the story of our flight from Mogontiacum and of our struggle in the forest snowdrifts.

Then I told them of their kinsmen who had captured us and treated us as if we were animals, plundering our meager possessions like mere bandits and disdaining as a coward a man who was as brave as any in Europe.

Somehow when I spoke, a great maudlin pathos moved through the ranks of my listeners, and as my story ended, many of the men and women were weeping and blubbering. By acclamation it was agreed that we would be set free and that we would be given back our possessions. My magic box—my radio—was brought forth and it and my guns and most of my small store of ammunition were restored to me also, being piled on the floor at my feet. The headman decreed that we should be allowed all rights of passage and protection that the Hermandurii could provide.

After that had been decided in our favor, we all took a much-needed break. More beer was brought in and we were welcomed as friends. Finally, and still not yet sated, they bid me to speak again, and I told them I would. As many of the torches had burned low or gone out, there was an eerie, campfire-like atmosphere in the hall. The place was packed and I stood quietly upon the dais between the thrones of the Priest of the Sky and Priestess of the Earth. My lover sat again in the large chair beside me so that I could rest my hand upon his shoulder as he continued to translate for me where necessary. The effect of it was purely magical, for our voices melded into a sort of spoken duet.

When all was ready for us to begin and the servants had filled the drinking horns and skulls and found themselves seats, I turned to the priest beside me and asked in a loud voice of what they would have me speak. He said "Truth!"

So I turned to the priestess and said loudly to her that Truth was too bitter a pill for many to swallow, and that now when we were all so content to be with one another, I should not want to introduce discord. She said that anyone present who could not face the truth was free to leave before I spoke it. No one left.

Then in deference to the secular leadership, I turned to the headman, who was also there upon the dais behind us. Loudly I said to him that Truth was often a matter of interpretation. I asked him if I had his leave to speak the truth as I knew it? He said I should, repeating the priestesses' admonition that anyone was free to leave, and showing by his demeanor that he was proud to have been deferred to.

Then I spoke to them for another hour, prophesying the future of the German people as best I could remember it, and embellishing it where I couldn't. I told them of the future of Rome and of France and of England. Without belaboring dates or speaking too much of religion, I told them of the rise and fall of nations as if I was in some sort of a trance during which I had revelation after revelation. Through it all, I flattered them and led my story of their descendants' future through almost 2,000 years of triumphs and tribulations. That, I told them, was as far as I could see.

My stories made sense to them in that they could readily understand how their national characteristics might lead them into the sorts of accomplishments and disasters that I prophesied. They were proud of the artists, inventors, soldiers, and statesmen that I told them their descendants would be, and they beamed when I spoke of how their distant offspring would someday build iron ships and airplanes and great factories and cities. And I told them about wars that would last for hundreds of years and of how the nation would so long resist its ultimate, albeit brief, unification. They themselves could see how people of their blood might well blindly follow first a chancellor, then a king and then a criminal dictator and his henchmen. They could imagine how, together with all the other Germanic people, such people as themselves might attempt to take on all the world in a time when men could fly and hurl thunderbolts. They could imagine great ships of iron that would fight upon and beneath the seas, and great battles upon the land. And I told them how after all the centuries of disunion and war among them, there would come a short time of union, power, and war. I said final war would end in a great defeat after which Germany once again would be divided by those against whom it had waged its wars of aggression.

But that division, too, I told them, would someday end even as all things end and even as my story and their story would end. Being a prophet is fun—except in your own country.

****

XXII

Through the Mountains & The Forests

My narratives astounded my lover as much as they did our barbarian audience. He thought I had overstepped the bounds of credibility so far that our captors-turned-hosts might be offended and turn upon us. On the other hand, he had heard the testimony of mushroom eaters and knew how purposefully mysterious I had been with him. He, too, felt the powerful and repeated resonance of truth in my words.

I myself was rather surprised by my ability to address the crowd, for I had never been much of a public speaker. My words seemed unforced and natural, though, and even my fumbling in both German and Latin added to my message, for it gave a natural series of pauses and repetitions that had an unusual and emphatic cadence that I enjoyed.

When I finished speaking the headman pronounced the assembly closed, and we were immediately given a small, wood-walled room that was sumptuous by comparison to the various cells and lofts in which we had previously been confined. Servants brought in those of our belongings that had been recovered.

By that time it was well after midnight, and though we were very tired, we were exhilarated, relieved, and alone together at last. We disrobed in the chilly air, washed ourselves in the basins of warm water that had been brought in for us, and got into bed together.

In the light of the single candle, my lover held my face in his hands and studied my eyes, looking to find in them the hallmarks of truth that the priestess had found. But he did not have The Sight, and even if he had, he probably wouldn't have been able to see much: Love is blind.

"Who are you—really?" he asked at last.

"I am the woman who loves you forever," I answered him with a vehemence that surprised me.

But I knew what he meant. When he asked me who I

really was, I knew that with this man there would be no more holding back, no more trying to protect myself by not letting him know the truth.

"And what I told them tonight," I continued, "was all true— at least allegorically—and the prophecies that I told them will all come to pass.

"If the gods allow us world enough and time—which I fear they may not—I shall answer your every question, for there is nothing about me that I shall keep hidden from you if you ask: not one thing. Only be careful what you ask. "

I held him close a moment as I wept with tears of joy. I looked into his mature and slightly lined face, and kissed him gently. As I did, the slight, electric, offsetting truth came in upon his breath. Suddenly I knew that nothing so beautiful as the love we had for one another could long endure.

More than that, I knew that it would be he—my beautiful and virile man, my savior and my companion—who would not long endure. I knew that he was going to die soon. I knew it as surely as I know that I shall type the next word after this one.

This was not the mature premonition of an adult-- which is not a premonition at all, but a weighing of probabilities and a consequent feeling of dread. No. I knew at that moment that the lady in Gaul was right. I had at least something of The Sight, and I knew that it was a beautiful and terrible gift, just as ours was a beautiful and terrible fate.

So I cried like a baby in his arms. I cried with joy because I had him and with sadness because I would lose him. I cried, in short, because I was alive and I knew it, and I was happy that my life could be so full and I could know such tender love and complete devotion.

He stroked my hair and held me close and—at my urging—made love to me while I cried. Then, safe at last if only for the moment, we slept entwined in one another's arms.

In the days that followed, as we traveled east by sleigh through the dense forests, winter clung to the earth despite the approaching spring. Occasionally we were mired in icy, wet tracks and had to get out and walk, and sometimes when there was freezing rain, we hacked along on paths lumpy with solid sheets of ice. For the most part, we traveled alone, and in spite of

238 THE EVANGELINE MANUSCRIPT

the apparent hardships, we were happy just to have our freedom, our health, and each other. It helped, too, that we at least had some money, a few of our possessions and our sleigh, not to mention plenty of food, dry clothes, boots, and furs.

For countless hours we talked about our favorite subject—ourselves.

He asked thousands of questions, taking everything I said as true no matter how fantastic my answers and explanations might seem. He was open-minded enough to accept practically anything as possible, even travel in time. He was intelligent enough to be able to probe for elucidation and verification. Having been raised in an age when fantastic stories, myths, and legends were the stuff of daily life, it was easier for him to believe me than it had been for me to believe Mark or—I would imagine—for you to believe me.

We sometimes stayed in lovely cabins by ourselves, cuddling against the cold in front of open fires. Other times found us well-fed guests in the beautiful, fitted log lodges of German headmen who had heard of our coming from runners who went out before us to warn of our inviolability.

We lived as people are seldom given to live—joyous in the fullness of the day. So thoroughly were we sharing ourselves with one another that I found myself longing to be pregnant once again, and that added yet another flavor to our lovemaking. Prior to meeting him, I had never really wanted to have a baby.

Even though we were headed a generally southeastward direction toward the Danube, our travel was rather aimless at first. We could have stayed among the Hermandurii, but thought that we might once again find ourselves at odds with them. With them, things could get nasty quickly. Therefore we traveled east through the lands of the Marcomanni, who also permitted us to pass without hindrance.

What few plans we made for the future were necessarily vague. In considering the possibility of returning to Rome or to his parents' estate in Eastern Italy, we had to assume that there would be some sort of proscription against us both. We decided that we would write letters of explanation from the border, detailing the reasons why we had left Mogantiacum and asking that his family do what it could to get any bans against us lifted. On the other hand, we were not exactly desperate to go back into the Empire, pardon or no pardon.

Since crossing the Rhine, we had thought of ourselves as stateless persons without countries. We had no friends or family to whom we might turn for aid. There was, of course, Mark, but I had last contacted him on the night before we left the frontier. After I got the radio set back from the Hermandurii, I had to wait until a full moon to try to transmit, but when I did there was no answer. I signaled the letter *M* over and over monotonously in the night. Since no answer came, I could not be sure if the set still worked or if Mark was still trying to listen, or, for that matter, whether he was still alive. It seemed logical enough that if someone had tried to kill me, that person might also have wanted to kill Mark.

Who would such a person be, I wondered? Tiberias's henchman, Sejanus? Or could it have been the other way around? Could it be that Sejanus wanted to prevent Mark and I from meeting Tiberias or from supplanting his power in any way? I didn't like the man, but no one else did either—including, it was said, his own wife, his mistress, and his parents.

The other possibilities were endless. That neither my army doctor nor anyone else in Mogantiacum had diagnosed poison made us suspect a group plot to get rid of me.

The only regrets that my lover ever expressed were these: that he had not recognized what was going on earlier, that he had not been able to write to his parents on the night we left, that in his haste he had overlooked one of my money-belts, and that he hadn't tortured Propea to find out what she knew. The Romans were big believers in torture. I was not convinced of its efficacy.

We often thought about Propea, and wondered whether or not she was in on a plot and what had become of her since we left. I actually missed her, too, for I had been fond of her. I knew, however, that if I ever found out she had betrayed me, I would kill her. That was The Code: I owned her and her loyalty was supposed to be beyond subornation.

Oddly enough, though, both my lover and I admitted that had I not been ill, we might never have come to such a complete understanding with one another. We could have gotten married and had a family and grown old together without ever having been so truly honest or so deeply in love with one another. Couples do it all the time.

We tried not to think of the future, contenting ourselves with life in the present and spending long hours talking about who we were and how the Fates had brought us together—talks that more often than not ended up in sweet lovemaking and blissful sleep.

Eventually, too, we declared ourselves married and performed our own ceremony one night when we were alone in a mountain cabin. Marriage is not a secular thing, though, is it? This was something that we thought about as we knelt together before the small fire as the rain pounded down outside.

To whom—or what—did we pray? We prayed to God. My husband was a worshiper of Mithras. I had been a Presbyterian, but what did that mean in 28 A.D.? But my tattered Christianity and his religion were practically indistinguishable. Both of us shared the same general beliefs in matters of basic morality—and mortality. Both of us were Deists and thought of the various myths of our respective societies as allegorical. We also had begun to understand and be aware of a myriad of wood nymphs, spirits, and goblins that surrounded us. Who could pass through the Bavarian forest in a sleigh and on foot and not sense them? The horses certainly could. Who could have been raised in religious families, seen the things we had seen and experienced the things we had experienced, and still be an atheist? Certainly not us! So we prayed, and held hands, and practiced to our satisfaction our polymorphous religion. By all that was holy we were married.

Life was for the living, and tomorrow was a possibly dangerous place that did not bear thinking about too much. When I did think of making some plan, though, I found myself thinking of the Short and of how, bereft of fuel, it was useless. With fuel we could have flown away—but where or, for that matter, when?

Before we reached the Danube, we had to give up the sleigh and ride horses or lead pack donkeys, for the roads finally thawed and turned to mud. Without either pavement or dry weather, carts were quite useless. We were not disheartened, for we still had some silver and gold, we had our supplies, we had each other, and spring was arriving.

Around what must have been the first of April, we arrived near what must be modern-day Linz. There we stayed for several days in a fortified town that was maintained as an armed camp against the Romans and their allies who themselves had a camp somewhere just across the river.

The German military commander there welcomed us into his quarters with a show of transparent generosity and tried to keep us amused and impressed by treating us to constant displays of his men's athletic and military ability.

Our movements were politely restricted. The fact that my husband was a Roman officer made our presence very awkward, for although we came with good recommendations and he was purported to be a renegade, he nevertheless could well have been a spy with a good cover story. He was, after all, an experienced intelligence officer who spoke fluent German, and it was second nature for him mentally to survey military fortifications and terrain features.

All along the frontier things were tense, and it was obvious that there were many in the garrison who wished to expel or kill us because he was a Roman. Others probably wanted to do away with him out of caution.

On our very first night there, the moon was full and I tried again to raise Mark on the wireless—and succeeded! The signal dots and dashes came in well and as my lover watched with rapt attention, I keyed out and received messages through several long hours. It was a laborious process since I was so slow, and Mark and I made many, many mistakes. It was actually rather hard to remember how to communicate in English, since neither of us had used it in seven or eight months. Sometimes we lapsed into Latin, but at any rate we finally adjourned our efforts just before dawn when we were too tired to go on.

We kept our messages short and to the point, as in his *"Told by Claudius you ran off with a deserter."*

To which my response was something like, *"I think I was poisoned. Almost died. He took me away to Germany. Saved my life."*

He agreed to tell Claudius that I was still alive and that my lover was with me and had not in any way gone over to the Germans—nor had I, for that matter. We agreed that he should formally protest as an ambassador, being officially offended that his fellow emissary's life had been endangered. We agreed to be in touch the next night.

That adjournment gave him the time he needed to have a talk with Claudius, who was, I presume, duly impressed with this amazing evidence of a technology that allowed us to communicate with one another over great distances. To him it must have been obvious that we could also communicate with our homeland. What might our nation do if its favored emissaries should be killed or silenced? Our power and our safety lay in the Romans' ignorance. On the other hand, Claudius might have thought Mark was just hoodwinking him.

On the second night, our messages got right to the point:

"Claudius to investigate possible poisoning. Advises you stay put."

"Must move soon. How about gas project?"

"Going poorly. Refining equipment sent to oil seep region. I must go there to tend it. Why do you ask?"

"To be prepared for anything. I could go try to do the job, but need safe conduct for us both."

"Understand. May take time in his case. He could stay there and wait."

"I will never leave him."

Mark took a long time to reply to that.

"Understand," he signaled.

"Thought you would," I replied.

"How much does he know?"

"Everything. We are married."

He took an even longer time to reply.

"Understand. Best Wishes. "

On the third night, Mark radioed me that Claudius had arranged a full pardon for any charges that might have been proffered against my husband and said that messages to that effect would be sent to Norricum at once.

I was not sure whether or not we could trust Claudius, Tiberias, or Sejanus. For that matter, I did not know whether we could trust Mark. He might reason—correctly—that his own safety was now compromised by my having revealed everything to my husband. What, if anything, Mark might do about that I could not guess, for the possibilities were endless.

On our fourth night at Linz, a servant warned me that the headman in command of the fortress meant to take us into custody the following day. At that time we would be examined— perhaps under the influence of torture—to determine whether or not we were, in fact, spies. Being forewarned, we were able to slip away in the night with only our money, my weapons and radio, and the clothes on our backs. It could have been worse.

From the banks of the river we stole a heavy boat that was little better than a coracle, it being a dory-shaped contraption made of hides stretched over a wooden frame— probably the same sort of craft that had been used along the Danube for 10,000 years. It was so heavy that had it not been beached on a set of slick, peeled logs, I doubt if we could have launched it.

Although the locals were able to navigate such boats with apparent ease, the one we took was over 20 feet long and very beamy. We could barely manage it and were immediately swept down river and bobbed along out of control in the dark. It was very cold.

After a harrowing night on the spring-flooded, swift river—a night that seemed to last forever—we managed to land on the southern side of the river many miles downstream from Linz. We pushed the boat back out into the river and struck out southward overland.

It took us over two months to travel down to the last great escarpments of the Dinaric Alps that separated us from the Adriatic Sea—a distance of only 175 miles by air. We crossed high mountains and forded swollen rivers and creeks, camping out in the open or in caves. Using false names when we had to, but avoiding people when we could, we traveled disguised variously as peddlers, exiled Romans on holiday, and displaced persons looking for farm work. Every day was a new adventure and presented new challenges. We borrowed, begged, bought, and stole what we needed and, for the most part, we managed to travel with almost reasonable comfort.

As we had reason to think there might be treachery on Marks's or Claudius' part, we decided it best to avoid contact with the Roman authorities and their lackeys, and didn't cross over into the empire. It also happened that I was not able to contact Mark by radio during those weeks travelling down from the Danube. Although I ascribed that failure to atmospheric conditions, I knew that it might have been that he didn't chose to communicate with me or that something had happened to him.

During that time, we decided that our well being might best be served by living with Marcus in southern Mauretania. I described their situation to my husband who agreed with me that it sounded like a suitable place. At least there the climate would be warmer, and I had friends I could trust. Somehow or another we could get a place of our own where we could live out our days in the relative peace and security of that out-of-the-way land.

In the meantime we had half the Roman world to traverse were living from day to day on the edge of disaster. All it would take would be one surprise attack, one encounter with barbarian troops, or, for that matter, one bad fall or failed river crossing.

Once again I became pregnant. It's no wonder, for by that time my health was completely restored and we made love with a frequency and an urgency that was astonishing. As we were almost constantly on the move, we quickly got used to outdoor lovemaking, and found that the late spring in the mountains of Austria was a perfect setting for such practices.

Sometimes we traveled on foot; sometimes we had horses or only a pack animal. For one reason or another we seemed to lose animals almost as soon as we acquired them. The main reason, of course, was theft. We developed a rather carefree attitude about having our animals stolen from us while we slept—and a similar attitude about stealing other people's stock.

As we approached the last mountains between us and the Adriatic, though, our attitude about losing our pack animal changed when we came into possession of a very cute, surefooted donkey which we had actually purchased—not stolen— from a farmer. I was terribly fond of her, for as we traveled she never complained, and she amused us by her antics— especially when we came to even the smallest of streams, which she hated and refused to cross unless she was blindfolded. It was her quirk and was another man's undoing.

That undoing—and ours— came when we were high up in the mountains and uncertain of which pathways we should follow toward the main pass that was said to be the only one in that particular locality which would allow us to cross over onto the Adriatic or western side. We weren't exactly lost, but neither did we know our way. That was unfortunate, for it was a region that was rough and rocky and wild— a region whose few inhabitants were— predictably enough— bandits. On several occasions we had been shadowed by individuals or groups of two or three, but had not been attacked. As always, we advanced cautiously and always watched our back trails, sometimes taking punishing detours in order to avoid narrow, rocky defiles where ambushes might be prepared for us. Our weapons— which my lover had learned to use— were always at hand even though we had very little .22 or .45 ammunition. Therefore, in addition to my weapons we had acquired swords, two javelins and a couple of bows with a large collection of arrows. If all of this sounds insecure and terrifying, let me say this: security is an illusion anyway, and danger adds spice to life.

Because of the elevation, it was very cool during the nights, and when we were just a few miles short of the crest we were going to attempt to climb, we made camp on an exposed, rocky knoll. There we snuggled together under our furs, weary but happy, in the lee of a circle of boulders. My husband always tried to be very careful in his selection of camping places. There was a half-moon that night, and it was lovely. We whispered endearments, and kissed, and made love. Then we dozed off.

In the middle of the night— at a time that I was supposed to be awake but wasn't— our donkey began to bray. It was obviously being led off by someone and was objecting. I sprang up, .45 in hand, and was ready to rush off in pursuit when my husband woke and held me back long enough to arm himself and to take stock of the situation.

Rather than going straight out in the direction of the donkey's noises, we slipped out of the little campsite and circled around. We were not as quiet as we had hoped to be, though, and suddenly found ourselves being rushed in the moonlight by a group of four or five men armed with clubs and short swords. They came bounding at us as quietly as they could, hoping, no doubt to take us by surprise. I was too astonished to be frightened and as I had done in Mauretania, I just stood there, frozen in place. They came on and were almost on us when my husband coolly cast a javelin straight into the foremost man and I, who had hesitated almost too long, began firing wildly in their direction with the .45. As the first one went down silently with the javelin through his neck, another screamed and threw up his hands when a couple of .45 slugs hit him. The others turned about and scampered off. My hands were shaking wildly and it was amazing that I hit anybody, but I did. Taking my left hand, my husband, sword in his other hand, led me forward in a counterattack of our own, and we raced down the trail fifty or sixty yards to where our stubborn little donkey was refusing to cross a tiny brook no wider than a cubit or two. A bandit was jerking on her lead rope, but to no avail. She had sat down on her butt, and as we came on him the thief couldn't seem to make up his mind whether he should let go of the donkey, fight, or run. His hesitation cost him his life, for my husband, having told me to reload and guard our back trail, leaped across the small stream and stumbled. Swearing fiercely, he got to his feet and cut the horribly screaming man down with a single swipe of his sword. Then he killed him with a heavy thrust to the heart.

He stepped back across the brook and nearly collapsed. Much to my dismay, he had a broken or badly sprained ankle from having landed wrong when he jumped the across.

Gathering up our faithful donkey, we made our way back up to the campsite without further trouble, my husband in pain and limping badly. We made ourselves comfortable, and I was able to go back to sleep.

In the morning we found ourselves surrounded not by a small band but by a large one numbering some thirty or forty men and boys who stood off from us at about a hundred yards in every direction. This time I was truly frightened. I thought, *This is it*, and that my life was at an end. Carefully I counted my ammunition. I had no more than twenty .45 rounds and 100 .22s. At least I had a rifle even if it was one of such an inadequate caliber.

My husband faced what lay before us with a calm and soldierly equanimity that was heartening, if not reassuring. He made a fire and started cooking us some porridge for breakfast, carefully keeping an eye on our foes and avoiding moving about in any way that would show them he was limping.

When we had stopped the night before he had selected our position so well that there was no way we could be approached without detection, and the large boulders around us gave us and the donkey some protection from arrows—

protection upon which I improved at his direction. I also tied the feet of our trusting animal and forced her to lie among the rocks. At least they could not sneak up on us by daylight. On the other hand, neither could we leave.

There were so many of them that I fully expected them to attack us within the hour regardless of the danger to themselves. I assumed that they could merely overrun us in one charge, and so I really assumed that I would soon die. I said as much to my husband.

"That is not likely," he said as he passed me my share of the porridge, "for they are cowards, And they have tasted of your gun," he added with a sweep of his hand.

We were calmly eating in full view of our foes and in sight of the bodies of the two men we had killed at first the night before. They were sprawled out in two bloody heaps some forty yards away. I asked what he expected.

"First, like sensible men anywhere, they will try to negotiate with us. I would imagine that the loss of three or four men last night was enough for them."

"Four?"

"Oh, yes! Didn't you notice that you hit one of the two who got away?" he asked. "Look at that trail of blood," he said pointing out something I had not noticed—a huge bloody splatter on the side of a boulder, followed by smaller marks of blood leading off down the hill. "I think you hit him in the left shoulder or arm."

I was astounded that he could have been so observant in the dark and in the midst of such terrifying action.

"He looked like he was about twelve years old," he added callously.

I distinctly remember that at that point I got a weird feeling in my stomach and thought that I would throw up. In little over a year I had killed two men and, probably, a boy. I told him how horrible I felt.

"Not as horrible as you would have felt if they had captured you," he said grimly.

His remark was loaded with meaning. I realized that unless we could fight our way out, we might even be forced to kill ourselves rather than to submit to capture. The thought of being at the mercy of a band of men was more than I could bear.

248 THE EVANGELINE MANUSCRIPT

Under those circumstances I clearly preferred death to rape, and I would rather have died than to go on living without my husband.

"If the moment comes, and I am too cowardly," I told him, "take me to heaven with you. Do not leave me behind." I felt quite Roman at that moment of truth.

He smiled and tears came into his eyes—a most unRoman look—but he smiled at me.

"No man was ever happier," he said, "and I would not leave you behind—not to them."

Then the first arrow fell nearby, and frightened me terribly, for it hit the earth hard and stuck up. I imagined how it could just as easily have stuck into me. I almost leaped up and ran away in sheer terror, but my husband was ready and held me with just a soft touch of his hand.

"You won't let them think ill of us, will you?" he said gently.

Then the peace of God which passes all understanding descended on me. Perhaps it would be more accurate to say that it came into me from my husband's fingertips. Those men couldn't have frightened me with Greek Fire, for it was the hour of our death, and I was with the man I loved, pregnant with his child, and he was as calm as the stones about us. His question was not a question, but a command to my soul. I kissed him lightly and shook my head for him, biting my lip to keep from crying. I smiled for him my bravest smile.

"Good, my angel. Now here comes the man to parley. Get your rifle ready."

So I re-checked the little Ruger semi-automatic and prepared to shoot at a distant bowman that my husband pointed out to me.

He was about eighty yards off and was standing in plain view, arrow nocked to his longbow, which was lowered. As all of the other bandits we saw carried smaller recurve bows, it was obviously he who had fired that first shot just to show us that he could dominate the situation. The other bandits obviously thought that they were safe at that or greater distances, for if we started to fire arrows at them, given our slow rate of discharge they would be able merely to dodge them or to take cover. Alternatively, their main archer could back off and shoot at us as long as their arrows lasted. Sooner or later he would be bound to get a hit. And then another hit.

Their negotiator came forward wearing a battered, old cuirass of some sort. At his side was a sheathed sword. Sleazy looking, with long, greasy hair done in buttered, black ringlets, he stopped twenty yards from us and spoke to us, finally, in Latin. In order to hide his injury, my husband did not stand up, but lounged back eating porridge while I tried to keep a casual lookout in every direction.

The negotiator told us that we had killed his chieftain's oldest son.

The boy and his friends were thieves, he was told.

The chieftain demanded indemnity.

And what was the amount? my husband asked, explaining that we were poor people, lost travelers, but would give a gold coin for the boy and two silver coins for each of the others.

The bandit laughed and said that they wanted all of our money and then we could leave with our lives. Naturally we did not believe him. We said we had a right to be left alone.

Rights are for those who can defend them, he told us.

We could defend ours, my husband told him.

The woman—they would take the woman—the bandit demanded. My husband told him that I was a daughter of the gods, and inviolate, to which the man spat on the ground and made a series of crude sexual gestures and said that all women belonged to them and they would take me over his dead body, if necessary.

Then, with an apparently casual lifting of the arm, my husband pointed the .45 at him and shot him. The slug blew a big chunk out of the center of the man's back and pushed him backward over a rock where he flopped like a fish and died.

I was amazed at my husband's quick decision and his unerring aim. He had only shot two or three of our precious bullets before. "Why did you do that?" I asked with a grin as we dove for cover from the shower of arrows that began to fall on our position.

"What is it you say?" he said with a grin. "Oh, yes: he just 'pissed me off'!"

We laughed together a moment and he explained to me a very rational group of reasons he had shot the guy. First, he knew that he probably couldn't hit anything beyond that range and he didn't want our foes to know it. Second, he wanted to frighten off the rest, if he could. Therefore publicly, if treacherously, shooting the man had a fourfold purpose: intimidation, demonstration, practice, and murder. That was good enough for me.

Of about thirty arrows that fell about us only two or three came close. Then there was no firing at all for a short period of time.

The second volley came in much more accurately than the first, and one of the big longbow arrows hit the donkey near its throat and made it begin to panic. Another, smaller shaft hit my husband in the left arm, entering it in the main muscle area just above the elbow and passing almost all the way through. He jumped with the sudden pain of it, then turned rather white. "Break it and jerk it out," he told me, and I did. I bound up the wound.

Then I took the .22 up to a firing position I had picked out, and found that I was trembling too badly to be able to aim it. More arrows fell in about us, and I heard my husband say to me, "Please, Honey: just do it!"

So I aimed as best I could and shot first at the longbowman who had hit my donkey. I missed him twice. He seemed to look about in the air in an apparent effort to figure out what the *"whiinnngggg!"* of the passing bullets signified. Then I remembered that when shooting downhill one should aim lower than one thinks one ought. I did that and saw my third bullet strike in front of him. On my fourth shot I hit him, and he threw up the bow and screamed, then grabbed his crotch. Apparently I had hit him in the testicles or somewhere close.

I would have felt squeamish about that, but for the fact that now I hated those men--those murderers who were attacking us and who would not relent even in the face of gunfire. They were the men who had wounded my husband and who could have simply left us alone in the first place.

So with a fine, white anger and a rush of adrenaline that made my nerves steady and my eyesight improve, I shot at them deliberately round after round. I reloaded and kept on shooting. And I kept on hitting them even though it often took several misses for every hit. As I was shooting only .22 hollowpoint, except for a couple of head and upper body hits I was only wounding them. I wished I had the .308 with the scope, and I thought I knew almost how Mark had felt at the fight on the road when Ned was killed. The difference was that after the first attack of that fight he was just shooting at men who were fleeing. I was shooting at men who were still trying to kill me.

Since they were in a ring about us, no matter how many hits I was getting in on the attackers in one direction, those off in another sector were unaware of their danger and kept on shooting, standing up in plain view and launching their shafts in high arcs. I had been firing at men on the eastern and southern sides of the ring. Those on the west had more favorable terrain over which to advance and they had at least had some cover. As a group of about eight of them got to some boulders about fifty yards away, they began to shoot directly at me as I took up a standing position behind a boulder and rested the gun on it. I just knew I was going to get hit in the back by shafts falling in from the other sides, but I had to face the men on the west. They saw me and began shooting at me.

The sensation of having the short, black arrows fired straight at my face from such a distance was amazing, for they flew toward me with an incredible rapidity and flashed past me: *Death! Safety!...Death! Safety!* they came. Some hit the rocks in front of or beside me and ricocheted off somewhere. Some passed just over my head. One went right by my bare right shoulder and sliced a fine, quarter-inch deep line on it that I didn't notice until later. I hit and killed the man who had shot it at me. He yelled and grabbed at his chest and began to stagger off, then fell to his knees while the fight went on behind him. Finally he pitched forward and died.

I was not afraid—I can say that— for my blood was up. I quit worrying about getting hit in the back and felt invulnerable— which maybe I was. Had I a bayonet on the rifle I might have charged them if had I run out of ammunition, but I had not yet gotten to that point. I reloaded and was eager to get at them. I willed the bullets into them, and they were easy targets.

The barrel was hot from shooting, but it was a good gun and in ten or twelve carefully-aimed shots I had hit or grazed every one of that closest group despite the fact that they began trying to hide from me. In addition to the one whose arrow cut my shoulder, I killed two others outright with shots to the head and hit a third in the eye. The wounded ones all tried to retreat, and as they did, my husband— who had crawled forward to a position where I was unable to see him—potted another one in the back with the .45, rolling him head over heels down the hill. With that final shot the entire attack came to an end and the other bandits all backed off and regrouped in a ravine a quarter of a mile away.

Of all of those we had seen since daybreak, my husband killed two and I killed or wounded some fifteen more. It was at once horrible and exhilarating, but we paid a price, too.

When I went to my husband I found him standing up, smiling at me weakly and holding out his arms for a hug. He had been hit a second time: an arrow had entered the small of his back and was sticking out of him at an odd angle. His standing up for me was his way of trying to put a brave face on things and show me that he was not too badly hurt. It cost him a lot of pain to do that for me, but he was, after all, a soldier. He had been wounded in combat some five or six times before.

Satisfied that our attackers had all backed off, he sat down on a rock and bid me to care for our poor donkey first, which I did, bandaging it with some woolen cloth from our blanket.

I went back, then, to do whatever he asked me to do. I would have jumped off a cliff for that man.

He pointed out that I, too, was wounded, and for the first time I noticed that the wound on my shoulder had bled all over the back of my tunic before it clotted. Although it caused me a great deal of discomfort in the days that followed, I still could barely feel its sting. It was obviously not much of a wound. His in the small of the back was a different matter.

Upon close inspection we realized that we could at least hope that it was not going to prove to be fatal. Aware of the danger of blood poisoning, we knew that for better or worse the arrow had to come out right away.

It had passed through him only enough so that we could see that its small, metal tip was just under the surface of his skin about seven inches to the left of his navel. Although there was little bleeding where the shaft had entered and it hadn't hit bone, it looked bad enough, for there was surely plenty of internal damage. We knew that I would have to get it out right then.

I immediately restarted the fire, put on the little metal porridge pot full of water, and sharpened our smallest knives. I was thankful that I had at least some experience in that kind of thing— first in field dressing deer and other game and, second, in doing the dissections in Rome. I was as ready to do what I had to do as I could have been on such short notice, and I had the additional incentive of knowing that we might have to move out within an hour or two, for our foes had not quitted the field entirely. As tenacious as they were, they could be expected to come back either to collect their dead or to renew the attack.

Oddly enough, my husband admired them now, and told me that they had not been cowards at all, but brave men who we had at least temporarily daunted but not yet defeated. He did allow that they were stupid not to have backed off sooner.

So with much less effort than I expected it would take, I cut the damn arrow out by making an incision over its point, pushing the shaft forward, breaking off the head, and sliding the blood-slick shaft out backward. It was over in less than a minute, but a lot of dark blood followed the main shaft out the back.

He didn't even grimace—much less cry out—as I worked. I thought about trying to do some exploratory surgery, but I didn't have any needles or thread for suturing and wouldn't have known what to do if I found problems. I could only hope that nothing vital had been hit.

I made compresses of moss and wool, bound him about with blanket scraps, and then went out to where the man lay dead from the night before. I jerked the javelin out of his throat. It being lodged in the bones of his neck somehow or another, I was obliged to put my foot on his chest in order to be able to get it out. I wiped it off on his filthy clothes, then took it back for my husband to use as a walking stick, for he could barely stand up. I put him on the donkey and strapped on the .45. Then I picked up the .22 and made sure it was fully loaded— something I should have done before.

Before we left, though, and saying that a girl could never have enough money, he told me to go strip the dead, which I did. It turned out to be a good thing because among the bodies I found a surprising amount of silver coins and I scared up a youngster who had been left behind to spy on us. He scampered away among the rocks as I shot at him with the rifle a few times. I only had about twenty rounds left after that— too few for any serious fighting.

One of the men I searched was still alive but was unable to move at all, for he had been hit in the upper spine. I took out his own knife and plunged it into the ground beside his neck, then took his purse. I had enough killing for one day.

My husband tried to be cheerful in spite of everything. Had he not been so badly wounded, and had I not loved him so, I should have found it a most amusing picture, for we looked like beaten up versions of Don Quixote and Sancho Panza as we limped away from our little redoubt. At least we were alive, I told myself.

We turned to continue along the trail leading up to what appeared to be a gap or saddle between the tops of two mountains.

By the late afternoon we had almost reached the top of the pass but we came to an area of rocks and escarpments that stopped us. My husband could not go on, and so as night closed in we huddled together for warmth in a cleft among the rocks. I tied the donkey's lead rope to my ankle and made her stand beside us, which she was willing enough to do.

My husband bled more during the night, and although I worried and fretted, I was too exhausted to stay awake. I slept and dreamed dreams of Austrian mountain meadows, of college, of South Carolina, and of savage men shooting arrows at me.

When I woke up, my husband was already awake, looking at me with such tender affection that I began to cry. I gave him some water to drink. We knew that the end was near.

We talked rather calmly. He then told me that as soon as the second arrow hit him he knew he was going to die from it.

"A seer, when I was young— before I knew about the love that men and women feel for one another— once read my palm and did some other works of divinations which I forget. From it all, though, he told me that someday I should be a great soldier and fight in many battles. He said that I would be wounded several times but would not die of any of them until such time as the gods would grant to me a great love such as few men ever know.

"I remembered all of that and I have been, I suppose, something of a decent sort of soldier.

"But you: when I first met you I remembered the

prophecy, but I was not afraid for myself, for death is such a certain thing. I was afraid only that the prophecy might *not* come true and that you would not come to love me and that it would be one of those situations when love is unrequited.

"But you requited me, and then you almost died. Who would not have left his legion for such a love?" he asked in his deep, melodious voice.

I wept as he spoke. He put his hand on my head.

"The seer also told me that the wound that would kill me would be down there on my back. He told me that it would not be a coward's wound, and he told me that I would die in another country.

"So when the arrow hit me, I knew.

"Most men die ignominious deaths. I die a great one."

To hear him tell it made it less sad, somehow.

He held his chin up and looked me in the eye and told me that his only regret was that he could not see the future to know what might become of me and of the child of his I carried. I cried, and he comforted me.

It was a beautiful, sunny day. He wanted to die, he said, looking out toward Italy and knowing that I was safely over the pass.

We made a final effort to get around the obstructions. In doing so, we found a path to the summit, a path worn by millennia of animals and people but which we had not been able to see in the failing light of the previous, bloody day. So with him on the donkey we went on up the last half-mile or so to where a rocky meadow formed the saddle between the two mountains. There we found a stone shepherd's hut at the very crest, situated so that from it one could watch the trail up from the wild country to the East while on the West it overlooked the meadow where I picketed the donkey. From time to time I looked back down the trail behind us to see whether or not we were followed by those who had tried to kill us, but the paths were empty. Apparently they had enough.

To the west was a gorgeous panorama of lower hills and valleys. In the distance were farms, and through the summer's haze we could see—or thought we could see—a great bay of the Adriatic Sea. Sitting and reclining on our blankets at the edge of the meadow as if we were having a picnic, we rested throughout the day. I refilled our water bags at a spring and tried to nurse him as best I could.

In the afternoon, he lapsed into a coma. Without regaining consciousness, he died just after dawn the next day. I was prepared for it, of course, but I still went into shock or something. Yet I was able to do what I had to do.

With an iron hoe that I found in the shed, I spent the whole day digging a grave in the rocky soil there on the edge of the meadow. By late afternoon, I was ready to put the body in the ground. I couldn't seem to do it, but realized that I should go mad if I stayed there digging and digging as if the depth of the hole made some sort of difference.

I knew that I was not the cause of my husband's death, but what roils through the heart is not the voice of reason. I had to finish the job or lose my mind.

Finally, crying out with grief and horror as I did so, I rolled the body into the hole and covered it over. I say "it" and not "him" because like most bodies, it was no longer him—it was just a corpse. Nevertheless, I cried as I worked. Finally, after tamping the soil down with my bare hands, and covering the raw dirt with my blanket, I fainted there on top of the grave, for it was all too much to bear. I slept.

When the next morning came I awoke with a start to find that someone had covered me over with blankets and furs. Nearby sheep grazed, and not far from me sat a wiry old man with a long beard—obviously the shepherd who had covered me up.

His name was Ovinin, and although I was not proficient in it, we spoke to one another in Greek. I told him about the fight and who it was I had buried.

He took care of me. He washed and treated my shoulder wound, which had become stiff and sore, and he fed me well from a large pot of lamb stew which he kept on a low fire hour after hour. After the first day and in spite of my grief, I was ravenous.

In the afternoons when his duties with the sheep were done, he sat on a nearby hilltop and played melancholy tunes on a sort of bagpipe, the sweet notes of which drifted past me as I sat near the grave and thought about my husband day after day.

In such simple ways he helped me get over my grief

during the time I spent there in the high meadows with him. He was a wise and kindly man—an angel, perhaps. He never intruded upon my thoughts, never tried to cheer me up, and only spoke when I first spoke to him. Having lived a long life, he, too, had known sorrow and loss. Gently, gently, he helped me through those days in the Dinaric Alps.

At his suggestion, during the first week he and I built a substantial cairn over the grave. The process of working loose stones from the earth, and carrying them to the site, and fitting them together with love was a helpful one for me—as he had known it would be. At first I felt like I would gather stones forever. After a few days even my heart knew that I had piled up enough there. After all, there were not enough stones in all the world, nor enough tears, either, and so at some point, the gathering of the one and the shedding of the other had to come to an end.

So I buried my own husband and prayed over his grave stone by stone, thinking how he was becoming a monument in my own mind. He had been the quintessential Roman—far nobler than many who would have held themselves to be his betters. I think sometimes of how perfect he seemed to me: how brave, and gentle, and intelligent. In moments of candor, I think that my love for him made me blind to his faults and that it was possible that I held him in such esteem merely because he loved me so much.

I am sure, for example, that throughout the United States, there are thousands of men who might be just as tough, as brave and as resourceful as he was were they to find themselves in similar circumstances. But who that I loved so much would ever love me so much in return, I wondered?

****

XXIII

The Adriatic

On that morning when I had first awakened and met the kind Ovinin--the morning after I had buried my husband—the birds had been loudly singing, oblivious to my loss. And on that same morning I had again felt the queasiness of morning sickness. The world was going on with or without me. Life was for the living.

As the Fates would have it, once again I was not to be a mother. About a week after the shock of my loss—or because of it—I miscarried. I was plunged into despair.

The thought that I would bear his child had given both of us comfort during my husband's dying hours, just as that hope of having his flesh be born anew from my flesh had carried me through some rough moments in the days following. All is as God wills: What might I have done had I borne that child?

Ovinin helped me through the sorrow of that, too. During the second week following my husband's death—after I had recovered my strength and come at least a little way our of the stupor of depression in which I had been enmeshed—once again we went to work. We built a table-like altar of large, flat stone next to the cairn we had made over the grave. When it was finished, my new friend sacrificed a large game bird that he had snared, putting the plump little body on the pyre that the breeze soon made hot.

"A good sign," he told me, as we stood back and watched. Of what, I asked him, caught with curiosity. I had seen sacrifices performed before, but I had never felt myself to be a participant in them—certainly not in any emotional sense. It occurred to me later that sacrifices were like funerals. The process of catching the bird, piling the stones, and kindling the fire occupied the hands and made me feel I was doing something in the face of great loss.

"The sign is good," Ovinin said, "because the fire burns steadily and with sufficient heat to consume the offering whole. The gods take away that which is theirs and that which is yours—your grief—in great swallows that blow off to the southeast."

I said that as far as I knew of such things his sacrifice was successful.

"It is not I alone who sacrifices." He corrected me. "Did you not also carry the stones and wood? Did you not also hold the bird and calm him and bring him to me? Did you not also hand me the firestone and striker? It is we who sacrificed to the gods."

And who are the gods, and what significance is the direction in which the smoke is blown? I asked him.

"We do not name the gods and goddesses for fear of offending any we might leave out." he said, making me shrug my shoulders.

"No. You are a foreigner even as I am a foreigner. This very place may or may not be special to a particular god or goddess, and how would either of us know? Therefore we offer sacrifice to all of the gods—even those whose names we do not know. Together we give our thanks and ask blessings, and stand in awe as our offering is sucked away.

"And there," he said with bony arm and finger pointing outstretched across the blue mountains where the smoke was carried, "lies your destiny. I think I see it somehow, somewhere out beyond Hellas."

"Could you go with me and be my guide?" I asked him, filled as I was with respect for his wisdom and competence.

"No. I am too old for such journeys as lay ahead of you, and I belong here even as he belongs here," he said, referring to my husband. "But you are young and destined to travel far.

"We will be there with you, though, he and I. We will have gotten there ahead of you, borne by the wind. For the rest of your life, when you smell smoke of this type, you will know we are there with you and you will be here with us in peace on this mountain top."

Now who could ask for more? It was all true—or so it seemed. I would go on living. I would adjust, and I would live out my life as the Fates had decreed I would. My husband—or the strong memory of him—would come to me from time to time just as Ovinin said he would.

During my stay in the mountains, I once again established radio contact with Mark. His signal came in clearly. To my chagrin, I could almost feel his relief when he learned of my husband's death.

He wasn't callous, but his single sentence, "You have my condolences," was just not enough. It had the same ring to it as his "I understand" of two months earlier, when I revealed that I had told my husband everything.

He could have said a lot more, even by Morse Code, but he didn't. As a person will, I had a fleeting suspicion about him just like the one I had about the boy, Bilau, when Ned was killed. Just as then, though, there was no possibility that Mark had anything to do with the bandit attack. Nevertheless, his insensitivity to my loss made me feel I was really alone in the world.

On reflection, of course, that wasn't true. By that time I had friends in several different places—people who I could trust and who admired and trusted me. Most importantly, I had for a friend the old shepherd, Ovinin, to comfort me and to help me adjust to the world. He was more than just a friend. He was a protector, a counselor, and guide.

In Italy I could number among my friends the physician, Aechelus, and his two colleagues who had worked with us on the dissections. I knew I could trust Messalina, too. Not only had we been together through a lot, but by sharing her escapades with me she had made herself vulnerable—hardly the actions of a spy.

I now had friends in Gaul, not doubting for a minute that I would be more than welcome in the villa where we had stayed during the grape harvest. For that matter, uncompromised by a Roman husband, I could have traveled back among the Hermandurii. There also would always be a welcome in Mauretania with Marcus, Naadia, Constatus, and Marillia.

With Ovinin's guidance, I thought back over all of my travels and realized that during the past year, I had met hundreds of friendly people along the roads, on the ships, and in the villas and towns of Italy and Gaul as well as in the holdings of Germany. Throughout my travels, I had met people who had been open and friendly and without guile. There were hundreds along the ways I had gone who would have been glad to have me back: children, working people, old people. There are always people in need of a smile or who appreciate a story.

Even without my telling him about all those people, my friend the shepherd knew. He knew so much about me, in fact, that I often wondered whether or not he was real. I do not mean that in the sense of questioning whether or not he was an hallucination, for that was not the case. He was definitely real, but the question is this: was he really an angel?

So with him I could count more friends made in a year than many people make in a decade, and I had done what the good wife in Gaul said that I would: I brought them happiness in return for their kindnesses toward me.

Once Ovinin spoke on the subject of friendship. He told me a story that was almost exactly like one my grandmother would tell me 1940 years later. They both spoke of a woman who moved to a new town with her husband. On the very first day, she went to visit with the old woman who lived next door and asked, "How are the neighbors around here?"

"How were they where you came from?" was the reply.

"Oh, they were just terrible!" the younger woman replied.

"Well," judged the old woman, "I think you'll find that they're pretty bad around here, too!"

In telling me that story, he reminded me of my father's adage that "to have a friend one must be a friend," and so I resolved that in the months that followed I would set about remembering many of the people who had been kind to me. I would write to as many of them as I could and let them know of my gratitude. I also decided that I would write to and perhaps even visit my husband's family some day.

In short, I did not get over my grief, but I found that I had the fortitude—and the friends—with which to face life. There was strength in remembering that I had friends and strength in remembering that twice in combat I had overcome my foes.

For those who are in times of stress and inner turmoil, perhaps the best way—if not the only way—to get well is through increasing one's devotion to others. I guess that's one of the reasons why dogs who have homes seem so happy: Their duties are clear and simple. They must love their masters, know their places in the pack, and protect their turf.

Naturally, I also had to think about my enemies and potential enemies. There was, first of all, the praetorian Sejanus who reminded me of the pet snake that the boy next door used to keep. Like many men of the time, power was the only thing he thought worth pursuing. As long as he thought we could benefit him, we were safe from him, but not, on the other hand, from his enemies.

Then, too, there were many people who had been outwardly friendly and helpful but had reasons to deceive me. I had to assign these to a gray category. Foremost among them were Claudius, Propea, my husband's brother officers in Morgontiacum and—last but not least—Mark! For all I knew, he could be under the power of others who wanted to lure me back to Rome. There were an infinite number of possibilities— including even the remote one that he missed me and wanted me to come back to him.

We communicated for several nights running, and as we improved our use of code, our messages became more lengthy and fluent. There was much to do.

Although he told me that I was welcome back in Rome, I had no desire to go there, and I believed that whoever had tried to kill me would try again. Also, having seen Rome, I knew it for what it was, and knew I would one day want to see the rest of the world. In the meantime, I just wanted to do something constructive for a while and to stay in one place with a roof over my head—a place with a real bed and a bathtub. After that it would be time to follow my smoke to Greece.

I offered to go down the Dalmatian coast past the land called Illyricum to Macedonia—or at least the part of it that is now called Albania. At the oil seeps near the city of Apollonia, I could take the refining equipment that Mark had sent ahead and do what I could to make fuel. The whole project would take months, if not years, but I was looking for something to do until I was ready to travel for pleasure, and if we ever wanted to fly the Short, it had to be done. I also supposed that since I needed money, I might be able to generate some cash by producing kerosene and gasoline.

While I was in Germany, Mark had tried to hire a mining engineer in Rome, but most of the really competent miners of the time were out in the provinces—mostly in Spain— and few of them knew much about petroleum, much less how to refine it. For that matter, Mark didn't know much about it either. It was I who had learned about working with oil and I knew how to get men to work.

For one thing, Mark couldn't just explain what he wanted to accomplish to somebody else. That was practically impossible as well as politically undesirable if we were to keep the Short a secret. Finally, I agreed to go see what I could accomplish, and he agreed to send the technical manual that I would need, as well as money so that I could rent a villa and get things going. I began to look forward to the trip.

Bidding farewell at last to my old shepherd friend, I led the donkey down into the little port city that was just a one day walk to the west. Disguised as a mountain woman with matted, darkened hair and blackened teeth, I determined not to make any sort of display of myself that might attract the attention of the authorities. I did, however, manage to find an inn where I indulged myself by taking a long, hot bath—my first in about five months.

Using some of the money I head left, I bought some serviceable clothes, and took a ship south on the first of July in the second year of my stay in the Ancient World. I took my little donkey with me.

When we arrived at last at my destination—a steamy seaport bustling with every manner of trade as well as crowds of people going back and forth to Italy—I felt almost as if I had found some sort of home. To the best of my knowledge, the town was approximately where the modern city of Vlone stands, but I'm really not sure. Since I rarely saw good maps and since at any rate many landforms have changed since those days, when I look at modern maps I can't be certain of much. Yet if I could retrace my journey through the rugged hills and mountains of Yugoslavia, who knows but that I might find the very hill where we made our stand? I might be able to find the cairn of rocks that Ovinin and I set up over my husband's grave two thousand years ago. On the other hand, maybe earthquakes or human interventions have broken up those rocky landscapes, and at any rate I don't have a need to go there. The place goes with me in the surprising smell of smoke.

For the next 12 months, I established a Macedonian base

and began to process petroleum. The project went well—better than we could have hoped—and I soon found that I really enjoyed being field engineer, chemist, magician, contractor, draftsman, and CEO all at once. At its height, my enterprise had 50 workers, including cooks, gardeners, secretaries, engineers, coopers, wrights, smiths, laborers, draymen, brick masons, stablemen, and housekeepers. I personally oversaw almost every aspect of the location, production, and refining of crude oil.

As in modern times, government was an impediment to success. At times it seemed that all the men with local and provincial power had their hands out. They always had to have their cut, their "taxes" and "fees." On the other hand, we had laws to protect us from the locals, and Roman legions to protect us from the "barbarians." As long as we shared some of our wealth, our refinery seemed to be safe.

With surprising ease, I had a successful well dug on some property I bought that held some major seeps, and from it we obtained a purer and more abundant supply of crude oil than was available on the surface. Using a "sinking shaft" of specially curved brick, a continuous-chain pump and a bellows-type breathing apparatus—all of my design--my men dug down 90 feet or more.

Although Mark had sought to arrange cooperage and pipefitting, his efforts had been sporadic and destined to fail. It was obvious to me from the first that the quality of the drums and vats that his subcontractors supplied were inadequate to the safe production or transportation of gasoline. I soon had smiths working at my direction who were able to develop soldered copper tins, funnels, and pipes equal to the tasks for which they were needed.

The basic stainless steel distillation and vacuum distillation columns and their interconnecting pipes that we brought in the Short were quite small—practically of laboratory scale. It had such a limited capacity that we had to run it 24 hours a day once we got started. The most difficult problems—at least from the chemical standpoint—were those related to refining the appropriate additives. Fortunately I understood the processes involved and had testing supplies and experience.

Although we had worried about the possibility that any fuel we produced might not have sufficient octane to be satisfactory, it turned out that what we produced was quite good and that with proper leading it could be made to have sufficient octane for potential use in the Short. Within six months after I arrived, we began shipping fuel in tins out to various places in the Mediterranean where Mark wanted it stockpiled, and even prior to that, I was producing lower grade diesel, kerosene, undifferentiated oil and asphalt.

Needless to say, I foresaw the serious dangers of fire both on site as well as in shipment and storage. These problems were overcome one by one while suffering only a few mishaps. An example of such a practice is how I had all of our marine shipments put into small, covered dories that I insisted be towed 50 yards astern the merchant ships that towed them. Whenever a captain objected to such precautions, I demonstrated the explosive possibilities of a single, leaky tin and how the nearly invisible fumes could spread out from it in search of a flame. Seeing what could happen was convincing enough to the typical captain.

I never met one who refused to ship fuel for me. Ships have always carried hazardous cargoes. Our gasoline was not considered much more dangerous than the various petroleum products and tars that were already being shipped in those times, and our tins, although expensive to manufacture, were remarkably safe containers.

After the first load of 500 gallons went out toward North Africa, I found that I could not stand to worry about how it was handled and whether or not it was stored safely upon arrival. I sent along one of my men with every shipment as a sales agent as well as a cargo master. Of the 27 shipments we made to various destinations, only two were lost, and I never found why.

The refining enterprise made me a quick fortune just as I hoped it would. Parceled out in small amounts—quarts and gallons—I sold kerosene and gasoline to magicians, priests, ship's chandlers, oil merchants, and weapons dealers, all of whom we suitably impressed with both the dangers and the uses of our products. At a kerosene-fueled kiln at the refinery, we began making ceramic lamps, fuel containers, and incendiary projectiles. We bought a small catapult with which my men amused themselves and impressed visitors by their ability to shoot earthenware Molotov cocktails at targets 200 to 300 yards away. Our nighttime firings were particularly impressive.

By my estimate, over the period of a year we produced about 15,000 gallons of gas and kerosene as well as hundreds of gallons of motor oil.

That was a busy time in my life. One way and another, I worked 15- and 16-hour days, seven days a week, and I had little time to sit around feeling sorry for myself. I was, in fact, pretty happy because I was producing things—often with my own hands—and experiencing a lot of success. I had my little donkey, my servants, and my foremen for company. I read a lot, rode horses, and dictated letters to many of the people I had met. I lived alone, kept cats, had a nice villa with a hot bath, ate well, and got plenty of exercise. For the most part I was content, but I often thought of how I would never again do things like hear a symphony, drive a car, speak English with anyone other than Mark or see a movie. My dreams were often disturbing and multilingual confusions of the past, present and future—confusions from which I would think that I had awakened only to find myself in yet another dream..

In the late autumn, I took a short trip over to Italy to visit my husband's parents. Travelling in disguise, I arrived at their place unannounced. It was not a particularly successful visit. Although his father was civil to me and appreciated that I did my best to help them come to terms with their son's death, my husband's mother could not forgive me for the disgrace she felt I brought upon the family, and she blamed me directly for his death. Had I been with child, things might have been different. They did not invite me to stay even for one night.

In the middle of the winter, Mark came to visit. He had become completely romanized. His dress, manner, and even his now-caustic wit made him seem more Roman than the Romans.

He looked as rich as any Roman of the day, and he struck a better pose than I might have expected, arriving as he did one afternoon, driving a nice chariot at the head of a small troop of cavalry and wagons.

He looked fit, tanned, and confident, and wore a shiny brass lorica that made him look stronger and more broad-chested than he had been when I had last seen him more than a year before. He wore a short sword on his left side and his .45 on the right in a new holster that matched his lorica. He wore a leather-and-wool kilt with sporran as well as beautifully engraved and polished greaves. He looked as if he was ready for battle.

Perhaps he was. I soon learned that this new style was no mere affectation of military prowess on his part. Quite to the contrary, he had accustomed himself to wearing heavy armor and practiced regularly with sword, pilum, and spear. In this he was not unlike most Roman officers of the time who knew that peace was only a temporary condition and that they might be called upon on very short notice to march, fight, and lead.

Naturally, he could not have been expected to equal men who had been raised to the military life, but then, he didn't have to: he had his modern weapons.

Always close at hand, the heavy Thompson submachine gun with its sinister, slotted snout made him look like an Italian mobster posing as a Roman general. He looked a little like Benito Mussolini, but he didn't have the full, fat face or body of the "Duce," nor was he given to ridiculous posturing. He looked, rather, like what he was: a raven-haired Englishman in his prime, a Briton or a Saxon, perhaps, in the service of Rome.

But for the guns and a few other modern things he had with him, he looked for all the world like a high-ranking officer riding with his staff. I gathered that the government had bestowed upon him a commission to tour Macedonia, Greece, and Illyricum as some sort of free-ranging adjunct of the Inspector General's office. Upon closer observation, though, his men looked and acted like a rich man's hunting party. They were: their quarry was men.

I don't exactly know what I had expected, but I wasn't too surprised. From our first meeting that winter, I could tell that in spite of his half-hearted attempts to play the man with me—which I most tactfully and to his relief rebuffed—he had almost completely given himself over to a homosexual lifestyle that he only briefly tried to conceal. As soon as it became plain to him that we were not going to resume any sort of conjugal intimacy, his relationship to his main traveling companion, an effete twenty-eight year old named Janus Publius, became obvious.

I can easily recall the fellow's name. Janus was the name of the god of gods who was most often depicted as having two faces, one looking forward and one looking backward. That was rather apropos in young Publius' case. The Janian face was often put on Roman coins, and Janus was thought to be the god of gateways, including the gateway to heaven.

I had seen all that coming, but it certainly didn't bother me. After having known my husband, I could never have gone back to Mark.

Once things were settled between us and I had introduced Mark to my crews and foremen, my secretaries, books, and records, we got along very well, for he had an eye for business and a love of money. What he really loved was the power and security money can buy, and one thing was certain: we owned a moneymaker.

The estate was large and rather isolated. I had a huge villa and workshops that were only a hundred yards from my main oil well. We had stables, fenced pastures, farm fields, and bunkhouses, and I was the mistress of it all. I liked that.

Mark liked it, too. So impressed was he by the financial and military prospects of the place that he practically moved into the villa with me. After a short time he began—quite naturally for a man, I suppose—to usurp my authority.

Once again we resumed speaking English with one another just for the pure pleasure of hearing our native tongue as well as for secrecy. Janus—who was with us quite a lot of the time— complained at first about our using English. He said he was Mark's friend as well as his secretary, and he felt left out and less able to do his work. Naturally enough I assumed that his "work" included keeping tabs on us, and I suspected that other fellows in Mark's retinue were spies. I said as much to Mark.

"Of course they are," he agreed. "And why not? Do you think they in Rome have no business watching us? We could be out here fomenting revolutions. We must be realistic and enjoy our lives at the same time. This is not a perfect world—but we didn't come from a perfect world either."

He didn't have to remind me of that. I had lost a husband to bandits, but I could still remember the world of 1980 and all the constant paranoia I had felt then.

"Sometimes I wish that we hadn't left that world," I told him.

"Sometimes I wish that Ned hadn't changed everything for me. I would have stayed where I was in the world of Hitler, Churchill, Roosevelt, and Stalin.

"But you know what?" he queried rhetorically, as he leaned forward holding a golden goblet of my very best wine,

"1939 or the 791st year of Rome: they're both superior to 1980. At least that's what I think." Then he sat back to let me mull it over.

I thought long and hard about how things were for me before I met Mark, and how it might have been had he not appeared in my life. I had been just drifting along.

Now my life was sometimes frightening, but it was interesting, thrilling, unique, and bold. I thought of all we had gone through together, and of our trip to Rome and mine to Germany, of my husband, and of our escapes and misadventures and pleasures. I thought of our love and of his grave high on the mountain, and I felt full with sorrow and joy. I reached forward and tapped his goblet with mine.

"Right. So right!"

Mark stayed for about three weeks, during which time he learned not only a great deal about my operations, but also of my trip through Germany and of the life and death of my husband about whom he had been grossly misinformed. He had been told conflicting stories from various sources and was forced to reach his own conclusions based on logic. For example, from sources connected to Sejanus and the Praetorian Guard, he had heard that my husband was a cad, a womanizer, and a dissolute gambler who had long been under suspicion for possible double-dealing with the Hermandurii. One soldier who had allegedly served under my husband told Mark that the man had shown cowardice on the battlefield so many times that the soldiers had called him by a Gaulish name meaning "Fleet Foot."

From Claudius he had gotten an entirely different picture of a man of impeccable military and familial background, one second in esteem for valor only to the illustrious Caius Chaerea who had fought so boldly at the Teutoborg Forest and at the Rhine bridge shortly thereafter. Far from having been at the brink of failure—as the Praetorians had reported—my husband had been in the front ranks of those men slated to command legions.

A third group of reports on my husband had come to Mark from an unlikely source, an old woman whose name was often connected to Livia, the widow of Augustus, mother of Tiberias, and reputed poisoner both of Germanicus (who had been beloved of the Roman people above all of the Claudians) and of Agrippa (her former husband who had been a partner of Octavian)—and there were others.

Her servant—the one who reported to Mark—was another old crone, Urgulania, a woman said by many to be both a witch and a poison-maker. The story she told was that my husband was a man of low character and that he had seduced me through the suborning of my slave. Supposedly he had induced her to introduce into my food a potion made from the crushed bodies of certain green flies from Spain—a potion that had made me at first sexually anxious, then sexually ravenous, and led to his having had his way with me. She told Mark that the effect of the drug was such that, if long used, it cause the eventual wasting of the victim. It was possible, she told him, for a doctor to discover the cause of death through a simple postmortem procedure. It was thought that rather than face a possible murder charge, my husband had fled with me to Germany to cover up his crime as well as to take my money and property.

Mark told me that he had listened carefully to all of those stories as if he had believed each of them, keeping his own counsel. He had been, he told me, most persuaded by the first one, for it seemed authentic enough, but he knew that it might have merely been the most subtly presented and best-orchestrated of the three.

When he found out that we were alive and that I had told my husband about our time travel, he could only fear for the worst. When he had learned of my husband's death, he could only feel relieved.

"You would not," he pointed out, "have been the first intelligent woman in history to have been deceived by a man. Or the last."

Who knows but that some of those negative stories about my husband might have been in some parts true? Maybe our flight was part of a plan to get me to level with him about everything.

From Mark I also learned something of what had become of Propea, for he had hired a private investigator to look into the matter even though he knew that the man he hired could have been induced or ordered to give him false reports. But what could he do? Mark felt that he could trust no one, and he was right. Even I cheated him some, for with the refinery, I had made more money and spent less than I told him about. I kept two sets of books and put aside a private stash of money before he arrived. I couldn't trust him either.

His detective reported that right after I fled into Germany, Propea moved in with a rich young legate who simply took over the lease on the house I had occupied. Some three or four months after that, Mark's source reported, she left town heading south—apparently with plenty of money. It was obvious that either she had found my second money belt or that she had received some sort of cash payment. She was last seen at Massalia. The mystery surrounding her remained.

Mark and I got on well enough while he stayed at my place at the refinery. His men spent the time hunting and fishing, and when at last they left, they were all happy to be on their way—which was eastward into the wild country. Although he didn't say and I didn't ask, I assumed that they were going off on a manhunt, for in those days many Romans treated the border areas like hunting preserves— particularly if those areas were wild and sparsely inhabited. Hunting men, Mark's lieutenant boasted, was "the most dangerous game," for the quarry often hunted back. It is little wonder that the wild mountains on the outer borders of Illyria and Macedonia were the scenes of so many battles during the years of the Roman Empire. The expansionist Romans were a constant threat to those who bordered them, and many of the border raids came as a response to incursions by groups like the one Mark was leading. Such raiding was so much a part of the times that there was hardly any reason to complain about it. That's just the way things were. If not busy at war, men always seem to be playing at it in one way or another--or planning a new one.

For that matter, the men who had attacked us in Mauretania and those who had killed my husband were not particularly deserving of my hatred. In a very real sense, neither group was more morally culpable than a pack of wild dogs. They were just doing what came naturally to them: kill and be killed. Take or be taken from.

By the same token, I learned that self-defense came naturally enough to me, particularly once the mental practice of it became routine. One wonders whether those moderns who advocate the abolition of guns are really aware of what it is that they propose to do. Incredibly, some weak people—and I include women—think they will be safer if everyone is disarmed. What an astonishing proposition! Only a fool would want to part with the equalizer that keeps her somewhat on a par with her enemies. Presumably the gun control advocate insists that she and the man who tries to rape her should both be disarmed so that they will have to fight it out as "equals," but I will keep my Colt.

After an uncomfortable amount of nagging and importuning on my part, Mark very reluctantly parted with some of his precious ammunition, giving me 300 rounds for my .45 Colt Combat Commander and a .45 derringer he threw in. He also gave me 2000 rounds for my trusty .22 semi-automatic rifle. He also relinquished my .35mm Leica with 20 rolls of black and white film and all of our powdered chemicals and photographic paper. He was not being generous. Only I knew how to use them, and it had actually been I who had bought the film, camera, paper, and chemicals. When I left for Germany, though, Mark acted as if everything I left behind for safekeeping had become his by default. Maybe it sounds like a small thing, but it was indicative of some of the real frictions which had grown up between us.

Be that as it may, as you may recall, my father was an amateur photographer and taught me how to take pictures and use a darkroom, and as a teenager I had also been a photographer on my high school yearbook staff. I knew how to make do with limited equipment, and one of the first things I did after he left was to develop my first roll of film which had upon it pictures of Naadia, Marcus, Ned and the rest as well as some shots of Rome and the views from the Rock of Gibralter.

I practically had to force Mark to part with some of the medical supplies that I had most fortunately neglected to take to Gaul with me. In addition to bandages and antiseptics, we had some dental and surgical tools as well as penicillin, morphine, and tetracycline, and a year's supply of birth control pills which, even though they were out of date, I was glad to have. Sooner or later, I might wish that I were using them.

Through having worked with the physicians in Rome and doctoring my workmen and several of the local women—work that included setting two broken arms, delivering two babies, and sewing up several wounds—I had become something of a makeshift healer that year. I had learned something, too, of the prevalence and signs of various venereal diseases that one sometimes encountered. It was enough to make anyone have second thoughts about casual sex. I suspected, for example, that many who were considered to be leprous were in fact syphilitic, but I had no way of testing that hypothesis. We had neglected to bring with us on the trip that most wonderful of instruments, the microscope. Without one I could not check blood samples for syphilis.

In cults predominant at Corinth and Babylon where ritualistic prostitution was mandated, it was common for the priests and priestesses to check—in the guise of ritual—both the women and the men who entered the temples for signs of infections. Given the sexual nature of Mediterranean life, it seemed that venereal diseases and unwanted pregnancies should have been far more common than they were. There again, Greek and the Egyptian physicians knew treatments that seemed to prevent and even cure most infections, including, if I am not mistaken, syphilis. There were also herbs and potions to prevent pregnancy and to induce abortion, but I believe it would be safe to assume that most of the ancient cures and medicines have been lost on the shores of time.

Rounding out the belongings that I pried away from Mark were three magazines— we're talking *Ladies' Home Journal* and *Vogue* here—which were very valuable because of the pictures in them that could be cut out and bartered individually.

Prior to Mark's arrival, I had once again bought a handmaiden—this time a strong, pleasant Greek girl four or five years younger than I. It was necessary for me to have a servant who was skilled in doing my hair and helping me dress and apply makeup. Although she was nice enough, I did not become friends with her as I had with Propea. On the other hand, I did permit her to prostitute herself in her leisure time—but not in my house or in any way that would interfere with my business or the smooth operation of the refinery.

During the first year I had let my hair fall long and curly, straight down past my shoulders, and like a good American girl of the 70s I usually had forsaken makeup. During the time that I spent in the refinery business, when I was working outside or in the workshops, I wore leather skirts, sandals, gloves, and vests over linen tunics. When, on the other hand, I was conducting business or doing office work, I dressed in much more contemporary Roman styles and wore my hair in an elaborate pile of curls, pins, and ribbons, often topping it with a silver comb. To make myself appear more powerful, more mysterious, and less foreign, I began to wear rouge, a sort of lipstick, and heavy eye makeup.

I was quite a powerhouse in those days, and men feared me.

****

XXIV

Hellas

A whole year passed by—a year which began on the day I buried my husband and ended when I woke up one morning and realized that it had gone by. The birds were singing just as merrily as they had when I buried him. I was over the worst of my grief, and it was time to be on my way.

After putting my affairs in order once again and placing my foreman in charge of the business, I hired my own ship—a double-masted, rowable 100-footer with a 23-man crew much like the one on which I had first sailed from Mauretania. We were going to head south toward Greece and the lands beyond.

The captain and his Greek crew were men I trusted, for they had handled cargoes for me several times before, and they kept a neat ship. They seemed loyal and daring and were willing enough to go where I bid them. I can't really remember how much it cost me for the ship and crew, but it was probably about a half pound of gold.

As in other ships throughout the ages, in addition to his wages each sailor was allowed to have his own "ventures," which usually meant the trade of merchandise that each carried in personal sea-chests. A ship would often carry only certain types of principal cargoes for the owners or shippers and would enforce a shipboard monopoly on those cargoes so as to reduce the temptations to pilferage. The captain might have a certain amount of hold-space allotted to him—on the theory that he was going to do as he would anyway. When ports were reached, the captain or a factor for the shippers or owners would carry out any necessary bargaining in connection with the main cargoes while the men would make their own little trades and deals ashore when they were off duty. Each member of a crew had a specialty. One man dealt principally in carvings, one in mushrooms, one in cloth, and so forth. It was a system that worked well, for not only did it encourage teamwork when it came to matters of sailing, but it also provided opportunities for common men to make good money—if they were sharp enough.

Thinking that I might not be coming back to my villa for a year or more, I took practically all of my worldly goods with me, and that was plenty. From having only the ragged clothes on my back and the money I had taken off of the bandits I had killed in the mountains, I had made a small fortune.

In the process I had naturally accumulated a rather respectable wardrobe of clothes. It consisted of various outfits, most of which looked downright matronly—more so than one might have expected a still-young woman to wear. I had heavy stolas made of wool as well as lighter ones made of linen, and a distinctive golden pallium or cloak that was lined with green linen. I also had two or three very well made, more fanciful Grecian dresses of silk. I took one of my leather work outfits which consisted of a vest and skirt with matching boots and gloves, but even though it fitted well and flattered my bust, I think I was the only person who thought I looked good in it. I wore it anyway when I was aboard ship. It made me feel as if I were a buccaneer.

Although khakis, tans, and whites had been my colors of choice when I was younger, in those days when I dressed casually I tended to choose pastels most often, for they seemed more reflective of my own nature and experiences. For business and public appearances, though, I usually wore a formal, scarlet stola with pink borders that looked wonderful when I was decked out with gold chains and jewelry.

A small chest of tough traveling clothes—leather britches and shorts, a chamois shirt, a pair of riding boots, socks, underwear and what was left of my original clothing—

completed my wardrobe. I also carried bedding and toiletries in other chests and bags that filled my cabin aft, and, naturally, I had my weapons and the radio, as well as my camera, medical supplies, gold, silver, and letters of credit.

That was everything portable that I owned except for my interest in the camping gear and survival equipment we had left in the Short in Mauretania. I still owned a half-interest in the refinery, and although I could expect it to keep on making money, it might be taken over by someone else or by Mark. Many a fortune in those days was won or lost overnight, and I was glad that I made enough hay while the sun was shining. I had made so much, in fact, that I felt guilty that I had not divided it more evenly with Mark.

He and I kept in touch by radio from time to time, but our correspondence was always brief and covered only the barest outline of business. After leaving me, he had led his gay retinue eastward on adventures that remained undefined and disquieting. Later on, he visited Alexandria, then returned to Rome.

It was a rainy day when my ship sailed out with the tide from our home port, towing behind us one of our covered boats laden with fuel. Rounding the great northward-pointing peninsula, we turned south and caught a fair breeze that pushed us toward the Ionian Islands.

"The sea will define our course," I had told the captain, "for the boat is my home." The feeling of the rising and falling wood under my feet felt as familiar as the floor of a South Carolina country church.

We took care of our floating home by avoiding dangerous shortcuts and wearying passages—such as the one which would have taken us in to Corinth but required a long row back out. There was a sort of rail line across the isthmus upon which boats could be transported, but our ship was too large for it and so we were obliged to go the long way around the Pelopennese.

We passed the site of the battle of Atticum and went ashore to visit the shrine that Augustus had set up to commemorate his great victory over the fleets of Antony and Cleopatra. We visited Corcyra, Nicopolis, Sparta, Argos, and a score of little ports and islands along the way. I was only a little lonely, for although the captain and I were the best of friends, we were not lovers, and I am the kind of woman who needs a man from time to time, if only for physical reassurance. As I have said, enough time had passed—and I was in Greece!

During those summer months, I became quite accustomed to seeing nude men and boys, both aboard ship, swimming in the sea, and in athletic contests. It was something that I got used to rather easily—rather like one might get used to seeing—and appreciating—stallions. I also visited in Sparta on the day it held an annual festival during which the single, young women of marriageable age paraded down the streets wearing nothing but sandals. It was a sight to see and was a quasi-erotic and popular carry-over from an earlier, more militaristic age which had promoted fertility and female fitness by making unmarried girls display themselves in that fashion at least once a year. Under the influence of the wine I had drunk as well as the encouragement I had gotten from a multitude of Spartan admirers, I was tempted to throw off my clothes and join in the girls' parade even though I was older than they were. I resisted the impulse.

Be that as it may, I should also point out that such processions as well as the widespread depiction of female nudity and sexuality in Greece operated as a sort of counterbalance to the homosexuality prevalent throughout most of Greek society. It would probably be more accurate to say that bisexuality among men was the norm. The absence of women in the public life of most cities as well as the system of military and educational segregation that had been practiced for hundreds of years gave rise to a virtual celebration of same-sex relationships not only among men but also, I gathered, among women. During most of that era, the birth rate in urban Greece was astonishingly low, but on the farm and in the small villages the usual proclivities of men and women were more likely to prevail and to produce the normal results.

Greeks generally allowed the practice of both infanticide and abortion, the latter being performed almost exclusively by midwives and not by physicians. Infants defective in any way— particularly in Sparta—were ruthlessly exposed or smothered, whereas those who were otherwise healthy but were unwanted might be given up for adoption through the simple expedient of being left in large jars on temple steps. Callously, perhaps, I learned not to concern myself with such jars on the few occasions I encountered them.

An awareness of female nudity in Greece went beyond the rare public displays and the arts. Summer clothes, for example, were little more than shifts or shirts, usually worn without underwear. The common summer dress of the younger women was mostly light linen or thin wool gathered at the shoulders and knees, so that the arms and calves were bared. As in Spain and Italy, practically everyone wore light straw hats during the summer to ward off the intense sunlight.

On many occasions during that trip, I went swimming with other women, either in the sea or in small streams or rivers, and we usually swam nude. To have done otherwise would have seemed silly or pretentious and, for that matter, I had lost my "famous" tank suit in Mogontiacum and had not bothered to have another swimsuit made.

Sometimes, of course, we were watched as we frolicked, for although by custom men and women seldom swam together, it was not uncommon to find ourselves swimming in the presence of men, be they servants, members of my crew, or mere appreciative spectators. In any event, I couldn't let my fading modesty come between me and swimming for it had always been my favorite sport.

Most of the Greeks I met were fair swimmers, but no women and only a few men could beat me in a freestyle race. The crawl was not commonly known among the ancients, and it was not a stroke that they had refined and perfected, mostly being used in the face-out-of-water way that is so ungainly and tiring. I had gained a fair amount of weight during the preceding year and probably weighed 160 pounds, but I was in terrific shape and had a shameless desire to win. I would bet on myself and offer outrageous handicaps. I seldom lost.

In mid-August, we arrived in Piraeus, the port of Athens. At that time we intended to stay in Athens for three months, then sail south to Alexandria for the winter. For the first two days in port I stayed aboard ship and sent my captain ashore as my agent to make suitable preparations so that we might trade effectively and get the most out of our time in Athens. We rented a large house situated on a hill overlooking the harbor of Zea where our ship was anchored. That house was probably the most beautiful place in which I have ever lived. It had a small gardens, a bath, and magnificent views, including one to the northeast where at a distance of about four miles, the Acropolis glittered in the morning sun. As the day progressed, its hues and colors changed a thousand times and commanded one's attention and devotion.

Everywhere in both Piraeus and in Athens, there were colonnades, statues, alcoves, tablets, carvings, gardens, and flowers. There were temples ranging from tiny one-priest affairs to the colossal Temple of Olympian Zeus beside the river Ilissus. There were theaters, markets, homes, paved avenues, adornments, colorful and educated people, seats of learning and houses of pleasure. In fact, Athens was such a wonderful place that banishment was considered as severe a punishment as death. There were stories of old men who, having been banished when young, disguised themselves and worked as sailors so they could see their native city from time to time. Made ever more beautiful through many generations, Athens was thought to be one of the wonders of the world, and no one I ever met thought Rome was more alluring.

It was too varied and great a city for me to storm by virtue of my personality, even had I wanted to do so, and of course I had learned my lesson: the powerful in Rome had apparently been jealous of anyone who might threaten *their* suzerainty. It was reasonable to assume that the leaders of Athens might not welcome me either.

The people, on the other hand, did celebrate my arrival after their own fashion. Word of my having taken up residence in the port spread rapidly.

Like Ostia in Italy, Piraeus was the principal district for brothels--mostly those in which the lowest order of girls, the *pornai*, plied their trade. They were everywhere and could be seen standing around outside the portals of their compounds or in the windows of their rooms. Almost always dressed in filmy shifts, they seemed to be surprisingly cheerful despite the nature of their work and their clientele.

The next highest class of Athenian prostitutes was that of the *auletrides*, or "flute-players" who provided more educated companionship to embellish the same basic product. In a sense, they were the work-a-day women of the merchant class.

The highest class of prostitutes was the *hetairai*. It was made up of women who were held in relatively high esteem due to their surpassing beauty, independence, or accomplishments. They usually owned their own homes, ruled their own households, and took such lovers—and money—as opportunity and skill permitted. Almost all of them were dyed blondes, and for that reason alone, during my first days in Athens I was thought to be a new, foreign *hetairai* who was setting herself up in business in the port. Even before I set foot in the city itself, many men who had heard of me made the long walk out to my house to call upon me and see for themselves if the stories of my beauty were true. All of them were turned away by my crew without so much as an audience. As I discovered later, that, too, was a famous *hetairai* interest-building tactic.

It was almost a week before I went into Athens. When I did, it was at the invitation of the priests of the Temple of Athena on the Acropolis, for they had discovered that apparently I was not a whore after all. Furthermore, they had heard that I was favored of Athena—a rumor my crew had most conveniently helped to spread. The comparison suited me well in those days. Similar to Athena, I was armed, vigilant, educated, virginal (well, after a fashion), and civilized. Moreover, I was something of a patroness of the industrial arts and thought to be rather good-looking. What more could one ask of a goddess?

On the appointed day I went forth in my best lavender Grecian dress that fit the midriff and hips rather closely. When I first bought it, it dropped away in narrow pleats almost to the ground, but since it looked a bit dowdy like that, I had my girl cut it off and hem it to knee-length. By Greek standards, it would have given me an almost boyish look but for my bust, where criss-crossed ribbons of deep purple silk held the thin cloth so tightly against me that little was left to the imagination. At that time I must have weighed about what I did when I lived with you, which is to say, heavy by your standards, perfect by theirs. As you will recall, under normal feeding conditions, I'm a big girl. With the help of the woman from next door, we did my hair up that day into a large mass of golden ringlets that were pulled back from my face to flowed out behind a lacy gold-wire hair band and tumble down to my shoulders.

My sandals were simple, open flats with long, soft leather thongs that wrapped and twined around my calves up almost to my knees, and I realized that Athenian men really liked a pair of shapely legs—so much so that they often shaved their own.

We went out just at dawn, travelling on foot with four or five of my men and a sort of impromptu honor guard of four priests. We had to go only four or five miles, but we stopped many times to greet people and to admire various works of art and architecture. It took two hours to get to the Acropolis. By then the day was bright and clear and the air was already beginning to warm up as we mounted the many ramps and stairs that led to the top of the famous rock which dominated the city. After we looked about the other buildings, and took some time to appreciate the panorama spread before us, we came at last to the temple of Athena, the Parthenon.

Even then it was almost 450 years old, but it was built to last and was incredibly clean and new-looking. The fluted columns were white as snow in the morning light and seemed to grow lightly from the perfect base of the building. They rose gracefully up to their leafy capitals above which the carved frieze of happy people walked in proud procession around under the eves toward the pediments where, sheltered by the newly renovated roof, the gods sat and stood in majestic splendor high above we puny mortals. It was awe-inspiring, but nothing had prepared me for what I saw in the cella, or interior, of the temple.

I entered with the sun at my back, and I was startled by my sudden encounter with the famous statue—or idol, if you will—of Athena that had been made by the great Phidias hundreds of years before. Some 20 feet tall, made of ivory, gold, and stone and gleaming in the various lights, she was fully armed and altogether glorious. Immediately my attention went to her face and I was instantly aware that she was looking back at me through her crystal and amethyst eyes with an inescapable and emotionally compelling gaze that took my breath away. Hers was the look of absolute judgment, and suddenly I felt naked before her, all my sins and shortcomings exposed to her relentless vision. This was not unusual: everyone felt that way when they came into her presence in the early part of the day. It was called, appropriately enough, her *Morning Look.*

At other times of the day and night other emotions arose when one gazed at her face. For example, at dawn when the low rays of the sun struck directly into her internally faceted eyes, radiant streams of lights beamed from her eyes and danced on the walls in joyous spectrums—her gift to the day. Gradually that turned into the very serious Morning Look. At midday, she gave forth feelings of power. It was then that the industrial and war-making aspects of the goddess were paramount. In the afternoon one felt intelligence, art, and beauty. Usually, but particularly so on moonlit nights, the haunting love of friends and family was said to be felt emanating from her.

The Parthenon was never closed, and it was rarely empty. Aged and infirm Athenians hoping to die there in the cella were allowed to stay overnight, but they were always removed before dawn whether or not their wishes had been granted by the goddess.

As I have said, I arrived in the midmorning when the sun could still get into the cella and find its way into those jeweled eyes, and so the dominant impression that I got from Athena was one of judgment. She as much as asked me, *What have you done with that which I have given you? How do you measure up in comparison to your own capacity? Have you done your duty? Have you served me and how?*

Such demanding questions often were too much for people to bear. Over the years, many morning worshipers had left the temple terribly distraught, and more than a few had thrown themselves from the steep parapet just beyond the edge of the temple. They had judged themselves and been found wanting. Miraculously, no one who ever leapt from that wall was ever injured—all were killed instantly. That, too, was understood as being yet another sign to the Athenians of the mercy of the patron goddess of the city.

As a Protestant raised in the South, I had shared with all of my contemporaries a general contempt for idolatry and the various religions of the ancients. The picture books we used in Sunday School had always depicted ignorant, intolerant people in silly costumes worshipping in front of lifeless, crude statues of stone or wood. The accompanying literature always heaped scorn upon people who were, after all, our ancestors. In hindsight it is obvious that the authors of such books displayed their own ignorance and intolerance of those systems of belief that had been part and parcel of human consciousness for millennia.

In reality, the pagan worship practices I saw and

experienced were altogether different from those the lifeless prejudices of my childhood might have made me expect. There was as much intensity and emotion and foresight put in pagan worship as was ever invested in any Christian worship I had seen. For that matter, whether it was a wedding, festival, or funeral, ancient worship seemed have *more* impact upon the participants than modern worship does. Obviously, I have had an opportunity to compare such things. The vehement worship services in the mountains of North Georgia and the Low Country of South Carolina where my grandparents lived were shallow by comparison to things I saw in '29 and '30. I can safely say that the anti-pagan propaganda with which I was inundated when I was a girl proved to be so much bunk. In hindsight, the Sunday School teachings were not so much anti-pagan as they were anti-ancestral. Apparently, the modern religionist mocks not only that which is ancient but also much of that which predates his own experience by more than a few generations. Such attitudes hardly speak well for one's belief in a God who is alleged to be eternal and unchanging. My own rather ambivalent attitudes toward the "old time religion" of my grandparents would have reached a full flower of contempt in the Temple of Athena had not the presence of the goddess prevented it with her gentle touch.

I don't mean to suggest that I was a pagan or pantheist at that point in my life. I'm still not sure what I was, but I was certainly totally immersed in a pagan society. I was no longer some neutral observer from another world. I walked on the same land and ships' decks, sailed the same seas and braved the same dangers, ate the same food, and slept in the same places as everyone else did. Is it not natural, then, that I perceived the same gods and felt the same forces they did?

It seems to me that the fears and aspirations of a people dictate the gods they worship. The actual, physical statue or idol of Athena embodied what Athenians wished for themselves and their posterity. She represented not so much a being as a collective wish for a permanent sense of the loftier possibilities of the human condition made possible through the intercessions of the gods. What went on in the cella was not idolatry. The worshipers no more thought the statue to *be* the goddess than a Catholic thinks of a wooden Christ as actually *being* his god, though the emotion each object might evoke would be the same, I suppose. The statue of Athena certainly had an emotional effect on me.

Standing in front of her for fifteen or twenty minutes, I was spellbound and yet, though judged, I was not daunted. In looking into myself through her eyes I could see my life—past, present, and, to some extent, future. Like a person falling from a great height is said to have her whole life flash before her eyes, so mine seemed to spin before me, the bad and the good passing rapidly on some sort of cosmic tally sheet, the changing balances of which left me staggered. By this I mean that I saw it all: how I had argued with my mother in high school, lost my virginity in a rushed and ugly way, protested the Vietnam War. I saw my sister, parents, schoolmates, you, Brad, grad school, Mark, the Short, Gibraltar, Rome, Gaul, Germany, my husband. Judgment, you must understand, involved everything significant that had ever happened to me. What I saw at that time came so rapidly and furiously that for some time its overall meaning was vague. It is clearer now.

What was clear to me, though, was that I had measured up somehow under Athena's penetrating scrutiny. With a growing feeling of power I knew that I could live without regrets for what had happened in the past. Suddenly I could feel the warm blessing of the goddess, and I broke into tears of joy as I stood there before her and spread my arms to embrace the emanations of goodwill that I felt pouring out over me.

Recognizing that mine were tears of reunion and joy, at a sign from the high priest, everyone else withdrew from the cella and left me alone there for private communion—a rare privilege indeed.

"May I touch her?" I asked of him as he was leaving.

"Since she has first touched you, you may touch her."

I washed my hands in a golden basin beside the door. Then I felt the smooth surfaces and flawless junctions between the various materials of which she was made—mostly gold and ivory—and found that she seemed to be not hard and cold but warm and smooth. Touching her, I also felt what might have been an electrical or ethereal current that was as subtle and graceful as a mother's touch of her sleeping child's lips.

The ivory was white, yes, but it was old and had an undertone that made it seem like flesh—flawless, female flesh that set off with studied perfection the golden, majestic, masculine armor and armaments that she held as she stood there eternally vigilant, poised, and self-confident.

Studying her there in private, I realized that after I had gone through those initial feelings of awe, judgement, relief and joy, my dominant emotional response to her was one of pride. I was proud to be a fellow human being of those who had made the great building and of the artist who had breathed such life into the sculpture. And I felt pride in being, like her, a woman. I got out my Leica and took some pictures of her, but she seemed indulgently to laugh at me and to say, *"Puny mortal: my silly child."*

So wondrous was the statue of Athena that one was supposed to look at it only once or twice a year, and madness was said to come to those who would not restrain themselves from more frequent visits. Even the priests who officiated averted their eyes from her on all but the holiest of days. When they cleaned her with damp cloths each week, they divided the work so that each would handle only a portion of the figure and could avoid looking into her eyes.

"A priest gave in to his weakness just last year," a guide told me later that day.

"One day while cleaning her face, he began to talk to himself—or to Her. We could not tell which. When we tried to get him to leave the cella, he said that the goddess had spoken to him and that he was to remain with her.

"What can we do when such a thing happens? Who are we to say that She did not speak?

"As time went on—only a few days as I recall it—his moods fluctuated wildly between elation and depression on the one hand and anger and love on the other. 'She wants me to stay with her always,' he would say. Or 'She's mad at me today,' which eventually was a thing he said more and more often. He ignored the entreaties of his wife and children to leave the Acropolis, and his business as a wine merchant failed.

"We knew better than to argue with him although we did consider binding him up and putting him on a ship. That, too, has been done before, but a day out of port, the man to whom it was done leapt overboard and drowned trying to swim back to Athens.

"So we knew he was doomed. One can only take just so much of the divine at one time. Finally he hated Her—or said he did—as each day She was the same as the day before: radiant, perfect, majestic, and calm, like the Goddess Herself. *Onward She goes through time while we like leaves in autumn fall*, says the writer. This building and that statue can be destroyed by man, but would that change anything? Perhaps: if only in that such a disaster might let the Athenians forget the goddess who made their city great.

"I must correct myself. I said that finally he hated Her, but that is not accurate. What happened was that finally he recognized that he had loved Her, but having done what is forbidden to man, he had worn out and lost that which had been most precious to him. He babbled all the time, explaining and revising his views constantly.

"One day he rose up from his place, walked outside, and jumped off."

Dominant as was the worship of Athena, however, she was only one goddess among many. To put it another way, she was but one of the many aspects of god. On the Acropolis and throughout the city, there were other temples to other divinities. Foremost among the other temples—at least in size—was the great temple of Zeus at which there were always, it seemed, great throngs of people. They used the temple precincts to carry on all sorts of business dealings that had to have some kind of special moral or equitable aspects attached to them.

During the months that I lived in the house at Piraeus, I took several side trips into the countryside and to places offshore, and I met most of Athens' leading citizens, including many of the guild or collegia of physicians and surgeons. Before I ever arrived, my friend in Rome, Aechelus, had written to several of his Athenian colleagues about me, and they asked me to meet with them. By that time, I spoke Greek rather well, it having been the main language I used during the entire preceding year. Naturally, though, my Greek was not entirely adequate to the demands of the lecture hall, but nonetheless the collegia asked me to give a series of talks on medical topics. For what it was worth—and surely many rejected as preposterous most of what I said—I told them what I knew about the workings of the circulatory, nervous, digestive, and lymphatic systems. In response to their questions, I spoke to the best of my abilities about the nature of matter, bacteria, and viruses. We were all disappointed by the painfully obvious gaps in my store of knowledge. On the other hand, I was once again treated not as a woman but as a colleague—a colleague who was both divinely beautiful as well as divinely sent.

I often wore slacks and a white blouse while I was in Greece, for at times I felt uncomfortable dressed as either a Roman or a Greek. Romans were unpopular in the Hellenic world, not because they were conquerors but because generally they were stiff, artificial and domineering. On the other hand, Rome's status as the dominant world power was not too abhorrent to most of the Greeks I met, for it had imposed order and peace upon a region that had long been plagued by a prolonged series of wars and civil disturbances. The Peloponnesian War and the wars of conquest led by Alexander—wars that established a Macedonian empire that had rather promptly fallen apart---had left a deep impression on the Greek psyche. It was widely believed that the city-states of Greece could no longer manage their own affairs and many people—particularly the merchants--were content that Rome should rule so long as the local customs and religions were respected.

On the other hand, after a very short stay in Athens, I did not want to be thought of as a Greek either—not because I disliked the people but because I felt it best to maintain my individuality and mystery. In a sense, the choice was forced upon me. To dress like an Athenian woman I could either wear the free-flowing shifts of the pornai, the styles of the hetairai, or the long, formal clothes of rich men's wives. Dressed in any of these styles, I could not have expected to get much respect.

Most of the respectable women of Athens, both married and unmarried, were kept in virtual seclusion in their homes and were rarely seen in public places. Their shopping was done by their servants, or merchants brought samples of their wares to their homes. Their husbands and fathers, on the other hand, had the run of the world and were expected to frequent prostitutes. Why the women put up with such slavery seemed beyond comprehension until a lady who became my friend and confidante explained matters to me. Like many a teetotaler throughout the ages, she and many of her friends feared their own weaknesses. They were afraid of their own sexuality, which is to say, of home-wrecking nymphomania. After all, they were Greeks, they were in their 20s and 30s, and they were separated only by a fine, bright line of gender from their brothers and husbands who were, in a word, concupiscent.

Not only were the men pleasure-seekers and lusty, but they were also jealous and possessive, and so the double standard reigned supreme. A man had the right to kill any child of doubtful paternity his wife might bear, and it was not unknown for a man to murder his wife upon the accusation—or the excuse—of adultery.

A fair number of respectable women settled upon the solution of lesbianism—which their husbands often not only tolerated but also encouraged. In any case, women usually cultivated long-standing friendships with other married women that allowed them the freedom even to travel—in groups, of course—outside their homes and cities. Many women, I think, adopted lesbianism simply as a means of getting a little freedom and enjoyment out of their lives.

On the other hand, there were stories of women who used their sisterhood to help one another hide their extramarital affairs. I heard many tales of ribald pairs or threesomes that might put on masks at Delphi and become quite active in their searches for male companionship.

So it was that I decided to dress once again as the American college girl I once had been. I had some pretty little flats made and, in spite of the heat of late summer, I went back to wearing long-sleeved blouses. Self-confident in my native clothes, I drove the boys crazy.

I liked being the object of so much fantasy and lust. During my medical lectures in front of 30 or 40 raptly attentive men, I could feel the old, familiar stirring in me inspired by the presence of all those healthy, attractive men and their transparent wishes. Many of those men were very good-looking.

At the end of the first month, feeling I could trust my servants faithfully to protect my home and my possessions, I decided to take a trip. My best Greek friend, Thetia, and I went with a large group of women and servants to Delphi, the center of worship and pleasure on the side of Mount Parnasus some 75 miles northwest of Athens. With our possessions loaded on two large oxcarts, we walked all the way to the sacred city, a trip that took three days 'though we could have done it in two. Each day we stopped and swam two or three times. At night we slept in the open or in straw-filled barns or sheds, and we bought our food along the way at cafes, wayside bakeries, and produce stands.

We stayed at Delphi for three days, attending plays, lectures and athletic contests. The primary object of our trip was to visit the temple of Apollo where I would consult the Delphic Oracle.

When the time came, and after having made my homage and offered a sufficiently magnificent animal for sacrifice—a ram—I prostrated myself before the alter and asked my question. I came back the next evening for my answer—which was read out to me. A written copy was given to me afterwards. It read:

> *Changing from girl to woman to queen*
> *To goddess to goddess and back again,*
> *From humble to humble and all in between,*
> *Searching for someone known but unseen.*
> *Thou wilt listen to air and heeding the call*
> *By earth and by water will rush toward the fall.*
>
> *Unbeliever, believer on Apollo's wings flying*
> *Uncertain, yet certain in all you are trying,*
> *Crossing the sun and crossed in turn*
> *You on the wheels and by the sea shall learn*
> *Coming in time, but in time too late,*
> *Free you are not, but an arrow of fate.*

I kept that prophecy until I had every ambiguous word of it memorized, and my translation of it is as close as memory and my knowledge of ancient Greek can make it. In time it became less ambiguous.

About three weeks after we returned from Delphi, I was invited by the priesthood of Demeter to participate in a religious experience known as the Mysteries. Held each autumn in a large complex of caves and buildings at the small city of Eleusis, the Mysteries were at first blush rather like a course of philosophical studies in which one participated. It was akin, for example, to rituals such as those of modern day Masonry wherein the participants through study and the passing of examinations progress along a pathway to knowledge by stages or degrees, there being, if I remember my uncle's words correctly, 33 such degrees.

Normally only those who had taken part in the Lesser Mysteries in the Spring of the year and been found morally and intellectually fit were invited to become initiates of the Greater Mysteries. In earlier times, non-Greeks were seldom invited to attend, but inevitably a certain amount of commercialism had developed around the yearly rites. They were famous throughout the ancient world and it would have been uncharacteristic of the Greeks to turn away those who had traveled from afar to attend—and who had gold in their purses. To some extent, The Mysteries—particularly the Lesser ones—had degenerated into something akin to a spiritual Disneyland.

My new friends in Athens, Thetia and her merchant banker husband, Alcibidee, kept me abreast of the city gossip and what was being said of me both on the streets and in the governing council. I might note that not only was Alcibidee's financial house the one that Naaida had recommended, but I sensed him to be both honest and straightforward and more interested in maintaining a decent family life and a good name than in getting stinking rich. In business matters I felt that his firm had dealt honestly with funds gained from our fuel exports, and I never had the feeling from either him or my friend that I was being cozened. They were just a decent, hospitable couple with three kids who liked me and who were flattered that I, in turn, liked them and graced their home from time to time with my increasingly famous presence.

Of course, my patronage of Alcibidee's business was good for his reputation, but why shouldn't it be? In the commercial circles of Athens, it was apparent that I was wealthy, and it was known that I owned and controlled some rare and valuable commodities. My choice of his factoring house reflected credit upon it.

"Trust all men," my father had advised, "but always cut the deck." Often thinking about his words, I did not entirely rely upon my friends for news, for I also used my men and my handmaiden to keep me informed of the things of the city. Being at leisure most of the time, they all acted as my eyes and ears in the city and developed a knack for garnering information about private as well as public matters. I didn't want to be taken in again as I had been in Mogontiacum.

At any rate, from the beginning I was considered by the priesthood to be somehow important to the religious life of Athens. At the same time, though, I had managed to make it clear that I posed no threat to the political stability of the city, despite my weapons (which I never displayed or demonstrated) and my wealth. This is indicative of how secular a society it was—unlike so many others before and since. The religious people in the city seemed to be in a distinct minority and had few pretensions to political power. They recognized me, one must suppose, as one of their own.

The priesthood of Demeter made an exception for me that allowed me to forego the Spring's Lesser Mysteries on the condition that I prepare myself by doing what was, in effect, "makeup work." Thetia and Alcibidee—neither of whom were initiates—were impressed that I was being offered such an opportunity and urged me to accept it.

I somewhat reluctantly committed myself to the priests of Demeter and was taken to a temple garden in Athens. There I took the sacred oath not to reveal the secrets to the profane. That oath bound the initiate not to speak of what she learned "for a thousand years." I am actually free to report what I will without fear of reprisal from Demeter or her successors.

For two days I was inundated with discussions concerning the philosophies of life that the Mysteries would reveal and celebrate. A series of priests and priestesses tried their best to teach me many things, including some of the basic ritualistic gestures, songs, and movements that were said by them to be essential in evoking the comprehensive experience known as The Way.

Initiation was not just a ceremony. It was a process that included attendance upon the Lesser Mysteries followed by a course of further emotional preparation throughout the summer until two days before the final trip to Eleusis. At that time religious banquets were held in honor of Persephone and of those who had been the founders of the Eleusinian cult. Such meals never featured either meat or fowl, but consisted almost entirely of breads and pastries derived from wheat. We drank very little wine either, and the gatherings ended early with solemn ceremonies and pledges.

The day of banquets was followed by a day of fasting, abstinence, and leisure during which time most of those who were to be initiated into the mysteries bathed together in the sea near Athens and retired early.

On the day set, up before dawn and dressed in the white, Greek garments of the day, my new-found priestly guides, friends, and I walked the 12 or so miles west to Eleusis. As we went there we became part of a converging, growing crowd that eventually numbered some two or three thousand cheerful, singing people, many of whom I had met since I arrived in Athens.

Not having eaten anything but a thin barley drink the day before, I was rather hungry and a bit light-headed that morning, but the walk was excellent. The air was crisp and clear and we all shared a feeling of calm anticipation and the gentle eagerness of those who were at least somewhat prepared for what lay ahead. Along the way we refreshed ourselves by drinking from various streams and wells that were beautifully kept and had been in continuous use for hundreds, if not thousands, of years. Water never tasted sweeter nor air felt fresher than on that morning. Even stepping out of the procession to relieve oneself had its elements of pleasure.

Arriving near Eleusis, we washed our hands and faces a final time in a sacred stream. Then the crowd separated into three groups: those who were already initiates, those who, like me, were to become initiates, and those who for whatever reasons simply either chose not to participate or were not qualified to take part in the Greater Mysteries.

Outside the temple of Demeter was a large courtyard into which we candidate initiates flowed. There we put down our various little bundles and took off our boots and sandals. Bareheaded and dressed in simple, white tunics as was the custom, we made a pretty picture as we sat down upon the grass and waited for things to begin.

Then the priestly initiates, dressed in various shades of green, the color of life, entered the courtyard in single file, singing in unison, and took up places in rows on low steps and rostra in a circle around us until they looked like a line of human trees. After a short while they quit singing. All was quiet. We waited a few minutes more. I thought how much I felt like a girl waiting for a first kiss from a new love.

Then the high priest came forward and said a prayer and performed a ceremonial libation of what was called the White Drink. I presumed it was sanctified goat's milk.

Then the graduate initiates or guides stepped down from their places around the courtyard and mingled among us for some time to help us to break into small groups—which was done with very little talking on the part of any of us. Somehow or another we quickly coalesced into groups of five to ten initiates. On the walk to Eleusis we had already pretty much coalesced into little groups and so the process went smoothly. In my group there were three men and four women, all but one of whom were about my age. I should point out that the rites at Eleusis provided a rare exception to the public segregation of the sexes.

From the courtyard each group began meandering almost aimlessly around the extensive temple precincts, looking at paintings and art objects as we discussed the philosophical matters we had already talked about during our initiations into the Lesser Mysteries.

Just when one began to wonder whether such desultory conversations and musings were going to be the sum total of the new level, and just when one began to feel seriously hungry in the midmorning, our little group found itself standing before a larger-than-life-size statue of Demeter in a grotto lighted by sunlight from a single hole in the domed ceiling. On either side of the alter were two particularly handsome, bare-chested priests and two lovely, bare-breasted priestesses. All had necklaces made of woven wheat tops and all were dressed in white, Minoan-style skirts that touched the floor. They were standing beside large basins filled with milky, white liquid into which they dipped golden ladles. As one by one we stepped forward, they offered us the liquid, saying, "This is the milk of understanding—drink it all."

One by one each of us drank, draining the ladle that was measured out according to one's size. It was the White Drink, of course, and tasted like coconut milk with a distinct flavor of grass in it, and I suspected that it was sweetened with honey. I drank without hesitation, knowing that it must be an hallucinogen of some sort. I was right.

It would be an oversimplification for me to say that the Greater Mysteries involved mass hallucination, for they did not. They involved revelation. There was, however, a Key, and that Key was then and it is now: lying there in the dust of centuries, resurrected partially in recent times. It was the Key of the Wheat—more specifically, of the wheat rust from which The White Drink was made. I understand now that the fungal rust from rye is the primary source of the lysergic acid from which LSD is synthesized. But what we did that day bore little resemblance to the heavy acid trips I had experienced in college—the Eleusinian experience was one of psychic union and enlightenment, and not one of disunion and confusion. The emotional grasp of the Mysteries that the drink facilitated was not transient, and the concepts that one pondered were not soon forgotten.

Those revelations can hardly be shared—at least not in words as I sit here so much later—indeed almost 2,000 years later. Who knows? Perhaps the Greater Mysteries may not be within the grasp of modern man even if the White Drink and the setting could be duplicated.

I met a man in modern times who seemed quite normal, calm, and intelligent who told me that he had done acid 200 times during the late 60s and early 70s. I asked him when was the last time he had done it and why had he stopped. He said something that will always remain in my thoughts.

"The final time was just last year," he said (the year being 1977), "and it was like lifting my sails again only to find that there was no wind."

Maybe the Greek wind has also died out. Maybe it died so long ago that even the White Drink could not help one lift her sails into its glory to be borne along toward knowledge.

"May your spirit soar forever," the young woman said to me as she took the dipper back from me.

"And yours forever with mine," I ritually replied as I looked her in the eye and touched my hands to my forehead. So it has been: I can remember her face as clearly right now as if I had seen it this morning.

Then the mysteries truly unfolded to us in the caves, plazas, grottoes, and temples of Eleusis during the rest of that day and into the night. The guide took our small group to various places and directed our attentions and thoughts as we experienced each. We always seemed to have enough time at each stop, each statue, painting, exhibit, or choral presentation, and yet we always seemed to leave each station just as another group was arriving and just before the wonder of it began to lose its luster.

At each station we seemed to maintain an amazing confluence of thoughts and feelings such that even though we did not necessarily do the same things at each place, we shared the same sensations and experiences. One of us might drink from a cold-water marble fountain; all of us would be refreshed. Another might sing a song learnt during the Lesser Mysteries, and the rest of us would know why he sang it; some might join in. It was acceptable also just to watch. There was no pressure to do anything.

The White Drink helped us to have the ability to understand one another. If a man spoke to me in an unknown tongue, I understood what he was saying to me and I could converse with him. Perhaps research in the future will lead to a similar development, to a psychoactive drug that facilitates translation and true intercourse among people. Perhaps there is in fact a common human language or an inherent ability to understand one another that transcends language itself but which is unlocked with the White Drink.

We arrived at the Chasm of The Souls in the afternoon when the effect of the drink was at a peak. The pit or transverse crack itself was in a large, dimly lit room or grotto some 40 feet in diameter that was divided into two halves by a seemingly bottomless crevasse that ran across it from side to side. Across from us on the other side some 12 feet away, stood three priests in their 30s. From the pit that separated us from them, coming up from the unfathomable depths, we could hear—or thought we could hear—the murmuring calls or songs of the spirits of the dead, the dead who had once themselves been initiates of the Mysteries.

I had an overpowering urge to cross over the bridgeless void to be with the priests who stood smiling and whose arms and hands reached out to me in a universal gesture of invitation, beckoning me. Dressed like us in white, wearing bracelets of gold, they looked so perfect that I felt they could give me the power to walk on air and I began to step forward. My guide restrained me with a gentle touch of her hand, then pointed out a simple wooden bench covered with fleece that was before us on the edge of the precipice.

"There is a Way," she said, gesturing toward it with a sweep of the hand that eloquently told me that I should lie upon it. For some reason I unfastened the shoulder ties of my white garment and let it fall to the floor around my ankles. Stepping forward naked, I lay down on my back on the soft fur. I felt very secure, clean and cool, and I looked up at my fellow initiates who stood there smiling and looking at me with approving nods. They Understood.

Then I floated across the chasm on the bench. It must have had some sort of a mechanism concealed beneath it, but I never saw it and could have cared less. I was not the least bit afraid of falling off. When I got to the far side, two of the priests lifted me from the fleecy bed as if I were a patient. Carrying me at chest height, they took me to the third man. I recognized him at once as being the High Priest of the Mysteries. With touches of his hands he positioned me very precisely above a certain spot on the floor. With his finger he touched my breastbone just above my heart, then raised his other hand as he spoke an exhortation in an ancient Doric dialect that I clearly understood, calling upon Apollo to use his power upon me. Suddenly a brilliant ray of red light came down through the semi-darkness from a hole in the roof far above us. It shone upon my chest at the exact spot where he had touched me.

Although it was not very hot and lasted only a short time, the red ray felt as if it could have melted a circular hole in me. It was as wonderful as—or it caused—an orgasm, and my mind went blank as I was suffused with pleasure and a sense of absolute well being. I might have fainted.

Then I found myself back with my group, still naked and kissing a fellow I had met in Athens the week before. I wrapped my arms around him and let my hands feel the smooth, strong lines of his muscles, and I responded to the touch of his lips upon mine with long, deep kisses. He was a man; he was all men. One or two others in our little group went across and were given the ray also, I think, but I was not watching them and did not see how it was done. I was too busy kissing Man. There was no past and no future. There was only the Present and in it I was melded into another human.

I probably didn't put on my shift for another hour. When we left the Chasm of the Souls I just walked around nude holding it. As in some of those college experiences I had known, that afternoon I didn't know or care what naked *meant*. I finally put it back on just so I wouldn't have to carry it.

It was a day of metaphor, allegory and mythology. It was a day, too, of laughter and comradeship and deep emotions. It would have been a good day to die.

At sunset, still under the somewhat declining influence of the White Drink, we went back out to the courtyard where we had begun our journey. From there we all walked out to a large grassy field beside the sacred stream which had a large swimming hole built into the middle of it. We were coming down and felt tired, so many of us napped on the grass or lay there thinking about all the things we had seen, felt, and thought. Even though the water was cold and we had few towels, most of us stripped down and bathed a bit in the pool. I was rather surprised—and a bit disappointed—that there was not at least a certain amount of spontaneous lovemaking, but there wasn't—at least none that I saw. My friend that I had kissed at the Chasm stayed close by me, and we held hands some, but we, too, did not indulge in that sort of thing out there in the fields. For that matter, there were very few conversations that afternoon.

After an hour or so of such leisure, we returned to the plaza to find a sumptuous vegetarian meal that had been prepared for us. While eating we watched the sacred drama of the abduction of Persephone by Pluto and of the subsequent search for her daughter by Demeter. The partially reclaimed Persephone, happy to be allowed to live on the surface of the earth for at least half a year and thankful for her mortal admirers, searches for ways to make the earth tolerable for mortals in her winter's absence. She consults all the gods and at last Athena tells her:

"Give them wisdom, for it will last when food is gone. Only with wisdom will people be happy in the long run."

"Maybe so," counters Bacchus, "but give them wine. Give them fun and pleasure when they want it."

"No," says a voluptuous and sultry Aphrodite, "give

them love without which life hath no lasting taste."

"Give them war" says Aries, "so that the men may know valor and through heroic exploits rise above their petty existences. Give them war so that their women will cherish them while they have them and not take them so much for granted and harass them about petty things."

But he is shouted down by all save Aphrodite, who agrees with him and says why she will agree to become his lover.

"Give them all of it," Zeus finally says, "but not too much of any of it. Give them something that is not quite complete, that they can puzzle over all their days. And give them the White Drink for their understanding's sake so that at least those among them who are pious and just will know that there is a Way. Those people can then lead the others to understanding and in prayer."

The gods and goddesses all agreed. Then they came out among us with silver pitchers and the golden dippers of the morning from which we sipped more of the White Drink. After all were served, we returned to the labyrinths and the experiences and the Mysteries which now we knew.

At midnight we all gathered for a third and final time in the big courtyard where we had begun the day, and there we spread out our blankets and lay down on our backs. In total silence we began looking up at the stars, it being a cloudless and moonless night. All of our guides and all of the priests and priestesses extinguished their torches, and in the darkness, we began the final ceremony. As one we welcomed among us the souls of those former initiates who at least for a while came back into material existence to join us there in the plaza. It was an experience that was at once both comforting and eerie. It felt like having a few hundred more people snuggle down amongst us, causing us to have to shift about to make room for them, and I could not tell whether those people who were touching me on either side were the living or the resurrected dead. At last, though, we were all united there, lying on our backs, looking out at the universe.

Once "they" were settled in, the priests and guides led us all in a final hymn of praise that lasted 15 minutes or more and cast over the entire assemblage a final feeling of peace and unity. As it trailed off, we in our hundreds went to sleep and dreamed scenes from the lives of others who had gone before us. I dreamed of England and Scotland and of picking berries with other deerskin clad girls in the Appalachian wilderness.

In the morning, happy, we walked back to Athens, chattering and singing.

Such was my stay in Athens, a city whose rich blend of natural and man-made scenery as well as whose cultural and religious experiences made each day a wonderful one for me. It was all so special that I decided I would settle there or somewhere nearby in Attica should I meet the right man and get married again. As things turned out, my visit was cut short after only two months by what was, in hindsight, the call of destiny.

****

XXV

At Sea

On the night of the autumn's first full moon in early October, I took out my radio and began to listen for Mark with whom I had not had contact in a month. As I waited for midnight alone on the roof of my rented home, I was particularly struck by the beauty of the views of Athens, Piraeus, the hills, and the sea. Even at that late hour, there were sounds of girls and young men laughing, playing musical instruments and singing.

Out in the harbor there were lights showing on my ship. Half of the crew stayed in the compound ashore while the others slept aboard, ready to sail at short notice if ever the need arose. Oil being fairly expensive, our kerosene lighting was a constant display of our wealth and a reminder of our power. We always had the best and the brightest lights in any port.

We had just returned from a two-week cruise that had taken us through Salamis, to Marathon, and along the western coast of Euboea. Along the way we sold oil, kerosene, and small bottles of gasoline and made a killing. We visited historical sites, temples, and small seaports, and on the trip back, we weathered a short but powerful gale off the eastern tip of Attica. One of the men was washed overboard and lost.

"We are not downhearted," the captain explained the next morning, "for when Poseidon calls, no man can ignore him, nor any man escape. To die at sea is the true sailor's wish."

I knew what he meant, of course, for I could see in their faces a love of the sea and the sailing life. They were a manly but gentle group of seamen, and we worked well together.

Mark was almost a memory to me by that time. It was like having had a lawyer who once handled an important matter for you, a case, perhaps, that dragged on and on, during which one had grown close to him if only out of necessity. One paid the bill, but who wants to see him again? At any rate, it had been almost seven months since he had visited with me at the refinery.

The radio messages I had exchanged with him after that time had been entirely businesslike and thoroughly boring, but they seemed important enough to make me look forward to the communications. Using the radio and my fading English gave me contact with the world that I had left behind, and in a world of many languages and many cultures, one's own becomes more precious.

I waited for his call and wondered how he was doing and where he was, and I wondered why he had missed the last new moon.

At last, almost at midnight, the tiny di-dah, di-dah, dit-dah started coming in through the earphones, and I keyed the reply, "*O.K. Send.*" Immediately I knew that something was different, wrong. Slowly, almost painfully slowly, a message came in: "*Go slow. Have hard time this end.*"

"*W-h-a-t i-s w-r-o-n-g?*" I keyed slowly. I waited a long time for a reply.

"*N-o-t-h-i-n-g. I-m-m-a-n-u-e-l !*" came the deliberate reply. It took me a long minute to figure out what the second word with an exclamation mark after it meant. Then it hit me.

It was Julian! He hadn't identified himself, but the fact that he couldn't send code well and that he was obviously using the most compressed message he could made it obvious it was he. I was quite shocked. I had long before assumed he was dead.

"*Where are you?*" I asked slowly.

After two or three suspenseful minutes, he replied,

"Israel. Who is this?"
　"Eva," I keyed.
　"Where?"
　"Athens."
　"Together?"
　"No."
　"Where Mark?"
　Before I could answer, another signal—Mark's—broke
in: *"Spain,"* he sent.
　I was doubly surprised!
　So for that night and the night that followed, we three
were once again united, if only via the thin tracery of the
messages we sent. Working slowly through long hours, we
pieced together our stories and brought one another up to date
with what we had been doing and what our plans were.
　Mark reported that he had become bored in Rome and
had decided to go traveling once again, this time to the West and
to Britain. I could tell by reading between the lines that he was
jaded and disillusioned, perhaps even afraid of being too much
at the mercy of his new-found friends. At any rate, his plan now
was to go once again to Mauretania where he would visit our
first friends and attempt to get the Short to fly again using a load
of gasoline that he would take with him. He said he missed
flying, and I believed him. It was hard for me to abandon the
notion of at least going up once more and, as your author
Vincent Sheean quoted, *"to ride the high road/ between the
thunder and the sun."* Nevertheless, I doubted that he would
ever be able to fly the Short again, aircraft being so complicated.
　As to Julian, it turned out that shortly after his last
contact with us, two years before, he had been imprisoned in
Egypt and Arabia. His captor had been a local ruler who merely
delayed him at first, then held him for a full year for no apparent
reason other than ransom.
　He had been deprived of all of his goods, including the
radio that he later—much later—recovered.
　Most of his imprisonment was spent in some sort of
small fortress or compound in the Sinai where he suffered
terribly during long months from poor food, boredom, cold, heat,
and fleas. It was the first time in his life that he suffered
prolonged physical discomfort and deprivation, and he was

severely tested. He also perfected his Hebrew and Aramaic through endless conversations with his fellow prisoners who were Jews.

We could surmise that the satrap who held Julian was afraid to kill him yet was equally afraid to let him go. After all, he must have known enough about Julian's background to have heard wildly exaggerated stories about the power of our weapons. There was also the possibility that Julian's captor may have been acting under the orders from Rome or from some other power.

Whatever the case might have been, he finally managed to escape. Penniless and almost naked, he walked to Palestine, travelling mostly at night and using a false name. He begged and worked for his food. Eventually he made it to Galilee.

There his luck changed and his quest ended, for it took him no time at all to find the man he sought and to join his little band of followers. They roamed the land preaching, teaching, and taking on occasional jobs. He became their amanuensis and their treasurer. He was with Jesus—or so he said.

Who was I to say he wasn't?

Through a combination of luck and incredible persistence, he had managed to save up enough of the group's money to hire an agent to go to Egypt to locate and purchase his long-lost radio. Miraculously, it still worked. He had just managed to get it from the agent during the preceding month and had anxiously awaited the night of the full moon to begin his attempts to communicate with us.

He wanted money and, naturally, we promised to send some right away. I got the feeling that he needed to replace the cash that he had perhaps embezzled in order to hire the agent and buy the radio—either that or he was under some pressure to show that it was money well spent.

To be fair to Julian, though, his motives in making such an extraordinary effort to regain the radio were not primarily mercenary, for his main messages were ones urging Mark to come to Palestine right away.

"The hour of God is now. He walks the earth as a man," he stated. *"How can you stay away?"* he asked. It was a good question, and even through the medium of Morse Code and Julian's abbreviated sentences, one could catch his sense of excitement and urgency. He didn't ask me to join him. I am sure,

though, that he was more than happy to learn that I would send a letter of credit he could draw upon.

For some reason, I decided to leave Athens at once and make straight for Tyre. From there I would go overland to the Sea of Galilee where Julian said their group was helping with the autumn harvest. I figured that it would only take me about 20 days to get there—25 if I made a few stopovers.

Mark, on the other hand, said that he would not join us—at least not right away. He was already so close to Mauretania that it made sense for him to go there first and, if possible, to fly back using the fuel he had and what was stockpiled in North African ports along the way. That really was the best plan, for the Romans—or whoever our enemies were— needed further proofs of our god-like powers, and surely the vision of Mark taking off and landing in the Short could fill that need.

On the third day following Julian's first message, I went to sea once again, telling my willing captain and crew to head directly across the sea to Tyre. They were up for anything.

Straight through the Cyclades we sailed, looking for all the world like some brave merchant ship hastening to take supplies to our countrymen besieging Troy. It started out marvelously, and although I was headed toward Julian and a meeting with the man who he said was the Christ, my thoughts lay not upon that distant shore and its problems and promises. I thought, rather, only of the present and the past, for there on the Aegean, they were fused. Each island and each rock we passed had a myth attached to it, and a member of the crew to tell of it. As soon as one such place passed astern we would espy another and talk about its history, its monsters, and its nymphs. It was as if Odysseus was alive and sailing with us.

In fact, there *was* a man in the crew who was called by that name who could recite from memory the entire Iliad. Many an hour we spent listening to him retell the crew's favorite parts of the old story. Having heard it many times before, many of them would join with him in reciting the most familiar and beloved lines. Poetry was as much a part of their lives as was the sea, and it was then that I most strongly thought of you, remembering very well that you were yourself something of a would-be poet back when I knew you. I often thought of how you could recite Poe's *To Helen* which had been, as I recall, the name of your first real girlfriend, saying:

> *Helen, thy beauty is to me*
> *Like those Nicean barks of yore*
> *That gently, o'er a perfumed sea,*
> *The weary, way-worn wanderer bore*
>   *To his own native shore.*

> *On desperate seas long wont to roam,*
> *Thy hyacinth hair, thy classic face,*
> *Thy Naiad airs have brought me home*
> *To the glory that was Greece,*
>   *And the grandeur that was Rome.*

> *Lo, in yon brilliant window-niche*
> *How statue-like I see thee stand,*
> *The agate lamp within thy hand,*
> *Ah! Psyche, from the regions which*
>   *Are holy land!*

I remembered how back in those days, I wished that I was your Helen, and maybe I could have been, had you the vision and I the mantle. But what could we have seen anyway, being so young and so blind? I thought of you and how much like my crewmen you would someday be, your atoms not yet assembled and your nation not yet founded.

Many a time, standing on the ship's windward rail, my hand holding the rigging as the breezes carried my hyacinth hair and pressed my short, Greek clothes against me, I felt as if I was my crew's very own Helen off on a quest, the goal of which was beyond even her far-seeing ken. They told me repeatedly that they felt privileged to be on such a journey with me and that they would go anywhere and face any danger in my service.

As things soon worked out, they proved their willingness to fight when we were beset by pirates just at nightfall off the island of Kos. Coming at us in two double-banked craft that were longer but narrower than our own, they made no pretense of being anything other than what they were. They counted, I suppose, on overawing their victims by speed, audacity, and strength of numbers. Each ship held about 50 men, and they came on fast.

They were not fast enough, though, to prevent us from preparing for them. This we did first by wearing ship. With the full force of the wind aft, we could move as quickly as possible and extend the time that it would take them to overhaul us. Seeing us turn, they increased their rowing tempo and began to close the distance between us, slicing through the swells like sinister sea serpents. Although I did not show it, I was very frightened, and I hurried to my cabin to get my rifle and .45, spilling bullets everywhere in my haste to load the .22's magazine. My crew set up and loaded our aft catapult.

When I went back on deck with my rifle, I was surprised to find the captain and crew as happy and excited as schoolboys even with death just three hundred yards off and closing. Immediately I knew why: they were preparing to use the catapult and had every confidence in it and in me. Ignorance in that case truly was bliss, and they were looking forward to the fight not as an ordeal but as an opportunity. When the pirates were about 200 yards off but looked much closer, we were about ready to begin firing. For my part, I had decided to wait until they were much closer before using the .22.

They fired at us first, using a bow-mounted balista that sent a heavy spear with a line on it rushing up over us and through the sail. With his razor-sharp knife a topman cut the line before it could damage anything. I asked the captain why he had not yet fired at the approaching boats.

"We were waiting for your command," he explained calmly.

I assured them that further delay was not necessary and so, waiting for the rise of the ship on a swell to begin, the mate ordered the first fire jug lighted. As it whoofed into flames, he jerked the release. With a loud "Knock!" the machine threw the copper, spherical shell in a high, graceful trajectory of fire that ended in the sail of the nearer of our two pursuers. Instantly a splat of fire burst in the sail, illuminating the astonished crew below. Worse soon came to them as the half-empty sphere rolled down through the decks spilling gasoline. All rowing amidships stopped and the boat began to lose way. I watched with astonishment at the immediate destruction and suffering that my own invention was causing when the second ship fired a flaming ball at us. It passed over our heads and fell into the sea. My crew fired two shots at the second boat, but neither struck it. Then they loaded a clay pot shot, lit its rag fuse and launched again at the first boat, striking it near the waterline and causing the sea to appear to burn as the flames leaped all along the side of the hapless and almost motionless ship. The second boat went to the aid the first and broke off the engagement. As my crew cheered, we came about to our original course and sailed away. The stricken ship burned brightly in the falling night.

Shortly thereafter we arrived at Rhodes in the Dodecanese, gliding gracefully into the smooth harbor. On the shore, looking like the rusted hulks of midget submarines, lay parts of the great statue of Helios, the Sun God, that had stood beside—but not astride—the entrance to the harbor for over 100 years. It had been toppled by an earthquake many years before and yet, even in ruins, was a magnificent thing. I wondered why it had not been restored. I suppose that the port—which was still prosperous—no longer worshipped whatever quality the statue had once personified.

We remained in Rhodes for two nights, selling fuel from the lighter and enjoying such hospitality as a rich city could afford. Mentioning to no one our brief sea-battle, and bandying it about that our next major port of call would be Antioch, we sailed on the tide before dawn on the third day.

By the time the sun rose we had almost passed completely beyond sight of the port. As was my practice, I went aloft with my secret binocular half and scanned the horizon. From the perch I had on the masthead I could see that a red-sailed ship was rounding the headland and entering the port. That gave me a bad feeling, for the red sail meant only one thing: that it was a Roman warship, and there were so few of them at sea in times of peace that I concluded that it was looking for us. After what I had been through, it was hard not to be paranoid. The Romans, after all, were the cops of the sea, and all day long I thought of that ship and remembered the 60s rock song, *I Owe It*, in which the singer notes his fear of "...looking into my mirror and seeing a po-lice car."

I also thought of how, when I had complained to him in North Carolina about the extremes he took to avoid getting caught or even questioned, Mark had said, "It isn't paranoia if you habitually stand on railroad tracks, hear a familiar rumbling, and fear getting hit by a train."

I should explain, too, that other seafarers feared the Roman galleys, too, for they not only represented the law, but also each boat could be a law unto itself. Graft, extortion, theft, and impressment were so frequent that most decent ships—as well as all pirates—would go well out of their way to avoid contact with the Romans on the high seas. By Roman law, all ships other than Roman warships and revenue cutters were required to have wide beams so that they could not outrun the Roman galleys. Generally speaking, it was an effective and popular edict that promoted commerce even if it slowed it down a bit.

The military ships, then, were much faster than the cargo ships they were set to police, and the few pirate ships that were built for speed along the lines of the narrow galley stood out like icebergs on the open sea. Raiders were therefore usually lightly and cheaply built and could easily be hidden in small bays and estuaries.

In times of political instability or civil war when the general sea-lanes were ineffectively policed, piracy and pirate ships multiplied magically. Every coastal village would to produce its own craft and crew to join in the plundering of wayfarers.

Therefore, Roman rule of the seas was somewhat tolerable under the circumstances. Despite its levies, taxation, and civil wars, Rome did impose order and peace on the seas when it was not otherwise distracted, and once it had its own house in order it could be counted on to send its navy out to suppress any piracy that had sprung up during its absence.

My own ship was a cross between a cargo vessel and a private yacht—although with its twin-masted, fore-and-aft lanteen rig and its 14-oared single banks, it could hardly be thought of as such by any modern standards. Like many similar cruisers of its day, it was built for as much speed as the Roman formulae allowed. On that morning, I longed for more.

Consequently I requested that the captain do what he could to speed us away from Rhodes. He pointed off to leeward and once again we ran before the wind. We also broke out spinnaker that I had ordered made in Piraeus. The new sail put considerable strain on the foremast and made the bow bite into the water more, so it only slightly increased our speed. Everyone worried aloud about the mast's strength, and although I could not have actually ordered the captain in matters concerning the sailing and safety of the ship, he never refused any request of mine. He would have sailed us upon a rock had I ordered it done.

All of our efforts were in vain, though, for by late afternoon, the Roman warship came into view off our stern and made straight for us. From the foremast perch, I could see that it was making all possible speed by employing both of its large, square sails as well as its long, double-banked oars. They were being stroked at a fairly brisk pace which must have been hard on the slaves.

I figured that we had about an hour before it got to us— two if we ran. Even with the naked eye, we could see the fiery signal that it launched in a high arch from one of its two foredeck catapults. That was the signal telling us to heave to and wait. Coming back down to the deck I was greeted by the worried faces of my captain, maid, and crew, all of whom looked to me to decide whether we should stop, flee, or fight. To flee or to fight would have branded them all as pirates, and might have even condemned their home villages near Corfu to punishments. They were waiting for my orders.

"Whatever the goddess bids us," the captain said for them over the sounds of ship and wind and sea, "we shall do. Just tell us!"

"Strike the sails!" I told them without hesitation. "It may just be a message they bear."

The crewmen released the mainsails and started taking in the spinnaker.

"But should we prepare for a fight in case they mean us harm?" the man named Odysseus asked.

I was standing on a coaming over a hatch. I could feel the ship rapidly losing way.

"No," I told them all in a loud voice, "even though I think we might be able to beat them as we beat the pirates. You should all know that I appreciate your willingness to fight. And yet I think we must all realize that our only hope is in submission—either that or we would have to kill every one of them. I am not willing to try that. So be it!"

I went below and packed a bag of my most important things and told my maid to pack hers. I had to work fast and I forgot several things I later wished for, but I remembered the most important ones: gold, derringer, rifle, ammunition, and radio. When I was finished, I sent my maid to bid the captain to come to my quarters.

He came into my tiny cabin and closed the door. There was only a bunk and a chair and they were taken up with my bundles, so we just stood there face to face. He looked very distraught, for he was as worried as I.

There was little time for making speeches, so I showed him where the rest of my money was stashed and bid him make straight for Tyre and wait there for at least a month. He knew the name of the merchant banker we used, and I knew that I could count on him to deliver Julian's letter of credit and not to make off with my cash.

There were only scant minutes left before we would be required on deck. Suddenly there was an awkward silence into which it seemed my duty to fashion some special words for this man who had so loyally served me for over a year. Reaching forth to hold each of his hands lightly in mine, and looking down into his dark, watering eyes, I said something to the effect of:

"My Captain, I do not know what will happen to us, but I fear that we shall be parted. You have been a true friend, a wise counselor, and a comrade-in-arms. More than that, you are a man in the finest sense of the word. May you go with God and my blessing."

Immediately, he dropped to one knee and lowered his head as if before a queen.

"Your blessing has been upon me and this ship from the moment I first saw you," he said. "I shall serve you forever."

I thought he was going to cry. My brave captain was going to cry! Quickly I raised him up and grabbed him by the shoulders.

"Cheer up!" I said with a smile. "Don't make us glum in front of the Romans or our men. And here:" I added for good measure, "don't take all of this so seriously! After all, I'm just a crazy foreign woman who likes you very much."

And with that said, I surprised him with a warm kiss upon his lips, holding him against me long enough to let him know that it was no token peck, no empty gesture. It may have been more sisterly than anything else, but it conveyed my love.

He was too astonished to respond and as I came away, he smiled a knowing smile. He turned and swaggered out upon the deck before me. I patted my derringer to make sure it was still in place in its little holster under my clothes in the small of my back, and then followed him topside.

It was bright and sunny. The Roman ship was just pulling up along the port side in a flashy yet poorly executed show of seamanship. They had halted just a bit too far off for a man to leap across. The boats rocked broadly in the swells and with a gesture of command and a loud snap of his fingers, my captain had our crew scull the starboard oars so as gently to bring the ships closer together. I noticed that my crew could not help but show pride in their obviously superior abilities. I wished they were not so obvious about it.

As the breeze was coming in from the starboard quarter, we were most fortunately to windward of the stench coming from the rows of slaves who powered the large boat. The craft was of a smaller type than the one on which I had journeyed from Nova Carthago to Ostia, being a bireme, or two-rowed, 80-oared ship with a short, tough ram front and three or four catapults and ballistas on the deck. It was painted a bright pink with red trim and red sails. By modern standards, its color scheme would be considered to be very gaudy, but by the Roman ones, it was held to be sharp, indeed. The ship itself was quite new, very up-to-date and in perfect condition, all of which indicated that its captain was a man of importance.

In addition to its hundred or so slaves, it carried a sailing crew of six, fifteen marines, four or five orderlies and cooks, a captain and two or three officers. Although it was certainly large in comparison to our boat, it was so lightly built that one could see daylight clear through it, giving me the distinct impression that it could not withstand a really big storm.

Since all of the leather oar compartment flaps had been let down to open the decks to the cooling airs. I could plainly see that in addition to all the men on the main deck above us, some forty or fifty pairs of eyes gazed hungrily out at us from the dirty faces of the chained starboard oarsmen. What freedom we must have represented to them! So near and yet so far and—Lo!—a beautiful woman dressed in strange trousers and a shirt, wearing soft boots: perhaps a German, her straying reddish blonde hair floating on the wind. A low moan of desire, despair, and envy came out from between the decks and a voice shouted in Latin "Be quiet!" as a whip cracked loudly. Somewhere a man wept.

The soldiers on the deck were orderly and quiet, but one could see that they, too, were envious captives aboard the pink cruiser. The Roman ship's main deck was eight or ten feet higher than ours, and the tarriffrail was another four feet up from there, so we were forced to look up into the faces above us, although truth be told, the sight of the poor oarsmen down at our level was more compelling. It is a bad thing to be helpless in the face of such evil.

A boarding-port opened in the galley's side, and as the boats touched, to our astonishment a tall, unarmed Roman officer—a beautiful man dressed in a light, thigh-length green-and-gold toga—leaped nimbly down to our deck with cat-like grace. Instantly coming to his full height—about 6'1"—and ignoring my captain, he bowed slightly to me in the manner of a gentleman, which is to say, without breaking eye contact. He smiled at me in a friendly and familiar way that made me feel almost at ease with him.

What beautiful eyes he had! A rich, reddish brown beneath long, dark lashes, they were the sort of eyes that speak for themselves of power, will, and passion. They smiled with self-confidence.

He had a well-shaped, powerful head, too, with a firm chin, square jaw, and perfect teeth. His muscles rolled easily beneath the toga. His legs were long, strong, and elegant, and his thick, deep auburn hair glistened in the sun. It was—for a Roman's—rather longish and had a bit of curl in it so that it looked almost boyish and made me long to touch it.

Like all officers, he was clean-shaven, but he was so hirsute that the shaving simply stopped at an arbitrary line around his neck just below the Adam's' apple. His skin was lightly tanned and he looked like a most magnificent specimen of a man. He was two to four years younger than I was, and although I had never met him before, I knew who he was.

"Lady Evangelica Atlantica," he said, as his slight bow ended and he squared back his shoulders, "I am..."

"Casius Chaerea, if I do not miss my guess," I interrupted sweetly, trying to pour on the charm as much as I could, and wishing that I was dressed in my best Greek costume rather than in my more practical shipboard trousers and white blouse. I could feel that my blush was giving me away.

I knew who he was because his father was the very famous officer under whom Marcus had served and with whom he had survived the battle in the Teutoburg Forest 20 years before. That same elder Chaerea had been prominent in other famous actions on the German frontier as well and had fought in the gladiatorial arena in Rome to defend the honor of the city against a famous German captive.

The son—who had been away in Africa at the time I was in Rome—was widely reputed to be the most handsome man and the most eligible bachelor in Rome. His effect on women was becoming legendary—so much so that it was practically considered *de rigueur* for both married and unmarried women to offer to sleep with him. It was said that he often left Rome just to be away from the pressures of celebrity as well as the unremitting female attention that he received there.

Knowing his reputation, throughout our initial conversations I tried to be on guard against his charms, but that was almost impossible, for he assumed a disarming, relaxed manner that made me think he was not the least bit interested in me. That, of course, makes a woman twice as interested in such a handsome man.

"At your service," he admitted with another half bow. "I am so happy that I was able to find you in these dangerous waters," he continued. We both knew that he had not just "found" me but that he had pursued me. A cat-and-mouse game began—he, of course, was the cat.

I suggested that the waters were not too unsafe for us. He insisted that they were, as evidenced by the attack upon us of which he had heard. I responded by pointing out how handily we had beaten off the pirates. He complimented us upon our pluck as well as our luck. I attributed our victory to our superior seamanship and weaponry. He pointed out that we had sunk but one of two ships—thereby indicating that he already knew of the details of our little sea-fight. I told him rather pointedly that we were capable of defending ourselves against ships of any size.

He spoke of an outbreak of piracy in the local seas and said that he was ordered to suppress it. I pointed out that we would soon be safe upon more open waters where there were few handy harbors and bays whence pirates might sally. He told of how bold brigands were even then venturing farther away from their islands and the mainland. And so it went.

He invited me aboard his ship; I had chairs brought and invited him to have wine with the captain and me, insisting that we could claim the privilege of being the first hosts. For the first time, he addressed my captain politely and made small sea-talk with him as we took our seats in the shade of the sail that my crew had awning-pitched ten or twelve feet off the deck. We drank to one another's health from silver goblets. My crew sat on the deck around us at a respectful distance—not too close to be obtrusive, but close enough to hear every word. All was quiet aboard the galley, too, where slaves and sailors alike strained to hear our words. For the benefit of our audiences, we spoke rather loudly—a practice one can easily adopt under those circumstances.

If he felt in any danger by being surrounded by my men, Cassius didn't show it, and though my captain and his crew were all fine, healthy men, it was sadly obvious that they felt themselves to be quite clearly in the presence of a man who they acknowledged as being their superior. He was practically of noble blood, famous, and beautiful. They were not.

It was therefore up to me to try to meet him on equal terms if I could. But under the circumstances—having the lives and fortunes of my crew to think of and without a detachment of armored marines at my immediate beck and call—all the real power lay with him.

So it was that he insisted that I go aboard his ship and put myself under his protection. He did this in such a way as to make it obvious that I had no choice in the matter and yet allowed me to save face by accepting the pretext that it was a duty imposed upon him that he had reluctantly accepted. I was, he said, too treasured an emissary to risk being lost on seas that were under Roman protection. Were I lost, he pointed out rather unconvincingly, my country might think Rome had a hand in it.

Cassius also noted that we could cruise the Aegean and see the sights while he carried out his mission of extirpating such pirates as might be attempting to prey upon legitimate commerce. It was easy enough to see where that sort of proximity to one another might lead, and with a little start of the heart I realized that maybe he was interested in me. With the kiss of my captain hardly cold on my lips, I looked at Cassius' mouth and thought how those lips of his that spoke so nonchalantly were sensuous and full.

I said that I had important business in Antioch and was on my way there, and he responded by promising to take me there as soon as possible, but in any case, to have me there within a fortnight even if he had to kill the oarsmen to do it.

With that comment, I changed my tack and tried to beg off by saying that I preferred never again to set foot on a slave-rowed galley. A murmur ran through the bireme's oar decks and a whip cracked. At that point both he and my own captain expressed their astonishment that I should say such a thing since most rich people would have preferred to travel in the fast, elegant galleys rather than the wallowing merchantmen. It was the first time that I felt like I had even slightly thrown Cassius off, but I continued talking without sufficient forethought—always a foolish thing to do.

"What then drives your ships forward against the wind in times of war?" they asked me.

I should have said, "Free men!" but instead said something to the effect of "powerful gasoline motors," but it lost a lot in the translation so that it came out something like "strong burning-fluid gizmos." I could tell that everybody there thought I was lying, for they were almost all seamen of one sort or another and had heard tall tales before. I should have told them we had teams of whales pull out boats. They would have believed that. At any rate, my gizmos remark hurt my credibility—a fact that I recognized right away. So much for a foolish utterance! It reminds me of a story about an Eskimo who sailed to New York with a whaler in the 1890s. Upon returning to Greenland, he told his friends about tall stone buildings covered in glass and about iron rails upon which ran huge iron machines belching smoke. Naturally, he was dismissed as a liar or a lunatic, and he died an angry, bitter recluse.

After an hour, the skies began to darken and the wind began to pick up enough to make it imperative that the ships soon part. Cassius took adroit advantage of the obvious necessity to bring matters to a close, and as it was obvious that he would resort to force if necessary, I agreed to go aboard his ship. After a brief address to my crew, my maid and I left our ship. The man named Odysseus went with me as my manservant, lyricist, and personal bodyguard, and we waved farewell to his brother and our friends when at last the Roman galley cast off and got under way. Out went the oars and forward to the catch. Then we pulled strongly away to the east—which was to windward—leaving my precious floating home and its devoted crew and captain in our wake. I always seemed to be leaving somewhere or losing somebody.

****

XXVI

Cassius & Company

Cassius gave me his luxurious cabin aft, removing his things to the second officer's quarters in a part of the ship which in later times would be called the fo'c'sle. Being a passenger by compulsion rather than by choice, I was not the least bit reluctant to take the best accommodations aboard. I did not even have to share my room, for my maid had her own place on the deck below mine. My manservant slept with the marines in their part of the ship.

As often as not, the boats being so crowded, biremes and triremes put ashore practically every night so that the men could sleep on the ground and bathe in the sea.

Our ship was no exception, and during the night we made a landfall in some little bay which was surrounded by rocky hills and cliffs which tabled back as they rose like some old, worn ziggurat dropped into the sea. Into the solid rock were cut hundreds of small caves which I later learned were essentially little rental vacation rooms for both local and foreign tourists. Usually quite shallow—say no more than ten feet deep—they had curtains for privacy as well as gaily-colored awnings to keep out the sun and rain. As the trails that connected the cliffs with the village in the back of the bay all followed the natural dips and strikes of the rock, the pathways all sloped with the natural formations. By daylight a typical section of the cliffs forty feet tall and a hundred yards long looked like some buff-colored Holiday Inn which was sinking by the stern, taking with it the immigrants who had just settled in. There were people of all ages almost constantly coming and going on the paths, and there was always something happening—a fight, a song, an argument between spouses. Down where the sea beat lazily against the base of the cliffs, there were several pools which had been cut into the living rock so that the crippled, the young and the timid might wade or soak without fear of drowning or shark attack. There were children running all about and the smell of wood smoke, fish, and cooking food was everywhere. Cassius ordered the boat to be rowed backward toward the shore and beached with its prow pointing seaward some hundred yards down from the village quay. The tide was beginning to ebb.

In their clanking chains the lines of slaves and convicts filed ashore by torchlight amid their marine guards, leaving only the sailors and cooks aboard with us. We had a late dinner of roast lamb, vegetables and sweet wine out under the stars on the open main deck. Cassius was as charming as ever, studiously avoiding giving me the sort of looks that some later writer might describe as "bedroom eyes". He was my captor and he was a Roman, but I can't say honestly that I did not try to be as attractive as I could. I was aware of the fact that all of the other men constantly stared at me with undisguised looks of lust or admiration. I could not be sure about what Cassius might be finding in my eyes.

Finally saying it had been a long day, he excused himself and retired, leaving the empty deck to me as the half-moon rose high above the harbor and the few remaining lights ashore went out. Feeling very safe, slightly drunk, and more than a little horny, I went to bed but could not sleep, for I thought of men—of talking with them, and looking at them, and of feeling them as they felt of me. I thought of my having kissed my captain that afternoon and of how his lips felt surprisingly soft. I pondered how I liked the way a man's chest hair felt against my breasts, how furry Cassius looked, and how he was so incredibly masculine, attractive, and intelligent. As you know, I always had a soft spot for intellectual men of action. Lying there alone in my cabin, that soft spot began to bother me.

Having no man to please me, I pleased myself. Reclining on my soft bunk and looking through the sash at the risen moon, recalling how I had kissed and been with Man during the Mysteries, my body remembered how much my husband had pleased me. Swimming in the liquid moonlight, I thought back—'way back—past even Mark to another who had pleased me, and to you who had pleased me, too, with your soft mouth and insistent caresses. Then I sped back to the present as the pleasure came over me in a series of waves. I had a vision of the sea, felt the hard but soft way that a man feels when I touch him, smelled the masculine scents all about me, heard my own soft animal noises and remembered how much like the sea a man tastes.

That night, finally, I slept like a kitten. I dreamed of seas and of people swimming. I dreamed of my house in Piraeus and of someone knocking on its doors, of getting up, and of going back to bed. The knocking persisted.

I awakened shortly after sunrise to the sound of a score of hammers beating away somewhere and realized where I was. Getting up, I quickly knew that not only were we not afloat but also that the boat was leaning slightly to port and was dipping toward the bow. I assumed that the tide was out and that we were aground.

Calling for my maid, we dressed me up as a Roman lady—and not a particularly drab one, either, if I do say so. Rather I appeared to be something of a cross between an unmarried girl and the hard, cold, widowed businesswoman I had been the year before. Wanting to carry some weight with Cassius Chaerea and his officers, I dressed in the ancient equivalent of what is now called a power suit. In my rich clothes, high-piled hair and heavy makeup I rather looked like one of those strange, Republican women we saw in Miami in '72.

Coming on deck I suddenly found myself amid an unbelievable flurry of activity and could immediately see that the ship wasn't going anywhere. Everybody—crew, marines, slaves and officers alike—was engaged in all kinds of work. The sails were spread out on the beach being refurbished. Lines were being uncoiled, inspected, and recoiled, and a team of carpenters was busy doing something to the starboard side down near what had been the waterline. When I overcame my matronly dignity and leaned out over the tariffrail to look, I could clearly see that they were carefully removing a couple of boards from the hull. It didn't look like we were going to be able to leave for several days.

On the small, rocky beach not far off I could plainly see Cassius Chaerea stripped to the waist working alongside a gang of slaves and marines. They were doing something or another with part of the mast, and even at a distance I could tell it was him, for he towered over them and seemed to be doing the work of two men. He had great, big shoulders and muscles that rippled as he worked.

I was rather put out that there wasn't anyone on the deck to impress, and I was downright miffed by the apparent fact that we were certainly going neither to Antioch nor pirate chasing. I felt as if I had been cozened. Standing there feeling overdressed and foolish, I began to get angry. Studying our position, I was frankly surprised that the bow was still in the water. Accordingly I called down to the young third officer who was standing on the beach below me and facetiously asked if we were going to be pulled completely out of the water.

"Yes, M'Lady! We'll have that done in a minute, too," he said with a grin. Practically as he spoke a cry rang out and a huge, many-voiced heaving song or chant broke out astern, which is to say, shoreward. Looking back, I saw two long lines of naked, wiry men laying into long cables tied to a harness around the ship. Others labored at the spokes of several vertical Spanish windlasses into which the main lines ran. Men from other parts of the beach, Cassius among them, ran to join themselves to the lines, and they all pulled away lustily. The ship began smartly to move beneath our feet up a long series of greased oars lying crosswise on the beach and in a few minutes we were totally out of the water. The men gave a weak cheer, then went back to their other tasks.

The sweating, muscular Cassius grinned like a schoolboy and waved up to me. Without thinking I waved back. Then I put my hands down on the tariff rail and found out that it had fresh paint on it. My stola was ruined with two big red spots on the underside of the breast area and I was a mess—a disconcerted mess.

Fortunately, a small bottle of gasoline I had helped to get the paint off my hands and, what the heck! I thought: I didn't like looking like a fussy Roman woman anyway. Changing into my only pair of shorts, socks and boots, I put on a simple, short, white tunic and tucked it into the waistband. Then I gave the Roman outfit to my maid who was glad to get it even if it was too big for her and had the two paint blotches on it.

When we reemerged on deck, I was a lot more careful about fresh paint and other such worksite pitfalls. Needing to recover my poise and to assert myself as best I could, I tested a rope that hung over the side, then went down it hand-by-hand like a true sailor.

On the ground I found my erstwhile protector and immediately tried to express my displeasure at his having delayed my travel plans.

In a gesture of extreme gentlemanliness, he dropped what he was doing, wiped his hands on his little leather miniskirt-sort of wrap, and talked to me with as much naturalness of manner as he might have employed were he fully clothed in parade uniform and lorica. He really had a gift for making me feel uncomfortable, for there I stood looking relatively weak and clothed while he drank water, wiped the sweat from his face, and patiently explained the repairs they were making. He stood there, almost naked: handsome, capable, healthy, and in charge. In short, he looked as sexy as a man could look, and somewhere back in his eyes and behind the polite facade of words, I could feel his animal nature. Like a barely tamed lion, he seemed as if on a moment's notice he could have eaten me—or mounted me, for that matter.

He was aware of the effect he was having on me. As we talked his wry smiles gave him away even as my own signs gave me away, no doubt. I could feel my breasts stiffening.

Telling me that all the repairs were necessary for both seaworthiness and speed, he assured me that we would probably sail on the next forenoon's high tide. I didn't believe him, but I didn't say so. I continued to assume that he was operating under some sort of orders to detain me.

Finally, strangely exasperated, I turned on my heel and left in a huff, and began walking toward the little village at the end of the bay, my two servants trailing along behind like ducklings.

We went for a walk—a very long walk—to the other side of the island. I didn't even bother to go back for the .22 rifle aboard ship but just walked on and on until I was both tired and, once again, happy. After all, it was truly a beautiful island, and October seas, though cooling, were glassy and clear. We even found a stream were my maid and I bathed and washed our hair.

When we arrived back at the top of the hill that overlooked the bay at the end of the day, we were astonished to see that the refitting was almost completed. The sails, though furled, were reset, all the stores and supplies which had been strewn about the beach had been put up, and there were two men painting the patched part of the hull with fresh paint. It restored my faith in the word of man. Happily we walked down to the shore.

That night Cassius and I were invited by the local Roman magistrate to dine at his villa outside of town. Leaving before sunset, the two of us walked by ourselves the mile or two out to where the house stood atop a high hill overlooking the sea.

Our host was a portly, older man who practically fell over himself in his efforts to be hospitable to us. His wife, a darker-skinned woman hardly older than I, was even more obsequious than he. But who could have blamed her, poor dear, being so isolated from the world as she probably thought herself to be? To my embarrassment, she repeatedly told us that we were the most famous and the most handsome people she had ever entertained. Obviously, she knew that it was a moment for her to savor and retell in the years ahead, and I could not help but like her and do what I could to make it a memorable evening for her.

They served us a wonderful seven course meal rich with the best seafood imaginable, all cooked to perfection. They served us their best wine and we ate their delicious repast as if we were gluttons. We asked them about themselves, listened to their children sing and play the lyre, and complimented them on their home and their cuisine. Obviously knowing of both Cassius Chaerea and his famous father, they knew that he had dined at many of the finest tables in the Empire. Therefore when he complimented the fish sauce or the honey-cakes, our hosts practically died with pleasure. Finally, in a gesture that bordered on going a bit too far, he insisted on having the cook be sent for. I rather suspected that our hostess herself had done a good deal of the cooking but was perhaps a bit ashamed to admit it. To do so probably would have seemed to her to be an admission of their being middle rather than upper class, although truth be told, in republican days even the richest Roman ladies had prided themselves on their skills as cooks. Livia, wife of Augustus Caesar, and mother of Tiberias, for example, spent many hours in hot kitchens even after her husband had become master of the world. In the early mornings she often went forth to the markets with her servants and haggled over prices like any other housewife.

The cook duly presented herself and Cassius, showing at least to me his full understanding of the human sensitivities involved, said a few kind but very sincere things to her and gave her a tiny, gold coin. It was probably more money than the woman had ever had at one time in her life, but she accepted it with a polite word of thanks, bowed and left.

As was the custom, Cassius was called on to sing, recite a verse, or tell a story, and he chose to tell a story which he had probably told many times before, for it was artfully crafted, true, and memorized— all that and it had a moral, too.

I for my part sang a song in English. It was, as I recall, "Joy to the World" and I sang it passably well, although it irked me not to be able to remember more than the first two verses. The third verse, which I la-laed through, I recalled latter and thought of often thereafter:

No more let sins and sorrows grow,
Nor thorns infest the ground;
He comes to make His blessings flow,
Far as the curse is found, Far as the curse is found,
Far as, far as the curse is found.

Never having been a particularly musical person, I often have wished that I had learned more songs when I was young. As you may recall, I had a rather decent singing-voice that was strong, if not quite lovely. If I do say so myself, it improved greatly with the daily use that living in the ancient world gave it, for not having music available with a touch of the hand, people had to make their own. It was not unusual for people to sing while working, playing, or even courting. I must say that most of the ancient tunes I heard and learnt were not as pleasant to the ear as were those with which I grew up.

Modern songs and tunes fascinated those who heard them, even though no one else could understand the lyrics. So there I was, singing songs with wonderful melodies but few words, and many a time did I wish that back during high school and college I had developed a real repertoire like you did. I always thought that it was incredible—and unnecessary—that you knew so many songs. In that world, though, where we made our own music and called on one another for entertainment, I came to feel that to sing is to help the soul to breathe.

It was a delightful evening. Our hosts importuned us to stay longer, even to spend the night. Having refrained from drinking too much—though not from eating too much—we politely declined their invitation and took our leave well before midnight. As we walked slowly along in the moonlight back to the village and the ship, I felt almost like a teenager again, walking home from a hootenanny with a boy I liked. Like such a girl, I was wondering when—and if—he was going to try to hold my hand and to kiss me, and I was wanting him at least to try. I hadn't decided what I would do if he did, but that didn't matter— he didn't try. Mostly we just walked along quietly. I resisted the impulse I felt to reach out and hold his hand.

The scene back at the beach beside the ship was very lively. There were several bonfires burning and there was meat roasting on each. There were fires for the free men and fires for the ankle-bound chains of slaves, and at each there was laughter, merriment, and a lot of wine, for Cassius had rewarded them all for their speedy completion of the refitting tasks of the day. Many a song was sung that night and many a man got as drunk as he wanted to get—some for the first time in years. Some fights broke out—mostly just drunken nonsense—and my industrious handmaiden—alluringly enough dressed as a Roman lady in an expensive garment with round, pink marks over her breasts—collected many a silver coin from the eager sailors and marines who visited her in a little tent they set up for her down the beach away from the village.

Some of the local women, too, came down to the beach to earn money, have a good time, get drunk, and dance. It would be fairly accurate to say that before we arrived back at the beach after dinner there had been a whole lot of shaking going on all over the place, but the mood had settled down by the time we got there.

For our part, Cassius and I went to every fire—even those of the slaves—and at each we were greeted with cheers and thanks. At each I was asked to sing, and it being a small enough thing to do, I sang—usually hymns or folk-songs in English. I gave brief descriptions or translations of them in Greek or Latin before I began.

By midnight, I was a bit drunk myself. Sharing in the ambiance of the waning parties, I was feeling very emotional and melancholy when we came to the last fire—one by which some thirty or so slaves sat and talked, mellowed out with satisfactory food and copious drink. About ten of them were passed out or asleep, and two or three older women from the village were snuggled in with those who weren't. In the dying firelight they all asked me to sing one last time. It was almost heartbreaking to look at all those forlorn men dressed in rags and chains, but alcohol did its thing to hold real compassion at bay and to let forth the obverse feeling: self-pity.

I gave them a long translation of the song I would sing—one that made me think of my husband lying in the cold ground in the mountains. It was also one of the few songs to which I knew more than one verse. I sang "Danny Boy", and though they could not follow the words of that haunting Irish ballad, many a man was blubbering by the time I was through— and so was I.

I could have cried more, but quickly I dried my tears. I smiled at them all, then Cassius walked me back to the nearby boat where we went aboard by climbing up the rope ladder to the sally port.

There on the empty deck, I wanted very much for him to hold me. I felt lonely. As I stood looking across the water, I thought of my husband and felt that somehow it wasn't right for me to be standing there, warm and healthy beside a gorgeous man while he—my husband—lay in his grave so far away.

"Are you not thinking of him?" Cassius gently asked, breaking the stillness of the night. I assumed he meant Mark.

"No. Of someone who is dead." I replied.

"I meant your husband," he said, speaking his name. Few people, including my husband's family, ever referred to him as having been my husband. I was surprised. I nodded and began to cry. He put his arm around my shoulder to comfort me.

"I knew him rather well," he said quietly, " for we served together for more than a year in Spain. He was a better man than I," he concluded wistfully.

With that I wept, and I leaned into his soft chest to do it. It felt good—the weeping that is—for there is nothing like a good cry sometimes. Knowing that, I let myself go in an orgy of self-pitying, albeit quiet, lamentation.

Naturally, I was crying for myself, which is to say, for my own mortality, and I knew it. I was only a little ashamed of being so self-indulgent. How we humans are that way!

I went on for a while, and Cassius indulged me by being there and holding me without—well, without trying to make a pest of himself or to importune me and take advantage of my vulnerability. He even had a clean cloth or handkerchief of some kind to lend me when I toned down into the sniffle stage.

Embarrassed, I knew that although I had begun crying when the sudden impulse to cry came upon me, I had gone on a bit long and was beginning, quite naturally enough, to be enjoying it and the embrace with Cassius too much.

So I came away from him, and dried my tears. Agreeing that we would talk of my husband at some other time, we said good night, parted, and I went immediately to bed. Sleep quickly came, and I would have dreamed of my husband if I could have, but the morning dreams were of Cassius climbing into my bed in the dorm back in my college days.

We did set sail the next day after all. The blocks were knocked out from under the ship and it slipped back into the water as prettily as could be. The oars were taken up and cleaned, the men put aboard, and the sails hoisted while the slaves—many of them still hung over—rowed slowly toward the waiting sea. We drew well away from the little harbor and Cassius set our course back westward toward the area where the pirate attack had taken place. The wind being fresh and from the East, the oars were shipped so that the crew could sleep. It was a leisurely beginning, and as I walked on the deck near the stern and looked at the large, handsome Cassius talking happily with his first officer up in the bow, I thought that perhaps mine was not such a terrible fate and that Palestine could wait.

For a week we sailed about among the islands of the area, but never did we spot any pirates. We did, however, stop several merchant ships, whereupon the second officer would go aboard to question the captains and inspect the cargoes. He brought back several reports of pirates operating to the northeast along the mainland coast of Asia Minor, and so we sailed thither. I was getting rather restless with the whole process and was becoming increasingly insistent that I be put aboard the next eastbound merchantman. Frankly, I missed having my own ship and my own crew, and I detested being aboard a slave-powered ship.

I seldom saw my manservant Odysseus, for he was usually either drunk, hung over or sick. I had little contact with my maid, either, due to the fact that she was so often in another part of the ship being either the center of attention for a group of marines or was otherwise occupied quite privately. By the end of the week she probably had almost every silver coin on the boat. I was tiring of her. She was becoming surly and even a bit insolent. I decided to sell her when and if we ever got to Tyre. She could probably have bought herself at that point in time.

My relationship—whatever that might mean—with Cassius had grown warmer and yet stranger and more tense over that week. We were together for twelve hours or more out of every day, and though we talked for hours on end and seemed to discuss everything under the sun, I could not open up to him. I couldn't just tell him who I really was and where I came from or, in the final analysis, any of the really important things about myself that the painful formality of our relationship mandated.

I use the word painful because I could tell that he was attracted to me and yet would not—or could not—act upon his impulses. I knew, too, that if not in love, I was at least in lust with him, and I could not help but look at his face and body the same way that men looked at mine. I knew that all he had to do was ask. I was taking my pills regularly.

On the morning of the eighth day, I chanced to wake up at dawn to use the head. Hearing some commotion on the main deck, I looked—peeked, actually—through a very small "captain's shutter" forward in my cabin and saw Cassius getting exercise by boxing and wrestling with the largest of the marines. Both men were wearing only a sort of strap that covered the genitals but left the buttocks completely bare. They wrestled, fought, and struggled some thirty feet away from me, their muscular bodies beautiful in the fresh, cool air and first rays of sunlight. I could not quit looking at them—particularly at Cassius, and I could feel myself being warm with desire for him as I watched and wished that it was with me that he was expending so much effort. I knew that I would have to take matters in hand and overcome his reluctance or his duty or whatever it was that was holding him back from me. I felt as if I had to have him.

Then the exercise was over. Both men toweled off and cooled down, yet still I watched. Then Cassius took off his little girdle so that a sailor could douse him with bucket after bucket of cold seawater in which he vigorously washed himself. I could see from that distance that although the cold water made him shrink up as men do, his member was still large and healthy. Or maybe that was just my imagination that was large and healthy, but it wasn't just my imagination that made me realize that I was breathing rapidly, that my breasts were sensitive, and that my nipples were hard and swollen. Something had to give.

It was the weather that gave first. After days of smooth sailing in perfect winds, that day clouded over and strong winds came, causing the ship to rise and fall sluggishly upon the following seas. Never a particularly seaworthy craft, the bireme was not designed to weather heavy seas and the amount of its roll when wind or wave caught it even partially abeam was most alarming. Anyone could plainly see that it would be difficult—if not impossible—for the ship to turn or come about if the seas grew any higher.

Although the third officer—the young one—assured me that we were safe, I could nevertheless see worry on the faces of all of the men except for Cassius. I put my nebulous plan of seducing him on temporary hold. I had to think of saving my people and myself if there was an emergency.

Accordingly, I packed a large bag which I thought would float, decided which of my heavy things would have to be left in the event of a capsize, and so forth. I was worried, and I went on deck to where Cassius stood like a rock staring over the stern into the wind and oncoming waves.

"I am afraid," I yelled at him over the sound of the wind. "Are we going to sink?"

He turned to me. He was close, very close, and he took my shoulders in his hands and looked me in the eye. His were calm and warm and there was something else in them, like a sparkle or a flame of decision.

"No," he said almost quietly but so I could hear him nonetheless. "We shall not sink—not while I'm alive! We are even now headed to harbor. The wind will soon abate. You should know me well enough to trust me. Do you trust me?"

I could feel the warm places where his hands were holding me and realized that his thighs were touching me, too. Suddenly that storm which had provoked my uncertainty and terror was reduced to a mere spectacular, romantic background for my certainty and my lust. My voice came out thickly. "Yes, I trust you," I said.

"Then wait for me in your cabin," he whispered in my ear. " I like it when it's wild like this! Let's bring this game to a conclusion. I can't wait any more."

"Yes! Yes!" I whispered back, brushing his ear lightly with my lips. I slipped away to the cabin beneath us.

The wind did abate, and it began to rain in sheets just as I was going to my cabin. It was late afternoon and dark, so I lit a lamp, straightened up a bit, and changed into a thin shift over which I wore my wool cloak. I waited for him to come, but knew that he would probably try to be subtle about it. He also had to make sure the ship was in good hands before he came below to be with me. I thought about how safe he made me feel, and how alive, and how weak in my stomach. My breasts stiffened. I got under the covers of my bunk and waited some more.

It wasn't long, though, before I could feel him coming, and hear his footsteps. Then he slid the door open and stepped in, closing it behind him. He came through the curtain that separated the main cabin from the servant's alcove, dripping wet. In his hand he held a flask of wine and two goblets.

There is no point of telling you what each of us said—although I can remember practically every word. I'll tell you what we did, though.

First I got out of bed and took him a towel. I undressed him and dried him off and watched him grow. He was ready to go and so was I.

Then he undressed me, and we stood there and kissed, touching each other all over until, finally, he led me to the bunk. He felt around in it, found a lump, and tossed my derringer over onto a chair. That was O.K. with me—I sure didn't want it to dig into my back while we were making love. My breath was rapid and I was clasping and unclasping my hands on his shoulders and arms as I pushed myself against him and rubbed him and felt that part of him I wanted so much. He lifted me onto the bed as if I were as light as a feather.

Then he tied me up.

For the first moment or two I thought he was just being kinky or something and I was game, but he moved so swiftly and brutally that it was quickly obvious that it—all of it—had been a hideous plan he had all along.

Who would not have fallen for it, though?

I still can't tell you how it felt to be betrayed like that. It was worse, I suppose, than having a good friend betray you by getting you busted. What he did was essentially the same thing: he had bided his time, made all the right moves, and taken me completely unawares. I should have fought him when I still had my own ship, my weapons, my crew, and my wits about me. But no: I was naked, tied up, totally defenseless and totally intimidated. It was terrifying—far more terrifying than any of the three fights I had been in, for in each fight I had been armed, had comrades, and could at least try to defend myself. Woe be unto her who lets herself be disarmed by her enemy!

Naturally, I was in shock. My hands were tied in front of me and my feet were bound together. Snatching me up off the bunk, he pushed me down roughly on the privy-closet seat, dressed himself, and picked up my derringer, shoving it into his belt.

Crazily, I cried, cussed and screamed. I said all kinds of things that I cannot remember saying. I suppose that for a few minutes there I went totally mad. He called in the second officer to bear witness to his words and acts.

"Second Officer," he said loudly enough so that he could be heard by those other ears which were undoubtedly listening intently nearby, "you will duly note in the ship's record that I have this day effected the arrest of the witch, Evangelica Atlantica. I have done this under the orders of Caesar and the Senate of Rome. Let no man touch this witch except to move her about, upon pain of death."

The second officer saluted and said, "Yes, Sir!" and acted very military, but he looked at me with wonder. Cassius' move obviously had taken him as much by surprise as it had me. From that I could assume that none of the other crew knew of his plan, either. I covered myself with my hands as best I could.

At a motion from my captor, the second officer sat down at the little table that was folded down from a recess in the wall of the room. Taking out my writing materials, he took notes while Cassius spoke.

"You will now give me true answers to any questions I may ask you," Cassius said to me rather matter-of-factly, "or I shall cut off your nose and have you chained at an oar."

I was terrified—too terrified even to speak. The ship's deck rose and fell beneath me, and I felt sick, horrible fear. Leaning over, I threw up on my own feet. They called in a man to clean it up. Kneeling at my feet to work, he looked up into my eyes with astonishment and fear. I must have gone crazy— crying and screaming and so forth. I hardly remember any of that. I think I passed out.

When I came to, Cassius began questioning me. Having recovered my wits somewhat, I told them the general story Mark and I had agreed upon two years before—a telling that took 20 minutes or more.

It was obvious to me that Cassius already knew our whole story as well as its contradictions and deliberate ambiguities. He began to cross-examine me in a very careful, systematic way. He asked about the size of our armies, our fleets, our weapons and so on. I could hardly think what I should tell him. My main fear was that he would not believe me and would start maiming me. That went on for about another hour.

All this time I was still bound and naked, and the only concessions they made to my comfort were to give me water to drink and to raise the lid on the commode I was sitting on so that I wouldn't soil the cabin. They watched my every move, even when I relieved myself. They were afraid to take their eyes off of me. I was cold and my bottom and wrists were sore. It was terrible, but I was getting used to it and had time to try to think, despite the rapid-fire questioning.

All this time the wind was picking up and the waves were growing ever larger. The ship rose and fell and bucked in twisting rolls.

We were being interrupted from time to time by reports from the deck as the weather developed into almost a full gale. Biremes weren't made for that.

Cassius may have been good at many things— particularly at seduction and deception, the two being oft so closely related—but he was not a particularly skillful interrogator. As he went on and on it became obvious to both the second officer and me that he was actually not particularly bright. I guess that means, ipso facto, that I am an idiot.

One sign of his lack of skill was that he began to let me ask questions and then bothered to answer at least some of them.

The first I remember asking had to do with why hadn't he gone ahead and made love to me, then betrayed me afterwards.

"That would have run the risk of falling under your spell—so much so that, like the man you called your husband, I might have betrayed my country," he explained.

Shortly after that, other things became clear when my silly maid came in and took up a place behind Cassius. Even though I was an idiot, I could plainly see that he had been sleeping with her so as to pump her for information as well as for pleasure. That explained how he knew about the derringer's hiding-place as well as the fact that I rarely was without it.

I would have felt doubly betrayed, but actually felt sorry for the girl. She was too stupid to realize that her usefulness to Cassius was almost at an end. For that matter, her own life might possibly be in jeopardy if the elimination of witnesses was also part of his plan. She had a pathetic, chin-in-the-air posture that was her way of reveling in the fall of one of her betters.

With her hands touching his shoulders, he smiled at me in triumph, lounged back in his chair and drank from a goblet of wine. The brass lamps—which hung from chains and were by then lighted—swung crazily about the cabin, making the shadow patterns race about chasing the patches of light. Outside it was getting dark and the sea was getting rougher by the minute. He set the goblet down and as soon as he let it go it leapt from the table. Outside there was a terrific noise, a crashing sound, and the crack and snap of lines breaking.

Immediately there was a banging on the door.

"Wind increasing, sir!" yelled the young third officer. He sounded worried. "Please, sirs!" he begged. "Come on deck! We've lost the front mast!"

"Mithras!" Cassius swore. He pulled out his dagger and cut the bonds from my feet, then pulled me up by the hair. At first I could hardly stand up, my legs being so cramped and the deck rolling about so, but he held on and snatched me about so that I had no choice. He found my shift and some other thin clothes and made a sort of rope out of them, tied it around my neck, and led me, still naked, up to the deck, telling my maid to remain in the cabin. It was obvious that he did not want to let me get out of his sight, lest I kill myself or suborn one of his men while he was on deck. That, too, was indicative of something about him, the nature of his mission, and how he distrusted his officers and crew.

During the long interrogation I had regained a lot of my nerve and composure, and when he snatched me roughly through the gangway to the deck what I felt was not fear but anger. It was a deep, murderous anger, full of cunning, and unlike any I had ever felt before.

Just as we came out on deck the wind abated just enough so that shouting was not necessary, but it was still blowing in hard over the starboard beam. There was almost no light left in the sky and two or three glazed-in, oil-fed lanterns on deck illumined the carnage we found.

The scene that met my eyes was this: The mainmast and square mainsail were down and were trailing over the leeward rail that had been neatly smashed in. At the point of impact lay a sailor's lifeless body in a huge pool of blood. The very fact that the sail had not been taken in or properly and tightly furled prior to the blow was indicative of the poor seamanship of the crew and marines, practically all of whom were standing about on deck waiting for someone to tell them what to do. They had been caught out on the open sea and were running for some safe harbor and hadn't made it. Now it was them and the sea, and they knew it. Obviously they were what my uncle referred to as "fair-weather sailors", and in Cassius' absence they couldn't decide whether or not to cut away the debris alongside, without which clearage the port oar banks were almost useless. Coming up from below over the sound of the wind were the shouts and screams of oarsmen. They knew what had to be done even if the marines and third officer didn't.

The short mizzenmast behind us still stood, but the tatters of what had been its sail snapped in the brisk wind. So it was that the boat was not moving under its own power and thus could not be steered. It was beginning to wallow in the troughs of a sea that was rolling in from abaft the starboard beam. Depending on how we wallowed, the waves on that side either raised us up or slapped heavily against the hull, sending shots of water through the various leather-covered oar-ports below. As great splashes of water leaped up above the starboard tarriffrail the wind caught and flung them across the deck like birdshot. The boat was listing to port and it was only a matter of time until waves would be coming in over the rails on either side. There was no sign that any bailing or pumping had been started.

It was raining again, too, the drops hitting me like needles. I have never liked having cold rain hit my bare skin, and I was totally exposed. My hair was either matted down or straying off into the wind, and I was covered with goose flesh from the cold. The men stood about and gawked at us. Stark naked with the cloth leash around my neck, I must have looked like Hell.

Cassius was clearly shocked, but he was a courageous, if stupid, officer. He jumped up onto a hatch and tried to start issuing orders. I say he tried to start, but of course he still had hold of the garments he had tied around my neck, so I was right there beside him.

"Stop!" I shouted over the din. I pushed him off the hatch. Taken unawares, he let go of the cloth as he stumbled into the crowd. My hands still tied, I stood up on the hatch.

"You have offended the gods," I yelled in Latin quickly before he could stop me. "The very sea rises against you! You will all die if you do not throw this man overboard right now! Only I can save you! Make your choice and be quick about it!"

Cassius leapt back up on the hatch and angrily grabbed me by the knotted cloth around my neck, giving it a vicious twist that choked me. Then he shook me as if I were a puppy. As I have said, he was a big, powerful man.

His voice boomed, "Listen not to the witch who I have arrested, but fall to your duties! You there, Fabius! Take your men and cut away all that rope there! You..." he said, until I managed to hit him square in the mouth with the back of my hands. I had to do something: I couldn't breathe. He lost his grip a bit and I stood up on my tiptoes to avoid the choking. Then a huge bolt of lightning flashed directly overhead with a great *Crack! Boom!* that startled the hell out of everyone. He let go of me. Just as the bolt flashed I was looking across the port rails and saw that we were hard by a coastline. It was only half a mile off and we were being driven toward it. In the near distance was a headland toward which the ship had been making when the mast had broken. If the ship could only round it she might be saved.

More lightning flashed. Before Cassius could jerk me around again, I drew myself up to my full height and gestured with my chin and outstretched hands, pointing off into the distance. I shouted "Look!" and as one they turned and looked out over the port bow at the promontory beyond which might lie safety. Beneath it the long, rocky coastline ended where the lines of heavy waves were crashing madly against three huge rocks that were less than a mile away.

Not a man moved. All of them—even Cassius—looked off whither I gestured and knew that I was pointing out where I thought or was foretelling that the ship would wreck. If left to the force of the wind and waves alone it wouldn't make it even that far. It was obvious—at least to the true sailors and me—that because of the ship's high freeboard and light construction the only thing to do was to get the oars out, come about to starboard in spite of the risks, and then try to fight for what is known as sea room. The classic dilemma in sailing is being too close to a lee shore during a heavy blow and watching helplessly while, relentlessly, one's ship is driven onto that shore. It becomes only a matter of time before the wrecking and the drowning commences.

They were running out of time fast. When I say "they", I meant all of them, because I had disassociated myself from all of them. Their fate was different than my own, and I suddenly thought that it was not my day to die. Perhaps that was just the arrogance of youth. On the other hand—hindsight being clear—I was right!

"Let her go!" A man shouted. "Let Aphrodite go!"

The call was taken up by others and another voice shouted, "Throw him overboard!" Obviously, the shouter meant Cassius.

A man reached out and snatched the cloth line that held me out of Cassius' hand. Then he slipped up to me and cut the bonds on my wrists with a razor-sharp knife. I looked back and realized that it was Odysseus, the bard who had come with me as a manservant but who I hadn't seen in days. On each of his wrists were manacles, but the chain was broken in the middle.

Somewhere off to my right the second officer was getting a line of marines in order. They had their swords drawn.

"That man has mutinied against the Senate and people of Rome," Cassius yelled, pointing at Odysseus who stood beside me and was probably the fellow who had yelled first. "He has mutinied against the ship and will die! But first, and with her own weapon, the witch shall die!" he boomed out as he pointed his finger at me, still confident of his own abilities even in the teeth of adversity and rebellion. His mouth was bleeding where I had hit him and hate filled his eyes.

With that, and standing not more than eight feet from me, he pulled out my derringer, cocked the hammer back, and held it out at arm's length in my direction. I grinned at him for I could tell what was going to happen, but not because I had The Sight. I smiled because I could see that he was going to make a big mistake, for he had put his thumb in the derringer's trigger guard. He held it up dramatically. Then he promptly shot himself in the face.

The loud report frightened everyone but me. The chunky .45 slug entered his left cheek just beside the nose and went on through, taking out a hole the size of a baseball in the approximate area of what had housed his medulla oblongata. The force snapped his head back and spun him around. He hit the deck face down, kicking like a pig as blood poured out of the grotesque wounds. The men all drew back in amazed, silent horror. The ones who had been standing behind him realized that they were spattered with bits of bone and brain of one of the most famous men of their time. The wind howled.

God help me, but I had a sudden fit of laughing. After all, I was almost hysterical and it really was about the funniest and most appropriate way for Cassius to end his illustrious career. As in so many other things he had done in his brilliant life, his timing was perfect. The lightning cracked again and lit the whole scene. I laughed in triumph.

The crew and idle marines about would have joined me in my laughter, but we were cut short by the second officer who, having recovered his wits, stepped forward, pried the derringer out of Cassius' still-twitching hand and threw it overboard. That sobered me up quickly, but not fast enough for me to gain the advantage over him. He and his men moved in on the disorganized crew to hustle them off to their tasks.

At his order, one marine grabbed me by the wrist and started to haul me back to the cabin. I felt that I had to act fast or I would either find myself on a sinking ship or, worse, find myself once again a prisoner threatened with unremitting torture. We went a few steps into the gangway back to the cabin, but I twisted away from him and ran back out on the deck amid the shouting and confusion. Quickly I climbed up to the mizzenmast stays on the edge of the port rail and went up a step or two into the shrouds. I tore off the clothes that had been tied about my neck. Instantly they were carried away by the wind. Below me the sea was greenish-gray and cold looking, but I was so full of adrenaline I felt as if I could conquer the world. The lightning struck the ground on the land less than a mile to leeward now, and I shouted out over the rising wind, "This is your last chance! Give me command of the ship right now or you will all die!"

Half the men had already begun to let themselves be marshaled into work parties and the others looked to one another for leadership. None of them took any initiative, though, and it was obvious that the second officer was going to hold his command. He was standing beside Cassius' bloody corpse giving orders.

"Cut her down!" he yelled to the man from whom I had broken free. The marine responded immediately and with short sword in hand started clambering up toward me.

"Then to Hades with you!" I said as a big wave began to pass under us and the ship rose up and leaned out to port.

Naked, I leapt into the sea.

Hitting the water was not nearly as bad as I thought it would be, for I was still pumped up and was already cold. It was actually rather warm by comparison. Moreover, it was an amazing experience, for my world changed instantly from one involving men, wind, a ship and death into one of silence and total immersion in the dark water. What changes there had been in the preceding two hours! I thought of them all in just those long seconds that I was still under the surface, and it occurred to me that perhaps out on the deck I had been wrong and that I really was going to die right then and there. The thought did not frighten me in the least. I came up for air, glad for the first time in over an hour that I had no clothes on, for clothes drag one down.

I gasped frantically for air amid the tumultuous whitecaps. Treading water for a moment, I could tell from its cabin lights that I was still only forty or fifty feet from the boat. It still had not yet gotten under way. At least the men were beginning to work. The rigging and mainmast remnants were being cut away and some of the port oars were coming out. I thought about waiting around to get a spar to cling to, but I realized immediately that I couldn't last long in that water before hypothermia set in. I knew that I had to get to shore as rapidly as possible.

The oars that could reach the water began laboring raggedly to get the ship going, but to little avail. Although it is impossible to tell in such circumstances just what is moving where, when I looked it seemed that the ship was continuing to move toward shore. It seemed, too, that it was sluggish and riding too low, which made me think that it had already taken in too much water.

Before I quit looking at the ship, I saw men pointing at me from the rail and just before a wave swept over me I thought I saw one of them leap over the side, which didn't surprise me at all. In my opinion any of them with any sense would abandon ship now while there was at least a chance of getting to a beach.

Turning my back on the ship, then, I began to strike out for the shore with a rather casual but strong breaststroke. After a hundred yards or so, I looked back a final time, but could see nothing in the darkness until lightning illumined the ship again. It was rowing slowly parallel to the shore. A second flash showed that she was obviously having a hard time of it and was still wallowing in the troughs of the waves and was not trying to turn to windward.

I swam another hundred yards and looked back again, but the waves were too high and there was no lightning, so I saw nothing.

Swimming on and on, I was thankful that I at least had put on some weight during the last year, for I needed that fat. I started thinking all sorts of things and my teeth began to chatter. I thought I might die of exposure and had morbid thoughts of my body lying dead and rotting on the shore—forgotten then, forgotten now. In my mind I repeated prayers both ancient and modern, starting with the old standby, *"Our father, Who art in heaven...Thy will be done, on earth as it is in heaven..."*. When I got to the part which went *"and deliver us from evil..."* I realized with almost a leap of joy that even if I was going to die I was happy, for I had just been delivered from evil. I was on my own again, and in no man's power.

I prayed to Athena, Poseidon, and Apollo, too,

mentioning in my mind to them my attendance upon their worship both on land and at sea. I would have gone through the whole pantheon, but that seemed a bit pointless and inappropriate: when you really want help, you don't ask for it in general, you get specific.

Suddenly I felt lifted up as if by a hand from below, and then I rolled down a moving mogul of water. I hit hard upon a sandy bottom and was dragged backward again, then shoved forward in the darkness and slammed onto the beach again.

I staggered up onto the land and would have felt completely saved but for the facts that the wind and rain were about to freeze me, and I couldn't see a thing.

Then when the lightning flashed I saw a cleft in the rocks above the high water reaches of the waves. All along the beach lay a heavy line of seaweed where the waves were finally exhausting themselves. As there was nothing more promising about, I went forward in the dark until I felt the line of stuff. Picking up armfuls of it, I stumbled on up in the direction of the cleft and found it just as there was another flash. I laid down the weeds and went back for more, arriving there in time to see another long series of flashes illumine the sea just as the long bireme was reaching those three great rocks off the headland a mile farther up the shore. It was sad to think about all those men chained together at the oars, as well as the others who had done me no harm. Only a few nights before I had sung for them and visited their bonfires, and now—well, now I had to get back to my little cave or die. Let the dead bury their dead.

Obviously I survived the night. Not only did I get warm enough half buried down in the sand and covered with seaweed, but I was even able to sleep a bit, curled up in a fetal position, as the land seemed to roll beneath me and thoughts and dreams interwove. Little animals and bits of grit tickled, bit and chafed against my skin and I was pretty miserable. But I was alive.

****

XXVII

Shipwrecked

When the morning came the storm had passed and the skies were clearing. The wind had died completely.

I was loath to move, for although wet, my little nest was almost warm, and I needed more sleep if I could get it. My hiding place was well concealed if there weren't any of my tracks left on the sand. As far as I knew, the second officer and his men might have swam to shore or the ship might not have sunk, for that matter. In either case, soon he would send out search parties to find me or my body and to step out into the open might be to court recapture. From my narrow crevice I could look off down the fifty or so yards of beach which ended in a line of boulders which trailed off into the water.

From the brief views of the shoreline that I had gotten the previous evening, I guessed that this was either the last or next-to-last of a series of the little crescent-shaped beaches between the rocky outcrops that jutted out into the sea like shark's teeth. There was a moderate fog that morning and since from my position I could not see the area of the headland where the three great rocks stood, I could only guess at how things stood. I was almost certain that the ship had wrecked, but I could not be sure that it had not somehow escaped total destruction.

Although the sea was still rough, it was not driving nearly as far up onto the shore as it had during the night. There was a heavy cloud cover that made the morning gray, still, and uninviting. I kept dropping off to sleep and awakening.

Finally, about midmorning, the sun came out and burned off the mist. In just a short while it was a beautiful, bright day with the temperature in the sixties and rising. I decided to get up and about—but carefully. I had no idea where I was and whether or not the country was inhabited or whether the Romans were about.

Gradually I crept from the hiding place and scouted about that particular cove, taking care not to leave footprints in the sand even if it meant hurting my feet on the rocks. Finally I clambered up the little wall of rocks that had blocked my view of the headland. Carefully I peered around a boulder to check things out. I discovered that I was at the western end of an even smaller inlet than the one in which I had landed. The little stretch of sand before me was empty, too, and I still could not see the big sea rocks. I had already begun to call them The Three Sisters.

Just as I was about to leave my little observation-place and cross the beach, I saw a man appear on the other side of the cove about a hundred and fifty yards off. He was coming my way, obviously searching for someone or something. Dressed in Roman clothes and carrying a sword, he nevertheless looked familiar, and I hesitated just long enough to recognize who it was and to determine that he was alone. I could tell who he was by the manacles on his wrists. I stayed hidden until he was only ten yards away then stood up. It was my Greek crewman, Odysseus.

"My Lady!" he exclaimed with totally unaffected joy. *"You live!"*

He rushed forward and threw himself at my feet, putting his forehead on the sand and averting his eyes from my utter nakedness.

"Did you ever doubt it?" I asked almost imperiously.

"Surely you are a goddess!" I heard him say as he began to cry and laugh. I thought about how he had left me alone too much aboard ship, and how he had taken to drinking shamelessly, but I was glad he was alive anyway.

"Now up, Odysseus!" I said, cheerfully unabashed by my nudity and the fact that I was a sandy mess covered only in bits of seaweed and goose flesh. "Enough of this blubbering! Let us be about the business of the morning. What of the Romans?"

He looked up at me, his eyes glistening with tears of joy. He could hardly speak.

"Dead. All dead! Even the whore:" he said with a sound of awe in his voice, *"just like you said."*

So it was.

He handed me a heavy, damp, wool cloak in a matter-of-fact sort of way, and I put it on, delighting in its instant promise of warmth. Just as I finally started to get warm, my stomach protested that it was hungry, and as if hearing it, he handed me some waterlogged bread. It tasted soggy but wonderful. He also gave me some sandals which I appreciated even more than the cloak.

We walked inland a bit, found a path eastward and walked toward the site of the wreck. As we went he told me many things that I hadn't known: about how he had been kept from me and was told that I did not want him around me while I was courting Cassius. He told me that he had drunk some, but the marines had urged him to drink all the time. Finally they had put him in irons just shortly before Cassius had captured me. He explained how he had gotten free, cut my bonds, and dived into the sea after me even though he thought that the ship had a chance of clearing the headland.

Almost drowning in his attempts to find me in the dark , he, too, had saved himself by making a nest of seaweed in the small cove to the east of mine.

He went to the scene of the wreck at first light, and then went back looking for my corpse or me. Optimistically enough, he took with him an extra wool deck cloak, the sword, and— most blessed of all—some sandals. I would rather be naked in cool air than barefoot on sharp rock.

The term, "the scene of the wreck" is somewhat misleading, for there was almost no sign of the ship itself. The Three Sisters being some two hundred yards off shore and the waves still dashing madly against them, their final mastication of the big cruiser was almost completed, and bits of wood—few of them being longer than ten feet—were everywhere. So were the bodies, of which we counted about twenty-five, including those of the second officer and of my maid, who was floating in a strange, inverted position. Only the soles of her feet were out of the water, and upon dragging her out we found that the reason she floated that way was due to the small sack of coins still hanging around her neck—the silver coins of the sailors and marines she had serviced.

We cast about for any possible survivors' tracks and, finding none and assuring ourselves that we were on a long, narrow, uninhabited island, we lay to the matter at hand with a will—namely, the stripping of the dead and the salvaging of everything we could.

I was going to write that we "worked like dogs" that day,

but thought that inappropriate, as would be the expression "worked like slaves" as neither dogs nor slaves work so hard . We worked like free people, which is to say, as rapidly and efficiently as possible. Our efforts were rewarded, for we salvaged rope, wood, clothing, coins, food and many other things. Most miraculously, we even managed to find the bundle of clothes and other items I had made up when the storm first rose.

In the middle of the afternoon the Three Sisters, having finished tearing open the after cabins, spit the bundle out, and it floated in toward us rather sluggishly. Recognizing it by the vivid color of my beautiful palium which was its main covering, I swam out and got it. I was glad that I had possessed the foresight to put several airtight bottles in it so that it wouldn't sink despite the weight of the thirty gold coins and fifty now-useless .45 cartridges I had wrapped in it. The .45 automatic as well as the .22 rifle were gone.

Be that as it was, it is difficult to describe how, arising from the sea like Quequeg's coffin, that little bunch of stuff buoyed me up. We had spent the day taking all of the clothes, rings, and accouterments off of the dead, and rigging clotheslines with various ropes we found. It was grim but necessary work, for we had no idea of how long we might be there or how cold the winter might become.

We hiked back down the beach to where the mainmast and its bits of rope and sail had come ashore and salvaged it so that we could make a tent. Odysseus tried—but failed—to make a fire, and again we ate soggy bread. We had only a half-bottle of wine to drink. By day's end we were exhausted. We camped that night on the high ground barely a hundred yards or so from the naked corpses on which scores of birds were already feeding. Wrapping ourselves in such clothes as we had managed to dry during the day, we slept the sleep of the dead.

In the morning there was still much work to be done. We located a better place for a camp and made a tent out of the sail. We strung up clotheslines and gathered more of the ship's debris. After hours of effort, Odysseus finally succeeded in making fire by friction and we roasted three sea birds I killed using a bola. As we ate them I could not help but think about how they had been eating on the bodies of our former shipmates right before I brought them down.

When we finally settled down as the sun began its early setting on our third night ashore, I got my makeshift float out and opened it with a sort of Christmas-present joy of a ten-year old. I had practically forgotten what I had packed in such haste. Would it surprise you if I told you that the things I found that made me happiest were the last bra and panties that I owned? They were both on their last legs or whatever: ragged and buff-colored from lack of bleach and proper washing, their elastic was almost shot, and they were both in need of mending. But they were mine, and we had been through a lot together even though I only wore them occasionally. Much to Odysseus' astonishment, as soon as they were dry the next day I put them on. He had never seen them or their like before and could not help but gawk. For some silly reason, they made me feel great.

I also had some toiletries: a hairbrush, toothbrush and a small mending kit with needles, thread, and a small pair of scissors. I did not, however, have the radio, for I had assumed—perhaps wrongly—that if the ship went down it would be ruined anyway.

In a way I didn't think of the loss of the radio as being nearly so bad as the loss of the .22 rifle, the .45 pistol and the derringer. After all, the radio was an almost abstract thing that yielded some funny little noises through a headset whereas the guns had been vitally important to me. Without them I was practically defenseless in a world which—like any other world—was full of dangers. I thought again of the saying *God made all men, but that it was Colt who made them equal.* Bereft of my modern weapons, I was no longer an equal. I was just a woman. I knew that I would have to learn to use the bow, the sword, and the dagger, but who could hope to accomplish much against powerful men already skilled in the use of such weapons?

Although I had been forced to fight the bandits in the mountains and the pirates near Kos, after my experience in the cabin of the cruiser I certainly didn't think of myself as being particularly brave, and I didn't want to face having to live without my weapons. Therefore, and against Odysseus' advice and my better judgment, I swam out to the Three Sisters on the fourth day in what proved to be a vain effort to find my rifle and its shells. Halfway out I was scared. When I got there I was terrified, for the sea surged heavily about among the rocks, and there were three half-eaten corpses tangled up in some cordage there. There was no ship, though, and none to dive to. Whatever could not float away must have lain spilled on the ocean floor far below, but I could not see that deep—only deep enough to see a few large fish and what I thought to be a huge shark. I went back to shore empty-handed and in a big hurry.

We stayed on that island for about two months, and as it was winter, it got really cold many times. I would surely have perished there had it not been for my companion's brilliance as a survivalist. For one thing, although there was plenty of driftwood to burn, I doubt whether I could have ever gotten a fire started on my own. There is a real science to making fire by friction—a science Odysseus patiently taught me.

We recovered a few food items from the ship. They lasted a few days, and together we found some edible wild plants and trapped an occasional skinny bird. Mostly, though, we lived off rainwater and fish—so much fish that we got really tired of it after a few weeks and even began to make jokes about wishing that we had cut up and dried some of the dead Romans while they were still fresh. As it was, Odysseus did use a few cuttings from one of them to use for fish bait, but he was polite enough not to tell me about it until some time later.

Because we had the foresight to save all the Romans' clothes, and because we had salvaged plenty of rope and some big pieces of the sails, we did not suffer too much from the cold even when we had to go outside of the shelter we made. Dressed in layer after layer of all kinds of clothes, we looked absurd but stayed warm. At night we slept right next to each other on top of and under all the clothes we had.

Of course, there was no privacy, but after a couple of weeks, when we settled in and started getting enough to eat, we didn't need any. It was just that sort of thing, and my only regret is that although I learned to respect Odysseus from the very first day, I could not love him or make him think that I did. It was all right, though, for at least each of us was not shipwrecked alone on that forsaken isle, and who needed to talk about the future anyway? It was enough just to meet the challenges of each day—and there were many days when we went hungry. Only when we lucked out and caught something big and feasted did we turn to one another for other comforts. I worried some about getting pregnant, but I didn't. I did, however, lose a lot of weight—twenty or thirty pounds, I suppose, which is to say, practically every spare pound I had. My once-snug undies no longer fit me and I missed my fat as I would have missed a friend. Both of us dreamed of rich food heavy with hot grease, and huge salads. Above all, we thought of peas and beans.

During the time we were together I memorized a lot of Odysseus' version of the *Iliad,* and I learned a little about how to fight with a dagger, sword, and javelin as well as how to fish and to make and cast nets. I learned a lot about Greek history, too, for although he was illiterate, he had a terrific memory and taught me some of the mnemic arts he had studied before he undertook to learn the *Iliad.*

I for my part taught him some of the things that I knew, including a couple of tricks which I would hope he took home to a grateful wife when finally we went our separate ways in Tyre.

Eventually we were saved by an eastbound merchantman that was passing nearby and saw our signal fire. They were glad to take us aboard. As I have said, we had some money—which was a good thing because by the use of it I was able to bribe the captain who rescued us to give us his own cabin, change his plans, and feed us well. I also paid him to land us some five miles outside Tyre at night, then continue on to Egypt so that if the my enemies—whoever they were—were looking for us and questioned his crew, we should have enough time to get away.

It was reasonable to assume that I was still in danger. In the hour before his death Cassius had refused to say for whom he was working. So far as I knew, he had never presented to anyone any proof of his authority to arrest me. By invoking the authority of the senate and people of Rome, though, he gave us all to believe that he had official sanction to capture and to mistreat me. On the other hand, he might have been working for someone other than Tiberias or Sejanus, and may have been exceeding his authority even if it was they who had sent him. Many a field commander in those times went beyond his orders only to find that his superiors not only forgave him but also congratulated him for his audacity.

Our sea captain rescuer did tell us, though, that in every

port there were lost ship notices posted that described the missing cruiser and offered a modest reward for information. Our presence aboard it had not been mentioned in the dispatch. Therefore we lied to the captain, telling him we had been put ashore by Cassius who had then proceeded eastward in heavy weather contrary to the objections of his third officer, the youngster who had been so nice to me but who had died with them. We also told him that we were being hunted by our creditors, and thus had a need to get ashore unannounced. He understood completely—or thought he did.

It was about the middle of February when we strolled into Tyre, which is, as you probably know, a port now known as Sur in southern Lebanon. In those days the city had two harbors, the northern or Sidonian and the Egyptian harbor on the south, the two being separated by a narrow, fortified causeway which connected Old Tyre ashore with New Tyre on the small island offshore. The city was reputed to be about 1300 years old, and through that time it had for the most part flourished and acquitted itself well through many sieges and wars. Some three hundred and fifty years before it had been conquered by Alexander the Great whose siege engineers had greatly widened the causeway by tearing down Old Tyre for the very fill materials that were used in the project.

But that which is torn down can be built up again, and so it was. By the time I arrived there it was a bustling place indeed, and three hundred years had more than sufficed to endow the place with new temples, walls, and factories. The city was famous for its silk works and the distinctive dyes that were compounded and refined there. The natural entrepreneurial prosperity that was possible under the Pax Romana was everywhere evident. I was amazed at the tempo of commercial activity and said so to Odysseus who told me that Antioch and Alexandria were more hectic still.

Entering disguised as two brothers, we quickly found the merchant banker with whom I had done some correspondence business in the past and to whom I had sent the letter of credit for Julian. An old Jew, he was the same man who had once owned Naaida before selling her to Marcus. It was, indeed, a small world.

The old man was good at keeping secrets, and he kept ours. From him we learned that our ship made port and hung about for nearly four weeks, during which time our captain communicated secretly with him daily in an ongoing quest for information concerning our whereabouts. Finally, the port authorities made him leave since by custom a ship was allowed to stay in the tiny harbor only five days.

Finally our captain had given up hoping that we might show up in Tyre. He sailed north as far as Seleucia Pieria, the port of Antioch, and then back to Tyre in hopes of finding us in one of the other coastal towns along the way. According to the Jew, he had not thought us dead even when the ominous "lost ship" notices about the Roman cruiser were posted in all the ports.

Borrowing a tidy sum of money without security of any sort, we stayed in the city two or three days, resting up and making preparations for my overland journey to Tiberias on the Sea of Galilee. We also ate a lot, for we couldn't seem to get enough. Four or five times a day we went to eat in the shops and cafes along the waterfronts and in the old town. Even now my mouth waters to think of all the delicious roasted lamb, chevron, goat, figs, dates, honey cakes, salads and, of course, beans, that we wolfed down during those few days. A few pounds came back slowly but surely.

Our disguises were as simple as they were appropriate: we passed for two out-of-work Greek mercenaries—one of whom was quite obviously a bit effete: two men who had money to spend but closed mouths about where they had gotten it. We cut my hair back and saved some of it with which to make fake mustaches. We bought me a hardened leather, chest-flattening lorica, a leather-fronted kilt and light brass greaves to disguise my figure and make me look more like a man. I liked being dressed like that.

In spite of his offer to accompany me on my journey south, we both knew that Odysseus had to get back to his wife and children on the island of Corfu. He had spoken of them quite often, and missed them greatly. His wife was, like him, in her early forties, and he assured me that she was very beautiful. Because of that and her reputation in the community for industriousness, he was sure that upon the receipt of any notice of his having been lost at sea with the Roman ship, a myriad of suitors would have emerged to vie for her attentions.

"She is very fond of the couch and every one knows it," he had said worriedly on many occasions, both on the island and after we were rescued, "and she cannot be expected to wait long."

"Write her a letter. Tell her you're on the way."

"She can't read. I can't write. Most important: she can't wait."

"She'll wait."

"You don't know my Chloe! She's no Penelope waiting for me and her with no comfort. Oh no!" He was totally irrational on the subject of his wife.

Such remarks displayed a side of him that would have been comical but for the fact that they revealed a tender, possessive regard for his wife I found admirable. On the other hand, it vexed me to no end to have him say such things in my presence—usually just after we had done the sort of thing which he feared that she might herself be doing. It was as if I was living proof of the faithlessness of women. The "faithlessness" of men, of course, didn't count. It was almost funny— particularly in view of the fact that we had started out as man-and-goddess. How could he, I wondered, fret for his wife ("with the cutest, big, dark mole on her nose: just here") when he was with the most beautiful woman in the world, the woman men had walked miles merely to see? It was ludicrous! I was amused by my own jealousy of a woman who was so far away. Then I realized that what I was jealous of was not her, but of the fact that this good, kind man who had saved my life and who had jumped overboard into a cold, dark sea to swim to me, actually loved her so much that he was not bewitched by me. She was a lucky woman. No man loved me like that. The only one who had was gone.

But we got through a lot together, he and I, and I liked him very much, particularly when he quoted the Iliad. His pet name for me was Circe.

****

XXVIII

Palestine

Having become wary of the perils of traveling, and with only the arms that a man of those times might carry—dagger, short sword, and Parthian cavalry bow—I decided that I should not travel alone even though it was only 50 miles to Tiberias on the western shore of the Sea of Galilee. Still disguised as a man—a man with long, dirty blond hair and thick Gaulish moustaches that fell an inch below the line of his jaw—I attached myself to a small, Greek-speaking caravan that was headed there. Leaving Tyre on the fourth day after I had arrived, I bought and mounted a small horse and served as an outrider on the flanks during the first two days of travel. I kept to myself.

To my dismay, I soon learned that it was very slow going. The carts kept stopping and the people plodded along so listlessly that it was almost as if no one but me was in any kind of a hurry at all. Even my horse was champing at the bit with frustration.

We also seemed to go through endless hassles and troubles. There were little guard-and-tax stations to go through, that is to say, little shake-down points manned by two or three Phoenician, Syrian, or Galilean cops waving little seals of office. They plagued the entire trade route from Tyre, down through Gischala and all the way to Capernaum. At each stop travelers were required to open their bundles if called upon to do so since the so-called "taxes" levied or extracted were based upon the various types and values of the goods carried. To challenge authority was to invite a beating—or worse.

I should know, for it happened to me on the very first day out when I tried to talk back to one of the dirty little men who had stopped us just a couple of miles inside the Tetrarchy of Herod Antipas.

Using my best mannish voice, I was saying in Greek, something like, "See here! We were just stopped two miles back!" to the leader of the three men who stopped us when—

suddenly and without warning—he hit me deep and hard in the stomach, knocking out my wind in spite of the leather lorica. I went down gasping for breath. I hadn't had that happen to me since I was a child, and for a long 40 seconds I thought I was going to die right there on the ground at the feet of my cursing, smiling attacker. Desperately trying to get my body to start breathing again, I hardly felt it when he kicked me four or five times. It hurt like hell, but I was lucky that I had on the lorica because otherwise he might have broken my ribs. It was a lesson to me, all right.

He liked my dagger and as I finally got to my knees trying not to throw up, he took it from its sheath.

"Your crossing-tax," he said in Greek, smiling. "I know you won't object." I shook my head. I was too shocked and too vulnerable to do otherwise. It is a horrible thing to be at the mercy of such cruel people—particularly when they have the trappings of authority.

The people with whom I was traveling acted as if nothing had happened. Totally indifferent to me, they gathered up their stuff and started off. Catching up with them, I addressed an older woman with whom I had spoken a few times. Still in pain and feeling deeply ashamed, I asked her if her people were so callous that such injustice did not offend them.

"Shut up, you fool!" she snapped at me. "He could have robbed you. He could have killed you. They could have used it as an excuse to plunder us! Don't speak to me of injustice!"

"But he took my knife. It was very valuable," I added weakly.

"Yeah. Rich knife for a poor soldier. Lot of us saw that," she said with a heavy note of suspicion. Maybe they thought I, too, was a thief.

I rode on off. I shunned the caravan and they shunned me, but I didn't really need their pity. I had my hate.

I had never really hated anyone as I hated that guard. I would have hated Cassius more had he lived long enough. But that guard was a man whose face I would never forget, and in the days that followed, I thought of him a thousand times and determined that I would return someday and kill him. So easy is it to contemplate murder! I would give him a month or two— maybe three. My ribs' bruises sustained me like no food could.

On the third night out, when we were camped in some

hills outside Capernaum, someone stole my horse while I slept. I suspected that one of the caravan had a part in it. By that time, I was so totally sick and tired of those people and that dusty, cold, villainous land that even the views of the Sea of Galilee that opened before me on that fourth morning failed to inspire me with any feeling of awe or history.

Sea! I huffed to myself, *We had reservoirs as big as that back in South Carolina—and prettier, too!*

I was sick to death of my boring, uncommunicative, and untrustworthy traveling companions, my ridiculous disguise, the slow pace of travel and the constant fear of harassment by "tax-collectors." I simply left the group and struck out on foot by myself without even entering Caperneum, the now-famous little dump that in those days had a reputation for being a filthy, crime-ridden backwater.

Forced to carry my belongings in a big bundle, I almost threw the half of it away after the first five miles. Around noon, however, and still dressed as a man, I came upon a small farm where I found a young man who could speak some Latin. I negotiated with him to buy his donkey and some food, and he seemed to be a most pleasant sort. For that matter, since he and his wife were the only nice people I had met since Tyre, I decided to hole up at their place for a day or two in order to get my bearings. I also wanted to nurse my grudge and plan my revenge upon the man who had treated me so badly.

My initial plan was simple enough. Knowing that I might not be able to come this way again, I decided simply to double back in a different disguise—probably as a woman. I would scope out the situation, find out where he slept, and cut his throat. I tried to consider every angle, including the getaway, but knew that until I spotted him again I would not be able to size up any such attempt.

The farmer and his wife spoke no Greek, and I no Hebrew or Aramaic, so we were compelled to converse only in Latin, of which the husband—an earnest 20-year old— knew quite a bit from having worked for a year on a Roman construction project.

Aramaic was the dominant language of the region, but it would be more accurate to say that there were many similar languages being spoken in that area—Galilean, Samaritan,

Hebrew, and Judean and many other Aramaic dialects. Consequently, there was a certain ability at least to understand if not to speak the similar languages, much as is the case in Scandinavia or as between English and modern Scottish. There was at that time a formal, written style of Hebrew that was used in the synagogues, but the broad masses in Palestine used their various Aramaic dialects and, if that failed, they used what I came to refer to as marketplace Greek.

Like practically all of the rest of the common folk of that region, my hosts were quite poor. They were, however, decent, clean, and apparently trustworthy people—of whom that region seemed otherwise bereft. The girl was about 19 and very pretty, with dark features and eyes that sparkled when she laughed, which was often. They had been married six years, had two children, and lived in a two-room stone house on a 20-acre farm that they leased from a big landholder.

They were very happy when I asked to stay on at their place for a couple of nights—particularly when I paid them a silver coin in advance.

As soon as it was appropriate for me to do so, which is to say, late in the afternoon after we had talked and negotiated for a couple of hours, I revealed to them that I was a woman. I had fooled them completely and they were both astonished. For one thing, I was taller than either of them and, of course, I had been disguising my voice. The wife chattered like a bird to her husband and thought my disguise wonderfully entertaining and even did imitations of me using my lowered voice. The farmer, on the other hand, was upset because he was very religious. He kept worrying about whether or not it was proper for them to have me—a foreigner, a gentile, and probably a whore—staying in their recently-resanctified dwelling. He wondered aloud whether or not I might not be on my way, but his wife put her foot down. To her I was very special: a prostitute perhaps, but most importantly, I was someone who was utterly fascinating. I was a window upon a world she would never see. I could tell all of this was running through her head and was behind her insistence that I stay.

Naturally, I wished that she could speak Greek or at least a bit more Latin, but she couldn't. She had to content herself with her husband's translations as well as with an increasingly complex vocabulary of sign language and gestures that she and I developed.

I stayed with them for two nights. The husband slept out in the shed while I shared the sleeping pallet with the wife. The very small gold coin that I had gave them, they assured me, was more than enough to pay for the food I ate, the donkey I took, and resanctification rites for the house that my stay necessitated.

I can still remember how utterly amazed the young mother was when I removed the men's clothing in front of her. Naturally enough, I had no modesty at all about undressing in front of her. After all I had been through, I could have undressed in front of a legion without blushing, and in front of her, I thought only of getting out of the restrictive, corset-like lorica and the dirty soldier's clothes that had not been washed in four days and probably had lice. No wonder I had fooled her with my disguise: I even smelled like a man.

Almost desperately I wanted a bath, and with signs I told her so. In a flash she produced jugs of tepid water, a pottery basin, and drying cloths. Overcoming her own embarrassment, she watched, open-mouthed, as I took a thorough cat bath right there in front of her in the little ten-foot square main room. To assure her that it was all right for her to watch, I chatted away as I washed my hair and my whole body and wondered whether or not she had ever seen another grown woman—particularly a big one like me—nude. I soon realized that she was fascinated not by my forthrightness and nudity so much as she was by my tattered panties, red-blonde hair, large stature, and pale, white skin. Had she not been so modest—which is to say, had she been more like most of the women I had met—I think that she would have stepped forward and touched my hair and skin to see if they were real.

After I was clean and refreshed and dressed in my most modest clothes, we called her husband to come in. He was utterly astonished at the transformation I had undergone, saying things like "Night has become day!." I asked him whether his wife had ever seen a blonde.

"Oh, yes," he said, "for there are many gold hairs who pass through along the Roman roads or live with rich men in the cities and in places like Capernaum." The inference was unmistakable, but he was polite enough about it.

"Honored host," I told him, "please understand that I am

from a far country where many women have light yellow hair as well as hair more red than mine. I do not make my living being with men. I have my own money."

He blushed and was confused, for he had not meant to embarrass or accuse me. I made everything all right by laughing and being cheerful. Nora brought food and we ate. I felt secure and that night I slept more soundly than I had for several days.

The farm was quite isolated, and was not even near a main road. I had stumbled upon it by coming on a footpath over the hills, and there were no other houses in sight. Nevertheless, during the day I mostly stayed inside so that I might not be seen by passersby. While I slept, Nora washed and boiled my clothes and prepared lots of food for me.

Nursing my hatred while I was awake, I spent a lot of time sharpening my short sword as the three of us talked. I was going to get my dagger back: it was the principle of the thing.

From my hosts, I learned some of the things I needed to know in that hostile country. To begin with, I learned that the quasi-legal thieves along the trade routes and the cutthroats that infested the towns and byways constituted one end of an awful spectrum of injustice. At the other end, a religion-cloaked oligarchy of high priests and lawyers ruled the land in league with their totally corrupt leader, Herod. The latter was known locally as The Great Thief and was widely despised as being one who sat on his bloody throne by leave of the Romans. "At least he is a Jew!" people would foolishly exclaim, as if that were a virtue in itself and had nothing to do with how they were being treated as individuals. As far as they were concerned, Herod's rule was what passed for Jewish sovereignty in the region, even though the net result was one of rabbi-dominated oppression.

I remember that you once held that one of the measures of a decent society could be found in the price of its beer, for those prices reflected how common folks are treated. By that measure, you found Western Europe somewhat oppressive. Well, if you think Sweden was bad, you should have seen Palestine. They didn't have any beer, nor did they have dope or opium. All they had to relieve the monotony of life was the worst wine and the sweetest water in all the world. It is a wonder that there were not more drunkards than I saw, and I saw plenty. Every crossroads had a farmer selling his wine, and every roadway revealed men and women staggering under the burdens of care and the influence of wine.

Contrasting with such scenes were the kinds of displays of piety that we used to hear about in South Carolina's Sunday schools. People made a show of avoiding work on the Sabbath, avoiding foreigners, and following strict dress codes. They were an uptight bunch of people, eager to condemn and to stone.

Except for their hands, they were also a comparably dirty people. The homes generally had no baths and I almost never saw people bathing in the shallow streams and rivers that watered the land. I was under the impression that few non-Greek denizens of that region could swim, and even among fishermen I almost never saw public nudity like I had in Greece.

I quickly noted that there was less slavery there than elsewhere in the Roman Empire. This was probably because so many people were serfs already.

I learned, too, that there were many religious teachers with bands of adherents roaming the land. Each had his own agenda and his message concerning personal or national salvation—the two concepts being so often interwoven as to be indistinguishable.

My host, though, had met the group I sought. He described Julian with unmistakable clarity—more clarity, in fact, than he used to describe the prophet who was the group's leader and spokesman.

That prophet, whose name he pronounced "Yeshu'a," had been preaching in the area for some time and was said to travel with men who were thought to be immoral and impious. He was quick to point out that the rabbis who ran the synagogues always said such things of the independents and he himself had no knowledge of whether or not Yeshu'a and his men were, in fact, immoral. He did say that he had heard the new prophet speak several times. For that matter, he had heard several of the other travelling rabbis of the region speak, too, for he was, as I have said, very religious.

He did not think that this prophet who Julian followed could be the Messiah. Pressed on the point, he said that his knowledge of the prophecies was limited by his illiteracy, and he therefore depended on readings and interpretations of holy texts that he had heard in synagogues. Based therefore not upon what he had read but upon what he had gleaned, he held that the true

Messiah who was expected would be not only obvious but also powerful and a natural leader of men. Moreover, the Messiah—when and if he came—would be a proclaimed savior of the Jewish people, leading them militarily to an overthrow of foreign domination and internal corruption. Jerusalem, he said, was to be rebuilt in fine stone, gold, and precious woods.

When I asked him why Roman rule was so hated, his answer was at once vague and vehement. "They are different than any who have subjugated this land before," he said, "for they bring with them not so much a pantheon of false gods as they do roads and armies and techniques of war impossible to ignore.

"They are vile, ignorant, and coarse," he concluded as I suppressed a smile. He said what ignorant people of all nations always say about foreigners they do not understand or like. It was just what the people of Rome and Greece said about the inhabitants of Palestine. It's close to what a lot of French say about Americans.

Apparently, the hatred of the Romans was a visceral, chauvinistic emotion prevalent throughout the land. Practically everyone felt that revolt was imminent, waiting only upon a leader or group of leaders, if not a Messiah. There was no doubt that when the call came, the men would be ready—if not to fight, then at least to die. Like my host, most of them would be untrained, untried, and yet not undisciplined. Their lives were already dominated by the discipline of the plow and the landlord, and their common religion and their adherence to centralized authority guaranteed that they would be fanatics.

Not all Jewish soldiers would be untrained. There was a very small standing army loyal to Herod as well an underground paramilitary movement of which my host was reluctant to speak but which is known historically as the Zealots. They were in training for revolt, and as I soon realized, they represented one of roughly five segments of Jewish political society.

The first, led by the Zealots, were those who believed in the immediate and complete overthrow of the "Roman yoke," which was, in my opinion, less onerous than the "Jewish yoke." To their credit, those advocating revolt knew from experience and observation that the Jewish people alone could not defeat the Romans. To win they would need either the help of allies such as the Parthians or of the unqualified help of their Almighty

God, in whom they had enough faith to take on even the Roman Empire if only He would give them a sign.

"The sign" kept coming to isolated groups who would "begin" the divinely-inspired revolts only to find themselves quickly defeated not by the Romans but by the troops of the tetrarchs. The Zealots, on the other hand, were rather like the IRA of Palestine, and the Jewish tetrarchs found themselves in political postures similar to those of the modern governments in Dublin and London. It was painfully obvious to them that the Zealots' ideal future did not include a continuation of the Herodian dynasty.

The second major group in Palestine—and by far the most numerous —was comprised of those who wanted or said they wanted revolt and national independence but were totally unwilling to do anything to further it except to watch and wait. Like modern Americans who want liberty but will do nothing to regain it, they would not risk hearths and homes by becoming involved with the Zealots or similar groups. This, needless to say, was the group into which most of the pharisees, sadducees, and scribes fit. Nothing changes.

The third group usually gave lip service to the goals of the others. It was comprised of a growing community of Jewish and gentile merchants, tax agents, and government officials who were quite content with the existing political system. After all, it provided them both their authority and their incomes. In this they, too, were indistinguishable from many modern businessmen, bureaucrats, soldiers, and police.

A fourth identifiable group was what one might have called "the indifferent peasantry": that broad mass of perennially cynical people who always fear for the worst, disdain the present, and fear the future but feel themselves totally powerless to influence anything. This group—with which I feel a great deal of sympathy—is present in all societies, I suppose. I think of the French peasantry with their characteristic shrug, or the Russian proverb: Who of whom?—which translates more accurately into "Which S.O.B. is winning out over the other?" I am reminded, too, of the contention that a third of South Carolinians fought for neither King nor Independence. They just wanted to be left alone.

The fifth group—and apparently by far the *least*

numerous—was made up of those who could be described as being the strict religionists. It was they who became monks, hermits, and cabalists and who were, like the fourth group I have described, outside the political turmoil of the day. In addition, they were—insofar as possible—outside of the turmoil of daily living and were for the most part generally respected by society for their choice of the aesthetic life. I believe that the Essenes were one of the sects representing this last group, but I knew of them only by reputation and never visited in one of their communities. It may well have been that their reputation for passivity was merely a front for their connections with the Zealots. Both feared and respected, the Essenes were thought to possess supernatural powers as well as an intelligence network from which no secrets could be hidden. If an Essene called upon someone to give over his son or his daughter to them, he did so no questions asked, for it was considered an honor and the youths were free to return home whenever they wanted. Few did.

On the second night of my stay, my host and I discussed the group I was seeking. I was still quite a mystery woman, and I suppose they assumed that I was a Greek or Roman who was escaping from a husband or from the authorities. In any case, it did not seem to be in my best interest to disabuse them of the errant-wife theory so I made up a story about how I was fleeing an abusive husband to be with my brother who was with the Roman garrison in Judea.

"For a decent woman on the run, you seem to be carrying too much baggage," my host said to me quite out of the blue.

"But I have the donkey I've bought from you," I answered .

"That is not the point," the bearded young man said to me quite earnestly. "It may be none of my business, but it seems that the weights you carry are on your heart and in your scabbard. I think that there is someone for whom you sharpen that sword," he said of my blade, the sharpness of which I was feeling with my thumb. "It is too heavy a thing to carry. Perhaps you should leave it here," he concluded, his earnest, brown eyes pleading the truth he had ascertained.

I bit my lip, and suddenly I felt like crying. For days the humiliation and pain and the subsequent hatred I had suffered because of the tax-soldier had been gnawing like an animal in my guts. I had nursed my pain, and plotted my revenge. I was planning to go back the next day to get my revenge if possible. Something seemed to be turned around on me. I had not cried about it. I had hated. I wanted to explain everything to this simple farmer but couldn't, for the murder I was contemplating would occur not more than 30 miles from that farm and even the simplest investigation might point to me. As it was, even if I said nothing to the farmer, it might well be obvious to him that I might be sought-after culprit. I realized that I would have to postpone my revenge.

I was at once relieved and frustrated. I found it difficult to turn my back on my project, but on the other hand, I knew that if I went on my way without the revenge I craved, I would be free of the danger that murder might entail. I was ashamed of myself for being happy to be off the hook, if only temporarily.

So I cried. My hosts were amazed, and the wife came over and put her arm around me. The simple, straightforward kindness of those people deeply touched my heart. I suppose they assumed that I had been raped, and in a way, I had been.

"Maybe if I wash the blade in blood, it will be lighter," I offered finally when I quit crying.

"Maybe so!" the farmer said, cheerfully trying to lighten us all up. "But it might make it heavier, too. It is a serious business to try to clean something that way. It takes a river of water to wash even a little blood from a garment. How much more, then, from a sword?"

Later on I began again to inquire about Julian in a reasonably subtle way, and my host once again spoke about him in even greater detail than he had before. Julian, he told me was the tallest, baldest and oldest man in the group. Julian did not speak in public very much, he said, and when he did, it was with an accent that marked him as being a foreigner. When he mentioned that the older man had also been the rudest in the group, I knew for sure that he was describing Julian. My host had even spoken to him for a short while—a few minutes only— some six months previously, and even from that brief interchange had determined that Julian was not a Jew and not even a foreign Jew whose education had been neglected. I was impressed by the young farmer's powers of observation.

Naturally enough he wondered why I was so interested in that particular little sect and I replied that the prophet Yeshu'a had once helped my brother, the Roman officer, who had in turn spoken highly of him.

"Well, maybe he can help you, too," he said. "All of us have things—wounds—we need healed, and maybe if you have some he can heal yours. I've heard that he can heal the sick and drive out demons, but I wouldn't know for sure. There are always lots of such stories about holy men."

He went on talking about prophets, and for the first time since leaving Rhodes in the Fall, I was beginning to be excited about this journey or quest. If what the whole society of my youth believed was true, and if the bumbling Anglican priest Julian had not latched on to the wrong group, I was on the verge of stepping into history, perhaps even shaping it. I might be, for that matter, just a few miles away from them! I might meet Yeshu'a on the morrow! I exulted inwardly.

But I had learned to be on guard. The miles could be terribly long ones. Casually, I asked where they were.

"Oh, they went south a couple of months ago. I think they were headed to Samaria or even on to Jerusalem. I think they wore out their welcome here."

Gone! It was a shock to me, for he had no idea where they went or on what mission. I felt like a kid the gypsies had left behind.

I asked him what he meant by "worn out their welcome".

"Well, you know how it is," he patiently explained. "These groups come and they always go--like traveling actors. If they get unpopular, they go elsewhere to find new patrons and new audiences. On the other hand, if they get too popular, first thing you know the pharisees and rabbis start cooking things up against them and drive them out."

I asked what kind of things, and he explained.

"Oh, you know: stolen funds, frauds, witchcraft, blasphemy, unmarried girls with child—let's see: what else? Oh, yes: violations of the Sabbath, adultery, tax cheating, thievery, and that great catchall, 'being an enemy of the king.' Of course, nobody likes the king, but that's beside the point."

I left the next morning before dawn so that I might

minimize the chance that someone might see I had been at their home. After stuffing down a huge breakfast and giving them money, I put on my freshly washed soldier's disguise and my moustache, packed the donkey's bags, and took up my arms. I was heading south, and I was eager to leave. I hugged the girl and kissed the sleeping children. On an impulse I gave their mother a silver coin for each of them—coins, I suppose, that my foolish maid had earned from the sailors and marines. I had no doubt that had she stuck by me as Odysseus had, the gods would have spared her, too.

Putting my hand on his shoulder and looking my host in the eye to impress him with my sincerity, I warned him.

"Someone very powerful wants my death, but I do not know who that person is. In the great world outside this region I am widely known, and it may be that many are seeking me, perhaps for a bounty. This is not for any crime I might have done, because I tell you that before God I have wronged no man.

"Those who seek me may offer you gold and silver for information about me, but they might just as easily torture you and your family to get what they want. They may abuse you even for the pure pleasure of it, for they will be wicked men.

"Therefore, if someone seeks me, say only that you met me, that I bought your donkey, and I went on my way toward Caesarea. Do not go looking for trouble or it might find you. And tell your wife that although she will want to speak of this visit to her friends, your lives may depend on her silence."

"I will do as you wish," he said, wincing uncomfortably under my touch and making me aware that this was the first time I had actually touched him. I had spoiled his attempt to keep *kosher* or whatever by avoiding touching me, and I had spoiled it. I took my hand away but it was too late. He smiled anyway.

"Be careful, Lady," he said to me, "and accept the advice of a poor farmer that swords belong in scabbards if they are to be kept clean and sharp."

"What does a man of peace know of arms?" I asked as I hitched up my weapons harness.

"I only know what I have been taught and what I have learned from observation. So don't ask me: Go ask that question of the prophet you are seeking. And may your God go with you."

"My God is your God," I replied.

"I know," he said with a smile as I turned to leave.

****

XXIX

On Foot

Palestine is a small place. Depending on just what one considers to be the boundaries of that region, it is still only roughly a third the size of South Carolina. The so-called Sea of Galilee, for example, is about 35 miles from the Mediterranean Sea by air. From Tiberias on its western shore to Jerusalem is only 60 miles. On the ground the distance was considerably greater, particularly given all the twists and turns of the roads one encountered traveling through the low mountains and towns of Samaria.

Following the slow progress I had made since leaving Tyre, and excited by a fresh sense of adventure, I was eager to get going. After striking out westward from the farm so I appeared in fact to be heading toward the sea, and after cresting the high hill beyond the little valley, I headed south toward Mt. Tabor, the town of Nain, and points beyond.

Looking back upon it, I realize that my journey into Samaria was a bigger undertaking than I had anticipated, but something in me made me do it. For several days I traveled light and fast, avoiding the main roads and ignoring those people who would have detained me or tried to sell me things. When I found people who could speak Latin or Greek, I asked for directions and for information. For the most part, though, I kept to myself. I detoured around the police stations that all too frequently lay astride the main roads and trade routes.

I kept heading south until I was not more than a few miles north of Jerusalem. I saw the city in the distance and found myself thrilled at the prospect of seeing Solomon's Temple.

A traveler I met on the road, however, told me that I would have to go east past Jerico to Peraea to find Julian and his prophet. He was so certain and clear and so enthusiastic concerning the prophet Yeshu'a--who he said could even raise the dead--that I found myself caught up in his fervor. Without regret, I turned east as the man told me I should. Jerusalem could wait.

Descending into the great rift valley with its barren, broiling wastes and crossing over the Jordan just north of the Dead Sea, my donkey and I wandered about for several days in a vain attempt to catch up with the prophet Yeshu'a and his disciple, Julian Parker-Lane. On more than one occasion, I tracked down a likely group only to find that it was not the one I sought.

Wearying of subterfuges and the uncomfortable lorica, I quit using my masculine disguises except when they seemed absolutely necessary. Dressed most often in a tunic, knee-length skirt and cloak and wearing boots and my last pair of white socks, I suppose that I looked more like a modern hiker than anything else. My legs and arms burned, then tanned.

On my head I wore a flat, straw hat that could be tied down by silk ribbons. At that time my hair was a bit less than shoulder length. Generally I kept it combed out straight, but when it was hot I usually tied it up or at least caught it in a small ponytail. I walked at a blistering pace, dragging the not-too-heavily laden donkey along.

Impatient also of detours and of hiding when others passed by, I found that I could get by all manner of people through the simple expedient of walking straight ahead through roadblocks or past slow caravans with a determined look on my face and a drawn sword in my hand. Most people probably thought I was a crazy German, but I was ready. Although obviously a woman, when I came striding down on a station or little group of people with that sword in one hand and towing the trotting donkey in the other, most people were daunted. Issuing commands in English or Latin to "Step Aside!" I astonished most everyone. In that way I had some funny moments from time to time, but there were some things that were not so amusing.

On my fourth day out from the turning away from Jerusalem, for example, I walked through a scene of horror in a little village in some rugged hills east of the Jordan. Every single person in the place had either died from some plague or had fled for his life. The six-day old corpses of 30 or more people lay scattered along the one pathetic street, and the flies and stench were terrible. But for the fact that it was located in a narrow pass, I would have given the place a wide berth, but such a detour would have taken me a half-day out of my way, so I just marched on through with a scarf to my nose and mouth. It was horrible.

Although I didn't mind all the walking and loneliness, my temper and patience grew shorter each day. It was not a comfortable time of year to be traveling. It was too hot during the day and too cold at night, and sometimes it rained hard. Fortunately I was equipped with a tightly woven, lanolin-rich sea-cloak that shed water and doubled as a sleeping wrap as well as a sort of small tent. And I had the little donkey for company.

One day when I felt particularly ill-natured—out in the middle of nowhere with no other people in sight—I walked rapidly toward two men who acted as if I should stop for them. They were talking back and forth with one another excitedly as I approached and I didn't like the looks of them at all. For one thing, they reminded me of the sort of men who had attacked me and my husband in the mountains of Yugoslavia.

One of them held up his palm in the universal sign meaning "halt." I already had my short sword out, but I was carrying it concealed in the folds of my cloak so that he couldn't see it. Almost involuntarily, I laughed aloud since he looked like a frowning, Bedouin version of the Coca-Cola tin cop that stood in the street near my grammar school in the 'fifties. My laughter was a mistake. It made him really angry. When we were still some distance apart I yelled out *"Move aside!"* in Greek.

"Stop!" he responded.

"Why?" I asked as I kept on coming.

"Because *I* say!" he said when we were only twenty feet apart.

Acting as if I did not understand what he wanted, I made to pass him by on the right so that my donkey would be between me and the two of them.

If he was a King's Man he should have said so or held up his seals, but he didn't. At that point I half expected him to let me pass, but you know the motto: Be Prepared. When I came abreast of them I was instinctively ready and tense with anticipation. The older, larger man was neither amused nor deterred by my boldness or my laughter, and he lowered his hand and shifted his weight to prepare to stop me by force. His hand tightened on his cudgel. When we were still some eight feet apart he was jabbering at me in Aramaic. I could see plainly in his eyes and by the wicked smile that came upon his lips what he intended to do with the arrogant, foreign Amazon who had laughed at him. If he could have hidden that look he might have lived a while longer, but he couldn't and so he didn't.

He stared into my eyes trying to transfix me. He should have paid more attention to my hands.

Stepping quickly to his left so he was right in front of me, he started to swing his club at me with his right hand as with his left hand he grabbed hard for my right wrist. He caught hold, instead, to the razor-sharp, double-bladed sword. His cudgel caught my donkey on the side of the neck just as he began to feel the bite of the blade. I yanked it free, almost severing his dirty fingers. He hardly had time to begin to say something when I shoved it forward, right through his heart. His scream was cut short by his loud "Whuff!" He staggered back a half step, taking my sword with him.

It happened so quickly that the other fellow—a wiry bastard with one eye—had no time to shove past the donkey to help his companion or to see exactly what was going on.

I tried to jerk the sword free, but it was stuck in the man right below his sternum. Avoiding a vicious swing of one-eye's heavy staff, I let go of the panicking donkey's lead rope and the sword and sprinted toward some boulders 40 yards away. I never ran so fast in my life and was gone in a flash, exalting in my triumph over the big man and planning what to do about one-eye. He was as good as dead, but he didn't know it. I did.

By the time he checked on his pal, gathered his wits, and ran after me, I was behind a rock waiting for him with an arrow. My heart was racing wildly and I could hardly hold my bow steady and the arrow in place. When I heard him running along the path I had taken, I drew back and waited, confident that I could get the second arrow in place if my initial shot missed.

The first one, however, was enough. It caught him by surprise as he came around a large boulder and found himself hemmed in a narrow little crevice without protection. Intent upon the chase and noting my footprints in the sand, he looked up just in time to watch as the arrow sped to his throat and went out of the back of his neck. Somehow or another and in spite of the wound, he screamed a lot right at first. I turned my head and walked away to wait for a few minutes. I did not want to watch him die.

At that moment, I almost wanted a cigarette. When I went back, he was dead.

In case the two men actually had some sort of authority to stop people, I used some rope tied to the reluctant donkey to drag their bodies behind the rocks. There I rolled them both into a small depression and covered them with the hot sand. Although I had them buried in record time, there were flies everywhere before I could finish—another of the little miracles of the desert.

Before I buried them, though, I plundered the bodies. Between them, they had no more than ten little silver coins, and I actually felt disappointment. After all, I had done better before. Erasing my footprints with some brush, I backed away from the rocks, gathered up their weapons and continued on.

Just off the roadway a bit farther along, I found their camp and was again disappointed, for they had nothing worth taking. From the looks of things I surmised that in fact they were police or tax collectors of some sort and knew I would be in for trouble if their bodies were found and the killing was connected to me. I did what I could to obliterate my tracks and left in a hurry.

Buoyant from my victory over the two men, I moved along at my usual fast clip and saw no one at all for the remainder of that day. Arriving at a small river just before dark, I led the donkey out into the water, then went upstream for nearly a half-mile to camp for the night. As the light faded, I began to feel very peculiar and began hearing things. I heard—or thought I heard—distant screams, cries for help, voices, men searching for me, wild animals, the rustling of the spirits of that place. I had not lit a fire that evening for fear of attracting unwanted attention, but now I wanted one—a big one to keep the terrors of the night at bay. I didn't feel lonely: I felt threatened and was beginning to get hysterical. One word in English came into my mind and would not go away: *murder*.

In the last of the failing light, I went to the stream and began trying to wash the blood off of my sword and the arrow I had used, but it was too late. Neither would come clean, though I used a bit of soap that I had as well as lots of sand to scour them.

The blood had irreparably stained the metal. *Murder*.

In the afternoon I had been so exuberant. I thought about the man who had hit me up north and how I had hated him so badly. These two, I tried to reason, had died for him, and yet I was not satisfied.

The attempt to clean the once-shiny sword became an obsession. Almost desperately, I tried to clear the dark lines and discolored areas, not wanting to admit failure. That sword had never been bloodied before, and I had treated it with uncommon care to make it as sharp and flawless as possible. In my hand, it had seemed substantial, yet light and quick—a real work of military art. Now, having accomplished its purpose, it was as if I had ruined it.

Sadly I put it away, knowing that something about me was stained, too, and might not come clean. Lying on my back and looking up at the stars, I began to feel shame and sorrow—not that I had killed them, for as I have said, I had killed men before. I felt shame because I had felt so good about it, and I thought about Mark and how he had so quickly become inured to and even fond of killing. I thought of what Hemingway would someday write: that a thing is moral if you feel good after doing it. By that standard, what I had done was moral—if only right at first—but it did not make me clean. I would have bathed again in the river, but it wouldn't have done any good. Somehow I was finally able to sleep fitfully, but I dreamed of soldiers chasing me.

All the next day as I trudged westward toward Judea, I thought about what the young farmer had told me--*"Swords belong in scabbards if they are to be kept clean and sharp."*

Oh, well: mine was no longer clean, but it was still sharp. I remembered with a mixture of pride and revulsion how easily it slid into my enemy.

I kept turning these matters over in my mind, retrieving even the silliest aspects of the encounter as well as the young farmer's admonitions. I thought of the cop's look and of my laughing at it. I could not forget the look of hatred and rape that had condemned them, or the sounds of the second man's imminent death.

Had I become "a cop killer"—beyond the pall of the law, outside of explanations or defenses if my crime was detected? That thought gave wings to my feet. To have come so far and endured so much only to be hunted down before I could find Julian and the prophet Yeshu'a would have been terrible.

What was I doing wandering alone through that arid country, I wondered?

Finally in the late afternoon of that day, I came to an overlook along the pathway. Out ahead of me lay a panorama of arid land split by the last sinuous ribbon of the Jordan River where it entered the marshy backwaters of the Dead Sea. I was hungry and tired. The word murder would not leave me. I was alone. As far as the eye could see, there seemed to be no one.

I knelt down and prayed. I wish I could tell you what or to whom I prayed, but I can't. I do remember I prayed for guidance. No answer came to me, and I felt that I was alone even though I wasn't. Suddenly weary with life, I rose and looked out on the barren, beautiful scenery. Then the land itself spoke to me. It seemed to say, "You are searching for God. God will find you."

Later that same evening, dressed as a man and having changed donkeys as well as shoes, I entered a small town east of Livias. There I learned that those I sought had left the area just the day before, heading to Jerusalem for the Passover feasts.

The Passover! It was the first time that I had heard it mentioned. Was it not at the time of the Passover that Christ was to be crucified? And which year might this be, I wondered? If something terrible was going to happen, were we powerless to prevent it? Confronted by the question, I had to admit that I had always questioned the crucifixion story. I knew—and Julian knew as well—that most, if not all, of the Gospels would be written 50 years or more in the future, and who were we to know if they were accurate?

As I walked toward Jerusalem, the philosophical themes that dominated my thoughts were similar to those we had argued many times. Could history be changed or is it immutable? What is history?

I knew something was about to happen—something momentous or terrible or both. But whether such a thing was to be personal or public, I didn't know. My skin crawled as I thought back about all the fortunetellers I had encountered in the ancient world and what each had foretold. The words of Delphi came back: *"Coming in time but in time too late:/ Free you are not but an arrow of fate."* What did they mean? If I had the Gift of Sight, why could I not see what lay in store for me?

I wondered if I was having premonitions of my own death—perhaps my own crucifixion. I was certainly afraid of being charged with murder, and while on the road, I was always looking back to see whether or not I was being followed. It was easy to picture myself being caught by the men of Herod Antipas, or those of the Judean leaders, or even by some Roman operating under the same orders if not the same warrants that the dead Cassius had alleged in support of his capture of me at sea. The 1970s world had seemed peopled by my enemies when I met Mark. How much more so for me the ancient one of 30 A.D.!

"Anno Domini" I thought: The Year of Our Lord. Well, maybe somebody's lord but not mine, I thought grimly, looking back along the road. I looked back often, but there were no pursuers. Not yet, anyway.

I remember distinctly wanting to blame men in general for causing the feelings of panic I was fighting back. I blamed Mark for being weak (which he really wasn't), Sejanus for being power-mad, Cassius for being a tool. I thought of the various bandits, chieftains and pirates who had attacked me. I blamed the guard who had struck me and the guards I had killed in self-defense. Most of all, I blamed Julian who had made us come here instead of going to the Golden Age we would have chosen. I was about to go crazy, I thought.

Then I remembered other men who were good, kind, and decent—not perfect, perhaps, and not without faults. Some were lovers. Others, like Ovinin and my ship's captain were companions. There was my father. I thought of my minister, my uncle, and my high school chemistry teacher, and I thought of you.

As I strode toward Jerusalem thinking of the world of men, I remembered my husband and all we had been through during our seven months together. All that seemed far away on the one hand and like last week on the other. It was as clear as a teacher's metaphor and as worthwhile as was that long climb that you and I took up the mountain on our last day in the Smokies. And I thought of the world of women, too, of my sister, mother, cousin, roommates, friends—even of Julian's mother—and of the love that I had known from all manner of people.

Then the peace of God descended upon me as I walked, and the future suddenly no longer mattered. I was lucky to be alive, lucky not to be chained to an oar or feeding fish amid the Three Sisters. I was lucky that I was not being held and raped by the two men in the desert, and lucky to have had a man like my husband who had loved me so much. I had lived an interesting life, and each day had been so distinct from the next as to fill volumes in the libraries of memory. In fact, I had lived already more than I could ever have hoped to live, and it was mostly because of the way that Mark had looked at me that day in Greek class.

Once I came to terms with my insecurity that day, each further hour seemed to be a blessing, even if I was tired, dirty, and thirsty. The dangers I feared or faced did not go away, yes, but had I not surmounted many already? It may have been, for all I knew, that I would fail in some way, but it didn't matter. I could take what came, be it for better or for worse and I had every reason to be optimistic. Apparently I had a mission. Truth to tell, I could not have defined what it might be. Perhaps the thing driving me on was an instinct such as the one that drives a salmon upstream. I only knew that I had to try to find the benighted Julian and the man Yeshu'a he followed.

****

XXX

The Meeting

My mind and purpose grew clear and I began to sing as I walked—seeming, I am sure, quite insane to fellow travelers on the increasingly crowded roads. By-passing Jerico for the second time, I set my sights on Jerusalem. Only then did I first remember the Apostles' Creed.

Each Sunday for at least 15 years I had spoken it with the my family at church, first mumbling the patterns, then throwing in a few words, then proudly repeating all that I had learned. I can still remember listening with only mild embarrassment as my father perfected my rendition of it with a kindly correction, telling me the name was *Pontius*, not *Conscious*, Pilate.

Now having come so far, I knew exactly how Julian must have felt when he had arrived in Palestine over two years earlier. I could barely imagine all the trials and tribulations he had been through to get here and how he must have enjoyed a growing confidence and joy working toward that initial message he sent to us: "Emanuel!"

I recalled how Churchill, having attained at last the supreme power of England in 1940 during its darkest hour, took up his duties with something akin to pleasure, having by his own account trained himself all his life for just such a call to duty. I knew that Julian must have felt that way: self-trained to step perfectly into that niche for which he had been created. How empowering!

I almost felt that way myself, but other than what I had learned in my childhood, and other than that which I had experienced and learned among the pagans, I was untrained. I had no idea what to expect, but I was ready.

In English I repeated as much of the Creed as I could remember on the morning I entered the city dressed in my final disguise of a local woman in modest, long garments with a cowl to hide my fair hair and tanned face. In spite of my attempt to blend in, I'm sure that I didn't, for not only was I taller than any of the local Jewish women, but I was leading a donkey and speaking quietly in a foreign tongue, saying,

"I believe in God the Father almighty, Maker of Heaven and Earth..."

Well, yes I did. But had He not spoken to me through the goddess Athena, and did He not penetrate my heart at Eleusis, and contact me at Delphi? And yes, had He not kept me safe through so many "toils and snares"? And had He—or She or It—not fashioned each minute of time since that first day in Greek class when I saw Mark looking at me? Had She not worked in many mysterious ways, Her wonders to perform?

... And in Jesus Christ, His only Son,...

"Where is the man these Jews all talk about—the guy from Nazarus, Soldier?" I asked the first Roman I saw. He was an off-duty soldier who was walking along with a young prostitute. He was surprised to have me step forward from the crowd and address him using the sort of jargon I had learned when living near the Rhine. He took me for a Gaul or a German, but he answered me straightaway and with respect.

"Lady, if I'm not mistaken, the guy you're looking for came to town yesterday. He's been here before, but you'd think he had won a battle or something, 'cause he came right up this here street, and crowds of people were cheering him and waving palm branches. I only caught a glimpse of him from a distance, but I have seen him before."

"Come, hurry, hurry!" the girl was saying in Latin. She didn't speak much Latin, and she may have been afraid that I was trying to take her customer. I pulled out a small silver coin that might have bought her for a whole night, and I gave it to her. "Now you be nice to this soldier in a little while," I told her as I handed it to her. The soldier smiled as he translated it into Aramaic for the girl. Astonished, she quieted down. She was going to get paid no matter what.

So it was that I made a friend of Apius Strabo, a Roman soldier who dropped what he was doing, told the girl to meet him there at dark, and helped me find my way about the city.

First we went to an inn where I could board my donkey, get a room, clean up, and get something to eat.

I was famished, and we sat down to that midday meal like young soldiers who had long before been comrades in arms. I had walked far and had not eaten well in several days, so we ordered the best meal the place could lay out and packed it in until I was stuffed.

Fascinated by me and undoubtedly hoping to bed me, Apius talked up a storm. Although he didn't know where the prophet was staying, he told me that he was at the temple every day and that the crowds there were getting larger and larger as the Jewish feast-day approached.

Apius was a sort of sergeant and had several times been assigned to lead small units of men in various duties outside the temple. The local Jewish police—controlled by the pharisees and sandhedrin—bore primary responsibility for such duties throughout the town, but the crowds felt free to push them about, if not to throw rocks at them out of pure contempt. They didn't do that with the Romans, though. When the Italians were called out, they went in full armor with pilums ready and swords sharp, tolerating no disorder whatsoever. A person who threw a rock at a Roman could be killed on the spot, and even a small unit of such determined, disciplined men could quell a big riot.

Apius told me that he had seen the so-called prophet, Yeshu'a, several months before in the streets outside Solomon's temple. The man was said to be "beautiful beyond men" by the women of the town, but he himself had been too preoccupied with his duties to notice anything special about the fellow.

We talked some about how the street life in Jerusalem was different than that found elsewhere. He, too, had been in Athens and several other major cities, but never in Rome. He knew of it by reputation, though, and over goblets of wine, we agreed that in Jerusalem the flows of public talk and rumor were more frenetic than even those of Rome. We wondered why, but now I know that such emotional turmoil stemmed from the constant spiritual and political currents that reverberated down the narrow streets and across the plazas and courtyards of the city. The answer lay in the weight of conversation in the respective cities. In Rome, all talk was shallow, for the final questions of public order and public belief were at least temporarily settled under the reign of Tiberias, whereas in Judea one slept on a powder keg—particularly in Jerusalem, which was the focal point of the nation. An idea, a movement, or a regime had to prove itself in Jerusalem. It was widely thought that a revolt initiated without support from the mass of Jerusalem's citizenry would be doomed.

Like the farmer up north, Apius was quite specific in describing Julian. He was referred to as The Big One or The Oaf around the Roman barracks. All of the wandering religious groups were objects of derision in the barracks. Strabo himself had never heard Yeshu'a or any of the others preach nor did he care to. For that matter, he had only been in the temple's Court of the Gentiles once, and then only to chase a thief who thought—mistakenly—that he could find refuge there.

Apius drank a lot of wine and tried to move on me, but I spoke to him as I would to a friend. "Apius," I said, touching his hand, "you are a good man, but it is not for us to be together. I can see that you know that in your heart. Now go find that girl who waits for you and enjoy her. I have to be going now. "

He got up to leave. I rose and took his hand the way

soldiers did in those days—wrist to wrist—and he said, "Eva, now you call on me if I can do anything—anything at all for you. I do not know who you are, but don't forget this promise."

"No, I won't. And I won't forget you, Apius Strabo. We shall see one another again—I know it."

"So be it!"

"So it shall be!" I responded in the way of the camps, and we parted, he heading down to the gate to find the girl and I out into the streets to go to the Temple of Solomon less than a half mile away.

Outside the walls of the temple courtyard throngs of people had gathered amid scores of little shops that made the whole place look like a flea market. I stood and studied the area and the movements of people before approaching the temple.

Passing through its gates at last, I found myself in a courtyard far larger and less intimate than the one at Eleusis was. It, too, was thronged with people although supposedly all commerce save the sale of holy objects and animals for sacrifice was excluded from the yard. The tone was more subdued than that of the streets outside.

Along one side—perhaps the one they called the Royal Cloister—there appeared to be a number of shops or businesses that I soon learned were Jewish banks. Vast fortunes in gold and silver were stored in ancient vaults below ground level. I learned, too, that the bankers had more control over the governing of the temple environs than even the High Priest and his rabbis.

Scattered about the courtyard, groups of young men stood or sat in circles studying together or listening to lectures on religious subjects. It wasn't quite like London's Marble Arch. There was no shouting and little vehemence, and there were always priestly listeners in every crowd who were quick to correct or censor.

There were not many women about, and those who I saw were all shuffling in and out of one side of the Court of the Gentiles into the Court of the Women—a sort of theological back door for the help, I suppose. The main Temple of Solomon was built of white stone and rose behind an intervening wall in the northern part of the overall enclosure. It was all quite new from having been totally rebuilt during the reign of Herod the Great some thirty years before, and though rather unimaginatively designed by my tastes, it was reputed to be a beautiful building on the inside. Naturally, I wanted to get a look at it and to go in and find Julian. Knowing that I would have to use the side entrance, I shuffled slowly off toward the Court of Women with bowed head and covered face, intently watching and listening for anything unusual. I wasn't the only one doing that: from time to time, those of us out in the courtyard could hear shouts or angry words coming from within the temple, as if some domestic dispute was going on in there.

Finally arriving at the gate where the women entered, I started to go in, only to find my way blocked by a pleasant-looking, old fellow who spoke to me in Hebrew or Aramaic. He obviously worked there and was a guard or guide of some sort. I answered him in Greek, in which he was fluent, and he told me that Gentiles were not permitted in the Court of Women inside the actual temple. He was so nice about it I didn't even think to argue the matter. I hadn't realized that there was further segregation of worshippers.

Then I stood about for a while just talking with the man and looking around to take in the scene. After a while, I asked the guard about the one called Yeshu'a. He shook his head as if in mild regret or disapproval.

"Inside," he said, jerking his thumb back over his shoulder to indicate the building behind. "They're all inside, arguing about something or another, probably about whether they get to "teach" in the Priests' Court or whatever: making trouble, as usual. I just wish they'd all get out of town. This is supposed to be a place of worship."

"Have you listened to him?" I asked.

"Some," he said, "but for the most part, I just mind my own business."

"Kind sir," I said, "perhaps his business is your business."

"Well, maybe," he admitted, "but I'm too old for all that trouble and strife. You know, I've got a job to do, and I can't keep it by adhering to every convincing rabbi who wanders in from the Styx."

I was surprised by his mythological reference and would have kidded him about it, but at that time, a great commotion began on the other side of the temple. Practically everyone looked toward the south side of the temple and moved in that direction. Excited, I moved that way, too.

As I rounded the corner, I saw what was at the center of the attention of the crowd. There, about 200 feet away and coming out of the temple, I could see Julian. I knew it was he by his height and by the way he moved—slumped over slightly at the shoulders, but with his chin thrust out in his perpetual look of challenge, the chip, somehow, still on his shoulder. I could recognize him even though I could not clearly see his face, even though he was dressed as a Jew and had a thick, black beard, and even though he had lost forty or fifty pounds since I had last seen him.

I pushed forward through the loose crowd until I was within 30 yards of the elevated portico that was crowded with men. I had been right: Julian was unmistakable. Naturally enough, he did not see me even though I was so close. I was wearing a hood that partly covered my face and hid my hair completely, and dressed in such dull clothing as I had on I blended in with the crowd. Naturally, too, he was not expecting to see me there. His attentions were focused on a group that was pushing forward to meet him and I was not too surprised to see that he was beginning to "work" them like some politician's bagman, holding out a leather purse into which they put contributions as he wrote their names down on a tablet. Well, I thought, even prophets have to eat. I decided to wait and get his attention when he left the Temple.

Then there arose a renewed commotion, and other men came out, several of them huddled in a knot around a single man who I knew was Julian's prophet, Yeshu'a.

The crowd in which I was standing became more agitated and voices cried out imprecations and questions in Hebrew, among which were shouted queries such as "When will be the hour of our deliverance?" and "What is the will of God?" and "Give us a sign!"

The tangle about Yeshu'a cleared and he stepped up on a block so that he could address the crowd. That was the first time that I saw his face. O, *he* was a man! Whoever says that Yeshu'a was not handsome has never seen him. His eyes that day were the light of the sky—just as I had heard they would be.

Watching him as he spoke in a forceful, resonant, kindly voice, I soon realized that his demeanor seemed to be without conceit or affectation. His histrionic gestures and movements, though effective, were subtle enough so as not to bear the imprimatur of the formal schools of rhetoric of those days. His large hands described his words with motions that were fluid and open and inviting.

It was obvious to me that he would be judged to be beautiful to different people in wildly different ways. It might be said that he was a human mirror in a relentlessly narcissistic and needy world. The man who wanted a military leader, a priest, a Messiah, or just a trustworthy carpenter, could find him in Yeshu'a. Similarly, the woman who wanted a husband, brother, son, father, or lover could find him in the beautiful Galilean. For lack of a better term I shall say that he had charisma.

Not all men and women found what they sought in him, for the man or woman of greed or oppression who looked for a kindred spirit in that face would probably come away dissatisfied—if not wordlessly rebuked. There were plenty of people in the world, then as now, who would have felt that way.

Transfixed as I was by studying him, I could plainly see that there were many about who held him in respectful disfavor. Like lawyers during a skillful opponent's opening statement, they were looking for flaws and contradictions. No: they were more like the gladiators I had seen in Rome. They were looking for an opening in their opponent's armor and would gladly run him through intellectually if given half a chance.

Interrupted occasionally by questions, he spoke for 20 minutes. Naturally, I understood nothing of it since I had picked up so little Aramaic. I could, however, pay careful attention to things like his delivery, tone, volume, and appeal. I could also study the effect he was having on his audience.

I was standing in a respectfully listening crowd of some four hundred men and twenty-five or thirty women, the latter of whom would normally have been hustled out of the main court yard by the rabbis or their security forces. Apparently, though, it was not a normal day, and as long as we kept ourselves covered up in the required drab, dark clothes, we were being left alone.

Every now and then a man—presumably a Pharisee—would posit some sort of question or make a comment, and Yeshu'a would answer him. When either man spoke, there would be all manner of head shaking and whispering.

Finally a group of older men in fine robes came out on the portico and tried to break up the meeting. Shouting and pushing started breaking out in the crowd, and it was obvious to me that those who had initiated the disturbances had done so in response to orders and that they most probably were *agent provocateurs* of the establishment rabbis.

Suddenly there were two men standing in front of me with angry looks on their faces. They jabbered at me loudly and it seemed that all of the attention in the courtyard shifted away from the rostrum and onto me.

All of the people around me stepped back a pace or two and I was left alone in a circle some eight feet in diameter. My two accusers were pointing fingers at me and shouting. They seemed to be urging someone else to lay hold to me, but no one would. Apparently I stood exposed as an untouchable foreigner and, probably, a whore, for a tendril of my hair had escaped the corner of my cowl. I assumed that they were trying to start a disturbance in order to distract the crowd.

All the men around me were shorter than I, and as it was easy to look over their heads to the rostrum, I looked up at the men there and caught the eye of he who had been speaking. Raising my hands with fingers outstretched in a call for quiet, I waited until the hubbub died down. Suddenly there was silence all around me. Everyone was curious about what I would say or do, and those closest to me stepped back even more as I squared back my shoulders and stood at my full height.

Once again I looked to the rostrum and to the face of Yeshu'a . Even before I spoke I could see that he had a look that was almost one of fear upon his face. Like everyone else, he could not take his eyes from me.

Please understand that I had no idea what the crowd might do to me. For that matter, I was not even sure that gentile women were permitted within the walls of the temple nor what might happen to trespassers. I had already seen the place outside the city walls where women were stoned to death for various offenses. Even then, though, I was not afraid. I had arrived.

With a regal gesture, I took off my cowl and shook out my hair, abandoning the hunched, submissive look that had hidden me in the crowd. I held my chin up. An audible gasp seemed to arise from the crowd. All of them—probably even Julian who was out of my line of sight—must surely have taken me for an apparition.

I lifted my arm in a slow, deliberate, and theatrical manner and pointed elegantly at the astonished Yeshu'a whose look was turning into one of recognition, and said loudly in Greek, "This is the man who I have sought, and to whom I have been sent by God!" I don't know why I said that. It just came out.

As my words were translated, all eyes shifted to him.

"No man can escape his fate," he replied in a strong voice that could have been heard for 60 yards. There was a note of fatalism in his surprisingly perfect Greek. The whole crowd, not wanting to miss anything, spoke in low, excited tones. "Nor can he set the hour that the Angel of the Lord shall come unto him," he added with a warm smile.

The pharisees who had managed to disrupt his teaching realized that their moment was slipping away, so they started up a new series of cries in Hebrew, and the whole courtyard was soon in an uproar once again. Yeshu'a and I were still looking at each other, separated as we were by 50 feet of angry, talking men. It was then that I saw Julian step up behind him and stare at me with an unfathomable look on his heavily bearded face.

A kindly man about my age shouldered forward to the edge of the circle around me and spoke to me in passable Greek, telling me that no non-Jewish women were tolerated in the courtyard and that many of the ongoing arguments concerned what should be done about me. Apparently, I was considered to be unclean as well as unwelcome to the powers there. He told me that he feared for my safety and asked that I leave at once.

I thanked him for his concern and told him to give the prophet and his band the message that I would wait for them outside the main western gate. Then I turned and left, bare head held high, hoping that the crowd wouldn't decide to stone me right then and there. For the first time since entering the temple, I was somewhat afraid, and it was all I could do to walk—and not run—to the gate.

Once outside, I crossed the broad, noisy plaza of little shops, bought something to eat and a small bottle of wine, and sat on some stairs. By that time, I was calm and I was happy. I felt as if I had "bearded the lion" and come away alive, and although I had not the slightest idea what would happen next, it didn't seem to matter. I knew that I had accomplished a major feat in getting to Jerusalem from Athens. It had been, as your father would have said, one hell of a trip.

Naturally enough, I did not go unnoticed as I sat on the stairs, for I hadn't put my cowl up. For comfort's sake, I reached up under my clothes and removed my belt and short sword and strapped them on around my waist in plain view. Swords in Jerusalem were rare in those times, and women never carried them. To be quite honest, I never heard of a woman being attacked in that or any other city in Palestine, for the penalty was always death, and trials were rare. Of course, who knows what all went on out in the countryside. There, as I have shown, things could be quite different.

People stared at me, but they left me alone that afternoon. Surely an armed Gentile woman was a rare sight. I left my dagger hidden in my boot.

Led by Julian as a sort of oversized bouncer, the group finally came out of the temple about an hour later and made straight for me through the crowd. I stood and walked down the steps to greet them, briefly meeting Julian's eyes to confirm that he agreed with me that we should keep our relationship a secret if possible.

"You have sought me?" the man Yeshu'a asked me in Greek.

"Yes," I replied as his men crowded around us, "for I have heard about you for many years—more than you might imagine. Having heard, I have traveled many miles to get here—across seas and mountains and wilderness."

"Quite a trip for one so beautiful," he replied, with a smile that could melt ice, "but what could a gentile want of one such as I?"

I smiled back and looked around to include his men with my words.

"What could you want of one such as I?" I responded.

"Oh, who knows? Maybe your soul," he laughed. "There again, maybe you have come for mine!"

"That may be so," I said, adding happily, "All as God

wills!"

"Let's all talk about things somewhere else, Master," Julian broke in irritably in rather rough Greek, "for it looks bad—us standing about here..."

"...consorting—no, negotiating—with a blonde woman, my friend?" Yeshu'a finished for Julian with a smile for him and a quick hug. "Then let's get away from here!" he concluded, "but let's take her with us, Julian. All right?"

I could see that it wasn't really all right with Julian for them to take me with them. It looked too much like they had emerged from the temple, gone straight to a shameless woman, bargained with her, and taken her away. But what was I to do under the circumstances?

Just from that brief interchange between them I could tell that Yeshu'a respected and liked Julian, probably deferring to him in many things. This seemed to be particularly true regarding money and other matters in which the older man's advice might be welcome, if only as a counterbalance to the youthful excesses of the others. He turned to the eight or so of his other comrades and spoke to them in their own dialect, telling them a joke, I suppose. They chuckled and elbowed one another in the ribs, and looked at me furtively.

I could see right away that they were not the least bit somber. For the most part, they were all younger than we were— early to late 20s—and full of pep. Wiry and strong, all but one had pleasant, homely faces and resembled a bunch of Jewish fraternity brothers dressed in brown woolen dresses that were caught at the waists with bright, woven sashes.

The standout was a man named Judas who was very handsome. I was sure that most women would have preferred his sharp, flashing eyes, strong jaw, jet black hair, and animal magnetism to the more profound, though subtle, beauty of his leader. He was also the best-dressed man in the group, wearing various almost-new leather accouterments, including a wide belt with brass-studded, polished bands across his chest and a long dagger on his left side. I met his level gaze only briefly and could feel his eyes stripping me—but not quite in the sexual way. He was obviously the group's number two man. At least that was my first impression of the situation.

I turned back to Yeshu'a and Julian.

"Perhaps, Sir," I said, when the chatting died down,

"your friend is right. Maybe it would look bad for me to walk off with ten men. Few things can be hidden from the professionally curious," I added as a reference to the gossips and spies who undoubtedly would be watching them and reporting to the authorities. "But appearances can be maintained. Let this man," I said, pointing to Julian, "accompany me to where I left my donkey and baggage. No one would think we were up to something."

With a big smile on his face, he translated my words to the group and they all chuckled and made jokes—at Julian's expense, no doubt. Even the handsome Judas joined in, but I could tell by his eyes that he was still looking me over and weighing things in his mind.

Julian, on the other hand, took the hint, and concealing his impatience with the others, readily volunteered to go with me. Yeshu'a explained to me that Julian could lead me to their lodgings later so that I could join them for dinner. Julian said nothing to that, but I could tell that he was displeased. Amid more kidding, we parted company with the group.

"This was a mistake," he said to me in a slow, halting kind of English as soon as we were alone. I would have thought he would be glad to see me, and yet there was a bitter tone in his voice.

"You should never have come here. I should not have urged you," he added. "This is not your place."

I was too astonished to be offended. "It was not I you urged, Julian. It was Mark. I came because I wanted to come. And, pray tell me: just what is my place, Julian?"

"I don't know, but it's not here," he blurted out, and again I was astonished. After all the time we had been apart, and all the hell each of us had been through, the first thing he could say to me when the opportunity arose was that I shouldn't have come.

Then I realized that something had him agitated and confused, and it was something so palpable that it was enough to keep me from being angry with him. Speechless, I looked at him and knew that he couldn't help himself. He was just a natural asshole, and no amount of divinity school or even exposure to Yeshu'a could change that. I felt sorry for the big bastard--sorry enough that I felt I should be gentle with him. At least he was not a bandit or a murderer. I touched his forearm gently to emphasize my words and looked him in the eyes.

"Don't be so sure about what is my place, Julian," I told him, "or yours, for that matter. I do feel one thing for certain. You and I are here for a reason."

"I'm beginning to wonder about that," he said despondently. With that mere remark, that admission of his own confusion, he began to relax, and we started to get along a lot better.

We stopped in at a sort of cafe and I bought Julian a light meal. We talked for two or three hours, catching up on all that had transpired during the years since we had last seen one another and gently overlooking our differences. He told me all about his lengthy captivity, and obviously appreciated my sincere expressions of sympathy for his travails.

For my part I told him about the poisoning on the Rhine and our subsequent flight through Germany and the Balkans, my marriage, and the death of my husband. I told him about the refinery, and of Mark's visit there, and of my trip to Athens.

When I spoke of Athens he looked wistful, and asked me all about it, saying that it was his intention to go there— perhaps soon—so that he, too, might enjoy at least for a few weeks the beauties of that place. I could tell from the way he spoke that the life of a lowly and dirty pedestrian was beginning to get to him, and, in fact, when he spoke of his life as a disciple he did so with remarkably little enthusiasm.

After a couple of hours during which time we had spoken little of either Mark or Yeshu'a, our English had straightened out some and found its way back into its natural cadences. This was not particularly easy for either of us, but more so for him as he had not spoken it for nearly three years. Often neither of us could quite remember the correct grammar or even the correct word to use in a particular instance, but we managed, and in that multilingual ancient world in which we clearly had our enemies, the use of English was more than just an unpracticed skill. It was a security measure. Then, too, there was another thing at work that I am sure you will appreciate—a thing that was true for both of us there that afternoon. It was this: when one comes right down to it, the English prefer their own kind, and as you may recall, there's nothing but English and Scot in my lineage. We were each the best the other could find, I suppose, although from Julian's standpoint I was still quite deficient, being both an American and a woman.

When we finally talked about Mark I was surprised to learn that Julian had had no contact with him for two and a half months. Of course, neither had heard from me since I left Athens and after that they had had contact with one another only three times. Julian said that those transmissions had been perfunctory and increasingly pointless but he did say that Mark had arrived in Mauretania after all and was working on the Short. The report was that he had been unable to start it even though he now had the fuel he needed.

I could picture him at Marcus' villa, working on the plane and trying to get it to run, dealing with all the details that have to be attended to in order to make something so complicated as an airplane operate. I knew, too, that there could always be something missing—some little thing or tool without which further repair or flight would be impossible. I wondered what problems he had encountered and, of course, whether or not he had eventually gotten the Short to fly.

Our radio night was just a few days off and I was surprised to learn that Julian did not have his set in Jerusalem. Most of his things, he said, were in Cesarea on the seacoast some 50 miles away. Naturally, I asked if I could go get it or if he could send for it. After a certain amount of excuse-making he flatly refused to do either, and from the way he spoke, I got the idea that all of his important stuff—if not the group's embezzled funds--was in one strongbox in a bank. It was obvious enough that he wouldn't trust me or anyone else to go into it on his behalf nor would he tell me the name of his banker. I did not press him on the issue even though he was indebted to me already for the amount of the letter of credit I had forwarded to him through Tyre--a fact he conveniently ignored. For that matter, he pointed out quite convincingly that it was unadvisable to have any modern things on hand as he traveled around in Palestine because their band was being spied upon constantly and had continually warded off charges of witchcraft. Finally he promised me that he would go to Cesarea during the next week and bring it back for me. I had to be content with that.

For better or worse, the subject of the radio was settled,

and so finally I decided to bring up the second of the two
subjects we had thus far avoided.

Taking a deep breath, I said something to the effect of,
"Now let's quit beating around the bush, Julian: tell me about
this man, this Yeshu'a. He seems quite remarkable. I assume you
think that he's the right one. What does that mean for us?"

He didn't start trying to answer me right away. I leaned
back and poured more wine. He drank some of his, twirled the
goblet around between his fingers and looked at me. At least I
was someone he could talk with about things. He began slowly
and deliberately. "Oh, he's the right one, all right, but other than
that, I'm not so sure about much these days. It's one thing to
grow up with notions and teachings and dogma, and then in due
course, to start repeating all of that to congregations and
confirmation classes. It's quite another thing to accomplish the
impossible as we have done, and to go meet a man who you can
only suppose is the very subject of all that teaching and to live
with him and his friends. It's different to be there when they go
out drinking and then roister off singing, not pausing even when
they relieve themselves on the side of the public road. How can
one possibly judge a man—or a living god, as it may be—who
one has seen pick at his nose or suffer from diarrhea? How can
one think in terms of human perfection, when one sees a man
going off with a woman—practically a stranger—for an
evening?" he asked as he looked into his goblet almost with
shame.

"Julian, lest you forget, I'm a woman. We're people, too.
People have needs and wants, you know—for companionship,
affection, love, respect... even pleasure," I added rather gently.
"Even him."

"Like animals!" is what he might have said three years
before, but life had taken hold of him like a terrier with a rat, and
it was still shaking him. I'm not sure that he really knew what he
thought anymore.

"Please forgive me. I meant nothing personal," he said.

I told him that was probably the nicest thing he had ever
said to me. He was embarrassed.

"While I'm at it," he continued after a moment, "I may
as well apologize for many of the things I have said about you to
your face, to others, and—worst of all—within my own heart. I
had no right to judge."

"Judgement is the price of knowledge, Julian," I told him. "We must all make judgements."

"Perhaps. But should then I judge my master? By what standard should I judge Yeshu'a of Nazareth?"

"Don't look at me. How should I know?" I said with a smile and a shrug, trying to lighten things up. "I guess that God judges us all—perhaps daily."

"Surely—if nothing else—then this is so," he readily agreed. "But can I judge God? That is the question."

I looked him in the eye to see how he would respond to my next question. "No, Julian, the question is this: is he God?"

"Yes, I think so!" he said with rather too much vehemence. But the slight downward flicker of his eyes told me that he was lying. The only question I had was whether he was lying to me or to himself. Perhaps he was profoundly uncertain but incapable of admitting his uncertainty. I could see how much the very question bothered him. What suffering the world has seen in that willingness to lie, that false profession of certainty, and the concomitant unwillingness of self-professed believers to tolerate uncertainty in others!

Then I asked whether Yeshu'a had raised the dead or cleansed the leprous, and like Christians ever since, he confessed that he had never actually seen it done. "But I have been away a lot attending to group business, and Peter, John, and Judas have told me he has done these things. They have seen the miracles."

I inquired about the handsome Judas. Will he attempt to betray Yeshu'a, I asked?

"Now listen, Evangeline," he said in a low voice, although none present could have understood him anyway, "I want to warn you about him. He's a very dangerous man, a Zealot, and he has friends in high places. You must be careful not to let on that you suspect any disloyalty on his part. On the other hand, for the time being, we need him. He is our connection to the most militant wing of the Zealots. They want to use us and, in a sense, we dare not ignore them. Therefore, as I hope you see, Judas is very important to us right now. But," he said, "when the time comes, I have a plan that will thwart him."

I looked at him for a long moment and saw his eyes shining in a way that was familiar but hard to place. Then it dawned on me. I had seen him look that way twice before: once on the pulpit in Brighton and once in the cottage in North Carolina. It was the look of the convinced fanatic, and I wondered whether he was sane or, for that matter, if he ever had been.

"Julian! Of what are you thinking?" I asked finally, "Intervene in some fashion? It can't be done!"

"Oh yes it can!" he said. "We are the proof of that. We've already done it! Look at us: we're here, aren't we? We've brought with us our few possessions—most of which we've lost, yes, but we have something greater than mere material possessions. We have knowledge of their future!

"It may be," he continued, warming to the subject and obviously glad to have someone to talk with openly, "that we can not 'change history,' but what is history? Just a report of what one supposed happened.

"Listen: I have prayed over this a lot, Evangeline. What if we can't change the history, but we can change the facts? What if things work themselves out differently? Maybe we *can* change everything!"

"And maybe we'll get murdered on the way to the house tonight and nothing will be in the least bit affected by the fact that we came here," I countered.

He looked me straight in the eye. "Do you *really* think that will happen? Do you actually believe that God would call us home right now before this matter is ended?" he asked.

I had already thought about that very question. "No, Julian. I don't think that we are here only to watch and to die. Whatever else may happen our presence here was decreed before the seas filled their basins.

"So now, Julian, what shall we do?"

"Not *we* Eva. *I. I* have a plan and some certain contacts, but I will not share them with you or with anybody else."

"Not even with your Master?" I asked.

"No. Not even with him."

Whether he realized it or not, that was Julian's admission of his disbelief in his master's omniscience, but I saw little need to point that out to him. In his heart he knew it, but he would never have admitted it to me.

So I asked how far along he had gotten with his plans to thwart the Zealots' efforts to transform Yeshu'a's group into a more militant role, but he would not be led into further discussion except to say that a showdown was fully a year off. Yeshu'a and the Zealots, he said, were headed for an inevitable schism.

"And when the time comes," he said excitedly, "I shall steal a march on them. You'll see."

So I asked him what he intended to do in the meantime and learned that it was his plan to continue to work to solidify the financial and political bases of Yeshu'a's little group.

It was late in the afternoon when we finally left the cafe and stopped by my tavern. He waited down the street while I went upstairs and refreshed myself and changed into some clothes that were a bit more attractive than the dour stuff I had been wearing. I didn't look the least bit flashy, but when I came down I could see Julian's look of disapproval. Convinced that I would be on my way within a week or two, he said nothing.

We talked very little as we walked out of the city toward a large villa where the group was staying. When we were still a hundred yards out, we could hear loud voices and snatches of songs coming from within the compound's walls, and we stopped to listen. It sounded like a party going on—the first such sounds I had heard since that night on the beach with Casius some five months before.

Then I broached the subject of what he thought should be my own role in things should I chose to stay in Palestine for a while, and he told me in no uncertain terms that there was no place for me in the group. He said that he wanted me to leave as soon as he let me use the radio, and it was obvious that he wanted me out of the picture. Truth to be told, although there were good reasons that I should have gotten out of the country as soon as possible, I resented his suggestion that I be on my way. I realized that if he found out about the incident down in the desert, he might use it to blackmail me.

"So what's the real problem if I stay on for a few months, Julian?" I asked as I looked him straight in the eye. He looked right back at me without flinching.

"You're a bad influence," he said without hesitation.

I've thought about his remark a lot since that evening, but at that very moment, his judgement seemed at once absurd and possibly true. It also seemed entirely like the old Julian.

"Maybe *you're* the bad influence, Julian," I said rather

angrily. "Ever thought of that?"

But I didn't wait for an answer. I had had enough of him for one day and so suddenly I turned and broke into a run that left him standing there speechless behind me. I was eager to be at the villa where there was singing, food, merriment, and—best of all—young, healthy men.

****

XXXI

The Villa

As Durrell might have said, many people need to have their gods and heroes "pure, symmetrical, and intact: like the sterile hyphen which joins, in a biography, the years of birth and death."

As I consider the next thing to write, the metaphor of an operating room stays with me and I think of how so many people mistake sterility for purity. Why should they do otherwise? After all, if my writings attack the sterility of their conceptions, would it also not thereby admit the possibility of infection, and, yes, corruption of the ideas that they hold? Well, if this report brings with it germs of thought, then physician heal thyself! Even as restricted as my accounts of him will be, they will get no sterile Yeshu'a from me. Better that they should turn away and read something else.

And if a man wants perfect apostles, he should stop reading now. If a woman wants her Yeshu'a to be less than a man, let her put this down and read elsewhere of the sort of sterile eunuch who lets her feel most comfortable.

Except for Julian and, to a lesser degree, Judas, Yeshu'a and his followers were a merry bunch, and it was their very joviality that set them apart from practically all of the other Jewish teachers of their day. Somewhat justifiably accused of licentiousness and holding Hellenic thoughts, they were shunned by the established political and religious leaders and ignored by the Romans. Like many such men through the ages they enjoyed an ever-growing popularity among the average people among whom they worked and taught.

Most of them were pretty straight, and for the most part all of them liked their wine, their women, and their songs. It should be remembered that as I have said, in those days much of the wine was drugged and had illuminating effects, and though I had heard the disciples described as a bunch of drunkards, they were not.

The established authorities, however, accused them all of being sexual debauchees or even deviants. Those men—most of those men, that is—became my friends, and like all healthy men with enough to eat, they had their share of sexual urges and appetites. It is simply not my place to write down any details of how they satisfied, transmuted, or otherwise dealt with such needs. For one thing, it was none of my business. It is sufficient to say that various women hung about the villa. Julian, again, was an exception: I never saw him eye a girl in a way that made me think he was interested in her. I should have let that be a warning from the start. As you may have determined by now, Julian was quite unusual.

The principle girl who traveled with the group was she who I would imagine history remembers as Mary Magdalene. She was short, good-looking, and buxom, and the men called her a name that sounded like "Martha" which is what I shall call her in this narrative just as I shall call all the men except Yeshu'a by their anglicized names. Be that as it may, Martha was a friend to all of the men in a way that reminded me of my sister, who in college had a whole web of platonic relationships based upon her being a fraternity "sweetheart." Martha's heart was "as big as a room and as soft as her breasts," according to her most ardent admirers. In addition to being a good listener, she managed the day-to-day domestic affairs of the whole group just as Julian managed its financial matters. Not more than 22 years old at that time, she was very capable and was a good cook. It was my understanding that Yeshu'a had found her when she was at rock bottom, outcast, and raving mad, and he cured her somehow. Out of pure love and gratitude, she had begged to join his group, and he let her stay. Even Julian liked her. I would imagine that she was one of the few friends he ever had.

The villa or compound was but a short way from the city and had been loaned to the group by its wealthy owner who lived in Jerusalem proper. It was a sort of walled mini-fortress similar to Marcus' in Mauretania. Already ancient when I visited it, the place had undoubtedly been used by armies many times before, most memorably by the army of Pompey. It had served as his headquarters some 87 years before when the Romans besieged and conquered Jerusalem.

In addition to all its other amenities—which included to

my delight an unusually sheltered, private, and sanitary outhouse—the compound had within its walls a Roman-style hot bath as well as a thirty cubit square, four cubit high, raised irrigation pool or reservoir that we used as a swimming pool.

The place provided both security and privacy for what was, relative to the general society, a very Bohemian group, and although I kept my room at the tavern, at Yeshu'a's insistence and over Julian's objections I moved in on the second day I was there. I was given a tiny room to myself in what we called the women's wing. In that way I was able to spend all of my time observing the daily life of the group and talking with the master himself.

Customarily he spent a good portion of each day reading and meditating, but during those days his time was more taken up by incessant talks with his men and with me. He also made daily visits to the city to deliver his messages of peace, toleration, joy, and self-sacrifice—which, of course, was and still is anathema to warlike, bigoted, and greedy people. Such people didn't like him in those days and their modern counterparts wouldn't like him now.

Quite frankly, I was fascinated by him and spent many hours talking to him in Greek. Always carefully choosing his words, he described his life and his thoughts with the utmost humility and reserve to the point that I almost had to drag information from him. On the other hand, whenever during our talks he recognized any reluctance on my part to reveal secrets about myself, he changed the subject. Unlike anyone I have ever met, he did not pry into my past. Consequentially, I told him almost nothing about myself: nothing about Mark, the plane, our weapons, my relationship with Julian, or even my fame and possible notoriety as the woman called by the Romans *Venus Atlanticus*. Somehow or another all that didn't matter to him anyway. He accepted me at face value, and for what I was right then, not what I had been or what others might have said that I had been. Among the many things we did talk about, I did tell him about my husband just as he told me about his wife. We could sympathize with one another's losses. He never seemed to criticize me or question my motives or judgements in any way.

For that matter, in all things he was superhumanly gentle and tactful and always did his best to avoid offending people—

but his best was often not good enough. This fact should not be attributed to his lack of skill as a thinker or an orator, but rather to the environment of religious fervor and ethnic intolerance into which his messages were being delivered. There in Jerusalem, for example, he had one strike against him from the start, for he and his followers were mostly Galileans, which is to say, they were practically foreigners in Judea. The northern areas that were once controlled by the tribe of Zebulun were held in contempt by the Judeans in much the same way and for as little reason that Yankees hold southerners in contempt. It should be noted that in the Book of Isiah it was written that *"from that region would come greatness by way of the Sea of Galilee."*

That being said, though, he was different from his men in much the same way that a European-educated intellectual from our South is different from his countrymen. That is to say, superficially he was very different while at heart he was much the same. Or as my Daddy used to say, "You can take the boy out of the country, but you can't take the country out of the boy." Like most Galileans, Yeshu'a was independent-minded, physically fit, unselfconsciously brave, and taciturn.

Like most Galileans, he and most of his followers were admirers of things Greek, including the love of sea faring, athletics, public speaking, drama, and debate. They were also much more comfortable with the acceptance of life's pleasures than were southern Jews.

Another major cultural influence that set them apart from the southerners was their use of a different Aramaic dialect and of at least a passing familiarity with a certain sort of "magic mushroom" imported from the East. The occasional use of such mild hallucinogens was not exactly commonplace in the region but was altogether prohibited in the south. That prohibition was, I think, justified by the Judean authorities not on the grounds of public safety but rather because the use of hallucinogens was thought to promote paganism. To be quite frank, I think that they do. I personally never used that type of mushroom, but I saw it being sold in a market in Tyre and am certain that it was quite different from the dangerous woodlands mushroom of Germany. Based on what I heard, I rather suspect that the Middle-Eastern mushroom's effects were similar to those of the psilocybe cubenisis that we used to find in middle Georgia. Out beyond Parthia and the Euxine or Black Sea, the potentially lethal Fly

Agaric mushroom was the dominant hallucinogen, at least among the priestly classes, but I never experienced that one, either. Be that as it may, I stick to my theory that societies' standards can be judged at least partially by the drugs they use.

From the Parthians to the East, the Galileans also derived a strong pride in physical stamina and toughness, as well as an affinity for the use of the short, powerful recurve bow such as the one that I had bought in Tyre. It was their weapon of choice and most of them were quite accomplished archers.

As I have said, Yeshu'a spoke Greek very well, and through long hours spent with him during the following days, I learned a lot about him that surprised me. It soon became obvious to me that he was one of the most educated and cosmopolitan men of the age, having been singled out as being special in infancy. As such a child, he and his family received special stipends and support from a variety of sources, particularly from the Essenes, the secret Jewish cult centered in the hills above the Dead Sea. Even though he had grown up in humble surroundings, he had learned to read early and had many tutors who taught him not only of the religion of the Jews but also of those of most of the rest of the world. He spoke six languages as well as all of the Aramaic dialects of Palestine. As a child and a youth, he had traveled over much of the oriental world, going as far east as Burma and as far north as Tibet and the southern shores of the Black Sea. He had spent a year in an Essene monastery by the Dead Sea and nearly two years in Egypt. In all of the places he went he studied the religious beliefs and practices, customs, architecture, societal traits, and military tactics of the peoples he encountered. As an observer he had taken part in military campaigns in southern Egypt and Parthia. He was an excellent archer.

To the disappointment of his sponsors, tutors, and family, at the age of 21, he had taken his own path, disappearing from sight for more than a year before showing up again in Galilee with a wife in tow. They were deeply in love with one another, he told me, but she died in childbirth just two years later. Those two years were, he said, the happiest of his life, and during that time he had made a very good living as a carpenter, a builder, and an architect, mostly in Tiberias on the west side of the Sea of Galilee.

His wife had not been Jewish. According to him, she was as learned as she was beautiful, and they had lived happily, entertained little, and worked hard to build his business and to refurbish the small farm that they rented. They had looked forward to the birth of their first child.

Naturally enough, he was devastated by her death and he told me how he had gone through a period of deep despondency and had blamed himself for not having taken her to the Greek physicians at Tyre when her time approached. Shaken to the foundations of his soul and racked with guilt and grief, he went out into the desert for a month and nearly starved to death. There he prayed and listened. Gradually he recovered, but not enough so that he could take up his trade and his farm again. His heart was no longer in it. So it was that he left Tiberias behind and became what was called in those days a walker.

A word of explanation is in order. A wealthy man like the writer, Virgil, for example, usually had friends and colleagues all over the world but might be too busy or too old or even too lazy to visit them all. In his stead for a very modest sum he might hire a pleasant young man to "walk" for him. The better looking and the better educated the walker, the better would be the patron's image among the friends with whom the walker would visit, and naturally enough, a sponsor tried to hire someone who seemed to be the kind of man he thought of himself as being or having been. Upon being retained, the new walker might spend two or three weeks in the home of his patron, soaking up as much knowledge of the patron's friends, interests, family, and history as he could before setting out to represent him.

Almost invariably, walkers traveled by boat or by foot, since such travel bespoke something of the way Greeks and Romans liked to think of themselves as being stalwart, virtuous, humble, friendly, and independent men in the prime of life. The sons of those same rich men might make the same rounds, but rarely would they have walked, choosing instead fast chariots, ornate ships, and elegant clothes, and thus rich sons often could not represent them half so well. In fact, the walkers often represented the patrons better than the patrons themselves could—particularly with the ladies of the house.

The typical visit of a walker lasted for four to six days. The host would put him up as an honored guest and dine with him regularly, inquiring about the health, prospects, and doings of the patron and his family and reporting on his own conditions and outlooks. The walker was expected to have a good memory for all details he might pick up during a visit and would usually rely on notes and shorthand to preserve and relay as much information as possible to the patron by letter or at year's end.

If the walker was particularly charming and pleasant, a host might give a generous tip or gratuity to him at the end of his visit, but mainly his support was borne by the patron. Walkers were expected to send letters and simple accounts every month or so, although that was seldom a requirement of the job.

After a year of travel, the walker would wind up his trip with a second visit to the home of his patron. There he might spend as much as another two weeks telling his patron all about his friends as well as about the walker's own adventures along the way. Sometimes young men were adopted into the families they had represented or visited, often replacing a son who had died or who had failed to turn out as his parents had wished. Sometimes the young man might be kept on or recalled later to provide a respectable husband for some niece or neighbor's daughter who had fallen in love with him.

In the three years of his walking, Yeshu'a, travelling under a Latin name, had improved his foreign language skills. He had been to Spain, Britain(which was not part of the empire at that time), North Africa, and the Rhine frontier, and had visited with many of the wealthiest people in the Roman Empire.

At the end of those years he had returned to Palestine following a spiritual experience of which he would not speak, but which made it easy for him to fit back into the provincial, narrow-minded, and relatively uncultured society into which he had been born. Thus he who had been raised to be a great rabbi had returned at last to his destiny

Since he could discuss practically any subject in perfect Greek and almost perfect Latin as well as in four other tongues, it was often necessary for him to go to great lengths to conceal his accomplishments. This was because on the one hand he did not want the common people to think him arrogant, and at the same time he felt it was important that he keep a low profile when dealing with the authorities. In a nation where rampant conformity was almost a legal requirement, discordant teachings and attitudes often provoked fear and retaliation.

The Jews of Judea in particular were very leery of foreign influences. In many ways they looked askance even at those among their own people who had traveled, thinking that such travels provided rich opportunities for otherwise pious people to be seduced away from the religious observances of their forebears. Of course, they were right. It is hard to imagine a farm boy from Judea being very impressed with Jerusalem if he had seen Alexandria, Athens, or Rome.

The Judean social and religious codes promoted insular behavior and an almost rabid abhorrence of intermarriage across national bounds. For a Judean's daughter to marry even a devout Samaritan, for example, might subject the father to quiet contempt, whereas if she wed a Galilean or, worse, an absolute foreigner, she invited open ridicule.

Into such a milieu, then, returned Yeshu'a with a mission and a duty he would not shirk. With little or no effort, he gathered followers and began to teach. What kind of men followed him?

As I have said, they were cheerful men, and men who could in good conscience leave their families—which is to say, single men. Once outside Galilee they must have seemed like American G.I.s did to the British when they arrived in England during World War II: happy-go-lucky, rowdy guys who sang in the streets, stirred up the common folk, and seemed to laugh at many of the customs of the local societies. In short, in Judea and Peraea, the cult from up north was disdained for being "overbearing, oversexed, and over here."

For his own and his men's safety, Yeshu'a tried—often unsuccessfully—not to seem to be overbearing or arrogant, but it was almost impossible for him to avoid besting his detractors at every turn. If it came to a disputation on the streets or in the temple, he could confound them. If there was a battle of wits, the wits won. If a town needed a song, he and his men sang one. Through his demeanor or even his silence, he seemed always to stand as a living rebuke to hypocrisy, deception, and self-righteousness. Then, too, his reputation as a chosen child preceded him. Among the scholarly men at the various synagogues and temples, the extent of his learning and intelligence was known by one and all. Among such men there was always the unspoken question: *Well, here he is. Now what?*

What, indeed, does one do in the presence of a Special One, an acknowledged child of God? It is well known that if a man does not love and respect his better he will hate and envy him, and it took little more than Yeshu'a' unflappable demeanor to evoke strong waves of envy, if not hatred, among the priestly class.

It was widely thought that the most powerful Jew in the city of Jerusalem was the High Priest, and it was said that he was practically a sworn enemy of the Galilean leader. If that was the case, one wonders whether such feelings were rooted merely in the man's mundane fear of losing his position or if there was something more momentous at work. After all, revolution and not just revolt, seemed always to be a stone's throw away, and whoever was the High Priest was standing in the eye of an inchoate storm.

It was not unreasonable to think of Yeshu'a as being the potential leader of either revolt or of revolution. For one thing, a common spiritual connection and a shared sense of a political mission bound his disciples and supporters together, and in Jewish society as a whole there was a constant feeling that something ought to change. Yeshu'a seemed to be calling for change, too, but he had not yet sounded the call to arms.

His being an effective religious leader made him all the more dangerous since in that area political and social arguments were always couched in terms of the national religion. Naturally enough, that religion was interpreted in ways that either supported or opposed the status quo—depending, of course, on who was doing the interpreting. At any rate, Yeshu'a's own political positions and plans were unclear even to his followers.

As I shall describe, Judas was the worst. He could speak Latin fairly well, and from the start he complained to me that Yeshu'a seemed to be advocating one day an overthrow of the existing order, the next an acceptance of it, and on a third yet another course somewhere between the other two. He wanted an immediate revolt.

It was hard for me to believe that a revolt against the Romans and their Jewish puppets would be in the best interests of the mass of the people. I would have thought that some sort of revolution or radical change such as a redistribution of land might have held more apparent benefit for them, but such was not the case. What most people wanted was spiritual change. While some demanded more social and legal strictures and some demanded less religious regimentation, dislike for the Romans was a common bond among them all. It was a bond that Yeshu'a himself did not share. After all, he spoke Latin and had Roman friends, and he judged people as individuals and not as representatives of any group, race, or nationality.

Nonetheless, most of the men in Yeshu'a's group wanted revolt—or so I was told. I should explain that only Judas, Julian. and Yeshu'a could carry on conversations with me, because all the others spoke only Aramaic. What Yeshu'a said to them and to the people of the city, I can only report second-hand.

Although he was shorter, Judas looked a lot like Mark except that he was more masculine, more perfect, and more powerful-looking. His eyes were light, liquid brown, and conveyed at his command a whole rainbow of emotional qualities beneath thick, black lashes and brows. Overall he had the animal grace and broad shoulders that one sees in an Olympic diver, but to me he looked a bit too handsome. He reminded me of the kind of good-looking college boy to whom girls and money came all too easily. Maybe I was prejudiced against him, for I thought I knew his future and he reminded me too much of Cassius.

All of that, I thought, might be another year or two off— if ever it occurred, for that matter. When I used to listen to Odysseus recite the *Iliad* with all the passion and self-confidence that made him seem like an eye witness to the siege of Troy, I had wanted it to be true even if it had occurred a thousand years earlier or even if it was a myth. And yet, and yet: *did not Achilles sulk in his tent and did he not slay Hector?* Who are we to say he did not? And who but Julian or I could have known what treachery might or might not come from Judas?

As it was, Judas was second in command of the group, although the term "command" is somewhat misleading. No one either "joined" or "left" the group. He was either there or he wasn't. In a sense, only Judas, Julian, and Yeshu'a were constantly involved in the teaching and the tramping about and visiting regularly with people. Other men might come and go at will, and often the disciples returned to their homes or jobs in order to support their families or just to take a break from the constant, restless travel.

Of course, Julian had no home to which he could go. To his credit, though, although he was often plagued by discomforts, doubts and embarrassments, he stuck to his original purpose. Being with Yeshu'a *was* being at home for him even if like many another cleric, he buried himself in his financial and amanuensis duties.

Despite his age and his obvious education, he was not a leader of men. As a foreigner, he would never be considered to be a possible successor of Yeshu'a, and although he himself had strong theological views which included a barely concealed worship of Yeshu'a, his views on spiritual matters were never asked. Oddly enough, on several occasions he as much as told me that he and Yeshu'a often conferred privately on matters of the deepest religious and philosophical concerns, and he openly implied that the younger man—despite his alleged divinity—relied heavily on Julian's judgment and reasoning.

I never saw any such thing. Quite to the contrary, during the days that I spent at the villa and on an evening when the three of us went to a tavern in Jerusalem for a private dinner, I could see that Yeshu'a was merely being patient with Julian. Yet he disguised his patience so artfully that Julian did not feel patronized.

One might think that under the circumstances, Julian and I might have made a clean breast of things to Yeshu'a right away. Of course, there was a possibility that the master had already figured out everything about us or otherwise knew all that there was to know about us, but that didn't seem the case. At any rate, it did not take him long to figure out that we were in league with one another—a fact which was unsuspected by the others.

Even though he had deduced almost from the start that we were countrymen or something close to being countrymen, he feigned ignorance of it until the night we dined with him apart from the group. As I have said, we went to a very nice tavern—even prophets like to go out from time to time—and it was there that he introduced the idea that he had noticed we were probably from the some country and had known each other in the past. We were almost dumbstruck and he watched our faces intently. In that world of powers and spies and treacheries, it occurred to me immediately that he might think we were spying on him for the Romans. I blushed with shame when I thought that he might think I was on such a mission.

"Fear not, Eva," he said with a smile over our rather elegant dinner. "I don't think you're a spy. In fact, I know more about you than you might think I would.

"You see, I, too, have friends in the wide world—more friends than perhaps either of you might imagine. A walker meets many people in his years on the road—people who report to him on the unusual and the miraculous.

"And you:" he said to the confounded Julian, "what an unlikely sort of spy you would have been, stumbling upon us with your scraggly clothes and strange accents and ideas!" Julian blushed, but he was not offended. He beamed like a big, old dog, for his master was speaking to him with obvious love and affection.

"Julian, I thought you were unique in the world: a man of no country, yet educated, but neither Roman nor Greek nor of any other discernable nationality. Yes, but I felt you had come to me for a reason, and that you were sent by God for a purpose He had for me."

We listened with rapt attention, and though I translate and paraphrase, I can remember those explanations as if they were given yesterday. I can still picture the whitewashed buildings in the evening twilight as we sat at a small table with silver goblets and platters of meat and bread. From that second-floor dining room, we could look out toward the Temple and the Antonia Fortress to the northeast of us.

I saw the look on Julian's face—astonishment and relief that he had been seen through by his master, the man for whom he had left one world and crossed another. Then Yeshu'a turned to me.

"But then you came, Evangeline," he said. "There you were all of a sudden, standing out from that crowd like the lighthouse beacon at Alexandria, and I could plainly see that you were sent, too. Then you spoke, and I knew that something soon would happen, for when the messenger knocks, the door is opened no matter what the tidings might be.

"I listened to you talk and watched you closely, even as you watched me and studied all the others carefully since you've been here. You have studied them one by one—all except for Julian—and then I knew. It was then that I remembered a letter from a friend written two years ago: a letter telling of two foreign men who had come to Nova Carthago—apparently from across the Atlantic. One was fat and kept to himself. The other had with him a beautiful woman, tall and blonde, who spoke some Greek. They were possessed of strange clothes and amazing weapons. The fat man went toward Alexandria, and the younger man and the woman went to Rome.

"Another friend in Italy wrote about how the couple came to Rome, but the beautiful woman went off to Germany. I couldn't remember what else, if anything, he had written about the subject, but I prayed about it last night, and it was revealed to me. You, Julian, are the man who was fat before his unfortunate captivity, and you, Evangeline, are the beautiful woman!" A kind smile lit his face.

I nodded my head. "In my country I was not considered beautiful," I said at last.

"Nor in this one," he said, chuckling, "for is not beauty in the eye of the beholder? You certainly don't look Hebrew—or even Galilean, for that matter, and the men here are mostly too provincial to see you as the Greeks and Romans must have seen you. How they must have raved!"

I was looking at him as he spoke, and I blushed. Then I glanced at Julian. In his eyes I saw something I recognized at once: jealousy.

"But the question I have is this, my friends:" Yeshu'a said, "Where is the other man?"

"Gone beyond the Pillars of Hercules, the last I heard," Julian said, looking him straight in the eye. He avoided mine and I knew why. Even then, even in that hour of truth, he was not going to mention the radio, the airplane, or anything he didn't have to mention. I wasn't either, and I can't exactly explain why not. Perhaps it was no longer a part of our incredible lives. We had not a thing on us of the world we had left. Everything we had in Jerusalem was of that ancient world and we were, too. Or so we felt.

Yeshu'a did not need to ask me what my relationship to the missing man had been, for he was wise. I would have claimed Mark if I had wanted to, but I didn't.

"Will he return?"

"Who knows?" Julian responded. "He has left people before without saying good-bye. He may try to return to his own country," he concluded.

That had never occurred to me. Suddenly I realized that if Mark had gotten the Short aloft, he might have gone someplace else in time and I would never see him again. Then again, I asked myself, did I care?

"Is the other man important?" I asked.

"Well, the 'other man' is always an important part to the understanding of any equation, isn't he?" Yeshu'a asked, employing the mildest of innuendoes as a sort of joke that, although subtle, made me blush a bit. He smiled the smile of a conspirator.

"In this case," he continued, in a lighthearted manner that made him seem like a character acting out a mystery novel, "he may prove to be very important, indeed."

"Why?" Julian and I asked simultaneously.

"Because things—particularly the things of God—come in threes so often. First there is the message, then the action, then the result.

"Think of the history of the people of Israel, for example. The pattern for them is like the pattern for us all: We are warned, then we are acted upon, and the new result is obtained, whether it be our downfall, or our salvation, or our illumination.

"So you see, perhaps you, Julian, are the messenger who came and has been with us. Now you, Eva, show up here—the second character—and the action—whether it be good or bad—is upon us. Will the third one of you come here, too, in completion of a pattern, the design of which is beyond our ken? I think maybe so. And I think so because one thing is obvious, is it not?"

Julian looked ashen. "And that is?" he asked.

"And that is," I said, repeating my earlier remarks, "that all of this—our every movement and moment—was set out to be lived from the foundation of the world, and we are powerless to alter or amend it."

"But you are powerful, Master," Julian blurted out without thinking.

Yeshu'a smiled at him and laid his hand upon the older

man's hand. "Any power I may have is not mine but is the power of God working through me. The same is true for each of you."

"Then you have the power, do you not, to protect yourself from evil," Julian asserted.

"What is evil? Who can call the will of God and even one's own suffering an evil thing when it is seen only from a mortal perspective?"

His words were simple and elegant--particularly so in the Greek constructions and words he used--but in his words there was a blending of philosophy and blood as well as a premonition of things to come. I thought of Death and felt a constricting tightness in my chest that made breathing difficult and I felt the same dread I had when Cassius captured me. It was difficult not to feel panic. At any moment the terrible events that I had feared might begin almost at once and I started looking about at the other tables as if they held armed agents of the Romans or the Jewish leaders. Paranoia swept over me. Automatically I closed my knees together under the table and felt the short sword that I carried strapped against the inside of my right calf. It was an awkward arrangement, but I could not bear to go about unarmed even when I was having dinner with Yeshu'a himself. I wished I had my derringer.

I was afraid for my own safety, of course, but that was not the cause of my distress. I realized that what was frightening me at that moment stemmed from the fact that I already felt great love for the man who sat across from me even though he was in so many ways still a stranger to me.

There he sat—perhaps the greatest man in the world— sipping wine and smiling at me with mischief in his eyes as he calmly accepted his fate. A man, yes, and one I had seen joking with his followers, holding a crowd spellbound by the power of his personality and the force of his words. A guy I saw wolfing down food when he was hungry. Here sat the savior of the world? Was he not one of the men with whom I had swum in the pool at the villa that very afternoon? Had we not competed in rough games of water polo? Had he not roughly held me under the water until I gave up the bladder?

There he sat: the aesthete who frankly and unashamedly enjoyed eating a decent meal in a tavern that catered to wealthy travelers. There, calmly wiping apple juice from the corner of his mouth, was the man who might someday be called, among other things, the Hope of the World?

I had never heard of him throughout the ancient world until I got to Palestine, and even there his name and reputation were not without tarnish. Yet to meet him was to love him, for he asked nothing and demanded nothing. He smiled and laughed and met your eye with his eye and your mind with his mind. Is the love one feels toward a man like that the love of a sister for a perfect brother? I will say only that it made me feel very protective of him.

Was he right? I wondered. Was I the herald—or even the cause--of what he had called "the action?" I felt the hair beginning to rise on the back of my neck as if the Angel of Death had swept into the room in a draft of cold air. I was almost terrified—too scared to turn around. Someone shouted something in Hebrew, then another in Latin: "*Shut the door!*"

I turned expecting to see Death, but saw only a man and a woman sitting down at a corner table. Something about them seemed familiar, but I was snatched back to reality by the sudden touch of a warm hand on my knee under the table.

"Fear not," Yeshu'a said to me. I looked into his eyes, for he had leaned over close to speak in low tones. I was very conscious of his hand. It felt warm and soothing on my leg. I covered it with my hand and began to feel under control.

In a low tone he told me that I should neither speak again nor turn around until we left, and I assented. He and Julian began to converse in Aramaic about some sort of business while I finished my wine. Then we paid for the meal and stood up to leave. I wrapped the veil around the lower part of my face. As we went out of the dimly lit room, I stole another glance at the rough, ugly man and the woman who had entered the room a few minutes before. She looked at me. Although she had her head and face partly covered and was dressed like a Samaritan matron, I felt that I had seen her before. The man was a total stranger.

Once outside, I asked them who the newcomers were. Neither of them knew.

"What would they want of us?" I asked.

"What does anybody want? Money? Power? Revenge?" Yeshu'a posited. "But in addition to the fact that neither was a Jew and they weren't a couple, I did notice that one thing else about them was different."

I asked what that had been.

"Well, mainly this: they weren't spying on me. It was *you* they were interested in."

Seeing my fear coming back, he threw an arm around my shoulder and hugged me.

Why me, I asked.

"Maybe as a way of checking up on me," he said, "or upon Julian. On the other hand—and this is serious—there is a story going around that the authorities are looking into a murder of two tax gatherers out in the wilderness beyond the Jordan. A woman is suspected."

He didn't need to say any more, nor did I. My knees buckled and they had to help me stay up. Since it was obvious that I was the one who was being sought, I told them what had happened. Julian was incredulous and started criticizing me in Greek and English, telling me I should never have been traveling alone in the first place and implying that I shouldn't have defended myself.

"On the other hand, Julian," Yeshu'a interrupted with a sly smile, "Maybe they shouldn't have gotten in the way of a girl from South Carolina!" I had only mentioned the name of my country only once to him, but he hadn't forgotten it. I laughed out loud, and he joined in as we walked along outside the city walls on our way to the villa, arm in arm. Julian was not mollified and huffed on off ahead of us. It was a beautiful night and the stars were out in all their glory.

"Maybe you'd better leave Judea," Yeshu'a said to me quietly as we walked.

"Maybe you should leave, too," I told him. "You could go with me."

It was dark, but we could see one another's faces by the light of the moon. My remark just came out and we stopped in the middle of the empty road and faced each other. He took my hands in his. I thought he was going to kiss me. He didn't.

"There is a difference," he said in all seriousness. "You can leave. I won't."

****

XXXII

Judgement

On the morning that followed, two more followers as well as Yeshu'a's mother and his younger brother joined us. Coming in from Galilee on foot and leading two heavily laden donkey carts, they brought food, wine and news. Their arrival brought the crowd at the villa to 20.

In the courtyard there seemed to be more than that number of conversations going on, and it was obvious that at one point or another each group talked about Julian and me. Seated apart from the others at a slight distance, I could tell that they were discussing us by the sidelong glances we were getting, but I felt no animosity emanating from anyone, just curiosity.

Yeshu'a introduced his mother and his brother to me using Greek, but as they knew only a little, I could not speak with them beyond a few phrases. I could tell from the way that their eyes widened when he spoke to them further in Aramaic that he was telling them amazing things about me. They stared at me with unconcealed awe.

His mother was quite nondescript, though not unattractive. She was very trim and wore a plum dress with a heavy, wool overshawl that was used as a cape. I wore just such garments myself, and I noticed that hers was very well made and had a rather understated elegance about them.

She looked her age. Her hands were rough from common work, and her face was lined from worry and the effects of the sun. About 45 years old, she had a kindly though forced smile for me, and it was obvious that as a mother she was worried about my relationship to her son.

The brother was as tall as Yeshu'a, but lighter of frame and milder of face. His eyes were almost identical to those of his famous sibling—eyes that arrested men's words and held women's undivided attention. This brother, whose name was Joseph, was cultured and exceedingly friendly toward me. He and his mother already knew Julian.

In fact, he seemed to be on downright friendly terms

with Julian. They laughed and spoke with each other in the Galilean dialect almost as if they were old friends. I could not shake the feeling that there was something amiss in the way they related to one another—as if each had a secret agenda of which the other was aware. Like Judas and a couple of the others in the group, they seemed to be jockeying for subtle advantage over one another, and it was hard not to compare them all with the group of people around Claudius that I had observed when I was in Rome.

For all the games and joking and singing that went on that day and into the night, there were—as you might imagine— many serious undercurrents of political and religious conflict. The approach of the Passover feast was bringing matters to a head.

Some of the group wanted increased confrontation with the authorities who controlled the Temple. They insisted that the group should hold its feast in the streets outside the Temple as a show of their challenge to the moral authority of the High Priest and as a show of confidence in their own popular support.

Others—the followers of Judas, mostly—believed in using the Passover season to forge stronger bonds with the Zealots and, according to Julian, they were trying to maneuver Yeshu'a into becoming the leader of their group. They wanted him to begin at once to organize a movement which could within the next year or two begin the longed-for drive to push the Romans and their Jewish allies out of Palestine. I had spoken to Judas about that very thing earlier in the evening.

"It's a thing that can't be done," I told him as we sat on the edge of the irrigation pool and polished off a bottle of wine. I had rarely been alone with him, and it seemed like there were things we needed to talk about. It hadn't taken Judas long to get to the point. He seemed to think that I could wield a great deal of influence with Yeshu'a, and he spoke of the necessity of immediate action against the Romans. He didn't want to hear me say his plan was impossible.

"All things are possible through God!" he said.

"Not only that," he continued, "but I know more about you than you might imagine I do. I know, for example, that there was another man with you when you came from your country.

He was your lover."

I blushed with shame, for although the term sounded proper enough in Latin, we were in a country where it sounded dirty. Does that make sense? It also occurred to me that he was threatening to blackmail me, although his face betrayed nothing of the sort. I also realized that he did not suspect that there was any significant connection between Julian and me.

He went on to say that he knew that my lover and I possessed formidable weapons and that I had produced and sold the flaming projectiles and "magic naphtha," of which there had been some talk within military circles throughout the eastern Mediterranean. What he wanted of me became obvious enough. Here was no great plotter. Here was a soldier, plain and simple. Here was a man of action who, although he said that all things were possible through God, was actually more interested in achieving victory through the use of technologically superior weapons.

So it came down to this: he wanted—no, he demanded-- my help. Even though I was a foreigner and a woman of questionable morals and background, he said he thought I had been sent by the God of Israel to insure its triumph. Somehow, he said, I was the key to victory and that Yeshu'a was or could be the successor to Alexander the Great.

Let me assure you that I felt like no key. In fact, I felt vulnerable and completely helpless. Without either the weapons or the status that had protected me in the past, and with the possibility of arrest hanging over me, I really didn't have much idea of what to do. I was like a person borne along on a flood in the night, not knowing in which direction I might strike out—or why. I thought about taking a ship to Mauretania on the one hand, but on the other, I began to accept on faith that I was exactly where I was destined to be. I was, after all, with Yeshu'a in Judea. Where else could a person go? If I fled, would I not have felt like Jonah? And would I not have deserved a similar fate—or worse? Therefore, staying right there made a lot of sense, and rearming myself and those about me made sense, too. But the idea of being some sort of consort-in-arms to the new King of Israel didn't seem the least bit desirable. I could imagine as well as anybody how a small, determined army might break up Roman formations in battle by using incendiary catapults, crude flame-throwers, and similar weapons, but the thought of being the authoress of such suffering was certainly not a cheerful one. Then, too, for every weapon sooner or latter there will be countermeasures.

In the end I tried to put Judas off with promises to consider what we had discussed. I gave him the disappointing news that it might take years to equip ourselves so thoroughly that we would have an assurance of ultimate success against the Romans. What I did not tell him was that I was beginning to be certain of the immutability of history. He would not have accepted such a view anyway. He wanted action.

So when I spoke in terms of years and not of weeks or months of preparation, the handsome, young enthusiast gave way to the hothead, and as if I had lied to him, he said too loudly, "This is not so! It cannot be! You have no right to withhold power just because you are afraid! We must act now!"

"And why is that? What's so important about right now?" I asked, with growing anger of my own. Who was this man? What right did he have to talk to me that way?

"Because the hour of Our Lord is at hand. It is written!" he said vehemently. "So gird up yourself and prepare," he told me. "Prepare to win with me—with us—or prepare to lose! There will be no middle road, no escape! You will stand with the savior of Israel or you will die! Think about it!"

He turned away and started to walk off. The words came to me.

"I will stand with him," I snapped, "and you will wait for that which God has in store for you, Judas, not dictate to him or to me or to God!"

He stopped and turned to me with an angry look in his eye. I kept talking.

"And neither of us shall live a moment longer than he should. It is written!" I concluded.

Others in the group—the men who I presume are known to history as John, Thomas, and James—were all for continued proselytizing in the countryside for another year. It was they who were urging Yeshu'a to leave Jerusalem at once, which is to say, before the actual beginning of Passover. To stay around the city challenged the Judean authorities and the Romans.

They had a good point. In those days there was no such

thing as probable cause or due process. If a governor wanted he could send out troops on short notice and on any pretext. *Agitation* was just such a pretext.

According to Julian, it was John's group that most strongly influenced Yeshu'a, for it was comprised of the men who were the most loving and pacific. With the exception of Julian, truth be told, they were also the most fun-loving and free-spirited of the men around him. Though obviously devout, they were quite apolitical, and as I have said, that was a rare thing in Israel. Theirs was an attitude of casual but sincere indifference to Jerusalem and its masters. Some of them were quite frankly homesick.

So it was that as the Passover week began, there were three factions in the group: those urging confrontation, those with revolt on their minds, and those favoring departure. The disputes, though never ugly, were constant. Only Yeshu'a seemed serene throughout and it was obvious at least to me that he was not at all inclined to take up arms and lead a revolt. As to the matter of whether he would stay or go, he seemed reluctant to take a definite stand, but at any rate he made no move to leave town. So the men argued on and despite their differences with one another, they stuck with him. Clearly, had it not been for his leadership, the group would have splintered into its components the way that all such sects do.

Tensions in Jerusalem were also mounting. I went into town several times either with small groups, with the women, or by myself. Where I could find those who spoke Latin or Greek, I asked questions. I spoke with merchants and soldiers and women getting water at the pools, and continually I wondered whether the political and social foment I sensed was extraordinary or commonplace.

Finally it seemed that some decision had to be made, which is to say, that the group seemed to need either to assert itself or admit its weakness by backing off. At last, Yeshu'a decided the group would hold its Passover feast in Jerusalem, but in a private home and not in the streets outside the Temple. It was a compromise that seemed to suit only Judas, and after it was decided on, I heard talk of dissention but not rebellion; all of those men were loyal to their master.

Julian was probably the least satisfied, for he wanted to be gone from the city as soon as possible. As easy as it might be for me to attribute his attitude to personal cowardice, I cannot, for I think his was simply a difference of opinion. His imprisonment had hardened him, but, naturally he never wanted to find himself in that sort of predicament again. He wanted to get out of town, but his advice went unheeded.

For his part, Yeshu'a was led by no man. He was led only by the answers he found in prayer, and on those he based his decisions. Over the years of his ministry, his reputation for infallibility had grown because time after time his decisions were seen to have been correct when viewed with the benefit of hindsight.

One may ask, how did they practice their religion? How much did they lecture, study, and pray? I write this account through my own eyes, and that's why I have not focused so much on prayer as on play. After all, I could play with them but I couldn't pray with them. But I once asked Yeshu'a how to pray.

"I think that at first one should cover the elementary, which is the acknowledgement of God's existence and omniscience. We follow by supplication, acknowledging that all we have comes from God. That we follow by an attempt to ask God's help in purging ourselves of sin—or at least not to gloss over its commission in such moments of absolute truth. As we do that we freely acknowledge the need for God's help in overcoming our mere humanity. Then we usually end with a simple powerful paean adapted from the Greek, recognizing again God's omnipotence and eternal presence."

So I asked what sin was.

"It is whatever separates us from the love of God."

And I asked him if this or that prohibited act was sinful, but he would only say, "Only if it separates one from the love of God."

What normally separates us, I asked.

"Worry, mostly: worrying about food or comfort or acceptance. I try to help people not to worry."

"Do you not worry also?" I asked.

"Yes, but mostly for those I love, and as God leads me

and helps me to love so many people, I am actually left little time to worry about myself. The main thing I worry about anyway is whether or not I am doing the will of God."

How does one know if a given interpretation of that will is correct or if it one's own will or choice and not God's? I wondered aloud.

"Ah!" he exclaimed, almost laughing. "That's where practice and application comes in. Just as a musician must train herself to listen so that the tones she plays are correct and blend with those whose voices or instruments she accompanies, so we must train ourselves to listen for variance and discord within our own hearts."

And what then, is the hallmark of discord?

"In the harm that it does or might do."

"Do you mean, to people?"

"No, I mean to existence. To the will of God and the harmony of the universe. It would seem that we need to test our answers against such a scale."

Is to kill a sin?

"Two men from two countries met in a combat which neither in honor could avoid. The second defeated the first and the first was slain. It is not held to be murder, but why not?

"A shepherd chooses which of his flock will be shorn and which bred. He chooses also which will be butchered and which will become an offering. He does his best with that which is under his control, and his flock prospers. But what of the lamb which is slain or given over to the priests?

"Is not the will of God like that of the shepherd? Is the soldier or the shepherd a sinner? Would it not be true to say that if either has sinned and has known God, he will know that he has sinned?"

One could not argue—indeed, one did not wish to argue—with him.

Three days after that meal at the restaurant the Passover finally arrived. In the early morning of that day I strapped on my sword and dagger, dressed in my dark wool traveling cloak, and walked into town with the women to help prepare the feast. Without drawing attention to ourselves, we went directly to a large house, the use of which had been donated by yet another patron.

Never much of a hand in a kitchen, and more in the way than a help, I finally decided to walk around the city *incognito* and see the sights. I strolled by Herod's Palace and all through the Upper City. I went down into the Lower City and the Pool of Siloam, then walked to the Pool of Bethesda. It was a very pleasant day.

In the late morning, I arrived at the Antonia Fortress. On a whim I sent a message in to Apius Strabo, the legionary soldier I had met a few days before. The messenger went off and in no time at all, my new friend and I were united and were walking down the street laughing and talking. It felt natural to be with a soldier and to be on something of a break from the villa. On an impulse I took his hand and we walked along like a man and his sweetheart. He was very happy to see me and to be seen with me. Together we strolled about, drank some wine, and talked. He told me that he had thought about me constantly—even when in the arms of the girl who I had paid for him. He still wanted me, but he wasn't an ass about it.

"Well, did you get my money's worth from that girl?" I asked him.

"Oh, yes: she tried so very hard to be better than she thought you would have been. By Mithras, she wore me out that night!" he bragged. Well, that was all right with me. I was glad she did.

When Apius and I got back to the Antonia in the early afternoon, his comrades high on the wall laughed and yelled things down at him. Undoubtedly they thought that I would not understand. I was wearing the cowl and they assumed that I was an oversized local woman.

"She's a big 'un!" one yelled.

"Got any there to spare, Primus Pilum?" another called out. The name represented Apius' rank and meant *first spear.* Thus it had a sort of vulgar double meaning. I resisted the urge to call back something tart and witty in soldier Latin.

Turning to him, I looked my friend in the eye and said, "Let's give them something to talk about." I pulled back my cowl and shook out my hair and stretched myself so that the fullness of my figure was more obvious. The men on the wall quieted down at once. Even from the ramparts above us, they could see that I was quite a beauty.

Then I kissed Apius with a long, loving kiss as the catcalls died into the silence of envy. It was pure theater and he knew it, but that was all right. I even remembered to lift up one of my feet. When we parted lips, Apius shook his head and, with a wry smile, thanked me.

"I have never kissed a goddess," he said. "Now I can die a happy man."

"I had never kissed Apius Strabo," I said, smiling back at him. "Now I can die a happy goddess!"

I went by the stable where my donkey was being boarded and talked to her a while. Then I strolled toward the Temple. As I approached the market outside its gates, I noticed a familiar couple shopping from booth to booth. It was the couple from the tavern.

Moving along in one of my best Old Woman shuffles, I approached them carefully. The woman had her back to me, but I could see the man's face quite clearly. About 45 years old, he was an ex-gladiator or a professional enforcer. He was exceptionally ugly, but he looked intelligent and utterly ruthless. He was frightening looking.

Both of them were dressed in clothes that gave them away as being either Romans or romanized occidentals, and when the woman turned around to talk to the man I recognized her immediately. It was my former servant, Propea!

She had come up in the world. Better dressed than ever, she had her hair and makeup done professionally, and had the look of money. By their body language, it was easy to see that the man with her was not her lover. Perhaps, I thought, he was her manservant or bodyguard. Maybe she had a husband somewhere who employed this mastiff to guard her.

Husband! How could she be married? I still owned her. I realized that I could have gone to a magistrate and had her seized and held as a runaway. It was something to think about.

It had been more than two years since I had seen her, and as I stood in some shadows and watched her, it all came back to me.

I remembered the little house she and I had shared on the Rhine and how we had been more like sisters than owner and slave. We had traveled up from Italy together, had shared little secrets and slept in the same beds and tents. She had helped me dress a hundred times, and had quietly slipped away when my lover came to me and we wanted to be alone. I remembered my "illness" and wondered whether she had had a hand in it.

A commotion over at the gates made them stop their aimless puttering and look intently in that direction. Then it became obvious: they were looking for me. They thought they had found me once—or maybe they weren't sure if the lady in the tavern had been me. Of course, it was possible that they were just trying to keep tabs on me for someone, but it seemed more likely that they were hired to capture or to kill me.

Soon they left the market. I followed them to a small inn that was almost empty due to Passover since the tourists were out seeing the city or worshiping at the Temple. The two of them went in, but the man left almost immediately. I could sense by his purposeful stride that he was on his way to business.

I slipped in by a rear door that led out onto an alley. Making sure that no one saw me, I crept up the servants' stairway and found Propea's room easily enough, for I heard her singing behind one of the doors. Peeking in, I saw that she had her back to me and was standing nude in a large metal basin taking a little cat bath of her own. I slipped in silently, bolted the door behind me, and came up behind her undetected.

My little dagger was not nearly as fine as the one that had been stolen from me on the road from Tyre, but it was considerably sharper. I had seen enough movies to know what to do, so without hesitation I reached across her shoulder and clamped down on her mouth with one hand and held the knife across her throat with the other. In Latin I told her to keep quiet or die. Feeling the kiss of the knife against her young skin, she quieted right down. In fact, she fainted. I pushed her down on the bed, tied her hands behind her back and put a gag in her mouth. As she came to, I turned her over and covered her nakedness with her shift. She was completely terrified.

When she calmed down, I questioned her. It was such a good start that she told me everything she could, and I had no doubt that what she said was true.

To begin with, I was right about the man, for he was some kind of detective working for someone in Rome. He had hired her to travel with him and identify me, and she said that unless there was an emergency, he would not return for her until the next morning.

When my husband took me away into Germany and she heard no more from us, she assumed that both of us were dead, and after an initial investigation, the Roman authorities left her alone in the little rented house near the Rhine. She found my money and kept it and all my other belongings, selling off some and keeping the rest. Soon she had something of a modest fortune, and for the first time in her life, she was free. Under the law, there was no one who could claim her as part of my estate, even had it been known that she was a slave. She tore up the ownership papers I had on her.

She had been very careful with my money, and had concealed the nature and extent of her new-found wealth so successfully that no one even knew she had it. In the spring that followed, she traveled down to Aquileia at the northern end of the Adriatic. There she started a small tailoring business that catered to wealthy ladies. It prospered.

Upon some urging, she admitted to me that during the time I was running the refinery she had heard a rumor that a woman fitting my description was living down the coast from her. Naturally, though, she had not run to me so as to become my slave once again. I could hardly blame her, but I didn't say so.

Some months earlier, the detective had come to her shop and had more or less requisitioned her to go with him to identify me. Telling her that I was wanted on various charges including witchcraft, murder (of my husband), and treason, he revealed to her that I was a devil from across the sea. As they traveled to Palestine together they heard that after being arrested on the open sea, I had made an entire ship and crew vanish without a trace.

She and the man had set out arrived in Athens just days after my departure. There it was variously rumored, she told me, that I was a *hetairai*, the daughter of Pesephone, Athena in the flesh, and so forth.

"And just who do *you* think I am?" I asked her at that point.

"I don't know, M'Lady, but some say you are a demi-goddess and some say you are a witch," she replied, instantly regretting her words and thinking that she might have offended me. After all, I was sitting on the bed beside her and the point of my knife was near her throat. "But I think you are the most wonderful mistress in the world!" she blurted out foolishly. Obviously, she thought I was a witch. At any rate, she feared me. I insisted on the truth and got it.

I found out from her that she had indeed been the person who put a white powder in my food when we were in the Mogontiacum, but she had done so upon the order of the camp physician who claimed that the powder was a sedative. It was only after my husband took me away that she realized there might have been a connection between the white powder and my declining health, but what could she do about that?

From her I learned the name of the man who was looking for me and where she was to send for him if she saw me again. Although she had been positive that she had seen me in the tavern, the man wanted her to be certain before he made his move. He pointed out to her that if I could escape from an armed ship of war, perhaps something more subtle than force would be necessary if I were to be brought to justice.

She had money—lots of money—in her purse and sewn in the hems of her clothes. It was more than she had gotten from our house on the German frontier, and she still had her business in Aquileia. I was impressed and took only what was mine. I thought I might need it, and it turned out later that I was right.

Then I offered Propea her life if she would leave town immediately. Naturally, she accepted, and within 15 minutes, she was dressed and we were off. We went straight to a livery stable, got her a donkey and went to the western gate. I left no doubt that I would find her if she betrayed me.

When we were a half-mile beyond the gates, she tried to ask my forgiveness. She was so sincere that I was able to forgive her even though her foolishness and duplicity on the Rhine nearly killed me and forced my husband to give up everything he had—including ultimately his life. Begging to let her own remorse counterbalance my bitterness and sorrow, she said kind things about my husband and used his name in a way that made him alive once more in my mind's eye. Finally, we hugged each other and cried—for we had been good friends once.

"What shall I tell the Roman if he catches up with me and asks why I left?" she asked from atop the donkey. "He is very clever and tenacious. He always finds whomsoever he seeks, he says."

"Oh, act like you've been drugged or bewitched and tell them I did it," I told her, "and when I hear that you are safely in Aquileia I will send the papers to free you."

When she rode off, I felt that I had lost yet another link to the past. For some reason, I thought of my husband and our love-making in the beautiful upland meadows south of the Danube, and what he said to me as we lay in one another's arms. I had protested that I would never love another.

"No," he had said, "when I am gone you will love many another, for your heart is big, and you mind is open.

"It's all right," he said, touching a finger to my lips to silence my protest, "Venus is not expected to be faithful. It is enough that she has loved me."

It was late afternoon when I went back into the city still disguised as a local woman shuffling from one duty to another. Heading back to the house where we were going to have the feast that evening, I passed by a woman's shop. There I traded in my old garments for new ones of different colors so that the thug who had brought Propea to Jerusalem might be further deceived if he came looking for me. As I changed clothes, I realized that I should have killed her to be really safe. I was disgusted with myself that I should even think that way. Once again I started on my way, but I was dizzy. The noises and stenches of the alien world were all around me. My ears pounded. My vision blurred.

Stopping on the side of a busy street, I put my hand against a wall. I was sure I would vomit. I had a vision of how horrible it would have been had I driven the knife into Propea's flesh. All the other killing I had done or seen washed before me like an open sewer. I envisioned the heap of dead men in the road on the day Ned was killed and how the javelin drove through him. I could see the mess Cassius had made of his own head, of the bodies in the surf, and those of the bandits in the mountains. I could see how my husband's body and the bodies of the two tax-men looked when I buried them. It was awful and enough to make me feel as if I were going crazy.

Suddenly I wanted to go home—back to the South and drive-in movies and necking in the back seat. I wanted to watch TV and listen to rock music. I wanted to be safe and have a family and a brick house in a subdivision near a shopping center. I wanted to drive a car. But I had no home and nowhere in the Roman world to hide from men like Cassius and the thug who traveled with Propea—men who were being sent after me by some person or agency whose decision to take my life had already been made. How long could I hope to continue to escape them, I wondered. *Not long*, was my conclusion.

A man was speaking to me at my elbow. I turned to face a short, elderly Hebrew man, who was obviously trying to be good to me. He was poor, dirty, and disheveled, yet his face was one of pure kindness. I asked him if he could speak Greek, which he could. He asked if I was ill, and I assured him that I was all right. He spoke on a little, not saying anything important, but only as a way of soothing me and letting me know that I could depend on him, whether it might be to fetch my friends, get me some water to drink, or just to have someone to whom I could tell my troubles.

I could see something wonderful and shining in his eyes, for although he was ragged and had only one good arm, and although he was old, skinny, and looked as if no one was caring for him in any way, he nevertheless seemed calm and content. I could see that he cared more for others than he did for himself. As a result, he was happily indifferent to his own poverty. Such decency in the midst of an indecent world choked me and I began to cry.

Again he asked if I needed his help. I shook my head. His offer of assistance would have been ridiculous had it not been so sincere and had it not revealed the great disparities in our stations in life, for had I not more of everything in life than that old man had: wealth, health, beauty, fame, and more? I was embarrassed that it was he who was offering to help me and not the other way around. I had passed thousands like him. He stopped for the first like me.

He reminded me of Ovinin and without forethought words came to me: *How many of these messengers of God will be sent to me?* and my gloom dispelled as quickly as a spring storm. Collecting myself, I thanked him and insisted that he take some coins from me.

"No, I just wanted to help," he said, trying to refuse the

money.

"And you did—more than you know," I assured him. "Please allow me to help you in return," I said as I closed his good hand around the coins. "You have given me courage. What is a little money compared to that?"

He looked me in the eye and said, *"Go with God. Do not be afraid to do His will."*

Even as he spoke, I smelled wood smoke coming from a nearby house, and it stirred a memory—a memory of something more than the fact that I was hungry and had a big meal waiting for me. I kept trying to place the smell and the memory. The old man and I parted ways, and I turned back toward my path. I stopped to let a boy driving sheep go past, and I smelled the same smoke coming from another house. It came back to me how Ovinin had spoken to me of the smell of smoke when we were sacrificing the bird beside my husband's grave. I recalled him telling me how the smoke was blowing off to the southeast and there my destiny would be and how there they, too, would also be. It was true. I was not alone.

I took a few steps back down the street to find the old man, but he was gone. The smell of smoke lingered.

****

XXXIII

Evening

It had been a long day and one that was draining for me physically and emotionally. Tired and dirty, I went back out of the city to the villa. When I arrived only the ancient gatekeeper was there to let me in; all the others were in town. I went to my little room in the rear building where the women stayed and took off my clothes. After carefully laying my short sword and dagger where they would be close at hand, I stretched out, face down, on my straw mattress. Instantly I fell asleep.

When I awoke, it was almost sunset, and I knew I should

get going if I was to be in time for the feast. I lit a small oil lamp, dug through my things and retrieved my toiletries and some fresh drying cloths. Taking stock of myself and of my stuff, I looked at my last little bar of soap bought in Tyre for an exorbitant price. The irony of that purchase had been that the little scented bar was actually part of a batch of soap that I myself had made in Albania the year before. I had started making it there first out of necessity and then for profit. Altogether we sold about two or three hundred pounds of it and were getting orders for more all the time. Doubtlessly I could have made a second fortune manufacturing soap had I stayed at it. As you may be aware, the Roman world had no soap, bathing being performed with powders and oils and something called a *stirgil* with which the skin was scraped after oiling. Lots of people swore by the method, but I always found it left much to be desired—particularly where washing my hair was concerned.

It was almost dark and no one was around when I walked out to the irrigation pool and jumped into the cool water for a quick bath. Immediately I remembered diving into the sea at night from the Roman ship, and it was hard to believe that had happened only five months earlier.

I stayed in only for a moment, then got out, stood on the top of the wall of the tank facing the water, and lathered up my hair and body with that precious little bit of soap. As I washed myself I sang a tune in English.

"What's that language?" asked someone in Greek who was standing down on the ground right behind me.

"*Jesus Christ!*" I shouted in English as I jumped up and whirled around, oblivious of my nudity.

It was Yeshu'a. Even in the gloaming, I could tell it was he by the shape of his head and the sound of his voice. He was standing on the ground at my feet, looking up at me. It was almost too dark to see his face.

"I'm sorry!" he appologized, " I didn't mean to frighten you, but what did you say?" he asked, "and what's that stuff with which you are smearing yourself? And what language was that? And do forgive me for sneaking up on you like that, but you looked so beautiful!"

I realized what I had said and it all seemed so unreal that I started to laugh. For a moment I thought that perhaps nothing was real and that I was only living in the throes of an infinitely extended hallucination.

There he stood: the wise man who was Julian's master and who was in some way becoming mine. He was certainly more that just a new-found friend. I didn't know what to think of him as he stood there patiently waiting for me to answer his questions as he looked up at me towering above him, clad only in soap suds.

I covered myself with my hands. I had not been nude around him before because all of us had been wearing at least some clothes when we swam in the tank together. This was different, for we were alone, and I stood before him as I had not before. As usual, I could not fathom what he was thinking and in that brief instant we said nothing.

In a way it was a rather ordinary setting. In the quiet evening, a bird was calling and insects made noises as they had before, and a man and a woman who knew each other stood conversing at a pool. He had the advantages of surprise and clothing and she had those of height and nudity. But here was no ordinary man, she remembered: Here was a man before whose penetrating gaze and insight all people stood naked.

I squatted down so that I could see his face in the growing darkness. In his eyes, I saw merriment, some hint of the unanswered question. I thought I saw, too, the look of a man close by a woman he admires. I felt my heart heavily beat once, twice, three times. He smiled.

Then I smiled right back at him and reached out and touched his cheek lightly with the back of my soapy hand. Then I stood up and stretched my arms out wide and threw back my head and laughed with joy. For an instant I was a white cross of flesh against the dimming sky. Of what use modesty before such a man?

"*Soap! English!*" I said as I turned around and dove into the smooth embrace of the water. It didn't feel nearly as cold as it had before. I held my breath and swam underwater in the silence. I heard him when he dove in behind me.

We swam around for a few minutes, ducking about and playing tag in the semi-darkness, and, naturally, he touched me. I touched him. Then we got out, dried off and dressed in silence.

Neither of us needed to say anything about the pleasure

of being alone together for the first time. Those sorts of things were, in the final analysis, trivial. There were other less obvious understandings and questions that needed to be answered, and we both knew that there wasn't much time for us to talk. We were expected in town. We sat down there on the wall of the pool, very close to one another and spoke in low voices.

"You know what is going to happen, don't you?" he asked me, leaving no room for equivocation.

"Yes. I think that I know what will happen, but not exactly how or when it will happen," I said to him as I placed my hands upon his hands. "Maybe next year..."

"Maybe next month." he finished for me. He knew.

"Nothing is certain, My Dear One," I said, in what I hoped was a soothing tone.

"You know, Evangeline, that term *'Dear One'* is often used by Boetian shepherds to name their chosen lamb—the one that goes to the priests at year's end."

I told him that I hadn't known that. As he always seemed to know what I was thinking even before I did, his next question came as a surprise to me, for it was something that he had not asked before.

"Who are you, Evangeline? Why have you come to me at this particular point in my life?"

"I'm not sure," I replied, "but I have thought about it a lot. I think I am some sort of agent of what in my country is called *Divine Providence*—or at least I am a Witness."

"And you don't know which?"

I admitted I didn't. My heart felt as if it were in my throat.

"Then perhaps your purpose is to be my deliverer—my savior of some sort?"

I looked at him and thought of how I hadn't saved Ned and I hadn't saved my husband. Here was a man destined for a violent death. He knew it, too. I shook my head, "No. I don't think so. Not even if I wanted it more than anything."

"How can I be your savior, when you yourself are supposed to be the Savior of the world?"

He did not contradict me. "It's a big world for one man to save," he said quietly.

"When I was a child," he said after a moment, "I would go into the synagogue to read—for I was invited to do so by the Rabbi. I opened the book at random, and I would read. One day a great weight of understanding fell upon me and the elders when I opened and read the passage which says:

'I will declare the decree: the Lord hath said unto me, Thou art my son; this day have I begotten thee.

Ask of me and I shall give thee the heathen for thine inheritance and the uttermost parts of the earth for thy possession.

Thou shalt break them with a rod of iron; thou shalt dash them in pieces like a potter's vessel.

Be wise now therefore O ye kings: be instructed, ye judges of the earth.

Serve the lord with fear, and rejoice with trembling.'"

He looked wistfully off toward the western clouds. "We all knew it meant something about me that I should read such a thing, and we were afraid in some way, for such a destiny is one that must involve suffering.

"But now, all these years later, I sit quietly with you, a poor man in a poor country, with something in all nature speaking to me of endings and not of great struggles and great triumphs. How could such a one as I—unwilling as I am to take up the sword and carve some glittering bit of empire—hope to claim the inheritance of which the singer sang?"

What could I answer other than to say, "You needn't wonder. God will accomplish all of that."

"And how do you know?"

"Like so many other things, it is written in the books of my people. The victory will be yours."

I squeezed his warm, strong hands that I held in mine.

"I'm afraid," he confessed to me in the dark.

"You wouldn't be human if you weren't," I responded.

He smiled a wry smile and looked at me, his eyes gentle and tender.

"Are you sure you're not supposed to carry me away from all this?" he asked in a kidding sort of way. "If not, then why are you here?"

"Maybe just to love you....and to comfort you," I said, and with that we looked into each others' eyes and I felt a wave of emotions so complex and so strong sweep through me that I could not speak. I tightened my grip on his hands. Again I was acutely aware of the slow thumping of my heart. It felt as if it might break. He raised my hands to his lips and kissed them as if in benediction. We sat in silence.

"I'll go up to my room now," I finally said.

Arriving there, I prayed. I prayed right through the confusion of the pagan world and the situation I was in, through the tunnel of imminent destruction and into the light of present joy. Then I lay quietly on my pallet, listening for the slip of sandals and the even more subtle padding of feet, and waited quietly for the touch that shocks but does not surprise.

****

XXXIV

The Feast

As we prepared to leave, I put on the rather pretty new dress that I had bought that afternoon. It was an almost-Hellenic, cheerful sort of long, vee-necked lavender shift that fitted my bust snugly but was neither too tight nor too low-cut. On the other hand, it wasn't too drab, either. Over it, I wore a loose, dark blue half-top to cover me as we went through town as well as my boat cape since there was a chance of rain and the night was going to be cool. As usual I took my short sword despite the fact that it was irritating to have the scabbard slapping against my thigh every few feet as I walked. If I wore it under my outer garments it made me look lumpy and less attractive, but if I wore it openly it marked me and could bring trouble. I thought about leaving it behind. After all, I was happy and felt that even if I was not safe then at least whatever lay ahead of me was so predestined that no mere sword could have protected me. I took it and the dagger anyway.

As I was putting them on, Yeshu'a asked me whether I really thought that carrying the weapons might be necessary. I was in a very good mood, and he didn't say it to criticize me.

"They have been before," I replied. I hadn't told him about having used the dagger just hours before to intimidate and interrogate Propea.

"Maybe they weren't as necessary as you thought they were," he suggested.

"Maybe not, but at the times I certainly thought so," I replied.

Then he said that he shouldn't complain, for if I was to be his protector I might have need of arms. I told him of the double entendre that the use of the term "arms" had in my native language and we laughed.

Picking up on the theme of my native language and demonstrating once again his incredible memory, he then asked about "soap" and inquired about "English". After I had explained the former I told him how the latter was derived from the land known as Britannia. I was surprised to learn that he had even been there for a few weeks and that he had visited Stonehenge.

"And everywhere you traveled you went unarmed?" I asked, incredulous.

"Everywhere."

I asked him if he had ever said that he had "brought not peace but a sword."

"I think I did," he said, "but I meant a different kind of sword—one that divides families and even nations."

"Apparently I, too, bring not peace but a sword," I said, "but mine is made of iron. It is not a metaphor," I concluded, "and I feel safer if I have it with me."

"I am sure," he said, with not a shred of criticism in his voice, "that the Angel of Death feels the same way."

"Particularly if she finds someone who needs killing," I agreed. I thought we would have time to talk about all that later, but it was then that someone yelling out in the courtyard interrupted us.

"*Master!*" cried out a voice in Greek. It was Julian, and he sounded either angry or worried. "We shall be late! Where are you? All are waiting!"

"You sound as if you are backstage at a theater, Julian," I said heartily as we emerged from a doorway and entered the yard where he stood waiting impatiently. "You sound as if the curtain is about to go up and the lead actor is missing!"

"And what, pray, is a curtain?" Yeshu'a asked, for I had used the English word. I explained.

I wish I had been able to see Julian's face so that I might have seen his expression. As we had neither lantern nor torch I could not, however, even though he was but ten feet from me. His voice sounded strange.

He started to say something, but broke off his half-begun question and huffed, "Let's go!" and the three of us left the villa together and broke into a jog that soon got us to the city. As we loped along, I found myself admiring the new Julian. Unlike the pudgy, pasty priest he had been, hard living and constant walking had made him fit and active. The old Julian had not been like that at all.

It was a beautiful night and we ran like healthy horses,

not talking but snuffing in the cool air. I wanted it to go on and on. Even with the irritating slap of my scabbard, the sweat forming in the small of my back, and the occasional rock that punished the foot, it felt good to be so healthy. It felt good to be alive.

By the time we arrived at the house in the city, the dinner had already started and everyone had gone on ahead with the ritualistic services without waiting for us. Julian was clearly miffed. Without his saying anything I knew that he felt that our being late was my fault and that the others should not have proceeded without Yeshu'a. We had missed some sort of prayers or something and the wine was already making its second round when we came through the door. The rowdy clamor died down and everyone turned to look at us.

Judas, who was more or less presiding over the group in our absence, stood up from his chair on the opposite side of the room and spoke to Yeshu'a loudly enough to be heard over the subsiding noises. Julian translated for me as things were said, but I hardly needed it, for the tenor was obvious.

"I hope you haven't eaten already and spoiled your dinner," Judas said loudly.

"Not at all! I have a great appetite," Yeshu'a replied. I noticed that there was an uncomfortable silence in the room and realized that it had something to do with me. Someone else said something.

" 'You always have had great appetites,' he said," Julian translated into Latin for me. It had been a criticism, not a joke. I could tell that some agreed with the speaker and some took offense with his implication. Maybe it was just the wine talking.

Leaving us, Yeshu'a walked over to Judas' table. He put his hand on the shoulder of the man who had made the comment, smiled at him, and spoke a few words that all in the room could hear. The lad smiled sheepishly and blushed, and the tension in the room subsided.

Then another fellow at the far side of the room stood up and started asking a long question, indicating me as he did so, and all the people watched him respectfully as he spoke. He was obviously speaking for most, if not all, of them.

Taking up a goblet of wine from a tray that Mary brought him, Yeshu'a began speaking in a strong, deliberate, melodious voice, accompanying his words with graceful gestures. Julian whispered to me. "The question was, Does the Law not say that strangers are unwanted at the Passover feast?"

I thought of how I must have seemed to the people in that room. I was more than just a stranger. I was a foreigner. I couldn't even talk with most of them. I was not a Jew, and I was probably a whore. I carried a sword and came in suspiciously late with their leader.

I whispered back. "Maybe I should just leave." Julian shook his head violently. I asked him what Yeshu'a was saying about me, hardly noticing how upset Julian was as he spoke.

"He said that you love him. He told them that anyone who loves him is not a stranger to him, and asked several of them one at a time if they love him, too." He paused and listened.

"He says that he loves us all...and he asks the question, 'Who would we be... if we were to send someone out into the night...when the Angel of Death is abroad?'

" And he says that you are a ... that you have been sent by God..."

At that point they were all looking at me, some in awe and some—particularly those sitting with Judas—clearly with skepticism. The latter probably thought that Yeshu'a was either rationalizing his attachment to me or that he was losing his mind.

"... And who are we," Julian was whispering to me, " to say that God's messengers...should all be Jewish men...with dark hair?

"He invites anyone to question his...authority."

One of the disciples spoke up, uncertainly at first, but with growing confidence.

"This fellow asks whether it is unwise to have you here. Do you not, he asks, have a reputation for being a...prostitute. He asks if that will hurt their...credibility." Julian fumbled for the right Latin words, but his facility with languages was still as impressive as ever.

Yeshu'a spoke.

"He says that they have all been around prostitutes before and tax collectors and thieves..."

Everyone in the room—including Julian—laughed or

smiled.

"...and lawyers." Julian hated lawyers.

Then the girl, Mary got up on a stool and beat on a brass tray to get attention. Everyone quieted down and looked at her. She spoke slowly and they listened with rapt attention. I had never seen her or any other women, for that matter, addressing a group of men in that country. All of the other women were in the room by that time, too, and they looked almost shocked that she had interrupted the Master, but it was obvious that all the men including him were very interested in what she was saying.

I suspect that several of them loved her more than just as a sister, and in the light of the many lamps of the room, she looked beautiful. Julian smiled and I saw in his eyes that perhaps he had something for her, too. He translated.

"She says that if anyone has a right to complain about you it would be her." People were murmuring and nodding their assent.

"She is pointing out that a woman feels bound to protect that which she thinks is hers, the same way that men protect their homes and countries. She was jealous, she says, when she saw you take off your clothes and swim like a fish in the pool with all these men." They shifted about nervously. It was obvious that this was the first time that the newcomers—including Yeshu'a's mother—had heard about our all swimming in the tank together.

He continued translating. "...when she herself cannot swim at all. She says that she was jealous of your..." Julian hesitated as cries and protests broke out in the room, "...your big body and real blonde hair when she herself is so plain."

It was obvious that her men didn't think she was plain—not the way they carried on. She smiled sweetly, then continued speaking.

"She is saying," Julian continued, "that if having a whore around hurts our reputation then we should demand that she leave." There was a stunned, shamed silence. She got down from the stool and came across the quiet room to me. Taking me by the arms she hugged me tightly to her in a warm welcome that almost made me cry. Then she kissed my cheeks and turned to say a final few words. The men cheered and stomped their feet. Everything was all right. She went to the kitchen.

"What did she say?" I asked Julian.

"She said," Yeshu'a said coming up behind me and whispering into my ear in Greek, "that she will love whosoever loves me, even beautiful foreigners!"

"She said something else, too, didn't she?"

"Sure. She said, 'Let's catch up on our drinking!' and an old toast: *Full Cups and Happy Hearts!"* It had, he explained with a wink, a double meaning.

The party got increasingly boisterous until it was time to give proper deference to the lamb that was served as the main course. Yeshu'a lead the group in a long prayer followed by what passed for a hymn. Then they dug in with a will. I wasn't particularly hungry so I helped with the serving. The mood was definitely festive.

While they ate—and at Yeshu'a' urging and insistence— I sang several songs in Greek and in English. As before, I was not averse to singing. I sang *Greensleeves, America the Beautiful*, and a hymn you sang when we lived together: *We Gather Together*, of which I knew only one verse that I translated for my hosts before I began.

"*We gather together*," I sang, " *To ask the Lord's blessing./ He chastens and hastens His will to make known;/ The wicked oppressing now cease from distressing./ Sing praises to His name: He forgets not His own.*"

Then Julian took over and led me onward through the second verse with a baritone that was stronger, more emotional, and lovelier than I thought it could be.

"*We all do extol Thee, Thou Leader triumphant,/ and pray that Thou still our defender wilt be,/ Let Thy congregation escape tribulation;/ Thy name be ever praised! O Lord make us free!*"

Judas was not the only one in the room who noticed that Julian knew the same song in the same foreign language.

The party went on until late in the night, but full of food and wine, the mood became more serious and subdued. Conversation broke up into little groups about the room. I was out of the main room most of the time as I was helping the women serve and clean up. I could hardly expect the men to translate for me constantly.

I am tempted to go into a long aside about how mediocre the food was, and how I would have given a gold coin for a gallon jug of sweet tea, a few bags of ice, some fried chicken, potato salad, and a cold beer, but I won't.

We had eaten some of the traditional bitter herbs, and it seemed impossible to get the taste of them out of my mouth. I kept drinking water and wine until finally Mary, noticing my distress, gave me a small honey cake. All the women laughed and patted me sympathetically on the back as I felt the honey take over.

Toward the end of the meal, on one of my trips back into the main room, I noticed Julian quietly but vehemently arguing with Judas and two others in the far corner of the room. I assumed it was yet another disagreement over money.

When, however, I returned several minutes later, Julian was going out in a huff, and the three Zealots were happily pouring themselves more wine down at their end of the tables.

After their long day, all of the other women, tired and sleepy, retired to the roof, leaving me as the sole representative of womanly charms. In that respect, several of the men looked sheepishly at me in ways that made me know that they wished they could speak more than just fishmongers' Greek with me. Foolishly, I wished that I were as pretty as Mary. What woman is ever content with her looks?

By that time in the evening, I felt that I was fitting in pretty well. Having lived in the ancient world for so long and having no hope or expectation of returning to this one, I felt as "normal" as any well-adjusted foreigner might have felt in such a setting. Happy with the evening and tipsy from wine, I imagined myself quite a good fellow and looked forward in a vague way to whatever good things the future might hold. How I could have so easily freed myself from the various concerns and worries that had surfaced that very day is in hindsight quite amazing, but there it is. It had been less than eight hours since I had driven Propea from the city with a bare bodkin, and less than that since Yeshu'a and I had admitted to one another our shared premonitions of disaster.

But I wasn't concerned about all that. I wasn't thinking at all, just feeling good about things like bathing in the cold water and having a nice body that turned men's heads and gave me pleasure. I took off the half top and I could feel myself swinging my hips just a bit more as I walked about pouring wine for all the men in the room—nothing too obvious, but something self-confident, a bit brassy and, I should add, not particularly out-of-place or unwelcome.

Finally I found a place for myself in a corner of the room where I could watch the men and they could watch me. There I sat, grinning what I suppose was a foolish grin and thinking about singing another song and about how I looked in my new clothes: evidence, I suppose, of the efficacious, mind-numbing qualities of wine.

Around what would have been about eleven o'clock, Yeshu'a called for everyone's attention and the room fell silent as he began to talk in a friendly but earnest manner. Sulking in the far corner, Julian had just come back in from somewhere. Judas, ever the Jewish chauvinist, was near me sitting with his buddies, but he didn't offer to translate for me. That was all right, though, for I was content to be a fly on the wall and to be off of my feet. Propped up against the wall on some rugs, I dozed off for a few minutes and began to dream of Eleusis, and of the room and the magical ray and of being in the arms of Man.

"Wake up! Wake up!" Julian said to me in Greek. I wanted to stay on the sheepskin with Man, though. "Get up!" Julian said, shaking me.

I came awake with a start, grabbing at the hilt of my knife underneath my cloak that I was using for a pillow. With the other hand I seized Julian's wrist. If the knife had been outside the cloak I'd have gotten it out. I had been sleeping with weapons to hand for three years, and the reaction was immediate. The knife was there, its reassuring, narrow oval handle under my cloak. I let go of Julian.

Had the men not been in such a serious mood, they would have laughed at us: me, the big hellion coming up from her nap with a knife, and Julian jerking backward as if from a striking snake. As things stood, though, those who saw it only smiled at the little scene.

I rose up from my slightly elevated resting place, stood up and stretched, then shook the sleep off of my face and pushed back my hair with my fingers. I must have looked rather formidable—like some great cat that someone had brought in.

Everybody was looking at me as if they expected something of me—a speech , perhaps, or a song—and I felt like someone who had been caught sleeping in church and was expected presently to make an explanation of herself. Julian broke the silence.

"Our master has asked that you say something to us all," he said to me in Greek. "He has told us that you are very special," he continued, barely suppressing some sort of inner rage, jealously and hatred with which he was obviously struggling. "Some of us have....questioned that," he added.

He stepped back as if to leave a stage—or a firing wall—to me.

So that was it! I thought. Julian wanted to be first among equals, and he had striven to merit whatever preference Yeshu'a might have given him. So to see me come in suddenly and be proclaimed special must have greatly rankled him. It must have appeared to him that I had gained immediate acceptance because I was a woman who had caught the master's eye, if not more.

Julian obviously aspired to some kind of leadership role, and when he spoke to me it was not without reason that he had used the term "us," thereby claiming allegiance with the group and setting himself apart from me. Judas translated Julian's words for his friends, then came over to where I was and said that he would translate for me.

Julian turned away physically. I could feel that somehow he was turning on me politically, and that he would do worse if he could and if he dared. I was only mildly surprised. After all, we weren't even from the same country and, after all, I used to sleep with his father.

I scanned the faces of the men in the room as I gathered my wits. I could see that some were open and innocent, honestly curious about what I might say about the implication that I was trying to gain influence within the group. Those who shared these thoughts looked skeptically at me as if I was poised to rationalize my actions. Only Yeshu'a looked calm and at ease even though he had no earthly idea what I might say. I had been on the spot before, though, and only had to think a moment before I spoke.

"What can I, a woman," I asked, as Judas translated, "say to you about this man who men shall someday call the Son of God? I have just met him. You have known him for years, some of you for your whole lives."

That astonished them all—all except Julian, I suppose. They started talking excitedly among themselves. Yeshu'a was calm and stared at me and smiled.

I had the floor.

"One and all, you want to know who I am. Well, let each man judge for himself," I began slowly. Judas used his beautiful voice to give inflection and emotion to my words as he translated them. That gave me confidence.

I told them that from beyond the Pillars of Hercules I had come, traveling by ship, horse, foot, and donkey through Rome, Gaul, and Germany. I spoke of my husband and our flight through Norricum and Pannonia, of his devotion, and of his death. I told them of the old shepherd, Ovinin, and of the fire we had made. I told them about the smoke of which had blown toward Palestine.

I told them in brief terms of other gods and goddesses, of Delphi, the Parthenon, and of Eleusis, and how I had experienced some of the wonders of those places. In conclusion I told them something to the effect of:

"And then one night when I was in Athens, the call came, saying *'God with us!'* and urging—no *telling* me—to come here in haste, which I did.

"But at sea, a Roman captured me and made me come aboard his ship. He kept me and treated me well until I lost my fears of him. I weakened, for he was beautiful, and then he betrayed me. A great storm arose and drove us toward a lee shore violent with rocks.

"In the story, Jonah was thrown overboard to save the ship and was swallowed by the fish. In my case, I jumped overboard and the sea swallowed up the ship with all hands save my loyal servant who had jumped into the winter sea to save me.

"Finally we were rescued and I came to Tyre and then here. Again I passed through dangers and followed after the news of you until I finally found you all here in Jerusalem. Here I smell the smoke of the fire that was lit in the mountains above the Adriatic Sea. Here is where I am destined to be."

All but Julian nodded in acknowledgment of my conclusion. I went on.

"You are more fortunate than I: You have been with this man longer than I, have heard and understood his words and seen his wondrous works. Let me stay here, too. Let me live among you for the next year—just one year! See if I can learn what you have learned. Let me love him as you have loved him."

"We have heard with our ears," Judas said to me, as if speaking for all. "Only time will tell if we have heard with our hearts.

"But it is not our place to permit or not to permit you to stay among us—only his," he said, gesturing at Yeshu'a, who was sitting quietly amid loudly whispered conversations.

"Judas," I said, as I stepped down from the raised floor on which I had been standing and placed my hand on his shoulder, "tell them all this:

"Friends, a certain rich man in a far country....had two wives, each of whom he dearly loved. While on a trip in another land he met another woman who he brought home, saying to her, 'here is my house: live in it with me.' To that she replied, 'Do not misspeak, but say, 'this is our house, live in it with us.' And then I will say, 'First let me talk with your wives who have been loyal to you all these years. Let us get to know one another, and let me learn from them whether or not I am welcome to become one of them.' The man did as she asked, and the family lived harmoniously."

As he finished translating for them, the men nodded their heads in assent or at least acceptance of the idea that their ranks might expand once more.

I looked at Julian and saw that he was shaking his head bitterly in the corner. Perhaps I should have gone to him right then, but I didn't. Instead, I went and sat down next to Yeshu'a.

"The hour is late," he said to me, squeezing my hand affectionately.

"Is this not the hour when the Angel is abroad and passes over?" I asked.

"He doesn't always pass over, you know," he said. "Sometimes he stops."

"But not tonight, Dear One," I replied, knowing that once again I might possibly come to feel unconditional love for a man. I presume that my eyes were blazing with affection.

"Who knows the will of God?" he said, lowering his

eyes from mine to kiss my hand.

"One more thing I must do," he said. "Please go see to Julian. Now I must lead us all in the final ceremony."

"Anything you say," I told him, as I got up to honor his request. *Anything you say.*

But Julian would not be consoled or mollified even when I told him that it was not my idea but Yeshu'a' that I should sit by him. "Hush!" was about all he said, "The Master is asking us to pray."

We bowed our heads with the others and Yeshu'a led the group in a prayer that ended up in their praying of a prayer in unison. It reminded me of being back in church when I was a girl, and a chill ran down my spine.

Yeshu'a spoke. Julian and all the others listened with rapt attention. Presently Yeshu'a held up a new brass flagon and a cup and said something as he filled the cup. Then he drank of it.

Julian got up quickly and walked over to him and took the proffered cup and drank from it, too. He wanted to be first.

He made a face at the taste of it, then handed it to the man named John who sat next to Yeshu'a. Then he looked about almost wildly, but I was the only person in the room who noticed, for the others were looking at John who was having the cup filled for him by Yeshu'a. Then Julian backed away in my direction shaking his head and sat down near me.

The cup was refilled each time a man drank. Finally it was my turn. I was the last. Yeshu'a filled it and passed it to me. I looked in it and realized that it was not ordinary wine. I wasn't even sure whether or not it was appropriate for me to share it with the men. After all, I certainly was not kosher.

"Drink it if you wish, Evangeline. It has in it the White Drink. If you drink it, drink all of it," Yeshu'a said to me from his end of the table. I looked at Julian sitting beside me, still fuming and shaking his head as he looked at his feet and mumbled. I drank it all and passed it back to the center of the table.

Yeshu'a spoke some more and passed some bread around. They all sang a hymn and started filtering out of the room. Yeshu'a left the room.

I got up, cleaned up a little and prepared to go outside into the cool night for some fresh air. Eventually I found myself wiping down a table near the door next to Julian. He was standing like a blank statue staring off into space. Fascinated by the texture and feel of the wood, I realized that the effect of the drink was coming on. I therefore surmised that Julian was under its influence, too.

Judas came over to him and spoke to him in Aramaic, tearing him from his reverie. I couldn't translate his words, but I understood what he was saying, which was "It begins! Are you with us or against us?"

Julian glared at him and bit back a few words and turned away from him, colliding with me when he did so, knocking me back. He glared at me.

I wasn't hurt or the least bit upset, and I told him—in English—that I was sorry I had been in his way.

"You don't know the half of it, young woman!" he snapped at me, also in English. "You have always brought disaster with you. You lead your life from orgy to bedpost! You deceive, you dissemble, you pollute! You take the fine and make it coarse, and debase the noble. Get thee from me, Satan!" he snarled, pushing past me for the door.

Perhaps I should have felt guilt or anger, but I felt neither. Rather, I perceived our little interaction as if I were merely an actress saying her lines.

"What have I done to you, Julian?" I asked after him.

He stopped and turned to me, saying, "Perhaps I should thank you, woman. I who had dedicated his whole life to serving the Lord, who sacrificed and studied and worked, who lived in the slums and bore the disgrace of my birth while my father was smuggling drugs and chasing whores! Perhaps I should thank you for being the instrument of Divine Providence by which I have come here.

"But no blessing is unmixed. What have you *done*, you ask?" he said, eyes wide, pausing for effect. "Precipitated crisis, brought with you the smell of death and Roman suspicion, made us look cheap in the eyes of the nation, undermined all we have built up..."

I cut him off by asking what crisis I had precipitated. I

really hadn't the slightest idea.

"Go ask that fool, Judas," he said, as he turned to leave.

"Don't leave, Julian!" I said. He hesitated. "Speak with Yeshu'a," I urged him.

"There is a time for every purpose under Heaven:" he paraphrased, holding his nose up in the air, "...a time to talk and a time to act. A time to embrace and times, young woman, to refrain from embracing."

"And just what do you mean by that, Julian?" I heard myself asking, only vaguely aware that everyone who was still in the room was listening to us, even though we were speaking English.

"I mean that I am willing to give him my heart and soul. You have only your body to give him!" he said in angry triumph.

Unlike the time we had parted in Spain, I had no desire to slap or to hurt him. I felt sorry for him and as I have said, none of it seemed real. I felt compassion for him and that we were just acting out some scene that had been written long before. His words might have made me angry at some other time, but coming from him as they did, all I could say in English was "Oh! That is so pathetically sad! Poor Julian!" It took him a few moments to remember what the word meant, but when he did, it was as if I had slapped him hard across the face. I hadn't even meant it as an insult, but he apparently thought I had.

"You will live to regret everything," he threatened. Then he threw on his cloak and left the house.

There were only six of us left in the room by that time. The men were speechless. They had understood almost all of what we had said to one another.

I turned to Judas and told him that Julian and I had spoken in anger and I hoped our words would soon be forgotten.

"Such words are not soon forgotten," he said with his small group right behind him. "Amazingly, we understood them all even though you and he spoke in your native tongue. I think we understand a lot more about the two of you now.

"But now I have words for you," he continued.

"You have said that you will withhold your power and

your magic and your weapons at this important time in the life of our country. You may not be able to do so any longer, for I shall ask you the same thing I asked Julian: the time is here. It begins soon. Are you with us or against us?"

"What *'begins'*?" I asked.

"The long awaited casting off of the Roman rulers and their collaborators and the establishment of the Kingdom of God."

"I am neither with you or against you," I said, right away. "I shall walk any path Yeshu'a walks or fight any battle he tells me to fight. I shall help him any way I can. There has never been such a man.

"But beware, Judas, of any trouble you may start, for if he is not with you, neither shall I be with you. Nor shall God himself be with you."

He would have translated my words for the others, but they understood me perfectly well even as they had understood the essentials of what Julian and I had said. They accepted my words at face value and nodded their assent. I could see that Judas was losing their support.

"Well, if that's settled," I said to them cheerfully as I belted on my sword and dagger and put on my half-top and cloak, "let's go on outside and catch up with the rest of them." And so some of us did. Judas stayed behind with two others.

It was a beautiful night and like a bunch of Spartan soldiers-in-training, those of us who had gone out walked along the dirty, almost empty streets without lanterns, lamps, or torches. All around us, the city slept and in shuttered homes its citizens hid from the Angel. For the most part, we were silent. Yeshu'a had been standing outside talking with some of the fellows when we caught up with them. He took my right hand and Simon Peter held my left, while others in the group held hands with one another so that the feeling of comradeship traveled from one person to the next. In that friendly manner, we went forth, pausing occasionally to get our bearings in extremely dark places. Shortly we came to a small walled-in brook. Knowing it to be from a jealously protected source, we drank from it with relish by getting down on our hands and knees to suck it up like horses so that no one's hands would dirty the water. Some of us got the hems of our garments wet or muddy, but the water tasted wonderful. I thought fleetingly of how my father and I drank from streams that way when I was a girl pretending she was Bambi.

It was the sweetest water imaginable. All the earth throbbed with sleeping life and insect sounds, for we were in a large garden. We wrapped ourselves in our wool cloaks and stretched out on the ground to look at the stars and to rest. There were about eight of us at that time, and I thought nothing of it. It was so late by then that we were all tired and it felt good to lie down and get off our feet. Some of the men dropped off to sleep. After a while, Yeshu'a got up from my side and walked down the trail.

After some time had passed, I went looking for him and found him sitting on a stone bench. To my amazement—for it seemed out of character to me—he was weeping.

Sitting next to him, I put my arm around him and pulled him to my breast. What could I say to his weeping? This was a man I had known only a week but with whom I thought I might be capable of falling in love: this rabbi, miracle worker, teacher, water polo competitor, laugher, world-walker, mind reader, person-lover: this Man.

"I am afraid," he said simply, sitting up and facing me in the darkness. All in innocence, I asked him of what.

"Of dying. Of suffering. Of losing you—all of you—and of being severed from this world that I love so much and from my friends and family."

He spoke not as a coward but as a man who values what he has in the way of friends and family and thinks more of the pain of others than he does of his own.

"Each of us has his destiny," I said, "but, do not worry: You will not lose me," I told him. "I was sent to be with you, was I not?" Then I thought with a pang: *so was his wife.*

"Yes, you were," he said matter-of-factly. "But why only for so short a time? It seems so unfair.

"I have a premonition," he continued, "and it's not just the White Drink speaking, for this premonition has been with me from the time I set eyes on Jerusalem two weeks ago. I have been here many times, of course, but this time it was different.

"Sometimes I am uncertain about what I should do— whether I should teach a certain way or not, whether I should do what the people call "performing wonders," and where I should lead my followers.

"At other times, what I must do and how I must express the word of God is clear. I must say what I say and do what I do even if it angers some people and seems as if I am a Zealot trying to manipulate the people in preparation for the inevitable revolt. And—mark my words—revolt is inevitable and probably undesirable.

"But I must say what I say and go where I go even if it leads me to my death."

"Don't say that," I whispered. "Nothing is inevitable."

He told me not to talk in that way, for many things about our existence—if not all things—are inevitable and that he was almost certain that the high priests and financial power brokers were so afraid of his rising popularity that they would soon act against him.

"We shall soon be separated. I know it," he concluded.

"Don't say that. It's a beautiful night—all nature sings to us and the stars are our coverlet," I responded. "I'm not going anywhere. I shall be with you for many more years."

"You're the angel. Therefore tell me, if you can: how many more years?" he asked, his words soft on the night.

"Maybe two, maybe 20. Who knows? Maybe thousands," I said, and though I was trying to be brave, I couldn't. The emotion, grief—which is seldom more than self-pity—welled up in me and my eyes were blinded with tears. For all I knew, whatever was going to happen to him was going to happen to me, too, and that was a terrifying thought. I knew from experience that I would leap into the sea or kill rather than let myself be taken by my enemies.

It was his turn to comfort me. He kissed my tears away. "Let us be brave," he said. "Others will look to us for their examples."

"To hell with bravery," I replied with a wry smile. "Let's get out of town, and let's do it tonight! Who needs all this?"

I knew that there wasn't a chance in the world he would flee with me.

He did not reply but held me close. I laid my head upon his chest and he stroked my hair.

"There is only one thing to do at a time like this," he said finally, "and running away is not the answer."

I sniffled in assent, and we got off the bench, and together we knelt down side by side and prayed aloud, each in his own native language. I prayed as I had always been taught to pray when I was a child, first thanking God for the many good things with which I had been blessed my whole life—parents, my sister, health, friends, education, lovers, adventure, wealth, and perhaps most importantly, gratitude for those blessings.

I prayed for forgiveness of my sins and thought of some of those, too. Then I got down to cases and prayed for bravery and fortitude and guidance. Then something strange happened. I felt the warmth of something moving within me and what must have been the voice of God or just a childhood memory said to me once again, "*Fear not, for I am with you!*" and I had a quick vision of all that I had been through so far. I could have stood up and shouted. Hurriedly, I finished with a final note of thanks that not only was God with me but also that I had heard His voice.

Yeshu'a put his arm around my shoulder and drew me to himself and kissed my ear playfully. "Now let us go and take our friends home. It's been a long day. Tomorrow will take care of itself."

We walked back up the path to where our friends were fast asleep. Yeshu'a went about rousing them, joshing with them, and carrying on. Groggily they got up and we all fumbled around in the dark to pick up our robes and other things.

When we were about ready to leave we heard the sound of men and saw the flare of torches. Along the road from the city gates came a band of about Jewish men who headed straight to the place where we were. Naturally I assumed that they were looking for us to tell us something—bad news, probably—and when they got to us I noticed that several of them were men I had seen in the Temple. I could remember them primarily by their costumes and by the various ways they styled their beards.

They began talking to those of our group who were standing in front of us, and suddenly an argument broke out. Yeshu'a made ready to push through to talk with the new arrivals, when suddenly Julian appeared from their ranks. He shoved forward through to us and greeted Yeshu'a with a formal hug rather like the one Frenchmen give. Everyone fell back away from the three of us who stood in a circle of light. Julian spoke to Yeshu'a in Aramaic, but I could understand it. It was a simple greeting. Yeshu'a spoke to Julian, telling him that all was well with us, and asked why Julian had brought all those men with him.

Then, almost quicker than I can express it, two or three of the newcomers stepped forward, shoved Julian aside and seized Yeshu'a by both arms and began to pull him toward their group. It took me totally by surprise, and I got ready to step forward when unexpectedly I felt someone pulling at my clothes on my left side. I turned just in time to see the disciple John draw my sword out of its sheath with his left hand, transfer it to his right, and swing it up and then down against the side of the head of one of the men holding Yeshu'a.

I think he meant to hit the man with the flat side of the blade, but instead it simply sliced off the fellow's ear. It would have killed him had it not been stopped by the top of his leather cuirass. The wound was white as a sheet for an instant, then blood leaped from it in many places. The man began to hop about and scream, bleeding everywhere. The other man let go of Yeshu'a, too, as John raised his arm to strike him.

Yeshu'a stayed the second blow by laying his hand upon John's arm and saying something to him. John lowered the blade but kept it pointed at the other men. I had my hand on the hilt of my dagger, but Yeshu'a touched me, too, and said, "Peace!"

Another man in the new group—one of those from the temple—stepped forward and said something to Yeshu'a in a demanding voice. He was arresting him.

By this time, Julian had pushed forward and started talking, saying, "But this is not the man!" Everybody ignored him. He was very agitated, and finally turned to me and asked where Judas was. I told him that I didn't know or care and asked him what was going on.

"These men are here to get the Zealots and to escort them from the city," he said. "John thought they were trying to take all of you and now they're talking about taking him in. You and your damned sword..."

The scales fell from my eyes.

"Look again, Julian!" I said to him. "Look what you've done!"

The men who had come with him were taking Yeshu'a and John away. Julian stared dumbly as a man came up to me and started talking to me in Hebrew in a bossy, demanding manner. I ignored him. I was trying to decide whether or not to try to fight to free Yeshu'a despite his telling me not to.

Julian pushed the jabbering man aside and grabbed me by both shoulders. We were face to face in the torchlight. I could plainly see his eyes dilating with growing, obvious madness as he tried to stammer out some words of explanation or apology, but they only came out like a jumble of rocks from an overturned wheelbarrow: English, Greek, and Hebrew rattling against one another. He started shaking his head and frothing at the mouth and I thought he was going to have a stroke. Finally, his hands lost their grip and fell to his sides.

In a final burst of clarity, I saw it all and so did he. I took his violently trembling hands in mine and looked him in his demented eyes.

"Julian," I said, "it would have been better for you had you never been born!"

Perhaps I shouldn't have said it, but it just came out. He looked at me and shook his head sideways in negation and then vertically in affirmation, and said that he was just trying to save things, to change things.

"It is written, Julian," I said. Then I thought about everything else that was written. It became clear what I should do.

"Now before you fulfill your destiny, Julian, tell me the name of the man in Cesarea who I must see," I told him.

He blinked his eyes with incomprehension. Then he understood me.

"He is in Joppa," he said with sudden, similar clarity of mind. "His name is Simon of Bethany in the House of An-Ra— the big one by the quay. Here, take this ring:" he added, removing a silver signet ring from his left hand, "it will give you complete authority."

And so, staggering a little, he parted from me for the last time, that poor man. I shall leave it for you to decide whether he was a simple victim of fate or whether he was yet another victim of that latter-day Pandora whose curiosity once took her down to Brighton.

When I last saw him, the insanity had taken hold again, and he was yelling in English, saying "*No! Wait! You don't understand!*" as he tried to run off and push his way through the confusing crowd that had closed in behind Yeshu'a and John when they were lead off toward the city. I watched as two men grabbed him and heard him shout and scream after the departing group and struggle against those who held him.

Then two men grabbed me by the arms and I was hauled off, too, but in a different direction. The raving Julian was simply thrust aside into the darkness.

I did not struggle. The men held me in such a way that rendered me incapable of getting to my dagger even if I had wanted to. One of them had a big club, and I had no doubt that he would use it on me if I gave them any trouble. Figuring that escape was impossible and captivity inevitable, and afraid but resigned, I was suddenly tired to the point of exhaustion.

Neither of my captors would talk to me, ostensibly because they did not have any Latin or Greek, and so I had no idea of what charges, if any, were against me. None the less, I stumbled along with them willingly enough until we came to a building that looked like a blockhouse. It proved to be a place used to house women—female slaves or prostitutes, I supposed—and I was turned over to two tough-looking Jewish women who frisked me in the presence of my captors and took away my dagger, empty scabbard, and coin purse. Fortunately enough, I was allowed to keep my belt, for they did not realize that it held in it a secret coin compartment. The purses' contents were counted out on the table and I was given a receipt for the money written on a small piece of leather that went around my wrist.

Then they took me up several flights of narrow stairs and put me in a small, clean little room with a tiny window, straw mattress, some blankets, a pitcher of water and a slop jar. It was obviously their nicest cell, and they treated me with a lot of deference, for they bowed to me as they left the room, closing and bolting the heavy oaken door behind them. The bed looked great. I went straight to sleep.

****

XXXV

Good Friday

When I awoke it was about 7 a.m. Sunlight poured through the window, and I could hear a bird singing nearby. For just a moment I felt very refreshed and happy—until I realized where I was and remembered all that had transpired the night before. It all seemed like a dream within the general hallucination of life.

On a table by the door were a pitcher, basin, towel, and some food and fresh water. Since I had long before learned to make the best of even bad situations, I ate all of the food and bathed myself as thoroughly as I could.

Pulling the table over to the window, I got up and looked out past its single cross of two iron bars, and found myself looking over the rooftops of most of the nearby houses. Here and there were women working at looms as their children played nearby. In a small courtyard across the alley a teenager nursed her baby. On the surface, all seemed right with the world, and I felt a sudden pang of regret that I had never nursed a child of my own.

I looked about the cell and tested the bars just to make sure that there was no way for me to escape. Clean and fed, I laid down on the cot and thought about babies and families, about the abortion I had my second year in college and how my boyfriend had pretended that he bore no responsibility and how he refused, finally, to take my calls.

Then I remembered how it was when you and I lived together and our life was made sweet by the feeling that perhaps someday we might get married and have children. I thought of my two miscarriages with tears and a heavy heart, recalling how much my Roman husband wanted me to bear him children, and how we might have lived out our lives happily on his family estate, surrounded by our family as we grew old. I stared at the ceiling.

My reveries were cut short by the loud sound of someone drawing the door's bolt. I got up and assumed my most commanding posture.

A woman—but not one of those from the night before—came in and without a word, made a bowing gesture indicating that I should precede her from the room and down the stairs. Chin high, and towering over her, I gathered up my half-top and cloak and went out.

She directed me not into the bare little room of the previous evening but rather into a spacious, carpeted room where two Roman soldiers—a Centurion and a non-com, were waiting for me. It was with the greatest relief that I realized that the later was none other than my friend, Apius Strabo. I was so happy to see him I could have kissed him again, but since he was cold and formal and acted as if he didn't know me, I said nothing to him.

The Centurion—a man perhaps ten years older than I—spoke to the woman jailer in Latin, directing her to bring out all of my things. She complied promptly and tried to take the little receipt from my hand, but I held on to it. I took the purse from her and counted out the money on a table. It was two gold coins shy. Not bothering with excuses, she handed them over to us. I handed her the bracelet.

The Centurion signed another receipt, put my weapons and purse into a bag that he handed to Apius, and led me out into the bright, sunlit street. We walked quickly away.

As soon as we rounded the corner, Apius and the Centurion became friendly and talkative, but none of us were happy. They had obviously taken a big chance to help me. I quickly learned that as soon as Apius had come on duty that morning and found out that I had been arrested the night before, he went to his Centurion, Lucius, and devised a plan to get me out of the city. Lucius—obviously a brave and resourceful man—had readily agreed to try to help me. He did it because he had heard that I was Yeshu'a's "woman." During the previous year, when he had been stationed in Capernum, Yeshu'a had saved the life of a servant whom he dearly loved.

"I would do anything for that man," he said in a tone that was at first serious, "and at any rate the risk is not great," he added in a happy voice. "We can always make up some story about how we got our orders mixed up and you were able to escape since—as everyone knows—you are a sorceress. Were I five years younger, you could certainly bewitch me like you have Apius here."

I touched his rough cheek with the back of my fingers and smiled at him with as warm a smile as I could manage. "I'm sure I could try, Lucius," I said. He grinned and looked those five years younger.

I asked if either of them had heard about Julian.

"Dead," they told me with long faces. "Suicide." It certainly came as no surprise to me. I told them that it had been written.

I asked about Yeshu'a.

"He has already been judged and condemned," they told me. "He has been before Pilate, and the sentence that the Jews imposed has been confirmed."

"That, too, was written."

What a horrible thing it is to hear that someone you love is to be executed, however much you might have anticipated the sentence! It was horrible, but I was calm about it. I asked them to take me straight to Pilate. Oddly enough, they agreed to go, and within minutes we were at the Procurator's palace demanding entrance. Things being reasonably informal, we were admitted almost at once. I wished that I was dressed in one of my old Roman outfits so as to appear more competent and powerful, but it couldn't be helped. As it was, I tried to wear the cloak in a way that made me look more imposing. I must have been succeeding, for by the time we entered the audience chamber, Apius and Lucius seemed to be acting not as my guards but as my escort.

The chamber was a spacious hall with a single seat or throne behind a long, solid table at one end of the hall. Behind it hung a floor-to-ceiling purple curtain. There were five or six other men standing about in the room, but I took no notice of them. To do so might have inferred that they were my political and social equals.

The provincial governor, Pilate, was seated and did not rise to greet me. The beautiful, gilded writing table was piled high with papers, wax tablets and scrolls.

About 40 years old, thin, balding, and dressed in a toga, the governor looked at me with the heavy-lidded eyes of a man who has seen too much of the world to be impressed by anything in it, even a beautiful woman. He examined me with a cold, calculating look and did not even offer me a chair. He pushed aside some papers and leaned forward so that his forearms rested on the table's edge. He touched his fingertips together and looked at me as if I was of almost no consequence.

"You're the young woman who wants to see me, are you?" he asked in Latin, his voice surprisingly resonant and powerful. "Who are you?"

"Called by some of the Romans *Venus Atlanticus*, I am the messenger of Pallas Athene who wants to warn you, Pontius Pilate," I responded, "that if you don't countermand your approval of the execution of the prophet, Yeshu'a, your name will be infamous throughout the ages."

"A true Roman prefers infamy to obscurity, young lady," he said in a way that told me he trusted no one.

"What is this man Yeshu'a to you?" he asked. "Your lover?"

Normally I would have blushed at such a question, but having anticipated it, I was ready with an answer.

"This man, Honorable Procurator, speaks the wisdom of the gods, which all men know in their hearts. And yours will be the name that people will remember when they think of how the man they will call the Lamb of God was slain."

"I found him to be a wise man," he said, as he stifled a yawn, "but not wise enough to get out of this benighted province and away from these blood-thirsty Jews. But you say that he will be called the Lamb of God. Tell me, are not lambs meant to be slaughtered?"

"Not all of them. What kind of a shepherd would kill all of his lambs, with never a one kept..."

"For breeding, young lady?" he finished.

"Now look here," he continued, "I really haven't the time to talk to you all day. Look at all this work I have to do, and more coming in all the time!

"Then you come in here and prophesy the condemnation of my name.

"So what? A man can be honorable all his life—and capable, brave, and even brilliant. He may be revered of men and beloved by wife and family and nation.

"Then let one misfortune befall him or one bad decision be made or one falsehood be told and the glimmer of fame is lost and all abandon him and revile his name."

I could see his point. He lifted a golden goblet and a

servant filled it with cold water. He lifted an eye, proud of his almost oriental power.

"I have responsibilities here. My wife came in and told me that in her dreams I was not to condemn that fellow, but the Jews will have their blood and they surely wanted his. It was the first hour of the morning and yet just outside below the balcony, there was a mob of them waiting and yelling. As I am entitled to do on their religious holidays, I gave them a choice as to which one to free—your man or a common criminal. And you know what they said, those believers in their One God? They wanted me to let the criminal go! So be it! That's the way these Jews are. They would rather have murderers among them than blasphemers. It is not the Roman way to interfere in these local concerns. I tell you the matter is done. I have publicly washed my hands of it."

There was no point in arguing with him.

"I knew that you would not change your mind," I said to him.

"Oh? How did you know?" he asked, skeptically.

"Because it is written."

"Where is it written?"

"In the books of my people since long before my birth."

He looked amused and, of course, he did not believe me. "Then why did you even try to talk to me."

"All the books could have been wrong about you, and I owed it to him and to you to make that effort."

"Well, apparently those books were not wrong," he said, with a dismissive wave of this hand. "But there is yet another matter with which I must deal—namely, you. What is to be done with you?"

One of the men in the room stepped forward and I recognized him immediately as the one who had been in the tavern with Propea. He was as ugly as a bulldog.

In formal terms the man Silvanius claimed that I was a witch, a murderess, a traitor, and something else that involved the disappearance of Propea, I believe. He claimed the right to arrest me and take me back to Rome in chains. It was obvious to me that I would never make it to Rome alive, but at that point—fit, tanned, and rested—I was only a little bit afraid, even though he was a brutal-looking son of a bitch.

The centurion and Apius stayed beside me, but I could feel them shrinking back from this new man's authority. It was obvious that he was some sort of member of the emperor's secret police, against which neither of them could hope to prevail. It was obvious, too, that they were beginning to regret helping me to escape from the Jewish prison and bringing me before Pilate.

I looked at my accuser and the procurator. *Why argue with them?*, I thought. Obviously a man who liked to shift responsibility to others in order to have a free hand elsewhere, Pilate was going to hand me over to Silvanius no matter what I said. I would have gone willingly enough without further ado, but felt that I owed it to Apius and the centurion to set the record straight.

There was no point in challenging Silvanius' authority or jurisdiction. Instead, with an expansive gesture that embraced all the men in the room and particularly my two supporters, I spoke, saying that although I knew it would avail me naught to say so, that I was innocent of all charges. I told them that I was "the daughter of my country" and that it was a very powerful nation. I claimed diplomatic immunity. If harm befell me, I told them, their country would be laid waste by great ships of ours that would rain fire from the skies—fire, I told them, that would make the Greek Fire that I had created seem like candles by comparison. I didn't tell them that it would be another 1900 years before that would happen, and that my father would someday fly a bomber over Foggia and other targets along the Italian boot!

Therefore, I told them, since the destiny of nations was involved, I demanded the right to be judged only by Tiberias himself, and not be imprisoned or murdered by some henchman working under orders from "those who only think they rule Rome"—an obvious reference to the temporary nature of Sejanus' *de facto* dictatorship.

That gave them pause.

Then I defended my husband's honor in the face of their countrymen's perfidy in trying to poison me. I spoke of his bravery in taking me across Germany. That went well with the soldiers in the room and with my two-man escort, for honor was the virtue they placed above all others.

"And then, all other dishonor by my faceless tormentors having failed," I continued, for I was in fine form, "someone

from Rome sent the once-famous, now dead Cassius Chaerea—
famous son of a more famous father—and a whole ship to
capture me." I watched them blanche, for they had known the
man, and they knew that the ship was missing. "The gods were
so angry with them that Neptune caused the sea to swallow up
that whole ship so that not a man of them survived—not one
soldier, or cook, or slave."

"Now do with me as you will, but do not say that I have
not warned you both. And through you all, I have warned your
country!" I concluded. At that point I was no longer afraid. Had
I not surmounted those other difficulties? Even if my luck had
run out, had God not spoken to me in the Garden the night
before?

"You will go with Silvanius Prato," Pilate said to me
after a deferential pause to make sure that I had finished talking.
Then he directed his attention to Apius and the centurion,
Lucius.

"And you two men will return to your barracks and
remain there under house arrest for one week," he said to them.

"And you will be damned if you do not change your
mind about that innocent man, Pontius Pilate," I said rather
gently.

My men stiffly saluted the Procurator and looked at me
for some word.

I saluted them in the casual, don't-give-a-damn way that
soldiers on the Rhine saluted. "You men are dismissed," I said,
"And don't worry about me—I'll put in a good word for you at
headquarters."

I turned to Silvanius and walked out with him and two
other men who went as escorts. None of them said anything to
me or to one another, and I realized with a certain thrill of
perverse pleasure that they were afraid of me.

Within an hour, I had been strip-searched by two women
who relieved me once again of my purse as well as of my
money-belt. I was led before an armorer who put some light leg
and wrist chains on me. They were unbreakable, but being
designed for women, they had lambs' wool covers to prevent
chafing and cutting—which is to say, damage to the property—
and unlike the shackles I had seen on men in many places, they

were not riveted together but actually had locks. The leg chain was about a cubit long and made running impossible.

Then I was put into another rather clean tower cell in the Antonia Fortress. They removed my wrist chains and left me alone. I looked about the cell, but found nothing hopeful.

From the room's iron-barred little window, I could look out toward the north, where I could see a barren, rocky hill, atop which I could plainly see that three men were being crucified—just like it was written. I had no doubts who was the one in the center. A crowd of people, looking like ants in the distance, seemed to cover the hillside. It was early afternoon, and the sun was shining brightly.

I watched for a few minutes, but what could I do? I did what I had learned to do in times of crisis: I prayed, I ate, and I slept.

That afternoon I dreamt I was in the Short once again, flying high above the sea, and Mark was in the co-pilot's seat, talking to me in Latin. He was smoking a joint and saying something about getting to class on time. Then he opened the window and squeezed out, pausing to take one last hit before he handed it to me. I sat there dumbly as he let go and in my dream, I saw him falling toward the sea and then deploying a parachute. I yelled but nothing came out of my mouth.

Then I was riding a horse once again, plodding through a little dusty village like the one I had walked through—a village where all were dead and rotting at the roadside. I spurred the horse, and we ran up and over a hill where we came upon a roadblock of South Carolina State Patrolmen with squad cars and flashing lights. "What's that in your hand, Sweet Thing," one of them leered from behind his silver sunglasses. I looked down, and there in my hand I saw the burning joint that Mark had handed me. Smiling and glad of the excuse to abuse me, the trooper reached up to pull me down…

I awoke with a start, thinking it was almost night, for it was very dark in the room. I went to the window and looked out. The crosses were still there. A huge, black thunderstorm had come up and was getting ready to cut loose.

It is reported that when Christ died, an earthquake hit the city and other marvels happened. I don't think that there was an earthquake, but the first rip of lightning and thunder sounded like the very Crack of Doom. It shook the walls and reverberated around the city and down the ravines like an artillery barrage. I looked to the distant hill and saw that what was left of the crowd was dispersing quickly, for even in those days, the propensity of lightning to hit higher objects and hills was well known.

Lightning then came again and again, mostly high, cloud-to-cloud bolts, but occasionally a bolt would hit the ground. One hit the cross on the left of the three in the distance. It disappeared from view.

Then came a downpour so heavy that even buildings in the foreground were screened from view by the gray cascade of water.

After 20 minutes of rapidly slackening rain, the sky cleared in time for the glancing rays of the afternoon sun to bathe the distant hill with a final, beautiful light. By that light, I could see the body on the center cross being let down and carried away. The third and final sufferer remained behind as most of the small crowd drained away from the place of execution.

To look on that sad scene did not make me cry or even feel particularly bad. Because it was happening in the distance, I felt emotionally distant from it at least at one level, for in that tidy room looking out on a lovely cityscape and up into the cloud-filled, sunlit skies, I couldn't hear the laments of the women. I couldn't hear the moans of the men's sufferings, or smell their blood and see the filth when they soiled themselves.

No, what I saw reminded me of a great painting by Bruegel in which the announced theme is depicted only in some part of the background, totally overwhelmed and rendered insignificant by the mass of other actions and other values which appear on the rest of the canvas. From where I stood, it was all so beautifully sad!

At dark the guards brought me a rather sumptuous dinner—a meal, I suspected, that was being paid for either by my own money or by Apius and his Centurion friend. On the other hand, it did occur to me that it could have been some sort of last meal or even be one laced with poison. Since I was ravenous by that time and the wine was good, I made quick work of it and went to sleep once again.

The next morning Silvanius came for me dressed in a

military officer's uniform complete with a bronze lorica and a helmet that he carried under his arm. Even dressed like that, the 41-year-old Silvanius Prato looked like an assassin, not an officer.

Accompanying him was a tough-looking, 50-year old matron. While he watched, she made a final, thorough strip search of me to make sure that I had no concealed weapons or lock picks on me. I have said elsewhere that I could stand naked before a legion and not blush, but that is not true. Exposed to Silvanius' evil looks, and bent over with the irons back on my wrists and ankles and with my tunic thrown up over my head so that my bottom could be checked, I blushed hot with shame and humiliation. It took me down a notch, and I could tell that it worked him up one. If the matron hadn't been there I have no doubt but that he would have raped me on the spot if only to satisfy his lust for domination.

A man of few words, he took me down to the courtyard and put me aboard a four-horse riding chariot that we shared with his two heavily armed guards. We drove slowly through the city and out of the northern gate, for we were headed to Cesarea, a seaport on the coast some 60 miles away.

That sort of chariot was designed to make good time, but we traveled mostly at a walk. Silvanius forced himself to make polite conversation with me. We spoke in Greek since neither of the guards could understand it. I began to have some hope of escape, for I saw that he was giving me an opening. Men can be so weak when they want a particular woman.

I tried out different styles of relating to him until I finally found one that seemed most effective. That is to say, I found a conversational style that seemed most calculated to have him eating out of my hand before he put me on the boat to Rome or finally decided to kill me and have done with it.

I played the part of a high-born woman with a deep-seated desire for rugged men of action. That wasn't too difficult a roll for me to play. The problem was that he was not a stupid man, and although it was obvious that he was not too familiar with the ways of wealthy, foreign women, he distrusted me thoroughly. Trying to entice him to remove the chains seemed entirely out of the question. That would have raised the suspicions of even the most obtuse man, and certainly no veteran policeman would have fallen for such a trick.

As we talked I considered many options—including, naturally, the one of going to bed with him and killing him in his sleep. I was hoping I wouldn't have to do anything so desperate. Curiously, I never even considered suicide.

By nightfall we had only gotten some 20 miles from Jerusalem. At that rate, it would take us some three days to get to Cesarea, and so I thought I'd have time to work something out. Silvanius had other ideas.

We stopped at a rather nice tavern north of the town of Bethel. Giving them some wine money, he sent the two guards off to sleep in the stables and sat me down to what he must have thought was a terrifically romantic dinner.

I was weary by that time, for the enormity of what had happened began to seem real to me. Just two days before, I had bathed at the villa with Yeshu'a, had enjoyed the Passover feast with him, and had gone with him to the garden. I had felt love and kindness and, yes: the presence of God. Now, just two days later, he was dead and Julian was dead. I was sitting with a stinking man—hardly better than a pig—who wanted to have sex with me. He was buying me a meal with my own money while I wore padded chains and pretended to like him so that, if necessary, I could catch him off guard and kill him. I was so tired I began to cry. After all, I was just a girl from South Carolina, I thought as I surrendered to a wave of self-pity. How much could I take? I couldn't help myself.

Silvanius watched and waited, embarrassed as the other diners grew quiet and surreptitiously watched us. He was looking for artifice on my part. He found none.

As if my tears were a magical solvent, something in my crying infiltrated his hard heart and touched him. He reached forward and placed his hairy hand on mine in a gesture that was actually human. Looking at the table, I cried some more. When I finally finished, his hand was still on mine and I looked up at his face and for the first time felt some normal, human sympathy for him. He seemed to understand my pain, and I saw that even in him there was some hope of redemption. But Oh, he was ugly!

Slowly I took away my hand and managed a weak smile. "Sorry," I told him, "but I have been through a lot."

He nodded and gulped. Brute that he was, he nevertheless recognized sincerity when he heard it. When the main course came I had surprisingly little appetite—at least at first.

Reverting to his nature, Sylvanius dug right in, talked with his mouth filled with food, and tried to cheer me up with a forced kind of jocularity that he thought might get me willingly into his bed. I knew that was where I was probably going to end up anyway, and the only real question was whether I was going to be raped or was going to pretend to go along with him long enough to make my move. This was not a man who would get too drunk nor be talked out of having what he wanted. I was getting nauseous just thinking about it.

Then I saw that a new waiter had appeared in the half-lit room. It was Judas the Zealot! He had shaved off his heavy, black beard and was wearing a foreign-looking garment that marked him as a gentile.

I had never in my life been so glad to see a person before. Obviously, he had followed us out of the city and was now prepared to do whatever it might take to get me free, including murder the Roman right then and there.

Standing behind Silvanius and swiping a finger across his throat, he indicated that he could slice his throat right then, but I nodded him off, indicating the shackles and rolling my eyes to show that I didn't know where the key was.

Then he held up a small vial and I shook my head in agreement and watched as he deftly poured all of it into two empty goblets. I assumed that it was either the White Drink or an opiate, and so I winked my assent.

I called him over to the table with a gesture. "Do you have any Latin?" I asked. He indicated that he spoke some, and I continued, looking at Silvanius as if I were resigning myself to spending the night with him. "Bring us some special brew that will cheer our hearts and warm our blood. The night is young."

Silvanius smiled. He had won—or so he thought.

Telling us he had just the thing—something brewed with an herb from the Black Sea that would, he said, "make you both wish for nothing but one another for half the night, then sleep like babes 'til dawn." He said it with such a convincing wink and sneer that I wondered how so fine an actor could have given two or three years of his life to wandering around Palestine with a preacher. He went back to the kitchen and returned with a flask of wine that he poured into the cups.

Silvanius sniffed the cup and sipped it. Then he put it down and took up the other and did the same. Convinced that both were of the same stuff and of equal potency, he then—just to be doubly safe—told Judas to drink of it, on the grounds that he was a Roman officer and charged with the duty of safeguarding the prisoner.

"With pleasure," Judas said lifting one cup after another and drinking from each of them. "Only beware: You wouldn't want to miss out on your own pleasure would you? Sir, if you let me and this beautiful lady drink all of this, I'll safeguard her all night for you and make quite sure she doesn't get any sleep."

With the leering wink of a co-conspirator, Silvanius assured him he could "safeguard" me himself. Then, raising his cup in a very crude army toast, he bade me drink. One upping him with an even cruder toast, I drank mine down and watched as he followed suit. It was the White Drink.

My good spirits and my appetite returned together, and I jockeyed with Silvanius and even started to like him a bit—particularly as I felt his power over me slipping away. At first I ate like the wench in that famous scene from the movie, *Tom Jones*, and made sure that from time to time Silvanius could see broad expanses of the tops my breasts. I faked a cramp in my leg so that he could watch them as I rubbed myself, and so forth. It was ludicrous, but I kept it up for about 30 minutes until the other diners had all cleared out. Silvanius was still ostensibly engaged in the courtship ritual, but the reality of it was slipping away fast, and finally everything wound down to a halt.

Then I pushed aside the plates and stuff and took his hands and looked into his eyes.

"Silvanius," I told him, "we are not going to be sleeping together tonight."

"Oh, yes, we are," he protested unconvincingly. I could see that his resolve was gone. "I can take you whenever I want to."

"That may be true," I said, "but tonight you don't want to." He looked blankly at me. He knew that was true.

"Sorceress! Witch! What have you done?" he asked not with anger but with amazement.

"I have saved your life, Silvanius Prato," I told him, which amazed him even more. "I have helped you to see truth even as the Jewish prophet they executed yesterday helped people see truth."

"He was a blasphemer—or so I heard. You are my prisoner," he added rather confusedly.

"No," I told him, "You are your own prisoner. I have the key—or one of the keys—to your shackles, and you drank that key. Do you wish to be free?"

"I wish to bed you. I know that," he said, looking at me no longer with command but with something that was almost akin to begging.

"Silvanius, listen!" I said to him in all earnestness, taking his hands more closely in mine. "I don't want you to say anything more. I want you to listen. Listen to what the gods say to you. Then you will know that what I say is true.

"The man who you used to be was planning on bedding me tonight and killing me later. The new man that you are could not do such a thing. In fact, all of the evil is draining away from you. The lightness you feel is from your shackles falling away to the bottom of the sea."

He closed his eyes and almost fell into a trance. I looked up and saw that Judas, who had an aura around his head, was sitting behind him in the dark, patiently waiting.

After several long minutes, Silvanius opened his eyes and looked into mine. "You are right, of course," he said. "What must I do?"

I told him what Yeshu'a had said: "Love God with all your heart and with all your soul and with all your mind. Do unto others as you would have them do unto you. Love your neighbor as you love yourself."

Without my asking him to, he took two keys out of a secret pouch and unlocked the shackles from my wrists. Then he got down on his knees and with my hands resting on his greasy hair, he unlocked the leg irons. Then he completely prostrated himself and kissed my feet.

When he got up again to his knees, he was crying from emotion.

He looked at me and seemed almost reluctant to let me go. "But you are so beautiful! I thought that, for once in my life..."

"I could never have given you what you wanted," I said gently, "but I have started to give you what you need. Your road will not be an easy one, but you are a strong man. And with God's help, you can be a beautiful one," I concluded, my hands still upon his head. "Now rise up and greet your new brother and sister."

It was only then that he realized Judas was still in the room and had been sitting behind him. In an instant he could see what had happened and how rather than committing violence upon him we had committed love. He stood before me and tears came to his eyes. To his astonishment I rose up, hugged him, and kissed him lightly upon the cheeks. He took my kisses as I meant them—as a blessing. He knew straightaway that he would treasure those kisses for the rest of his life, not because it was me who gave them, but because they were given in love, acceptance, and forgiveness.

Then he turned to Judas who, to his credit, was able to overcome in that instant all his chauvinistic aversion to foreigners and to step forward and embrace him, saying "Brother, I give you the love of Yeshu'a."

"He who was slain?"

"He who was slain."

We sat down. The White Drink was not terribly strong, but it was strong enough to give us clarity of thought and vision.

"I was there when he died, you know," Silvanius told us after a few minutes of silence. "It was rather like....part of my job." He looked down at his hands and then as if seeing the blood upon them, he put them in his lap out of sight and asked, "What will become of me?"

I smiled, for with the sight that was given to us the answer was easy enough to see. "You will," I said, "be our brother and you will go forth with us happy that you have a family. You will help us help other people to find their way to the same light you now enjoy."

Within the hour the three of us were in the chariot and headed back to Jerusalem, leaving the two drunken guards soundly sleeping in the stables.

****

XXXVI

Sunday Morning

Just before dawn we arrived at the Hill of Tombs. According to Judas, it was there in the tomb of one of his rich patrons that Yeshu'a's family had put his body.

The cemetery covered an area of ten or twelve acres, and although most of the graves were dug from the stony soil, there were also a number of above-ground, stone boxes as well as niches or even small caves hewn into outcroppings of rock. It was not a tidy place. Rank weeds grew unsuppressed wherever some spot of soil to support them could be found. Here and there a tree fought its way up amid the rocks or directly atop an old grave.

Cemeteries have always given me the creeps. As a child, my friends and I had a panoply of superstitions, tales, and practices concerning them that would have done justice to Tom Sawyer and Uncle Remus. The black kids I played with in the low country were even worse and knew chants and Geechee incantations to ward off evil spirits. Even when I was in college, I would go blocks out of my way to avoid passing graveyards at night.

Particularly since I had buried my husband with my own hands, I had assiduously avoided burial grounds. Almost invariably they reminded me that he was lying in the cold earth. I could remember the smell of the dirt, the tight resistance of the rocks, and the way the cold, heavy body didn't quite fit into the hole I had dug. I may have been exhausted and upset that day, but I remember it as if it were just last week.

Yet even in the face of all that, we went there.

If you ask why we did it, I can only ask this in reply: if you were in that area on that day, where would you have been?

It would have been an easy thing never to return to that city. I could have gone on to Caesarea with Silvanius and Judas as my loyal bodyguards. On the other hand, I had to go to Joppa first in order to get the radio, and the main road thither was back down the road to Jerusalem.

We were aware of the dangers of going back. After all, I had been arrested there twice and had managed to get free both times. How could my luck hold out?

For that matter, there were dangers to the men, too, but when I told them why I thought we should go back, they readily agreed to accompany me. I told them about the prophecy that Yeshu'a would rise from the dead. They were astonished, but as both of them thought me semi-divine or at least divinely inspired, neither of them questioned me about the origins of such a prophecy.

It was hard to say which man had changed more. From an undercover agent and a hired assassin, under the influence of the White Drink and our quick tutelage, the ugly Silvanius had become a friend and a protector. Like a bulldog who had quit snarling at us long enough to be petted, he didn't even look so bad anymore. It is amazing to see the power of love—and the White Drink—at work.

In a way, Judas had changed even more. When Yeshu'a was alive, he was the second-in-command, the probable successor, and the one so handsome that men gave him their automatic respect and women gave him their unrestricted affection. As the "first among equals" he had been arrogant and proud, and although a loyal follower of Yeshu'a after his own fashion, he had his own personal agenda. It was easy to imagine Judas as king of a revitalized Israel—a king who had taken up the scepter from Yeshu'a, the fallen leader.

He seemed eager to atone for his presumptuousness. I have little doubt that had things been slightly different, and but for the intervention of the White Drink, the old Judas would have almost welcomed the death of the seemingly indecisive and now-martyred prophet. It would have cleared the way for him to assume leadership not only of the disciples and their allies but also of his friends and supporters among the Pharisees and scribes—of whom there were many—for he was less offensive and less threatening to them than Yeshu'a had been. Moreover, since Judas had strong family ties in Judea (and thus his name, "Judah") and could speak and read both Greek and Latin, they might have seen him as an acceptable successor to the Herodian dynasty. Unlike Herod, he would have been a true religious Jew, a Zealot, a man of action and military capacity, as well as a person with strong ties to the common man.

But he had changed. From a talker, he had become a listener. From one who made plans and outside contacts and who considered himself better than practically everyone he met, he had become humble, quiet, and focused not on that which would help him but upon that which would help others. Fortunately for me, I was the one who he had decided to help first. He had to walk and run the 20 miles out to Bethel to overtake us. Then he had to concoct and carry out his plan.

So it was that we three drove back in the dark to the Hill of Tombs. Not knowing what or who we might find lurking about, we stopped the chariot a quarter mile from its entrance. Judas stayed with the horses and walked them around to let them cool down and yet stay ready for precipitate flight if that became necessary.

From him we had learned that we might encounter two or three guards posted near the tomb as a precaution ordered by the Sanhedrin to assure that there would be no tampering with the grave. So informed, Silvanius and I were able to proceed with some confidence. I had planned for us to hide nearby and see what might happen, but as we passed the gates of the inner cemetary in the faint pre-dawn light and saw up ahead of us the embers of the fire that the guards had made, we decided to go forward. There were only two of them and both were asleep— probably because they were drunk. Had they been more alert, they might have awakened to the startling sight of a grim and terrible Roman officer accompanied by a giant woman. They might have thought their own days were numbered. As it was, though, they snored on amid the bits of camp litter. I could smell wine, sweat, and burnt beans.

Without asking me what he should do, Silvanius went straight to the mouth of the small cave and began to try to move the big rock that blocked it. I stepped forward and whispered to him and asked him what he was doing.

"You want to make sure it's his body in there, don't you?" he said. I tried to shush him.

"Don't worry about those two," he said with a disdainful

nod. "They're going to be out for a long time yet, and even if they do wake up, I'll chew their asses out for sleeping on duty."

"What if they don't speak Latin?" I whispered, wishing he'd pipe down.

"My Lady," he said in a quieter voice, "when I chew men out, it don't matter what language them and me speak: They'll understand!"

I had to agree with him. After all, I don't speak bulldog, chow, or rotwieller.

He couldn't move the stone by himself. I asked again if we ought not leave it alone. I was really getting the creeps.

"I'll do whatever you say, M'Lady, but if you don't see his body in there, you may never know the truth of things."

I was really getting cold feet about all of it, and as I have said, I hated seeing corpses. At funerals here in your world, I never looked into the caskets. Dissecting the bodies of people I didn't know in front of the physicians in Rome had been different. That had been more like cutting up deer.

I asked if he thought Yeshu'a was dead.

"Yes, Ma'am," he said, as he studied the rock. "He was dead all right. Like I say, I was there."

"Look," he continued, looking up into my face in the increasing light, "We've come this far. Let's satisfy ourselves that there's a body in there and that it's his body. If you want, I'll tote it off for you so that these two guys'll catch hell for it— kinda like a joke, y'know. It's up to you."

He may have been a new, transformed man, but he was still a practical and cynical soldier with a soldier's macabre sense of humor.

"What the hell!" I said with a grin to mask my queasiness. "Let's do it, Comrade!"

I picked up the two stout spears that were laying on the ground and with them as levers, we soon moved the rock aside. A musty and moldy odor—but not a putrid one—emanated from the cavity. "Eva Weathers:" I thought, "grave robber."

The pre-dawn light was sufficient for us to see into the cave—a small affair, no more than 12 feet deep with four shelves for the dead cut into either side. Two were occupied by wrapped corpses, but the one on the upper left had obviously been there a long time, for it was dirty and sunken in.

On the right, however, lay a fresh occupant carefully wrapped in a linen sheet. I looked back at Silvanius and nodded as if to say, "Well, there he is. We've seen what we came to see. Let's leave!"

He looked at me, and prodded me in the direction of the corpse.

I stepped over to it—or rather slouched over to it because the ceiling was only five and half feet high—and looked it over quickly. Going to my knees I studied the wrappings. My stomach turned when I saw what were obviously small bloodstains that had emanated from within. I felt that something about it was odd—the wrong size, I thought. At least it wasn't going to be a big mess like some of the other bodies I had dealt with. I thought of my husband and suddenly felt my curiosity give way to a wave of grief. I thought of Yeshu'a—not as an object or a story but as a friend and a living, breathing man— and the grief was heavier still. It was so sad, knowing him to be so innocent and yet to be dead—he who had been in the prime of his life, who had swam in the pool with me and who had held me and talked with me just three days before.

The truth be told, I had known my husband so much longer and through so many more trials and pleasures that even at that moment I missed him more than I missed Yeshu'a. I reflected, though, upon the thought that he had been a soldier, and during a life of service had killed many a man in combat and had enforced the Roman rule wherever he was told to. He had many regrets about those years, he said, and few about the months he spent with me. When his hour came, he died of wounds suffered in battle and in the arms of the woman who loved him—the fate, he said, that satisfied him.

But the enigmatic man who had animated the corpse before me—if in fact it was Yeshu'a's corpse—had suffered alone among enemies who reviled and beat him and staked him to a cross. What had he done to deserve that? It was crass and pathetic, and as I began unwrapping the body, my eyes were filled with tears.

Silvanius kept watch while I worked quickly, starting at the horribly wounded feet. In a very short time I had off the outer wrapping and peeled back the shroud from the face. It was Yeshu'a. His face was bruised, cut up, and white. Instantly I turned away, wishing I had not looked, but it was too late. I knew that I could never forget how he looked at that moment and would have preferred those other views of him that had been in my mind's eye: views of his looking at me for the first time, of his triumphant smile when we played water polo, of his looking at me as a man looks at a woman. Now rather than those scenes, my paramount memory would be the brutal look of death. With my head against the side of the shelf, I wept.

"He lives!" Silvanius said loudly, startling me so badly that I leaped up quickly and banged my head against the rocks. It hurt like hell and I swore in English. Then I looked down.

Yeshu'a' eyes were open and he blinked, then smiled at me weakly.

"My angel," he said quite frankly in Greek, "I should have known it would be you!"

As I stood there hunched over him in the half-light with one hand up on the top of my head rubbing the spot I had hit, my mouth was hanging open in astonishment. Some would-be physician I was! I had thought he was dead.

"My Lord!" said Silvanius, dropping to his knees beside him and bowing.

"Who are you?" Yeshu'a asked weakly. "I have seen you before." He could barely move.

"You saw me from the cross."

"Ah, yes!" Yeshu'a said. "And in the tavern with that pretty girl."

Silvanius went out and brought back a skin of water which he held up so that Yeshu'a could drink deeply.

I told him I thought he was dead.

"I think I was," he said, "or maybe death is only a dream. I descended into Hell or the Underworld and saw many people there, and heard the calling and singing and wailing of many others. Then I came back out—up the long, dark pathway, led by an angel toward a bright light that was the face of God. And I was made to understand that it was not over. Then all was peace and quiet and some dull pain and restriction.

"Then I heard the shuffle of feet coming toward me, and felt the loving hands gently unwrapping me and lifting my shroud. I felt the chill air and heard the weeping of a woman.

"And I opened my eyes and saw an angel," he continued

feebly, looking at us, "and her assistant. I knew that I was back among the living." He closed his eyes.

"But you were dead!" said Silvanius, with a note of pleading in his voice, wanting an explanation. "I saw it! I was there."

"I remember you now," Yeshu'a replied to him with an outstretched hand that Silvanius took in his own great paws, "and you were dead, too, soldier of Rome. I saw it in your eyes, but now I see that you, too, live. Thanks be to God."

Silvanius began to weep. "It is true! It is true!" he said.

"Weep not, my friend," Yeshu'a said, "for now you are alive. Is that not a great miracle? You even travel with an angel and have become one yourself."

I cannot describe the confusing tumult of my emotions. It was almost as if it were all an hallucination that was complete with feelings, smells and words and even the sharp pain of the place where I had struck my head. I could feel the hair on the back of my neck beginning to rise eerily as if the body behind me was also coming to life or reaching out to grab me. As Yeshu'a quit talking and Silvanius composed himself, I knelt there rubbing the sore spot on my head, half-expecting to wake up somewhere else.

"With all due respect, M'Lady," Silvanius said after a minute or two, "if we want to keep in the land of the living, we'd better get out of here. The change of guards can't be too long off."

"So be it!" I said as I shook off the unreality of it all. "Do you think you can walk, My Dear One?" I asked Yeshu'a. He shook his head, *no*.

Silvanius lifted him gently, but as the position was so awkward, he needed my help to do it. Once outside the cave entrance, Silvanius was able to manage on his own, for he was very strong, and he started off down the path, carrying Yeshu'a in his arms. I looked about quickly, placed the spears back as I had found them and ducked back into the tomb. I folded up the shroud and took it with me, leaving the other windings laying loose upon the bench. I turned to go. The sun was only a few minutes away from overtopping a thin layer of clouds on the eastern horizon, and I prepared to hurry away lest the guards trap me.

At that moment someone moved into the cave entrance.

Screwing up my nerve and hiding my dagger in the folds of the shroud-cloth, I ducked down and went out.

It was the girl, Mary! I almost shouted with relief. She was so astonished that she didn't know what to do or even what to think.

Placing a finger to my lips, I took her hand and led her off down the path Silvanius had taken. After about 50 yards, she looked back and said something to me. Using what little Hebrew I could speak and smiling as much as I could, I told her, "He is not there. Come with me. He lives."

My words astonished her so much that she would have fainted had she not been such a strong-willed woman. She didn't believe me, but there was one thing that was as plain as the coming of day: she had loved Yeshu'a very deeply and had been coming there that morning so that she might be permitted to pour ointment on the wrapped body a final time. She turned and went away with me.

Farther down the trail we came upon another woman from the villa who had come with Mary but feared the guards. The three of us went off toward the chariot.

Right before we got to it, we came upon Yeshu'a. He was seated on a rock and leaning on another, wrapped in Silvanius' cloak. The others were nowhere to be seen.

The women fell to their knees in front of him and kissed his bandaged hands. He spoke to them briefly in a stronger voice than I would have thought he could manage, and then they arose to leave. After she stood up, Mary looked up into my eyes. Hers were filled with tears, but I could tell that they were tears of joy through which she was smiling. I held my arms open to her and she stepped forward to hug me, saying "Thank you," over and over, and I held her tightly to me, for I was deeply moved. She may have been jealous of me in the past, but it was obvious that she deeply appreciated everything I had done. As I held her head to me and ran my fingers in her hair, she hugged me and cried against my breast until I could feel the moisture penetrate my tunic. Then they left.

Silvanius and Judas came out of hiding and the four of us left and went to the tavern where I had been keeping my donkey all along. The keeper was already up and gave me a suite of three rooms that had been vacated that very morning. It must have looked to the inn keeper as if I had taken up with a Roman officer and that he and I wanted some serious privacy for which we were willing to pay generously. When he went to the kitchen for hot water and food, we carried Yeshu'a in and put him in one of the two bedrooms.

While Judas went out and fetched fresh cloth for bandages, Silvanius took care of the exhausted and irritated horses that had been in harness for about ten hours. He fed them and my donkey and made sure that the groom curried them all. Then, like a good soldier, he worked on the chariot and greased its wheels before returning to the rooms, eating and going to sleep.

I tended Yeshu'a' wounds and fed him. He was ravenously hungry, but as he was still very weak, we spoke little. He dropped off to sleep. Using some fresh, deliciously hot water, I bathed myself, lay down beside him in the bed, and was soon asleep, too.

*****

XXXVII

Hiding

We awoke in the late afternoon to Judas' gentle prodding and soft words. Silvanius' loud snoring in the other room drifted in through the door and had the comforting sound of a slowly idling tank—our tank.

My clothes were hanging all around the room to air out, and though I had on only a thin tunic, I felt very comfortable as I sat there with the two men. If only we had safety and a pot of strong coffee it would have been perfect. Big *ifs*.

We talked quietly with Judas as he wolfed down our leftovers from the morning. It felt so good just to be safe in a bed in a quiet room that I did not want to get up. As you know, I was never a regular smoker, but just then I wanted a cigarette—one of those rich, hand-rolled Dutch ones like you and I used to share late at night. For that matter, I thought about how good it would have been to have a record player and some classical music. Do you remember how we used to listen to Brahms when we took Sunday afternoon naps together?

But of course not everything was going well. For one thing we were all hiding out and the authorities might descend upon us at any moment. Also, of course, Yeshu'a had lost a lot of blood and, for all I knew, might soon die from his wounds or from infections. I could confirm that in addition to small cuts and bruises, he had at least one broken rib, a severe contusion on one of his shins, and a gash about half an inch deep and 15 inches long on his right side which, though it had clotted, still leaked a clear fluid. The worst of the wounds, however, consisted of ugly spike holes through the centers of both hands as well as through the centers of both feet, all of which I had washed out with boiled salt water that morning. That restarted some bleeding, but as I was there to staunch it, I felt it was worth the risk—particularly in that the feet are vulnerable to grotesque and complicated infections amid their various bones and cartilageous structures. I tried to flush out as much dirt and debris from those holes as I could. It must have been painful, but he never complained and only occasionally winced or groaned when I treated him. He was, after all, a Galilean.

About an hour before dark, Silvanius awoke and came in to join us, looking ugly and disheveled. I was worried that once the White Drink's effects had worn off completely he might revert to his former self and remember his former duties. I should not have worried. He greeted us so affably that I knew in an instant he was still the new Silvanius, and his loyalty was to us. All of us warmly greeted him and we all thanked him over and over for his help. He begged us to stop, dropping to his knee beside the bed and saying to the three of us, "No: it is you who have helped me, for not only have you all saved my life, you have brought me here to add my poor efforts to your service. Your God is my God," he added, "your friends mine, and your enemies mine."

"Alas," said Yeshu'a, putting his hand on the man's head and looking him in the eyes, "You'll just have to settle for having my friends. I have no enemies."

We were all astonished by such a remark coming from a

man who had just been beaten up and crucified. After a long pause, Judas said something to that effect.

"My dearest friend," he responded, "they knew not what they were doing and they were doing no more than they were supposed to do since the beginning of time. Perhaps they acted in the fulfillment of the scriptures wherein it is written."

"Then—if God wills—you will lead us at last?" Judas asked.

"If you mean with swords, then no. I told you: I don't have any enemies. Only those within ourselves need to be conquered and overthrown. Have I ever *led* you, Judas? I thought we were just friends who walked the same pathways," he concluded.

Judas seemed relieved, for in the space of a few days, he had given up on the ideas of national revolt against the Romans. After all, it had not been they who had demanded Yeshu'a's death.

Silvanius, always the practical planner, asked what we should do next, to which Yeshu'a replied that he had prayed over the matter and it was clear to him how we should proceed. Then we made our plans and decided what each of us was to do.

Even though he had been bled to the point of death—or beyond—Yeshu'a was nevertheless able to go downstairs to the tavern's main room that very night. We had reserved it that evening and as soon as we had, Judas went forth again and gathered all of Yeshu'a's followers who were still in the city. He got them to go to the inn in secret, each following his own route since by that time the city was abuzz with rumors and accusations that they had spirited the body away after drugging the guards. There was talk both of revolt and of the decapitation of revolt, and the streets were full of groups of men hastening about on various missions, the supposed urgency of which could be inferred from the looks on their faces. Men can be such funny creatures.

I went down the stairs at Yeshu'a' side, supporting part of his weight. He walked on his heels and could only breathe shallow breaths, and his face looked terrible from the beatings he had taken.

From the women the assembled followers had heard the

incredible news, but they had not believed what they had been told. Who would have? Of course they had heard all kinds of rumors around the city, but didn't know what to think of them, either. For his part, Judas had told them nothing save that they should assemble at the tavern two hours after dark, and so they did.

When they saw us coming down the stairs, though, all of them were shocked and amazed, and all but one of them fell to their knees. The one walked forward to where we stood at the bottom of the stairs. Yeshu'a held out his swathed hands to him. The man shook his head as if in disbelief. Yeshu'a reached over to his right side and lifted up the bandage so as to expose the spear cut, and the man stuck his finger roughly in it to see whether it was real or simply made up with wax and colorings. Yeshu'a flinched with pain as the man jerked back as if he had touched fire, then fell to his knees. Clasping his hands together, he begged his master for forgiveness that he should ever have doubted.

Then they all rose up and spoke to him, crowding around deferentially, many with tears in their eyes. Then all of us sat down on the benches, and in a gentle voice Yeshu's spoke with them for about a twenty minutes, and then he was worn out. Silvanius carried him back upstairs and I redressed his wounds.

Judas took charge of the group and enjoined its members to keep the matter secret lest the authorities get wind of what had happened. He gave specific instructions as to where they should go and when they might reassemble. But for the fact that all the lust for power was gone from him, he would have made a great officer in any army.

Aware of the dangers of our situation, I told Silvanius I wanted another sword, for I had vowed to myself never to be captured again. I had thought about it and knew, too, that I was willing to die in the defense of Yeshu'a if it became necessary to do so. What would it matter if I went down fighting? Anyway, my prospects of living out another year were none too bright. There would be more Cassiuses and other Silvaniuses.

Silvanius offered me his, but it was heavy and too long for concealment, and I declined it. Unlike me, he felt he no longer needed to be armed, but on the very next morning, he bought me a sword that was almost perfect. It was an expensive piece of work. The hilt and scabbard were of leather bound with golden wires and silver appointments. The blade guard was worked of polished brass and the blade was sleek. It wasn't very sharp, but I could soon fix that, and I thought of my old sword and what the young farmer had said to me about blood staining the blade. Well, I thought, this new one was the right size and weight. I vowed to myself to try to keep it clean. A master of many of the dark arts, Silvanius knew weapons.

At nightfall on that same day, Silvanius and I left by chariot for Joppa, which was only about 40 Roman miles away. Once again as we traveled I appeared to be his high-born prisoner, and we made great time. All of us—man, woman, and horses—were rested and wanted to cover some ground. We had things to do.

Silvanius was a good traveling companion and a skilled handler of horses—traits that I have discovered often go together. He respected the animals and they respected him.

He talked of his sorry childhood, of his years in the army and of many of the things that he had done in the service of the emperor. He explained the structure and practice of the department for which he had worked—one that was like a shadow government and, in some ways, resembled that of the tsarist Cheka and other secret police organizations. He had what was essentially a license to kill and told me with a mixture of shame and pride that he had worked on special assignments for the Empress Livia, the wife of Augustus. It all made my blood ran cold. I could just imagine this guy showing up with a warrant in one hand and a sword in the other.

I asked him what his duty had been toward me and who had ordered it. Disappointingly enough, he wasn't sure, but he had been given his instructions to find and dispose of me by an old woman through whom he had previously gotten such orders. For her proof, she bore a sealed instrument in proper form when she came to his ranch at Ortona in eastern Italy. Even though he had suspected at the time that someone had been exceeding his or her authority, he had gone on the mission anyway on the strength of the orders as well as the size of the retainer. As he told me quite forthrightly, he hadn't worried much about the validity of the orders to find me. As he had seen it, if mistakes were made and innocent people were hurt, what was the problem so long as he got his money?

At any rate, he had been told to find me and arrest me, then bring me to the island of Capri. On the other hand, the old woman had told him that if I died in transit, well, that couldn't be helped and might be for the best, anyway.

"You know," he said, over the noise of the horses and chariot as we hustled westward along the road, "the more I've thought about those orders, the more I think that the scamp, Germanicus' son, is somehow behind everything.

"That little hellion would piss in a dying man's wine just to see him make a face. I used to know his father on the Rhine during the good old days. We used to call the kid 'Little Boot' and we spoiled him rotten. Rotten"

That discussion led to others, and it soon came out that he had known our friend Marcus from the army days following the Teutoburg Forest disaster of 9 A.D. Like so many of the new men, Silvanius had held Marcus in high esteem for the valor that he and his companions had shown in fighting their way out of the great ambush. Years later he had been assigned to the office that investigated Marcus' embezzlement and his disappearance. When I assured him that Marcus the Fox was still alive when last I saw him, he seemed greatly pleased. Apparently, when it came to government funds, there was little moral opprobrium connected to embezzlement—just death or the galleys if one got caught.

We arrived in Joppa at dark and quickly found a place for the horses, ate a big meal and slept on piles of hay stored there in the stables.

As soon as we had some breakfast and tidied up the next morning, we walked around Joppa and out onto the quay. The sea felt like a huge magnet to us both, but its lure was easy to resist, for we had our duty and knew that a sea voyage might come soon enough if only we could persuade Yeshu'a to leave Palestine at last.

I should explain that at that point I was once again dressed in chains and a veil so that when Silvanius checked in with the port's police our outward appearances were still those of captor and captive. In case an investigation was undertaken, it would be thought at least initially that he still intended to take me to Rome in chains. He was a professional.

Then we made straight for the House of An-Ra—the most prominent merchant's exchange in town. He removed the chains at the door, of course. We knocked and were immediately allowed into the outer offices were I gave Julian's name and the press of his ring's seal in wax and asked for Simon of Bethany.

A terribly hunched man came straightaway to see us. About 50 years old, he seemed kind and honest, and undoubtedly—at least at that moment—he was more honest than we were. I told him I was Julian's sister and that Julian had given me authority to go through his accounts and to draw against them. I was sure he didn't believe me since Julian and I didn't look at all alike, and he said as much. I told him that Julian and I had different mothers—which was true.

Silvanius, dressed in his Roman uniform, acted his part and confirmed that Julian had authorized my access to the box. He readily agreed to sign an affidavit to that effect and also gave the names of two member's of the army secret police by way of confirming his own authenticity.

Realizing as I did that things could easily get tied up under Jewish inheritance law, and assuming that a power of attorney is revoked at death, I did not tell the old banker that Julian had hung himself the week before. We thought it might upset him—not to mention our plans. We wanted money and we hoped that Julian had set enough aside to last us for awhile, for we were running through ours fast.

After a long show of legalism, reluctance, and conservatism, Simon agreed to let us examine the contents of Julian's chest that he kept locked in his cellar. He also agreed to let us examine the books of account that he kept concerning Julian's investments. That should have given me a clue as to what we should expect. We called for the chest.

It was made of wood and bound in leather. To our surprise, it contained a small fortune in gold and silver coins, a .45 pistol without ammunition and, carefully wrapped in a square of fine goat leather, Julian's radio. He had obviously been busy.

There was also a thick folio on the cover of which in English was written, *The True Account of the Acts and Sayings of Jesus of Nazareth, The Christ, by Julian Parker-Lane, Eyewitness.*

I flipped through it. It looked like it hadn't been updated in more than six months.

While the banker looked on with an eagle eye, we carefully counted the coins on the table, setting aside the one-third of them that he said was the maximum amount that he would let us withdraw under the circumstances. Silvanius seemed unbelievably stupid and counted them over and over, arranging and rearranging the piles of coins, biting those he thought might have been only gold-plated and dropping the silver ones he thought might also be counterfeit. Finally he pronounced himself satisfied and I signed a receipt and placed the other coins and the .45 back in the chest. Over the half-hearted objections of the banker, I kept the radio and the folio.

I checked over the account log as best I could and signed a statement that Silvanius wrote out which said that Julian had made me his heir and named Judas as my first successor. I also gave him a sealed draft against my bank in Athens made payable to the Tyrian banker who had loaned me money during the previous month. After having worked with us for more than three hours, the man was glad to see us go.

Then we went out and bought writing materials and took over a table in a tavern. There we dashed off short letters to Claudius, Naadia and Marcus, my friends in Athens, Silvanius' overseer and the woman who had hired him to find me, as well as to several others of our friends and business associates. I penned a brief note of manumission to Propea in Aqueilia and sealed it with Julian's signet. Mailing them was as simple as going down to the docks and finding Roman equivalent of an official post office.

That evening—with my being dressed once again in chains—we had a big meal to celebrate our successes. After getting another good night's sleep in the stables beside our well-fed horses, we headed back to Jerusalem at first light the following day.

As we pulled out of town, Silvanius gave me a small bag of coins. At the banker's offices the day before he had managed to pocket some 20 or 30 extra of the more valuable coins through some magnificent sleight-of-hand maneuvers that he had perfected during a long life of crime-watching. The trick, he said, was to let the audience see what it thinks it is going to see, keeping up a patter of talk all the while. I remembered how dense he had seemed when we were counting and recounting the coins and going through the books of account. Obviously he was showing Simon what Simon wanted to see—a stupid army cop trying to be very, very careful so as to cover his own ass.

"Lawyers—particularly when they are trying to be smart—are the second easiest marks to swindle," he told me with a big, ugly grin as we rolled along eastward. "Doctors," he said, "are the easiest. But a shopkeeper? Look out!"

It felt good to be rich again. I had begun to wonder how long the money would hold out, for even though Silvanius said that he would sell his ranch in Italy, I hardly felt that any of us could ask him to do that. And at any rate, it would take months to realize any funds from such a source.

I was very impressed with Silvanius' investigative and acting abilities, and I told him so. He swelled with pride at my compliments, and as we drove along on that beautiful spring day, he treated me with scores of stories and anecdotes about his experiences. Through his years as a professional enforcer and an investigator, he had seen or heard about every dodge or swindle imaginable and had been able to amass quite a tidy fortune of his own merely by reaching various accommodations with the rogues he had caught through his police work. I asked him how Julian could have gotten so much money together in just a year or two.

"Well, it seems obvious to me that he was playing every side of every wall he came to," he said with a smile as he drove. "The other men in the group said he was from Kerioth in Moab—which is a place known for its avariciousness. That's what he let them believe, and they called him *the money-box man*."

I was astonished, for as he explained it to me, the term, "the money-box man", was used interchangeably with Kerioth or "out of Kerioth", the later being bastardized into "*iscariot.*" It was immediately obvious how the chroniclers would later remember poor Julian as Judas(the Money Box Man) Iscariot. Silvanius kept on talking about him.

"I would imagine that he was something of a miser—I know he was not extravagant with money. I could tell that by the way he dressed and that he had no jewelry or other outward show of wealth other than that common signet ring he gave you.

The ring itself, though, was an obvious but subtle sign of banking connections that he probably displayed to rich men as he talked to them on the Master's behalf. I also noted that he had ink-stained fingers—the sign of an accounts-keeper and a scribe. Then, too, he had the look of a hungry, greedy man as he kept studying other people."

He went on talking about various observations he had made of Julian in the half-light across a dim room in the space of no more than twenty minutes on the night he and Propea had spotted us at the tavern. That was the only time he ever saw Julian.

Fascinated, I asked him what he had observed about me and Yeshu'a that night. He was reluctant to say anything but finally yielded to my importunities, particularly when I pointed out that I might need to disguise myself better in the future. As he warmed to his subject—a certain foreign and mysterious woman who he had been engaged to track and to capture—his reluctance faded before the telling of his own professional abilities.

First, of course, he had secured by threats and bribery the services of a person who could identify me. Through weeks spent with Propea, he learned everything about me that she could remember. He knew about my weapons, formulated a good idea of my general appearance and knew practically every identifying mark on my body right down to a couple of small moles on my butt. He learned what sort of accent I used when speaking Latin, how I walked, and what sorts of gestures and other mannerisms I commonly employed.

From Propea and from other contacts he made on the trip in from Greece, he knew how I ate, the names of many of my workmen and sailors, almost everything about my husband and enough about my sex life to leave only a little to one's imagination or speculation. So thorough had been his study of me that when he finally heard that someone fitting my description had been seen first in Tyre and then later walking the roads of Palestine, and when he finally tracked me even to the restaurant and at last saw me, he instantly knew it was me. Even then he waited for Propea to identify me—which she did only on a tentative basis since my skin was darker, my hair was shorter, and I was considerably lighter.

It was all very interesting and, tactfully, he pretended to be concentrating on the road ahead at those points in his narration which were most embarrassing to me. Apparently he had been hired while I was still in Athens. That was, I suppose, at about the same time that Cassius was being sent out against me, and raised the possibility that it might not have been the same enemy who sent them.

At any rate, having arrived with Propea some three weeks after I left, he followed me east and had a pretty good idea that I was going to Palestine. On the way he learned that Cassius had probably captured me at sea, but there the trail went cold. The ship was known to be lost or stranded somewhere. On a hunch, and still dragging Propea along, he went to Antioch, Sidon, and other ports along the eastern Mediterranean coast until finally he got word that I might have been in Tyre. From there the signs had pointed toward Jerusalem and so he had gone there at once and used it as his base for further investigations. Carefully sifting through information gathered from several sources, he had surmised not only that I had traveled on foot east of the Jordan but also that I had returned to the city. My advent at the Temple being widely reported, he had only to check out the villa and to wait. When an informer came to him and told him where we were dining, he rounded up Propea from the market and took her to dinner at the same place. The quarry was in sight. Within a few days he had me in irons.

I told him more or less how Cassius had captured me and then how he had killed himself, and how the Roman galley had wrecked and I survived. As with Pilate, I did not mention that Odyseus had also survived. After all, someday someone might be sent after him, too, if only they knew.

I described how I had seen, followed, and captured Propea, and what I had done with her, and then it was his turn to admire me. Despite our worries, it was a nice trip back to Jerusalem.

In the days that followed, the disciples dispersed. Mostly they headed home to Galilee. Yeshu'a, Silvanius, Judas, and I also went North, traveling together in the chariot. It seemed to me that it was becoming as obvious as a stolen pink Cadillac would be on the Interstate in Wyoming. Silvanius agreed with me that it would be easy enough for investigators to track us down but was convinced that it would be several weeks before they would even begin trying. "Much can happen in even one day," he said. "Look what happened to me!"

From that chance remark made on the open road one beautiful Spring day we concocted a plan, and that plan was to subvert the nation to the notion of love and peace and acceptance. We would do it at the rate of one individual at a time. I say *we* concocted the plan, but it was really Yeshu'a's plan and it was the plan that he had been practicing for almost three years. During the course of that time he had "subverted" thousands of people to join in what had begun as practically a one-man revolution against the *status quo*. By the time he arrived in Jerusalem before Passover, thousands were willing to do whatever he asked—except, perhaps, to repent of their sins and to renounce the concept of a military solution to the problem of Roman domination. When he had said something to the effect of, "Render unto Caesar what is Caesar's and unto God that which is God's," he had meant just that. He had accepted Roman rule for what it was—just another government, just another form of force employed by one group over another.

His real threat to the men who ultimately had him crucified was not his antipathy toward them but his indifference toward their beliefs in Jewish racial and theological superiority. Those beliefs had long since led them to try to enforce on an increasingly cosmopolitan and indifferent populace a huge panoply of what were in effect racial purity laws—laws that incidentally tended to perpetuate their political power. It would seem that the great irony in the pronouncements of such people is in their assertions that God—or "the gods," as the case may be—"ordained" whatever notions they are forcing upon others in the name of law.

Writing that, I am forever reminded of how when I was in college, I would go home and visit with a good friend who lived next door. Without contradicting her, I would listen as she condemned the use of marijuana as being "against the laws of God." Her preacher and her whole congregation were sure that such was the case and had all enlisted their hearts in the great drug hysteria of the late 60s—all the while, smoking endless packs of cigarettes and drinking whiskey straight. I should have spoken up, but what good would it have done?

Of the ancient peoples I encountered, the Greeks were

the most laid back and open-minded—except, as I have said, where marriage was concerned. Their acceptance of what is currently called "multiculturalism" freed their creativity in so many fields that they were almost universally admired— even in parts of Palestine. For that reason, the reactionary ruling classes of the country were forever trying to suppress all things Greek— particularly Greek freedom of thought. They thereby put themselves in immediate and fundamental conflict with Yeshu'a and all the others of the growing body of Hellenized but still-religious Jews who felt that salvation was personal. The irony of the Judean discrimination is not lost on me.

Yeshu'a needed to convalesce, and although he was recovering from most of his wounds very rapidly, he told us that his days on earth were numbered. As I was with him all the time and had undertaken to treat his wounds, I was very worried. One of his feet would not heal and he was apparently losing the battle with infection. Not knowing much about such matters, I wondered whether I ought to operate on it in a blind attempt to extract whatever it was that might be retarding the healing process. I considered, for example whether or not I ought to attempt to cauterize and sterilize the wound by passing a red-hot rod all the way through it. Naturally, I knew that that might cause much more damage and seal in rather than drive out the infections. Not the least bit confident that such a cure would work, I delayed undertaking anything so drastic and painful. I knew, too, that I might have to amputate. Secretly I obtained a proper saw, opium, and some suturing needles and thread, though I doubted that I had either the skill or the nerve to go through with an amputation. He would not let us take him to Sidon or Tyre where a good Greek doctor could be found, and we were afraid to take him to any Jewish doctors—whose reputations were poor, anyway.

"It is my destiny and my wish to stay here in the land of my ancestors until comes the appointed hour of my leaving," he told me more than once.

Finally one day when I was kneeling down by his bed, I kissed his cheek. It was hot and feverish. Still hoping that he would go to Tyre where the most famous surgeon in the region practiced, I told him that I might be forced to cut off his leg if it got much worse.

He smiled at me and ruffled my hair with his fingers. "What is a leg to a man who has God? Would you still love me like you say that you do if I were short a leg or an eye or a tooth?" I nodded my head *yes* and began to cry.

"Of course you would, Eva!" he grinned. "You'd love me if I were dead, wouldn't you?"

I was a little puzzled but looked up at him through the tears and nodded.

"And you still love your husband, don't you?" he continued.

I nodded, sniffling and trying to wipe back my tears.

"And he still loves you, doesn't he?" he said, with a voice as soft as warm honey. His hand was on my head but I could not see him, for I shut my eyes, and his became my husband's hand that rested on me in a simple benediction of affection and love. Then it was the hand of Yeshu'a, and the hands of my father and my mother. Then it was yours, my sister's, my grandmother's and on and on.

What could I say? The man knew more than I did. Maybe he knew so much more about the basic nature of life and death than I did that my concerns about his feet were irrelevant. Maybe that infection, too, was part of the circumstances that would shape—or seal—our fates. How was I to know? After that I was much more resigned to accepting his judgment—at least so long as he could exercise it.

It's lucky I didn't know about what is called gas gangrene or I would have worried even more than I did, for it is a killer that comes quickly.

On the tenth night after my return from Joppa, the moon was full. We were staying on a farm in Samaria. If not hiding out we were at least keeping a low profile.

The farm was perched on the side of a large hill. In the quiet, warm night, Judas and I climbed the hill until we reached its crest. From there we could see for many miles across the silent land, and after spending a few minutes admiring the scene before us, we lit a lamp, set up Julian's radio and stretched out the antenna wire. I pulled out the papyrus sheet upon which I had written the letters and corresponding Morse Code that I would attempt to send.

The radio was in remarkably good condition,

considering that it was three or four years old and had been out of Julian's hands for many months. Although he had used it only a few months before, I had no way of knowing if it worked, even though it lighted up properly and made all the right noises.

That still left out the other side of the equation. Would Mark be listening? Into the middle of the night, I tapped out my first few letters.

We waited. Nothing. After another five or ten minutes, I keyed again and listened. We went on that way for almost an hour until, finally, Mark responded! His signal was very sharp and clear, for it came not from his radio but from the Short's.

For the next hour we sent messages back and forth, and I learned many things. First—and most importantly as it turned out— he had finally gotten the Short to fly, and although it was not operating well on the fuel that we had made for it, he had headed east, bringing with him the lad, Bilyau, and another man as crew. They had been gone from Mauretania for almost three weeks. Due to one mishap or breakdown after another they had only made it as far as the area now known as Tripoli.

I'm heading your way, he signaled, *but now out of gas. May not be able to continue.*

I was more than a little disappointed, for although the reality of the Short was a distant thing—practically a mere memory—in my mind's eye, it was a palace even if it couldn't fly. I longed to get inside it once again, and to marvel at all its parts and rivets and screws, its dials and switches and characteristics and smells that made it, somehow, representative of the paramount achievements of our civilization. I wanted to sleep in it, sit in the seats, and, if possible, rev up the engines and hear their power. I decided that if it could not come to me, I would go to it—at least some day.

Mark said, though, that more fuel was on the way from one of the small caches we had built up. Even if it arrived, he had no hopes of getting airborne within the next three weeks. *Political position here unstable. Flight unstable. I'm unstable. And you? Where have you been?*

It was hard for me to imagine what he was going through, and how he was getting by in the world. It was a matter I would have to think about later.

I told him—very briefly that I was captured by a Roman officer. Shipwrecked. Lost my radio. Without elaboration I told him that Julian was dead and that Yeshu'a lived and that we were together.

Stunned! he signaled. There was a long pause. *I shall come there as soon as possible.*

Bring the Short, I replied. *I miss her.*

I shall. New Moon.

New Moon.

In the days that followed we moved on north into Samaria. Being so near Tyre, I decided to go there and get either a good surgeon or at least some good advice from one. I had to know more about how to do an amputation and, more importantly, to know what signs would indicate the necessity of performing one.

Leaving Yeshu'a in the care of Judas, Silvanius and I went to Tyre in the chariot. Once again I traveled as his ostensible prisoner draped in chains. We passed swiftly along the same roads that I had traveled so slowly when I had entered Palestine just weeks before, and we were soon in Tyre. There we stayed for two days during which time I was unable to find a physician who was willing to make the trip down to Galilee with us.

I did find one, however, who was willing to spend several hours teaching me about infectious wounds and who gave me drugs and surgical clamps. I already knew some of the basics about amputations, and he helped build up my store of knowledge and confidence on the subject. He might have gone with us had I been willing to sleep with him. Under the circumstances, however, and handsome man though he was, he had to settle for the pleasure of my company and what knowledge I could share with him on topics such as the circulation of the blood and the characteristics of the nervous system.

While I pursued such medical interests, Silvanius devoted his considerable talents to sending out misleading reports to his presumed employers and to once again creating false leads to confuse anyone who might eventually try to follow us.

In that short time he also bought a Greek woman in her mid-30s who was on the market following the death of her owner. He did so with my encouragement, for I spoke with her first and thought that she might be useful to us. With my blessing, he took her back to Galilee with us. Her name was Ionica. Plain, sturdy, healthy, and cheerful, not only was she grateful to be with us but she was bright and good-hearted enough to appreciate Silvanius' intelligence and capacity, and I suppose she did what she could to perfect his loyalty to her.

That whole trip took about ten days, for we had some unexpected delays along the way—including a day-long stop during which we re-painted the chariot like one might have repainted a stolen car. I think the thing actually had belonged to Pilate.

By the time we returned to northern Samaria, we found to our dismay that Judas and Yeshu'a had hired a cart and driver to take them on to Tiberias on the western banks of the Sea of Galilee. Yeshu'a left me a letter in Latin detailing why they had left and where they could be found. We turned to the northeast and followed after them.

We reached Tiberias a day later, arriving on the outskirts of the town at sunset. As was our practice, we found a stable where we could sleep amid our horses and equipment. Once we were settled in I disguised myself once again as a mustached soldier and walked into town to try to find Yeshu'a and Judas.

I was worried more than ever about the condition in which I might find my patient, for I thought that the real reason they had gone on to Tiberias was to find a surgeon. Bolstered by my crash course in amputations, I knew that if it had to be done, I was probably the most qualified non-Roman person in that area who could do it. The problem, of course, with gangrene is that there comes a point at which it's too late for even amputation to be effective.

With only a little difficulty, I located the house in which I thought he would be staying. It belonged to some friends of his who had been close to him and his wife during the years he had lived in Tiberias. Like many another place in that part of town, it was a large, walled place on a quiet side street. In response to my knocking on the door, the owner came and, opening a tiny port, asked who it was at such an hour of the night. When I said, "A friend," he opened the door reluctantly. About my age and slight of build, I could tell that he was afraid; he had a club in his hand. Who was this soft-voiced, Greek-speaking man who came in the night calling himself a friend, he wondered? He took me back through the gloomy passageway to the main living room in which his wife and a female friend of theirs were lighting lamps. When I took back my hood and told them who I was, their relief was palpable and they greeted me with enthusiasm. Laying out cold food for me, they tried to make me feel at home. Yeshu'a and Judas had spoken highly of me, they said, and had told them I was a great physician.

But the men were no longer there, and after the initial flush of excitement, I learned that Yeshu'a and his brother, James, had gone on up to Capernaum the day before. My hosts didn't know where Judas had gone. I don't think they wanted to know, for that matter, since Judas' ties with the Zealots were well known to them. At any rate, we had a nice visit and by the time I left, it was rather late. Refusing a guide and donning my disguise, I sauntered off toward the stable.

As is best under such circumstances, I looked neither too rich nor too poor. I kept my face fairly well covered up and my long hair tied tightly back under my cowl which also concealed a metal skullcap that I wore in case someone tried to hit me over the head. As was my practice when dressed as a man, I wore my sword and dagger openly, and as I was taller than many of the men I passed, I looked like a formidable enough chap who one ought not cross. Muggings in such towns were not too common, but they did happened from time to time. It was a warm and noisy night.

My path took me through the section of town where most of the brothels and taverns were located, and for some reason—thinking myself a clever sort of spy, I suppose—I tarried there among the thin crowds of men drifting about in their searches for pleasure and diversion. Emboldened by my success in passing so effortlessly for a man, I went into a Greek tavern and ordered a goblet of wine, watching carefully as it was selected and poured to be sure that nothing was added to it. It was good wine and I savored its rich flavors and thought about how fortunate I had been in my life to have done so much—and to have lived through it.

Then I turned to study my fellow man and found myself

suddenly confronted with yet another dilemma, for in the corner, drinking with a whore, I saw the man who had beaten me, kicked me, and stolen my knife two months previously. I had no doubt that it was he, for he was wearing the same clothes he had on then, was missing the middle finger of his left hand, and was carrying my dagger.

The two of them were both a bit drunk. I watched them while they argued in Greek about her fee. She left. He went out into the back alley to urinate, so I followed him, realizing with a sinking feeling that he was totally off guard. I knew that there would be no better time to kill him and knew that God had delivered him into my hands.

But from the first moment I saw him, I knew one thing quite clearly: I didn't hate him any more. There again, he *was* delivered into my hands.

He leaned against a wall with one hand out in front of him, looking down dumbly as he held himself with the other. In a step I was behind him, my sword drawn, its point touching his back. In Greek I told him not to move and to keep holding on to himself. Naturally he complied, and he told me that he had no money.

"It is not your money I want, nor your apology," I said, unsure of what it was that I did want.

"I have never wronged you," he said, trying to get a look at me. I touched his cheek with the point of the sword so that he would not tune around.

"Oh, yes, you have," I corrected him, "for on the road where you stop people in the King's name you struck me and you robbed me."

He was man enough not to try to lie about it, but he was scared. He probably was the type who robbed and beat people all the time and had no idea which one of his victims I might be. He was, as I had hoped and suspected, a coward, and he began to cry. I am sure he thought that he would soon feel the hot thrust of the blade into his back. He begged for forgiveness and mercy.

"I have already forgiven you," I told him, "and it is from God that you should ask mercy. I have come to you in this way to tell you this: no sin is unseen. No sin goes unpunished." I pulled the sword away from him.

He fell to his knees in his own mud without looking at me. I suppose he thought I might thrust the sword into his back anyway.

"May I see who you are?" he blubbered. "Do I know you?"

"No, you may not see me. I am the messenger of the gods, and when I was on the road you struck me and stole from me. It will be your punishment never to have seen my face. That is fair."

"Yes:" he agreed, " that is more than fair." And he kept his head down as I backed away.

"One last thing," he called to me, "How will I know you if we ever meet again."

"My face is the face of every man and every woman you will meet upon the road," I replied in my normal, feminine voice. Then I left.

When I finally caught up with Yeshu'a, it was in the late afternoon of the following day. He was down by the shores of the lake around a campfire with eight or ten of the men and some of their wives and girlfriends. Two boats were drawn up on the shore and local fishmongers were hauling off the last of the day's large catch. Judas was not there, for in accord with Yeshu'a' wishes, he had headed back to Jerusalem to confer with various leaders of the Zealots and to prepare for what Yeshu'a called "the next step."

When he saw me, he stood up using a crutch. He opened his arms and I ran into them and kissed him.

The others, too, were happy to see me, for he had told them the same things he had told his friends in Tiberias. They no longer looked at me as a foreign interloper. Now I had brought miracles. They still didn't know what to think of me, though. I had, after all, been among them as a person. They had seen me talking with Yeshu'a, the disgraced Julian, and Judas. They had seen me eating, drinking, laughing, swimming, and going off to the outhouse just like Yeshu'a and everybody else did. They had seen me do all of those ordinary human activities. How then could I be considered by them to be more than human?

On the other hand, they now knew of my reputation in the Roman world, and that I was thought to possess fantastic weapons. Through Judas, they heard about my audience with Pilate, the wreck of Cassius' ship, and of the death of my husband. They knew, too, that with the help of Silvanius, Judas, and God, I had brought Yeshu'a back to them. It was all marvelous to contemplate—certainly a series of events that each of us would long ponder before drawing conclusions.

One by one, Yeshu'a went aside with each man and each woman, giving him or her some special words, some instructions, or some sort of request so that each would know that he, too, was special in the eyes of the master. As we sat with our backs propped against cut stones around the fire in our snug little grouping, one man even lay his head upon Yeshu'a' leg and stared at the flames with tears in his eyes while Yeshu'a stroked his hair.

Well after dark we heard someone coming from the north along the shore. We could hear the sound of a small group of running horses coming closer and closer until at last Silvanius and his woman appeared before us out of the dark in the chariot. He had been off on a scouting expedition of his own since mid-day, having left without telling me what he was up to.

He soon told us, though, and it was simple enough. Word had gotten out that a convicted criminal—a revolutionary—had escaped the cross through some sort of deception, and had come home to Galilee to hide out. Herod and Pilate had men searching the countryside for him and his followers. Just to the north of us, he reported, two squadrons of cavalry were already combing the region by day, while squads of soldiers were sweeping down the roads from Tyre and Bethsaida. They were already in Capernaum. By morning they would be in Tiberias.

Everyone turned to Yeshu'a and asked him what we should do, and without hesitation, he said that we should disperse once again and reassemble in Jerusalem. *Why there?* we asked him.

"Because that is where it begins and ends," he said vaguely, "and that is where it will begin again."

Far be it from me to question his wisdom, I thought—particularly with troops closing in.

We said farewells, then helped him into the chariot and trotted off into the night, leaving our friends scant hours to go and say their own farewells before they followed us on foot during the coming days. I gave each man some of the money.

I won't forget how Tiberias looked that night, for all the populace seemed to have turned out to see if Yeshu'a of Nazareth was still alive. Many had known him personally and had heard him giving talks in the synagogue, and many more had gone to the great open-air meetings that had been held on nearby hillsides or by the edges of the lake during the previous two years. Still others had known him as a local builder and a fellow citizen. He was greatly loved by the people and the town proudly claimed him as its own.

We let Silvanius take charge since he seemed to thrive on crisis and was used to issuing orders and making decisions under pressure. It was he who decided that Yeshu'a should stand in the chariot and I should drive it, while he and Ionica more or less hid under blankets at our feet. In that manner, he explained, not only might our connections be harder for the authorities to figure out, but also we would make a better impression on the crowds. That is to say, he explained, we would look like gods passing in the night and not like the fleeing refugees we were.

From every direction the people came out with torches in their hands. In the lurid lights we passed among them like a slow boat in a river of faces. There was some cheering and some crying, but mostly there was silence. Yeshu'a smiled and spoke to people as we moved slowly along. Sometimes a stranger would come up just to touch him or have him touch her. Sometimes a friend from the old days would walk right up and grasp his still-sore, scarred hands or just say something encouraging and pleasant. Every person he greeted and every person who saw us shared with us the tangible emotion, the weight of which lay in that we all felt we would never see one another again. His eyes were as wet with tears as theirs. Even Yeshu'a of Nazareth was moved by having people express their love for him. Two or three women put their arms around him and kissed him gently on the lips. Parents held up their children so that they might see the great teacher, and many a person pressed upon us small gifts of food, wine, and money. We thanked them and passed the gifts down to Ionica and kept moving.

I was too busy controlling the nervous horses to pay careful attention to everything that went on, and Yeshu'a was too busy with people to stop and translate for me, but it didn't matter. It was obvious enough what people were saying. It was obvious enough that they adored the man who stood beside me—the man who they had heard had raised the dead, but who they knew had been crucified down in Judea. Most of them hadn't believed that he was alive, but the news had spread like wildfire— particularly when the two units of cavalry had come through in the morning sprinkling word of their mission and asking where the false prophet Yeshu'a was hiding. That had electrified the town, for whatever one believed, the apparent fact was that Yeshu'a, the hometown boy with a national following, had clearly done something extraordinary. Now people wondered what he would do next, and they wondered if he would be caught and executed a second time.

Once out of the city, we camped for the night at the summit of a low pass where there was water and grass for the almost exhausted horses. It was a warm night and Yeshu'a went to sleep immediately. Leaving Ionica to watch over him and give oats to the horses, Silvanius and I climbed to the top of the hill and spread out the antenna wire in the dark, for it was the night of the new moon. Although I had explained basically what the radio was supposed to do, my friend found it hard to believe it actually worked. When at last I made contact with Mark and shared the use of the earphone with him, he was satisfied that what I said was true. He marveled at how technologically far ahead of the Romans were my countrymen. Perhaps I should have told him the truth, that it was a country that was nearly 2,000 years away, but how could I prove that? But the wonder of the radio was as nothing compared to the wonder that might appear, for when Mark and I signaled one another that night, he had great news.

The necessary fuel had arrived ahead of time, and since I had heard from him last, he had flown the next leg of the journey. He was in Alexandria some 370 air miles away, four hours away by slow plane, three weeks by foot.

Our skills with the code still rusty, we were brief with one another. I told him about the manhunt and urged him to come as quickly as possible. I could tell that he really wanted to come to our aid, but he told me that he was working on a fuel problem. We agreed to be in touch every other night.

In the morning as we left, we could see clouds of dust in the far distant north and assumed cavalry units were operating there. Silvanius was concerned but unruffled and assured me that there was little chance that they could catch us. I thought he was sounding overly optimistic. As things turned out, we were both right, and there were many times during the next five days that we were almost caught by one group or another.

Finally, however, we came once again to Jerusalem.

****

XXXVIII

Jerusalem

We arrived in the city after dark and went directly to the very inn in which I had stayed before. There Judas met us so that counting him and Silvanius' woman there were five of us.

The infection in Yeshu'a' foot had taken a turn for the worse during the trip down from Galilee, and though he could somehow take the pain well enough, the angry redness had given away to purples and, most dreaded of all, to patches of black. I noted, too, that telltale red lines of what I assumed was a pre-gangrenous infection were beginning to appear in the area above the ankle. It was my opinion that if it was to do any good at all, amputation just below the knew would have to take place within the next two to four days. I gave him enough opium so that he could sleep, and I worried.

Late that night, I went onto the flat roof with Silvanius and strung the antenna wire for the radio. As we waited for midnight, my friend coughed in the dark. I asked him what was bothering him.

"M'Lady, you know we can't go on like this, don't you?"

I asked him what he meant.

"Well, it's rather like a lion hunt using dogs. The lion may be smart and able to break out now and again, but when the hunters are persistent and the dogs are numerous, it's just a matter of time."

"Who knows when his hour will come, my friend?" I asked. "Back on the road from Tiberias, there were several occasions that I thought our time was up, but we gave 'em the slip. If worse comes to worse, we can run for Joppa or even to the East, can't we?"

"No," he responded flatly. "That's the whole point, M'Lady. Look here: I'm an old hand at this game. I've done it so many times myself that I can tell when the quarry's been run to ground. I can smell it. Well, we're the quarry—or rather, you and the Master are."

I put my hand on his hand. "You've done so much for us, Silvanius. No one could have asked for you to do more than you have done," I told him as my way of saying that even if we were captured again he should not blame himself or be caught up in it either, if that were possible.

"But I owe you all so much," he responded, "particularly Judas. Why, had he not caught up with us that night....well, it could have been bad. Very bad.

"But it was just like you said that night in the inn: you and he saved my life. I was lost but now I am found. No one loved me and I loved no one. No woman would touch me unless I paid her—or forced her," he continued in a wavering voice.

"Now I have friends, Ionica, and some kind of a cause other than myself to which I can give loyalty."

I agreed with him. He was almost going to cry with the emotion of the moment.

"Tell me something, though, M'Lady," he asked after he had composed himself a bit.

"Tell you what?"

"Tell me what *is* that cause, M'Lady—that cause of which I am now a part? Sometimes I am not sure what it is even though I do not regret having joined it. The Master teaches it and he lives it but he does not name it. Can you?"

"Yes, I think I can name it, my friend," I told him quietly in the night, "even if I can't always live it. It is the cause of Love."

"So, then, M'Lady: are you truly the daughter of Venus—just like they said? Perhaps the offspring of her union with Mars?"

"No, my friend," I said, "I am just a woman from a country called South Carolina, a country I shall never see again."

"Oh, don't say that," he said in a blustering sort of way. "You'll live a long life. You'll see your people again someday," he lied.

We were quiet as I thought about what he had said. Who were my people, anyway? You folks who I had left behind one evening when Mark told me who he was? Not hardly. Y'all were in a different world, a different, unreal dimension. No, I knew who my people were, and they didn't have names like Hamrick, Jones, Brown, Jackson, and Chandler. They had names like Judas, Marcus, Naadia, Ovinin, Odysseus, Silvanius, Ionica, Mark, and Yeshu'a. They were my people. We had shared bread and wine, joy and heart-stopping danger together. We had slept on the ground and in hay racks together, walked dusty roads, and spoken with one another in common languages. They were real.

"*You* are my people, Silvanius," I told him finally.

"But tell me something, Ma'am?" he continued after a few minutes. "If the cause is love, then why are we all in such danger?"

"Ah, Silvanius! You know the answer to that already!" I said. "Just look into your heart and remember the old Silvanius and how he acted and the things he did.

"That which is *not* love must suppress that which *is* love. The loveless know that they should be ashamed, and when a force like Yeshu'a arises, they lash out. Is it not easier to hate than to love and easier to destroy rather than to create?"

"So it is, M'Lady. So it is," he said sadly.

I tried to send a message. No reply.

"Is there really a man over in Egypt somewhere who can send you a message through the air using one of those things?" he asked simply.

I assured him that there was. I had explained it to him before when I had signaled on the mountain, but he obviously still thought that I might have been faking the transmissions.

"Well," he said, "I was just wondering. I remember once when we were in jam up in Germany, the officers told us all kinds of lies just to keep up morale. When I watched you use that thing last time, I thought maybe you were just trying to give us hope that the man with the iron weapons and thunderbolts would come in time to save us."

"He might," I said, "and he might not, but I wasn't lying when I said it was he who was using the other radio."

"Well, if he does try to come here it will be a waste of time. It will be too late."

I asked him what he meant.

"It's what I started out to say, Ma'am. I think you've only got another day—maybe two—before you're caught."

He could feel me beginning to be afraid.

"I didn't want to scare you, Ma'am," he continued, "but you of all people ought to know. I can feel them closing in. In the streets around here I have seen people who I suspect are working for Herod or for the Romans. This building is being watched all the time, and I can't figure out what it is they're waiting for.

"It might be that they're afraid of you and think you might have iron weapons of your own....or that you are a powerful sorceress or have divine powers. Maybe they don't want to start a war or a revolt by trying to grab you again and risk having you give a public demonstration right here in the city of your ability to defeat them. These Jews are very leery of losing their control over the multitudes, and I think the Romans must be truly daunted by you. By now they must assume that you are under the special protection of a particular god."

"I think that I am, too, truth be told," I said, "but sometimes such things end."

"Exactly, Ma'am, but what I mean is it might be one of *their* gods—one like Venus who might get revenge on them if they hurt you. Surely Neptune destroyed Cassius Chaerea's' whole ship. Why else would only you have been saved?"

"Maybe they will stay away," I hoped out loud. He shook his head sadly.

"No," he said sadly, "men are fools who will offend even the gods they fear if it suits them. I don't think they'll hang back much longer. I smell something cooking. They've got us in their pot."

"What shall we do, then?" I asked him.

"Let's try doing what the Master would have us do. Oddly enough," he continued half-embarrassed, "it's about the only thing that makes sense."

And so it was that we knelt down together beneath the

stars on that Jerusalem rooftop and prayed aloud side-by-side, taking turns. We felt like two soldiers facing an impossible battle on the morrow and we spoke the language of the legionaries. Then we silently waited for God's answer. It came to us both at the same time. There were no words, but what was said came through our hearts and ran something like this: "I am your God and always will be. Even when you die you will live, so fear not and do as I command you!"

I turned to Silvanius and I could see his face as clearly as if it were illuminated. "God spoke to me!" he exclaimed, astonished.

"And to me," I replied. "The trick will be to make sure that we follow His will and not just be forced about by circumstances--or our fears."

"Yeah, that's the trick, all right," he agreed, and in that moment dear Silvanius was made beautiful in my eyes.

Then we heard the tiny *di-dah, di-dah, di-dah*, from the earphones that were around my neck. I put on the headset, keyed a reply, and as Silvanius scrambled to light a lamp and get out the writing supplies, Mark and I began sending and receiving messages—a slow process since we had to write out letters as they were sent, then re-read the choppy sentences.

Time is short. I led off. *Js medical condition bad. Police army worse. Friend says 2 days to arrest. Weaponless.* I paused. *What about you, Pal?*

Short runs badly. Fundamental defects, he sent, *but will try tomorrow to fly there. What water?*

Tomorrow! He was going to fly to Judea the very next day!

It was unbelievable, but there it was. Of course he might not make it the whole way, but he was actually going to try it the very next day. I was astonished.

Great! I coded.

What water? he asked again. I didn't know what he

meant.

Then I understood. *Northwest corner Dead Sea.* I sent.

If I can, I will. ETA noon, he sent. Possibly last flight. Maybe possible return Alexandria.

Immediately, I thought of the phrase, *Flight to Egypt* and all that it meant. I imagined getting Yeshu'a and myself on the Short and of flying to the Nile.

Must go now. See u tomorrow, Sweet. he said *Will talk then.*

Yes. Noon. Be there or be square! I sent.

Well, that was God's message. Mark sent it and we recognized it. When with excitement in my voice I told him that Mark would leave Alexandria the next day, Silvanius said, "Well, he'll be too late to help us unless we can continue to hide for another two or three weeks."

To which I replied, "But my dear Silvanius, he is not coming by foot, or chariot, or sea. He is going to fly here in the morning!"

His eyes widened. "Then surely you are of God, and surely He will let me live long enough to see such a wonder!"

"Perhaps," I said, "but let us remember this: it is His will and not ours that will be done."

In silence we rolled up the wireless and packed up our stuff on the roof. Standing up, we faced each other and on an impulse I hugged Silvanius tightly to me.

"Thank you, Silvanius. Thank you for everything."

"Thank you , M'Lady—for everything."

Going downstairs, we made a plan, awakened Judas and gave him some instructions, then went right to sleep. One learns to sleep when one can under circumstances like those. It was going to be a big day no matter what happened, and if I was going to get killed, I at least wanted to be wide awake when it happened.

****

XXXIX

The Chase

We woke just before dawn and ate a big breakfast of porridge and fruit. Then I packed all of my things—which included half of what was left of the money from Joppa. The other half we had given to Judas before he slipped away in the night, figuring that it would be more prudent to divide it in that fashion in the event that our plan did not succeed. Then, too, it wasn't just Yeshu'a's money since Julian had gathered most of it for the group's use.

I had also told Judas how he was Julian's "heir" to the property held by the banker in Joppa and gave him written directions about how he might at least try to claim some of my assets in Albania and elsewhere should I be killed. My parents had been thoughtful enough to write a will, and I thought I should make one, too, so I had written something out the night before. I gave it to him.

In the courtyard of the inn, hidden from the street by a 15-foot high wall, Silvanius harnessed the horses to the chariot. They were well rested, frisky and ready to hit the road. After almost a month of daily use and regular rations of grain, they were in terrific shape and were probably the best team in the whole country. I knew each of them by name and went from one to another giving them tidbits of food, petting them and hugging their necks. They knew something was up.

And so it was. Yeshu'a, in spite of the gravity of the situation and the painful condition of his foot, smiled and kidded with us as we took him down to chariot. He urged us to leave him behind.

"I was destined to be in Jerusalem," he said.

"Maybe so," I agreed cheerfully, "but that doesn't necessarily mean that you are destined to die here. Not again, at any rate."

He didn't contradict me on that because he knew I was right. He was just worried about us and didn't want us to be caught in the nets that were being cast for him. He said as much.

Silvanius cut him off. "Think nothing of it, Master! They fear M'Lady as much or more than they fear you. I would think that she is the fish they seek.

"Even as they plan, though, we plan, and if God wills, we shall soon be safe from them. Soon M'Lady's friend, the man named Mark—borne on the chariot of Apollo—will arrive. He is bringing with him the weapons of iron before which not even an army can stand."

Yeshu'a asked if it was so, and I cocked my head to the side and smiled my crooked smile. "Who knows what may happen this beautiful day, My Love," I asked him, "whether it be for good or ill?"

While he sat in the chariot, we hustled around preparing to leave, putting aboard some skins full of water, our weapons, and, of course, our money and my precious radio. We were a little crowded, but as I have said, it was a big chariot.

Ionica was to leave in the direction of Joppa leading a donkey, and it was time for her to go. While I held the reins to the horses, Silvanius went to her to bid her farewell. They stood by the gate in one another's arms talking quietly, and though I didn't mean to stare, I watched as she kissed him, and I could tell by the way that she used her hands to pull him into her that surely it was as he had said: he had found love.

"So where are we going?" Yeshu'a asked me. By the tone of his voice I could tell that he was tired of our constant moving.

"I told Mark that we shall meet him down at the shore of the Dead Sea today at Noon, but to do that we must hurry," I told him as we strapped down the last of my possessions.

Suddenly it struck me that Yeshu'a did not own a single thing in the world. Even the clothes he had on belonged to other people. Yet penniless as he was, there was not about him the slightest hint of poverty or want, the condition of his foot excepted.

"Why there?" he asked.

"You shall see—I hope," I replied as I reined the horses around and pointed them toward the gate. Ionica went out, moving off into the city in the dark and passing from sight. Silvanius shut the gate behind her but stood by it.

"The man, Mark," Yeshu'a asked, "will he bring with him your famous weapons of iron like Silvanius said?"

"Probably," I replied.

"I hope that there will be no call for him to use them—at least not to protect me," he said quietly. "It has never been my way."

"I know, My Prince," I said, "but we did not create this world and many things happen that we do not wish. I myself have used such weapons," I admitted to him for the first time, looking him in the eye and watching a look of worry cloud his face. "I have killed men with them. For that matter, I have fought men with fire, and I have slain men both with the sword and the arrow.

"Without my telling you, you have known this, My Prince, and you have loved me anyway. I have come to you with blood on my hands and you have taken me in and cleansed my heart from some of its wounds."

"Yes," he said with a smile, "I have loved you—even with the blood on your hands. But every man has blood on his hands. If a man does not defend his brother or his neighbor when evil comes, he must share the blame for the evil. I have that sort of blood on my hands.

"But now?" he continued. "Can it be over now? Can it ever be finished?"

He was weary of life's troubles and worries. Suddenly I had the feeling that on that very day or some day soon, he would die. I knew that he could face it without fear, but my heart went out to him.

"I do not know what God intends for this day," I replied. "You are much more likely to have an answer than I, for I shall tell you this: Come what may this day, men shall call you the Son of God and the Prince of Peace for ages to come. This thing is certain. That is why poor Julian came here. That is why I came here."

Just then Silvanius whistled and swung the gates wide open. There was some light in the clear, graying morning, but the sun had not yet peeked from behind the distant horizon. The horses pranced forward and, as we turned into the narrow street, Silvanius leaped nimbly aboard and we were off, the three of us, with the Roman and I standing up and Yeshu'a sitting comfortably on some cushions to our right with his right elbow up on the rim. In a nearby doorway, two men stepped back as we squeezed past them. Silvanius grinned at me as I kissed the wall next to them with the iron tip of the axle as if to say to them, "Get out of our way!" We came so close to the wall that Yeshu'a pulled in his arm a little, then looked up at me sheepishly.

"In my country we are called 'crazy women drivers'," I said to them over the noise of the wheels on the cobblestones. Relinquishing the reins to Silvanius, I gripped the rim and let the cool, damp air wash my face and blow my hair back.

He was glad to take over since he was a much better charioteer than I. Looking back, I could see that three men were running down the street behind us while a fourth was trotting off in the direction of the Temple and the Antonia Fortress. We soon left them behind.

We came to the city gate leading to the east, and as it was a double-door affair and only the one on the right was open, the chariot could not pass through and so of course we would have to come to a halt. The two Jewish guards there had seen us coming down the street and had taken up positions barring our way. They held their spears upright as they awaited our arrival. As we had planned, I stood up, drew my sword, and threw back my cape so as to look as formidable and otherworldly as possible. Beside me Silvanius, still wearing the uniform of a Roman officer, looked as implacable as Pluto.

He stopped the prancing horses, and I raised the sword to the sky and addressed them loudly in Aramaic.

"Open the gates for the Son of God!" I proclaimed. They hesitated for only a moment, and, setting eyes upon Yeshu'a, threw down their spears and opened the other gate. They stared at us as we passed on through. It was obvious that they knew who he was.

"The man on the left was on the hill when they were crucified," Silvanius said.

Just then the sun broke out of its concealment within the gray cloud bank to the east. Its first weak rays struck our faces. There was promise in it.

Beyond the gates, Silvanius gave the horses some slack. They broke into a canter that quickly brought us down the Jerico road past the turn to the villa and onward two or three miles to the little village of Bethany at the foot of the Mount of Olives. There we pulled the still-eager horses to a halt alongside a large mud brick house in the center of town. We knew where to stop because as we came to the town, Judas, dressed in a red cloak, had been standing upon its uppermost parapet.

As soon as we stopped, several of Yeshu'a's followers as well as some 20 or 30 curious onlookers surrounded us. Silvanius and I got out and tended to the horses, calming them so that they might not dash off, kick out or otherwise cause trouble.

Bracing himself against the pain, Yeshu'a stood up in the car and spoke with his forceful and melodious voice to all who were gathered. They listened in silence to what was obviously his farewell speech to them, and I could see that both speaker and listeners were caught up in the emotions of the moment. The crowd kept growing and growing as the word spread through the town that the famous man who had been there so many times, the man who was the great prophet and had once been thought of as the possible savior of the country was again among them. They all knew that he had been crucified. Some of them had witnessed his being marched to the Hill of Skulls. Like most residents of the region, the people of Bethany had heard the rumors that he was still alive.

The commotion grew. When his speech was finished, we tried to get underway as we had about fifteen miles to go in the next three hours. We started pushing our way forward carefully. But people longed for a last word, a last touch, a last farewell. Yeshu'a's followers didn't want to be left behind and so we proceeded at a fast walk dictated in part by the eager horses that Silvanius had constantly to restrain.

Back in the car, Yeshu'a remained seated and greeted his friends and admirers with the kindness and warmth typical of him. I recall one man shoving forward a crippled child and demanding that Yeshu'a heal her. Yeshu'a laid his hand upon her and looked at me as if to say, "With a father like that this child needs help!"

The crowd around the car changed from time to time as one group gave up its place to another; people said what seemed appropriate or just walked along beside us content to touch his hands or even the hem of his garment. At one point we were surrounded only by his ten most devoted followers. I got down and walked beside Judas who translated for me some of the things that were being said.

The one called Peter spoke to him for them all, saying that he had directed them to come once again to Jerusalem, which they had done. Then he directed them to assemble there in Bethany that morning, which they had also done. Now he was leaving—into exile, no doubt. What were they to do now? Peter asked. They all nodded their agreement with his question—all, that is, except Judas, who always had a plan and two backup plans. It was he who was to execute Yeshu'a' plan.

"No man can stay beyond his appointed hour." Yeshu'a told them. "It therefore falls upon others to take that of a man which was good and pass it along, adding to it that which is good about them. In this way, what we have spoken will, like the water of an irrigation project, fan out across the thirsting human landscape. The problem is and always shall be this: though men are thirsty, will they drink? Will they listen long enough to know, and can they understand what we are saying? The walls that separate them from the love of God can be thicker than those of any city. And when a city is locked up all in fear, go and knock upon the gates, but don't expect the High Priest to order them opened. No.

"But if you have a key, then use it. If you enter by night or in disguise, then give men within the key so that they might free themselves.

"Go back to Jerusalem," he concluded, "and bide your time. Spend it in rest, meditation, and fasting. Counsel peace to all men, forswear the sword, follow Judas, and prepare for the festival of the Shabuoth when the town will be filled with men from all over the world. Invite all who will to sup with you and our friends in the early morning so that the whole day will be yours.

"If all goes right you will receive the power of the Spirit of God, and they will all listen to you and know what you say. Their ears will be unstopped and many of their hearts will open to you.

"You, Peter, shall have power you have never had before," he said to the oldest of the disciples. "Use it. Speak directly to those who claim authority and who will try to put you down. Cite them to the prophet who said that in the last days God has said that He will pour out his Spirit on all flesh so that the young men shall see visions and the old men shall dream dreams and their sons and daughters shall prophesy.

"And with the power that comes from God, all of you will bear witness to that which we have known together and all that you have seen and heard. With that power you will share our love both in the city, in Judea and Samaria, and unto the uttermost parts of the earth, such that men will know your names for centuries and will name their sons with your names."

After we had gone about ten miles in that fashion, and even after we had turned off the Jerico Road to head down into the Essene-controlled area, a crowd of about 150 people still accompanied us. Often a person would come up, say a final few words, stop walking, and watch as we faded off into exile. Not a few of them cried, for they were losing a friend or a hope—or both.

When we came within view of the Dead Sea, it still lay some five miles ahead down a long, rather smooth but crooked road. It did not look particularly inviting, but there it was. It was already Noon and it was warm. I could see nothing down there but desert and lake.

Upon hearing a commotion behind us, we looked back. Some of the stragglers at the bend some 200 yards behind us were running forward waving their arms and yelling. Their cries were soon relayed to us: *The Romans are coming!*

Around us everyone began yelling, crying, and even cursing. More information—probably inaccurate, I supposed— was shouted forward. There were 200 horsemen followed by 300 foot soldiers, the shouters reported.

Most of the men started picking up rocks the size of

baseballs. They were preparing to fight for us using only them. A couple of men had quarterstaves and four or five might have had slings, but only Silvanius and I had swords. A fight would be as hopeless as it would be short.

Coming through the small crowd, Judas came up to us saying rapidly in Greek, "Go! Fly! We'll hold them here as long as we can," and I knew that he was fully ready to give up his life to save ours.

Yeshu'a gestured with his hands as if to present Judas to us and said something to the effect of, "Better love hath no man than he would lay down his life for his friend." Then in Hebrew, he spoke sharply above the tumult so that everyone could hear him. Knowing it was he who spoke, the crowd quieted down and listened.

Most of them dropped their rocks even as he spoke, and some—mostly the grown men—started to weep.

He turned to us. "I told them that there would be no bloodshed on my account," he explained. "You two go on. I'll get down and wait for them."

I was dumb struck by the sudden turn of events. I should have expected disaster, but I had shoved it out of my mind so successfully that when the emergency came, I was unable to think clearly about our options. Only our Roman friend had no such problems.

"Begging your pardon, Master," Silvanius spoke up quickly, "but what about some bloodshed on M'Lady's account? They're coming for her, too, I'd bet, and maybe even for my worthless hide. Among other things, I'd also imagine that Pilate wants his chariot back by now."

I looked down the road toward Jerusalem but still could not see the Romans coming. All along the way, though, our people were running toward us in panic. It was getting to me: I was just on the verge of panic and flight. I looked to Yeshu'a.

He smiled at Silvanius and me and hugged Judas to him with his free arm. Suddenly he grinned and surprised us by saying in common Latin, "Hey! Who said anything about sticking around this joint? Whaddya think these nags have in 'em?"

"Piss and vinegar," Silvanius replied with a grin.

Yeshu'a turned back to Judas and spoke to him in
Greek, telling him with a wink, "Now I'm leaving you in charge,
O Son of Israel. Don't let our friends get hurt. Let the Romans
pass in peace. I wouldn't have any of you here harmed for my
sake. I am leaving now—perhaps forever—and I am leaving you
in charge. Be a man of peace for my sake!"

"I shall," Judas said, choking back his tears.

"But whatever happens," Yeshu'a said, with a hand
upon his shoulder, "Don't let them forget the truth. Break down
the very walls of Jerusalem with it if you can!"

Unable to reply, Judas nodded. Yeshu'a laid his hand on
his head and said a word to the silent crowd.

Then he turned to Silvanius and with more Latin slang
said something to the effect of, "Well, Silvie, let's see these
babies do the fast act!" and he grabbed the hand rail and straps
beside him.

"Yes, Sir!" Silvanius said, but even before he could
finish speaking, the horses threw themselves into the harnesses
so suddenly that I lost my balance and almost went over
backward--which I would have done but for Yeshu'a's strong
hand reaching out around my waist to steady me.

The horses wanted to run, but Silvanius, holding back
the reins with as light a touch as he could manage, kept them to
a trot over the first half mile so that they could warm up properly
after the three hours of walking that they had just done. I wanted
to get out of there, but he restrained them. Anxiously I looked
back to see the crowd of our friends and the local people
standing watching us disappear from sight. Some of them were
on their knees in postures of supplication and prayer, but most
just stood there, some weeping in one another's arms.

Behind them, rounding a bend, I could see the leading
elements of cavalry cantering into view. When they saw us,
though, they increased their speed and began to close the gap
between us. Still Silvanius held our horses back. He knew how
to get the most of out of them—particularly if it became
necessary for us to turn off and make the long run down into the
Wilderness of Judea where we might at least find refuge among

the Essenes. I looked up anxiously at the sky and down toward the salt lake but saw no sign of the Short. Obviously Mark hadn't gotten it going that morning, for it was already past Noon. It was hot and bright without a cloud in the sky.

I looked back. The fastest four or five horses had closed the gap between us and them down to about three-quarters of a mile and were still gaining. I turned to my companions and saw that they were both looking at our horses and had big smiles on their faces.

"If nothing else," I said loudly over the noise, "you madmen are enjoying the ride!" They grinned at me.

"Hold on!" Silvanius shouted, before he loosened up on the reins. "The ride is only beginning!"

Freed of the restraining command, the horses immediately picked up their pace to a canter. The ground started rushing by and the wind was in our faces, as we looked down the road ahead.

Sensing that Silvanius had no intention of slowing them down and feeding upon one another's excitement, the horses broke into a dead run. Glancing back I saw that we were widening the gap between us and our pursuers as if they were standing still. I thought about the Short, and about the past and the future for just a few moments until I looked at Yeshu'a' and Silvanius' faces.

Unlike me, they were intent only upon the ride itself. For them there was no past and no future, just the onrushing present. At any moment, the axle or one of the wheels could break, or a horse could stumble and it—the instant of horror, injury and death—could begin and I could be cast headlong beneath the hooves of the horses or amid the splinters of the breaking chariot.

But until the very instant such a thing might happen, we were flying. We were one with the horses, going so fast that our eyes watered. Bits of sand and tiny stones thrown up by the 16 hooves struck us or zipped by, and bits of foam and lather lifted from the horses and splattered against us while our nostrils filled with the smell of horses, desert dust, and the vague rot of the dead waters toward which we rushed. I remember hearing the sound of wind and hooves and the spinning wheels, but through it all, some song that later I realized was the one from Handel's *Messiah* wherein the woman sings *O Death, where is thy sting? O Grave, where is thy victory?*

And with the presence of death came, as always, the appreciation of life. It was as if the otherwise bright but uniform colors of the day became richer and more distinct from one another there in those wide-open spaces under the brilliant sun. We were part of a great palette of essential colors so that it was all gray, white, blue, and buff into which the black horses pulled us. My pink, slightly tanned arms, the white dress I wore, the men's flying hair and their white, grinning teeth in their tan faces were all of the moment through which we rushed. We were alive! Alive! Alive! and as always—but rarely so clearly—Death was right behind us.

Nothing lasts but change. Three people will forever hurtle down that empty roadway in glorious, precipitate flight followed by faceless men working for some king, some government, something that despises love and liberty. Two men and a woman, thinking their hour is at hand, will race down that slope until the end of time whether or not the world remembers what they did, and whether or not the world could ever care. Four horses will give their all for the pure joy of giving it and of having it to give, and a few hundred onlookers will forever be privileged to watch what happened to them all on that hot day in May and to watch them as they ran for one, last, great run before the change, the inevitable change, came.

Free at last of the pebble-covered road, we hit a long flat that trailed out to the water's edge some distance away, the wheels seeming to welcome the smooth kiss of the alkali strand. The road ended a few hundred yards short of the water's edge: Our flight had ended. Gently but firmly Silvanius pulled in the horses and brought them into a circling trot to test the strange, hot earth beneath our wheels. Just to the south of us, I could see where a wadi or creek split the hills and made its desultory way across the flats into the lake, possibly creating quicksand or bogs that might bar our flight in that direction. To the north, if one stayed along the shoreline, one would come upon the impassable, almost lifeless delta marshes of the Jordan River. We were 1200 feet below sea level, and the air felt like some leaden vapor as it pressed down upon us. Although we probably should have tried breaking away to the south along the western shore, we turned and waited for our pursuers with the water at our backs. I looked across it to the plateau of Moab rising some 4,000 feet high on the other side of that strangest of lakes. They were shimmering above the heat some four or five miles away, and I thought, *End of the line.*

There was nothing to say and so we listened to the labored breathing of the horses as we drove them slowly up and down the beach, keeping them in readiness for whatever we might decide to do.

Having seen us stop on the edge of the water, the leading horsemen among our pursuers slowed down and fanned out into a formation that was soon filled in by their comrades so that they formed a great semicircle with us being the center and the shoreline being the diameter. Altogether there were only about 40 of them, and I realized they were probably one of the units that had been searching Galilee and Samaria for us during the previous two weeks. Well, I thought, their search is over.

Either out of an abundance of caution or in response to orders, they stayed about 200 yards out and did not move on us. For all they knew, I might have a rifle or a machine gun. I wished that I did.

Off in the distance two large groups were coming on foot to join us. The first was a detachment of 200 Roman soldiers, double-timing along in the heat. In their van was a two-man, three-horse war chariot—obviously the commanding officer's.

Following right behind the troops was an unorganized mob of our friends and those of the Bethanians who had not turned back. We saw a few other people coming from other directions, too—white-robed men and women from the hills to the south and brown-clad farmers and shepherds from a road that led out to the   northwest. Undoubtedly they were people who wondered what was going on and what desperate criminals or loyal patriots had been brought to bay by the forces of law and order.

I was outwardly calm but inwardly nervous. I had come

close to death several times, but it was a thing I could not get used to. Remembering how it was when I was being poisoned, though, I knew that I would prefer it this way—wide awake and healthy in the sun, not lying listlessly in a cold bed in a cold room with the feeling that death might be an improvement in one's condition. For some reason, I started worrying about sunburn.

Ever the practical man, Silvanius was the first of us to speak up. "If we are going to do something, perhaps we should do it soon."

The horsemen were obviously waiting for the soldiers to reinforce their arc, and as we watched, the head of the infantry column a half mile away began dividing like a zipper centered on the stopped chariot, splitting into two single files that were going out to the wings. A great inverted "Y" that was rapidly becoming an inverted "U" was closing down on us. Even if the Roman soldiery was generally a crude bunch, one had to admire the precision with which they were trained to maneuver in the field.

Yeshu'a finally said that he was content to stay where we were for a while. He paused. "Hey!," he said brightly, "Maybe these guys are lost and just want directions."

And maybe it was a dumb remark, but it caught us by surprise and we laughed and laughed. "No, not likely," I said, when we stopped. "You know that men are too bull-headed and proud to ask for directions."

"That was certainly true in my line of work," Yeshu'a responded. "Same problem with pride, too."

The lines filled in and the cavalry moved back a few yards. Their shields held before them, the infantrymen advanced, closing the radius of the circle down to about a 150 yards. Then they rested their shield-bottoms on the ground in front of them so that we looked as if we were surrounded by a perfectly spaced line of posts, each of which had a man behind it.

Silvanius circled the horses back out into the water, then handed me the reins. Grabbing a canvas bucket, he got out and started to splash water on them. He spoke to each one and petted it and washed out its nostrils with some fresh water from a skin.

My heart went out to him. Here he was, probably only minutes away from his death, and rather than stay in the car with us, he got out and tended to the still-panting animals. Such a fine man! I thought. Shame on them who would so readily kill him!

Yeshu'a sat there calmly thinking and looking at the array of soldiers. My eyes filled with tears as I gripped my sword hilt. He put his hand on top of mine.

"Don't hate them," he said quietly. "What they do, they do in ignorance and in response to orders. Isn't that similar to what we ourselves have done? We all have our duties. I just wish that I could help you more. You've done all you can for me." He grimaced with pain.

I looked down at his foot. The bandages had mostly fallen away and were sodden with water. The wound in the broad daylight looked more horrible than ever, and I knew and he knew that his end was near. But it wasn't a time for tears. It was too beautiful a moment for that.

I got out and bathed his foot anyway, sloshing the tepid salt water over it to wash away the dirt and pus and fresh blood that was oozing from it. How he had managed to stand the pain for so long was a mystery to me.

The Romans had kept their distance, but we knew that wouldn't last long. Behind them the crowd of onlookers was forming. Judas was there, obvious by the red cloak that he was carrying. It was rather quiet, and the temperature was in the low 90s.

Silvanius came splashing back around to us. "I guess one of us ought to go out there and ask 'em what they want." He was volunteering.

Yeshu'a grinned. "Well," he said, "I'd do it myself, but I seem to have stepped on a nail somewhere."

I was exasperated. How could these men make more jokes!

"We could send M'Lady," Silvanius grinned, "but she might get rocks in their boots." It was an expression soldiers sometimes used.

Leaving us, he splashed forward and walked across the shore straight toward the commander. Stopping about ten paces short of the man, he saluted him. The officer returned his salute. They parleyed together for four or five minutes until the commander made a gesture toward our friend and two soldiers stepped forward to take him into custody. He did not resist. There was certainly no reason to.

For us the story was different. Now it was just them and the two of us. I was glad that Silvanius was out of it, for he might be able to claim he was bewitched or otherwise talk his way out of trouble or pull strings. On the other hand, they might just go ahead and crucify him.

At a word of command that was repeated around the arc, the soldiers all picked up their shields and advanced five or six paces, then stopped. The posts were closer together. Clearly they would get within pilum distance and it would be all over.

I looked at the man sitting beside me so calmly. I slapped the reins nervously on the horses' backs to get them ready. There was no breakout possible, but my Daddy taught me always to try to take one of the bastards with you at such a time, and so I decided that when the time came I would feint south, then rush straight toward the commander.

I ruffed my hand in Yeshu'a's hair and thought about how I used to do that with my husband, and how on his last day he was content, he said, about how he was dying with me. I understood how he thought, but standing there beside another man I loved, our backs to the salt lake, I felt what he understood. Better to face it right then and there and get it over with than to let them take me again.

A young horseman rode over to the officer then came forward to us, addressing me first in Latin.

"My commander requests that you give yourselves up peaceably," he said.

"My son, tell him that we request that he leave us in peace," Yeshu'a said to him, "for we have harmed no one."

The youngster, who was about 19, was not cowed or daunted. He would make a good officer someday. He spoke to Yeshu'a. "Let me make myself more plain. You are a convicted man, a subject of Rome, and have been condemned by the Jews. You have no rights at all. Legally you are a dead man."

Then he turned to me. "And you are a wanted person, a fugitive from justice, and an escaped prisoner. As a foreigner and an emissary of a foreign power, you may be treated leniently, but only if you give yourself up right now."

I told him to go back and tell his commander that I was not afraid of him, and that it was obvious that his commander was afraid of me—as well he should be—otherwise he would have not sent a boy out to deal with me but would have come himself.

"Surely you all know that I am under the protection of the gods," I added. "Surely you know that Cassius Chaerea and over 100 men died because he betrayed me and tried to kill me. Neptune himself sent three wicked sisters to destroy that whole ship.

"And soldier, surely you know that some unnamed Romans have tried to poison me and sent that assassin there to kill me. But I bewitched him and made him my slave. Tell your commander that the gods cannot be mocked nor their revenge avoided.

"Tell him that this man here is a son of a god and that not even death could hold him. You must all leave while you can!"

I watched him as I spoke and saw him shift nervously in the saddle. He knew he was in over his head.

"I shall tell my commander all that you have said," he replied. After saluting me, he rode back to their lines. A long conversation—almost an argument—between him and the commander ensued. Then he was sent back to join the small cavalry reserve. I noted with satisfaction that the commander still didn't come forward personally.

An order rang out and the men hefted their shields. Behind them the crowd of onlookers began to scream and wail and shout.

I flicked the reins and got the horses to start warming up by walking in a small circle. I kept looking as if I would attempt to break toward the south to save our lives. I wanted the soldiers to be at least a little off guard when I turned to run down the commander.

I pulled out my sword and held it above my head. Yeshu'a pulled himself up so that he could stand on one foot beside me. Grabbing the handrail with his left hand, he bent down and half-heartedly took up Silvanius' sword with his right. I'm sure he had no intention even to strike a blow when the clash came, but it was the thought that counted. I was proud to have him standing there with me as we readied ourselves.

"Such beautiful horses," he said.

I had a fleeting remembrance of my father saying of the deer I killed, "He's got his day to die. We'll have ours."

"Such beautiful horses," I thought, "but it's their day, too."

He tightened his grip on the sword and squared his shoulders back. "The race isn't over until the last dolphin falls," he said, referring to the six or seven brass dolphins that recorded each lap in a chariot race.

I wondered if he actually thought we had a chance of breaking through. I stopped the horses and looked him in the eyes. He kissed me. Then he smiled and said, "Quite frankly, I don't think that this is my day to die. Maybe tomorrow."

The soldiers started moving in cautiously. Obviously the commander was giving us an opportunity to change our minds and surrender, otherwise he would have had them advance at a dead run.

The crowd behind the soldiers wailed and shouted. Some rocks were thrown. My horses were keyed up and ready, and I think that they, too, knew that it would be do or die. The soldiers hefted their javelins and pilums. The circumference was approaching the center. Now it was only 70 yards away. The crowd pressed in behind, yelling and pleading hysterically. I readied the horses, but held them in check. Yeshu'a was beside me. I was not afraid.

Suddenly, above the pandemonium, the single shout of a young soldier off to my right along the water's edge could be heard over the tumult. He must have severely injured his voice to call out so loudly, and his shout was so extraordinary that all of us turned to him. He stood pointing off in the direction of Jerusalem. We all then turned our attentions to the west, not seeing what he was pointing at.

But then as one we all saw it. The Short was flying toward the northernmost end of the lake at about 3,000 feet! A

dead silence fell over the crowd, and only then did we realize
that had we been paying attention, we could have heard the
distant, heavy droning sounds of the engines.

Everyone spoke or shouted or cried out.

Like a hawk that has spotted prey, the Short shifted
course just slightly, banking so as to bear down upon us directly,
and although it was only going about 90 miles an hour, it came
toward us very rapidly. The soldiers forgot their attack. Many of
them turned about so that their shields were between them and
the oncoming, roaring monster.

On every side people were pointing, shouting, running
away or falling to their knees in prayer and supplication, many
probably having no idea what they were doing or saying. But I
knew what I was doing. I was grinning like an idiot. So was
Yeshu'a. He could see that whatever it was that was coming
toward us wasn't frightening me and so it surely didn't frighten
him.

Suddenly the well-drilled soldiers and the crowd behind
it resembled nothing so much as a flock of chickens upon which
a hawk was diving. In a matter of seconds there were people
everywhere—particularly out on the flats fleeing to the north,
west and south.

The Short looked ever so beautiful to me. It had been
three years since I had seen it, and its big body and long wings
made it look like some sort of huge, white pelican. On that day I
felt the kind of love for it that one might more properly feel for
her mother.

Having seen the assemblage of people as he passed over
the last hills on his way in, Mark came down at us directly,
bleeding off altitude rapidly and using lots of flap to steepen his
descent. He leveled out about 300 feet above us, raised his flaps,
waggled his wings and roared over us like gangbusters. More
soldiers—including the commander this time—began to flee.
My horses lunged and would have panicked but for my firm grip
on the reins and my calming words.

Mark completed his downwind leg, turned and turned
again, then brought the Short in straight toward us low and slow.

About a third of a mile out it touched down, neatly slicing the water with its bow. Then it settled down and came on in roaring and coughing. Mark was loafing the engines, and he throttled back even more until the engines were going at their slowest speed, then he killed them. They were loud engines and the noise died away quickly as the big, beautiful, gold-plated propellers spun out their momentum, flashing like everything in the bright sunlight. The sight of it was as magnificent as it was blinding.

As the big plane slid forward, a young man dressed all in white scrambled out of one of its hatches and stood on the nose with a coiled rope and a small aluminum anchor. It was young Bilyau from Mauretania. Like an old salt he swung and threw the anchor, then smartly hauled the plane to a halt just offshore in about three feet of water. He waved at me and grinned as idiotically, no doubt, as I grinned. The other Mauretanian waved at us from a window.

Then Mark popped out of the main side door and waded in to greet us, smiling broadly. Some people, led by Silvanius and Judas, and including a couple of young, curious Roman soldiers who had thrown down their weapons, walked toward us.

Mark and I hugged one another with joy. We may have parted on rather bad terms, but that was all behind us in the ecstasy of the moment. Looking back on that meeting I know that what we felt was the love a brother and sister have for one another, and that whatever it was that had come between us was forgotten. Since he had just saved my life, I was particularly forgetful.

I introduced him to my friends and I introduced him to Yeshu'a. Had he not been an atheist, Mark might have been much more impressed. He had not doubted that a Yeshu'a existed or that a man by that name or somebody like him had been crucified, but now how was he to be impressed? Here he was being introduced to a rather dirty man who was just days away from dying of blood poisoning. The man he was meeting was apparently not at all magical or powerful. He was, instead, quite real.

I drove the chariot's team out into the water so that we could talk under the shade of the wing, and there Mark and I tried to explain things to one another. Briefly he told of why it had taken him so long to fly across North Africa, and I described how we had ended up surrounded by Roman troops and were about to be killed just as he arrived.

We spoke in Latin mostly, but aware even then that our future safety might depend upon the Romans continuing to be at least somewhat mystified by us, we switched over to English and continued our discussions inside the plane. While Bilyau and another Mauretanian who I vaguely remembered from before kept watch outside and made sure that the Romans didn't re-form for an attack, we had the briefest of reunions. We brought Yeshu'a aboard and made him comfortable. Judas and Silvanius and some of the others took turns coming in and looking around while Mark and I talked.

I told him about Julian's death, and although he was not at first fazed by the news, as the story unfolded he became ever more fascinated by it. Then fascination gave way to distress of a most profound sort. He kept looking at Yeshu'a who, I must admit, was not a fair sight. By that time, the pain, the suffocating heat, and the stress had taken their toll on him. Despite his curiosity and his discomfort, he had dozed off or passed out. He was white as a sheet.

Mark asked me if Yeshu'a was the son of God and I told him that I wasn't exactly sure what that meant, but that I could vouch for his greatness, his character, and his mind. I told him about how Silvanius and I had gone to the tomb and how he had risen up and left the place with us.

He listened to me—amazed—as I told him of our trips to Joppa, Galilee, and Tyre. I spoke of the infection and of my intention to amputate. We unwrapped the loose, new bandages without waking him so that Mark could look at the wound. He was a tough man, but the wound was so vile he almost vomited from revulsion.

"Yes," he said, "you don't need to be a bloody doctor to know that it's got to come off, but what you really need is penicillin. I saw two cases like this back in '38, and neither of them looked this bad. One of the chaps died—after the amputation. At least the doctors had heroin."

I asked him if he didn't have some penicillin.

"We brought some," he reminded me, "but what's left of it is not any good. I've got a couple of sealed battle dressings in the first aid kit, though, and we can try those, but frankly, I think he's a goner." He looked down at him and shook his head.

"You sure this is Him, Sweets?"

"Yep," I said, "That's Him."

"Then what's next?"

****

XL

The Ascension

That was a good question and quite frankly I hadn't really thought of an answer. Of course I was anticipating that we would all fly away to safety in the Short. Where safety might be found was another matter altogether.

But the plane, he told me, was very unsafe, and he proceeded to tell me that Ned's theory of what he had called Cumulative Impossibility was proving to be accurate. Briefly put, Ned had postulated that in response to time travel, living organisms might carry out imperceptible but extensive replacements of the elements of which they were comprised; inorganic things would have no such capacity. Ned held that although it was theoretically impossible for a thing—an atom of iron, for example—to exist in two places at the same time, the newly-arrived future atom, to continue the example, would nevertheless have all the characteristics of existence despite the fact that it had not yet been mined on the other side of the world. After a passage of time, the item—a gun, a cylinder, or an instrument—might be expected to be considerably weakened at the molecular level. In time it might be expected to disintegrate.

Conversely, an organic collection of molecules such as a human being could not possibly exist—even as antimatter—in the same time space with itself. That postulate was embraced in his theory of Absolute Impossibility.

As Mark explained things, the aircraft and all the things we had brought with us were falling apart. "Anything could happen," he explained. "The wings could fall off, another cylinder wall could fail—I've lost two in the port engine—or the rest of the instruments could go out. The thing's really not air worthy anymore, and I don't want to die—not just yet if I can avoid it. I don't think it'll even make it back to Alexandria."

"Then let me have it," I asked him. "I want to go home."

"You'll never make it," he told me flatly, and in that instant I realized that I didn't believe him. The aluminum deck felt solid enough under my feet, the engines sounded good enough when he came in even though the left one was smoking badly, and there was something more: I wanted to believe that the Short had one more flight in her and that she could take me back to the future where I belonged. Outside Roman troops were waiting for me. Even though these had withdrawn a half a mile or so, Rome would send other men like Silvanius or Cassius until I was crushed.

"Will you let me have it?" I asked, looking him in the eye.

"No, but I'll sell it to you for you interest in the refinery," he said with a sad smile," but I don't think you'll survive if you take her up."

O Ye of little faith!

He let me have it. Immediately, he and the other men began removing things from the plane: guns, ammunition, food, and practically every non-essential thing that they might find useful for barter. Piling it in the chariot, they made trip after trip to the shore, and I was glad to see it go, for all it was to me was weight of which I was well rid. I did, though, talk three the Roman soldiers into giving me their helmets, swords, shields, and armor.

Mark and the other men then unrolled the copper mesh that was stored in the plane and slipped it on the wings and fuselage, a process that took over an hour. I had forgotten about the mesh, and as they worked I began to have serious doubts about the plane for the first time, for its motors were clearly weaker than they had been and the mesh added a lot of drag— perhaps enough to prevent lift-off. That's why Mark had removed it in the first place.

He made the electrical connections between the copper netting and the wave machine and showed me how to set the computer timer control so as to "aim" for the proper year. I kept asking him if he would go with me, and he kept urging me not to make the attempt but rather to go with him to Egypt—by land. I refused to be dissuaded.

That left only one real question to be decided. When Mark went outside to help the others with something, I woke Yeshu'a. It was very hot in the plane and we were both drenched in sweat.

"Arise, My Love," I bid him, "for you have a very important decision to make." He awoke instantly. As if expecting an imminent attack, he swung his feet to the floor to stand up, hitting his foot against a box. He yelled with pain and almost fainted.

He was soon alert, though, and concentrating all of his attention on the story that I was telling—very briefly—of who we were and how we had been forced to come to that era by Julian. He didn't ask, nor did I tell him—as perhaps I should have—how the world would think of him and worship him for the next 2,000 years.

He listened to what I said, though, and hardly knew what to think. After all, such a thing as our time travel was too much to contemplate. For that matter, the plane itself was too much to think about but for the fact that it was tangible with its smells of fuel and oil and rubber.

But I did tell him as best I could in Greek how Mark did not think that the Short should be flown any more and how I had decided nevertheless not only to try to take it up but also to set the time control and to throw the switch. I told him that there were so many ways that we could get killed that I could not name them all. In addition to the problems of immediate mechanical failure, I told him of the possibility that we might be trapped outside of time, or emerge into a mountain or over a trackless ocean or in a time wherein I could not exist and would therefore disappear, leaving him alone in the Short.

Without elaboration I told him that even if we got through, mine was not an ideal world and that although it had many comforts it also had many dangers I could not now enumerate.

"No one's world is ideal," he said, and he asked me what my heart was telling me.

"My heart says that I should die trying," I told him, "and it's pretty obvious that today at least is not my day to die. If I survived the chariot ride and the Romans, I'll survive flying this machine. Even if it won't jump time, at least I'll get to go flying one last time. This morning when I prayed, God told me to have no fear and to do what he commands me. He says, I think, to fly this plane."

"Well, He tells me to go with you," Yeshu'a said with a big smile, "and when it gets right down to it, I might as well. After all, I can't last much longer with this foot, and I truly think that my duty here is done.

"There's another thing, too," he continued, "and that is this: God sent you to be my guardian angel and to save me. If you don't save me by taking me away from here in this thing, how else will you?

"And there's a final point," he said with a weak grin, "if I don't go flying with you right now, I'll never get another chance."

So it was settled, and it was decided that only Yeshu'a and I would go up in the Short, for although Judas wanted to stay with us that day, it was upon him that Yeshu'a' leadership would devolve, and he took his responsibility seriously. He kept asking for advice from Yeshu'a and even from me, although I had little to give. Finally I took him aside on one of the many trips back and forth between the chariot and the airplane. I asked him to try to help Mark, and he was astonished that I should think that a man who could fly the Short and who had weapons of iron might need his aid.

"All men need aid, Judas, and Mark more than most. He lacks a purpose and a plan and even a friend. I am asking you to be that friend if he will have you. God has a plan for each of you, and that is for you to do as Yeshu'a said: Return to Jerusalem and wait upon His word. Take Mark with you. Get the other men to accept him and something will come up wherein he will help you all."

"I know this will be our last farewell, Judas," I continued, "but how will you remember us to those who come after you? How will you help to propagate that which Yeshu'a has taught? I do not know much but I will say this: There will come a man—I don't exactly know when, and he will be a Pharisee who will persecute the followers of Yeshu'a. His name, I think, will be Saul. You will be tempted to kill him, but I tell you this: If you can do with him and with others as you did with Silvanius, you will soon have many followers, and that man will become your greatest ally. He will write great things, and he will travel the earth spreading the good news of God's love."

"And Israel?" he asked. "Will it not ever have its Messiah?"

"The man inside the mechanical goose is he of whom the prophets wrote," I told him. "Rejoice that you have been blessed to have known him. Do not put your faith in armies and revolts and men. Put your faith in God and look outward at the world that is waiting for your message."

Right before we got ready to attempt the takeoff I gave Julian's ring to Mark and commended him to Silvanius who could take him to Joppa. I pointed out that the money there belonged to the group but that what I thought might be more important to him was the manuscript—his son's manuscript. I handed it to him. I knew that if I tried to take it with me, it might be lost forever.

"Study it, Mark. Publish it if you can," I advised him, "and add to it whatever you think is appropriate for folks to remember all of this by. Each of us has his purpose in life. Perhaps this is one of yours. Be sure to tell people that we flew away, and be sure to tell them the truth. Tell them that we shall be with you till the end of time."

So we finished saying our farewells to our friends who were there, and then I turned to the problem of flying the Short. Mark gave me a run-through of the gauges and controls and we pre-flighted the aircraft. As we did—and it took nearly an hour—I became aware of how accurate Mark's assessment of the Short's unreliability really was. Even in its prime, it used prodigious amounts of oil. Now it was worse and had only enough oil for a few hours more flying. The tires that had allowed the Short to operate amphibiously had gone bad, and Mark had stripped them and the landing gear off to save weight. Whereas in the distance the plane had looked white and efficient, up close, the fuselage was odd and discolored, and the control surfaces responded sluggishly to the yoke, wheel, and pedals. As we went through all of that, Mark kept imploring me to reconsider my decision.

Trying to take into account what we remembered of Ned's theories, we set the timer of the wave machine to target the year 1992, thereby attempting to give me a twelve year "cushion" that would lower the possibility of attempted contemporaneous existence. There was no way to check whether or not the wave device would work.

It was getting on in the afternoon. The shadows were lengthening, and everybody but Yeshu'a had started getting antsy. The Roman troops off in the hills were coming back and reforming, if only out of habit. Finally we were ready to go. With considerable difficulty, Yeshu'a got into the unfamiliar co-pilot's seat, and we strapped him in and got his oxygen mask ready. I made a final visit to the tiny head and said a last farewell to all. I took my place. I had never flown the Short by myself before. The men outside began rotating the props by hand to loosen them. Then I tried the starting procedure on the less reliable engine. It refused to fire time after time. I almost screamed with frustration. When it fired and caught at last, though, it coughed out a huge cloud of smoke, then roared in a way that made the people on shore back up again.

Not to be outdone, the right engine started right up. The noise was deafening. Bilyau took in the anchor and we started to drift out. With a wave and a grin, he and the other fellow jumped off into the shallow water and waded to shore. He had a wife and child to go home to, even if it would take him a year to get there. He had lost confidence in the Short to such an extent that he wouldn't have even flown with us to Alexandria had that been our destination.

Mark remained on board and helped me nurse the engines along and get used to some of the handling characteristics of the big plane as we taxied north then turned south for a run into the light wind.

I eased the throttles forward and we picked up speed. Yeshu'a was amazed by it all, as well might he be. I was amazed, for that matter. It had been a long time since I had done something like that.

We had gotten up to about 30 miles an hour when we passed the place where our friends were standing. With a grin and a final wave of his hand, Mark jumped out and I pulled on a rope that closed and secured the side hatch from the inside. Then I gave it the gas.

The plane picked up more and more speed, but I did not try to get it to lift it off, waiting instead for the airspeed indicator to assure me that we were going fast enough. It seemed that we were going well over a hundred miles an hour, but we weren't. It had been so long since I had gone fast that even 40 or 50 seemed terrifying. The engine power seemed, though, to plateau out before we had quite enough speed for lift-off, and so we skirted along for what seemed like miles. I became acutely aware of the rising cylinder head temperatures that the use of full power was causing, and I expected the plane to bust a gut at any moment. She just didn't seem to have enough power.

I kept my eyes on the gauges, and in brief moments, I prayed. I was trying to drag the plane airborne by the force of my will, but it was just too heavy and the mesh dragged in the water too much. Only by the grace of God could it have flown out of that valley.

Blissfully unaware of my agony, Yeshu'a stared with wonder out of the window at the rapidly passing scenery. All along the western shore people in white—Essenes, I think—stood at the water's edge and watched us roar by. Finally, desperately, I pulled on the yoke and we rose up. Then we fell back down, but not before we picked up a bit more speed.

"Can we go on up higher now?" Yeshu'a shouted over the noise.

"Sure!" I shouted back. "Let's go!"

We hopped again, and, free of the water's drag, the boat started flying and only just kissed the water when it fell back down again. Then we lifted up off the water a foot, then two, then eight. I eased off the throttles just a hair. Little by little I gained altitude, then did a long, shallow turn and headed north. The port engine was smoking and misfiring. I fiddled with the mixture controls and got more power out of the engines at a slightly lower RPM.

When we flew over the place where we started, we were not too high to see Mark, Silvanius, Bilyau, and Judas standing at the back of the chariot in the middle of a crowd of people. They all waved and I waggled the wings.

Then we passed directly over the remnants of the Roman detachment that had reformed. Bearing in mind that Mark might be right and the plane might not be able to take the stress, I resisted the urge to buzz them. They scattered anyway. I caught one last look at our friends down on the earth.

My heart turned over with the realization that I would probably never see any of them again. Tears filled my eyes and some small part of my heart seemed to be yelling out that it was not too late and that I could go back!

Then I felt Yeshu'a's hand gently come to rest on mine as it held the throttles. I looked at him, surprised to find that he, too, had tears in his eyes. Yet what we felt was not just sorrow but also *moment* and the high drama of it all as we sat there in the unbelievably loud, roaring present which might at any second end in our deaths.

"There's no turning back now," he shouted. His face flushed, the pain of his foot forgotten, he was smiling from the sheer adventure of our flying upward toward the clouds.

Let us therefore lift up our eyes unto the heavens whence comes our help, I thought.

We kept gaining altitude as we passed over the western lip of the great rift valley into which the Jordan flows and the salt sea sets. In no time at all we were back over Bethany, then Jerusalem. I circled to gain some more altitude and we went higher and higher. I pointed down at the city, but Yeshu'a was not interested in looking at it. Instead he looked all around us at the huge cumulus formations among which we rose. Looking out at their varicolored magnificence in the late-day sun, and looking at my companion's calm and trusting face, I knew that I had made the right choice about taking the Short up. Even though it was beginning to falter ever so slightly, as once again and westward flying we crossed the coast, I could not help but feel that she, too, was eager either to regain her home or to die trying. We put on our oxygen masks.

Then at last we reached the maximum altitude that Mark

said the old girl could make. It was not nearly as high up as we had been when we made the original jump, but that couldn't be helped.

We exchanged a final look with one another, for the time had come. I could feel a deep sense of ecstasy come over me. We held hands for a brief moment.

Then I turned off the engines and put the Short in a shallow dive to maintain airspeed. I reached forward and flipped the switch.

****

Epilogue

Now at last I end this writing down of my story that I began last Christmas, but it is not a story which has ended. It is one in which so obviously there are the seeds of new beginnings.

What a change it was for me to come back here you can well imagine, but one thing didn't change and that was the necessity for me to live the secret life again. I suppose that now I'm in greater danger than I was in back during '79 and '80. Then I was only a smuggler's girlfriend and someone who knew something about a time machine. Now I am the companion and the sole witness of the world's greatest potential revolutionary. Even the physician who treated his wound, who has become our friend and who has been told the entire story is not as credible as I am. Only I can vouch for him and offer the proof of what I have written here.

Soon enough, however, through his growing command of English and the two other languages he is learning, he will be able to vouch for himself. If he chooses to do so—a matter that is so far undecided—he will have some of the tokens that might be necessary to help you to believe it is actually him. He will have the small collection of almost-new gold and silver coins and the Roman armor that we brought with us from the Dead Sea that day. He will have a command of ancient languages second to none, he will be possessed of a depth of wisdom impossible to fathom, and he will have his scars to show you.

Can such things and talents be faked? Perhaps.

Will there be millions who will want to deny him—or even to crucify him once more? Probably.

Would not whole denominations turn their backs on him and adherents of other faiths want him silenced? Of course.

On the other hand, *if* the world accepts him, what then? Would there be any sort of real change in the daily lives and pursuits of people?

More importantly, perhaps we should ask ourselves—as he has—whether or not devout Christians would be willing to discard those long-practiced forms of worship that might not conform to the new reality of a living Jesus who might say, "Do not pray to me: talk *with* me! I am here."

For those who doubt as well as for those who believe, he may extend the cup. If extended to you, would you drink and run the risk that your comfortable life might change?

Then, too, there is this question: If the cup contains the White Drink, will your governments see to it that it is illegal to possess it or to use it? The answer to that question seems obvious, for there will always be those who from ignorance will demand the suppression of the truth. The political types of the world will readily take up their cries, for they will rightly understand that their own power will be eroded if people become able to see them for what they truly are. Both groups will seek to silence or even to kill the man with the cup. It has happened before. Who would say that it cannot happen again?

Look, for example, at your own state's government. Go into its legislative branch and look around. Their professed Christianity aside, is it not obvious that should someone run in and shout, *Jesus is outside and offers you the cup of salvation! Drop what you are doing and go to Him before it is too late!*, only a few would leave their seats? The rest would scoff and resent the interruption of their more important business, and the police would be sent to arrest him. They would take the cup and have it sent off to your state Crime Lab while back inside the capitol building the beat—or the beatings—would go on. Anyone who doubts me should study what they have already done regarding peyote.

No: the world--and particularly the political world--is not ready for him, nor he for it: not yet. Perhaps the two will never will be ready. And think, too: the modern world demands information even of the purely innocent, and the quest for it by the press and the government and the professionally curious is enormous. If he comes forth, what kind of pressure will there be for him to appear on radio and television? He would need an agent, would he not? To which I shout: *Not me!*

He would be asked to opine upon matters of public policy. If he reveals himself to you, how will he be able to exist with simple dignity in a world gone crazy with religious discord and celebrity publicity?

Perhaps what I have done—and I do take personal responsibility for it—was a mistake. It may well be that you live in a world too busy and too distracted to believe in the return or even the existence of a real Christ. If he steps forward he may well find himself locked into an insane asylum with others making similar claims. On the other hand, he could be shot by some Christian fanatic. Look what Julian did.

We have been "back" for some time now. When we set the machine for emergence in 1992, Mark and I did not take into account something Ned called *processioning*, and we emerged somewhat later than that target date. What a world I found! The Soviet Union dissolved and the Berlin Wall destroyed: who would have thought such things could have happened so quickly? What else? Oh, yes: computers! Computers everywhere and car phones, fax machines, satellite television for everyone and all of that stuff and information that was just beginning to come on the scene when I left. And, irony of ironies: a sweet-voiced girl singing a popular song on the radio, asking *What if God was one of us?*

I have been busy again. I checked to see if there were charges extant against me in North Carolina. There aren't. I visited the farm and recovered the cash, and I have gotten together money from other sources—including the sale of some of the coins we brought back. I have obtained all sorts of false papers for both of us, and, of course, I have written this account.

Especially now as I draw this writing to a close, I think of you with amazing frequency even though it has been—for me—some 10 years since I saw you last.

I doubt that you have thought of me very much since we were together. After all, you have your life now--your wife and children, your profession, home, and community. In your spare time, when you think about girls you have known, I am sure there are many others to contemplate besides the big girl who blew so hot and cold and made those strange scenes you said you could not understand. You haven't seen her now for almost 22 years.

If you could see her now, however, you might notice something beside the fact that her face and body are slimmer. You might at first think that she looks surprisingly younger than 48—if you were not otherwise aware that she has lived only 36 years.

But if you knew, on the other hand, that she was only 36 years old, you might look at the corners of her eyes and see the lines that years of living in the sun have already left. If you looked closer still you might see from the expression in those eyes that those years have left their marks upon her, too.

As much as you might have loved her, and as passionate as y'all were back then, you would still not think her beautiful. She would still have the same odd, straight nose, and a few unsightly pounds of fat around her hips and the same inelegant arms. You would not be able to see her as the ancients saw her, nor would you think of her—as some of them did—as one of the most beautiful women in the world.

That would be all right with her, though, for she has had her days in the world's eyes and amid its fickle judgments.

On the other hand, you might discover that she has found something, and that she can stand up and talk for herself even before strangers and crowds. After a fashion, she can tell stories, sing songs, and—most importantly—she can tell truths.

You would find, too, that she is in much better physical and mental shape than she was in when you knew her. You might be impressed—or intimidated. Or intrigued.

H. L. Mencken once wrote that when women find a new man the old one is *stricken from the minutes*. As I have related in this story, after you and I broke up, I went out and found new men. You were stricken from my minutes.

But when I found myself in the most unlikely places, like magic ink you kept reappearing upon the pages of those minutes even as my sister and my parents did. I attribute that phenomenon to the fact that you and I were more than lovers. We were friends, too, and that counts for much. As I have said several times through these writings, I thought of you many times during that great journey. When I sang for people I thought of you and your repertoire of songs and jokes and how you shared them with people and brought them some happiness. I thought of your quote from Whitman:

> ...*Each singing what belongs to him or her and to none else,*
> *The day what belongs to the day—at night the party of*
> *young fellows, robust, friendly,*
> *Singing with open mouths their strong melodious songs.*

When I was away I sang and heard sung many a strong, melodious song. Writing, too, is a song, and over the months of working on this—this manuscript—I have sung what belonged to me and to no one else and what belonged to the day.

I think often of the party of robust young fellows singing on their way out to the little villa near Jerusalem, and I contemplate how they would have been forgotten long ago but for their comrade. He sang with them and walked beside them into the pages of history and into the hearts and minds of a hundred generations. Someone wrote much of it down. Others went forth into the world and somehow what happened during those few years in those obscure places grew and spread a message of peace and love.

Of course that message that has been often distorted and used to justify theft, murder, and oppression, and in that regard, I often think that it was an act of cruelty on my part to have brought Joshua to this day and age. He can see what men have so often done in what they are pleased to refer to as *His Holy Name.*

It is obvious why I have not described Joshua's physical characteristics with any particularity. As long as he enjoys his anonymity he can pass along through the world dressed as you dress and speaking the languages you speak. With his false papers—and if he is not closely questioned—he may travel through the world learning and observing conditions for some considerable time.

He may be the man seated next to you on the bus or plane, or who drives through your town. He may be the newcomer, the foreigner, who visits your church one Sunday or who your police stop on some pretext and then arrest. He may be the man who is hitchhiking or is wandering down a side street asking for charity in this incredibly rich country or in some less fortunate land. He won't be asking for your help because he needs it. He'll be wondering whether or not you'll give it.

In your opinion he may be beautiful or he may be ugly. Although he has some little wealth, money means next to nothing to him. If you ask him to help you, he will.

The story is told; the paradigm shifts. God Is.

✝